D1014674

The Times That
Try Men's Souls

PRELUDE TO GLORY

Volume 1: Our Sacred Honor
Volume 2: The Times That Try Men's Souls

The Times That Try Men's Souls

A NOVEL BY
RON CARTER

BOOKCRAFT
SALT LAKE CITY, UTAH

Library of Congress Catalog Card Number: 99-72623

ISBN 1-57008-647-8

First Printing, 1999

Printed in the United States of America

This series is dedicated to the common people
of long ago who paid the price.

★ ★ ★

America was discovered, colonized, and made into a great nation so that the Lord would have a proper place both to restore the gospel and from which to send it forth to all other nations. As a prelude to his coming, and so the promised work of restoration would roll forward, the foundations of the American nation were laid.

—BRUCE R. MCCONKIE

This volume is dedicated to
Harriette Abels.
Wonderful person.

The Times That Try Men's Souls

These are the times that try men's souls: The summer soldier and the sunshine patriot will, in this crisis, shrink from the service of his country; but he that stands it NOW, deserves the love and thanks of man and woman. Tyranny, like hell, is not easily conquered; yet we have this consolation with us, that the harder the conflict, the more glorious the triumph. What we obtain too cheap, we esteem too lightly:— 'Tis dearness only that gives every thing its value. Heaven knows how to set a proper price upon its goods; and it would be strange indeed, if so celestial an article as FREEDOM should not be highly rated.

. . . My secret opinion has ever been, and still is, that GOD Almighty will not give up a people to military destruction, or leave them unsupportedly to perish, who had so earnestly and so repeatedly sought to avoid the calamities of war, by every decent method which wisdom could invent.

THOMAS PAINE
THE AMERICAN CRISIS I
DECEMBER 19, 1776

PREFACE

The reader will be greatly assisted in following the *Prelude to Glory* series if the author's overall approach is understood.

The volumes in this series do not present the critical events of the Revolutionary War in chronological, month-by-month, year-by-year order. The reason is simple. At all times during the eight years of the conflict, the tremendous events that shaped the war and decided the final result were happening in two and sometimes three different geographical areas at the same time. This being true, it seemed to this author that in writing a series of novels about the war it would become extremely difficult to move back and forth between locations without badly confusing the story line.

Thus, the decision was made to follow each major event through to its conclusion, as seen through the eyes of selected characters, and then go back and pick up the thread of other great events that were happening at the same time in another geographical area, as seen through the eyes of the characters caught up in those events.

In all this, the fictional family of John Phelps Dunson, with their friends and loved ones, are the principal people through whom we see these episodes. The reader will recall that in volume I, *Our Sacred Honor,* the story of the beginning of hostilities between the British and the Americans in April 1775 was presented through the experiences of John Dunson, his son Matthew, Matthew's dearest friend Billy Weems, and John's old and beloved friend Tom Sievers as they went through the battles of Lexington and Concord. From there, the first volume then followed Matthew, a ship's navigator, through the sea wars to the year 1779.

This second volume, *The Times That Try Men's Souls,* now goes back and follows Billy Weems, nearly killed at the battle of Concord in April 1775, from his recovery, through the heartbreaking battles in the area of

New York in the summer and fall of 1776, then through the terrible retreat across the state of New Jersey, and finally over the Delaware River to Pennsylvania in December, where General George Washington must face the fact that his army is destitute, sick, starving, freezing, beaten. The reader meets Eli Stroud, the white man raised as an Iroquois Indian, who becomes fast friends with Billy.

Subsequent volumes will cover the extraordinary battles of Trenton and Princeton, the engagements at Germantown and Brandywine, the pivotal battle at Saratoga, the entrance of French troops and ships into the war on the American side, the heartrending hardships at Valley Forge, and so on. Through it all, readers will get an up-close perspective on all of these events through the lives and experiences of the various fictional characters.

Finally, may I take this occasion to address a question that has reached the writer hundreds of times from distraught readers all over the country. Be patient. There is yet good time to tell the conclusion of the Matthew and Kathleen love story.

CHRONOLOGY OF IMPORTANT EVENTS
RELATED TO THIS VOLUME

1775

April 19. The first shot is fired at Lexington, Massachusetts, and the Revolutionary War begins. (*See volume 1*)

June 15. The Continental Congress appoints George Washington of Virginia to be commander in chief of the Continental army.

June 17. The battle of Bunker Hill and Breed's Hill is fought, which the British win at great cost, suffering numerous casualties before the colonial forces abandon the hills due to lack of ammunition. (*See volume 1*)

September. King George III of England and his cabinet agree upon a strategy for putting down the rebellion in the American colonies, as well as the British officers who shall command and the armed forces that will be necessary.

1776

February–March. Commodore Esek Hopkins leads eight small colonial ships to the Bahamas to obtain munitions from two British forts, Nassau and Montague. (*See volume 1*)

March 17. General Sir William Howe evacuates his British command from Boston. (*See volume 1*)

June. A plot to assassinate General George Washington, as well as other American officers, and blow up American powder magazines is uncovered. It becomes known as the "Hickey Plot" when Thomas Hickey, personal bodyguard to General Washington and one of the conspirators, is publicly hanged on June 28.

June 25. General Howe arrives in the New York area aboard the British ship *Greyhound* to take command of all British forces in the colonies.

July 9. On orders of General Washington, the Declaration of Independence (adopted by the Continental Congress on July 4) is read publicly to the entire American command in the New York area, as well as the citizens.

July 20. General Howe sends his adjutant general, Lieutenant Colonel James Paterson, to offer pardon to General Washington and all American Patriots if they will cease the rebellion and swear allegiance to the Crown. The offer is refused.

Late August. The British armada of over four hundred ships and thirty-two thousand troops having arrived in the New York area, a large portion of this force now moves from Staten Island to Gravesend Bay on Long Island, preparatory to attacking General Washington's forces at Brooklyn.

August 27. The battle of Long Island is fought, with disastrous results for the Americans.

August 29–30. General Washington abandons Brooklyn and moves the entire army from Long Island, across the East River at night, to Manhattan Island.

September 15. The battle of Kip's Bay on Manhattan Island is fought, resulting in another disaster for American forces.

September 16. The battle of Harlem Heights on Manhattan Island is fought, in which the Americans prevail.

September 21. An accidental fire burns about one-fourth of the city of New York.

October 11. General Benedict Arnold leads a tiny fleet of fifteen hastily constructed ships to stall the British fleet of twenty-five ships on Lake Champlain. The hope is that Arnold's forces can at least delay the movement of thirteen thousand British troops south until the spring of 1777 and thus save George Washington's Continental army. (*See volume 1*)

October 28. The battle of White Plains is fought, in which the Americans are defeated.

November 16. The battle of Fort Washington is fought on Manhattan Island, resulting in a catastrophe for the Americans, following which the Americans abandon Fort Lee, opposite Fort Washington on the New Jersey side of the Hudson River, surrendering the fort to the British forces without firing a shot.

Early December. General Washington leads the remains of his devastated army in a headlong retreat across New Jersey and crosses the Delaware River into Pennsylvania, opposite the small town of Trenton.

Mid-December. General Washington sends a secret message to John Honeyman, an American spy posing as a British Loyalist, and resolves to take the remnants of his tattered army on the offensive, back across the Delaware River to attack the British forces garrisoned there.

1779

September 23. Commodore John Paul Jones, aboard the *Bonhomme Richard*, engages the larger British man-of-war *Serapis* off the east coast of England in the much-celebrated night battle in which Jones utters the now-famous cry, "I have not yet begun to fight!" (*See volume 1*)

Part One

★ ★ ★

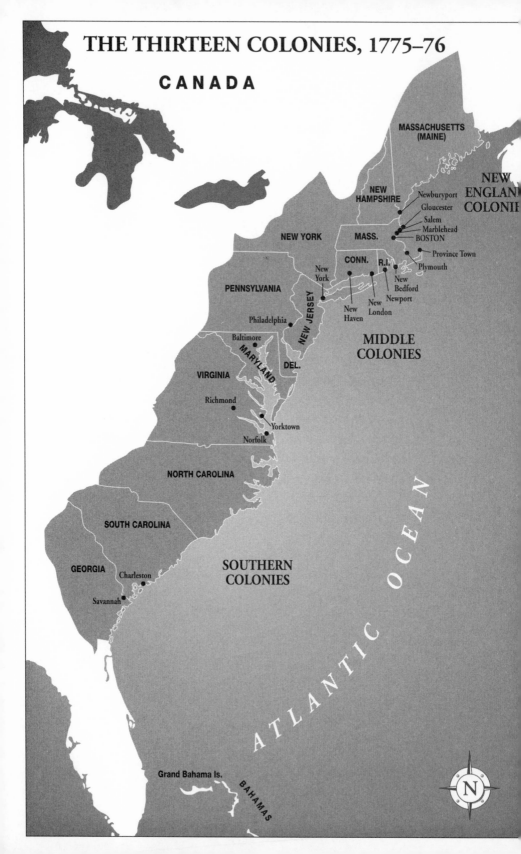

THE THIRTEEN COLONIES, 1775–76

CANADA

MASSACHUSETTS
(MAINE)

NEW
ENGLAN
COLONIE

NEW
HAMPSHIRE

Newburyport
Gloucester
Salem
Marblehead
BOSTON
Province Town
Plymouth

NEW YORK

MASS.

CONN.

R.I.

New
York

New
Bedford
Newport

New
Haven

New
London

PENNSYLVANIA

NEW JERSEY

MIDDLE
COLONIES

Philadelphia

Baltimore

MARYLAND

DEL.

VIRGINIA

Richmond

Yorktown

Norfolk

NORTH CAROLINA

SOUTH CAROLINA

OCEAN

GEORGIA

Charleston

SOUTHERN
COLONIES

Savannah

ATLANTIC

Grand Bahama Is.

BAHAMAS

N

London

September 1775

CHAPTER I

★ ★ ★

*C*hill rain fell heavy in the night, steadily drumming on the shingles and slates and thatches of rooftops before gathering into puddles that turned the countryside to mud and the dirt roads leading to the great river and London Town into rutted quagmires. The narrow, winding cobblestone streets of the city became channels of water slowly working their way to the Thames. A gray and somber dawn came creeping over the sodden land to find the incoming roads crowded with the great two-wheeled carts loaded with fresh farm vegetables and salted pork and beef for the ever-hungry ships on the deepwater seaport of the river and the merchants in town. By nine o'clock, golden shafts of sunlight came streaming through breaks in the lead-colored overcast; and by ten o'clock, the sprawling, throbbing metropolis was in full sunlight, with steam rising from the puddles and wet cobblestones in the streets.

At ten-thirty, trumpets blasted within the grounds of Buckingham to clear the streets, and the guards threw their shoulders against the massive iron gates. They yawed open, and the guards snapped to rigid attention, shoulders thrown back, chins high. They smartly presented arms as the flawlessly decorated blue and gold royal coach of King George III rumbled past, drawn by six matched white horses. Four of the elite palace guard mounted on the big-boned bay geldings preferred by all light cavalrymen led the coach, with four behind.

The uniformed officer in the driver's box glanced neither right nor left as he turned the lead horses toward St. James's Palace and the Whitehall district beyond, with the wheel horses following. The guards at the gate were at rigid attention, with only their eyes moving as they strained to see the king in the dimness inside the coach. The cushioned wheels of the royal coach made little sound as they rolled over the uneven cobblestones.

As if by magic the heavy traffic in the streets opened, and the barking of hucksters and merchants, the rattling of carts on cobblestones, and the sounds of protesting animals quieted as the opulent coach made its unhampered way towards the great tower and the broad stone bridge spanning the dark waters of the Thames.

Inside, King George III sat straight, mouth clenched as he stared unseeing out the coach window, tenuously controlling the hot rage that seethed within. Beside him, his aide sat clutching a large pouch filled with documents, while in the opposite seat were two of the king's personally selected bodyguards, uniformed, dashing, pistols on their laps while they watched every movement in the passing crowd. Two footmen stood at their posts on the rear platform of the coach, grasping the handrails against the gentle sway.

The coach rolled onward towards the half-mile-long complex of elaborate buildings and lavish courtyards and manicured gardens on the banks of the Thames that formed Whitehall, where those who had clawed their way to the top of the political and military heap lived and kept offices. It was they who made the crucial decisions of who in the empire rose and who fell; of which competing world powers felt the crushing weight of the British army or navy; of which of their colonies shared the wealth or felt the iron hand of discipline of Mother England.

As the coach rolled, King George stared ahead at Pall Mall, where Lord George Germain had taken up residence; St. James's Square, where Admiral Pallister of the board of Admiralty lived; Duke Street, where Lord Suffolk resided; and Cleveland Row, where the secretaries of the three Departments of State officed, where the commander in chief of the army once resided, and where the lord president of the council, the lord privy seal, and the lord chancellor carried on their business as members of the Royal Cabinet, suitably close to Downing Street and the Admiralty building.

The coach slowed as it approached the aging St. James's Palace, and King George started as though suddenly realizing where he was. He raised the blind on his window and peered outward as the coach swung left through the high black wrought-iron gates into the palace courtyard and continued on down to stop before the great double doors of the entry. Instantly the footmen dropped from their platform. One unfolded the three steps from beneath the coach while the other opened the door wide, watching while the two bodyguards concealed their pistols beneath royal blue capes and stepped down, heads turning, eyes darting. The aide followed, head bowed while he clutched the pouch of documents to his chest and turned to await the king, furtively watching the face and eyes of His Majesty, hating the anger in the slitted eyes and the white lines around the clenched mouth.

Not quite of average height, round face regular but fleshy, hands soft from a life spent largely in the rich halls and chambers of royalty, King George III descended from the coach. He strode wordlessly to the heavy carved oak doors, and he did not break his stride as the two door guards hastily hauled them open and the king passed through. He turned right and moved down the high-ceilinged hall, past the painted wall murals of scenes of England's glories, to a highly polished maple door. He pushed through into the room and stopped short while his two elite palace guards walked to chairs on either side of the room and stood waiting. His aide, still clutching the pouch, remained silently behind.

The chandelier above the two-ton polished marble table in the center of the room glittered with 240 candles, whose light was refracted by ten thousand pieces of cut crystal. The draperies were lush, the paintings adorning the walls lavish, the appointments rich. The monstrous fireplace at the far end was dominated by a commissioned portrait of the king, twelve feet high, eight feet wide. The eighteen chairs lining the sides of the table were upholstered with royal blue velvet and brass studs, each with the lion and the unicorn of Great Britain delicately carved in the high, arching back. Eight men in powdered wigs sat at the table, four to the left of the great chair at the head, four to the right.

At the moment of the king's entrance, all eight men leapt to their feet and faced him, each in resplendent court dress appropriate to his position, all with velvet frock coats that dazzled with gold braid at the shoulders and lapels and cuffs. All talk ceased and the room fell into total silence as the king stood stock-still, eyes moving from one man to the next, while the men breathed light, studying the eyes and face of their king. Not a muscle moved as they read the set of his jaw and the points of light in his eyes. King George removed his hat, and for long moments stood with his feet spread slightly as he studied the most powerful group of men in the civilized world—the cabinet of the king of England.

To his left was Frederick, Lord North, first lord of the treasury. His powers were exceeded only by those of the king, and on his shoulders rested the awful responsibility of moving the totality of the far-flung British empire in the direction dictated by the monarch and approved by the cabinet. Success in his position brought immortality and treasure; failure brought dismissal and inglorious anonymity. Large, prominent eyes, wide mouth, thick lips and tongue, heavy jowls, and clumsy movements gave Lord North the aura of a harmless bumbler; in truth he was as shrewd a politician as existed in England. But for all his brilliance in the subtle, deadly arena of world politics, Lord North was totally without qualification to wage war. He knew nothing of the refinements of massive military operations, and he hated them as much as he hated being accountable for the unending sucking of millions of pounds from the treasury to pay for them. Each year the approach of annual Budget day drove him to talk of retiring, and his murmurings had reached the king. Dark whisperings had lately been heard in the corridors of government: Lord North is inept; he has pushed the kingdom into decline—he must go.

In a line behind North stood the three secretaries of state: the earl of Suffolk for the Northern Department; the earl of Rochford for the Southern Department; and for the critical American Department, the newly appointed Lord George Germain.

King George considered Lord George Germain for a moment. Born George Sackville, he had lately changed his name to George Germain to receive a vast inheritance from Lady Betty Germain. At age sixty the man stood well over six feet, with broad shoulders, strong build, prominent nose, masculine face. He had been accused of cowardice years earlier in the battle of Minden, Germany, for executing an attack order later than expected. Incensed at how his reputation was being destroyed by subtle undertones, he demanded a wide-open court-martial to clear his name, and finally got it. The case against him failed, and he began rebuilding his image. Then, when Lord Dartmouth proved to be a failure as secretary of state for the American Department, King George had moved Dartmouth to lord privy seal in the cabinet, and turned to George Germain to replace him as the secretary of state for the American colonies. Germain had accepted only days earlier and had not yet been sworn in, nor would he be until two months later, November of 1775. No man in the king's cabinet was under greater pressure, greater scrutiny at that moment than Lord George Germain, and no man was more keenly aware of it than he.

Opposite, on the right of the table, stood the earl of Sandwich, first lord of the Admiralty, followed by the earl of Gower, lord president of the council; then the earl of Dartmouth, lord privy seal; and last, the earl of Bathurst, lord chancellor.

Though but thirty-seven years of age—and by his own admission not yet matured in the ways and wisdom of war—King George had no illusions about his place in the hopelessly complex inner structure of the English government. The political world where wild, cutthroat patronage allowed one to buy a colonelcy in the British army for five thousand pounds, and with it a seat in the House of Commons, had turned politics into a cauldron of bitter experience that had taught George the hard truth. His leadership was more visible than real, more moral than direct. He could set policy, and no more. The power to execute his policy and turn the wheels of government, and of war, lay in the cabinet. He could inspire the men who filled these positions, or cajole them, or order them, or frighten them, or he could replace them. But in the end, the machinery of the British Empire ground on only if the cabinet functioned. He knew that North was vacillating and indecisive regarding the crisis in America; yet the king chose to let him remain at the head of the cabinet simply because it was easier to struggle with North's inadequacies than to go through the wrenching experience of replacing him. As for the newly appointed Germain and the American Department of State, King George could only desperately hope that he had found the man for the most critical task of the decade.

King George's eyes flashed as he took his rightful position at the head of the table, settled onto the largest of the ornate chairs, and waved his hand. Only then did the cabinet members sit, each man on the front edge of his chair, backs like ramrods, faces turned to the king in silence so thick flies could be heard buzzing near the high cut-glass windows along the right wall.

"My lords," the king said.

"Your Majesty," came the instant chorus of replies.

The king's chin quivered slightly as he struggled, and then he lost his tenuous hold on his deep anger and bolted to his feet. "How dare they! How *dare* they!" His hot words rang off the stone walls and the high ceiling as all eight men flinched. "A century and more we nurtured, protected, defended, fed the American colonies! They have grown rich on British wealth and British blood! And what in return? They have wounded us!" His face was flushed, eyes alive, voice too high as he slammed his open palm on the table and repeated himself. "How *dare* they!"

He paused as his words echoed, and he trembled as he slowly brought himself under control. He drew and exhaled a great breath before he continued. "Today we are going to address the bringing of our errant offspring to heel. To do so will require what I calculate will be extremely frank and painful admissions of our own willingness to accept fiction as fact when it pleased us, and to remain blind to what was so plainly before us when it was convenient to do so."

Every man at the table felt the brutal cut. They blanched, and their eyes diverted as the king looked into their faces before continuing.

"I shall attempt to lay out some of the principal events that will provide an appropriate background for my conclusions."

His aide handed him a document, which the king quickly scanned and then laid on the table before him.

"For seven years we waged war with France and her Indian allies to save our colonies, and we won at a high price in lives and money."

His aide handed him a note and he glanced at the figures.

"The national debt was 122,603,376 pounds when the French surrendered. Bankrupt, my lords! We drove the empire into virtual *bankruptcy* to save our colonies, and our armed forces sacrificed thousands of lives."

He cleared his throat and went on. "They prospered because we brought them into the world trade centers, and under our protection they became strong, wealthy. The time came when it was just and fair for them to pay their share of the burdens of success, and Parliament was most benevolent in inventing the lightest tax levy in the entire empire for our young and tender colonies. And what was their response? They destroyed the tax stamps and hung the tax collectors in effigy!"

For a moment he struggled again for control. "We sought no reprisal. With the fond heart of a mother towards a stubborn but beloved child we abandoned the Stamp Act but felt compelled to pass the Declaratory Act, which stated that the empire retained the power to bind the colonies in all cases whatsoever. Accordingly we levied the Townshend Acts, which were but slight taxes on imports. We were forced to send troops to maintain the peace, and they attacked them with sticks and stones and snowballs, and when the troops defended themselves, they called it a massacre. 'The Boston Massacre.' Did they expect our soldiers to do *nothing* in the face of a maniacal mob intent on destroying them?"

He was breathing heavily, face flushed. "But again, in our compassion we repealed the Townshend Acts and left remaining only a miniscule tax on their tea. And what did they return for our kindness? They threw three shiploads of tea into Boston Harbor, and then defied Parliament when demand was made of them to pay for their insurrection."

His aide passed him another document, and he quickly glanced at it and bobbed his head violently. "Then we heard the radical voices raised against us, and they left us no choice. Parliament passed a series of acts that should have brought the colonies to their senses and made them realize that, until they came to heel, they would feel the consequences of their rebellion. We closed down Boston Harbor, and Boston ceased to function as a major port of commerce."

His aide passed him two documents, and as he scanned them, the eight men moved on their chairs and cast guarded glances at each other, uneasy, nervous, frantically trying to make sense of why the king had thus far said nothing that they had not known for months, years. He continued and they settled down, hanging on his every word, waiting for something, anything, that would suddenly burst forth to clarify what was so far meaningless rhetoric.

The king tossed one of the two documents onto the tabletop and it skittered to a stop. None reached to touch it.

"They called those laws the Intolerable Acts, and the voices of the radicals multiplied and fairly screamed, 'Tyranny.' Samuel Adams. John Adams. Hancock. Patrick Henry." His voice was raised, his jowls trembling as he paused to breathe deeply. The eight men did not stir, caught up in the sudden passionate explosion.

" 'Liberty!' they cried. They have enjoyed more liberties under the kindly hand of the mother empire than any colonies in history. If they are given any more liberty, they will *drown* in it. What did they do then to strike back at the empire? Lost in their own infantile world of political fantasy, they organized a Continental Congress! Recently they drafted and sent to us their Olive Branch Petition." He thrust out his hand and his aide placed a document in it.

"Here is a copy." The document went sliding onto the tabletop to join the others, and King George thrust his arm forward, pointing an accusing finger at the document. "With all their prating of 'liberty,' now they have the gall to pretend to approach me on bended knee, groveling before me, beseeching my mercy, begging me to intervene between my colonies and my own government in Parliament! How dare they! Do they think they can mock me to my face? They did not even have the integrity to declare that this document, this petition, is the work of their Congress! Their gimcrack Congress is nothing more than a gathering of men whose sole ambition is to jostle their Congress into my throne and pretend to rule the empire by my side!"

He paused to gather his thoughts. "But well before they sent this so-called Olive Branch Petition, in their state of delusion they began preparations to engage the empire in war. We, my lords, *we* concluded that if any sane man were given one hundred years, he could not invent a thought so far removed from the light of reason. We inquired into the hard truth regarding the radicals and were assured they were only a small but loud segment of the colonial population, certainly nothing to raise concern. We inquired regarding their militia, and were told the soldiers were rather effeminate, totally undisciplined, almost without musketry or cannon, ill-clothed, with officers who had been farmers and fur traders and merchants until the day they joined. We were told most of them were poor rabble who could never threaten our army and navy."

He paused, and North, and then Germain, suddenly sucked in air as the thought struck home. *He's going to crush them. He's going to send an army and a navy, and he's not going to stop until there are no more radicals or colonial militia left.* Their faces turned white with the sudden, sure conviction. At the sound of their gasps, King George studied each man for a moment, and he knew they had somehow divined where he was going with them. The corners of his mouth turned upward for one fleeting moment before he moved on.

"We accepted what we were told because we wished to accept it. Send over a few troops and flex our muscles—they'll come to heel soon enough. So we sent over some troops. They responded by preparing for war. General Gage executed our plan to take their arms and ammunition and capture two of their leaders, Adams and Hancock, and put down the insurgents before they had begun to fight."

His face dropped and he shook his head and spoke with quiet intensity. "Lexington. Concord. Their militia gathered overnight and took down Gage's army in a single day! The longest running ambush in the history of the North American continent."

For a moment his mouth clenched and then relaxed. "But was this the only consequence of our self-deception and indolence?"

He leaned forward, and his eyes were slits, points of light, cutting to the core of each man like a sword.

"Three weeks later forty-five colonials took Fort Ticonderoga from us without firing a shot." He spoke quietly but his voice pierced. "Benedict Arnold with Ethan Allen and his Green Mountain Boys." A look of cynical disgust flitted across his face. "How utterly quaint. How colonial. The Green Mountain Boys. A gathering of undisciplined, drunken illiterates, I was told. Fort Ticonderoga! Key to control of the vital Hudson River corridor. Lost in less than five minutes because we convinced ourselves the Green Mountain Boys were nothing."

Humiliated, stripped of any pretenses by the verbal assault of their king, not one man in the cabinet dared move.

King George stared at them for a full fifteen seconds in thick, stifling silence, then continued. "We learned of Lexington and Concord and of the fall of Ticonderoga, and what did this august body do about it? We let them fortify Breed's Hill and Bunker Hill near Charlestown, and then we unleashed the full strength of Gage's forces to annihilate them. And they nearly annihilated Gage! They chopped his army to shreds and then retreated from the high ground only when they ran out of ammunition—walked away on their own terms. General Gage sustained forty percent casualties at the hands of this gathering of rabble that could never become an army, or so we had convinced ourselves. Unbelievable!"

Every man in the cabinet dropped his head in shame to stare at his own hands while the blood drained from his face. They dared not raise their faces.

For a moment the king covered his mouth with his hand as he once again organized his thoughts. "And what are our current circumstances in the colonies? Their Congress has appointed a forty-three-year-old Virginia foxhunter named George Washington as commander in chief of the Continental army, and he has surrounded Boston, with General Gage's forces inside his circle—essentially laid siege to our armed forces. And thus far he has succeeded."

He rose and paced for half a minute before he settled back on his chair. The room wallowed in a silence filled with pain.

"George Washington has bottled up our forces! He has them surrounded—running short of all supplies and unable to break out of the circle to get more. And what did this ministry do about it?" His face was nearly contorted in rage. "August twenty-third I issued a proclamation declaring the colonies in rebellion, and then this ministry *did nothing about it!* With half of our army having becoming casualties at Lexington and Concord and Bunker's Hill, and with a proclamation giving this august body the official support of the Crown and of all England, *we did nothing!*" He thrust out his hand, his aide jammed the next document into it, and the king threw it skittering onto the table. "There it is! A proclamation that has thus far been absolutely useless."

His chest heaved in anger, neck veins extended, face red. The echo of his words died, and no one breathed while the king battled to regain control and then once again spoke quietly, with restraint.

"My lords, may I now come to the point. Twelve short years ago—February 10, 1763—we ended the Seven Years' War by the Treaty of Paris. We gained, and France lost, Canada and the colonies. The French were embittered, humiliated to the core of their national soul. Never have they forgotten or forgiven us for their loss of pride and national honor in the eyes of the world— Russia, Austria, Sweden, Prussia, Spain, and the others."

He paused and his aide handed him the last document. "I think I need not remind you of the predictions of the French leader the duc de Choiseul, made in 1765." He laid the last document on the table before him. "There is his writing. He predicted the colonies we won in America would rise against us in an attempt to break free. He proposed that at the moment they did so, if France would ally herself with Spain, those two powers in combination with the Americans could regain supremacy of the seas, defeat us, and regain the colonies they had lost."

He looked into the eyes of each man for a moment, until he was certain they all remembered. "The duc de Choiseul erred in but one thing: his time calculations. He thought the rebellion of the colonies would come soon after 1765. Time has removed him from the politics of today, but in his place has risen the comte de Vergennes—less brilliant than the duc de Choiseul but blessed with patience and a bulldog determination. He has clung to the duc de Choiseul vision relentlessly, and today, my lords, as we sit here, Vergennes is watching every move, every development between the empire and the colonies, and he has steadily strengthened the ties between France and Spain. Should the slightest hint of opportunity present itself, it is a certainty France will join forces with any power to regain her national pride and honor by avenging the losses she suffered to us in the Treaty of Paris in 1763. To do so, she will have to defeat us."

He settled back in his chair and waited and watched. All eight men moved in their chairs, faces a stunned blank, and for the first time low murmuring began and then subsided.

"May I put it in a nutshell, my lords. I believe France saw what we refused to see and has prepared to do what we have not. I am convinced France is prepared to join the colonies to defeat us the instant she can." King George rose to his feet and waited for absolute silence before he spoke again. "And, my lords, it is not going to happen."

North leaned back while he desperately struggled with the question of whether King George had essentially given him notice that he had failed in his leadership so violently that he was being replaced, and for a moment felt a sense of giddy relief at the thought of being free of the burden. Germain's chin settled as he pondered whether the king had just delivered some subtle message to him that he had somehow missed.

The king broke into their thoughts and spoke slowly, touching each word with unmistakable emphasis. "I now charge this cabinet with the total responsibility of raising a military force of not less than thirty thousand trained regulars, the same to be transported to the colonies with not less than thirty men-of-war for purposes of supporting the ground forces with their cannon. This shall be done during the winter season, and the armada and the ground forces shall be in the colonies no later than the spring of next year, 1776. As soon after their arrival as possible, our forces shall proceed to destroy this 'Continental army' and all resisting militia until their total and unconditional surrender. Once battle is begun, it shall not cease until our objective is reached. Am I absolutely clear?"

North closed his eyes as the weight of it sunk in, and he nodded his head in silence. Germain licked suddenly dry lips and swallowed hard.

"I leave the details to you, however. Your recommendations of who shall command and the general plan of attack shall be delivered to me at the Queen's House no later than thirty days from today. Are there any questions?"

North glanced about the table, then turned back to the king. He spoke slowly so that his thick tongue could enunciate clearly. "No, Your Majesty. There are no questions."

"Good. I thank you, my lords." He continued as though reciting a meaningless prepared speech. "May I add, you have my full faith, full confidence, full support. Each of you has been called to this because of your proven abilities. You are not to shrink from this work. Your success is assured if you pursue this with vigor and determination. And, with success, you will enshrine yourselves forever with glory and the gratitude of England."

He made a gesture with his hand and his aide quickly began gathering the documents on the table. He turned from his chair, and the two elite palace guards quickly walked to his side and then led him out of the great room, leather boot heels clicking on the marble floor, with the aide hurrying behind, working to force the documents back into their pouch. When the great doors thumped closed behind the king, North drew a breath and slowly released it through rounded lips. Every face in the room was white with stunned surprise, and shocked exclamations rolled out to echo in the room.

North raised his hand and the talk dwindled and died. "My lords, this cabinet meeting is adjourned until ten o'clock on Thursday. I trust each of you will consider what impact His Majesty's directives will have on your department, reduce it to writing, and be prepared to commence the discussions and debates that will be necessary to accomplish what now must be done."

One rose to political power in England by learning the ruthless art of replacing the man ahead in the chain that led to the king's court or cabinet. Having arrived in a powerful and coveted position, one retained such by learning the equally ruthless art of stopping the man below. Survival lay in one's ability to hide the treachery and deceit behind a facade of innocence and virtue. There were no rules. Men and careers were destroyed without conscience by any means necessary in the desperate, murky shadows of political intrigues. Each man in the cabinet knew the terms of the political combat, and none intended to allow his standing with the king to be lessened by the plan the cabinet must now create.

Lord North ordered in enough scribes to record the general text of every speech, every suggestion, and the precise details of every issue and every vote taken on it. He had long since learned that nothing is so potent in a showdown before the king as a well-kept "minute" in which the comments of each speaker were available in hard, cold print. And no member of the cabinet had illusions of why the scribes were there. Later disavowals of how they voted or what they had said and any convenient loss of memory would be denied them. North was forcing them to the wall. They would perform or face the wrath of the king.

For more than twenty days the cabinet worked through calculations of how many ships would be required to transport thirty thousand troops, together with their muskets, cannon, horses, gun carriages, gunpowder, uniforms, clothing, medicine, and food in sufficient supply to sustain them for one year. It would require three hundred transport ships. In addition, the king had ordered thirty men-of-war to support the ground troops. Total—three hundred thirty ships. That having been established, North systematically and methodically charted out the issues that must be addressed and resolved.

Troops? Where were they to find thirty thousand troops? Take them from those assigned in Minorca? Gibraltar? No, that would seriously weaken the British presence in the Mediterranean. India? No, there were too few troops holding India as it was. The West Indies? Impossible—the Indies needed more troops to protect the taxes derived from the thriving sugar and rum industry. Scotland? Yes, use the Black Guard. Hire Russian conscripts? No, Catherine the Great had refused. Then Germans? Yes, get Hessian conscripts! Hesse-Cassel and Brunswick had consented. Seven pounds per head. Get them—as many as you can. Raid the pubs and docks and brothels. Find more.

Ships? Never had the British Empire required three hundred transport ships for one military effort, with thirty men-of-war for support. Where were they to be found? Call in some from the fleet in Gibraltar. The West Indies. Buy some from the Dutch. Build some. Forget the cost—get them.

Food and supplies? Contract for the salt beef and pork now, pay later. Hardtack. Sea biscuits. Wheat. Beans. Rice. Cattle. Sheep. Chickens. Lime juice. Fresh potatoes. Horses. Cannon. Rum. Muskets. Gunpowder. Soap. Utensils. Shot, both cannon and musket. Medicines. Fodder and oats for the horses and cattle and animals. Determine the quantities that are needed and contract for them now, pay later. Ignore the cost. Get them.

All of the men in the cabinet knew their political futures would stand or fall on the success or failure of their master plan to bring the American colonies into submission. And that being true, the fulcrum question was simple: to whom would they entrust the awesome responsibility of making it happen? It was clearly the most critical and politically explosive issue this cabinet would ever face. Lord North spent tense days and sleepless nights pacing the floor, then assembled the men.

Solemnly he faced them. "My lords, we shall commission Lord Amherst to assume command of our forces in America. His abilities as a military leader are without peer, as evidenced by his unequalled victories in the Seven Years' War. His popularity, capabilities, and dedication are beyond reproach."

The vote was unanimous. Lord Amherst was summoned to Lord North's office on Downing Street. He listened intently, traced the proposed plan on the maps spread on the huge table, pursed his mouth in deep reflection while he paced on the marble floor with his hands clasped behind his back, and returned to the table.

"My lords, I must respectfully decline for at least the following reasons. I have grave doubts England can maintain so large a force so far from home long enough to conclude peace. Also, it would be difficult for me to return to the colonies to crush them, after having been the one who saved them from the French. And last, I would very much prefer to remain in England for the balance of my life and not in the rather . . . um . . . raw colonies. I am truly sorry."

Stunned, with growing misgivings, the cabinet resumed debate that raged for days before final votes were taken. The scribes finished their flawless, minute entries. Lord North closed the books, reached for his feather quill, and penned the single most vital message of his career.

"May it please Your Majesty: The cabinet has finished a proposal which I am prepared to submit to Your Majesty for your consideration, at your pleasure. Your most humble and obedient servant, North." He pressed his seal into the heated wax and sent the sealed message by his private courier with six armed guards. The courier returned within the hour with a message under the king's seal.

"His Majesty presents his compliments to Lord North and declares that it would be his pleasure to receive Lord North's report tomorrow morning at nine o'clock in the Royal Chambers at the Queen's House."

At nine o'clock A.M. two of the palace guard ushered Lord North down the long, lavish marble hall from the entry of the Queen's House, heels clicking in perfect cadence on the polished floor, to stop before a thick door ornately decorated with the royal arms of the sovereign of the United Kingdom. One guard rapped lightly and, upon invitation from within, opened the door and Lord North entered.

"Your Majesty," he said, and bowed deeply, clutching a locked box of documents at his side.

At ten-thirty the king called for his guard, and Lord North was led from the grandeur of the room and back down the hall, where he was introduced into a library wherein the walls were lined with polished white ash shelves filled with books in every language. He sat on an upholstered chair beside an immaculately carved and polished table, heaved a sigh, and settled in to await the beck and call of his king. At one o'clock a servant entered to set on the side table a silver tray with strips of roast mutton, fruits, cheeses, and a crystal flask of wine. At four o'clock the two palace guards escorted him back to the presence of the king.

King George sat down in one of two facing chairs, with a small, low table between them. The meticulously drawn maps and documents, with the minutes of the cabinet meetings, were spread on a tabletop on the opposite side of the room.

"Be seated."

"Thank you, Your Majesty." North eased onto the chair facing the king. The tight smile on North's face belied the tremble in his stomach as he peered intently into the face of his king, seeking something, anything, of his thoughts. The king crossed his legs and leaned back, elbows on the chair arms, fingers interlaced.

"Let me be certain I understand your plan."

North leaned forward, focused.

"Abandon Boston, and take New York?"

"Exactly, Your Majesty. Boston is of no military importance. New York is clearly the economic and political center of the colonies. Take New York and we control the center."

"Divide and conquer? You intend sending a large force from Canada, down Lake Champlain and the Hudson River valley to Albany, while another large force comes from New York to join them?"

"Precisely. Take control of the Lake Champlain–Hudson River corridor, and we have divided the New England colonies from the middle and southern colonies. With the support of those loyal to the Crown, it will then be a simple matter of bringing the New England colonies into subjection, then the middle colonies, and finally the southern section."

"You have reliable estimates of how much of the American population remains loyal to the Crown?"

"We do. In the New England colonies, perhaps ten percent. In the south, thirty percent. But in New York, Your Majesty, half the population remains loyal to the Crown and will rise to our support when we arrive."

The king considered the figures before he pushed on. "You

intend giving command of our forces to General William Howe?"

North knew what was coming next, and a faint quiver of panic came and went before he made his answer. "Yes, Your Majesty."

King George lowered his hands, leaned forward slightly, and came directly to the question North most feared. "My information is that General Howe is a Whig, not a Tory. His declared political position is in sympathy with the colonies, not with me. Am I correct, or am I deceived?"

North smiled feigned confidence and did not hesitate. "That is correct, Your Majesty. The cabinet did a thorough investigation. It is all there in the minutes, beginning on page 288 and—"

The king cut him off. "I know where it is. My question is, why is this man being trusted when his personal political inclinations are clearly contrary to the objectives of the command in question? Besides, wasn't he in command at the debacle at Bunker Hill?"

North met him eye to eye. "At Bunker Hill, General Howe faithfully followed the orders of General Gage, contrary to his own inclinations. He is the most dedicated professional soldier in the empire, Your Majesty. If he does accept this command, there is no personal consideration, no political leaning, no distraction that will color his absolute and complete commitment to following the letter of his orders. He has proven himself in the Seven Years' War and every major conflict since."

The king's eyes dropped for a moment. "You feel it prudent to give command of our support naval forces to his brother, Viscount Richard Howe?"

North did not hesitate. "Absolutely. No admiral in our navy stands higher in the eyes of his peers. Neither William nor Richard is a creature of politics. Each is a pure militarist. We can do no better."

"You intend using Brigadier General John Burgoyne? You have no question about his reliability? My information is he has a penchant for the ladies and champagne and high living. He writes plays—referred to as 'Gentleman Johnny.' Can he rise above those weaknesses?"

"Without question. I am certain Your Majesty recalls his heroic performance in defense of Portugal, when he led the surprise raid on Valencia d'Alcantara and defeated the Spanish." North leaned forward, eyes shining. "But his greatest asset is, he has served in northeastern Canada! He knows the country and the native Indians. He is uniquely qualified to lead our force down the Lake Champlain–Hudson River corridor. And, Your Majesty, he is ambitious. He wishes to rise and make his name, and perhaps secure honors in the bargain. He will do so in your service, and most energetically. His ambition will more than offset his penchant for dalliance and playwriting."

King George gathered his thoughts. "You recommend General Henry Clinton? A winter attack on the port of Charleston in South Carolina?"

"Yes, Your Majesty. General Clinton's father was governor of Long Island, across the East River from the city of New York. General Clinton played there as a child—knows the people and the geography from earliest memory. He understands the Dutch who settled Long Island. He will be invaluable in our plan to take New York. And by taking Charleston before we attack New York, we will have established ourselves in the south, preparatory to the divide-and-conquer action."

"I have no thought about General Lord Charles Cornwallis." Again King George paused and locked eyes with North. "Your estimated cost exceeds sixty million pounds. How do you plan to get the money?"

"Borrow it, at first, then recover it by levying taxes on the colonies commensurate with the taxes all of your subjects have been paying. Your Majesty knows our tax structure has long favored the colonies with the lightest taxes in the kingdom. When they are subdued, that will cease. They will repay the loans."

The king rose, face clouded in deep thought, and slowly paced to the far wall, then returned to his chair and leaned forward. "Draft an order for my signature, authorizing you to proceed with your plan. However, I want it understood from this moment that

General William Howe shall not have power to arrange terms of peace, should the colonies surrender. I and I alone shall have that power. Nor shall he have power to pardon, except on conditions that I shall dictate. You will see to it his written commission includes those limitations. Is there any question of what I have said?"

"None, Your Majesty. I understand and I concur completely."

The king drew a great breath of air and exhaled it as he stood. "Thank you for all your efforts. I commend the cabinet. Tell them. I will await the documents I must sign to authorize you and those you have recommended for command."

Relief flooded through North's body like a great wave. "Yes, Your Majesty. I shall begin today."

North watched as the king took his leave, with his entourage of personal bodyguards and his aide, arms loaded once again with all the documents; and then North closed his eyes and exhaled a great breath. He made his way to his own waiting coach, and laid his head back against the leather-covered cushion and closed his eyes as the coach swayed into motion for the return to his office. In the late evening twilight, he was seated alone in the gloom and silence of his own quarters before the awful realization materialized in his brain.

The mightiest armada in the history of the world must be assembled, and it must cross the Atlantic Ocean in the winter, to subdue an entire population in a raw, sprawling country many times larger than England, and it must be accomplished in less than five months. And should he fail, his political career would end, either by the pleasure of the king or by his own resignation. It was full dark before he rose and lighted a lamp.

Notes

Buckingham House—dubbed the Queen's House by King George III after he bought it for his wife—was one of the king's residences and was not far from the famous Whitehall district, Pall Mall, and St. James's Square, where many of the powerful men in the king's cabinet both resided and had office space. A description of this area and the persons who resided and officed there is found in Mackesy, *The War for America*, beginning on p. 54.

Also, excellent descriptions of the Thames River, the miles of docks, the important role the river played in England's history, the Whitehall area, and the other historically important places in London are found in Pool, *What Jane Austen Ate and Charles Dickens Knew*, beginning on p. 26.

The titles of the eight men constituting the cabinet of King George III are found in Mackesy, *The War for America*, in a freestanding diagram on pp. xxviii–xix following the preface to the book. The descriptions of the physical appearances and general personalities of both Lord North and Lord Germain are found on pp. 20–21 and 47–54, respectively. The limitation on the king's ability to force the cabinet to function is described on p. 23.

Buying military rank in England during the Revolutionary time period was common. Stuart, the son of Lord Bute, wrote that he had purchased the rank of major for 2,600 pounds, and later was buying the rank of lieutenant colonel for over 5,000 pounds (see Higginbotham, *The War of American Independence*, p. 124).

The British national debt in 1763, when Great Britain concluded the peace of the Seven Years' War with France, was 122,603,336 pounds (see Higginbotham, *The War of American Independence*, p. 34).

In 1776, England's empire included a presence in India, Africa, the West Indies, Gibraltar, Minorca, and the American colonies, all of which must be maintained at tremendous cost (see Johnston, *The Campaign of 1776*, part I, pp. 26–27).

The taking of Fort Ticonderoga on May 10, 1775, by Ethan Allen and his Green Mountain Boys, with Benedict Arnold, is described in Higginbotham, *The War of American Independence*, p. 67. See also Leckie, *George Washington's War*, pp. 120–21, for a somewhat whimsical report of the incident.

The titles by which people in all classes of English society were addressed are described in Pool, *What Jane Austen Ate and Charles Dickens Knew*, commencing on p. 38.

The hiring of mercenary soldiers by one nation from another was common practice in Europe in the Revolutionary time period. King George III attempted to hire Russian soldiers to fight the Americans, but Catherine the Great of Russia declined. The king then hired German soldiers from Hesse-Cassel and Brunswick, which soldiers were known as Hessians (see Higginbotham, *The War of American Independence*, p. 130; Mackesy, *The War for America*, pp. 61–62).

The general plan for defeating the Americans finally agreed on by King George III and his cabinet was to take New York City and have a major force proceed north up the Hudson River valley to meet a second force coming down from the north, which would isolate the northern colonies. The British forces would then conquer the colonies in sections—northern, middle, and southern. Despite his personal leanings in favor of the American cause, General William Howe was made commander of the British forces in America (see Mackesy, *The War for America*, pp. 58, 75–76; Stokesbury, *A Short History of the American Revolution*, p. 82; Higginbotham, *The War of American Independence*, p. 148 and following).

The estimates of the number of Tories, or Americans who remained loyal to the king in the various sections of the colonies, are found in Mackesy, *The War for America*, p. 36.

CHAPTER II

★ ★ ★

*H*e saw the red coats with the white crossed belts and the lowered bayonets breaking through the haze of gun smoke, and he frantically jammed the ramrod down his musket barrel to seat the ball on the powder and he knew it was too late—too late. In strange silence, orange flame spurtled from the British musket, white gun smoke blossomed, and the solid hit of the huge .75-caliber lead ball knocked Billy Weems down backwards. The scalding pain numbed his side, and he tried to gather his legs to stand and face the running British regulars, and he could not understand why his legs would not work. He realized he had lost his own musket, and he groped in the tall April grass and flowers and dandelions of the beautiful green field west of the Lexington Green but could not find it. He saw the sun glint shining on the British bayonet and he tried to raise his legs to kick it away, and they would not rise. He saw the sweat on the man's face and the kill-lust in his eyes and the silent shout as the man came upon him, and Billy cried, "Matthew!" but there was no sound as the bayonet plunged stinging deep into his middle, and then strong hands were shaking him and he was screaming, and then he saw his mother's face in the lamplight. She was shaking him by the shoulders and talking sharp to him. He shouted, "Matthew!" once more and suddenly sobered and stared wild-eyed into his mother's face, and could not understand how she got to the battlefield, where a thousand muskets were silently blasting and cannon were thundering without sound, and why he was seeing her in the dark when there was bright sunshine and it was midafternoon.

He lunged from his bed, threw his mother to the floor, and fell across her, shouting, "Keep down! Keep down!" He held her to the floor, and then Trudy was beside him, crying and jerking frantically at his nightshirt. He reached to grab her, and she cried, "Billy, Billy, it's me, it's me." He looked past her into the shadows in his room, and suddenly he slumped and all the air went out of him. He looked at his mother, and slowly his brain returned from the battlefield near Lexington to his bedroom. He reached to take her into his arms, and he held her while Trudy sobbed at his side.

Gently his mother pushed him back and put her hands on his sweat-streaked face. "It's all right, Billy. It's all right. It's all right. It's me. You're home. You're safe." He turned tortured eyes to his terrified sister and gathered her shaking eight-year-old body to him and held her tightly, and she threw her arms about his neck as she sobbed.

For a time they stayed in the yellow lamplight as they were, until Trudy quieted and drew back from him. He gently touched her hair. "Are you all right?" he asked. She nodded her head while her chin quivered.

His mother rose, and he stood, and she put her hand on his chest. "You're soaked with sweat." She threw back his bedcovers and felt the sheets. "And so is your bed. Change from the skin out and come out to the kitchen. I'll make coffee." She lighted the lamp in his room and turned to go, when he stopped her. "Did I hurt you?" She shook her head and motioned to Trudy, and they walked out of the room together, her lamp held high.

Billy slowly sat on the edge of his bed, hunched forward, head bowed. *Fourteen months. One year and two months. My side is healed. But when do the nightmares—the memories—stop? The killing—the dead men with dead eyes—I can still see their staring dead eyes. Accusing.* He shuddered and rose to his feet, still slightly favoring his right side where the British ball had ripped nearly through his body and the bayonet had gone deep during the running ambush of April 19, 1775. Fourteen months ago.

In the time he spent wiping sweat with the damp cloth, the memories rose clear as though it were yesterday. Eleven o'clock the night of April 18, 1775—the orders from Joseph Warren—the British are crossing the Back Bay to get Adams and Hancock at Lexington and then on to Concord to get our munitions—go to Concord to stop them. Running, trotting through the night with militia from Boston through fields and over hills and across streams to avoid the British on the roads—waiting at Concord for John Dunson and Matthew (John's eldest son) and Tom Sievers— John his neighbor and Matthew his most beloved friend from earliest childhood, the brother he never had. April nineteenth they lined the ridges that ringed the beautiful Concord Green, and they met the flower of the British army at the North Bridge. They faced them and the muskets blasted, and the British gaped in disbelief as the colonials stood their ground and poured a second volley into the red-coated column. Officers and regulars dropped all up and down the orderly lines, and the stunned British turned. Their retreat became a rout as they ran in panic through an eighteen-mile corridor of swarming minutemen and militia they could not see in the woods and behind stone walls and in creekbeds and behind trees at Meriam's Corner, the Bloody Angle, Parker's Revenge, Fiske Hill, Lexington, and Menotomy. The British reached the outskirts of Charlestown and Boston as the sun set, a decimated, beaten army, near total annihilation.

Billy reached for a fresh, dry nightshirt, and felt the slightest tremble in his hand as the bright, hot image of the muzzle flash of the British musket flitted before his eyes once again, and he felt the hit of the big musket ball and then the shocking sting of the bayonet, and then the jumbled snatches of senseless memories of John carrying him to a home in Lexington and Matthew staying with him, holding his hand, saying over and over, "You'll be all right, I'll stay, I won't leave you." Then six weeks of high fever, the dreams of rows of redcoats and muskets, and the deep ache as his body battled for life and wasted as it used all its strength to heal the bullet and bayonet holes. He still smelled the stench of bandages heavy with gray drainage from the wounds as they slowly closed and knitted. And always he could see the stolid face of his mother, and the strained faces of Matthew, his mother, Margaret, and his sister Brigitte, who came to bring meals for Billy's family, place cool hands against his hot forehead, and sit quietly.

And he remembered the times he awoke in the night to find Matthew in the deep shadows of a dimmed lamp, kneeling at the foot of his bed, hands clasped before his bowed head. "Almighty God, I beg of thee, please don't take Billy. Please don't take him."

The clear, piercing voice of a blue jay scolding somewhere outside his bedroom window startled him, and he glanced at the clock on the nightstand beside his bed. Just past four o'clock A.M. Dawn would break soon. While he shrugged into the nightshirt, he remembered the day the fever stopped and a ravenous hunger settled in. Soup, then vegetables, and finally meat. Never enough.

"Billy, are you coming?"

He walked down the hallway and through the arch to the kitchen, where his mother lifted the steaming coffeepot from the black stove, set the draft on the firebox beneath the plates, and walked to the dining table. They sat opposite, with Trudy at the end. Outside, the blue jay chortled again, and another answered, and then another as they argued territorial rights at the approach of a new day. Dorothy poured the pungent coffee into their cups, and while they added milk and sugar and stirred, Billy studied his mother.

Dorothy Weems was not pretty. Born Dorothy Pulliam, and raised in the fishing port of Gloucester, she was in her third year of school when she understood in her nine-year-old heart that her thin-lipped, broad-nosed face was plain, and her body was square, stout, unattractive, and she did not know how to move with grace. At age fourteen she understood the pain of boys averting their eyes when she passed and cliques of chattering girls falling silent as she approached. She wept in the secrecy of her own small room, confused and bitter at the great secret that would explain why she had been born plain in a world that rewarded beauty. At age fifteen she accepted the cross borne by all who are not beautiful, and stoically began groping for anything that would give release from the gray hopelessness.

Slowly she learned that excelling commanded respect, if not acceptance, and she exhausted her body and mind relentlessly at whatever she undertook. She learned that silent smiles and quipped compliments were welcomed by others. And then she learned that the beautiful people needed listeners; she became an adroit master of the art of listening.

At age twenty she was a respected friend of half the young men in Gloucester and sweetheart to none. At age twenty-two she passed into spinsterhood. When she was twenty-four, a north Atlantic hurricane slammed into the Grand Banks and sank four of a small fleet of twelve Boston fishing boats, leaving the surviving eight boats with rigging in shreds, mainmasts snapped, hulls ruptured. The survivors limped into Gloucester for repairs.

First mate on one of the battered boats was a bull of a man named Bartholomew Weems. Short, legs like oak stumps, arms that could hoist a 360-pound barrel of salt cod onto his thick shoulders and neck and carry it up the gangplank, Bartholomew Weems's square face was plain, homely. He was twenty-nine years of age, and his life on the sea had weathered his ruddy complexion. His beard was red, his hair sandy, his mouth too big, his teeth large and square.

The following Sunday he saw Dorothy Pulliam in the second row at the small white church. He worked his hat with awkward hands after the meeting, shifted his feet and looked at the cobblestones in the church walkway, and stammered when he introduced himself. One week later he faced her once again after church. His boat would be finished in two days and he would leave for Boston. Would she allow him to write to her?

Yes.

Six weeks and six letters later he once again fronted her after church. He had sailed from Boston to see her. He had a question. She met his eyes. Would she ever consider marriage? coming with him to Boston?

Yes.

When?

She would be packed in three hours.

The minister at the church married them before they boarded the boat for their return to Boston.

He had the peculiar, lonely ways of a bachelor and the crusty language and crude manners of a fisherman, but he loved her with all his heart. With wisdom born of her own loneliness, she was blind to his shortcomings, and lived for the time his fishing boat returned and they were together. She miscarried their first child; the second was stillborn. Their third was a husky, ruddy-faced, barrel-chested boy who came howling into the world with a shock of reddish hair, unmistakably his father's son. When Billy was eleven, their second child was born, a blue-eyed, dark-haired girl, Trudy. Eight months later a somber-faced man stood in Dorothy's doorway and refused to raise his eyes as he worked his hat with his hands and told her the fishing fleet had lost two boats in a storm off Newfoundland. Bartholomew Weems was among the missing.

She lived for Billy and Trudy. She threw herself into anything she could do to make an honest living. Under the watchful eye of crusty old Doctor Walter Soderquist, she learned enough about birthing to become a midwife and to do some practical nursing. She taught herself fine needlework and crocheting and to knit mittens so tight they were said to turn water. With an old quill and ink, she worked by candlelight after the children were in bed until she could write invitations, announcements, and business cards with the beautiful French scroll so perfectly done that the quality exceeded that of a printing press. Guided only by her eye and her rug hook, she could soon transform a pile of discarded rags into tightly braided rugs, oval or round, any size, with unbelievable designs. Slowly her work became known, then sought after. She trained Billy to help in all she did, and while yet an adolescent he developed a steadiness.

Their small brick home and their yard, with fruit trees and the flower garden, were clean, well ordered. The salt-sea air blistered the paint on the white picket fence, and every second year Billy scraped and repainted it. Inside, the small parlor was unpretentious but pleasant, and the dining room, with its great, open stone fireplace for heat and cooking, was immaculate. The old wood-burning stove in the kitchen was painted black every second year when the fence was painted white. They wasted nothing. They were not wealthy; neither did they want.

When Billy was thirteen, Dorothy knelt with him and Trudy for evening prayers, and with hands clasped before her face she turned to him. "Billy, in the name of Him to whom we pray this night, you must make a sacred promise to me."

He turned surprised, inquiring eyes to hers.

"You will never go to sea for a living."

He understood. "I promise."

One year later she acquired a position for him to clean the office of Potter and Wallace, who kept a counting house. Two years later he became a beginning apprentice.

Taller than either Dorothy or Bartholomew, plain, husky, strong as a bull, Billy was blessed with a carefree joy for life that was contagious. Before he could walk, his mother had become fast friends with Margaret Dunson, who lived two blocks away with her family, one of whom was Matthew, two months younger than Billy, taller, serious, intense. By age five Billy and Matthew had sensed that each was a rare complement to the other, and they became inseparable, each barging into the home of the other without announcement, accepted as one of the family. When Bartholomew was lost at sea, Matthew wept with Billy and slept on the floor next to him for more than a week. At school, bullies soon discovered the folly of picking on either one of them.

Dorothy raised her cup and tentatively sipped. "Nightmare gone?"

Billy nodded and raised his cup.

"Been nearly two months since the last one," she said. "They should stop soon."

"I wish they would. I'm sorry about them." He turned to Trudy. "I wish they didn't scare you so bad."

Trudy sipped at her coffee.

"Any pain left?" his mother continued.

"No. Only the things I see in my mind."

"With both armies gone to New York, those memories should go away."

Billy raised his cup. "I wish I could have seen the redcoats leave."

Dorothy nodded. "March seventeenth. Nearly three months ago. You were walking, but you couldn't stand straight. I couldn't let you walk that far."

"I heard them. And I guess I heard George Washington leave, too."

Dorothy sipped. "That was a little later."

"I don't know much about him."

"From Virginia. Plantation owner. He was a hero in the French and Indian wars. Surrounded Boston and drove Gage and Howe and their army out. They say he was made general of the whole army because he was from the south, and we needed someone who could bring the south and north together."

"I hope he can. Heard anything about what's happening in New York?"

Dorothy shook her head. "Some red-coated troops have already landed there, and rumor is they're expecting more. Many more."

Billy glanced at Trudy. Her hands were around her warm cup, while her head was bowed as she battled to keep sleepy eyes open. He looked at his mother.

"Let's get her to bed," Dorothy said, and pushed her chair back.

At the sound, Trudy's head rose. "Can't I sleep on the sofa? I hate being alone when you're both out here." Billy tenderly lifted her to the sofa and laid her down while Dorothy covered her with a quilt. She closed her eyes as they stepped silently back to the table. For a time they sat in the lamp glow, lost in their own thoughts. Outside, the blue jays again took up their morning disputes, and the robins joined in.

"Soon be dawn," Dorothy said. "Things will look better then. Things always look better in daylight than dark." She studied Billy for a moment, then finished her cup. "Want to go back to bed for an hour or two?"

He pursed his mouth. "No. I'll get a quilt and sit by Trudy. Somehow when I sleep in the rocker I don't dream as much."

"I'm going to lie down for a while." Dorothy brought a quilt from his bed, with his heavy felt house slippers, and watched as he draped the quilt over his shoulders and started to sit in the large rocker. "Put on your slippers. You'll get sick." She watched until he obeyed, then turned down the lamp and walked softly back to her bedroom. Billy leaned back and gently rocked in the chair for a time, watching the black curtains turn gray with the approach of sunrise. Gradually his head tipped forward and the rocking slowed, and stopped, and he slept.

He opened his eyes at the sound of felt slippers on the bare, polished hardwood floor and for a few moments struggled to understand where he was, and then he started and his head jerked up.

"Good morning," Dorothy said quietly. "Didn't mean to wake you."

The window curtains were bright. "What time is it?"

Dorothy glanced at the Dunson clock on the mantel. "Past seven-thirty. Beautiful morning. Don't wake Trudy."

He quickly pushed the quilt from his shoulders, stood, and glanced at the sleeping child breathing deeply on the sofa as he followed his mother into the kitchen. "Why didn't you wake me? I'll be late."

"For what? work? It's Sunday."

Billy shook his head, then exhaled a grunt and grinned. "Forgot the Lord's Sabbath."

Dorothy set the draft on the stove and thrust two more sticks of wood into the glowing coals. "The Almighty may forgive you this once if you will prepare for church. For now, get dressed and fetch four eggs from the root cellar. I'll get breakfast started."

They wakened Trudy, and with breakfast finished, Dorothy walked to the great fireplace with pine shavings in hand, used the small brass shovel to open the bank of coals from the previous night, and gently blew on them with the worn leather bellows until the first flame flickered. She added more shavings and then sticks of pine, poured water into a large black kettle on one of the swinging arms, added diced carrots and potatoes, replaced the heavy lid, and swung the pot back over the fire. Trudy helped rub thyme and allspice into a small shoulder of mutton, place it in a roasting pan, and carefully slide it into the wall oven built into the great fireplace.

At nine-forty A.M., dressed in his Sunday finery, Billy opened the front door and walked into the brilliant sunlight of the still, warm Boston June morning. He held the front gate for Dorothy and Trudy, then took his place, his mother on his arm, Trudy following, as they joined the parade wending its way to the church. Oak and maple lined the streets and yards, and overhead branches cast delicate filigrees of sun and shade on all who passed. Restrained greetings echoed across the narrow cobblestone street, and women turned to whisper to husbands and point.

They rounded the corner and walked up the brick entry and through the double doors of the white, high-steepled church to sit in their usual place behind the Dunson bench. Sunlight streamed through stained-glass windows high on the east side of the austere chapel, casting a wild patchwork of color inside. Margaret Dunson led her family to their usual bench, and Dorothy and Billy and Trudy leaned forward to exchange quiet greetings.

"Matthew?" Billy whispered.

"Still at sea," Margaret answered.

Billy touched Brigitte's shoulder. "Captain Buchanan?"

Brigitte turned enough to look at him from the corners of her eyes. "Ask me after church."

Silas's nasal voice stopped the buzzing. "Our opening hymn is on page thirty-seven of your hymnals, 'Now Thank We All Our God.' "

Billy quietly turned his head to study the vacant seats in the congregation. Ben Telford, captain in the militia, lost at Lexington. Joseph Warren, lost at Bunker's Hill. John Dunson, lost near Charlestown. Matthew, gone to sea in the service of the colonies. Tom Sievers, gone with the militia. Andrew Thomas, Jedediah Prowse, Albert Samuels, Daniel Cullens—all gone to New York with the militia. Gone to the fighting. He turned back and finished the singing, slipped the hymnal into the rack, and waited for Silas to announce his sermon.

In his Boston twang the Reverend Silas Olmsted offered a short prayer, then droned, "Our sermon today is from the book of Joshua, that great leader of the Israelites." He paused to open the cover of the huge Bible on his pulpit and peer through his spectacles, mouth pursed while he turned pages.

Without warning the tall double doors at the rear of the chapel burst open and everyone in the congregation started, then turned to peer. Silas jerked and then squinted into the rectangle of bright sunlight, unable to identify the silhouette of who had interrupted his Sunday services. Three men in militia uniforms had entered, and one marched down the polished hardwood of the center aisle, the sound of his clicking heels echoing slightly in the high-ceilinged chapel.

Silas's head thrust forward in recognition. "Lemuel, is that you?"

"It's me," the voice boomed. "Reverend, sorry to interrupt this way, but I haven't got much time, so I'll need to get straight to it. I am under orders of General George Washington, and I have to deliver this same message to other congregations in Boston this morning." On his shoulders were the gold epaulets of a general in the Massachusetts militia. He did not remove his hat with the gold braid trimming. He reached the podium and looked up at Silas. "May I talk?"

Silas stared down at him. "On what matter?"

"Here are my orders from General Washington." He thrust a folded letter up to Silas, who straightened it on his pulpit and read it, then nodded. "Go ahead."

The man turned, squared his shoulders, and spoke loudly. "For those of you who don't know, I'm Lemuel Hosking. I'm a general in the Massachusetts militia, here under written orders of General George Washington." He paused with the clear look of his own self-importance. "The general is in New York with the Continental army to defeat the regular troops of the Crown who are now gathering to *crush* us." He waited to allow the congregation time to savor the word *crush.* "I am ordered to raise a company of men from Boston to march to New York to drive the British into the sea. I intend doing it. You men in this congregation who are fit are expected to do your duty." He paced for a moment. "This war started right here in Boston. Brave men marched from here to Concord and Lexington, and to Breed's Hill and Bunker Hill."

Open murmuring and then talk broke out in the congregation, and Hosking allowed it to go unchecked for a minute, then raised his hands and it quieted. Dorothy glanced at Billy. He sat unmoving, eyes locked onto Hosking. Brigitte turned far enough to see his face, then straightened.

Hosking continued. "Some of those men gave their lives. It's up to us to carry on so that their sacrifice will have meaning. My adjutant will set up a table at the Old North Church tomorrow. Arrange your affairs. Come sign your name any time before you march out under the command of Colonel Israel Thompson. We have a list of the things you will need for the march and the battle. You leave Wednesday morning at eight o'clock."

He paused and gathered his thoughts, then turned to Silas. "Sorry I had to interrupt. Hope you understand." Silas bobbed his head once. Hosking saluted him, turned on his heel, and marched rapidly back up the aisle and out into the brilliant June sunshine. The doors thumped shut. For a moment silence gripped the chapel, and then open talk erupted. Silas patiently removed his spectacles and cleaned them with a handkerchief while the talk ran on, then mounted them back on his nose and raised a hand for silence.

"You all heard the announcement. Those of you who wish to go with General Hosking, sign up at the North Church tomorrow or Tuesday. Now, let's return to Joshua."

Billy leaned forward, eyes downcast, as the message from General Hosking settled in. *He was talking to me. Back to the fighting.* His face blanched as the scene flashed once more in his brain and the deepest fear he had ever known came surging. Meriam's Corner— crouched behind a stone wall with Matthew and John and Tom— leveling his musket—burying the sight in the midsection of a red-coated regular—jerking the trigger—the solid kick—watching the soldier buckle—the terror in his eyes as he died. The dead, accusing eyes! The horrible searing of his conscience—*I have killed— sinned against God and man.* And they had caught the redcoats again and again, and he had mechanically locked out all feeling as he loaded and fired and watched men die.

Sweat rose on his forehead, and he leaned back, moving his legs and arms, unable to sit still with the terrible torment inside. *I cannot do it again!*

Dorothy looked at him, saw his eyes, his white face, the sweat, and she sensed the pain that was destroying him. She did not move or speak. Silas moved on with his sermon, aware of the unrest in the congregation as they pondered and weighed the message Lemuel Hosking had delivered.

"And so it was that the great Jehovah chose Joshua to lead the children of Israel into the promised land." Silas closed his Bible, raised his head, and announced, "We will join in our closing hymn." The singing ended, and Silas bowed his head and pronounced the benediction on the service. With his loud "Amen" the sounds of chairs sliding and of benches creaking filled the chapel as the congregation rose and the undercurrent of talk began.

Billy stood and Dorothy touched his arm. "What's wrong, son?"

Billy shook his head and gestured toward the door, when Brigitte turned and faced him squarely. "You're white as a sheet and sweating! Your wounds again?"

"No, I'll be all right. Just need to get outdoors for a few minutes."

Margaret Dunson studied him with narrowed eyes. "It's something else, isn't it? What Lemuel said?" Billy locked eyes with her for a moment but said nothing as he started working his way out to the center aisle of the church. Margaret grasped his arm and stopped him. "Billy, will you tell me later?"

He looked her in the eye. She was his "second mother," who knew him for the happy, carefree, outgoing boy he had been until they brought him home from Lexington in a two-wheeled hay cart, more dead than alive. He had never withheld a secret from her, or from Matthew or John or Brigitte. He nodded and kept moving. Margaret exchanged glances with Dorothy, then spoke to Brigitte. "Bring the twins. Caleb, give me your arm."

With his mother on his arm and Trudy following, Billy worked his way out the doors into the brilliant sunlight. He answered tersely when spoken to as he made his way through the milling congregation and down the brick walkway, and turned the corner. Only then did Dorothy slow him and speak quietly. "Is it being wounded again, or maybe being killed, or is it doing the killing?"

Billy stared downward as they continued walking. "The killing. I don't think I could do it again."

As they continued, Dorothy said, "It's a terrible thing. We'll talk later."

Dorothy and Trudy set the steaming leg of mutton and vegetables on the table, and Billy came to sit silently at the head. Dorothy offered grace, and served portions on their plates. Billy picked at it but ate little. Trudy cleared the dirty dishes into a pan of hot, soapy water on the kitchen cupboard, while Dorothy put the remainders in covered bowls and walked out the back door, down the seven steps, and into the cool of the root cellar, where she placed the bowls on shelves.

A somber, gray sense of foreboding settled inside the house, and Dorothy sat down in the rocking chair with the Bible while Trudy went to her room. Billy moved nervously about, first to his room, then back to the parlor, where he read the titles of books on the bookshelf but selected none. He went out into the yard to wander about, looking first at the flower beds, then the green nubs of apples and apricots on the fruit trees; then he came back into the parlor. Dorothy watched and waited. With the sun settling behind the trees to the west, Billy sat down at the dinner table and stared unseeing at his hands as he slowly worked them one with the other.

Dorothy closed her Bible, rose from the rocker, and sat next to him. "Billy, you have to settle this thing."

He raised tormented eyes. "Kill again? I can't."

"There are some things more sacred than mortal life."

He shook his head. "I only know I can't bear the thought of taking a man's life again." An involuntary shudder ran through him.

"Could you do it if it were the will of the Almighty?"

He looked at her for long moments, then dropped his eyes without answering.

"Could you do it if there were something more valuable than mortal life?"

Slowly he formed his answer. "I know what I felt when I was hit and took the bayonet. The pain was bad, but believing I was going to die was a feeling no man should have. I saw it in the eyes of men I shot, so close I heard them whine and beg for their mothers. No matter what, I don't think I could do that to a man again. Taking the life of another human being is evil." He shook his head, unable to say it more clearly.

As with all true mothers, in her heart Dorothy Weems felt the deep stab of her son's fear, his pain, and more. She felt the sick dread that she had failed him. She had given everything that was in her to be both a mother and a father to him, but she had known all along that nature had intended a boy to have a father to teach him the male things a woman cannot. She buried her own anguish behind a calm exterior and continued. "I know. But are there times it's necessary?"

"I only know it's something I can't do."

"What do you think this trouble with England is about?"

"They say it's because we are ungrateful. We say it's for liberty. But no matter where the truth lies, the result is the same for me."

"Did you talk with Matthew before he left to go fight on ships?"

"Yes."

"What did he say about taking life?"

"He hated it."

"But he went."

"His father was killed by the British. He said he had to go."

"Matthew? Revenge?" Deep surprise showed in her face.

"No, not revenge. He's above that. He said he went to John's grave the night they buried him, and a powerful feeling came to him that he had to go resist the British."

"Even if he hated it?"

"Yes."

"What do you think your father would say?"

"I don't know. I can hardly remember him."

Dorothy straightened, and for a long time they sat, him staring at his hands, her watching him while in her mind she groped for someone, something that could give him what he needed and that she could not give. She stood. "Maybe you should go talk with Silas."

Billy raised weary eyes. "I don't know what he could say."

"Then go find out."

Evening shadows were lengthening when Billy opened the

doors to the church. His footsteps echoed in the deserted chapel as he strode down the hardwood center aisle and knocked at the door of the living quarters of Silas and Mattie Olmsted. The wizened little reverend with the large hawk nose swung the door open and for a moment stared. "Billy? Are you all right?"

"I need to talk with you. Do you have time?"

Silas pursed his mouth for a moment and lowered his face to peer over his wire-rimmed spectacles. "Done something wrong?"

"No."

Silas stepped aside. "Come in." He turned and called, "Mattie, I'll have company for a while." Billy heard a door close as Silas gestured to a chair in the small, sparsely furnished parlor. "Sit down." Silas sat on a straight-backed chair and faced Billy, and waited expectantly.

Billy raised pleading eyes. "You heard Lemuel this morning. He said if you're fit, you have a duty to go join General Washington. I'm healed in my body, but not inside. I can't take another human life."

Silas remained silent, studying Billy's face and eyes, and Billy continued, forehead wrinkled with intensity as he selected his words. "I know the feeling of dying, and it's something I can't do to another human being." He stared into Silas's face, hoping.

"Did your mother send you?"

Billy nodded.

Silas's eyes dropped for a moment. Then he stood, turned his back on Billy, and walked across the small room and back before he once again sat down. "You're caught between a sense of duty and a fear of taking another man's life? Is that it?"

"Yes."

"Let's get to the bottom of it," Silas said, and lifted a battered, scarred Bible from the table beside his chair and opened it. "Exodus, chapter twenty, verse thirteen. 'Thou shalt not kill.' " He watched while Billy nodded understanding. "Now let's look at the book of Joshua. Chapter eight. Jehovah told Joshua to lift his spear against the city of Ai and take it. And Joshua did. Verse twenty-six. 'For Joshua drew not his hand back, wherewith he stretched out the spear, until he had utterly destroyed all the inhabitants of Ai.' " Silas stopped, and for long moments Billy sat in silence before Silas continued. "Jehovah had Joshua kill every living soul in the city of Ai. What does that teach us?"

Billy spoke thoughtfully. "We can take life when Jehovah commands it. But Jehovah hasn't commanded me to do it."

"Let's go on. War has always been and will always be, because at the bottom of everything is the eternal conflict between light and darkness, good and bad. There are but two champions. Jehovah for the light, Satan for the dark. It's as simple as that, even in heaven. There was war in heaven, between—"

Billy jerked upright. "War in heaven?"

"You've heard my sermon on it before."

"I thought it was fictional, not a real war. In heaven? In God's presence?"

"Absolutely. The devil rose up to overthrow God, and there was war."

"Shooting? Killing?"

"Let's read it." He thumbed to a worn page. "Book of Revelation, chapter twelve, verse seven. You read it." He handed the book to Billy.

" 'And there was war in heaven: Michael and his angels fought against the dragon; and the dragon fought and his angels, and prevailed not; neither was their place found any more in heaven. And the great dragon was cast out, that old serpent, called the Devil, and Satan, which deceiveth the whole world: he was cast out into the earth, and his angels were cast out with him.' "

Billy raised his eyes. "That isn't a myth? a parable?"

Silas shook his head. "Open warfare between the evil ones and the good ones. They were real individuals, not mythical. One was named Michael. How many others were in that war and who they were, I do not know. I only know it happened, and I know the battle they fought will go on forever, wherever there are those who worship darkness and those who worship light."

Billy swallowed and locked eyes with Silas, mesmerized by thoughts so new he neither moved nor spoke, and Silas continued. "No good man ever took joy in war, but no good man ever failed to rise against evil when it threatened. At Bunker Hill, I saw good men—"

Billy's head jerked forward and he blurted, "You were at Bunker Hill?"

"I was twenty feet from Joseph Warren when he fell. I wept, but I kept firing."

"You killed men at Bunker Hill? you, a man of God?"

"I did." Silas's voice was strong, steady. Billy stared, incredulous, as Silas went on. "You were home with fever dreams and deliriums. I know because I visited you every day, but I doubt you knew I was there, or at Bunker Hill."

"You gave your life to God. How could you kill another man?"

Silas remained silent until he knew Billy was ready, hanging on his every word, and then he spoke with quiet intensity. "I went to war against an eternal evil called tyranny, not against other men. If I could have found a way to fight tyranny without taking life, I would have done it. But there was no other way. The men I killed had become the champions of tyranny and were here to force it on me. I had no choice. They had to die or I had to yield my soul to tyranny."

Billy shook his head violently. "They weren't the champions of tyranny. They were soldiers, doing their duty. They were good men."

Silas nodded. "Good men who had been deceived."

"Deceived?" Billy's eyes were wide.

"Deceived! It's been happening since Adam and Eve. They thought they were right to be here, following king and God, but the hard truth is, they were here to force us to submit to the will of their Parliament in everything we did. That's tyranny."

"No, no," Billy exclaimed. "They were soldiers, not tyrants."

"Think, Billy. There are some things every man has to face and decide, whether he be king or peasant. The important things. At the very bottom of it all is the plain, simple choice on which we will all stand one day and be judged by God. Did I choose good or evil to build my life on? On that choice, some kings will fall and some peasants be exalted at God's judgment bar."

"Those red-coated regulars didn't choose to be evil! They chose to be soldiers."

"They made a choice without thinking deeply enough. It led them here to take away our liberty. That was wrong. Against God."

Billy's face was a study in pain, indecision. "Is it worth killing for? liberty?"

"Ask Sam Adams."

"I'm here asking you."

Silas drew and exhaled a great breath, then locked eyes with Billy. "Maybe more than any other thing on this earth. The evil one wants to own you, Billy, body and soul. That's tyranny at its worst. God wants you to grow the good that's in you until it fills you. That's liberty at its best. I will fight tyranny wherever it is. And if I must take a man's life to do it, then I will, even if it is a British regular who doesn't understand what he's doing. If I have to give my life, I will. I can't think of a way to say it any better."

"Are you sure, Silas? Sure?" Billy didn't breathe as he waited for the answer.

"Certain. Do you remember the day the regulars came to this church—held me and Mattie under armed guard?"

Billy nodded.

"Before he died, did John Dunson tell you about that night?"

"No."

"He came here with Warren. We talked in here after the British left. Something happened. I saw this war coming, so plain and clear. We wanted to be loyal to our king, but Parliament was forcing us to submit to tyranny. I saw it then. There would be blood. Then when the king refused to intervene for us and control Parliament, it was beyond hope. We had to fight. This land had to be free! Had to be! We all felt it. Overpowering. We knew. There was no way to deny it."

Silas paused to swallow against a lump in his throat as a feeling came creeping into the room, gradual, sure. Billy felt his arms begin to tingle.

"John knew then he had to go. His head said stay home with Margaret and the children, while his heart said the Almighty wanted him to go. It rose above anything to do with this earth. I think he had a premonition he would be killed, but it didn't matter. He went."

Billy sat white-faced, wide-eyed while the tingling slowly spread. Silas moved his feet and rubbed the palms of his hands together for a moment while he gathered his thoughts. His voice softened as he spoke. Billy lowered his eyes to listen. "Billy, if the Almighty had blessed Mattie and me with sons, we would have wished them to be like you and Matthew. What I've told you tonight—it's a sorry thing that you had to learn these things so young, and in war."

Billy raised his eyes and asked the final question. "Silas, are you telling me God wants me to take the life of another man?"

The answer was instant. "God wants you to put down the tyranny that is now threatening us. If you can do it without bloodshed, then do it. If you cannot, then lives must be taken, perhaps your own." Silas reached deep inside, searching for a way to give Billy peace, and it came. "Think about God's own Son. Jesus went to the cross and gave his life to make us free from the tyranny of sin. He thought it was worth it."

The strange feeling strengthened, and Billy slowly straightened, eyes wide as it spread. Neither man moved. They sat for a long time while the room seemed charged; and then the feeling receded, and then it was gone.

Silas broke the silence. "It was right that you hated taking life. It was right that you had to find an answer. You're good, Billy. Stay close to God. Pray often. Learn to trust the feelings he sends to you. You'll be fine. A good man."

Billy swallowed and stood. Silas stood and faced him, and then the little man threw his arms about Billy, and Billy held him, and for a few moments the two men shared the embrace before Billy relaxed and they separated. Without a word, Billy walked from the room, and his footsteps echoed in the dark chapel as he strode up the center aisle and out into the soft, warm air of a beautiful Boston night.

Lantern glow showed on the drawn window curtains as he pushed through the front gate and opened the front door. Dorothy was seated in her rocking chair, Bible in her hands, when he entered.

"Trudy?" Billy asked.

"Asleep." Dorothy closed the Bible and rose. "Your supper's in the oven. I'll get it. You must have had quite a talk." Billy sat down at the table while his mother set the hot food before him, and he said grace. She remained silent while she waited.

"I didn't know Silas was at Bunker Hill."

"I thought you knew."

Billy broke off a piece of bread and began to chew it thoughtfully. "He told me about the night John Dunson and Joseph Warren came to his place—when the British came to his church."

"I heard about it."

"He said he saw war coming, like in a vision."

"He did. It came. It's here."

Billy added cheese to the bread and continued chewing while he worked with his thoughts. "He talked about good and evil. He said the choice all of us have to make is which one we follow. Everything else that happens to us depends on how we decide."

Dorothy nodded but remained silent.

He slowed and stopped chewing for a moment. "Sometimes we even have to decide about taking life."

"He's right," Dorothy answered.

Billy shook his head. "It's all too new. I'll have to think about it, get used to it."

They talked on, Dorothy listening, watching, judging whether or not Silas had reached him. He finished his food and pushed the plate back. "Thank you. Let me help with the dishes."

She washed, he wiped, and they blew out the lamp and left the kitchen. Billy glanced at the clock on the mantel and stopped short. "Past eleven o'clock?"

Dorothy smiled. "Lost track?"

He grinned. "Where did it go?"

"Time for evening prayer."

They knelt together beside the dinner table, and Dorothy bowed her head and offered her thanks and supplications to the Almighty.

They rose together and walked towards the archway into the bedroom wing, when Dorothy slowed. "Margaret and Brigitte came. They want you to go see them tomorrow after work."

"What about?"

"They saw you in church. They're worried."

The Potter and Wallace counting house rented street-level office space in a square, plain brown brick building on King Street near the center of the Boston Peninsula. They opened at precisely 8:00 A.M. daily except for Sunday, and closed at 6:00 P.M. Cyrus Wallace had retired at age seventy-one. Hubert Potter bought him out, along with the right to use his name in perpetuity to preserve the firm intact. At age sixty-four, Hubert had semi-retired from active accounting and was spending most of his days managing the firm. Under his strict eye, there was little meaningless talk, little idle time between the five employees. A fair day's work for a fair day's pay. Hardheaded, dour New England discipline.

At five minutes past six P.M. Billy wiped the point of his quill on a piece of paper, closed his ink bottle, and put a large leather-bound ledger in its place on a shelf. He was walking towards the door, when the high-pitched voice of Hubert Potter stopped him. "Billy, could I see you?"

The door rattled when Billy closed it behind him and sat down in an ancient leather-bound chair facing Potter in his office. "Yes, sir?" Billy waited.

Corpulent, balding, Hubert Potter leaned back in his chair, thumb hooked in his watch pocket. "Something on your mind?

You seemed distant all day."

Billy's eyes dropped for a moment. "Lemuel Hosking has orders from General Washington to raise a company of men from Boston. He visited the churches yesterday."

"You considering it?"

Billy drew and released a great breath. "I don't know."

"How soon?"

"They leave Wednesday morning."

Hubert's shaggy eyebrows rose. "That quick?"

"They're expecting trouble in New York."

Hubert leaned forward, arms on his worn desk, and remained silent for a time before he spoke. "It's going to be hard on the office if you leave that quick. You have some big accounts."

"I know. I haven't decided yet."

"You better tell me as soon as you can."

"I will."

"See you in the morning."

Billy rose and walked out of the small, austere office, made his way across the main floor of the firm, and closed and locked the street door behind him. The heat of the day sat heavy in the streets, and he slipped out of his coat for the walk home. At the sound of the door opening, Dorothy called from the kitchen. "That you? Wash for supper."

She wiped the light perspiration from her face before sitting down with Billy and Trudy at the table to cold sliced mutton, cheese, homemade bread, and vegetable soup if they wanted it.

Billy offered grace and poured cool milk. "Hubert talked to me about leaving."

Dorothy laid down her fork. "What did you say?"

"I haven't decided."

"Be as fair with him as you can."

With supper and the dishes finished, Billy went to his room to change clothes, and called to Dorothy, "Am I still supposed to see Margaret and Brigitte?"

"They're waiting."

The heat of the day was past, and a cool, gentle salt breeze from the Atlantic stirred the leaves on the oaks and maples that lined the familiar, narrow cobblestone street. The sun had reached the western rim of the world and cast long shadows in the yards and on the fences and houses. An unexpected, quiet sense of peace came creeping as Billy walked, and for a time the war seemed to fade. He turned through the white picket gate leading into the yard with the carved wooden sign, "John Phelps Dunson, Master Clockmaker and Gunsmith," and rapped on the door.

Margaret Dunson opened the door and exclaimed, "Billy! Come in."

Unexpectedly a thousand warm memories of this home and of Margaret and the family came flooding, and Billy felt himself relax, smile at the lift in his spirit. He sat at the dinner table and Margaret sat facing him.

"Heard anything from Matthew?"

"He's still at sea."

"Is he all right?"

"His last letter said so."

"Coming home any time soon?"

"He never knows."

Billy reflected on it for a moment before he continued. "Mother said you came by."

Margaret sobered. "Did I see something bothering you in church yesterday?"

They both turned at the sound of Brigitte's bedroom door closing, and she entered through the archway to the bedroom wing and came directly to the point. "Billy, what was wrong in church yesterday?"

He dropped his eyes to order his thoughts, and then poured it all out to them while they listened intently, scarcely moving.

"I thought so," Margaret said quietly. "Silas was right. We have to see this thing through with the British." She hesitated, weighing whether Billy could yet answer the single heavy question.

Brigitte barged straight into it. "Are you going with Lemuel?"

Billy pursed his mouth for a moment. "I don't know yet."

"If you decide to go," Margaret said quietly, "do it for your own reasons. Don't go because of what people will say."

Billy nodded, and for long moments they remained quiet before Billy turned to Brigitte. "Heard anything about Captain Buchanan?"

Brigitte's face lighted at the thought of Richard Arlen Buchanan, tall and capable, with a deep scar in his left brow and gentle, strong eyes. A captain in the command of British general William Howe, he had saved her from arrest in the shadowy side street beside the church the night the British regulars held Silas and Mattie in their own church. He knew that Brigitte and other women had smuggled into the church some militia muskets wrapped with quilting frames, but he had quietly ordered her to get away from the church—go home—and he stirred her heart as no one had before. She remembered the panic when he was shot twice in the catastrophic retreat from Concord, and she spent weeks frantically searching before she found him in a British hospital. She remembered the most unforgettable evening in her life, when she invited him to supper in their home, and he came, and then the black day, March 17, when the British vacated Boston, and he rode past with his column, peering down at her for long moments, and then he was gone. When Billy was able to hobble with a cane, she had begged him and he had helped her search, but Captain Buchanan had vanished.

"Nothing," she said, and her face dropped for a moment. "I'm still trying."

Billy sadly shook his head. "He has to be somewhere, maybe with their army in New York."

Brigitte shrugged. "I don't know."

Margaret served cool apple cider from the root cellar, and for a time they chattered about little things and laughed and basked in the warm glow.

Finally Billy rose from the table. "I better be going."

Margaret stood. "Promise you'll tell us how you decide."

"I promise."

The two women followed him out into the warm night and stood inside the front gate to wave at him until he disappeared in the darkness. As he walked, he raised his eyes to the black velvet heavens and the million points of light, and he slowed in wonder and awe. *So vast—so much. Is Silas right? War up there? No one can count the creations—are they all empty? just to look at? Besides the Almighty, who's up there? others like us? different? wiser? better? worse?* He could not comprehend the immensity of the endless reaches above, nor could his mind cope with the unanswerable question of who, or what, may be there. He pushed through the front gate and into the house.

Dorothy was seated in the rocker, reading a small pamphlet by lamplight. She studied his face for a moment. "Everything all right at Margaret's?"

He nodded and went to the water pail in the kitchen to dip and drink cool water, and she followed with the booklet in her hand. "You may want to read this," she said. "It talks about what Silas said."

"What is it?"

"*Common Sense.* Written by an Englishman who came here."

His eyebrows arched. "I heard about it. What was his name? Paine?"

"Thomas Paine."

"You said an Englishman?"

"Yes. Thetford, England. A Quaker's son. A common corset-maker. Ben Franklin sent him here. He wrote this earlier this year and it's being read all over the colonies—New York, Philadelphia, here."

Billy dropped the dipper back in the water bucket, took the pamphlet, and walked back to the parlor and turned the cover to the light. Philadelphia. Published by Benjamin Towne for William and Thomas Bradford. February 14, 1776. Without a word he placed the lamp on the dining table and sat down with the pamphlet before him. Twenty minutes later Dorothy said, "Trudy's gone to bed, and I'm going too. Shall we have evening prayers?"

Half an hour later, hunched over the booklet, Billy slowed, then retraced a line with his finger and read it aloud. " *'How came the king by a power which the people are afraid to trust, and always obliged to check?* Such a power could not be the gift of a wise people, neither can any power, *which needs checking,* be from God.' "

Ten minutes later he again slowed.

> To the evil of monarchy we have added that of hereditary succession. . . . For all men being originally equals, no *one* by *birth* could have a right to set up his own family in perpetual preference to all others forever.

A stirring began in his heart. Five minutes later he stopped and carefully retraced more lines.

> In England a king hath little more to do than to make war and give away places. . . . Of more worth is one honest man to society, and in the sight of God, than all the crowned ruffians that ever lived. . . .
>
> . . . This new world hath been the asylum for the persecuted lovers of civil and religious liberty from *every part* of Europe. Hither have they fled, not from the tender embraces of the mother, but from the cruelty of the monster; and it is so far true of England, that the same tyranny which drove the first emigrants from home pursues their descendants still.

His arms and fingers tingled as he continued.

> Is there any inhabitant of America so ignorant as not to know that . . . this continent can make no laws but what the king gives leave to; and is there any man so unwise as not to see, that . . . he will suffer no law to be made here, but such as suits *his* purpose? We may be as effectually enslaved by the want of laws in America, as by submitting to laws made for us in England . . . Independency means no more, than, whether we shall make our own laws, or, whether the king, the greatest enemy this continent hath, or can have, shall tell us, *"there shall be no laws but such as I like."*

Billy leaned back in his chair and pushed the booklet away. The king of England—the greatest enemy this continent has? Never had printed words reached into his soul as these did. In his mind flashed the image of Silas, sitting bolt upright in his tiny, austere parlor, eyes flashing. *Tyranny. I will fight it. If lives fall, even my own, so be it. More precious than life—liberty. Liberty!*

Hardly breathing, Billy read on.

A government of our own is our natural right; and when a man seriously reflects on the precariousness of human affairs, he will become convinced, that it is infinitely wiser and safer to form a constitution of our own in a cool deliberate manner, while we have it in our power, than to trust such an interesting event to time and chance.

The mantel clock read a little past two o'clock when Billy lay down on his bed and stared into the black darkness of his room. It was nearly four o'clock when he drifted into a dreamless sleep. At six-thirty Dorothy gently moved his shoulder. He sat up in his bed and swung his legs over the side as Dorothy waited.

"Mother, I have to go with Lemuel."

Dorothy looked at her clasped hands for a moment. "I thought you would." In an instant his life passed before her eyes. The red-faced, squalling infant—the happy child—the carefree youth—the square, blocky, strong young man—the wounded soldier—the maturing man. "You'll have to tell Mr. Potter."

At ten minutes before eight o'clock he was seated opposite Hubert in his office. "I am going to have to go, Mr. Potter. I'm sorry it came without much notice."

Hubert drew a deep breath and leaned back, studying his desktop for a moment. "It's all right. You go ahead. You can pick up your wages any time after noon today. I'll include your bonus, and some extra."

"I didn't earn extra."

"I don't pay my people what they didn't earn. Write to your

mother often and tell her to let me know how you're getting along. When you get back, come see me."

Billy stood. "Thank you, Mr. Potter."

Potter shook his hand. "God bless you, Billy."

By suppertime he had split nearly two cords of wood into kindling and stacked it against the back wall of the house. After supper he strung the line across the kitchen, draped the blanket, bathed in the wooden tub, then changed into fresh clothing and walked into the parlor to Dorothy.

"I promised Margaret I'd tell her."

Ten minutes later Margaret opened her door, and Billy sat at their dining table while Margaret sent Brigitte to get her younger brother, fifteen-year-old Caleb, and the nine-year-old twins, Adam and Priscilla. They all took their places at the table and waited, the children wide-eyed, wondering why they were there.

Margaret spoke. "Billy has something to say."

"I'm leaving Wednesday with the militia. We're going to New York with Lemuel."

Both Brigitte and Margaret dropped their eyes for a moment, and Margaret spoke. "Dorothy agrees?"

Billy nodded.

Margaret covered his hand with hers. "I'm proud of you."

Caleb's forehead wrinkled. "You're joining the army? You just got well."

Billy looked at him. "I'm going."

Caleb rounded his lips and blew air.

Adam looked at Margaret, lost. "Billy's going to war?"

"He's going to protect our liberty. If he has to fight, he will."

Adam nodded, then dropped his face to puzzle on it.

Priscilla was white-faced. "Will we ever see you again?" Her lip trembled at the remembrance of her father, who had joined the fighting. Now he was gone.

Margaret smiled. "Of course we will. Don't worry."

For a moment Brigitte remained silent while unexpected memories flashed. She could not remember the time before Billy.

Billy and Matthew. Three years older. There was nothing they could not do. Always, always they were there to protect her, shield her, slay all her dragons. For her, Matthew was not handsome, nor was Billy plain. They were simply hers.

She swallowed and spoke with unintended intensity. "Billy, you be careful. Promise me."

"I will." He turned back to Margaret. "Mother says if you need help with anything, go see her."

"Tell her the same thing."

"When you write to Matthew, be sure to tell him."

"I will."

He stood and started to speak, and couldn't find the words. Margaret walked quickly to him and threw her arms about him as if he were one of her own, and Billy wrapped her close and kissed her on the cheek. For long moments they stood in the embrace, and Billy felt the quiet sob shake her before he let her go and took a step backwards.

Suddenly Prissy bolted forward and Billy swept her up into his arms and hugged her and kissed her. "Be good while I'm gone."

"Come back."

"I will."

Adam thrust out his hand and Billy shook it, then gathered the boy into his arms. "Help Caleb."

He settled the boy back onto the floor and turned to Brigitte—the tagalong, tomboy, nuisance, and then overnight an emerging beauty, and then a beautiful, confident, opinionated, intelligent young woman. But through it all, always, always the little sister whom he and Matthew had looked after.

He drew a deep breath. "I hope you find Captain Buchanan. I'll see you when I get back." He didn't know what else to say.

She impulsively stepped to Billy and reached up to throw her arms about his neck. She had never embraced him before. For a moment he could not move; then he hesitantly raised his arms around her and she buried her face in his shoulder, and he felt the sob and the tremble. Then she released him and stepped back, and he saw the tears in her eyes. She tried to laugh and it became a sob. "Why am I crying?" she said, and laughed through her tears. "Billy, I don't know what I'd do if I lost you or Matthew. Promise me you'll be careful. Promise."

"I will." He thought he should say something else but nothing would come. He turned back to Margaret. "God bless you all."

"God bless you, Billy. Bless you and keep you."

He walked to the front door and opened it and then was outside in the shadows of late dusk. Past the gate, on the cobblestone street, he turned for a last look, and they were all at the gate, waving. He waved back, then turned toward home. He was unprepared for the strange new realization that rose in his breast.

She's become a woman, grown!

Notes

The character Billy Weems and his mother and family are fictional, as are all members of the John and Margaret Dunson family, including Brigitte, as well as the Reverend Silas Olmsted.

The insights or visions of the approaching war credited to Silas Olmsted were not uncommon. Many men of the cloth believed the Revolution was inspired of God, since many of the colonies were originally founded by religious leaders, such as William Penn of Pennsylvania (see Leckie, *George Washington's War*, p. 10 and following).

General Lemuel Hosking and Colonel Israel Thompson are fictional characters.

Thomas Paine's pamphlet *Common Sense* is credited with being instrumental in the movement toward the drafting of the Declaration of Independence and with inspiring countless thousands to support the Revolution. One author has dubbed it "the most successful political pamphlet of all time" (see Leckie, *George Washington's War*, pp. 244–50).

Connecticut

Early June 1776

CHAPTER III

★ ★ ★

𝒜t three o'clock A.M. low clouds came creeping from the Atlantic to cover the stars and the quarter moon hanging low in the east and turn the heavy, dead air sultry. A gentle rain quietly began pelting the 513 men in the Boston regiment as they lay on their blankets in the sweaty, road-stained clothing they had worn for the two days since they marched out of Boston under the command of Colonel Israel Thompson. Tall, hawk-faced, proper, precise, tough, he had marched them fourteen hours each day, south and west on the winding dirt road leading through the lush Connecticut countryside towards New York. They lay on a grassy knoll by the roadside, sleeping the sleep of men exhausted in body and soul, and they pulled their blankets over their heads against the rain without waking.

In the dead silence just past four A.M., twin columns of flame leaped a hundred feet into the heavens and lighted the underbellies of the black clouds for a mile, while the ground shook and the deafening blast and the concussion and shock wave rolled in all directions. Bits and pieces of wood and metal ripped through the camp and began falling from the sky. Those nearest the blast were thrown twenty feet from their blankets, splinters and shrapnel stinging as they drove home. Pickets standing night guard at the north end of camp were knocked backwards, stunned, staring at the smoke and flames to the south.

Stay down—don't move! The thought flashed as Billy Weems heard the broken pieces of metal and wood falling all around, and he lay on his side, curled, arms covering his head while he waited. For ten seconds there was no movement, no sound in camp other than the quiet rain and the falling debris; and then, above the ringing in his ears, Billy heard the moans and the pleading and the calling of the wounded, and of men searching for them in the rain.

He rolled onto his feet and stared at the place the cannon had been lined for the night, thirty yards from where he had spread his blanket. A thick, rank cloud of acrid gun smoke engulfed him for a moment, then passed; and he saw pieces of the two heavy gun carriages still smouldering, flames licking. The six-foot, heavy-spoked wheels of two cannon and the great oak cross members that had supported the two-thousand-pound guns were gone, blown to splinters. One cannon barrel lay on the ground ten feet from the wreckage, the carriage on which it rested gone. Another was jammed muzzle upward against the wheel of the gun next to it, carriage smashed beyond recognition, one trunnion missing. The remaining four cannon were askew, tipped crazily, one on its side with the wheel on top turning lazily.

Billy heard the strangled moan and the faint call for help, and he broke into a trot, then a hard run to the guns. In the darkness he stumbled over something and went down on his hands and knees and turned back and made out a dim shape lying on the ground. It lay face down, and the cloying smell of burned hair and flesh came strong as Billy turned the body to look. In the shadows he saw the open dead eyes, with the black blood running from the nose and ears, and he saw the stump at the shoulder where the left arm had been, and the blistered flesh on the left side of the face, and the hair, burned and melted. The clothing was still smoking. Billy recoiled, wild-eyed, and his gorge rose sour, and for a moment he gagged as he reared back on his knees, staring at the dead face before him while other men worked their way past in the gray-black, placing their feet carefully, probing.

From behind came a strained voice, pitched too high. "This one's alive!"

Billy swallowed against the bitter taste and for a moment longer stared at the still shape before him, then turned and was on his feet, trotting towards the place where men were gathered around a cannon and carriage that had been blown onto its side, one wheel up, the other down. He saw the man pinned beneath the spokes, with the axle hub driven into the midsection, and he realized the man was suffocating, unable to breathe or speak. Two men threw their weight against the cannon carriage trying to tip it upwards, but could not.

Without thought, Billy shoved the men aside until he was at one edge of the wheel, and he bent his knees and reached down. He grasped it with both hands, bowed his neck, and began to straighten his legs. The great muscles in his shoulders bunched, and the veins in his neck stood out like cords, and he clenched his eyes shut and his jaw muscles made ridges. The muscles in his thighs knotted, and slowly the wheel began to leave the ground. Men stood back, awestruck, as Billy's legs straightened and he stood there, his entire body trembling as he held one side of the great wheel three feet off the ground while strong hands grasped the injured man and slid him from beneath the spokes and the axle hub, and moved him onto the grass. Only then did Billy release the wheel, and the ground shook as the great gun dropped. Instantly he was at the man's side with the others as they gingerly felt the alignment of his arms and legs and then carefully unbuttoned his shirt.

Billy bit off a groan. The wheel had smashed into the man's sternum and separated two ribs on the left side. The ribs were still beneath the skin but were pushing the flesh outward, three inches out of line. The man's eyes fluttered open, glazed with pain, and his breath came shallow in short, quick gasps. Small trickles of blood showed from his nose and his ears.

"Get the regimental surgeon!" The call went out and someone sprinted, to return in seconds with an elderly, bespectacled, gray-haired man in shirtsleeves carrying a black leather case. He moved with a clear sense of authority and a path opened. He knelt beside the injured man, swiftly gauging the damage, and he raised his face to the knot of men gathered around. "I'm Charles Nolan. Regimental surgeon. What happened?"

"That cannon fell on him."

From behind came another frantic call. "Surgeon! Surgeon!"

Nolan's head pivoted, then came back to the man before him as he spat orders. "Get some rope. Wrap his chest tight and I'll be right back." He rose and was gone.

Someone slipped a musket ball between the man's teeth while someone else passed a coil of rope forward, and gentle hands lifted him. His teeth sank into the lead ball while quick hands passed the rope from one side to the other, tightening the coils as they went, until they had wrapped him from his outstretched arms to his waist. Then they tied it off and settled him back onto the grass. A piece of canvas tarp was thrust forward and spread, and men held it over him while the rain tapped. A coat was wadded and slipped under his head. Someone dug the lead ball from between his teeth, and his shallow breathing steadied and became regular. He raised a hand, weakly, and motioned, and Billy knelt beside him, and he felt the clutch in his chest when he saw the raw terror in the man's eyes. The man tried to speak, and could not, but his hand locked on to Billy's arm, and his mouth slowly formed the words, "Will I die?"

Billy grasped the hand and shook his head. "No. Don't talk. The surgeon's coming."

"Alive or dead?" The stern, piercing voice of Colonel Thompson came from behind Billy and he turned his head. "Alive, sir."

The colonel hunched forward to peer under the tarp. "Ribs?"

Billy answered. "Two."

"The surgeon?"

"Been here. He's coming back."

"What broke his ribs?"

"A cannon rolled on him."

"Was he close to the cannon when the explosions came?"

Billy shrugged. "I don't know, sir. I was over there." He pointed.

Thompson raised his head to look into the faces of the gathered men. "Anyone know this man? why he was by the cannon when the powder blew?"

"Sir, he's Private Darren McMurdy. Company Six. Assigned to the cannon. He sleeps there alone."

Thompson crouched down and winced as he studied McMurdy's chest. He gently touched his shoulder. "I'm Colonel Thompson. Do you know what made the gunpowder blow?"

McMurdy moved his mouth but no words would come.

Billy cut in. "I don't know if he can hear, sir, and he can't talk. He can hardly breathe."

Thompson saw the blood at the ears and he nodded and straightened. "Anyone know how this happened?"

No one spoke.

"Anyone see lightning?"

There was no answer. In the silence, rain tapped on the tarp and on their hat brims.

"Where are the pickets? They see anyone?"

A white-faced, wide-eyed young lieutenant spoke. "Only four have reported. They saw no one. We're looking for the other four."

Voices rose from behind, and Thompson turned as the surgeon made his way back to McMurdy. His sleeves were rolled up to his elbows, and his shirtfront was blood spattered and rain soaked. He faced Thompson, eyes narrowed, intense, and gave orders as though to an assistant. "Colonel, I'm going to need your tent and a big table, or the side of a wagon on barrels, and a lot of alcohol and sheeting and hot water, with some long, straight sticks and a dozen lanterns."

"Surgery?"

"Foot amputation, broken arms and legs, wood fragments to dig out, two dislocated ribs to set." He gestured downward towards McMurdy.

Instantly Thompson turned to his second in command. "Major Bascom, see to whatever Doctor Nolan requires. And I want a damage report within twenty minutes, and an accurate count of the barrels of gunpowder down at the magazine, and a statement of how gunpowder got up here near the cannon."

"Yes, sir!" Bascom barked orders and men jumped. Four of them quickly rigged a blanket between two poles, and while others raised McMurdy groaning, eyes clenched, they slipped it under him, lifted him, and followed Nolan, striding off to the command tent.

Thompson turned to the young lieutenant, still standing wide-eyed in shock. "Lieutenant Holgate, clear everyone away from this area and set guards to keep it as it is. At first light we're going over this ground inch by inch." He paused to collect his thoughts. "Then get to my tent all the pickets that were on duty, along with everyone who was within one hundred yards of these cannon when they blew up. I'll set up a table and we'll begin our inquiry immediately. Get fires going to light up this entire area. Understand?"

"Yes, sir."

Billy spoke and pointed. "Colonel, sir, there's a body over there. It's burned and one arm's missing. Maybe that man was close when it happened."

Thompson's response was instant. "Private, get some men and bring the body to my tent."

"Yes, sir," Billy answered.

Thompson pursed his mouth for a moment, then turned on his heel and walked off briskly towards his tent. Four volunteers gathered around Billy and he led them to the body, nearly invisible in the grass, and they lifted it onto a blanket and carried it to the side of the command tent, where they gently settled it onto the mud and grass and covered it against the rain. Billy nodded to them, then sat cross-legged in the wet grass next to the folded blanket, elbows on knees, to remain with the body until further orders from Colonel Thompson. The others disappeared in the

chaos of fires and men running to carry out orders barked by officers struggling to understand what had happened.

Billy sat motionless in the rain, staring without seeing, groping
inside to rise above the numbness in his brain and bring some
sense of order to his shattered thoughts and to the nightmare of
bright, grotesque images that danced in his memory of the past
twenty minutes.

Was it two? two blasts, one right after the other? Lightning struck the gun-
powder? Not lightning—none before and none since—not lightning. Gunpow-
der stored under the cannon? Never—only in the magazine—away from camp.
But I saw the gun smoke and smelled it. It was there. How? How?

He watched as men brought the wounded to the command
tent, and the shadows from inside played on the canvas tent walls
as Doctor Charles Nolan made the hard decisions. Billy listened as
men groaned and ground their teeth on a piece of leather belt
shoved into their jaws while Nolan cut chunks of wood and metal
out of their bodies, dropped the pieces clattering into brass pans,
and then stitched the incisions closed with catgut soaked in hot,
raw alcohol.

It wasn't to be like this. We were supposed to march to New York and fight
the British. Not this. Who? How? Why?

Outside the command tent, half a dozen men drove poles in
the ground, spread a canvas over the poles against the rain, and set
a table and chairs. The sound of voices approaching from the far
side of the tent brought Billy's eyes up, and he watched Bascom
march the eight pickets who had been on guard duty beneath the
overhead canvas. Thompson appeared from inside with two
lanterns and sat down at the table. A second young officer followed him with a large ledger in hand and sat beside the colonel,
pencil ready. Billy, thirty feet behind them in the shadows, cocked
his head to listen.

Bascom saluted and Thompson began. "Damage report?"

"Oral only, sir. No time to write it out yet."

"Speak."

"Two known dead. Six seriously injured and in my opinion

unable to continue. One foot partially amputated. Thirteen others injured but able to continue. Two cannon destroyed beyond immediate repair. The other four damaged but repairable. All twenty-two kegs of gunpowder accounted for at the magazine. No further damage of any consequence reported, sir."

"Did you personally count the kegs of gunpowder?"

"I did, sir. Twenty-two. Confirmed."

"You check that against the regimental ordnance record?"

"I did, sir. We left Boston with twenty-two kegs, twenty-five pounds each. There are none missing."

Thompson straightened in his chair. "Then what blew the cannon?"

"No one knows, sir."

The young officer beside Thompson was writing rapidly. Thompson clenched his jaw for a moment, then continued. "Those the pickets?" He pointed.

"Yes, sir."

"One at a time."

Bascom motioned and the first picket strode to the table, stopped, and saluted.

Thompson spoke gruffly. "Your name and company?"

"Private Zechariah Sherman. Sixth Company."

"What was your position when the powder exploded?"

"Northwest corner of the camp, sir."

"How long had you been there when it blew?"

"Just a few minutes, sir. Since four A.M."

"Was the previous picket awake when you arrived?"

"Yes, sir."

"What did you see or hear from the time you went on duty?"

"Only the rain, sir. Nothing else."

Thompson leaned forward. "After the blast, what did you see? anyone trying to get out of camp?"

"No, sir. No one."

"Any lightning during the night? at any time?"

"None I saw, sir."

"Do you have any explanation for what happened?"

"No, sir. One minute I was standing alone in the rain and the next minute the whole camp was light as noon, and then I got knocked backward a step or two and my ears were ringing and I heard things fly past and fall from the sky. I never been through anything like that before, sir." He paused before he added, "And I hope never again."

Thompson glanced at his scribe, head down, writing, then turned back to Bascom. "Next." The rain began to slack off as the next picket saluted and stood rigid before the table.

In the shadows, Billy listened to Thompson repeat his sharp, precise questions as he worked his way through the pickets, then other men who were within one hundred yards of the explosions. The answers did not change. Billy was aware when the rain stopped, and he could hear the steady drip from the edges of the command tent and the large canvas tarp covering Colonel Thompson's table. He glanced eastward, where the low, dirty clouds were separating from the skyline and the first hint of deep pre-dawn purple crept through. Billy listened intently as Thompson finished with the last man, and his forehead wrinkled.

They saw nothing, no one. No lightning. No missing gunpowder. Then how? He felt the hair on his arms rise as realization struck into his brain. *Someone inside the picket lines! We have a traitor in camp!* He started, then settled back, wide-eyed, with a quick rise of anger, then a sense of fear.

Thompson dismissed the pickets and turned to Bascom. "Where's that body someone found close to the cannon?"

"Here, sir," Billy called, and came to his feet at attention.

Thompson peered into the shadows beside the tent, seized the two lanterns, and walked rapidly through the sodden grass. "Your name?"

"Billy Weems, sir. Ninth Company."

Thompson held the lantern high and stared directly into Billy's face, then handed one lantern to Bascom, dropped to one knee, and threw back the blanket. He froze for a split second at the sight of the staring eyes and the stump of the missing arm. He leaned forward and held the lantern low while he examined the blistered face, the burned, singed hair, the battered remains. Then he rose, knee muddy, and turned to Bascom. "Recognize him?"

"No, sir."

"When we finish here, find out who he is." He turned to Billy. "Private, why were you the first to find him?"

"I was asleep with my company, sir. I heard men call from the cannon and ran and stumbled over the body."

"Show me where?"

Quickly Billy led Thompson and Bascom to the deep, soggy grass and pointed. Thompson turned and calculated the distance to the wrecked cannon, then dropped his head forward in thought. "Anyone find the missing arm?"

"I don't know, sir. I didn't."

Thompson spoke to Bascom. "When it's light, get a search party." In afterthought, Thompson turned to Billy. "Did you see anyone, anything that might explain all this?"

"No, sir. I was asleep until the blast."

Thompson turned to peer intently towards the east, where the break in the clouds was prominent with the first show of deep blue spreading. "We'll go over the ground in half an hour when it's full light. Private, go on back to your company." He turned back to Bascom. "We're going to talk to that man with the broken ribs." He turned on his heel as Billy spoke.

"Sir, I'd like to know if that man lived."

Thompson turned. "Why?"

"I helped him."

Thompson's eyes narrowed. "Are you the one?"

"Yes, sir."

"Come along."

The clouds in the east were showing pink fringes as the men approached the tent where Doctor Nolan was washing his hands. Bandaged men lay on cots or on blankets spread on the ground.

Nolan's assistants were scrubbing dried blood from the large table they had used for surgery. In one corner a man sitting on a chair rocked back and forth with his eyes closed. His foot was propped on the seat of another chair, leg straight, and at a glance Billy saw the bandaged foot was half missing. Other men sat on the ground, arms and legs splinted with wood sticks and tied.

Doctor Nolan turned as Thompson ducked his head to clear the tent flap and walked in, Bascom and Billy following. "Any more injured out there?" Nolan asked.

Thompson shook his head. "I need to talk to the man with broken ribs."

Nolan pointed with his chin. "Over there."

"Can he hear? speak? Is he going to survive?"

"He'll survive. His eardrums are ruptured but he can hear. His ribs are wrapped. Don't talk long."

The man lay on his back, unmoving, one arm thrown across his eyes. Thompson dropped to one knee beside him. "Can you hear me?"

The man moved his arm, his eyes slowly focused, and he nodded his head.

"Do you remember what happened?"

The man shook his head.

"Did you hear the explosions?"

Again the head shook.

"You didn't hear the explosions?"

The answer was almost inaudible. "No. Nothing until here."

Thompson paused, perplexed. "Do you know how gunpowder got over to the cannon?"

"No." The man was breathing rapidly, face flushed and drawn in pain.

"That's enough," Nolan said.

Thompson rose back to his feet, shaking his head. "Why didn't he hear the blasts?"

No one answered.

Still shaking his head, Thompson spoke to Doctor Nolan. "As

soon as you can, I'll need a list of the men we have to send back."

Nolan wearily nodded his head.

Thompson turned to Bascom. "Let's go look at the cannon."

They ducked out the tent flap into a clean, dripping world, with the eastern sky a kaleidoscope as the first arc of the rising sun cleared the skyline and set the underbellies of the breaking clouds on fire with a thousand hues of reds and pinks and golds and yellows. For a moment Billy felt an unexpected surge of renewal, and he breathed deep in the cool air, caught up in the humbling power of earth and sky. And the thought came, *Why war?* He marched on behind the officers, through the wet, knee-high grass, feeling the cold bite as it drenched his legs and shoes.

Thompson stopped in front of Lieutenant Martin Holgate, who snapped to rigid attention and saluted. Behind Holgate, men had formed a box, inside which was the cannon emplacement, exactly as it had been following the destruction by the gunpowder. The men carried muskets, and all came to attention.

Thompson spoke to Holgate. "Anyone disturbed anything?"

"No, sir."

"Open up."

Holgate gave orders and the guard lines opened to admit Thompson, Bascom, Holgate, and Billy. They walked to the tangle of cannons, thrown crazily, blackened, spokes cracked, broken.

Thompson spoke to Billy. "Private, which one was the man under?"

"There, sir."

Thompson dropped to his haunches and looked at the ground. The rain had washed away all tracks; there was nothing. He looked at the cannon, then at Billy, incredulous. "You lifted that gun alone?"

"Yes, sir."

Thompson rounded his lips and blew air, then pointed. "His blanket is over there, maybe twenty feet. How did he get caught under the wheel over here?"

Holgate broke in. "Maybe the blast."

Billy shook his head. "That would have moved him and the blanket the same direction, not apart."

Thompson stood and his eyes widened for a moment before he stepped to the shallow, powder-burned, muddy craters dug by the blasts, and once again he went to one knee, peering intently at the ground. He moved to the second crater and again leaned forward, missing nothing. He dug into the mud in the center of each depression and pulled out charred wood chunks and tossed them into a small heap between the craters.

"Keg bottoms. Driven straight down." He backed up and for two minutes studied the positions of the big guns and the scarred ground. "Someone set a keg of powder beneath each of the two center cannon and ignited them at about the same time. Maybe it was the dead man with the missing arm." He shook his head. "That leaves a lot unanswered."

He turned to Bascom. "Get a few officers and a dozen men and go over this ground one step at a time. Get me at the command tent if you find anything. And have the men begin the morning meal. We'll march as soon as possible."

"Yes, sir."

Thompson turned to leave, when the murmur of voices and then loud exclamations brought him back around. All eyes turned toward the rising commotion at the south end of camp. They watched two pickets, muskets at the ready, marching towards them with a man between them, while more than fifteen others crowded around and behind, faces contorted, loud in their anger and threats.

Billy studied the man. He walked with the peculiar in-line, swinging stride of an Indian. Taller than average, well built, he was dressed in deerskin hunting shirt, breeches, and moccasins. The sleeves of the shirt were fringed, and the breast and the moccasins were decorated with blue and white Indian quill and bead work. A leather thong held his long brown hair at the back. The nose was prominent, tended to be hawked, the cheekbones not high like those of an Indian, the chin firm, with a three-inch scar along the left jawbone. He carried a .50-caliber Pennsylvania rifle more than five feet long, and his powder horn and bullet pouch hung at his right side, looped over his shoulder. A second, larger pouch hung on his left side. The thigh-length hunting shirt was gathered at his middle by a weapons belt, with a broad knife scabbard on his right hip, and beside it Billy saw the black iron head and handle of a tomahawk.

Billy pursed his mouth. *Indian? Maybe. Maybe half.*

They waited until the pickets stopped, with the man facing Thompson. "Sir, he was at the south end of camp on the road. We thought we should bring him here."

For a full five seconds Thompson studied the man, and he did not miss the belt knife or the tomahawk. "I don't recall seeing you. Are you in my command?"

"No." The gaze was steady, the face noncommittal.

"Do you have business here?"

"Yes."

"State your name."

"Eli Stroud."

"From where?"

"Lately, Boston."

"Before that?"

The man hesitated for a moment. "A longhouse."

"Longhouse?"

"An Iroquois longhouse in an Iroquois village southwest of Quebec, near the Richelieu."

Thompson's eyes widened. "Are you an Iroquois Indian?"

"No. White. The Iroquois raised me after I lost my family."

Billy detected the slight accent in the man's speech and the flat intonation, like that of an Indian.

"Orphaned? By whom? At what age?"

"The Iroquois. I was two."

For a split second the colonel gaped, then continued. "Who taught you to speak English?"

"Jesuits."

"What's your business here?"

For the first time the man dropped his eyes for a moment, then raised them and made his answer. "Personal to me."

The colonel's eyes narrowed. "Are you a spy?"

"No."

"Someone blew up two of our cannon this morning and killed two men, and crippled others. Then we find you in camp three hours later. If you had anything to do with it, you'll hang. Where were you at four o'clock this morning?"

"About eighteen miles northeast. I heard it. I saw the light."

"You could have walked around us but you didn't. Why?"

The man measured his answer before he spoke. "I want to join your regiment." The words were level, calm.

Dead silence fell and held for several seconds while Thompson's mouth dropped open. He clacked it shut. "We're from Boston. Why not a regiment from the north? New Hampshire?"

"I have my reasons. Nothing to do with Boston."

Thompson began to shake his head, slowly at first, then firmly. "I don't like this. You show up at the wrong time and won't tell us your business. I think we better take you along with us."

The pickets reached for the man, and his hand rose to his tomahawk. The pickets gasped, startled, and involuntarily took a step backwards. In the instant tension no one moved for a moment, and the man lowered his hand and spoke directly to Thompson. "Before something bad happens let me ask, did you catch the guilty man?"

"No, but that has nothing to do with you."

"Let me take a look at the cannon."

"Why?"

Stroud shrugged. "Can't hurt. Might help."

For reasons known only to Thompson, he turned and pointed, and Stroud walked over to the ugly craters and the damaged guns. He knelt to study the ground, then the craters, then the blown guns. He pointed to the small pile of charred wood between the craters. "Bottoms of the powder kegs?"

"Yes."

A sergeant handed a slip of paper to Lieutenant Holgate and he glanced at it, then handed it to Thompson. His forehead wrinkled as he read the brief message, and then he spoke as though to himself, "The dead man with the missing arm was Corporal Oren Pinnock. He's a cook for Company Eight." He brought his focus back to Stroud. "You've looked. Let's get on with it. Pickets, take—"

Stroud raised a hand. "You counted your powder kegs?"

"Yes. None missing."

"What else you got in kegs?"

"What do you mean?"

"Flour? Rum? Dried fish?"

Billy felt a rise in the tension.

"Flour."

"I'd count my flour kegs if I were you."

Billy could hear the morning insects and birds in the silence.

Thompson turned to Bascom. "Check the flour kegs against the commissary inventory."

They stood in awkward silence while Bascom hurried away, then returned, face flushed. "Fifty-two kegs when we left, eight used, forty-two remaining. There are two unaccounted for."

Billy felt the hackles rise on his neck. *The cook. Pinnock.*

Thompson studied Stroud long and hard. "If you weren't part of it, how did you know?"

Stroud dropped his eyes for a moment, and Billy saw him form a decision, and then he spoke. "That's how I did it once."

"Did what?"

"Blew the gates off a French stockade forty-eight miles west of Quebec. The French sent in supplies that included ten kegs of rum. Four of us on the outside switched four rum kegs with kegs of gunpowder. Three of our people on the inside put it against the gates and set it off. From what I heard, a cook tried it here, but he either cut the fuse too short or it flashed. Whichever, it killed him."

Thompson was incredulous. He looked at Bascom. "Do you agree with that?"

Bascom swallowed and found his voice. "It would explain almost everything, sir."

Thompson stood stock-still for a moment, eyes locked with Stroud's. "For now I'll accept that, but don't leave camp without my permission. I have to think this over." He started to give further orders to Bascom, when Stroud interrupted.

"That cook didn't do this alone. He had help."

Astounded, Thompson's head dropped forward. "What do you mean?"

"He had to have a lookout somewhere while he was setting the gunpowder."

"How do you know?"

Stroud ignored the question. "Was there anyone else close to those cannon when you got there? maybe hurt?"

It took Thompson two seconds to remember. "A man was pinned under one of them."

"Alive?"

"Yes, over at the command tent."

"Can he talk?"

"A little."

"Mind if I ask him a couple questions?"

"About what?"

"A confession."

"You think you can get a confession from him?"

"Maybe. Nothing to lose by trying."

Thompson turned on his heel and led the way to the command tent. Stroud stopped him at the entrance and spoke quietly. "What's this man's name?"

"McMurdy."

"What's the dead man's name?"

"Pinnock."

"Let's go in."

Thompson ducked his head through the flap, with Stroud and

Bascom following, and Billy stopped outside, head cocked, listening. Thompson pointed, and Stroud walked to McMurdy, who had his arm thrown over his eyes, half asleep. Stroud dropped to one knee beside him and spoke quietly, gently, while Thompson and Bascom stood back watching, listening intently.

"Can you hear me?"

McMurdy uncovered his eyes and focused, then nodded.

"Much pain?"

Again McMurdy nodded.

"We got Pinnock. We know he's the one who blew the gunpowder, and we know you helped him. Smuggled it into camp in flour barrels. Looks like there was a third man, but we're not sure of his name. Want to tell us? You'll feel better if you confess and name that third man."

McMurdy's lips compressed, and he closed his eyes and turned his face away.

Stroud gently laid a hand on his shoulder. "You don't want to die with this on your conscience."

McMurdy slowly turned back to face Stroud, eyes panic-stricken. "Am I going to die?"

"By hanging."

McMurdy gasped and his frame shook with a sob.

Stroud waited a moment. "Tell us. At least they might put you before a firing squad. It's better than hanging."

Tears trickled from McMurdy's eyes, down the sides of his face, and his poise, his defenses crumbled. He whispered, "It's true. I was lookout for Pinnock. No third man. I swear."

"Ever hear the name Eli Stroud?"

"No."

"Was he the third man?"

"No third man. Never heard of Stroud."

"You brought the gunpowder in flour barrels?"

McMurdy nodded.

"You're sure there was no third man?"

"Pinnock and me. That's all."

"How about back in Boston?"

"A lot of Loyalists. Some helped. I don't know who."

Stroud nodded. "Anything I can do for you?"

McMurdy's eyes were pleading. "Tell my mother I'm sorry. Sorry."

"What's her name?"

"Beatrice McMurdy. Charlestown."

"I'll do it."

Stroud rose and walked past Thompson and Bascom, out through the tent flap into the bright sunlight and the scolding of blue jays and of bees working busily in the wildflowers, away from the smell of carbolic acid and raw alcohol and blood, away from the sight of men crippled and bandaged, away from a man who was broken in heart and soul and going to be executed before noon. He settled cross-legged onto the grass, laid his rifle across his lap, and bowed his head, sickened by the black evil of war and what it does to men and all that is good in the world.

Billy walked near him and stood silent, not moving. Thompson and Bascom ducked out the tent flap and started towards Stroud, then slowed. Thompson paused before he spoke. "Stroud, I think any questions about you have been answered. You still want to join this regiment?"

Stroud nodded his head without raising his face.

"Ever been in battle before?"

There was a pause while Stroud calculated. "Six years, eleven battles."

"Speak Iroquois?"

"Iroquois, Huron, Seneca, Onondaga, Mohican, Mohawk."

"The Mohicans are gone."

"Their dialect isn't.

"Ever live off the land?"

"For seventeen years." Stroud rose to his feet, rifle in hand.

"Do you want to tell us why you want to join?"

"No."

Thompson drew and released a great breath. "All in good

time." He turned to Bascom. "Assign this man to a company that's at less than full strength. Get the morning meal finished. Then get the list of disabled from Doctor Nolan and arrange wagons and a detail of men to return them to Boston. We'll march this afternoon." He looked at the ground for long moments before he continued. "And arrange a firing squad for eleven o'clock."

At ten-thirty, Colonel Israel Thompson convened a court-martial at the table outside his tent, flanked by two officers and a scribe. He appointed an officer to preside and another to defend Darren McMurdy. The bill of particulars was read to him by an appointed officer. McMurdy refused to enter a plea. A plea of not guilty was entered for him. McMurdy refused to testify or call witnesses. Eli Stroud and Lieutenant Holgate were called as witnesses to his confession. At ten minutes before eleven o'clock the three-man court conferred for one minute, and the scribe recorded their verdict of guilty of spying. The entire regiment was assembled and ordered to attention. At eleven o'clock McMurdy was tied onto a chair in front of them in the tall grass amid a carpet of red and gold and blue wildflowers.

Ten soldiers were picked by lots and handed muskets. At a range of thirty feet, they primed and cocked and held their muskets at the ready. McMurdy was asked if he had last words. He did not. Did he want a blindfold? He did not. Did he wish to make his peace with God? He bowed his head and spoke words known only to him, and then raised his head. His face was white, eyes wild, his entire body shaking uncontrollably, and he could not control a high, thin whine.

At five minutes past eleven o'clock, Major Bascom barked orders and the ten soldiers brought their muskets to their shoulders and aimed; and when the shouted command came and the sword dropped, all ten muskets blasted. McMurdy was slammed backwards in his chair. It nearly tipped over, then settled, and his head slowly slumped forward onto his chest. At 11:10 A.M. Doctor Nolan pronounced Darren McMurdy dead. A burial detail picked him up, still strapped to the chair, and removed him to a freshly dug grave one hundred yards west of the campsite, where they placed him in a hastily constructed pine box and lowered him into mother earth. Twenty minutes later they returned to the campsite with the chair. They had placed no marker on the grave.

A somber despondency crept into camp. The regiment felt little appetite for the noon meal. At two o'clock they gently loaded the wounded and three days' supplies into two wagons and hitched up the horses, and a ten-man escort led the small column back towards Boston. The regiment stood in silence, watching the men and wagons until they disappeared behind the thick, lush woods at the first bend in the winding, crooked dirt road, and then they turned to the work of striking camp and preparing to march.

Thompson slumped into a chair inside his command tent, drained, hating the killing and maiming of some of his command, hating the court-martial, hating a duty that required him to sit a man on a chair and kill him before the entire regiment. He drew and slowly released a great breath, then glanced out the tent flap. *Over six hours of daylight left. They could be twenty-four miles from this melancholy place by dark. They need the marching, the sweat, to fall onto their blankets tonight exhausted.*

Wearily he walked to the tent entrance and motioned to Bascom. "Get the regiment ready to march as soon as possible and then assemble them. I need to talk to them."

Thirty minutes later he stood ramrod straight before his command and raised his voice. "Men, today we all endured terrible events. Spies struck a blow against us; a court-martial tried and condemned the survivor, one of you, to death; and we all witnessed his execution. The man who died and the man who was executed by firing squad after a fair trial were Tories, allies of King George, and instruments of British plans to establish a tyranny over us and to deprive us of our God-given rights. I hope that there are no more such men in the regiment, but we all know the risks. We who are loyal to our country's cause will be vigilant. Any among the ranks who is a Tory and whom we discover will be dealt with severely but with justice. Any blow against this regiment, any act of violence, any deed of malice or stealth will be punished by legal means, but that punishment will be swift and final, as you saw it executed on McMurdy today."

He thrust a fist into the air and his eyes were ablaze. "Do I make myself clear?"

No one moved or spoke.

"We have many miles and many battles before us. We will drive the king's lobsterbacks from our soil—we will secure our liberties and our rights. These are the goals we must keep constantly before us. These are the goals from which no hardship, no tragedy, no calamity must distract or dissuade us. Remember your wives and your mothers and your sisters and your daughters at home, and resolve in your hearts that the cause to which we are committed is worthy of our every effort."

He paused to pace for a moment. "We're marching in five minutes. We must be at New York before the battle begins, and I warn you now, one-half of the citizens of New York City are Tories! Be constantly on your guard, ever vigilant."

Again he paused to collect his thoughts. "Now, put the events of today in their proper place, take courage in our cause, and conduct yourselves as befitting men from Massachusetts."

By midafternoon every shirt in the regiment was sweat-soaked. All talk had ceased. They marched mechanically, while in their minds they were again seeing flames leap into the black sky and hearing the deafening roar and feeling the shock wave roll through their rain-drenched camp. Then they were seeing a man sitting on a chair, ribs bound and bandaged, wild-eyed, mortal terror on his face, and then the blast of muskets and his head falling forward. In the mindless monotony of marching they could not push the bright images away. At dusk they silently made camp in a meadow beside a stream, ate fried mush and salt fish, and spread their blankets.

In the light of a flickering campfire, Billy dug a pencil stub and a paper tablet from his knapsack, smoothed the wrinkled paper, and placed the tablet on his knee. He gathered his thoughts and put pencil to paper.

My dear mother:

I take pencil and paper to inform you I am uninjured and in good health, and that you are not to worry about me when you hear the news of today's events, as you surely will.

He sensed a presence from behind and turned his head to look. Eli Stroud stepped forward, rifle in hand.

"I'm Eli Stroud. I was assigned to the Ninth Company an hour ago. Writing a letter?"

"Yes."

"Family?"

"Yes."

"Charlestown?"

"No, Boston. Across the river."

"When you finish, could I write a message to go with it?"

Billy's eyes widened in surprise. "You have family in Boston?"

"No. I promised McMurdy I'd deliver a message to his mother. I hope it gets there before she learns he was shot as a Tory spy. Her name's Beatrice McMurdy, in Charlestown. Anyone in your family who would deliver it for me?"

Notes

The character Eli Stroud is fictional, as are the characters Darren McMurdy and Oren Pinnock.

The event described wherein McMurdy and Pinnock use gunpowder to blow up two of the cannon of the Boston regiment marching to New York is also fictional. However, it is consistent with the actions of the Tories as described in a letter of August 1, 1776, by Henry Flint to his brother Josiah, wherein he writes: "They had undermined the magerzine [*sic*] in the ground Battery in York and General Washington's house and had got all things almost ready to give the fatal blow." The plot was discovered and undone (see Flint, *Flint Family History*, vol. I, p. 85).

Boston

June 1776

CHAPTER IV

★ ★ ★

An easterly breeze arose in the night and carried the tang of salt air from the Atlantic through the narrow cobblestone streets of Boston Town. By seven A.M. a thin skiff of high clouds moved steadily to the west, and dark smoke rose from countless chimneys to disappear in the light wind, as all proper Boston goodwives set great copper kettles of water on kitchen stoves or hung them on black iron arms and swung them over fires in dining room fireplaces to heat.

Monday was wash day. One hundred years of relentless custom required all Boston matriarchs to have smoke rising from their chimneys by breakfast time, heating wash water. Midmorning must find them in their backyards in ankle-length work dresses and heavy aprons, hair wrapped in scarves or linen caps, hunched over huge wooden washtubs, grinding bedsheets and pillowcases and the week's soiled clothing on corrugated washboards. By noon they must be finished with the hot-water rinse and hanging the finished wash with wooden clothespins on outdoor clotheslines, visible to all who passed by in the morning traffic. In bad weather they strung lines in the kitchen and hung the laundry indoors. Those who did otherwise felt the ostracism of over-the-back-fence gossip and stony stares in church.

Dorothy Weems reveled in the salt breeze on her face, and she did not realize she was humming an ancient fisherman's folk song as she set the clothespin on the corner of the last pillowcase and stood back for a moment to survey the morning wash, fluttering in the warm wind and the brilliant sunshine of a rare June morning. She smiled as women do at the soul-satisfying feeling of fresh wash on the line.

"Get the basket," she said, and Trudy dropped the last half dozen clothespins into the large wicker basket and followed her mother into the kitchen. She set the basket beside the stove, and they both worked with the tie strings on their wet aprons, then hung them on pegs on the back of the door.

Suddenly Trudy pointed through the parlor window. "I think I saw Abraham from the hardware shop at the front gate with a letter!" She ran to get it, and studied it as she brought it to Dorothy, who waited with clasped hands at the dining table. "Mama, it's from Billy!" Her eyes shined with excitement, and they both sat as her mother broke the wax seal with trembling fingers.

Dorothy quickly scanned the letter, and then her shoulders slumped as relief flooded through her body. "He's all right." She looked at Trudy. "I'll read it to you. '. . . I am uninjured and in good health . . . you are not to worry about me . . . terrible explosion . . . two men killed, several wounded . . . caused by two Tories in our regiment . . . one killed in the explosion . . . second one shot for spying.' "

Dorothy paused and studied Trudy's serious eyes for a moment before she continued. " '. . . marching on to New York . . . expect a major battle . . . regiment improving each day . . . eating well . . . letter enclosed for Beatrice McMurdy in Charlestown . . . message from her son the traitor, shot . . . will you find her and deliver it? . . . share this letter with Margaret and Brigitte . . . will write again soon.' "

Dorothy laid the letter down and picked up the second folded piece of tablet paper with the blocky printing on the outside, "Beatrice McMurdy, Charlestown, Massachusetts." It was not sealed, and she read and re-read the name while she pondered if she should unfold it and read the message. She carefully tied the letters together with string and raised her eyes to her daughter.

"We'd better change and go see Margaret."

The sea breeze tempered the mid-June heat and moved the leaves of the oak and maple trees lining the streets to make a shifting patchwork of the brilliant sunlight on the walkways and the streets. Dorothy felt a rise in spirit as she opened the gate of her small home and glanced back at the fruit trees and the grass and flower beds. Trudy slowed her skipping and reached for her mother's hand, and the two walked side by side the two blocks to the home with the white picket fence and the sign in the front yard, "John Phelps Dunson, Master Clockmaker and Gunsmith."

Margaret was wiping her hands on her damp wash-day apron when she opened the door. She knew instantly what had brought Dorothy and she blurted, "Is he all right?" She stood rooted, not moving.

"He's fine."

Margaret's eyes closed and her shoulders slumped as she exhaled, and then she reached to embrace Dorothy. "Come in, come in. I'll set some coffee."

She settled Dorothy at the dining table and spoke to Trudy. "Adam and Prissy are in back, raking up the chips in the wood yard." Dorothy nodded and instantly Trudy was gone and the back kitchen door slammed.

Margaret sat down at the head of the table, next to Dorothy. "You heard from him?"

"Yes. Today." She drew the tied letters from her handbag and handed them to Margaret. "He said I should share it with you and Brigitte."

"She'll be home from the bakery in an hour or two."

Margaret untied the string and looked at the two separate folded sheets inquiringly, and Dorothy pointed. "That one's from Billy. Read it first."

Margaret flattened it on the table, then held it as she read it silently, and then re-read some parts of it. Her forehead wrinkled. "Have you read the one marked for that poor boy's mother in Charlestown?"

"No. I didn't feel it proper."

The coffeepot suddenly whistled and they both flinched, and moments later Margaret set on the table a silver tray with cups and saucers, thick, rich cream, and sugar. They both silently poured steaming coffee, stirred in sugar and cream, and then picked up their cups to sip gently, avoiding the burn while they savored the first taste.

Margaret shook her head. "Billy's been through a bad experience already, and they haven't even reached New York."

Dorothy's eyes fell for a moment. "I'm just thankful he's alive and unhurt. That explosion killed two men and crippled more."

Margaret's face darkened. "Terrible thing. Terrible." She tapped the second folded sheet. "What about this one?"

"I think I'd better go to Charlestown and try to find her."

"Any idea how to do it?"

Dorothy shrugged. "I guess go to the post office and ask."

They were sipping at the steaming coffee when the sound of pounding feet brought both women around. They both recoiled as the front door was thrown open and Caleb burst in. At fifteen, he had nearly reached his full height of just under six feet, and the spread of his shoulders had begun. His knees and elbows were still too obvious; his hands seemed far too large for his arms, his feet too large for his legs; and his nose seemed out of proportion. He was still smooth cheeked, with hazel eyes and light brown hair, and his jaw had only begun to catch up. His shirtsleeves were rolled above his elbows, and he had forgotten to take off his printer's apron before his headlong run from the printing shop to his home. It was covered with ink stains, as were his hands and arms. It was clear the man he would become was going to be strong and striking.

"*Mother!*" Coming as he had from brilliant sunlight into the sheltered room, he did not see the women seated at the table for a moment, and then he saw them and slowed. He nodded to Dorothy, and his eyes flashed as he spoke too loudly. "Mother, a rider just told us at the print shop! Colonel Thompson's regiment had a Tory! He blew up half the regiment and . . ." He suddenly realized who was there and he paused. "I don't think Billy was hurt."

Dorothy smiled. "He wasn't."

Caleb plowed on. "He blew up a lot of things, and they caught him and they shot him! Just like *that!* Held a court-martial on him and shot him for spying! He had it coming. All Tories do. There were other men killed and some hurt, and the doctor had to set up a hospital and everything. The wounded are going to be here today or tomorrow!"

Margaret nodded and pushed the letter towards Caleb. "We just got Billy's letter. He told us about it."

Caleb's eyes widened. "Can I read it?"

Dorothy handed it to him and he stood planted, oblivious to the world as he read every word. He rounded his mouth and blew air. "Billy's all right. It isn't as bad as that messenger told." His forehead wrinkled. "Is there another letter?"

Margaret held it up. "It's for the mother of the spy. We shouldn't read it."

A thought struck and stopped Caleb in his tracks and his eyes widened in instant excitement. "Can I let Mr. Ingram at the print shop read Billy's letter? We're setting print, and Billy's letter would be something special! Mr. Ingram might pay me for it, or make me a reporter!"

Margaret looked at Dorothy and she nodded. "It's all right. Please don't lose it."

"Promise. I'll bring it back real soon." He turned on his heel, then stopped. "Can I take that other letter sometime?"

"That will depend on the boy's mother."

Caleb ran out the front door clutching Billy's letter, eyes bright in anticipation of what Mr. Ingram was going to say when he read it. In his mind he was seeing large print on the article in tomorrow morning's biweekly newspaper: "BOSTON REGIMENT DIS-COVERS TORY SPY PLOT." In smaller print: "Billy Weems a witness." And at the bottom of the huge article: "By Caleb Dunson." He broke into a pounding run, working out which words would be powerful enough to describe midnight explosions that devastated the Boston regiment in a rainstorm.

Margaret smiled ruefully and walked to close the front door, left standing open when Caleb made his running departure. "Last week he said he was going to join the militia. He has a lot of anger over losing John, and Matthew being gone. I worry about him."

"Why are they always so willing to go to war?" Dorothy said softly.

Margaret sat down. "I don't know. When do you think you'll go to find Mrs. McMurdy?"

"This afternoon, if I can." Dorothy shook her head thoughtfully, and there was pain in her eyes. "I hope the letter tells her about her son, before the newspaper comes out."

Margaret leaned back in her chair. "Do you want to take Billy's letter along?"

Dorothy reflected. "Maybe I should."

"I'll send Brigitte with it as soon as she's read it."

Margaret remembered the scarf holding back her hair for the morning wash, and removed it and laid it on the table. They finished their coffee, and both rose to go to the backyard.

The wood yard was to the right of the kitchen door, a small area inside a low fence where the firewood was stored. Inside, there were rungs of pine and maple stacked on one side, a chopping block with a large axe in the middle, and the split kindling stacked high against the back wall of the house. An abandoned rake lay across a partial pile of the wood chips that had fallen from the splitting of the kindling.

At the far end of the yard, beneath the great oak tree around which John and Matthew had built a circular bench, Prissy and Trudy squealed in mock terror as Adam threatened them with a large spider he swore was clasped between his rounded hands. He threw his hands towards the girls and separated them. Prissy and Trudy screamed and ran around the oak to stand with their hands clenched beneath their chins, thrilling in the horror of the fictional spider.

"Trudy," Dorothy called. "Come along."

Trudy thrust forward an accusing finger. "Adam had a spider!"

Adam shook his head violently. "Did not."

Prissy marched forward, hands on her hips. "Did too."

"Did *not*."

Margaret stepped into the yard. "You two come finish in the wood yard!"

The tone in her voice put an end to all arguments, and Adam pouted as he marched back to the rake, Prissy following with her chin high, face a mask of indignant superiority. Trudy trotted to Dorothy's side, and they walked back through the house, Margaret following.

Dorothy stopped at the front door. "Tell Matthew when you write."

"I will. Come tell me about that poor mother."

Less than twenty minutes later, once again wearing her heavy wash-day apron, Dorothy walked into her backyard and felt the bottom of the nearest sheet, then a pillowcase, and smiled. They were dry, slightly stiff, and they smelled of good, homemade soap and Boston sun. Systematically she pulled clothespins and stuffed them into her apron pocket, loaded Trudy's arms and sent her in, then gathered her own load and followed. They stacked the piles on the dining table for sorting into two stacks, one to be ironed, the other not.

Tuesday was ironing day for goodwives, and tomorrow at dawn Dorothy would sprinkle and roll and pack the ironing stack in the wicker basket, and heat six flatirons on the kitchen stove. When the sprinkled clothes had ripened she would spend four hours with light beads of perspiration on her forehead in the hot kitchen, rotating the flatirons from the stove to the ironing board, while Trudy helped hang or fold the finished articles. Then Trudy would iron all the pillowcases under Dorothy's sharp eye.

Dorothy started at the sudden, urgent rap at the front door, and she quickly hung her heavy apron and hurried to open it.

"Brigitte! You're early. Come in."

"Oh, Dorothy," Brigitte exclaimed as she walked in and untied her bonnet, "when Mother told me about the regiment I was so scared! Billy right there with explosions and men hurt."

"It frightened me too," Dorothy replied.

Brigitte held out Billy's letter. "Thank you for letting me read it. Mother said you have a second letter for someone in Charlestown?"

Dorothy's eyes fell. "The mother of the boy they shot for spying."

Brigitte shuddered. "How awful! When are you going?"

"Right away."

"Could I come with you? Trudy can go down with Adam and Prissy. Mother said it's all right, and she thinks someone should be with you."

The east wind moved their ankle-length skirts and tugged at their bonnets as they stood on the heavy timbers of the dock for the Charlestown ferry, watching the pilot bring in the squat, round-nosed boat from Charlestown loaded with wagons and livestock and people lined against the guardrails. The battered bow thumped against the baffles and the dock shuddered slightly, while the dock crew quickly looped four-inch hawsers over weather-blackened pilings two feet thick and secured the ferry into its port. The ferry crew opened the gates and began calling orders to start the unloading of the walking passengers, then the wagons and carts, and finally the livestock.

Half an hour later Dorothy and Brigitte stood against the guardrail as the sailors on the dock cast off the heavy hawsers splashing into the water, and the ferry pilot blew his horn. The boat, riding low and sluggish with its new load, started back towards the Charlestown side of the Charles River.

Twenty minutes later they braced for the jolt of docking, then waited their turn to walk through the gates onto the Charlestown dock, and up Deery Street towards the high white spire of the

Charlestown South Church. They walked in silence, awed by the many remaining burned-out homes and shops and the rubble of buildings destroyed by British cannon one year earlier. During the battle of Bunker Hill and Breed's Hill, with hidden American snipers in Charlestown maintaining a continuous fire, General Howe had ordered the guns of the British fleet riding at anchor in the Charles River, led by the *Somerset* and the *Lively*, to reduce Charlestown to rubble. The 168 heavy twenty-four-pound cannon joined with the British guns atop Copp's Hill to blast for hours, while Bostonians stood on housetops in grim silence, listening to the thunder, watching Charlestown burn and Howe's army sent reeling in defeat on the grassy slopes. New homes and shops were abuilding now, but the blackened wreckage of the old was a grim reminder of the terrible price paid by the city of Charlestown for the staggering losses the Americans inflicted on the red-coated regulars on June 17, 1775.

The two women walked to the tall front doors of the church, read the sign, and walked to the rear of the building to rap on the door. A moment later it opened and they faced a short, portly, balding man. "Yes?" he said, head tilted while he peered over his spectacles.

Brigitte spoke. "I'm Brigitte Dunson and this is Dorothy Weems. We're from Boston, looking for a woman named Beatrice McMurdy. Do you happen to know her?"

The round face puckered in concentration. "No, I don't think I've heard that name."

"Then could you help us find the post office?"

The rotund little man walked out and pointed. "Anchor Tavern. Down two blocks, turn right one block, on the corner. Polly Ambrose owns it."

"Thank you, Reverend."

Polly Ambrose stood just over six feet in height and weighed close to three hundred pounds, and Brigitte and Dorothy heard her laugh roll out into the street while still a block away. Her hair was piled on top of her head with strands hanging, her dress was loose and flowing, and her homely face was as round as a dinner plate, split by a great smile. The faint odor of rum lingered in the tavern, where four sailors sat at a table with a large flask and pewter mugs. They straightened to stare as Brigitte and Dorothy walked through the open door. Polly stood behind a small counter against one wall, sorting envelopes.

"Beatrice McMurdy?" she said. "Yes, seems like I've heard of her." She sobered for a moment. "You have business with her?"

"Yes. A message."

"Bad news?"

Brigitte shrugged. "We don't know."

"If she's the one I'm thinking of, she lives on Busey Street, down near the shore. Never comes outside her house. I don't know how she gets food. Come on outside; I'll show you."

The wind stirred her hair and billowed her dress as she pointed.

"Thanks so much," Brigitte said.

"Don't mention it." Polly grinned. "You two gave those sailors quite a start when you walked in." She chuckled as she walked back inside the tavern.

Brigitte blushed and hid a smile as she hooked her arm inside Dorothy's. They walked away together down the slight incline to a narrow street with a crooked sign with the single word "Busey" printed on it. The cobblestones ceased, and the women continued on the winding dirt street, past houses that became increasingly more derelict. They stopped at the one with no fence or gate and studied the unpainted, weathered boards and curtained windows that stared back like dead eyes in a dead building.

Brigitte felt an involuntary shudder as she rapped on the front door. They heard a slight rustle inside, but nothing more. Brigitte rapped once again, and from the corner of her eye she saw a slight movement in the curtain. She turned, but the curtain settled and did not move again.

"Mrs. McMurdy," Brigitte called. "Please come to the door. We have a message about your son."

A full minute passed with not a movement, not a sound, before Brigitte rapped again. Slowly the rusted door handle turned and the door opened three inches. The room inside was dark, and the two women could see nothing past the door. A high voice demanded, "Who are you?"

"Brigitte Dunson and Dorothy Weems, from Boston. We have a letter about your son."

"Is he dead?"

"May we come in?"

"Where's the letter? Show me the letter."

Dorothy handed the folded sheet to Brigitte. "It's here." She held it up.

"Hand it through the door."

"Mrs. McMurdy, we need to talk to you." Brigitte carefully weighed her next words. "I believe your son is dead."

For long seconds Brigitte waited, while the only sound was the lapping of the sea on the rocks two blocks down and the wind in the few trees and dried sea grass. Slowly the weather-cracked door opened, and a small, hunchbacked woman with an old, worn shawl clutched about her shoulders stepped back to allow them entrance. They entered the small parlor, blinking while their eyes adjusted to the dim light, and they breathed shallow at the rank smell of a house too long closed and too long neglected.

The woman faced Brigitte. Her face was sallow, cheeks pinched, nose hawked. Half her teeth were missing, decayed. "Give me the letter."

"May we sit down?"

The woman gestured, and they walked a path through the clutter to the dining table and sat on chairs that creaked. The woman opened one blind and thrust her hand forward for the letter. She sat down and smoothed it, and formed the words silently as she read the brief, undated message.

Beatrice McMurdy: I write to tell you today your son was found guilty of spying and was shot. He asked me to tell you he was sorry. He was not hung, because he was finally brave and told us what he done. I believe he was a good man who got the wrong friends. I am sorry for you. Signed, Eli Stroud, Boston Regiment.

In the single shaft of sunlight, her thin hands crumpled the letter, her gray head settled forward, and she buried her face in her arms. Her shoulders shook in silent sobbing. For two full minutes Brigitte and Dorothy sat unmoving, pain in their hearts for the grief-stricken mother. Finally Dorothy leaned forward and placed her hand gently on the bony shoulder. She could think of nothing to say.

The sobbing slowed, then stopped, and the woman raised her face and wiped at her tears with her sleeve, and Brigitte and Dorothy saw a change, a softening in her face and her eyes. "You were good to bring the letter. You should go now."

Dorothy spoke gently. "Did your son lose his life?"

The woman blurted, "Shot for spying. A Tory!"

Dorothy closed her eyes in pain for a moment. "Your son was loyal to what he thought was right. You must not condemn him for that."

"It makes no difference. He's gone." Her mouth trembled and she swallowed hard.

Brigitte interrupted. "When will your husband be here?"

She shook her head, and her expression again became hard, cynical. "Never. He ran off when Darren was two. Drank too much. Wouldn't be responsible. Didn't like me or the children." Her eyes became pleading, and she spoke as though she were trying to explain her life, justify herself. "I tried. Heaven knows I tried. It got hard when Madeline died, and I had to try to earn enough money to feed Darren and me. When he got older he knew his father ran off and he was so full of anger. So angry all the time. That's when he changed. I knew in my heart he would come to no good end." For a time she bowed her head, and once again her shoulders shook, and she murmured softly, "I just didn't know what to do . . . what to do."

"Who was Madeline?"

"My daughter. Beautiful little thing. Four years older than Darren. Smallpox."

She battled for composure. Suddenly her face softened once more, and she spoke as with a new voice. "You were good to come. I thank you. Do you want to read the letter?"

Dorothy read it slowly and passed it to Brigitte, and Brigitte read it and folded it. "It says your son died bravely in the end. He was loyal to what he thought was right. Remember him that way."

"Can I make some coffee?" she said eagerly. "I can make coffee."

Brigitte glanced at Dorothy. "If we come back another day, would you make coffee for us?"

"Another day? You'll come back?

"Yes."

"Soon? Yes. I'll make coffee. I have some coffee. I can make coffee."

"Thank you. We must be going now. We'll come back."

"What are your names? Where do you live?"

"I'm Brigitte Dunson, and this is Dorothy Weems. We live in Boston, not far from the South Church."

The woman repeated the names quietly, as though memorizing them. "Brigitte Dunson. Dorothy Weems." She raised her face. "You will come back soon?"

"Soon."

Brigitte walked to the door and opened it, and she and Dorothy turned. "Keep the letter in a safe place. Thank you for letting us come in."

The small woman walked quickly to Brigitte and threw her arms about her, and Brigitte held the thin body close for several seconds. Then Dorothy gathered her into her arms and held her and felt the wracking sobs.

"Soon. You promised."

"We promise."

The two women were half a block away before the old,

unpainted door closed. They walked back to the ferry in silence, each lost in her own thoughts, her own heartache for the small recluse whose pain of years ago had been so intense she had survived only by denying herself to love again, or be loved. They boarded the evening ferry and crossed the river, with the riffled water gold in the setting sun, and walked back to their homes in gathering dusk. Before they separated at Dorothy's front gate, they both involuntarily looked northward, towards the river, across to Charlestown, at the place where the small house stood near the water.

In deep dusk, Beatrice McMurdy lighted a single lamp and walked to a cupboard in her kitchen. She held the lantern high and studied the cans on the shelf, then selected one with faded colored illustrations on the sides, unscrewed the lid, and raised it to her nose.

"Coffee. I can make coffee when they come back."

She returned the can, then walked to another cupboard and carefully lifted down half a dozen dust-covered cups with hand-painted roses, and for a moment held them tenderly before replacing them.

The sudden knock at the door caught her by surprise and she stiffened for a moment, and then her heart leaped. "They came back," she cried aloud, and hurried to the front door and threw it open, lamp held high. She gasped and recoiled.

"He's not here!" she exclaimed. "He's gone." She tried to close the door, but one of the two men before her reached to hold it open. He was tall, dressed in the uniform of a ship's first mate, full beard, black cap in hand. Behind him the second man, shorter, wore the clothing of a dockworker. The two had been at her home twice before, both times to speak in hushed tones and exchange papers with her son.

The tall man spoke. "We know, ma'am. We're sorry to bother you at night, but before your son left we gave him some papers he was to return. He said you would be able to deliver them to us if he was not here." His smile was wooden.

"What papers?"

"Business letters."

"What kind of business?"

"Ships. Commerce."

"He took all his papers when he left. Go away." Again she tried to close the door.

"I'm sorry, ma'am. It's important I have those papers. Would you look for them?" It was not a question.

"Come back in the daylight. I'll look." She was trembling, her voice scratchy.

"I sail in the morning. I need them now." The forced smile was gone. His mouth was ugly, eyes narrowed.

She threw the door open. "His room is there. Satisfy yourselves." She pointed and stepped back to give them passage. In the dim lamplight they walked through the parlor and opened the door into a small room with a bed against one wall, a chest of drawers against another, and a small, scarred table and chair in one corner with pen and ink. The air was close, dank. The taller man lighted the lamp on the desk, and the two began a systematic search of the room.

They stripped the bedding from the old grass mattress and tossed the mattress on the floor to search the bed frame. The smaller man brought a knife from the inner folds of his coat, slit the mattress on both sides, dumped the dried grass onto the floor and scattered it, then threw the mattress back onto the bed frame. They emptied the tiny closet and turned out the pockets in the old coat and the two soiled pairs of trousers, then threw them and the old shirts onto the pile of bedding. The tall man struck the closet walls with his fist, listening for any hollow sounds. There were none. They took the drawers from the chest one at a time, sorted through everything, and threw it all onto the growing pile. Then the shorter man kicked the chest to pieces, searching every part before they shoved the splintered wood over by the bed. They turned to the table in the corner, swept the pen and inkwell onto the floor, turned the table upside down and searched the underside, then did the same with the chair. There was nothing. Hanging on the wall was an old, faded framed painting of a green valley bordering the sea in Ireland, and they pulled it from the wall.

"Leave it! It's my birthplace," the woman cried.

They ripped the frame from the canvas, then slit the painting to be certain there were not two pieces of canvas with something between. They threw the wreckage beside the bed with the smashed chest.

There was no place else to look, no other article of furniture in the room. The tall man turned to the woman, defiant in a corner. "Did he keep anything in the rest of the house?"

"No," she shrilled. "He kept himself and his business to his room. You've been there before. You know! He took your papers with him. I saw him. They're not here." She darted through the door, through the parlor, and into the kitchen, where she snatched up her broom. They followed and she met them in the middle of the parlor. She frantically flailed the taller man with the broomstick, shouting, "Get out of my house! Get out!"

He caught the broomstick and jerked it from her, then thrust his head forward and spoke low, thick anger in his voice. "We'll leave for now, but if we find out he didn't take the papers, we'll be back, and you'll give them to us."

"Get out!" she screamed.

The shorter man turned, and the taller man backed up one step, then turned and followed him out the front door into the night. The woman slammed the door and dropped the oak bar into the brackets, then slumped onto a chair at the dining table and buried her face in her arms. She sat thus in the dim lamplight for a long time before she raised her head and wiped her eyes. She blew out the lamp, then settled against the back of the chair, staring wide-eyed into total blackness, listening for every sound. There was only the whisper of the night breeze from the Charles River.

A little past midnight she lighted the lamp and silently entered her son's bedroom. She moved the bed frame and dropped to her knees near the wall. Then she carefully lifted a loose floorboard, set it aside, reached into the darkness beneath the floor, and lifted out a small wooden box. Inside were the treasures of her son's life—a pocketknife with a broken blade; a top with the string still wound; a small worn book about tall ships that sailed to China; a note passed to him from a girl in his fourth year of school; a bosun's whistle. She tenderly lifted them out one by one and looked at them through silent tears, until she reached the bottom of the box, and they were there. Six heavy brown packets tied tightly together with cord. She set them aside, replaced everything, and lowered the box back into its hole before she inserted the floorboard and moved the bed frame back to cover it.

Carefully she wrapped the packets in a cloth and clutched them to her chest. In her own bedroom she changed to her sturdy shoes and a better dress, tied her bonnet onto her head, and walked to her closet, where she opened a strong, small wooden chest on the floor and removed a leather pouch held closed by drawstrings. She opened it, counted the thirty-two gold coins, then closed the pouch and dropped it into her purse. She again sat at the dining table, put out the lamp, and waited for dawn.

At two o'clock her eyes closed and her head dropped forward. At two-fifteen she started, instantly awake. She sat motionless, staring, waiting to hear again the sound that had wakened her. Without moving, she closed her eyes and listened intently until she heard it again and knew whence it had come.

My bedroom! They're trying to open the window!

She battled an overpowering urge to scream, to run, and rose to her feet. Without a sound she clutched her purse under her arm, moved through the kitchen to the back door, and carefully lifted the bar, then the latch. It opened soundlessly, and she slipped out into the darkness of a sliver of moon and stars. Turning to her left, she moved away from the house on the dirt path through the unfenced backyard, over a small sandy rise, and on down towards the sea. She hid behind the wreckage of a longboat long since washed ashore and half-buried in driftwood and rotting seaweed, and waited. A little past four o'clock she saw a glow rise in the sky and she watched, and she knew. She settled back into her hiding place and bowed her head in tears while her home burned to the ground.

In the bright eight o'clock morning sun she stood and carefully studied the beach, the streets leading to it, and the people as they went about their daily tasks. Then she quickly walked to the nearest street, into the safety of the morning traffic, and hurried on, watching furtively, to the dock of the Charlestown ferry. At eight-thirty she paid her fare and boarded the boat, and obscured herself in the crowd crossing the river for business in Boston.

The tall white spire of the Old South Church in Boston shined bright against the clear blue of the midmorning sky. The front doors were thrown open to the fresh smell of the flowers and the sea, while the Reverend Silas Olmsted swept the hardwood floors and Mattie, his wife, patiently worked with cloth and compound to shine the woodwork on the pulpit. Neither was prepared for the small, bent figure in an ancient dress, an old, faded bonnet, and a shabby, worn shawl that intruded into the vacant chapel, heels tapping loudly as she hurried down the aisle. Silas stopped the broom and walked to meet her.

"Good morning." His words echoed in the cavernous chapel. "Is there something I can do for you?" He studied her cautiously.

Beatrice McMurdy glanced back at the doors nervously before she answered. "Is this the South Church?"

"Yes. I'm the Reverend Silas Olmsted."

Beatrice's eyes brightened with hope. "Do you know Brigitte Dunson? Dorothy Weems?"

Silas pursed his mouth for a moment. "Yes, I do."

"Can you find them?"

He hesitated. "Do you have business with them?"

"I do."

"Do they know you?"

"They were at my house yesterday."

"I see. Where do you live?"

"Charlestown. Can you help me?"

Silas raised a hand to stroke his jaw thoughtfully for a moment. "I can take you there."

"No!" Beatrice reached to grasp his arm. "Bring them here. I must talk to them here."

"Are you in some kind of trouble?"

Beatrice ignored the question. "Will you bring them here?" Her bony fingers were clamped onto his arm, face drawn, eyes like points of light.

"Now?"

"Now!" She turned her head to once again look back, then faced Silas, waiting.

He patted her hand. "Brigitte works at the bakery, but I can probably bring Dorothy. Wait here. What is your name?"

"It's not important. Tell her she visited me yesterday."

Silas called to Mattie, "I'll be gone for a few minutes. Could you make some coffee for this lady?"

Beatrice shook her head violently. "No coffee. Hurry."

Silas turned on his heel and walked rapidly from the chapel, closing the doors behind. Ten minutes later Dorothy answered his knock. Five minutes later she had her flatirons off the stove and onto the cupboard and had Trudy on her way down to Margaret's house. She hurriedly changed out of her housedress, and was tying her bonnet as she walked out the front door with Silas. Ten minutes later Silas swung the tall chapel doors outward and Dorothy entered and stopped. For long moments her eyes darted as she searched, Silas beside her, eyebrows arched in surprise.

"Where is she?"

They both started at the high voice from the corner. "Here. Is that you Dorothy Weems?"

Dorothy walked to her. "Yes. Why, Mrs. McMurdy, you're terrified! What's wrong?"

"I must talk to you alone. Is there a room?"

Silas nodded. "You can talk here. I'll leave."

Beatrice waited until Silas closed the door into his quarters behind the pulpit, then turned eagerly to Dorothy. She opened her purse and thrust the bundled letters into Dorothy's hands. "Here. You take them. They came after them last night."

"What are they?"

"I don't know. I only know that the men who came had been at the house twice before and they left them with my son. Last night they came back and wanted them and I wouldn't give them, so they ransacked my son's room. I sent them away. They came back in the middle of the night and tried to break in, and I left with these. Those men are evil. They burned my house."

Dorothy gasped. "They burned your home?"

"When they couldn't find me, or these letters, they burned it. These letters must be important. I think they have something to do with my son being a Tory and getting killed. You take them. You'll know what to do."

Dorothy looked at the packets in her hands in utter disbelief. "I can hardly . . . you want me to have these? I have no idea what they're about—what to do with them."

"Read them. Take them to the sheriff or to the army. You do it."

Dorothy forced her mind to settle. "You have no place to stay. Come to my home while we decide what to do."

"No! If they followed me, they'll come to your house and do damage. That's why I had you come here. When I leave here I'm going to the docks and get passage on the first ship going north I can. After I'm gone you watch for those men. One tall with a beard and a black cap, the other shorter, red hair, from the docks. If you see them, go tell the militia."

Dorothy hesitated a moment, accepting all Beatrice had said. "You're going north?"

"I have family in Falmouth, what's left of it. I can find some-one there."

"Falmouth? the one burned by the British?"

"Yes."

"You have no clothes, no money."

"I have money. I saved it." She held up her purse. "I have to go now. Promise me you'll take care of the letters. Maybe it's one way to get something good from what Darren did." Her lip quivered and she choked back tears. "Will you do it?"

"Yes. Of course. But won't you at least stay tonight?"

"No. I won't bring this down on you. I'll get my ticket and I'll hide until the ship sails. I'll be all right. I have money."

"I'll do all I can."

"Thank you. Thank you. Tell the young lady—Brigitte—that I thank her, too. Such a pretty thing—looks so much like my Madeline. You were both good to me. Don't think too bad of my son."

"Your son died bravely for something he believed in."

"Maybe. I'm going. Watch for those bad men." She turned from Dorothy and walked hurriedly to the front doors, with Dorothy following. With tears on her cheeks, she embraced Dorothy, and then she was out in the sunlight, hurrying from the church, head turning as her eyes darted everywhere.

Dorothy stood transfixed, the bundle of documents in her hands, watching the small, hunched figure until it was gone. She looked at the bundle for a time, while her mind struggled to understand all that had happened. She started at the sound of Silas's voice from behind. "Did she leave?"

Dorothy turned. "She did. Silas, I need to talk."

They sat facing each other in the high-ceilinged chapel, with the sun streaming through the stained-glass windows, making color patterns on the plain hardwood benches and floors, and for more than forty minutes Dorothy spoke in hushed tones while Silas's eyes grew ever larger.

Dorothy stopped and heaved a great sigh. "This is the bundle of letters. I don't know why those men wanted them."

Silas leaned back, struggling to gather his scattered thoughts. Finally he shook his head. "Maybe we better look."

For half an hour they pored over the documents, one at a time, and finally organized them into three piles. The first appeared to be a map showing a street and a house, but neither of them recognized the street or the house. On the back of the diagram was a tiny dot of ink, which meant nothing to them. Two documents had nothing more than two lines each drawn on them—one set of lines straight and parallel, the other curved and parallel. The other three documents appeared to be letters in which a business transaction was described involving freight rates for shipping hogsheads of salt fish to an unnamed port.

Silas shook his head. "They burned her house over these?" He gestured at them, baffled.

"She was terrified," Dorothy said. "That poor woman."

Silas stroked his chin thoughtfully. "Maybe there's a secret message in this somewhere. Code, maybe." He narrowed his eyes at Dorothy. "You said her son was in the Boston regiment. Should we take these to the militia office? Maybe they know about such things."

Dorothy shrugged. "Maybe they do."

Silas glanced out the door. "There's still time this afternoon."

"Let's stop at the bakery for Brigitte."

Brigitte walked with them in shocked silence as Dorothy talked. They stopped on the corner of Prince Street and Middle, before the old brick building with the plain sign "BOSTON OFFICE, PROVINCIAL CONGRESS." Twenty minutes later a uniformed corporal showed them into a small, plain office with a sign on the door, "COLONEL J. ROBERT PEARLMAN." The tall, sparse young officer motioned them to chairs and sat down facing them. His uniform was ill fitted, the blouse open at the throat.

"You have some documents you want us to see?" His eyes were steady as he studied the three civilians before him.

Dorothy leaned from her straight-backed chair to lay them on his desk.

"What are they? Why should the militia have an interest in these?"

"I don't know. I only know two men burned the home of an

elderly woman to get them, and that the woman's son who had these documents was shot for spying."

Pearlman's eyes came to sharp focus. "Was he the one with the Boston regiment on the way to New York?"

"Yes."

"I heard about it." For ten minutes he concentrated on the documents, then raised his head and shrugged. "There's something odd here, but I can't tell what it is. Can I show these to our experts?"

"Yes. Can they make copies?"

He nodded. "Come back tomorrow at noon. I'll return these to you."

At eleven-thirty the next morning Brigitte and Dorothy stopped at the South Church. At twelve o'clock, with Silas, they entered the militia headquarters. Ten minutes later they were sitting at a table in a private room with Colonel Pearlman, opposite a square, dour, iron-chinned major with a clipped beard.

"I'm Major Waldrup," the man said. "I got a few questions." He laid the map before them. "Any idea what street or house this is?"

All three of them studied it again. "No."

He turned the map and laid it face down. "Does that little ink dot on the back mean anything to you? We think it's a mistake—a spill."

"No, nothing."

He shook his head in frustration. "We've laid that diagram over every place on every map we can find of Boston and Charlestown, and it doesn't fit anything."

He laid one of the written documents before them. On it, parallel straight lines were lightly drawn through the center of the written message, corresponding to the parallel lines on one of the other sheets of paper. "Read what's between those two lines," he said.

As they read, their eyes opened wide in astonishment. While the parallel lines embraced only the center three inches of the letter, nonetheless the words inside the lines read as sentences, with a complete, clear message. Twelve hogsheads of salt cod from Nova Scotia would arrive in port on June twentieth, freight paid by receiver, same price as before. No price was stated, nor was the port.

He narrowed his eyes and spoke in his gravelly voice. "Know what salt cod has to do with all this?"

"No."

"May be code for something else. Any idea which port?"

"No."

He laid a second written document before them, this time with the curved parallel lines isolating words through the center of the page. "Read this."

Again the isolated words made complete sentences, and the message was clear. Two men would be in port with twenty additional hogsheads of fish, same price, freight paid by receiver, sometime on June twenty-fifth or twenty-sixth. If the fish was acceptable they would make a contract for another one hundred hogsheads for delivery in July and August.

"Mean anything to you?"

"Nothing."

"Those are signed T. Horton. Recognize the name?"

"No."

Major Waldrup carefully assembled the documents, then stood. "We have no idea what all this means, but we'll keep working on it. If you learn anything more, come tell us. We don't know how critical this is, so we must treat it as being very important. Understand?" He stared at them intently.

"Yes."

He gathered all the documents back into a bundle and handed them to Dorothy. "You wanted those back. Take care of them. We've made copies."

"There was one letter you didn't mention," Brigitte said.

"No part of that one could be isolated and still make sense. We'll keep working."

He looked at Colonel Pearlman. "Anything else, sir?"

"Nothing. Thanks for your help."

Major Waldrup slipped his copies into a folder while Silas led the two women out of the room, Pearlman following. At the front door, Pearlman offered Silas his hand. "Thank you. If we need you we'll send someone."

The three walked back to the South Church together, saying little, unaware they were watching the street traffic intently for a tall man with a full beard, in a black cap, and a shorter man with reddish hair dressed in the garb of a dockworker.

At the chapel doors, Silas spoke. "Be careful with those letters, and watch for those men." He pondered for a moment before he raised his eyes. "There is too much we don't know."

Three days later Brigitte hurried home from the bakery, changed clothes, and walked rapidly to the Provincial Congress office. Ten minutes later she sat opposite Colonel Pearlman.

"Sir, have you learned any more from the letters or the map?"

Pearlman drew and exhaled a deep breath, and Brigitte watched a decision forming. "Nothing." He paused a moment. "The question we couldn't answer was, which port did the letters refer to? Putting it all together, we knew that McMurdy was going to New York, that General Howe has the British army there, and that General Washington is gathering the Continental army there to meet Howe. It made sense that the port talked about in those letters would be New York port."

He paused for a moment. "So we sent those documents to General Washington in New York. I hope he can get to the bottom of it."

After the supper dishes were finished and Adam and Prissy were in bed, Brigitte sat at the dining table with quill, ink bottle, and paper.

My dear Billy:

She paused to look at what she had written, and her face

clouded in wonder for a moment before she wadded the sheet and brought another into position.

Dear friend Billy:

I take pen in hand to tell you of strange occurrences that have happened since arrival of your letter concerning Darren McMurdy . . . I enclose copies of letters, a map, and keys to coded messages . . . delivered by Beatrice McMurdy . . . mother of Darren McMurdy . . . home was burned to the ground by two evil men who were searching for these papers.

We took these to Colonel Pearlman . . . local militia . . . concluded that the port mentioned in the letters must be New York . . . sent copies to the military command there, and I send these to you hoping they may somehow be of value to you or to your regiment.

I now explain how to use the keys to read the coded message. The keys are numbered, as are the letters. Lay the key on the corresponding letter . . .

Notes

The designation of Monday as wash day had become a Boston custom by 1776. Most households also made their own soap. From fireplace ashes the colonists leached lye, which they then mixed with grease and boiled into soap (see Earle, *Home Life in Colonial Days*, p. 254; see also Ulrich, *Good Wives*, p. 28).

Letters were not usually placed in envelopes. The four corners were folded to the center, and a large lump of sealing wax was used to seal them together. The address was written on the reverse side. For an illustration, see Wilbur, *The Revolutionary Soldier*, p. 83.

Beatrice McMurdy, the tall man with the beard and black cap, and the shorter man are fictional.

A "hogshead" was a measurement common in 1776, and when used to measure liquid, it contained 54 gallons, the equivalent of about 1.5 barrels (see Pool, *What Jane Austen Ate and Charles Dickens Knew*, p. 24).

The hiding of secret messages within written documents—represented fictitiously here by the story of the McMurdy documents—was among the practices employed by spies during the Revolution.

Falmouth was on the coast of what was then Massachusetts, later to become part of the state of Maine. In 1775, Patriots of Falmouth tried to seize a British man-of-war lying at anchor. In retaliation, the British burned more than half of the town (see Higginbotham, *The War of American Independence,* p. 332).

The American officers Waldrup and Pearlman at the Provincial Congress office are fictional characters.

CHAPTER V

★ ★ ★

*I*n a forgotten millennium near the dawn of creation, a trillion tons of ice grinding its way south formed land masses and sculpted mountains and valleys before it melted to become the seas and oceans of this world and leave continents broken, fragmented. When the Dutch dared venture across the uncharted reaches of the Atlantic early in the seventeenth century, they discovered three islands broken from the mainland in the New World, clustered close together, each emerald green with nearly impenetrable growth of oak and maple and foliage.

One island was a twelve-mile long narrow finger of land that lay north-south, dividing the mouth of a great river so broad the incoming Atlantic tides reached 150 miles upriver; hence the native Indians called it *Manituck*, which means "The River That Runs Two Ways." The great river became the Hudson, or North River; the island, Manhattan; the east leg of the Hudson River that ran down the east side of Manhattan Island, the East River.

The mainland west of the Hudson River became New Jersey; the island and mainland to the east, New York.

The north end of Manhattan Island, facing New Jersey three miles across the river, rose steeply to a ridge one hundred fifty feet above the Hudson. Opposite, the New Jersey shore was sheer granite cliffs that rose to three hundred feet and were called the Palisades. Realizing that strategically the Hudson was the great highway to the northern reaches of the continent, the colonial Patriots built Fort Charles Lee at the south end of the Palisades on the New Jersey side and Fort Washington on the Manhattan side. The two forts faced each other, with cannon batteries covering all approaches, but particularly the river. Anything moving up or down the Hudson would have to come under the muzzles of the deadly colonial cannon on both shores. The result was, with both forts planned and under construction, in June of 1776 General George Washington and his army felt secure in the certainty that the two thick-walled forts, dominating the skyline on both sides of the water, could control the Hudson River.

Very close to the south of Manhattan Island, a second island, irregular and oblong, became Staten Island, with the smaller Governor's Island nearby.

To the east, and close to both Staten Island and Manhattan Island, was the great island called Long Island, lying east-west for 110 miles just off the mainland. The Dutch named their most prominent settlement on Long Island Breukelen, meaning "marshland," because of Gowanus Creek, which rose on the island to flow westward, making a large, marshy bog where it emptied into the waters of the Hudson. Breukelen later became Brooklyn. Nearby to the southeast, another lesser settlement grew on Long Island, Flatbush, and further south, on the coast, Gravesend, on Gravesend Bay.

By 1776, the city of New York, on the southern tip of Manhattan Island, boasted twenty-five thousand inhabitants, four thousand buildings, and the most prominent, busiest, and best deep-sea harbor in the colonies. And it had the frightening honor of being the city that the British had concluded to take first in their plan to crush the American rebellion. Being completely surrounded by water deep enough to accommodate the largest men-of-war in existence, each of the three islands was totally vulnerable to assault by sea. Thus, a naval blockade could strangle any of them. Clearly, he who had the dominant navy could take any or all of the islands at will. June of 1776 found Great Britain with the most powerful navy in the world, and America with not one gunboat in the New York navy. No one was more keenly aware of the fatal imbalance in naval power than the two opposing forces, the British and the Americans.

The five A.M. banging of reveille by the Boston regimental drummer rang clattering across the clearing where men had gathered to begin the endless digging for the foundations of Fort Lee atop the granite cliffs that fell sheer to the water on the New Jersey side of the Hudson. It rolled west across the river to echo from the bluffs on the Manhattan side, where men were trenching for the building of Fort Washington on the gray skyline.

Billy opened weary eyes as the camp began to stir, and he struggled for a few moments to remember where he was, how he got there, and why. He threw back his blanket, damp with heavy morning dew, and gritted his teeth as he stretched arms and legs stiff and kinked from sleeping on the rough ground. He was in a great clearing they had hacked out of the thick scrub oak and maple trees and foliage so dense a man could not be seen on the ground five feet away.

He swallowed against the sour morning taste and reached for dirty socks as he glanced out over the campground, calculating how many men remained. *Two dead back where the cannon blew eleven days ago, another shot for spying, six wounded sent back to Boston with a ten-man escort, four sent home with dysentery, four more from heat exhaustion, five known deserters, and one man—Eli Stroud—joined.* With the mental habits and instincts of an accountant, Billy made the calculations without thought, and then the deduction from the 513 who had set out from Boston thirteen days earlier amid shrilling fifes, banging drums, the cheers and shouts of the crowds, and the tears of wives and mothers. *Four hundred eighty-two of us remaining.*

He pulled on his socks, stiff from sweat and road dust, then his shoes, with the soles beginning to separate from the uppers and so thin he could feel the wet morning grass. He stood, and his nose wrinkled at the smell and appearance of his clothes, sweat-stained, filthy, wrinkled from living in them for six days and nights. He brushed them with his hands, then tucked his shirttail inside the waistband of his trousers and smoothed his shirt as best he could.

While he worked rolling his blanket he ruefully surveyed the campsite and the men of the regiment, and shook his head in wonder. There were two tents for the officers, but the remainder of the regiment cast their blankets on the ground at random, with no sense of organization or coherence. Rope lines were strung between poles and bushes wherever whim dictated, with an occasional blanket tied to form a lean-to or makeshift shelter. They had no military uniforms and had worn light summer clothing of every color and description, and it was draped everywhere on lines, or bushes, or trees, as though a hurricane had struck.

He studied the men for a moment. Very few had ever been more than thirty miles from Boston in their entire lives. There were fourteen officers and ten sergeants, two doctors, himself a keeper of accounts, but from there the men of the regiment came from every walk of life and every trade known in the colony of Massachusetts, the largest single segment being farmers. Those from farms came in all ages, from smooth-faced fifteen-year-old boys who whimpered in their sleep at night for mother and hearth and home, to grizzled old men with gray beards and leathery faces and hard hands. All were certain the war would be over and they would be home in time for harvest. A few men with sullen, shifty eyes spread their blankets alone and spoke to no one, and Billy understood they had joined to escape sheriffs and criminal arrest warrants.

Billy shook his head at the thought of the daily mandated drill. Almost no one in the regiment had even the beginnings of an understanding of military protocol, and Billy had to grit his teeth to endure the drill commands shouted by angry sergeants at men who looked back with blank faces while their brains struggled to conform action to command and their formations disintegrated. Disgusted officers walked among the frustrated companies carrying pebbles in their pockets, which they jammed into the left hands of men who could not remember their left foot from their right.

Billy tied his bedroll and sat on it, and reached for his wooden canteen. While he pulled the wooden stopper he noticed Eli Stroud thirty feet away, rifle across his lap, studying a small, thick leather-bound book held between his knees, and for a moment Billy stopped in surprise when he recognized the Holy Bible. He sipped at tepid water that tasted of pine pitch, rinsed his mouth, and spat onto the dusty ground. His eyes wandered over the rest of the regiment. *What will happen when the cannon shot and musket balls come hitting? Will they break? Will they?* He shook his head, fearful of the answer.

He glanced eastward across the smooth black waters of the Hudson, where a cloudless sky was bright with a sun not yet risen, and the men working on Fort Washington were etched in vivid detail. *Today we cross. Today we see New York.* He felt a nervous eagerness at the thought of the long march being finished and of finally confronting the British—as well as his own inner torments—in the great and final battle of the war.

"All right, you lovelies!"

Billy turned to see dour, bandy-legged little company sergeant Alvin Turlock, hands on his hips as he bawled, "Flag in five minutes. Then we go to the creek to wash. The colonel expects you to look like men from Boston when we march into New York. We strike camp and march at nine o'clock sharp. Get yer hardtack and pork cracklin's from the commissary, and be glad yer gettin' any breakfast at all."

Three minutes later, four uniformed soldiers from the Vermont regiment, camped near the digging with a regiment from North Carolina, marched to the flagpole. Two clipped the flag to the rope, the bugler raised his bugle, and the fourth man began the raising of the colors in the golden glow of the first arc of the rising sun. The red and white and blue of the Grand Union flag were radiant, and an unexpected feeling came stealing as Billy watched the colors climb into the clear sky. Every man in the regiment was at attention, saluting, and in the eyes and the raised faces of these citizens who were not soldiers was a strength and a commitment that humbled Billy.

The flag reached the top of the pole, the regiment dropped their salute, and Billy walked back to his bedroll and knapsack and rummaged for soap before he moved with the men of Company Nine to the large creek, 120 yards south and west of the timber stacked nearby for the walls of the fort. He took off his shoes and walked into the stream to his waist, gasping at the bite of the icy waters from the June snowmelt in the higher mountains, then stripped to his underwear and worked the soap into his shirt and trousers and socks. He rinsed them and hung them on the bushes lining the bank, then waded back in to lather his chest and face and hair. He ducked his head under and then threw a million droplets sparkling in the sun when he broke the surface, gasping, grinning, and he dug water from his eyes. He blew through rounded lips and was starting for his clothes when he saw that the man next to him was Eli Stroud.

Eli's weapons belt was on the bank with his rifle, and he was stripped to the waist, working water into his leather hunting shirt, without soap. Billy stopped, dripping, and turned to him, and Eli looked up. Without a word, Billy tossed the bar of brown home-made soap to him and he caught it, lathered his shirt, rinsed it, and slogged out of the creek to hang it on the bushes next to Billy's clothing. He waded back in to soap himself and duck under, and he came up throwing and spouting water. He walked sloshing to the bank and handed Billy the soap, nodded his thanks, and moved back to his hunting shirt and his weapons belt and rifle, still wearing his breeches and moccasins.

Billy laid the soap on a rock to dry and wiped his hand on his wet underdrawers. He was reaching to turn the wet underside of his shirt to the sun when the sound of the voices of five hundred men of the North Carolina regiment reached him as they came striding towards the creek.

The men of the Boston regiment watched them coming, and Eli's eyes narrowed as he spoke. "Looks like every man in that regiment has a belt knife. I hope all they want is a bath." He dropped to his haunches beside his weapons belt and rifle.

The southern regiment walked to the creek just north of the Boston regiment, and those in the lead plunged in fully dressed. The ones behind spread along the bank and began stripping off their shoes and boots, then their shirts and pants and socks, and then walked into the water to begin their wash. Those who had gone in fully dressed stripped their soaked clothing and wrung it out and then came splashing onto the bank, water streaming from their long hair and beards. They hung their wet garments on bushes and scrub oak until there was no more space. Then a few of them shrugged and began throwing the clothing of the Boston regiment from the bushes onto the ground.

The nearest Boston men recoiled in disbelief, then stepped forward. "You can't do that!"

The southerners turned towards them and each reached for his belt knife. One of them spat a stream of tobacco juice through his stained beard, raised his broad-bladed knife, and jerked more clothing from the bush at his side. Eli swept up his weapons belt and came trotting, Billy beside him, barefoot, in his drawers. Eli fronted the man, tomahawk in his right hand, belt knife in his left. The two regiments were now faced off but hanging back, letting the two men finish what had gone too far.

Eli smiled, both arms hanging loosely at his sides. "Ought not do that, friend. We'll be finished here directly and you can have the creek."

A wicked grin showed through the black beard and the man growled, "We'll just take it right now," and he spat tobacco juice onto Eli's chest.

The smile never left Eli's face. "If you've a mind, give it a try."

Instantly the man lunged and his knife flashed upward in a sweeping stroke towards Eli's bowels, and Eli twisted sideways. As the knife cleared his midsection traveling up, he swung the tomahawk down with all his strength and the handle struck the man's wrist, and Billy heard the muffled crack of the bone. The knife flew to one side and rolled in the grass as the man gasped in agony and grabbed his arm behind his broken wrist. A man with a drawn knife standing opposite Billy took a step towards Eli, and Billy's movement was a blur as he grasped the man's arm with his left hand, caught his broad leather belt with his right, and lifted him high and threw him down on his back, where he lay gasping, unable to move, while Billy stood beside Eli, eyes flashing, balanced, ready.

Eli straightened from his crouch and his words came low, guttural, to those of the southern regiment standing nearby. "If anyone else wants to throw our clothes in the dirt, let him step forward."

The crack of a pistol shot and the sound of a running horse turned everyone's head searching to the east. They saw Colonel Israel Thompson spurring a big bay gelding into the outer fringes of the regiment, scattering men, saber flashing over his head in the morning sun, face flushed with anger, and they opened a path. He pulled his running mount to a sliding stop, and the horse threw its head high, fighting the pressure of the bit.

"What's the meaning of this?" he shouted. He turned in the saddle, facing his command. "You men move back ten yards, *now!*"

He wrenched his horse back around facing the southern regiment. "*You men do the same!*" He was trembling, neck veins extended, and he leveled his saber directly at those nearest. "I swear I'll kill the next man who provokes trouble!"

A second horse came pounding in, and a brigadier general wearing a green uniform reined to a halt, facing Thompson.

"I'm General Ballantine," he barked. "What's going on here?"

"I separated the two regiments to avoid trouble."

Ballantine leaned forward, anger flashing. "I'll take command of my regiment, sir."

"Thank you," Thompson said, "and I trust you will bring them under control." He stared steadily into Ballantine's eyes, and

Ballantine broke it off and turned to his men. "You will continue as you were, but under no circumstance will you come within twenty yards of anyone from the Boston regiment."

Lesser officers from both regiments came running and moved in among their men, shouting orders, moving the regiments farther apart. Billy's shoulders slumped and he exhaled held breath as he moved back, warily watching the southern regiment moving back, surly, reluctant, wanting to fight.

In near total silence the Boston regiment finished their bathing and collected their damp clothing and moved back to their campground, eyes seldom leaving the sullen, rebellious faces of the North Carolina regiment. Eli walked behind Billy, weapons belt in place, wet shirt over his shoulder, the long Pennsylvania rifle carried in his right hand, light and easy. Billy was startled when he realized that from the first time he had seen Eli, the man had never been more than a few steps from his rifle and his weapons belt.

The men spread their damp clothes near their blankets, got their muskets and rifles, and sat down, eyes never leaving the men of the southern regiment while they waited for their clothing to dry and thought of breakfast.

The regimental commissary had lost one wagonload of food supplies in a rough river crossing six days earlier. Four days ago the remaining salted meat and vegetables and flour had run out, leaving five barrels of hardtack, so dried it had to be broken with a rock and soaked in canteen water to be eaten, and fried pork belly that was little more than the skin, fried crisp, like pork cracklings.

Three days ago the regiment had gleaned ears of corn from a cornfield near the road, and two days ago they had stuffed hard green apples into their shirts from an orchard across a split-rail fence. That night a dozen of the young had gorged on the green apples, and by three o'clock in the morning the camp was awakened by their moaning as they made their way out of camp, doubled over with stomach cramps, to retch in the grass while older men smiled cynically and shook their heads in the dark.

Billy shrugged into his damp clothes and walked to the

company commissary to get his ration of hardtack and fried sow belly, then returned to his bedroll and knapsack to soak the hardtack and chew on the crisped pork rinds, with small bites of the last green apple from his knapsack. A few moments later Eli approached and dropped to his haunches, hardtack and sow belly in hand. "You put that man down hard back there."

Billy shrugged and said nothing.

"Who taught you?"

Billy thought for a moment. "No one."

A wry smile passed over Eli's face. "You do things like that often?"

Billy grinned. "No. Just didn't have time to think."

"For a minute I thought I was going to have to take on that whole regiment alone. You mixed in and they changed their mind."

Billy laughed out loud. "I don't think I scared anyone. Colonel Thompson changed their minds."

Eli sobered. "Maybe. It's past."

He rose to go and Billy spoke hesitantly. "Did I see you with a Bible this morning?"

Eli looked down at him, and Billy saw him weigh whether he wanted to let anyone into that part of his life. "Yes. Why?"

Billy shrugged, hesitant to ask the question he so much wanted answered. "No reason."

For long moments Eli stared into Billy's face. "Because I was raised Iroquois?"

Billy was taken aback by the open frankness. "Yes."

"You want to know why a white man raised Iroquois would read the Bible?"

"Yes."

An intense look came into Eli's eyes. "Mostly Jesus."

"Jesus?"

"What he taught. There's no bottom to it."

"Who taught you about him?"

"The Jesuits. They taught from the Bible, but they wouldn't let us read it."

Billy was incredulous. "That's why you left the Iroquois? to read the Bible?"

Eli pursed his mouth in thought. "Partly."

Billy knew there was more, but sensed that Eli was going to keep it hidden and that the talk was over. "Sometime maybe we can talk about it," Billy ventured.

"You a reverend?"

"No, I'm an account keeper, but I'm a Christian."

Eli shrugged. "Maybe we can."

The high nasal voice broke in, "All right, you lovelies," and both men turned towards Sergeant Turlock. "Form up the regiment. The colonel wants to talk to us in five minutes, and then we march out of here."

The 482 men formed into a loose square of crooked rank and file, murmuring as they waited. Colonel Thompson came striding to stand before them with his spine straight, chin high.

"We leave in ten minutes. Transports are waiting to ferry us across the Hudson. You will make yourselves as presentable as possible, and you will march into New York smartly, in perfect rank and file."

Murmuring broke out.

Thompson bellowed, "You are at attention! There will be no talking in the ranks. We will be met in New York City and shown to our campground. For now, that is all. Get your packs and be in marching formation in ten minutes."

They marched south half a mile to a place where the primeval cooling of the great upheaval of molten granite had cracked the face of the Palisades, leaving a fissure half a mile inland. In single file the regiment cautiously picked its way down a steep, rocky, narrow trail that had been chiseled and blasted along the north wall of the fissure. At the bottom they came to the waters of the Hudson.

There were no ferries, no water transports waiting. Instead they loaded into square-nosed barges, longboats, and rowboats, shoulder to shoulder, and river men pushed off into the broad expanse of the river, running wide and fast and deep with the late spring runoff from the Adirondacks, the Appalachians, and the Green Mountains to the north. Every eye turned to stare across the three-mile gap at the squat, stubborn silhouette of the ridge on the Manhattan side, and when they reached midriver they turned to look back at the face of the Palisades on the New Jersey side, bright as a jewel in the green of the lush foliage and the morning sun. A sense of quiet confidence arose in their assurance that the forts, on the high ground, would be impregnable. Sweating, they unloaded onto makeshift docks and reassembled on the sloping shore where a trail slanted southward up the face of the ridge. They sat on anything they could, or in the dirt, to wait for the officers, who came last.

Billy shrugged out of the shoulder straps of his knapsack and sat cross-legged on his bedroll, wiping sweat from his hatband, when he felt the first movement of the dead, sweltering air and then the touch of a hot southeasterly breeze on his face. He squinted south, where low, lead-covered clouds were gathering on the horizon, and then he settled back to wait for the barge carrying the officers. It thumped into the dock, the river men looped hawsers over pilings, and the officers unloaded.

Colonel Thompson strode into the gathering of the regiment. "New York is ten miles south. You will form ranks immediately for the march."

The crooked, narrow trail angled upward through scrub oak and brush, and as they crested the top the stir in the air became a hot breeze. Thick clouds rolled in from the south as the column marched due east, then turned south once again on the much wider Post Road that ran the full length of Manhattan Island. Half an hour later the sun was hidden by big-bellied purple clouds, and ten minutes later the clouds flashed bright gold as lightning streaked inside and the deep-throated rumble of thunder came rolling. The first huge drops of rain splattered on their faces and made tiny volcanoes in the dirt of Post Road, and they watched the oncoming south wind whip the trees and brush as it moved towards them, while behind it the cloudburst came sweeping like a great wall.

The wind hit with a roar, and then came rain so thick they fought to breathe. They ducked their heads into the storm and held onto their hats and trudged on, with lightning lacing the clouds and thunder shaking the ground. The scudding clouds passed northward, and the lightning and thunder slackened to leave a heavy, steady rain falling straight down in hot, stifling air, and they slogged on through sticky red mud up to their ankles.

A little after eleven o'clock the first breaks in the purple overcast appeared, and before noon the rain thinned, then stopped as shafts of golden sunlight reached through breaks in the clouds to turn the world into a patchwork of light and shadow. They passed clearings with summer hay knocked down by the cloudburst, orchards, green pastures with milk cows, and cornfields with stalks seven feet high and ears formed and swelling in the heat and moisture of spring. Some farm families gathered inside split-rail fences to wave at them, while others got the children and disappeared behind closed doors and curtained windows. Half a dozen saddled horses stood hipshot, tied in front of the Blue Bell tavern, and four or five men walked out into the mud and sunshine to watch the regiment trudge steadily on, mud-caked to the knees, while the sun drew steam rising from the puddles.

"Break ranks for noon."

They stopped and moved off the quagmire in the road to find grass or brush to sit on and shrugged out of the shoulder straps to drop the weight of their knapsacks and bedrolls. They reached for canteens and sat tired in the sweltering heat, with water running down their backs and off their noses and chins, and they dropped their heads forward and closed their eyes to shut out the sodden world and all thoughts of plodding on.

"Form ranks."

They continued south in the rutted mud of the old Post Road, sweating in soaked clothing, and puddles began to sink into the soil and evaporate into the hot, humid air.

"There it is!"

The shout went through the column and every neck craned to catch the first glimpse of the city of New York, and it was there, rooftops and buildings in the midst of oak and maples. Farther south, above the Narrows, they saw the dim, low skyline of Staten Island and the masts of anchored ships. Excited talk broke out and their step livened.

They crested the hill on William Bayard's farm and then Jones Hill, where they saw the breastworks and muzzles of cannon at the Jones battery, and they continued down to the freshwater lake called the Collect, where Colonel Thompson ordered a halt.

"One hour to wash off the mud and dry your clothes." He paced before them, face stern, voice piercing. "We will march into New York City in clean clothing, with military bearing befitting men of Boston."

They took turns standing guard while others stripped their muddy clothes and washed them in the lake, then hung them on bushes or musket barrels to dry in the early afternoon sun. They fell back into regimental formation and straightened their rank and file, while those with hats put them squarely on their heads. They took proper interval, shouldered their weapons, and on command marched forward, shuffling until all left feet were coming down together.

They came in from the north, past Chatham Square where the old Post Road became Bowery Lane, and Bowery Lane became Broadway. They continued south through McGown's Pass, past the estate of Andrew McGown, then the great, sprawling estate of James DeLancey and the Rutgers mansion. In awed silence they stared at the rich DePeyster, Dyckman, and Stuyvesant mansions.

Off Broadway, on nearby streets and sections, they caught glimpses of other great estates owned by the Apthorps, Strikers, Joneses, Hogelands, Somerindkes, Harsens, and finally, Benjamin Vandewater. They drew nearer to inner New York City, and the streets narrowed as the estates were left behind and the homes diminished in size.

Suddenly they sobered and stared in disbelief as British flags began to appear in many windows and dooryards. Sullen-eyed men and women peered through parted curtains, mouthing curses as the regiment passed. A thrown egg splattered the hat of a sergeant, who held his face straight ahead, continued in stride, and did nothing about it. Shocked, angered, the troops looked at each other and marched on.

Billy glanced up the cross streets and understood that Broadway divided lower Manhattan Island. The streets to the right, west, led to the Hudson River; the streets to the left, to the New York shipping docks and, above Catherine Street, to the shipyards on the East River, where ships with foreign flags were tied, their masts towering above the rooftops of the brown brick warehouses and business buildings.

His eyes widened as he marched past Chambers, Warren, and Murray Streets, where he saw barricades of stone and heavy timbers and some of teakwood commandeered from some foreign ship. He began to count. Vesey, Partition, Deys, Cortlandt Streets—all with barricades and cannon, muzzles trained west towards the Hudson.

He stared in surprise as they passed Washington Street and he saw the Grenadier Battery, then the Jersey Battery on Reade Street with two light and three very heavy cannon, McDougall's Battery and the Oyster Battery south of Trinity Church, the Whitehall Battery, Waterbury's Battery, Bedlam's Redoubt, and Spencer's Redoubt, all on or near the docks on the East River.

Soldiers with muskets were stationed to guard each battery, and every street he had seen leading to the water on either side of the island had barricades thrown up. He had counted over 110 cannon trained on anything approaching New York from the Hudson River, the East River, or the bay south of Manhattan Island.

He gaped at the men patrolling and guarding the batteries. They wore at least fifteen different styles and colors of uniforms, and the regimental and company signs on poles read Oswego

Rangers, Fusiliers, Hearts of Oak, Grenadiers, Sportsmen, German Fusiliers, Light Horse, Artillery, Brown Buffs, Rifles, Hussars, Scotsmen, and half a dozen other names that meant nothing to him.

They reached the wide, grassy common at the foot of Broadway and Wall, where it met the water of the bay and the Narrows that opened into the Atlantic, and marched across to the great Fort George Battery, built on the ruins of the ancient Fort Amsterdam that had been destroyed years earlier by fire. The walls of the rebuilt fort were eight feet thick, bristling with the muzzles of heavy cannon that commanded the harbor.

They marched onto the flat flagstones set in cement on the north side of the fort and stopped on command, quickly realigning themselves, rank and file. Colonel Thompson took his position before them, ordered an about-face so that they were facing the common, backs to the fort, and addressed them briefly. "We are to wait here for our orders, and we will do so. You will stand at rest in regimental formation until such orders arrive. That is all."

They stood in the sweltering heat, waving off flies and mosquitoes and wiping sweat that trickled to sting their eyes and soak their shirts. Half an hour passed, and Billy felt the muscles in his legs begin to stiffen and set. He studied the people and the soldiers and the ebb and flow of traffic on the common and the side streets; he saw the British flags in some windows and the dark looks of some people as they paused to look at the regiment; and slowly the realization struck into him. *This town is divided against itself, half Tories, half Patriots! In a battle we'd have to fight half the people and the British besides! And with all those barricades and batteries, we're in the middle of a powder keg waiting to explode.*

Colonel Thompson called four of his officers with him back onto the grass of the common, and Billy watched an animated discussion before Thompson turned and walked north away from them. The other officers returned to the regiment, still standing on the flagstones, the sun beating down on their heads and shoulders.

An hour later Thompson strode rapidly across the common and once more took his place facing them, his face dark, sober. "You will come to attention!"

They brought their heels together, straightened their spines, brought their rank and file into alignment, and waited.

"We are going to move from here to the common, where we will camp for the night. When you dig your fire pits and latrines, save the sod. Within one hour, three hundred pounds of beef will be delivered to our campsite, together with two hundred pounds of fresh potatoes, three hundred pounds of carrots, two hundred loaves of bread, one hundred dozen eggs, two hundred pounds of coffee, and fifty smoked hams."

He paused and open murmuring broke out.

"You are at attention," he snapped, and continued. "There will also be two hundred plum puddings, three pounds each."

There was a spontaneous outburst, and Thompson ducked his head until it quieted, and then he continued. "I do not know when we will get our next rations, so I instruct you to be judicious. Beef stew will be in order tonight, with bread and coffee and a reasonable portion of plum pudding. Tomorrow morning, fresh eggs with ham and coffee. There is good water at the north end. I leave it to the officers and sergeants to arrange portions, storage, and transport of the unused supplies. Each company to arrange its own cooking facility. Theft of food will result in severe discipline. You men will share and share alike. While we are on this common we will be in plain view of the citizenry of New York City. You will conduct yourselves as gentlemen and patriots. Offenders will be publicly disciplined. Am I clear?"

His face was severe as his eyes met those of his troops. He turned to his officers. "That is all. Carry on."

They stood tall and their ranks were in line as they marched back to the lush, level grass of the common. They divided into companies, and the sergeants supervised setting up the tall iron tripods with the chains and hooks from which the fire-blackened stew pots were suspended. Officers led details of men to the docks and the barricades to gather scrap wood. Forty minutes later two freight wagons rumbled down Broadway onto the common, and the uniformed drivers quieted and held their mules while hundreds of eager hands emptied the wagons and officers and sergeants divided the supplies evenly among the companies.

In early twilight, sergeants stood at the kettles with dippers and filled pewter and wooden bowls to the brim, and grinned as they watched hungry men sit in the grass and scoop great spoonfuls of beef and diced carrots and potatoes, and stuff torn pieces of bread into their mouths and close their eyes as they washed it down with coffee. The men returned with plates to take their ration of rich, hot plum pudding. None of them touched it until they were once again seated in the grass, and then they ate it in small pieces, chewing slowly, savoring it as never before.

Lanterns were lighted in the deep dusk, when all heads turned to the clatter of shod horses cantering on the cobblestones of Broadway. The regiment rose to its feet as uniformed officers reined their horses to a halt near where Colonel Thompson and the regimental officers were gathered about a table at the command tent. The men saw the gold on the shoulders of the eight officers, and they watched Colonel Thompson rise to face them. The leader among the eight stopped a scant four feet from Thompson, eyes flashing anger in the light of the campfires and lanterns. "Sir, are you in command of this brigade?" he demanded.

"I am in command of this regiment."

"Your name, sir."

Thompson paused to examine the man's uniform and the gold epaulets on his shoulders. "Colonel Israel Thompson, Boston militia, sir, under written orders of General George Washington. And whom do I have the honor of addressing?"

"Colonel Jonathan Landon, New York militia, and I too am under written orders of General George Washington." His voice was high, piercing, and he raised his arm to point. "Under whose authority are you bivouacked here on the New York Common?"

"General Lemuel Hosking, Boston militia."

The man's head jerked forward and he fairly shouted, "A *Boston* general ordered you to camp on our *New York common?*"

Thompson didn't hesitate. "A Boston general executed the written orders of General Washington. We were ordered here expecting your General John Morin Scott to meet us with directions to our campsite. He was not here. *No one* was here! I went looking for over one hour and no one knew where he was, so I presumed your General Scott intended us to camp on the common. If you feel otherwise, I will be profoundly *delighted* to accompany you to settle the question as to exactly who in his command utterly failed to execute the orders of General Washington. My officers and I are prepared to do so right now. Your decision, sir."

Colonel Jonathan Landon puffed up like a giant frog, and he tried to speak but could not force a coherent sentence. Thompson stood facing him like something cut from granite, and waited. The Boston regiment silently gathered close by.

Landon spouted, "Were you responsible for the theft of two wagonloads of beef and fresh vegetables? Bread? Eggs? Ham? Plum puddings?"

"There was no theft. My orders stated we would receive rations and a campsite when we arrived and an assignment to assist in the fortification of New York City. There were no rations, nothing, so I concluded your General Scott intended we forage, which I did. I discovered the rations at a commissary near the docks. I filled out the requisition, signed my name, and had them delivered here. We thank you for your hospitality."

"*You* signed the requisition?"

"My own name as commander of the Boston regiment. Your men delivered."

"*Preposterous!* My men delivered on a requisition signed by a *Boston colonel?*"

Behind Thompson, half the regiment had their heads ducked with their shoulders shaking. Thompson's face did not change. "They did. I am not certain your man could read, sir. Perhaps someone should also bring *that* to the attention of General Scott."

From behind, Thompson heard sounds of men choking, strangling, and dared not look back. The veins in Landon's neck extended. His eyes protruded and he shouted, *"Criminals!* You have stolen government stores! The penalty is hanging! I'll return with a warrant—"

Thompson cut him off. "Stolen? No one in this command stole anything. *Your* men delivered the rations. If hanging is in order, perhaps you should begin with them. You swear out a warrant against anyone in this command and I'll have you court-martialed for bringing groundless charges."

"You forged a requisition!"

Thompson's eyebrows rose. "I forged nothing. I signed my own name and rank. I have my receipt, sir, if you care to examine it."

All the air went out of Landon and he stood silent, deflated.

Thompson spoke. "I will need your answer, sir. Do you want me and my officers to meet with you and General Scott right now to put this whole matter to rest? Or do you want to wait for a more opportune time?"

Without a word Landon turned on his heel and he and his men mounted their horses. Thompson called to him, "My compliments to your General Scott, sir. The plum pudding was delicious."

He watched the rigid backs of all eight men disappear in the firelight before he turned to walk back to his table among his officers. The faces of the men behind him were contorted while they fought a losing battle to stifle laughter. As he passed, Sergeant Turlock spoke. "Colonel, sir, beggin' your pardon."

Thompson stopped. "Yes, Sergeant?"

The tough little sergeant looked up into his face. "Sir, that plum puddin' was sure good, sir. It surely was."

Thompson showed no change in his demeanor at the spontaneous outburst of uproarious laughter and the remarks that followed from behind Turlock. "Fine pudding, sir." "The best, sir."

For a moment Thompson looked at his men, and the slightest hint of a smile passed before he spoke to Turlock. "Carry on,

Sergeant. Take care of your men." He walked on through the regiment to his own campfire and table, while Sergeant Turlock grinned his wry grin and murmured, "Yes, sir, sure good puddin'."

In the flickering light of dwindling campfires, the men of the regiment spread their blankets and one by one sat down to stare into the low, dancing flames and glowing embers. A quiet, somber, reflective mood seemed to settle in. The only sounds were those of crickets chirping out their nightly round and the throaty song of frogs near the creek at the north end of the common. Fireflies left tiny glowing trails, like shooting stars. Night insects buzzed, and nighthawks pirouetted on silent wings to catch them.

Billy lay on his blanket, propped on one elbow, staring into the ever-changing flames of a low fire, with others sitting or lying nearby, eyes reflecting the dancing light, each unexpectedly caught up in his own reveries, his own inner reflections.

Billy pulled a long blade of grass and for a moment glanced at the clean white root before he took it into his mouth and slowly worked it with his teeth, and let his mind run unchecked with its own thoughts.

The fight this morning—deadly—too fast—no time to think—Eli quick, sure—the broken wrist—the second man thrown to the ground—if that knife had hit Eli—maybe killed—too fast, too fast.

Without guidance, his thoughts changed.

British flags in the windows, on poles—some people staring ugly—trouble coming from it—certain.

He carefully pulled a second blade of grass.

How many different uniforms today? different signs on different regiments? Can Washington make one army out of thirteen different armies? different rules? different laws? different officers? Maybe—maybe—he better—he has to.

He shook his head.

Did mother get my letter? Did she share it with Margaret? and Brigitte? Brigitte—how is she? Did Mother deliver Eli's message to that other woman, Beatrice McMurdy? Are they all right?

In his mind he saw Matthew—tall, handsome, intense—and felt a rise in his breast.

Is he all right? God, please let him be all right. Kathleen—where is she? How is she? Can she rise above the shame of her father's treachery? Can she find her way back to Matthew? Can she? She has to—has to—their hearts are one— they've got to find a way back—no good without each other.

He moved his legs and settled back down.

We shot a traitor—hard to watch—was he the only one? Are there others in the regiment?

He was suddenly aware of a presence from behind and turned his head. Eli stood with the firelight making soft shadows on his shirt and face. His Bible was in his hand. "Could we talk?"

Billy swung to a sitting position and pointed, and Eli sat down, legs crossed, elbows on knees, and for long moments he stared into the glow of the fire, then spoke without shifting his gaze. "Did your mother deliver that letter to the woman in Charlestown?"

Billy shrugged. "I haven't heard. She'll do it."

"It will be hard for that woman. Son a spy, shot."

Billy read the pain and compassion in Eli's face and felt an unexpected stir inside, but said nothing.

Eli came directly to it. "Do you read the Bible?"

Billy paused in surprise at the abrupt change of direction. "Yes. Mother and I."

"Do you mind talking about it?

"No."

The purring sound of an owl call came from a distance, and Eli paused and his eyes narrowed as he listened. Then he drew and exhaled a great breath and continued. "Back there today, that man with the knife intended to kill me."

Billy nodded.

"I broke his arm, and you threw a man down hard. We were close to a fight, and their men had knives. Things could have gone wrong and a lot of people could have been hurt bad, some killed."

"That's true." Fascinated, Billy watched Eli's face intently, waiting to see where his thoughts were taking them.

Again the sound of an owl came in the dark, closer, and Eli

closed his eyes to concentrate. The sound stopped and Eli continued. "Did we do right?"

Billy's forehead wrinkled in astonishment, and for several seconds he did not speak. "I hadn't thought about that. It stopped some bad things long enough for Thompson to ride in. It was probably right."

Eli nodded agreement, then opened his small Bible. Billy saw the scarred, worn leather cover and the dog-eared, smudged pages as Eli turned them, then stopped and faced the book to the firelight.

"The book of Matthew, chapter five. Starting with verse thirty-nine—no, thirty-eight." His eyes narrowed in deep concentration, and he read slowly, sounding out each word with care. " 'Ye have heard that it hath been said, An eye for an eye, and a tooth for a tooth: but I say unto you, That ye resist not evil: but whosoever shall smite thee on thy right cheek, turn to him the other also. And if any man will sue thee at the law, and take away thy coat, let him have thy cloke also. And whosoever shall compel thee to go a mile, go with him twain. Give to him that asketh thee, and from him that would borrow of thee turn not thou away. Ye have heard that it hath been said, Thou shalt love thy neighbour, and hate thine enemy. But I say unto you, Love your enemies, bless them that curse you, do good to them that hate you, and pray for them which despitefully use you, and persecute you.' "

He stopped and quietly said, "I'm not sure what 'twain' means."

"Two. It means two. If someone asks you to walk one mile with him, walk two."

"That's what I thought." He turned directly to Billy, open, frank. "When that man brought that knife up, he meant to kill me. What would Jesus want me to do?"

Billy's eyes widened at the abruptness of the profoundly simple question, and he opened his mouth to answer, then stopped and did not speak for a time. "Stop him."

"Then what did Jesus mean in Matthew about turning the other cheek? going a second mile?"

"I think he meant try to avoid trouble. Go a long way to avoid trouble."

"Why didn't he say that?"

"He spoke in parables."

"Sometimes they're hard to understand."

"You have to work with them. Think on them."

Eli's forehead wrinkled in thought. "But two men can get two different thoughts from the same words."

"Not if they work with it long enough."

"Maybe." He reached to poke a fresh stick into the fire, and a quiet time passed while they watched the sparks dance and cascade. "What did he mean, love your enemies?"

"I think he meant hate is a poison that will hurt you. Don't hate anyone."

"He didn't say don't hate. He said love them. There's a difference." He reached to touch the scar on his left jaw with his thumb. "The man who did that to me was trying to kill me. I killed him because I had to. I don't recall hating him, or loving him. I only recall his tomahawk, and then mine." He raised his eyes to Billy. "Was I wrong?"

Billy remained silent, grappling with questions for which there were no ready answers. "I don't think it means you have to be foolish, but I do think it means we should have a feeling of charity for everyone. Maybe more for our sake than theirs."

Eli closed his eyes and for a time did not move. "I hadn't thought about what that would do for us inside. I'll have to think on it." Once more he looked directly at Billy. "What does God look like, the one in the Bible?"

Billy recoiled. He could not recall anyone ever asking that question, or answering it. "Do you mean Jesus?"

"No. Jesus says he's the Son. His Father is God. If that's true, then does God look like Jesus? and us?"

The profoundly simple reasoning and the provocative question stopped Billy, and he had no answer. "I don't know."

Eli shook his head and a look of disappointment passed

over his face. "Do you know God's name?"

"What do you mean, name?"

"Jesus is named Jesus. What's God's name?"

Again Billy pondered, searching for an answer, and none would come. "I don't know if he has ever said. I think he said once that he was the great 'I AM.' "

"That's a title, like King, but it's not a name."

Billy shook his head, confounded by the startling, clear reasoning that left him without comment or answers. "I don't know if he has a name."

Eli shook his head and remained silent, a sadness in his eyes.

The faint sound of another owl came drifting in the warm night air, far to the east, and Eli suddenly raised his head, face caught in deep concentration, the scar on his left jawline prominent in the flickering firelight. From closer, the louder answer of another owl, and then the distant sound came once more, and then there was silence. A full minute passed before Eli lowered his face to stare once again into the fire.

Billy broke the silence. "Owls bother you?"

"Those were not owls."

Billy started. "No?"

"Those were white men. White men learned night talk from the Indians, but not good enough. Two white men are out there now, more than a mile apart, talking."

"Saying what?"

"No way to tell. The question isn't what; the question is why." Eli reached once more to poke at the fire with a stick and watch the orange sparks rise and drift back. "We already shot one turncoat. I hope we don't have to do it again."

The implication slowed Billy. "You sure those were men?"

"Certain." He raised his face, and his eyes were points of light in the glowing embers. He rose to his feet, Bible in hand, adjusted his weapons belt, brushed the grass from his buckskins, and walked away with that peculiar swinging stride until he disappeared in the darkness.

Billy turned his face back to the dying remains of his fire, then glanced one more time into the darkness where Eli had disappeared. Inside he felt a strange rise of excitement at the brief time he had spent talking with Eli.

What does God look like—his name—where did he get those questions? What other questions are in his mind? What does he see that I've never seen—know that I've never known? What god did the Iroquois teach him about? What other reasons did he have to leave them and come into the white world?

Billy watched the orange glow of the fire embers blacken and die, and then lay back on his blanket, hands behind his head, staring into the endless blackness and stars above. From the north end of the camp came the quiet rattle of the regimental drummer sounding tattoo. Campfires out. Go to your blankets. Billy smothered his tiny fire with dirt, settled onto his blanket, and once more reflected on the strange time he had just spent with a white man raised Iroquois, whose simple questions about the Bible left him without answers.

We'll talk again, he and I.

Notes

The Dutch word *Breukelen* (pronounced "Brurkeler") is the original name for the city Brooklyn. It means "marshland," since the Gowanus Creek that runs through Brooklyn broadens to create a great marshy bog before it reaches the East River. The bog was known as Gowanus Marsh (see Johnston, *The Campaign of 1776*, part I, pp. 44–45).

Fort Lee on the New Jersey Palisades, Fort Washington across the Hudson River on Manhattan Island, and their strategic position as guardians of the Hudson appear on a map in Higginbotham, *The War of American Independence*, pp. 156–57. General Washington had boats filled with rock tied together and sunk in the Hudson River between the two forts, and a monstrous chain strung with them, intending to form a barrier against British boats in the river.

Buglers did not sound reveille and taps, morning and night, as they do now. A drummer pounded out reveille to awaken the soldiers in the morning and sounded "tattoo" to signal lights out at day's end (see Wilbur, *The Revolutionary Soldier*, p. 47).

The Continental army consisted of men from all walks of life who had joined to fight for home, country, and liberty. They were not professional soldiers; consequently their camps and their military conduct fell far short of that expected of soldiers. For an excellent description, see Johnston, *The Campaign of 1776*, part I, pp. 122–24.

The novel's description of the Boston regiment's march south from the site of Fort Washington on Manhattan Island to the common at the south end of New York City contains several references to historic sites, street names, regiments, uniforms, barricades, gun emplacements, and the general layout of New York City, including population and number of buildings, all of which are described in Johnston, *The Campaign of 1776*, part I, pp. 36–40, 84–92, 104–9. This source also includes an exceptional map showing the Post Road and many other roads.

The Iroquois longhouse and the role played by the Jesuit missionaries in the Iroquois culture are described in Graymont, *The Iroquois in the American Revolution*, pp. 330–31; see also pp. 5, 13, 17, 19, 26–28, 59.

Frictions sometimes developed between regiments from different colonies, resulting in arguments and, occasionally, fights, of which the clash depicted here between the Boston regiment and a southern regiment is meant to be representative (see Martin, *Private Yankee Doodle*, pp. 116–17, 135–36).

Sergeant Alvin Turlock, General Ballantine, and Colonel Jonathan Landon are fictional characters.

New York

Mid-June 1776

CHAPTER VI

★ ★ ★

*T*he heavy rattle of wide iron-rimmed wheels and iron horseshoes on cobblestones brought the heads of the regiment up from pewter plates heaped with scrambled eggs and ham strips, and they watched a column of eight New York militia officers lead a team of mules pulling a freight wagon from Broadway onto the thick grass of the common, wet with heavy morning dew.

In brilliant six-thirty A.M. sunlight Billy glanced towards the command tent, where Thompson and his staff ducked through the flap and stopped to study the incoming entourage. The leader had gold braid on his shoulder, but no one in the Boston regiment recognized the rank. He stopped his men twenty feet from Thompson, dismounted, and walked forward to stop before the Boston regimental command.

"My compliments to you. I am General John Morin Scott. I presume you are Colonel Israel Thompson." The man was average size, young for a general, energetic, charismatic.

Thompson's face was noncommittal. "I am, sir. At your service." The two shook hands perfunctorily.

"May I have audience with you in private?"

"Concerning what matter, sir?"

"Many things."

"Follow me, sir." Thompson led him into the command tent and gestured, and they sat down at the table. Thompson waited.

"My apologies for the fiasco last night about the common and the rations. I issued written orders that went astray. We think we have a spy somewhere. You did right by your men."

Scott removed his hat. His hair was already sweaty, stuck to his forehead in the muggy heat. He leaned forward, focused. "Some things you should know. Boston is strongly Patriot, but New York is not. About half the people you see out there are Tories, loyal to the Crown. There have been open battles in the streets between them and the Patriots. About one out of ten people in town, man or woman, is a spy for one side or the other. Our pickets have been shot at during the night. One or two killed."

Thompson leaned back in his chair. "What are your orders to your pickets?"

"At night, challenge once, then shoot to kill."

Thompson gaped. "That bad?"

"That bad. Check any rations you get. We found some poisoned flour and some bad turkeys and mutton." An unexpected smile flashed. "The beef and ham are all right."

Thompson dropped his face and smiled.

"We've received death threats. You'll get some if you're here very long. Keep pickets posted day and night, double if you feel the need."

Thompson pursed his mouth. "Is General Washington here?"

"He was at 180 Pearl Street, but moved a few days back. He's headquartered at the Mortier house, over near Richmond Hill, not far from McDougall's Battery and the Oyster Battery. You passed the battery coming in."

"I remember. Any death threats against him?"

"Every day."

"Do you have written orders for this regiment?"

"In a minute. First, about your cooking fires and latrines."

"We saved the sod. We'll leave the common in good condition."

Scott nodded his head. "Rations are short. Few blankets, no tents, little food. We'll do all we can, but we have a large force to maintain. Be prudent."

"What's your strength now? from where?"

"About twelve thousand, but we don't know exactly because some are coming and going all the time, from all over, every colony. Mostly without uniforms or supplies." He shook his head. "Different manuals of arms, different officers, different dialects. Sometimes it's total chaos. Been a few fights between regiments. You could be combined with a regiment from anywhere. Caution your men to be patient and tolerant."

"I understand. I noticed barricades and batteries everywhere when we came in."

"General Washington knows that the British plan to invade New York soon, but he doesn't know where. British regulars are on Staten Island right now staging. We have a force on Long Island digging trenches and throwing up breastworks if the assault comes there."

"What's the British strength?"

"We don't know. Much more than ours."

"Which side will the local population support when the fighting starts?"

Scott sighed and shook his head. "Probably half them, half us." His eyes narrowed. "Right now New York is hanging in the balance. There's open talk that whichever way the battle goes, the other side is going to burn the city to the ground."

Thompson rounded his mouth and slowly blew air.

Scott reached inside his tunic, and his demeanor sharpened. "Here are your written orders, signed by myself, according to my written orders from General Washington. Do you wish to see my orders?"

Thompson shook his head as Scott handed him the document.

"Your regiment is to report to the Jersey Battery at the end of Reade Street, just west of Greenwich. They've put two twelve-pounders and three thirty-two-pounders in there to cover the North River. Your men are to help haul rock and cut timbers for the breastworks. The map inside will show you where."

"The North River?"

"Hudson. West side of the island." He pointed.

"When do we report?"

"As soon as you can. I'll leave the wagon and some men and an officer to transport your remaining rations. The officer can help with any problems. He'll respond to your orders. Name's Jacob Truman. A captain."

Thompson nodded.

Scott dropped one palm flat, smacking on the tabletop. "General Washington has to make all this work. Try to smother any problems before they start. I think that about covers it."

"Thank you, sir."

Scott stood and ducked out the tent flap. Thompson followed as the general walked to his waiting horse, and as Scott mounted, Thompson called the regiment to attention. "Thank you, sir."

Scott looked down, a regiment of Boston faces looked up at him, and Billy saw him struggle with an impulse. His eyes crinkled and a grin spread and he said, "How was the plum pudding?"

Men grinned and there were stifled comments. Thompson said nothing, while Scott's shoulders shook with a silent laugh. "And you thieves didn't invite me to the party!"

Open guffaws rolled out over the common. Scott raised two fingers to his hat brim, then smartly reined his mount around back towards Broadway, followed by his officers.

Thompson turned to his officers. "Have the men strike camp and then assemble them on the common for orders."

At eight-thirty A.M. Thompson faced the regiment as they stood at rigid attention. "Our orders are to report to the Jersey Battery at the west end of Reade Street to assist in constructing breastworks for cannon. General Scott informed me of some things you need to know."

The regiment listened, eyes growing ever wider as Thompson described the chaotic conditions into which they had been thrust—Tories, dead pickets, spies, death threats, poisoned food, sabotage. Billy licked suddenly dry lips as the thought flashed,

Owls talking at night—about what? more dead pickets? more sabotage?

Thompson paused to organize his thoughts and conclude. "We will have double pickets at all times, day and night. Watch the rooftops and windows and all people you see. At night, challenge once, and then shoot to kill."

He looked at Major Bascom. "Move the regiment to the Jersey Battery."

They marched out, silent, watching the roofline, the side streets, everyone that moved. They passed barricades with narrow-eyed pickets holding primed muskets at the ready. Children darted out, some to wave, some to throw sticks and run. They turned left, with the rhythmic sound of their marching feet echoing slightly as they wound through the crooked, narrow, cobblestone street, and then they saw the broad, dark expanse of the Hudson where the buildings stopped. They crossed Greenwich Street and moved out onto the sandy, rocky shore of the Hudson near a regiment of men stripped to the waist, sweating with axes and picks.

Captain Jacob Truman led them to their campground, and they unloaded the supply wagon. Truman saluted and led his small detail back the way they had come. By ten o'clock they had established camp where the rocky beach met the grassy slopes at the end of Reade Street, and received their orders. By ten-thirty the regiment was divided into four work crews, stripped to the waist, sweating.

One trimmed and cut logs to measured twelve-foot lengths, sharpened at both ends. Another loaded them onto wagons to be hauled to the battery and set upright and packed solid in two trenches six feet deep, three feet apart. The third drove oxen or mules hitched to great sleds. And the fourth loaded the sleds with stones to be skidded back to the breastworks and dropped in the three-foot gap between the two rows of logs anchored in the rocky soil at town's edge.

They broke for one hour at noon, ate their ration of beef and vegetables, drank river water, and lay down in whatever shade they could find. At one o'clock they went back to their workstations and once again doggedly settled into a steady rhythm. Soft hands blistered on shiny axe and pick handles, and the water blisters broke to expose the tender pinkness beneath and leave small flaps of skin hanging loose in their palms. Men paused to pull off the hanging skin, then tear strips of cloth and wrap their hands; and they grimaced as they continued the relentless work. At three-thirty a wagon rattled to a stop near the battery, with six barrels of fresh cold water, and they took turns drinking from wooden dippers and pouring the chill water over their heads.

At six o'clock, with the sun dropping towards the New Jersey skyline, the order came to cease work and prepare the evening mess. Tired men walked to the river and stripped off their shirts before they dropped to their haunches to wash sweat and dirt, then get their shirts and shrug into them. Some walked to the commissary for lard to work into the raw blisters, and the farmers, with hands hardened by a lifetime of work with axes and picks and hammers, stopped them. "Not lard. Keeps them soft. Rub salt. Burns, but heals and hardens."

Billy rose dripping from the riverbank and pulled his shirt over his head and tucked it in. He smoothed his long reddish hair back as best he could and retied the leather thong. He paused to look at the twin rows of logs of the breastworks and at the stones he and his crew had hauled from the sleds to drop thumping between. The fortifications were taking shape.

He looked south towards the Connecticut regiment they had joined, where the men were moving into their established routine of evening mess and blankets, occasionally looking north at the Boston regiment. Almost no words had passed between the two camps throughout the day; each had done its work with no interference from the other. Billy drew and released a great breath. *Maybe there'll be no trouble.*

Driftwood cook fires were lighted beneath huge black kettles hung from chains on tall iron tripods, and river water was poured in from wooden buckets. The last of the beef and potatoes and carrots was diced and dropped into the steaming pots. Cooks grasped handfuls of salt and slowly sifted it in while they stirred with long-handled wooden spoons.

Billy walked to his blanket and knapsack, looking closely at the skin of his hands, roughened from hauling river rocks but not blistered. He got out his plate and spoon and sat down, waiting for the call from the cooks. It came and he waited his turn in line, then held his plate while the cook loaded his portion and laid a thick slice of bread with it. Billy returned to his blanket and sat down cross-legged. He took the first smoking spoonload and blew on it before he gingerly tested it with his tongue, then took it into his mouth and sucked air with it to cool it. He savored the richness as he loaded his spoon again.

The sound of an incoming horseman brought his head up, and he watched a rider with a large pouch tied to his saddle walk his horse from the end of Reade Street and angle towards the command tent. The man dismounted, untied the white canvas sack and settled it onto the tall grass, and spoke to the picket. "Mail for the Boston regiment. Is this the right place?"

"It is." The picket turned and lifted the tent flap. "Sir, mail has arrived."

Thompson came out immediately, signed the receipt, and asked, "Is there anything else?"

"No, sir."

"Thank you." Thompson gestured to the picket, who seized the mail sack and followed him into the command tent.

Most of the regiment had seen the incoming rider and the conspicuous sack and guessed that mail had arrived. They began putting down their plates and rising to their feet to gather at the command tent, hoping against hope they would have something from home. The boys from the farms lined up first, with both fear and hope in their faces, all thoughts of food lost in their deep longing for mother and family and home.

Billy raised his spoon and continued his supper. *It's too soon— no letter from Mother.*

Inside the tent Thompson quickly sorted out all the mail

addressed to him and the officers, pushed the remainder back into the bag, ducked out the tent flap, and handed the mail pouch to the picket. "Have Major Bascom distribute this."

Ten minutes later Billy jerked his head up, startled at the call of his name, and trotted to get a thick brown packet. He turned from Major Bascom and read the neatly written name in the upper left corner of the face of the heavy packet and stopped in his tracks, gaping. His breath came short and his heart leaped as he read the neat, beautifully scrolled writing: "Miss Brigitte Dunson." For a moment he was transported back in time and again saw her on the day of farewell when she had impulsively thrown her arms about him and held him as one dear, and he once again felt the lift into a world he never knew existed when he dared put his arms about her and hold her for a moment.

He broke into a trot to his blanket and dropped to his knees. With trembling fingers he broke the seal, opened the packet, and sorted through the maps until he found the letter written by Brigitte, and suddenly the thought struck him: *Why Brigitte? Is Mother all right?* He calmed his racing thoughts and read.

Dear friend Billy:

I take pen in hand to tell you of strange occurrences . . .

Slowly he read her letter, and his forehead wrinkled as he studied the map, the three documents written in an unrecognized hand, and the two sheets with the odd lines. He worked his way through Brigitte's letter again, handling the other six documents in turn as he began to understand the explanation and directions. For five minutes he stared at the documents while his mind pushed and tugged at them, trying to comprehend the unbelievable implications.

"Mail from home?"

Billy flinched and stared up at Eli beside him, wondering how he had gotten so close without a sound. "Yes."

"Mother?"

"No. A friend. Brigitte Dunson. Brigitte and my mother delivered your message to Beatrice McMurdy." Billy gestured and Eli sat down facing him on the blanket, rifle at his side.

"Mrs. McMurdy take it all right? about her son?"

Billy shook his head. "Read this." He handed Brigitte's letter to Eli.

For ten minutes Billy quietly finished his stew and bread, then drank from his canteen, while Eli studied the documents, sorting through them, putting the puzzle together. Billy scrubbed his plate and fork with river sand, rinsed them with canteen water, and set them on his blanket to dry.

Eli lowered Brigitte's letter and raised his eyes to Billy. "Who's Brigitte Dunson?"

"Our families are close. Brigitte is the oldest daughter. Her brother Matthew is my friend."

Eli saw that Billy's eyes softened as he spoke the name *Brigitte,* and something inside Eli stirred and for a moment he dropped his eyes. He raised them back to Billy and asked, "Can you make sense of all this?"

Billy shook his head.

"Ever heard of someone named T. Horton?"

"Never. And I've never heard of anyone buying fish with letters in code."

"Any idea what this map shows?"

"None."

"She says the military in Boston sent this to the military headquarters here. Suppose they're doing something about it?" Once again Eli studied the map intently, turning it slowly, peering at it from every angle. Baffled, he shook his head. "Maybe someone should ask."

"Maybe they should. I'll take the papers to Colonel Thompson in the morning. He'll know what to do."

Eli nodded and handed them back, and Billy folded them back into the packet as Eli reached for his rifle to leave.

Billy spoke. "Have any time to talk?"

Eli shrugged. "About what?"

"You said one of the reasons you left the Iroquois was because of the Bible—Jesus."

Eli nodded.

"Can I ask about the Iroquois god?"

Eli drew and released a sigh. "Which one?"

"You have more than one?"

"Several. Like in the Bible."

A look of surprise crossed Billy's face. "The Bible? There's only one God in the Bible."

Eli shook his head but said nothing.

Billy's forehead wrinkled. "No? Then how many?"

Eli drew a heavy breath. "I don't know. In the first part—Genesis, I think it is called—it talks about the Creation, and it says God said, 'Let us make man in our image.' Who is 'us,' and who is 'our'? Who was God talking to? And later, it talks about God the Father, God the Son, and God the Holy Ghost. Are they all Gods?"

Billy stared, then recovered. "I hadn't thought about Genesis, but the Father and the Son and the Holy Ghost are one God."

"How?"

"I don't know. It's a mystery."

A look of deep puzzlement crossed Eli's face. "All three in the same body?" He turned his face directly to Billy, and in it Billy saw a deep hunger to know.

He reached inside himself for an answer, and there was none. "I don't know about three in the same body."

Seconds passed before Eli spoke again. "That night in the garden, before they killed Jesus, it says he prayed to his Father for help. Was he praying to himself?"

Billy saw the irreconcilable conflict, and he saw the pain in Eli's face as he struggled, but Billy had no answer. "I don't know what that part of the Bible means. I only know that there is a God, and that the Bible is his book. What I don't understand I accept on faith. Someday I hope to understand it all. I don't know what else to say."

The sun had settled onto the cliffs across the Hudson, casting long shadows eastward. The men of the regiment moved about, weary, subdued, doing only those things necessary to bed down for the night. Eli and Billy paid no heed, lost in their thoughts.

Eli spoke quietly. "I've read that part so many times. Why do they say we can't understand it?"

"Did the Jesuits explain it?"

"No. They said what you said, but that only confuses what the Bible makes plain. God the Father has a Son named Jesus, and he sent Jesus to this earth." Again he faced Billy. "Is that too simple?"

Billy put wood chips in his small fire pit, struck flint to steel, and gently blew until a flame flickered. He added more chips, then small twigs of dried driftwood, and for a time they watched the flames spread in the twilight. "I don't know. I've never thought of it that way. It's like God being everywhere all the time. I'm not sure what that means, either."

Eli shook his head, and a look of great sadness came into his eyes, and he spoke with quiet deliberation. "White men have lost something in themselves. They can no longer hear and see from inside." His hand made a slow, wide, sweeping gesture at earth and heaven. "Everything has its place in the plan of God, and its own message. The sun and stars and moon, the rocks, the rivers, the woods, the animals—everything. He created it and gave it to us. He made it all, and it all tells truth to your soul that your mind cannot understand, and that truth is God's, if we will only learn to listen." He shook his head and his face dropped.

The power of the simple faith and reasoning struck into Billy, and for a time he remained still, reluctant to speak. Then he asked, "Do you understand the Iroquois god?"

"Yes, most of it. Enough of it."

"Does he have a name?"

"Which one?"

"The highest one."

"Taronhiawagon."

"What does that mean in English?"

Eli thought for a time, working with a translation. "He Who Bears the Heavens on His Shoulders."

"Are there gods beneath him?"

"Yes."

"Who are they?"

"The Twin Brothers. The Good Twin and the Bad Twin. And some others."

"Twin Brothers?"

"The Good Twin brings us all good things. The bad one all that is evil."

Billy's breathing slowed. *Jesus and Satan! They have their own Jesus and Satan! Did they get it from us, or we from them?* "Where does the Iroquois god stay?"

"At his home in the heavens, but his spirit is everywhere. He made everything, and his spirit is in all he made."

"What does he look like?"

Eli looked at Billy with his frank, open expression. "Us. We are all his children."

"If we are his children, does he have a wife?"

"Yes. First Woman of the Earth."

"Where is she?"

"With him, where she should be. A woman descended directly lives today."

"Who?"

"Ji-gon-sa-seh."

"What does that mean in English?"

Eli's forehead furrowed while he struggled to translate. "The Mother of Nations."

For a time Billy stared into the fire, fascinated, absorbed in thoughts so new he did not think to speak further.

Dusk gave way to moonless darkness, and still the two men sat on the blanket, elbows on knees, the firelight playing shadows on their faces, lost in an exchange of thoughts that obsessed them, left them unaware of time and place.

Finally Billy asked, "What name did the Iroquois give you?"

Eli smiled. "Skuhnaksu."

Billy grinned. "What does it mean?"

Eli shook his head. "It translates directly as the One It Skin Bad Is. In your language, the Bad-Skinned One, and it means 'fox.' They say it that way because foxes have red fur and it looks like the sun has burned it."

Billy chuckled and Eli grinned, and Billy quietly tried to pronounce it. Eli corrected him, and within a few seconds Billy had it right, with the peculiar glottal stop at the end.

"Why did they name you Skuhnaksu?"

"Because I was white and each spring my skin would sunburn before it became brown."

They chuckled together as a soldier walked by, lantern in hand, and nodded to them in passing.

Billy pointed after the soldier. "What's the word for *lantern?*"

"Yachihri thrat'ah."

"What is the translation?"

Eli dropped his face to think. "One drags light with."

Billy shook his head in wonderment, and then he sobered. "You lost your family?"

For a long time Eli stared into the fire. "Not all. I was two when the Iroquois came. I can remember small bits of it. I remember Father dead at my feet and Mother dead in the bedroom, and the heat in the cabin when it burned. I remember them taking me."

He stopped, and Billy saw a faraway look steal into Eli's eyes and a longing that made Billy's heart ache.

"I have an older sister. Golden hair, blue eyes. I remember her pushing against the door when the cabin was burning and the Iroquois came through the door." He licked his lips and shook his head as though to rid himself of unwanted memories. "I think she tried to save me. I don't know what happened to her. The Iroquois never said, and the Jesuits couldn't find out. Most of my reason for leaving the Iroquois was to find her. I will look for her until I find her, or know she's dead."

"Do you remember her name?"

"Only what I called her. Iddi. I know that's not her name, but that's what I called her, and that's all I can remember."

"After you left the Iroquois, did you go back to your home?"

"Yes. There's nothing left, after seventeen summers and winters. No one within a hundred miles knew anything. I asked. I learned about George Washington and the war and that regiments of men were gathering from all over. I thought maybe some man in a regiment from the north might remember something, so I came looking. A traveling preacher told me they were all gathering to New York, so I came south and heard this regiment was marching to New York, so I joined. I hope someone from the north can remember something."

"Do you mind if I ask around?"

"That would be good. I thank you."

The night song of bullfrogs had begun, with the crickets adding to the sounds of flying insects. Fireflies left their signatures in the velvet blackness. Dwindling fires glowed up and down the camp, and fresh pickets marched to replace tired ones.

"You mentioned George Washington. Was there a reason?"

Eli nodded. "He's special. I want to meet him once before I die."

"What do you mean, special?"

"There is an—"

Without warning Eli's head jerked up, eyes narrowed, every nerve instantly taut. Billy started to speak and Eli raised a hand to silence him, and then his eyes closed as he listened intently. Billy heard nothing but the frogs and crickets and the usual sounds of a military camp coming to the end of a hard day, but he remained motionless, silent, waiting for Eli to move or speak.

Eyes still closed, Eli's hand pointed, then shifted to point again another direction. His words were whispers, nearly inaudible. "Hear it?"

Billy closed his eyes and concentrated and only then did it come to him. The distant call of an owl. He started to speak and again Eli raised a hand to stop him, still locked in deep concentration. Again the distant call came floating, and Eli did not move.

Suddenly an answering owl call much closer came loud and Eli's eyes opened wide. It came once more, and then stopped.

"Authentic?" Billy whispered.

Eli shook his head. "The first one, far, was a white man. The second one, close, was either an owl or an Indian. I think Indian. I think there's a white man and an Indian out there talking."

For five seconds the two men locked eyes while their thoughts ran wild to explain what they had heard. In one easy, fluid movement Eli came to his feet, tall and unreal in the firelight, face like stone, eyes points of light, and Billy was stunned to realize that in an instant the white man Eli Stroud had become an Iroquois warrior named Skuhnaksu—the Fox—once again.

"Watch my rifle. I'll be back."

Billy rose, alarmed. "You don't have permission to leave camp. There're pickets. They'll shoot to kill."

"Watch the rifle."

"You be careful."

Eli strode to the edge of camp and disappeared beyond the campfires, while half a dozen men turned their heads to watch him. One followed him, calling, "You got no permission to leave camp—you'll be shot." The man stopped where the light stopped, shrugged, and came back to his blanket.

The tip of a quarter moon rose above the New Jersey cliffs behind Eli as he silently worked his way north and east in the blackness, through grass and brush and scrub oak, and onto the grass behind the scattered houses near the end of Reade Street. Window shades glowed, and he avoided the light as he moved between houses. A dog growled and he froze and backed up and moved to his left and continued. He stopped and dropped to his haunches, listening, eyes wide in the blackness, and the music of the frogs and the crickets continued uninterrupted. He moved west onto a crooked dirt road, then worked north again, slowing, and then stopped again and waited. Minutes passed and he remained motionless, waiting, and then it came again, closer—the call from the distant owl. He gauged distance and direction without moving, and waited.

Where's the answer? There's got to be an answer.

Minutes passed, with only the frogs and crickets sounding in the silence, and then the answer came, very close, and Eli had to make up his mind.

Indian. It's an Indian. He doesn't know I'm here yet. Wait. He'll move. Wait. Wait. Seconds became a minute, and he felt the hair on his neck and arms rise. *Did he see me coming in? Ambush?* Without a sound he placed his right hand on the head of his tomahawk and opened his mouth to breathe silently, missing no sound, no movement in the night, and by force of will he did not move.

He sensed it before he saw it, and through slitted eyes he watched a silent shadow move quickly from half a dozen scrub oak to a growth of bushes, crouched, head turning every direction.

Indian! He missed me!

The quarter moon hung low over the western skyline, casting only enough light to faintly reveal the nearly hidden outlines of trees and buildings. But for those who had spent a life dependent on sensing what could not be seen or heard, the light was enough. Eli counted twenty breaths, then quickly moved across the open space and dropped behind bushes. Ahead, to his right, some crickets momentarily silenced, then continued, and he soundlessly drew his tomahawk from his belt and moved in that direction. Minutes passed as he continued tracking the man ahead, steadily working through the dark streets and houses, north and west, across a narrow, crooked dirt street, past an abandoned, crumbling barn, onto a cobblestone street, and then straight west. The houses became larger, then mansions, and Eli stopped.

Close. This has to be close to where the first owl call came from.

On the corner ahead, light glowed from many window shades on both floors of a large house outward towards the street. In the dim light, Eli made out half a dozen men in full uniform standing in a line near the street, and he understood they were soldiers and bore muskets with bayonets. He settled down behind bushes and began a patient study of the men and what they were doing.

Pickets. Who lives in that house?

Without warning a shadowy figure, also in full uniform, appeared from beside the house and walked unchallenged through the line of soldiers and angled west directly towards Eli. Eli moved his feet, ready for a silent retreat, and he began gauging distance in the dark.

Fifty feet. At fifty feet I move.

At seventy feet the man suddenly stopped, turned to look at the soldiers behind, then motioned with his arm. From nowhere a crouched figure appeared and they exchanged objects that Eli could not see, and then the figure disappeared, moving south as quickly as it had come. The uniformed man turned on his heel, strode back to the house, moved through the line of soldiers, and vanished beside the building.

Eli made the instant decision and moved silent as a cat towards the place the men had met, and then he turned south into the bushes, where he stopped, listening. There was nothing, no sound.

I lost him!

He wished he could strike flint to steel and make a light and look for tracks, but he dared not. By dead reckoning he moved on, covering open spaces at a run, gambling he would find the man ahead before the man discovered him. Ahead a dog barked and Eli dropped to the ground, then sprinted, crouched. He stopped, worked past the dog without a sound, and ahead caught a blur of movement beneath a lighted window at the side of a large brick house. He saw more pickets in the street in front.

Got him!

He waited for three seconds while the man crouched beneath the window, did something Eli could not see, then turned to his right and moved northwest, through the yard of the neighboring house. The pickets had seen nothing, raised no alarm.

Eli counted twenty more breaths, then moved, crouched, tom-ahawk in hand, following the man back towards the Hudson. Two hundred feet short of the river, past the last of the houses and buildings, the man turned north onto a footpath through the weeds and sea grass and broke into a ground-eating trot, showing no caution, no concern of being seen or heard. Eli followed one hundred yards behind, as the dirt trail wound around outcroppings of rocks and clumps of oak and maple. They passed the large lake called the Collect far to their right, and the man veered west once more, down to the river's edge, where he threw brush aside and dragged a hidden canoe to the water's edge. He paused to look behind and listen for a time; then, satisfied he was alone, he shoved the canoe scraping into the water and stepped in. Eli watched as the river current caught the light birch-bark Indian craft and drifted it south as the man dug his paddle into the black water, driving towards the far New Jersey shore.

Eli pushed the handle of his tomahawk through his weapons belt and turned back south on the dirt path, moving at a trot, unconcerned about being seen or heard. The path ended near an old abandoned shed, and Eli continued on south, moving through the streets until he came to Reade Street, where he turned west. He slowed as he came to the regimental campgrounds, located the nearest pickets, and silently passed between them. He worked his way to Billy's blanket, where Billy sat before the remains of his fire, the rifle across his lap, waiting. As Eli settled beside Billy, he glanced at the moon and judged the time to be after one A.M.

"Are you all right?" Billy whispered.

Eli ignored the question and spoke in hushed tones. "Strange things happening out there." Both men lost track of time as Eli chose his words, and Billy sat like a statue, groping to believe the wild story. Eli fell silent, and still Billy said nothing while his mind struggled with a hundred questions, each getting in the way of the other.

Eli shook his head in the darkness. "I don't know if the Indian was Iroquois. If he's Mohawk, then maybe Joseph Brant, or maybe Red Jacket or Blacksnake of the Seneca, are with the British. If Joseph Brant's with them . . ." Again he shook his head.

"Who's Joseph Brant?"

"Mohawk shaman. Earlier this year he went to London with General Howe to visit the king. They made some sort of agreement."

"London? An Indian went to London to meet the king?"

Eli turned his face to Billy and spoke with emphasis. "Don't underestimate Joseph Brant. He's likely smarter than King George, and may be the most powerful leader in the northern tribes."

"What's a shaman?"

"Medicine man. Joseph Brant's a shaman, but he's also a great war leader. He'll get the Mohawk or the Iroquois to do things no other leader can. If he's the one in command, George Washington has a lot of trouble he doesn't know about."

"Isn't Joseph Brant an English name?"

"Yes, but he's full-blood Mohawk. His Mohawk name is Thayendanegea, but his baptized Christian name is Joseph Brant, and he speaks good English. A long time ago he sided with the English against the French. He's the one Mohawk with enough power and leadership to make real trouble."

"Who's Red Jacket?"

"An Iroquois leader. He's a hothead, but he's no Joseph Brant."

Silence held for a time while Billy let his mind settle and organized his racing thoughts. "We better report this to Colonel Thompson."

Eli shook his head. "Not yet. At first light I'm going to be back at that big house where that man met the Indian, and then down to the second house before anyone's in the streets. I got some tracks to look at. When I'm sure, we tell Thompson."

"You're going back?"

"I'll leave about four o'clock."

"There're pickets everywhere."

Eli ignored the comment and stood, and Billy handed him his rifle. "Thanks for watching the rifle. I'll see you before morning reveille."

A little before four o'clock a sleepy-eyed picket thought he saw a shadow move forty feet to his left, and he brought his musket around and opened his mouth to challenge, but there was nothing there. He yawned and settled his musket back onto his shoulder.

At fifteen minutes past four o'clock Eli stopped at the place the two men had met and exchanged something, and he dropped to his haunches behind bushes to study the house. Six pickets were still in a line across the front, and there was still light behind drawn shades, one on the first floor, one on the second. He settled into a sitting position and watched, waiting for first light. Minutes passed while the eastern sky changed from velvet black to deep purple and the morning star dimmed. The roofs of houses and tops of tall trees became defined, and Eli could see bushes in yards, and then white picket fences.

He moved low and fast to the place where the earlier meeting had taken place in the dirt street, and dropped to one knee. Quickly he examined the prints, one set of moccasins, one of square-toed, flat-heeled boots. The man wearing the moccasins weighed about 170 pounds, the man in the boots about 130 pounds. The moccasins walked toed-in slightly, nearly in-line, authentic Indian. The boots were slightly toed-out and walked side by side. The man came down heavy on his heels, military, and the right foot showed uneven pressure on the outside of the foot, like a crooked leg—a man who had broken a leg earlier in life and got a bad set on the bone.

Eli glanced up the street. He could see the pickets individually, the color of their uniforms, and the bayonets on their muskets. He drew and released a big breath, then stood and walked rapidly up the middle of the street, rifle held loosely in his hand.

He was sixty feet from the nearest picket before he was seen, and the man frantically jerked his rifle from his shoulder and pulled back the big hammer. "Stop or I'll shoot," he shouted, and the other pickets came running to his side, muskets at the ready, bayonets lowered at Eli.

Eli raised both hands above his head, holding his rifle loosely, and stopped in his tracks. He opened his eyes wide and his mouth dropped open. "I'm stopped. Don't shoot."

"Who are you?"

"Eli Stroud of the Boston regiment. I was sent out last night to find General Scott and got lost. Didn't dare move for fear of getting shot, with all the pickets in town. Can you tell me where the Boston regiment is?"

The command came sharp. "Move over here."

Eli walked forward, hands still up, holding his rifle high. The picket with the cocked musket held it trained on Eli's chest.

"Boston regiment?"

"Yes."

"When did you arrive?"

Behind him a second picket set his musket on the ground and began searching in a sheaf of papers.

"Two days ago."

"Who's your commanding officer?"

"Israel Thompson. Colonel Israel Thompson."

"Who's his aide?"

"You mean Bascom? Major Bascom?"

"Your sergeant?"

"Turlock."

"Why aren't you in uniform. You look like an Indian."

"None of us have uniforms. Only the officers. I'm white."

The man with the papers raised his head and nodded to the man with the musket and he exhaled nervously. "All right. I don't know where the Boston regiment is, but whatever you do, don't come back here in the dark, and don't come back unless you're sent on military business by a general."

Eli recoiled and lowered his rifle. "Why? What's in there?" He gestured at the house.

"General George Washington's headquarters."

For a moment Eli's breath came short. "No one told me that. I'll be more careful." He turned around and walked rapidly west, turned south at the first corner, and slowed while his mind grappled with the shock.

Washington's headquarters? An Indian at night?

He put it in the back of his mind and set out at a trot, working south and east, watching the surroundings and streets, looking for the second house, where the Indian had stopped before going to the river. Five minutes later, with the purple fading into gray, he stopped behind a house and peered towards the front. The two pickets were still there, backs towards the house, faces to the street. Eli crouched and moved quickly, silently to the wall of the house where the man had stopped four hours earlier and left something in the bushes beneath a window.

There was nothing. He studied the ground, the bushes, the grass, and other than faint moccasin impressions in the long, dew-covered grass, he could find nothing. The single sign that someone had been there was one small broken branch in the bush beneath the window. He glanced at the window two feet above the bush, and it was dark, the shade drawn. He dared not test it to see if it was locked.

Still crouched, he circled the neighboring house and walked calmly into the street and turned east, directly towards the pickets forty yards ahead, leaning on their muskets, more asleep than awake. He was nearly upon them before their heads snapped up and they jerked their muskets from the ground, fumbling with the hammers.

"Halt," one commanded.

Eli stopped.

"What's your business here?"

"No business. I'm looking for the Boston regiment."

"Who are you?"

"Eli Stroud."

"If you're looking for the Boston regiment, why are you here?"

"I'm lost. Can you tell me where they are?"

"They're not here. Move on. And don't come back in the dark. You could be shot."

Eli's mouth dropped open. "Why? What's here?"

"The mayor of New York City."

"No one told me. I'll be careful."

He turned on his heel and trotted away, south and west, down to where Reade Street met the river, and stopped behind a high outcropping of sea-worn granite boulders. The eastern sky was showing gray-blue, and Eli could see the pickets clearly, and knew they could see him if he moved. He waited until the camp drummer rose stiff from his blankets, slipped on his shoes without socks, tugged on his shirt, and walked to camp center. He pounded out the five o'clock wake-up, and all the pickets flinched and turned to look, and in that instant Eli sprinted. When the pickets turned back, all they saw was a man walking between them, digging sleep from his eyes, yawning.

Billy was waiting by his fire, blanket pulled over his shoulders as he sat poking sticks into the low flames. He saw Eli coming in and spread his blanket, and Eli sat down with his rifle across his lap.

"What happened?"

Eli shook his head. "I don't know. The big house where the Indian met the soldier? George Washington's headquarters."

Billy's head jerked forward.

"The place where the Indian left something in the bushes under a window? The mayor of New York."

"*What!*" Billy gasped.

"I stopped at both places. The pickets told me." Again he shook his head, trying to bring his reeling thoughts to a focus. "The Indian weighs about one hundred seventy pounds and walks strong. The white man wears military boots and weighs about one hundred thirty pounds. He walks deliberate and his right leg is a little crooked."

Billy started. "How do you know?"

"Their tracks."

For thirty seconds neither man spoke, both working with thoughts that staggered their minds.

Billy broke the silence. "We've stumbled into some sort of plan, British or American."

"Which?"

"I don't know." Then Billy locked eyes with Eli. "I think it has something to do with the papers I got from Brigitte."

Eli straightened, waiting.

Billy continued. "McMurdy and Pinnock were spies headed for New York. They blew up two cannon. Two men came to McMurdy's home to get papers, and when they didn't get them they burned his mother's house. The papers went to my mother and then here. Next we have an Indian and a white soldier talking owl code at night and exchanging things at Washington's head-quarters, and at the mayor's home."

Billy paused, and an inner assurance rose to stand the hair on the back of his neck on end. "I can't connect the two yet, but it's there. Somehow it's there."

Slowly Eli's eyes narrowed as the thought settled in. "You may be right. It could also mean nothing."

Billy reached for the packets. "Either way, we better go see Colonel Thompson."

Eli touched his arm. "I got a hunch you're right. Give him the papers, but don't tell him the rest."

"Why?"

"Wait one more day. There's one thing I need to know."

"What?"

"Who comes and goes at night at Washington's headquarters."

Notes

John Morin Scott was a brigadier general in command of his own brigade at New York (see Johnston, *The Campaign of 1776*, part I, p. 127).

General George Washington took headquarters first at 180 Pearl Street, then at the Mortier house in New York City (see Johnston, *The Campaign of 1776*, part I, p. 86).

The Jersey Battery was at the end of Reade Street and mounted two twelve-pound and three thirty-two-pound cannon (see Johnston, *The Campaign of 1776*, part I, p. 85).

There was an often bitter division in the civilian populace of New York City between the Tories, who remained loyal to Britain, and the Patriots (see Johnston, *The Campaign of 1776*, part I, pp. 80–81, particularly the footnote thereat).

The Iroquois words for *fox* and *lantern* are *skuhnaksu* and *yachihri thrat'ah*, respectively (see Graymont, *The Iroquois in the American Revolution*, p. 8). The Iroquois name for their highest god is Taronhiawagon (see Hale, *The Iroquois Book of Rites*, p. 35). The figures known as the Twin Brothers play a signifcant role in the Iroquois creation story (see Graymont, *The Iroquois*, pp. 16, 17).

Joseph Brant was a Mohawk Indian chief and shaman whose Mohawk name was Thayendanegea. He assisted the British against the Americans in the Revolutionary War. Red Jacket and Blacksnake were Seneca chiefs (see Bolton and Wilson, *Joseph Brant*, pp. 11, 19, 86).

CHAPTER VII

★ ★ ★

*L*ieutenant!" Colonel Israel Thompson wiped sweat from his face and neck and dropped the towel onto his table in the stifling heat inside the command tent.

The flap opened and a young, smooth-cheeked lieutenant entered, snapped erect, and saluted. His dark blue Boston regiment tunic was sweated black between his shoulder blades and around his arms. "Yes, sir."

"Go find the Ninth Company and bring back two privates named Weems and Stroud."

"Yes, sir." The man ducked out the tent flap and trotted south through camp, past exhausted men still dripping from their evening bath in the river and cooks slicing the last of the beef and carrots into steaming stew pots. He worked past the stack of cut timbers at the back side of the Jersey Battery, where men had used sledgehammers and wedges to split logs and lay the inclined ramps for the big guns that had not yet arrived.

He angled up towards the place where Company Nine was camped and found Sergeant Alvin Turlock. "Colonel Thompson wants Privates Weems and Stroud, right now," he panted.

Turlock's eyebrows rose. "What they done?"

"Colonel didn't say. Where are they?"

Turlock pointed. "You let me know what they done." The tough little sergeant turned his head to look at Eli and Billy, and he added, "Sir," as the young lieutenant trotted away without realizing Turlock's breach of military etiquette.

Billy and Eli followed the lieutenant as he picked his way back through camp to the command tent, ordered them to stand, and ducked past the tent flap. He reappeared in five seconds and held the flap. "Colonel Thompson will see you now. I'll take the rifle."

Eli reluctantly handed his rifle to the young officer and followed Billy into the tent. They stood at attention before the table and Billy spoke. "Privates Weems and Stroud reporting as ordered, sir."

Thompson picked up the tied bundle of brown packets from one side of his desk. "Those documents you gave me this morning were returned by General Scott late this afternoon. He said he got copies about six or eight days ago from an officer named Pearlman in Boston, and Scott's men have gone over them half a dozen times. They know something's going on but don't know what. Scott said to return these to you. Take care of them."

Billy picked up the bundle. "Thank you, sir."

Thompson's face puckered for a second. "Scott said there are a lot of things like this happening right now on both sides, and he doesn't expect much to come of it, so keep it quiet. Understand?"

"Yes, sir."

"That's all. Dismissed." He watched them duck out the tent flap, then reached for the towel to wipe sweat and wave away mosquitoes and flies.

Eli took his rifle from the young officer, checked the pan, and followed Billy picking his way back through the blankets and men and evening fires of the camp. A faint, distant rumble brought his head around south, and low on the horizon, far past Staten Island, he saw the purple clouds building.

Weather before dark.

They got their plates and stood in line for the thin, watery beef and vegetable soup, waited while the cook handed them two pieces of hardtack, and made their way back to Billy's blanket. They ate in silence, lost in their thoughts, then scrubbed their utensils with river water and sand and returned to prop them up to dry at the edge of Billy's blanket. A soft, hot south breeze stirred the grass and then died as they sat down.

Billy shoved the bundled packets into his knapsack. "You still plan to go back to that house tonight?"

"I think so."

"Storm coming."

"I saw." Eli rose and picked up his rifle. "See you sometime later." He walked away.

Billy gathered his supper utensils and packed them in his knapsack, then sat down on his blanket, cross-legged, arms over his knees. In the golden glow of a sun settling towards the skyline across the river, he watched the men of the regiment shake sand and dirt from their blankets, spread them for the night, and sit. They moved slowly, talking little, exhausted, gathering their strength and their resolve for the coming day in which they would swing the heavy axes and sledges, and lift the river rocks onto sleds, and drain their bodies and souls as they had done today.

His thoughts drifted and he let them run unchecked. *Is Mother watching the sunset across the Back Bay right now?* A faint smile tugged at the thought. *Are the apricots turning? What did Mother and Trudy have for supper? ham? Ham and greens. Sweet potatoes. Custard.* He saw his mother rocking in her chair with her Bible, and deep longing welled up for a time, and he swallowed and shifted his feet. *Did Mother and Brigitte ever see that woman again—Beatrice McMurdy? I'll have to answer Brigitte's letter—when I know how things turn out. Has Brigitte heard from Richard Buchanan? Is he well? Is she well?*

Idly he reached for the bundle of papers in his knapsack, unfolded Brigitte's letter, and read each word slowly while the breeze fluttered it slightly between his hands. He glanced south where the rain clouds were billowing, their tops golden in the light of a sun already set. The rising breeze fanned his small fire, and he laid on more sticks of dried, aged driftwood and picked up one of the written coded messages. He read it without thought and refolded it and dropped it on his blanket with the others.

For a time he watched the storm moving in from the south. Clouds covered the fading sunset, and early dusk changed to full darkness and the breeze stiffened in his face.

A movement from behind brought him around. Eli stood there, rifle in hand, and then settled onto Billy's blanket. "After the rain starts, I'll go." He reached to pick up one of the maps and unfolded it. He held it between his hands in the wind and leaned towards the fire for light to study it one more time. The wind stirred the other papers, and Billy gathered them. He glanced at the back side of the map Eli was reading as he wrapped the tie cord around the bundle, and suddenly Billy froze.

Eli lowered the map. "What's wrong?"

Billy snatched the map from his hands and held it with the diagram towards the fire, staring at the back side. "Look! The ink drop on the back side! Look where it is when you hold it to the light!"

Eli seized the map and held the face of it towards the firelight, peering at the ink dot on the back. It was at the rear of the building, near one corner. Eli's head jerked, and he breathed, "That home! I've been there! The diagram was backwards until I saw it from the wrong side." He lowered the map and his eyes locked with Billy's. "That's General Washington's headquarters!"

Far to the south, lightning streaked the clouds yellow, and seconds later the deep rumble of thunder rolled past. The wind began to moan in the trees and brush, and tug at their hair, and fan sparks from the fire. Eli thrust the map back to Billy. "Put that away and don't let anyone near it. Watch my rifle. I'll be back."

Billy grabbed his arm in a grip like iron. "Eli, you're walking into trouble. I'm coming."

The firelight played on Billy's face, and Eli sobered at the mortal concern he read in Billy's eyes. For a split second Eli's face softened, and he reached to place a gentle hand on Billy's arm. "You've got to stay here to tell the story if I don't get back." A smile formed for a moment and the scar on his jaw was prominent. "I'll be all right. It's hard to catch an Indian in a storm at night."

The first huge drops of rain came slanting on the wind as Eli stood, and he moved north, peering into the darkness. He paused at camp's edge to locate two pickets, moved out between them, and turned northeast at a trot, with the wind driving rain against his back and lightning flashing as the storm rolled in.

He came in on the two-story building from the east side and dropped to his haunches behind bushes to wait for lightning to show him where the pickets were. Two minutes later the city of New York was bright as midday as lightning streaked ten miles through the clouds, and in that instant the six pickets in front of the house and the two at the side were there, blurred in the cloudburst. Eli calculated the time between the lightning flash and the thunder, counted two breaths, and sprinted in the howling wind, crouched low, directly towards the space between the two pickets at the side of the house. Thirty feet before he passed between them the thunderclap shook the house and the ground, and Eli slammed against the wall and dropped to lie flat in the mud, watching, listening to see if either picket had seen or heard him and was going to raise the alarm. There was only the singing of the wind and the roar of rain and the thrashing of the trees.

He crawled on his stomach to the rear of the house and lay in the mud, peering desperately into the darkness, probing. *Where're the ones in the back? Where?*

He felt heavy planks stacked against the house, moved away two feet, drew his knees up, set, ready, and waited for the next lightning bolt. It came, and the three pickets were there, standing in the mud across the big yard twenty feet in front of a row of great maple trees. Their heads were ducked into the south wind as they clutched their hats onto their heads and sheets of rain pounded them. Again he counted two breaths, and as the thunderclap struck he sprinted between two of them and dived sliding in the mud behind the massive trunk of a maple and lay still, again waiting and listening for a challenge or an alarm, and there was none.

He stood and seized the lowest branch and swung into the

pitching, flailing tree and climbed ten feet, facing the back of the house. He could see nothing in the blackness nor hear anything above the howling storm, and he waited. Again and again lightning flashes showed the pickets rooted in place, heads still bowed against the wind, drenched by the torrential rain. Minutes became half an hour, and no one came, no one left.

Was I wrong? Nothing here? Wait. Wait.

The storm center roared overhead, ripping branches and leaves from the tree while Eli clung to the swaying trunk. Lightning flashed white so close he could smell the acrid taint, while thunder cracked above the treetops. Slowly it passed northward and the wind slackened. The lightning flashes dimmed and the thunder rolled in the distance. The wild motion of the trees settled, and the rain fell straight down, drumming. In the house, two lights, both on the second floor, showed blurred through drawn curtains and the rain. Nothing moved. No one had come or gone.

I was wrong. Wrong.

Eli dropped one foot to a lower branch to drop from the tree, when a long sliver of dim light suddenly showed at ground level near the left corner of the house, and he froze.

The dot on the map! That's the corner!

He watched the thin shaft of light widen, and he understood that someone had opened a cellar door and lighted a lantern that was burning in the cellar. He watched a man cautiously emerge upward on the cellar stairs, pause to look, then quickly motion with his arm. The three pickets in the backyard walked splashing through the mud to the cellar door, stopped for a few moments, and then turned to their left, towards the corner of the house, and Eli lost them in the rain blur and the blackness as they left the light. Seconds later they reappeared, laying planks in the mud from the corner of the house to the edge of the cellar door. They disappeared once more into the darkness, and he heard sounds of men straining. Then he saw two of the pickets rolling a large barrel. It was tipped on its side, and they worked it carefully on the planks from the darkness to the light at the cellar door. They heaved it up onto its bottom; then one stepped into the cellar stairwell, and they lowered it downward, one step at a time.

Eli's mind raced, remembering the bundle of papers he had left with Billy. *Barrels of salt cod? at night? in General Washington's cellar?*

The two figures blocked the light as they walked back out of the cellar, and then they stood to one side while the other picket and a new man rolled a second barrel on the planks to the dim light of the cellar door. They moved it down the stairs, and suddenly Eli tensed.

That last man—a beard? black seaman's cap? He narrowed his eyes, peering in the darkness and the rain to be certain.

The two men emerged upward on the cellar stairs, silhouetted by the dim yellow lantern light below, and Eli's breath came short. *The black seaman's cap, and that beard. Is he the one who burned that woman's home in Charlestown! Delivering salt cod here at midnight in a storm? No. Not fish. Then what?*

The thought struck into his brain and he stopped for a moment. *Gunpowder! It has to be gunpowder!*

The pickets disappeared for ten seconds with the planks, then moved quickly back to their posts. The fourth man disappeared in the blackness at the edge of the house, while the man who had opened the cellar door lowered it into place, and blackness closed in. The dim light of the two windows on the second floor showed through the rain blur, but there was no other light, no other movement.

Silent as a cat, Eli dropped to the ground and worked his way east behind the trees to the side street, crossed it, angled south until he was past the pickets in front of the house, then broke into a run, headed back in the steadily falling rain towards the regimental camp at the end of Reade Street.

The instinct and the whisper of sound from behind came in the same instant, and he dived to his right, rolling splashing in the mud of the street and then back onto his feet as the thought flashed, *The Indian, I forgot the Indian.* He took the hurtling body head-on, frantically reaching down for the knife that had to be coming up looking for his bowels, and he felt the quick shock on his left forearm as he locked onto the wrist of the knife hand. He went down backwards, pulling the knife hand as he went, reaching across with his right hand to wrench the knife around, twisting, and as he hit splashing on his back in the mud he drove the twisted hand upward and the blade sank to the guard under the ribs of the body as it fell on him. He heard the gasp and the whine, and he felt the knife hand jerk and the man's body convulse. The struck man tried to rise, and then he relaxed on top of Eli.

For a moment Eli lay in the mud and the rain, and then he heaved the body to one side and rose to one knee, flexing the fingers and wrist of his left hand to be certain the slash had not severed tendons. He rolled the body onto its back and felt the throat and there was no heartbeat. In the dark he drew the knife from the chest and shoved it back into its sheath, then unbuckled the weapons belt from the body and looped it around his own neck. He systematically patted the shirtfront until he located a large lump underneath, then pulled the leather hunting shirt up and reached to draw out a flat package wrapped in oilcloth. He shoved the package inside his own shirt, then dragged the body through the mud to a ditch and rolled it in and covered it with tree branches broken and scattered by the storm.

The heart of the rainstorm had rolled north, leaving a heavy drizzle falling. Eli gauged the time to be around midnight and turned southwest once more at a run, back towards the regimental camp. Not one campfire had survived the rain, and one hundred yards before he reached the outer picket line of the dark camp he began calling, "Friendly coming in. Don't shoot. Friendly coming in." The pickets challenged, and he paused long enough to be identified, then continued on, picking his way in the dark, stepping around men sleeping in drenched blankets until he found Billy.

Billy sat up and Eli didn't hesitate. "Remember the man with the full beard and the seaman's black cap? the bad one in the letter?"

"Yes."

"I think he was there tonight. The dot on the map marked the basement door to Washington's headquarters. They put two barrels down there about an hour ago."

Billy's mind began to race. "Barrels of what?"

"It has to be gunpowder. I started back here and the Indian tried to kill me, and I don't think he'd do that over two barrels of salt cod." Eli drew the oilskin package from within his shirt. "He had this."

"Where is he?"

"Dead."

Billy swallowed. "You killed him?"

Eli ignored the question. "We got to see what it is."

Billy struck flint to steel, blew on the tinder, and lighted a lantern, and together they unwrapped the oilskin. Inside was a packet. They ripped it open and unfolded the document. With Eli holding the oilskin against the rain, Billy read it. "It's like the other ones we have. Same handwriting, I think."

"Know what it says?"

"Talks about more barrels of salt cod coming into different ports."

"If I'm right about the gunpowder, it sounds like they're planning some bad surprises in a lot of places. Is this a big plan to try to stop the war by killing the American generals?"

Silence held for a moment as both men let their thoughts run, while raindrops hissed on the hot lantern chimney and the light cast strange shadows. Slowly their thoughts settled, and then a sure conviction crept into them, and they felt the tingle on their arms and the backs of their necks. Billy refolded the letter, worked it back inside its oilskin wrapper, and spoke. "We've got to take this to Thompson. Now."

Eli shook his head. "No time. When that Indian doesn't show up back at headquarters, whatever they put in that cellar could be gone before we get there."

"If we go back alone, those pickets could shoot us and tell everyone we were spies."

Eli stared at the lamp intently for a moment. "Let's go see Thompson. Bring your bundle of packets with the one in oilskin."

The pickets at the command tent stopped them at bayonet point and one spoke. "Identify yourselves."

Billy answered. "Privates Weems and Stroud. Life-and-death business for the colonel."

"Life and death?" the picket snorted. "Whose life? Yours?"

"General Washington's, and maybe others," Eli said flatly. "You better roust Colonel Thompson now, or I will." The purr in Eli's voice silenced the picket. While two pickets held their bayonets at the ready, the third one backed to the tied flap of the tent, loosened the strings, and ducked inside. Thirty seconds later a lantern glowed. Billy and Eli listened to muffled voices and watched the shadows play on the tent walls, and the tent flap opened. Israel Thompson stepped outside in his trousers, barefooted, hair awry, face dour, lantern held high. "What's this about life and death?"

"Sorry, sir," Billy said. "We have a story to tell and little time to tell it."

Thompson's face thrust forward, and he stared wide-eyed in the yellow lantern glow. "Aren't you the two who took on that North Carolina regiment back where they're building Fort Lee? and brought those documents?"

"Yes, sir, but this has nothing to do with that."

Thompson backed into the tent, holding the flap while Billy and Eli ducked inside. Thompson gestured to chairs beside his table, set the lantern down, and sat opposite them. "Go ahead."

Billy turned to Eli, and for three minutes Eli spoke. Billy laid the bundle of packets on the table, followed by the one document in the oilskin. Thompson unfolded the oilskin and read the letter and compared it briefly with those from Billy's bundle. Then he raised his eyes to Eli. "What's that around your neck?"

"The weapons belt of the Indian who ambushed me." He dropped it on the tabletop, and Thompson stared for a second, then noticed Eli's left hand. Blood was dripping from his finger-tips onto the dirt floor of the tent.

"How bad?"

"No tendons. It's all right."

"Orderly!"

The tent flap jerked open instantly. "Yes, sir."

"Get the regimental surgeon. Now." Thompson stood and reached for his socks and boots.

"Should we wait outside, sir?" Billy asked.

"You've seen a man dress before. Stay where you are." He shrugged into his tunic and buttoned it to the throat. "We've got to get General Scott into this. I have no command authority in New York."

The flap opened and the surgeon burst in, thinning hair awry, unshaved, thin, bony, a black bag in hand, pants held up by one suspender, and no shirt. "Who's injured?"

Eli held out his arm, and the surgeon examined the cut, five inches long, a quarter inch deep. "That'll take stitching."

Eli shook his head. "Not now, there's no time. Bind it. Stitch later."

The surgeon looked at Thompson, who nodded, and one minute later the surgeon pulled Eli's shirtsleeve over the white bandage. "That'll hold for a while. I don't know what's going on, but you be back here for stitching as soon as you can, under-stand?"

Eli nodded and turned to Thompson.

"Let's go."

The storm was only faint lightning glow and distant rumbles far north. The rain had stopped, leaving the world a sea of mud and puddles and water dripping from bushes and trees. Overhead, stars began to show through the first breaks in the fast-moving clouds, and the wind had dwindled to a chill, mild breeze. Thompson strode through camp, leading Billy and Eli past the picket lines, due east on Reade Street, then south towards the common. He approached the headquarters building of General

Scott and stopped when the pickets challenged. Five minutes later General Scott was working on buttons to his tunic when he gestured Thompson and Billy and Eli to chairs at his office desk, and sat down, waiting.

"General Scott," Thompson said, "Private Stroud has a story you need to hear."

Ten minutes later Scott abruptly stood and called, "Lieutenant," and a young lieutenant was in the door frame immediately. Fifteen minutes later Scott and Thompson strode rapidly north up Broadway, each carrying a lantern, splashing through the water puddled on the worn cobblestones. Billy and Eli were behind, followed by a squad of ten armed, uniformed New York militia, muskets primed, loaded. The weapons belt Eli had taken hours earlier swung from his right hand.

They turned left, and three minutes later Scott pointed in the starlight. "There it is. The Mortier house. General Washington's headquarters." It was just past two A.M. The heavens had cleared. Countless stars shined, and the quarter moon was high over the New Jersey Palisades.

The pickets challenged the tiny column as it approached, and General Scott came to a stop, lantern held high. "I'm General John Scott, New York militia. I must speak with General Washington now."

The pickets saw the gold on his shoulder gleaming in the yellow lantern light. "Sorry, sir, General Washington is across the river where they're building Fort Lee until tomorrow night."

"Who's in command here?"

"Brigadier Jonah Ulrich."

"Rouse him."

"Yes, sir."

The picket vaulted up the steps, boots clomping, and entered the house. Lights came on in the lower floor, then the upper floor. Minutes passed, and then the front door opened and the picket led Brigadier Ulrich out onto the high four-columned porch.

"General Scott?"

"Here, sir. I must speak to you now."

Ulrich stepped aside and gestured, and they climbed the stairs and wiped their wet, muddy boots on the bristles of a horsehair pad. Scott gave orders to his squad, and they stopped and took up positions on the front porch, while Scott, Thompson, Eli, and Billy followed Ulrich through the parlor into a large library with a great oak table, polished, carved, surrounded by matching carved chairs upholstered with velvet. All except Eli sat down.

Ulrich glanced at him. "Have a seat."

Eli shook his head. "I'm muddy. I'd rather not dirty the chair."

Ulrich shrugged and turned back to Scott. "What's so important?"

"Eli Stroud is a private in the Boston regiment. His commanding officer, Colonel Thompson, is here with him. Private Stroud has a story." Scott gestured to Eli, and Ulrich turned in his chair to face him directly and waited.

"Sir, I think you got gunpowder in the cellar of this building, and I think it's there to kill General Washington."

Ulrich's mouth dropped open and he slowly straightened in his chair, eyes wide. "Here? Now?"

"Yes, sir."

"How do you know this?"

"I was here. I watched five men put it there two hours ago."

"How do you know it's gunpowder? Did you go down and look?"

"No, sir. No chance. But I think you'll find the barrels marked 'salt cod.' The question is, do you believe five men are going to put two barrels of salt cod in the basement of this house at midnight in a bad storm? When I left, an Indian tried to kill me. I doubt he'd do that over two barrels of salt cod. It has to be gunpowder."

Ulrich's face sobered, and for ten seconds the room was silent before Ulrich spoke again. "Where were you to watch all this?"

"In a tree behind the house."

"What were you doing there? How did you get past the pickets?"

"That don't matter. What matters is I had to kill a man who was one of the bunch who did it, and when he doesn't show up, the others are going to get spooked and they might set it off now and kill who they can and run."

"You mean blow it up tonight?"

"That's what I mean."

"Shocking! We'll go down there right now and prove it, one way or the other."

"Sir, might be good to roust everybody in the house awake and bring them here while you go down there. Otherwise the guilty one is bound to know why you're in the cellar and he'll likely run."

Ulrich leaned back in his chair for a moment in thought, and Eli continued. "Those three pickets in back helped, and there were two other men. I don't know if your other pickets were in on it, but it won't hurt to have General Scott's squad here armed, watching your men."

Ulrich was incredulous. "Are you suggesting we have spies, traitors, here at headquarters?"

"No, sir, I'm not suggesting that. I'm stating it as a fact. We better be ready for trouble from any man you got here." Eli dropped the weapons belt on the table, and Ulrich stared at it.

"What's that?"

"The weapons belt I took off the man I had to kill. Part of the blood on the knife's mine, the rest his."

Ulrich started. "You're wounded?"

Eli shrugged. "On the arm." A smile flickered and was gone. "He was hurt a little worse."

Eli tossed the oilskin-wrapped document beside the belt, and Ulrich raised inquiring eyes.

"That's a coded message I took from him."

Eli turned to Billy, and Billy dropped his bundled packets on the desk.

"More?" Ulrich asked, startled.

"Yes, sir. There's no time now, but those letters and maps are all the same, and when you put it all together, and add what I saw tonight, and that Indian trying to kill me by ambush, I doubt we're dealing with salt cod."

Ulrich turned back to Scott. "What do you think?"

"I think it deserves at least a hard look."

Ulrich stood. "Lieutenant!"

The young lieutenant was instantly in the doorway.

"Assemble everyone in this library at once."

The young man's jaw dropped. "What?"

"Now, Lieutenant."

"Pickets too?"

"Everyone."

"Yes, sir."

"Sir," Eli said, "when all this starts, I think there's a way to walk the guilty man into a trap."

"How?"

"No time to explain it." Eli gathered his thoughts, then continued. "I know this is asking a lot, but sir, could I ask for a free hand to try to trap this man?"

Ulrich looked at Scott, then Thompson. "Is this man in your command?"

"He is."

"Would you trust him with this?"

Thompson studied Eli thoughtfully for a moment. "I would."

Ulrich shrugged.

Eli said, "Have your people leave their arms out in the parlor."

Lanterns came on all over the house, and men assembled in the library in twos and threes and stood silently, fearful, eyes darting in question. Eli took a place in one corner, Billy beside him, and Eli studied every man as he walked through the doors.

Ulrich spoke. "Every man is here." He turned to the lieutenant. "Take all the firearms out into the parlor."

Stunned silence fell over the room for a split second.

"Yes, sir." The lieutenant gathered the muskets and pistols and laid them clattering on a table in the parlor.

Eli turned to Scott. "Could your men come in?"

Two minutes later the ten-man squad from Scott's command stood in the crowded library, muskets in hand, bayonets mounted.

Eli looked at Ulrich. "Could you and I and General Scott and Billy—and those two men—leave now?" Eli pointed to two men under Ulrich's command, shorter than average, about 130 or 140 pounds.

Ulrich gave orders, the two men stepped out, and Ulrich led them all out of the library and into the parlor. He turned to Eli, again waiting.

Eli spoke. "Sir, is there a broom handy?"

Ulrich's forehead creased in wonderment. "A broom?"

"For sweeping floors."

Two minutes later Ulrich handed Eli a broom.

"Follow me." Carrying one lantern, and Ulrich another, Eli led them out the front door and down the side of the house, turned the corner, and stopped at the cellar. He lifted the door and said to Ulrich, "Wait here until I call."

He eased down the stairs, opened the lower door into the cellar room, and hung his lantern on the center pole. Quickly and carefully he swept the broom over the entire dirt floor until all tracks were gone, then called up, "Come on down. Billy, you last."

Ulrich led the other five men down, Billy last, and they ducked their heads to clear the low door frame and stood in the yellow lantern light in the dank smell of the chill cellar. The walls were cement, the ceiling was made up of the timbers supporting the first floor of the house above, and the floor was soft dirt. They stood looking at each other, mystified, struggling to understand the unexplained directions from Eli.

Eli pointed. Against the west wall were two barrels, still wet, muddy. He lifted the lantern from the center pole and held it close. Ulrich read the shipping bill tacked to the side aloud. " 'SALT COD. THREE HUNDRED WEIGHT AND TWENTY POUNDS. SHIPPED JUNE 12, '76, NOVA SCOTIA. BUYER PAY AT NEW YORK.' "

Eli drew his hatchet from his weapons belt and knocked the seal from the top of the barrel, then pried the lid loose. He drew a great breath and motioned Ulrich to step back with the lantern. Every eye in the room glittered in the yellow light as Eli raised the lid. He thrust his hand into the top, brought it out, and raised the fine black granules to his face to smell them, then touched some to his tongue. He raised his eyes to Ulrich and poured the stuff into Ulrich's hand. "Gunpowder."

Ulrich gaped, and for three seconds total silence gripped the room. Then Ulrich murmured, "Five hundred pounds of gunpowder, directly below Washington's bedroom."

Eli spoke quietly. "Nobody move."

Everyone froze while Eli took a lantern and carefully dropped to one knee. He studied the clean, clear tracks in the fresh-swept dirt floor until he sorted them out, then shifted his position to study the tracks of the two men he had asked to come with them. He stood. "Can we go back upstairs now to the library?"

As they cleared the top of the cellar stairs Eli called back to Billy, "Stay here and stop anyone who tries to go down in the cellar. Someone will relieve you soon."

The five men climbed the front porch stairs and passed through the parlor into the library, and Eli waited for silence.

"General Scott, could you send two of our men down and have Billy come up? Tell them to shoot anybody who tries to go in the cellar."

Scott gave orders and two men of the New York militia left.

Eli turned back to the others. "Which three of you were standing picket in the back of the house around midnight?"

Three men looked at each other and raised their hands.

Eli approached the nearest one. "What was in those barrels you took into the cellar?"

The man's face went white. "How did you know about that?"

"It doesn't matter. What was in them?"

The man stammered an answer. "Salt fish. Private Hickey told us salt fish for the general."

Eli looked at the other two men and they blurted, "Salt fish. Just like he said."

"Who's Private Hickey?"

The man pointed and Eli turned and looked. The man was one of the two he had called out to accompany them downstairs. Shorter than average, about 130 pounds.

Eli spoke to Ulrich. "What's this man's duty here?"

"Personal bodyguard to General Washington."

Eli paused for a moment, then spoke. "Does he have free run of the place?"

"Of course."

"Now it all makes sense. He could do all this and nobody would challenge him." Eli turned back to Hickey. "General Washington's across the river tonight. If you're his personal bodyguard, what are you doing here?"

Hickey stalled. "What is your authority, sir?"

Eli looked at Ulrich.

"He speaks under my authority, Private."

Hickey answered Eli's question. "He left me to guard General Ulrich."

A rap came at the door and Scott opened it, and Billy entered the room.

Eli spoke to him. "Watch the door, Billy."

Eli paused to gather his thoughts and took a stride towards Hickey. "How long ago did you break your right leg?"

Thomas Hickey's mouth fell open and he clacked it shut. "Sir?"

"How long since you broke your right leg and got it set a little crooked?"

"I don't know what you're talking about."

"Yes, you do. I tracked you two nights ago when you walked down the street to meet that Indian and trade messages, and I read the same tracks in the cellar tonight. You come down hard on your heels like military, and your crooked leg puts the right edge of your boot down a little harder than the left. I watched you and the others put those two barrels in the cellar tonight, and your Indian followed me. When did you break your leg?"

"This is utter nonsense!"

General Ulrich interrupted. "Private Hickey, did you break your right leg?"

Silence held for a moment. "As a child."

Eli stepped to the desk and picked up the weapons belt. "You might recognize this. It belongs to your Indian. He used that knife to try to kill me tonight. He's dead. Part of the blood on that knife is mine, the rest is his."

He lifted the oilskin-wrapped packet and laid it back down. "You might recognize that, too. I took it from him after he was dead." He pointed to Billy's bundle of packets. "We got those after your men burned the house of another one of your spies from Charlestown, trying to destroy these maps and messages. Remember the map of this house, with the ink dot on the back? Remember McMurdy? the turncoat we shot about two weeks ago?"

Hickey blanched, and Eli continued. "There was one more man, with a beard and a black seaman's cap. Big man, maybe two hundred pounds. The pickets know. Who is he?"

Hickey swallowed, and for a split second panic glinted in his eyes. "I have no idea. He was sent to deliver the salt cod. I swear, we all thought it was salt cod."

Eli nodded. "One more thing." He paused, and his eyes narrowed, and his words came low, distinct. "I followed that Indian to the home of the New York mayor. He put a message in the bushes by a window at the side of the house. When we finish here, we go visit the mayor. I thought you should know that."

Hickey clamped his mouth shut and his face was a blank.

Eli shrugged. "Where's your quarters?"

"What's that got to do with it?"

"We're all going to search them."

"No, you're not."

Once again Eli turned to Ulrich, waiting.

"Yes, we are," Ulrich said.

"You'll find nothing," Hickey said.

"I think you're wrong," Eli answered. "I think you exchanged messages with the Indian tonight, just like the last time, and his message said the bearded man was delivering the gunpowder tonight. I think your message told him where to deliver the rest of it. I think we'll find it wrapped in oilskin in your room."

Hickey spat defiantly, "Then go search!"

They left the armed militia squad on guard in the library, and the five of them escorted Hickey to his quarters next to those of George Washington. The small room was dominated by a great bed with thick, high, hand-carved oak posts on the corners. They began a systematic search, floor to ceiling, starting on one wall, moving towards the other, while Hickey stood near the center of the room, arms folded in defiance.

They came to the bed, and Thompson spread the great goose-down comforter on the floor and slit it open half a dozen times. There was nothing inside. He laid the pillows on top and slit each one open, and there was nothing.

"I told you there's nothing here," Hickey said.

The men worked on in silence. Ulrich ripped open the side of the mattress and found nothing, then the large box springs. With the bed stripped to the frame, Scott began knocking the sides from the great posts, when Billy saw the twitch at the corner of Hickey's mouth. Billy raised a hand and all work stopped while everyone in the room waited in silence. "It's somewhere in this bed frame. The only parts big enough are the four posts."

Hickey started, then settled.

Eli drew his tomahawk while the others watched. The blade cut deep into the large knob at the top of the first post. Thirty seconds later the post was in splinters, and Eli moved to the next one and drove the blade into the large knob. On the third blow the blade sank nearly to the handle.

"Hollow?" Ulrich asked.

"Felt like it," Eli answered. Fifteen seconds later the top of the post was gone, and Eli slipped his tomahawk back through his weapons belt. He reached into the exposed cavity and drew out an oilskin pouch. Instantly Hickey pivoted and bolted for the door. Billy caught his shirtfront in both hands, lifted him off his feet, and slammed him against the wall, and all the fight went out of Hickey and he slumped.

Ulrich unfolded the oilskin, and for twenty seconds no one moved in the silence as he read the document inside. He refolded the document and raised his head, and his face flushed with anger. His words rang loud. "Thomas Hickey, you are under military arrest for mutiny, sedition, and corresponding with the enemy. A court-martial will be convened as soon as I can assemble the officers this morning, and you will be tried. Should you be convicted you will be hanged in public. You will have an officer to speak in your defense." He looked at Billy. "Take him downstairs."

The two pickets at the library door stepped aside, and the six men entered. Everyone inside came to their feet, eyes wide, waiting.

"Hickey is under arrest," Ulrich said. His eyes were moving, watching everyone. "Every man who was assigned to duty at this building is under house detention until further orders. You will all be questioned about this matter. If you're innocent you have nothing to fear. If you're guilty you will be hanged."

He turned to Scott. "May I request that your pickets remain here until I can arrange some of my own?"

"Done."

"Could I further request that Privates Stroud and Weems assist the two pickets guarding the cellar in removing the gunpowder from under the house?"

Men gasped and exclamations erupted. Gunpowder? Under the house? How much? Who? How?

Billy led and Eli followed as they made their way through the parlor, where Eli picked up a lantern from a table, out the front door, down the front stairs, and around to the side of the house. Eli called, "Friendly coming in. Don't shoot."

The pickets helped open both cellar doors, then set two planks down the stairs. They tied the barrels with ropes, and with the pickets pulling the ropes from above and Billy and Eli pushing from below, they skidded the barrels up the planks to ground level, rolled them across the yard, and tied them behind two huge maple trees. The pickets took up positions in front of the trees, and Billy and Eli walked back to the parlor. Ulrich, Scott, and Thompson were waiting.

"Are the barrels removed?"

"Tied behind two of the big trees in back. The pickets are there on this side of the trees."

"Good."

Eli continued. "Going after the mayor?"

"Yes. I'll have ten men here in minutes."

Eli's face clouded. "I hope you get enough on him to arrest him."

Ulrich's eyebrows rose. "Why?"

"Unless Hickey confesses and tells it all, I doubt you'll get the mayor. The one man who I could tie to the mayor's house is dead." He shook his head in frustration. "I'm sorry about it, but I had to kill him." He looked at Ulrich, hoping. "Do you think Hickey will confess?"

Ulrich shook his head. "I doubt it. He refuses to say anything at all."

Eli drew and released a great breath. "I'm sorry about it. I know there are half a dozen others in this thing. I doubt we'll ever catch the man with the black seaman's cap. He's likely a long way up the river by now. I doubt we'll get the mayor. I only hope we broke this whole thing up enough to stop it."

Ulrich pursed his mouth, then spoke. "We'll need those documents in there and that knife and weapons belt."

Billy interrupted. "General Scott has copies of most of the papers."

"We'll work it out."

Eli spoke. "Do you want us to come to the mayor's house?"

"No need. Just be available to testify at his trial if it gets that far."

Suddenly Eli looked around as though surprised. "What time is it?"

Ulrich smiled. "About four-thirty. Daybreak in another hour. Been a busy night."

Thompson broke in. "I'll be needed back at my command."

Ulrich nodded. "I'll see that General Washington gets a written report on all this. Your names will be in it. I'll keep you advised."

"Thank you, sir."

Scott spoke. "I'll stay until my pickets are replaced."

Thompson bowed. "I'll take my leave. May I borrow a lantern? I would like not to be shot in the dark by one of my own pickets."

Ulrich smiled, Scott chuckled, the tension of the long night broke and began to drain, and they all laughed. Thompson led out the front door, lantern held high, Billy and Eli following.

Thompson spoke. "Where's the body of the dead Indian?"

Eli led them through the muddy streets and stopped at the ditch where he had piled the windfall branches and limbs. Thompson held the lantern while Eli and Billy pulled the branches aside, and suddenly the body was there, face down, one arm under the chest. Eli eased the body over onto its back to show the face. Thompson lowered the lantern, and a strange, unexpected feeling crept over the three men standing in the mud and water in the dark, peering into the relaxed face of a man who only hours earlier had been vital and alive. A man like them, who had weaknesses and strengths, hopes and dreams, and an allegiance to the British empire. A man who had tried to kill a sworn enemy from behind, in a storm, with a knife, and failed, and who was now beyond the cares and pain and sorrows and joys that bind mankind. Beyond the torment of a world that keeps the final mysteries of life locked safely away, just past the yearning reach of mankind. Who are we? From whence? To where? Why?

For a moment the three men were overpowered by the impression that they were but tiny players on an endless stage, playing out a miniscule part that had meaning only to them. For a few seconds they were stripped of their pride and vanities and illusions and defenses. They saw into the very core of their own being, and were overwhelmed by how little was left of themselves when all things that are of this world were stripped away.

They stood in silence, not moving as they stared at the dead man with the great black gout of blood on his chest and the face finally at peace. Eli dropped to his haunches and carefully, almost tenderly, reached to touch the face, and then he rose and spoke and the mood faded. "Mohawk."

"Know him?" Thompson asked.

"No. But he's Mohawk, and if Joseph Brant was his leader, General Washington has more trouble than he knows."

"You know Joseph Brant?"

"Yes."

"I'll tell General Scott. We better move on."

The eastern sky was showing deep purple as they approached the picket lines of their own regiment. Thompson held the lantern high and answered the picket challenge, and they worked their way through the sleeping regiment to the command tent.

Thompson spoke to his aide. "Get the camp surgeon."

Eli raised his bandaged arm. "No need. It's all right."

Thompson shook his head firmly. "We're not going to risk it."

Three minutes later the surgeon pushed through the tent flap, tired eyes blinking in the sudden light. In the glow of two lanterns he removed the bloody bandage from Eli's arm and washed the open wound with alcohol. He sat Eli down at the table, straightened his arm on clean sheeting, and drew a curved suture needle and six feet of gut from his black bag. He soaked the gut in alcohol, threaded it through the needle eye, and spoke. "Want something between your teeth?"

Eli shook his head.

For twenty minutes Eli sat with his head bowed, jaw clenched shut, and sweat forming on his forehead, while the surgeon took twenty-two stitches and slowly closed the deep gash, with Billy wiping the blood. The surgeon washed the arm with alcohol, shoulder to fingertips, waited for it to dry, then bandaged it.

He exhaled and began replacing his equipment in his black bag. "Not bad. Clean cut. You should be all right."

Eli flexed his fingers

"Too tight?"

Eli shook his head.

"If your hand starts to go gray or numb, come get me. Keep that arm dry and don't use it for a while. You tear out those stitches, we get to start over. I'll be back tomorrow."

Eli nodded.

The surgeon looked at Thompson. "Do I get to know what this is all about? Knife wounds at night, you gone, coming back at dawn?"

"You'll know soon enough," Thompson answered.

The surgeon picked up his black bag and stopped at the tent flap. "You start to feel light-headed, get some hot coffee."

Eli stood. "I'm all right. I better get back to my blanket."

Thompson grunted. "Reveille in less than an hour. You two tell your sergeant you're relieved of duty until further notice."

"I'm all right," Billy said.

Eli shook his head. "Why? I can still use my right hand. Rather be doing something than not."

Thompson shook his head and his rare smile flashed. "Sometimes you men from the woods don't have good sense. All right. Do what you can, but don't abuse that arm."

"I got to wash my clothes."

Billy interrupted. "I'll do that."

Thompson said, "Brigadier Ulrich may want you both at the inquiry. Be ready."

"Yes, sir."

Billy held the tent flap and followed Eli into the purple gray of a clear sky and a soggy, muddy, wet world. It took him half an hour to find enough dry firewood to build a fire to partially dry Eli's blanket. He turned to Eli. "Strip off those muddy clothes and wrap in the blanket. I'll wash the clothes and start them drying."

Eli dropped his weapons belt on his blanket and then bent forward, and Billy pulled the wet, muddy buckskin hunting shirt over his head. Eli straightened and began working with the leather thongs on his breeches, and suddenly he froze. He slowly raised an arm to point south, down the Hudson River.

Billy turned, and at first there was nothing, and then he saw. In the hazy distance, past the south end of the island, he made out the billowed sails of four heavy ships, riding low in the water, three masts each, and even at that distance he recognized three decks with black specks at measured intervals. He felt his breathing slow for a moment as he narrowed his eyes and shaded them to study the flag they were flying.

The proud red, white, and blue of the British Union Jack.

He turned to Eli. "British men-of-war. Big ones. Three decks of cannon."

They looked at each other and said nothing, and they both watched, mesmerized, fascinated. The great ships moved forward through the Narrows between Long Island and Staten Island into New York Bay, and the sails were furled and the ships slowed and stopped, dead in the water.

The bow and the stern of the second ship bore the name *Greyhound*, carved into the thick English oak hull and painted bold with royal blue and gold. Her captain extended his telescope and for several minutes studied the coast of Long Island, then the south end of Manhattan Island, and finally Staten Island. He turned and walked back to the officers' quarters and rapped on a door, then entered the sumptuously appointed quarters of his commander, and waited.

General William Howe was seated at a table in the center of the room, maps and books piled. He was tall, slender, angular, regular features, eyes slightly sunken beneath heavy brows. His speech was slow, artless, blunt, and totally unpolitical. He was dressed in his British officer's uniform, with his tunic hung on the back of a nearby chair. He raised his eyes. "Yes?"

"Sir, we have arrived. Perhaps the general would like to come look."

General Howe had endured the sea voyage from Halifax, facing the grinding daily monotony of inaction by sheer power of his will. He rose without a word, put on his tunic, and finished the last button as they walked out the door. He settled his hat onto his head in the bright, sweltering heat of the late-June sun.

The captain pointed and handed the telescope to General Howe. For a long time he glassed the islands to the north, then looked west at the New Jersey coastline, and finally south towards the protected waters inside Sandy Hook Bay on the New Jersey side.

He returned the glass to the captain. "We stay here and wait for Admiral Howe."

"Yes, sir."

The captain turned and gave sharp orders. The yards turned, the sails unfurled, and once again they billowed bright in the hot east wind. The great ships swung around and moved south, back through the Narrows whence they had come. They spilled their sails and lashed them to the arms and once again slowed and stopped dead in the water, and their six-ton anchors plunged into the still waters of Sandy Hook Bay, within sight of the New Jersey shores.

Notes

The plan to assassinate General George Washington by placing gunpowder beneath his quarters was discovered in time. One of the participants was a personal bodyguard of General Washington named Thomas Hickey. The plot is generally known as the "Hickey Plot." The plan to assassinate General Washington, as well as other American officers, and to blow up American magazines of gunpowder was largely calculated to cause Americans to abandon the Revolution and take up the cause for the British. The use of gunpowder to destroy General Washington appears in some reports, as well as poison in other credible reports. The "Hickey Plot" as depicted in this chapter has been somewhat abbreviated to accommodate this novel (see Johnston, *The Campaign of 1776*, part I, p. 92; part 2, pp. 129–30; Godfrey, *The Commander-in-Chief's Guard*, pp. 21–34).

On June 25 and 26, 1776, four British men-of-war sailed into New York Harbor, then retreated to Sandy Hook on the New Jersey coast to await further arrivals. One vessel was named *Greyhound*, and General William Howe was on board to take command of the British forces (see Johnston, *The Campaign of 1776*, part I, p. 94).

New York City
June 28, 1776

CHAPTER VIII

★ ★ ★

*A*ttention to the reading of the articles of sentence."
General John Scott's voice rang out over the New York Common.

In the late June heat the entire Continental army stationed on the southern end of Manhattan Island, seven thousand strong, came to rigid attention, jammed together, sweating in the eleven A.M. sun. Civilians from as far away as New Jersey crowded the side streets, silent, wide-eyed, unable to resist the tantalizing draw of watching a human being hanged by the neck until dead.

They heard the words of General John Morin Scott standing on the raised platform at the north end of the common, but their eyes never left the high scaffolding to his right, cut from pine and hammered and bolted together twenty-four hours earlier. They had counted the thirteen steps from the grass of the common up to the deck, and they had looked at the one-inch rope with the noose formed by thirteen windings dangling from the heavy cross arm. They looked away, then back at the deadly noose, again and again, high in the sun, moving slightly in the occasional stir in the air.

A dog barked and fell silent. A horse whickered and someone grasped the bit and it stopped. A child whimpered and a hand covered its mouth. An unreal silence settled over the entire common and into the side streets, where more than twenty thousand human beings waited and listened.

General Scott looked down at the large ledger he held and again raised his voice. " 'By His Excellency George Washington, Esquire, General and Commander-in-Chief of the army of the United American Colonies.

" 'To the Provost Marshal of the said army:

" 'Whereas Thomas Hickey, a soldier enlisted in the service of the said united colonies, has been duly convicted by a general court-martial of mutiny and sedition, and also of holding a treacherous correspondence with the enemies of said colonies, contrary to the rules and regulations established for the government of the said troops; and the said Thomas Hickey, being so convicted, has been sentenced to death, by being hanged by the neck till he shall be dead; which sentence, by the unanimous advice of the general officers of the said army, I have thought proper to confirm. These are, therefore, to will and require you to execute the said sentence upon the said Thomas Hickey this day, at eleven o'clock in the forenoon, upon the ground between the encampments of the brigades of Brigadier-Generals Spencer and Lord Stirling; and for so doing this shall be your sufficient warrant.

" 'Given under my hand this twenty-eighth day of June, in the year of our Lord one thousand seven hundred and seventy-six. George Washington. Headquarters, New York.' "

Murmuring broke out and Scott waited. Billy stared straight ahead, sweat forming on his forehead. He forced his eyes away from the hangman's noose and glanced at the men ahead of him, all in rank and file, all at rigid attention to watch the proceeding, as ordered by General Scott. The backs of their necks were red, and sweat was trickling from beneath hatbands of those who had hats.

As the murmuring died, Scott turned to his right to face four soldiers wearing the green uniforms of Colonel Lasher's New York brigade. They stood at rigid attention in the form of a square, muskets at the ready, bayonets mounted. Inside the square was Thomas Hickey, dressed in homespun. His face was ashen, but his head was high, mouth set, defiant.

Scott drew and released a great breath and nodded to the chaplain standing behind the soldiers. "The chaplain will attend the prisoner."

The chaplain stepped forward, taller than Hickey, stooped, gray haired, round faced, a large Bible under his arm. He faced Hickey and his words were soft, low. "Be at peace. You will soon be free of this world of pain. Is there anything you wish to say? any confession you wish to make?"

Hickey's chin trembled and he shook his head.

"Do you wish me to carry any last words to your loved ones? your family?"

Again Hickey shook his head.

Impulsively the old man reached to tenderly take Hickey's hand into his own, and suddenly the dam burst. Soundless tears streamed down Hickey's cheeks and onto his shirt. He gasped and battled, but said nothing. Half a minute passed, and then Hickey shuddered and shook himself and gained control. He wiped the tears with the backs of his hands and turned towards Scott and raised his voice, eyes flashing his defiance. "We failed to get Washington, but I tell you now, unless Greene is cautious, we will not fail to get him."

The chaplain returned to his place.

Scott spoke to the sergeant in charge of the soldiers. "Tie the prisoner's hands."

Hickey's hands were brought behind, and a rope was quickly looped and tied.

Scott licked dry lips. "Take the prisoner to the gallows."

The four soldiers climbed the thirteen stairs, their boots thumping loud in the silence. They stopped, turned, and looked down at Scott, waiting.

"Prisoner, do you wish to have a hood?"

Hickey shook his head.

"Bind his ankles."

Quick hands wrapped and tied a rope.

"Place the noose."

The soldiers moved Hickey squarely to the center of the trap. The loop settled over his head, and the sergeant pulled the slack out.

Billy stared, struggling to comprehend the enormity of the act he was about to witness. Eli closed his mouth and for long moments stared at the ground before he once again raised his eyes.

Scott exhaled and his shoulders slumped, and in that split second both Billy and Eli sensed in small part the price paid by those who bear the heavy burden of command. Scott stared hard at the sergeant, and then he drew a deep breath. "Execute the sentence."

The sergeant grasped the heavy lever and quickly shoved it towards the trap. The pin holding the trap in place withdrew, the door fell open, and the body of Thomas Hickey dropped out of sight into the yawning space beneath his feet, and a gasp swept through the common. The rope snapped tight, then began to swing, twisting.

Scott counted off three minutes while murmuring rose in the common, and people moved their feet and turned their eyes. He turned to his regimental surgeon and nodded, and the small, erect man walked behind the scaffolding and through a door into the chamber with the body. Thirty seconds later he made his way back to Scott on the platform, checked a large pocket watch, wrote down a time in Scott's large, leather-bound ledger, and signed his name. He laid the quill on the page, faced Scott, bobbed his head once, turned on his heel, and walked away while Scott closed the book.

Scott walked to the front railing of the platform and for a moment looked over the sea of faces peering upward, some at him, some at the rope that was still twisting. "Officers, take command of your regiments. Clear the common at once and resume your assigned duties after completion of the noon meal. That is all."

Orders rang out and the regiments worked their way through the crowded streets, trying to hold the cadence as they slowed from time to time while people made way for them to pass. Colonel Thompson moved the Boston regiment straight north, then west onto Reade Street.

Billy marched mechanically, eyes straight ahead, still seeing a man drop from sight and a rope jerk, then swing slowly back and forth. He was not expecting the sudden eruption of sound and action towards the front of the column, and he craned his neck to look. On the right side of the narrow cobblestone street, in the dooryards of two houses, civilians were clustered around something on the ground, shouting, angry, arms flailing.

Thompson shouted orders. "Hold your step. Keep moving."

The column marched on, heads turning to stare at the melee. Billy tracked with his eyes as the Ninth Company passed, and the crowd opened enough for him to see the battle. Two men had been thrown to the ground, terrified, kicking, stripped to their underwear. Angry hands held them down while four men with long-handled mops smeared them with hot tar. Billy saw open burlap bags filled with feathers being passed forward, while half a dozen men stood by holding long rails, waiting.

The regiment marched on, with the smell of hot tar in their nostrils, wondering what they had seen, who was being punished and why. At the end of Reade Street they turned to their camp-ground, Thompson shouted orders, and ten minutes later the companies lighted cooking fires.

The summer sun was directly overhead, oppressive, pounding down, as they lined up to take their ration of boiled salt pork, a boiled potato, and hardtack. Each man inspected his thin, brittle piece of hardtack for worms, knocked those they could see off into the sand and grass, and silently moved on.

A somber mood moved across the campground, and there was little of the usual banter and grumbling at food not fit to eat and at the stupidity and arrogance of officers as they moved back to their blankets and settled down cross-legged to work on their smoking meal with their forks and fingers. Men looked at their plates, or the ground, or the sky, but not each other as they groped to come to terms with the sight, etched forever into their memories, of a man dropping through the trap of a gallows, and then the sight of a mob holding terrified men on the ground while they smeared them with hot tar.

Billy sat on his blanket, split his potato, and watched the steam rise, then divided the chunk of salt pork into pieces with the edge of his fork and waited for them to cool. He broke a piece of hardtack with his teeth and tucked it in his cheek to let it soften while he waited for the potato and salt pork to cool. He glanced up when Eli sat down on the other edge of his blanket. For a time they remained silent as they worked with their food.

Finally Billy spoke, but not of the hanging of Thomas Hickey. He and Eli had been too close to it, too instrumental, and had not yet come to terms with their role in the grisly affair. "Any idea what the tar and feathers was about?"

"Tories and Patriots, I think. I don't know which was getting the tar." Eli fingered a piece of hot pork into his mouth and sucked air to cool it. "If we don't get on with this war with the British soon, we're going to have our own war right here in the streets."

The high, piercing voice of Sergeant Turlock interrupted. "Weems. Stroud. The colonel wants you at his tent. Now."

Billy looked at Eli, eyebrows risen in question, and Eli shook his head. They put their plates down on the blanket and rose to follow Turlock through the camp to the command tent. The officer at the flap took Eli's rifle, announced them, then held the flap as the two ducked inside and came to attention.

"Reporting as ordered, sir."

"Sit." Thompson gestured and the two sat down at his table opposite him. "Thought you should know. There are three more traitors that were in the plot with Hickey that will be hung in the next few days. Two on Long Island, one across the river."

He paused and rounded his lips for a moment, then continued, eyes cast down at a paper before him on the table. "We learned that the names in those documents were wrong, but they had the same initials as the men involved. T. Horton signed some of those papers. The real name was Thomas Hickey."

Again he paused as though weighing whether he should reveal more, and then he continued. "Some of the other names were A.

Taylor and H. Millman." He raised his eyes to Billy and Eli and spoke evenly. "Taylor's real name is Tryon. He's the governor of the colony of New York. Millman's real name is Matthews. He's the mayor of New York City."

Billy's face went blank, and Eli's mouth dropped open for a split second.

Thompson nodded acknowledgment of their expressions. "The plot included the royal governor of this province and the mayor of this city. At least eight other men high in government and commerce put up hundreds of thousands of English pounds sterling and all the power of their positions to put this plot together."

Billy exhaled pent-up breath.

"We're after them, but right now we don't know if we'll ever get enough evidence to convict them all. I doubt we'll get the mayor or the governor."

Eli shook his head. "I killed the man who could convict the mayor. I regret that."

"Don't worry. Even if we don't convict him, he'll never be able to do this kind of thing again."

Billy asked, "How far did the plan reach?"

"All over the colonies. Here, Boston, New Jersey, Connecticut."

Eli leaned forward. "On the gallows, did I hear Hickey say something about someone named Greene?"

Thompson nodded. "General Nathanael Greene. In command on Long Island. They had barrels of gunpowder over there to blow up his entire command headquarters."

"Any others?"

"General Putnam, General Sullivan, General Scott, half a dozen others."

"Anything besides the officers?"

"At least eight powder magazines. Four hundred thousand cartridges, over a hundred cannon, thousands of muskets—they intended to disable the entire Continental army over about a two-day period."

Billy eased back in his chair, face a blank.

Thompson picked up a pencil and idly twisted it between his fingers for a moment. "General Washington knows what you two did. He may never get the time to thank you personally, but General Scott says he was ordered by Washington to convey his thanks. I add mine." He raised his eyes. They were, as always, firm, direct.

Billy murmured, "Thank you, sir."

Eli said nothing.

Thompson laid the pencil down. "That's all. No need to spread this." He gestured to Eli's arm. "How's it coming?"

"Good."

"You resting it?"

Eli smiled, his eyes dropped, and he said nothing.

"That's what I thought. Stroud, I'm giving you a direct order. You put that arm in a sling within the next ten minutes and leave it there until the surgeon takes the stitches out. If I hear otherwise I'll have you in the stockade. Understood?"

"Yes, sir."

"All right. Weems, if he disobeys, you're to report it immediately."

"Yes, sir."

"Dismissed." Thompson busied himself with paperwork, and the two men rose and walked out the tent flap into the sweltering heat. Eli took his rifle, and they said nothing as they walked to the surgeon's tent, where Billy got a roll of clean, torn sheeting, and they made their way back to Billy's blanket. Billy tore off five feet of the roll of white sheeting, knotted a loop, and fashioned a sling around Eli's neck and left arm.

They ate the cold potatoes, picked at the cold, greasy salt pork, ground the hardtack between their teeth, drank from their canteens, and set their plates aside.

Eli spoke. "I can hardly believe what Thompson said about the mayor and the governor and those other men in high places. Out to kill General Washington."

Billy nodded. "Washington, Greene, Putnam, Sullivan, Scott—

it's like some fable." He raised his eyes to Eli. "A couple days ago, you mentioned you wanted to meet General Washington. Something interrupted and you never said why."

Eli sobered and he stared at his hands for a moment. "There's a story among the Iroquois. They don't think he can be killed by a bullet or cannon or gunpowder."

"What? I've never heard that."

"It comes from a long time ago, when he was young. The Iroquois were with the French when they ambushed some English, and Washington was one of the English officers. His commander got hit, and Washington tried to save him. Six or eight Iroquois got so close with muskets they couldn't miss, and shot at Washington. They hit his hat and coat, but they couldn't hit him, and it scared them. Washington got his commanding officer out of there but he died, and Washington buried him in the road and made the English march over the grave so the Iroquois couldn't find it. The Iroquois told their chief about trying to kill Washington, and the old chief said he had seen them shoot, and he told them, maybe like a prophet in the Bible, that Washington would never be killed by a bullet or a cannon, but he would live long."

Eli stopped, and Billy watched his face become sober, reflective, and he waited.

Eli concluded. "And he said George Washington would become the father of a great and free land." Eli raised his eyes to Billy, and in them Billy saw the deep need to see the man, to meet him, to feel his spirit, to be able to judge.

Was it true? Would George Washington live long? Would he survive the war? win? be the leader of a great, free land? Could an old Iroquois chief make such a prophecy? If he could, was it from God?

Billy's words came quietly. "Do you believe it?"

Eli hesitated for a time. "I don't know. That's why I want to meet him. Maybe I'll feel it. Maybe I'll know. I'd like to find out."

"What happens when you find out?"

"If I believe it's true that the Great Spirit—God—sent him to set this land free, then I do everything I can for him."

"And if not?"

"I leave."

For a time Billy fell silent at the profound simplicity. Eli rose and picked up his plate and utensils, and Billy followed him to the river, where they scrubbed them with sand, rinsed them, and returned to the blanket and set them to dry.

"If you ever meet him, do you think you'll know?"

"I hope so. I hope I'll feel something, one way or the other. Maybe enough." He looked at Billy. "Once before I said white men have let many things inside go to sleep. They don't feel. If I meet Washington, I hope I can feel his spirit try to speak to mine. I hope it will be strong."

"You're white."

"Raised Iroquois. Raised to feel. Like Joseph Brant. If he's with the British . . ." He did not finish the sentence.

Billy stuffed his plate and utensils into his knapsack and was rising when a rumble from behind turned both of them around to look. A great freight wagon built of heavy oak, double axled, wide, heavy-spoked wheels six feet in diameter, rolled from Reade Street eighty yards distant. Two pedigreed Percheron draft horses, eighteen hundred pounds each, in well-oiled, brass-studded harnesses, swung the wagon to the right, and the wheels sank eight inches into the sandy, stony soil as the wagon made its way around the encampment towards the command tent. The driver came back on the lines and talked the horses to a stop, and Billy peered, aware there was something different about the flat-crowned, stiff, flat-brimmed costly straw hat and the wrist-length sleeves shoved back to the elbows. A civilian sat next to the driver on the high seat, with a musket between his knees, and two other armed civilians were in the back, sitting on whatever was loaded behind the high, thick sidewalls. Their eyes never ceased moving, watching everyone.

A nearby officer spoke to the driver, who handed him a document, and the officer disappeared inside the command tent. A moment later Thompson ducked under the flap and strode to the

wagon. He handed something up to the driver, spoke, and pointed. The driver slapped the reins on the rumps of the horses and gigged them. The big bay geldings heaved into the harnesses and dug into the loose soil, and slowly the massive wagon lurched into motion, headed towards the powder magazine twenty yards past the north end of the encampment.

Billy and Eli watched it rumble past, and their eyes widened when they realized the driver, sitting high and straight on the seat, was a woman. She held the reins locked between the index and middle fingers of each hand, left foot thrust forward and out, riding the cleat of the brake pole, and she talked low to the horses, eyes straight ahead as she approached the powder magazine. The straw hat sat low and level on her head, held in place by a leather thong tied beneath her chin. Her long-sleeved, ankle-length calico dress was of high quality, with lace at the throat, down the front, and on the cuffs. Her dark hair was caught in back by a leather cord. Her eyes were dark, wide set, serious, nose straight, aquiline, mouth drawn as she clucked and talked to the horses, chin firm, with a hint of a cleft, and there was a slight gap between her front teeth. They saw perspiration on her forehead as the wagon rolled past. She did not look at them.

She rolled to within forty feet of the powder magazine, and the double pickets moved to meet her. She came back on the reins and the wagon stopped.

Wide-eyed in surprise, the pickets challenged. "Uh, ma'am, this is a munitions magazine. No one gets close without orders from the colonel."

She leaned to hand the picket the document Thompson had given her, and he studied it for a moment, then turned to the other pickets. "Colonel says she's got munitions. Let her pass. Company Nine will be here to unload."

She moved the wagon forward, near the heavy oak door that opened into a stairwell downward. The magazine was twenty-five feet by thirty feet, sunk seven feet in the ground, with a roof of heavy timbers covered by two feet of compacted dirt and rocks.

Behind her a young lieutenant talked to Sergeant Turlock, who was working at his hardtack. He handed a document to Turlock, who scanned it and then turned to look at the wagon beside the powder magazine. He stood, and Ninth Company watched him, waiting.

"All right, you lovelies. We got cartridges to unload, and a lady waiting. Follow me."

The men stood, brushing dirt and sand from their trousers, and fell in behind Turlock as they walked to the waiting wagon. Hard hands that had been soft and blistered only days earlier pulled the pins and lowered the tailgate. The soldiers glanced guardedly at the woman, who stood near the door to the sunken stairwell, tugging her sleeves down to cover her arms. The three armed men who had arrived with her stood silently nearby, muskets in hand, watching everyone.

"Weems!"

Billy's head swung around to Turlock. "Here."

Turlock motioned and Billy walked to him.

"You the one who keeps accounts?"

"Yes."

Turlock thrust the document to him, with a stub pencil and a piece of pine planking. "Here's the manifest on that load. Be sure everything on that manifest gets off the wagon. Any shortages or overages, stop everything until we figure it out. The lady's name is Mary Flint."

Billy nodded.

"Stroud around?"

"Over there."

"Get him. Colonel says he's not to lift anything with that arm. He's to help you count. He'll have to sign off on that manifest with you."

"I'll tell him."

Turlock called out orders, and four men climbed into the wagon bed. The others lined up shoulder to shoulder in a chain down into the magazine, and the men in the wagon began handing down the small, heavy pine boxes with handles on both ends. The boxes were labeled "TWO HUNDRED COUNT .75 CAL BALL PAPER CARTRIDGES," "TWO HUNDRED COUNT .60 CAL BALL PAPER CARTRIDGES," or "TWO HUN-DRED COUNT .50 CAL BALL PAPER CARTRIDGES."

Billy stood at the top of the stairwell, Eli beside him, and as the first box passed them, Billy's eyes narrowed and he read the stencil again, then turned to Turlock. "Those markings aren't reg-ular military marks like the ones we've seen," he said.

Turlock shrugged. "Take the count and ask about it later."

Billy took the count, making a mark on the manifest for each box that passed them. On the other side of the door, Mary Flint was intently making her own count, watching every box, marking her own copy.

The work settled into a rhythm beneath the relentless sun. Sweat ran dripping from noses and chins and soaked shirts. Mary drew a large handkerchief from a pocket in her dress and wiped her forehead, never losing her count. Turlock left and returned with two buckets of cold springwater and two dippers, and the work stopped for five minutes while thirsty men rinsed their mouths, spouted water, and then drank long. Steadily the load in the wagon dwindled, and then the men up in the wagon bed set the last box on the back edge and dropped to the ground. The box disappeared into the magazine, and moments later the men climbed back to daylight.

The heavy door was lowered into place, and the double locks snapped in their hasps. Billy quickly added the columns on the manifest and entered the totals, then watched Mary. She finished her figures and looked at him, waiting.

"One hundred eighty total," Billy recited. "Ninety-two .75-caliber, fifty-five .60-caliber, thirty-three .50-caliber. Thirty-six thousand paper cartridges."

Mary studied her figures for a moment. "That's what I have."

Billy bobbed his head. "Good." He signed his name, Eli signed his, and Mary signed hers and took her copy. She briefly checked it, then raised her face directly to Billy. "Thank you."

The open expression in her dark eyes startled Billy, and he answered, "My thanks to you, ma'am."

She turned to Eli, and for an instant her eyes swept his buckskins with the Iroquois quillwork, his moccasins, and then the weapons belt with the tomahawk. For a moment their eyes met, and in hers Eli caught a glimmer of frank directness that came from having lived with deep pain or sadness. He also saw compassion and strength, and he saw the unspoken question he had seen so many times in the eyes of others—how did an Indian come to have blue eyes and brown hair?

She gestured to the sling on his left arm. "Broken?"

"It's all right."

Turlock's voice rose to interrupt. "Back to camp. We have work yet today."

Billy and Eli both nodded to her and turned to Turlock. Billy handed him the signed manifest; then both he and Eli fell in with the company, moving back towards camp. Mary turned on her heel, climbed the wagon wheel, and used the step to climb into the driver's box, while her escorts took their places, one on the driver's seat beside her, the other two in the wagon bed. She unwrapped the reins from the brake pole, threaded the long leather lines through her fingers, and slapped the reins on the rumps of the two horses. They leaned into the horse collars, the traces tightened, and the big wagon moved. The men of Company Nine watched her make the tight right turn and slowly pass them as she returned to the Reade Street entrance and swung the team left, the empty wagon clattering when the heavy iron-rimmed wheels reached the cobblestones.

"Ten minutes rest, then we get back to the battery," Turlock called, and the men searched out canteens and dropped to their blankets. Billy drank and was forcing the wooden plug back into the spout of his canteen when he noticed a young, smooth-cheeked lieutenant make his way to Turlock, take the manifest, and speak briefly. Turlock nodded, then turned and motioned to Billy and Eli.

Eli looked at Billy inquiringly. "Was that paper all right?"

"I thought so."

They stood and strode to Turlock and waited. "Lieutenant says Thompson wants to see you two."

Billy asked, "What about?"

Turlock shrugged. "Lieutenant will take you. He's got the manifest."

They followed the lieutenant back to the command tent, waited while he disappeared for a moment, then entered while he held the flap.

Thompson dropped the manifest on his table, then motioned. "Sit." He looked at Billy. "I'm appointing you a corporal in the Ninth Company. I'll have the order written by late afternoon and delivered to Turlock. You'll assume those duties tomorrow morning."

Billy swallowed. "Sir, I don't have an idea what a corporal does."

"Neither does any other man in the regiment. Turlock will tell you. Is there any reason you cannot accept the rank of corporal? Health? Politics?"

"No, sir."

"Sergeant Turlock will deliver the order to you by morning. Take care of it." He turned to Eli. "I'm making you a scout for the regiment. You'll keep the rank of private, but you'll report directly to me when you're on scout duty. Otherwise, you'll remain with the regiment on their regular duties."

Eli leaned back in his chair, eyes narrowed. "Scout? Scout what?"

"I don't know, yet. But I see a battle shaping up between an untried army of farmers and merchants and the mightiest army on earth, and I don't mean to have this regiment walk into any surprises if I can help it. I'm aware of how you handled the Hickey plot, and you told me the British have Mohawk in their ranks, maybe Joseph Brant. I want you available."

Eli exhaled held breath. "Yes, sir."

"How's that arm?"

"Healing. Aches a little."

"You remember what I said. Until the surgeon pulls those stitches, it stays in that sling."

"Yes, sir."

Thompson dropped his eyes for a moment to gather his thoughts. "I think that's all for now. Any questions?"

Billy responded. "Yes, sir. I was surprised to see a woman deliver those cartridges."

"So was I. I asked about it. Name's Mary Flint." He paused to shake his head, and there was pain in his face. "Heartbreaking story. She's a widow. Her maiden name was Broadhead, and she married Marcus Flint, both prominent families here in New York. He was an officer in the New York militia. Fine man. She gave birth to a stillborn child about ten months ago, and three days later her husband was crushed in what was called an accident, down on the docks, unloading cannon from a captured British man-of-war. Some say it was murder by the Tories, but no one can prove it. A dark shame. She's thrown herself into the Patriot cause."

"That wagon was not military. It was expensive. So were her clothes."

"Both families, Broadhead and Flint, are wealthy. One of them owns the wagon."

"Those cartridge boxes weren't marked with regular manufacturer's marks."

"She provided them, too."

"Had we better check the cartridges?"

"No."

"Who made them?"

"Women. She's organized women. They tie cartridges and roll bandages, gather blankets, shoes, food, anything they can."

Eli broke in. "What was that fuss on Reade Street when we marched out at noon?"

Thompson pursed his mouth for a moment. "I asked. They

call it 'Tory-riding.' The Patriots catch Tories, tar and feather them, and ride them out of town on a rail. It's become a sport here in New York. Seems they caught about three at the hanging."

"Do we know what those British ships were that came in down south a couple days ago?"

Thompson leaned forward and picked up a pencil and worked it in his hands for a moment, then laid it down. He leaned forward and spoke quietly. "Yes. General William Howe was on the flagship in the squadron, named the *Greyhound.* They're anchored farther south now, off Sandy Hook. We know Howe's orders are to destroy the Continental army. We also know his brother, Admiral Richard Howe, is on his way here with a fleet and that the general is probably waiting for it to arrive. When it does, there will be a battle. We better be ready." He looked at Eli. "That's why you're becoming my scout. I've got to know some things about all this when the time comes."

Eli rounded his lips and blew air for a moment. "How many ships coming?"

Thompson considered for a moment. "We don't know. Dozens—hundreds."

Billy caught his breath and Eli straightened. "Hundreds?"

Thompson nodded but said nothing.

"When?"

"No one knows." He stood. "This needs to go no further than this tent. We'll all know soon enough. In the meantime, go on back to your duties with the regiment."

Billy and Eli ducked out the tent flap into the sweltering afternoon heat. Eli took his rifle from the picket, then paused to turn south and shade his eyes, searching for the four ships, but they had vanished. Eli followed Billy back to the regimental campsite, where they drank from their canteens, then walked on to the battery, where the last of the split logs were being countersunk to form the inclined recoil ramp for the big guns.

Billy settled into his assignment of swinging a pick to loosen the top eighteen inches of soil, while others used shovels to dig it out to form trenches thirty feet long. Others moved the split logs into the trench, flat side up, rounded side down, and bedded the logs in cement to form the ramp. Eli settled into a rhythm, swinging a hatchet with his right hand, trimming all branches from the logs until they were smooth, ready for the splitting wedges and sledgehammers.

At six o'clock Sergeant Turlock straightened from his shovel, wiped his dripping face with his sleeve, and bawled, "Supper." The men leaned their shovels and picks against the battery wall and walked to the river to thrust their heads under and come up spouting water, soaked hair flying, then wash the sweat and grime from their hands.

Ten minutes later the cooking pots were boiling dried fish and wild turnips. The men stood in line to take their rations and their chunks of wormy hardtack, then went to their blankets where they sat cross-legged with their faces turned from their plates to avoid the stench while they worked with knife and fork to cut the steaming food into pieces to cool.

Billy breathed shallow while he cut, and Eli suddenly set his plate aside and stood and walked towards the river. Twenty minutes later he returned with ten dark brown hard-shelled clams and some salt in the palm of his hand. He set the clams on a piece of firewood and settled them into the middle of Billy's campfire.

Billy looked at him in question.

"Quahaugs," Eli said.

"What's a quahaug?"

"Iroquois word. Hard-shelled clams. They dig into the mud. Not much, but with a little salt they're better than what we got."

Fifteen minutes later Eli poked the clams out of the fire with a stick, then used his knife to pry them open steaming. He grasped a pinch of salt between his finger and thumb, dropped several grains onto the gray meat on the shell, and speared it into his mouth with his knife. He gestured to Billy, who repeated what he had seen.

The meat was mild, nearly tasteless, but better than the bitter boiled turnips and fish. With the meal finished and their utensils washed and drying in gathering dusk, Eli picked up his rifle and started towards his own blanket, when Turlock came picking his way through the sprawl of men and blankets with a document in his hand.

"Weems, here's your appointment as corporal. Take care of it. I'm supposed to teach you. Tomorrow we'll start." He turned his eyes to Eli. "You're a scout, but when you aren't on orders from Thompson, you're still a private in Ninth Company."

"I know."

"That arm all right?"

"Fine."

"Weems, come find me in the morning after breakfast."

"Yes, sir."

"Don't call me sir. I'm no officer. I'm a sergeant."

"Yes, Sergeant."

Turlock bobbed his head, turned, and was gone.

Eli glanced down at Billy, nodded, and walked away towards his own blanket in the gathering gloom of night.

For a time Billy sat with his arms on his knees, staring into the firelight, and let his thoughts run. In full darkness he dug his pad and pencil from his knapsack, got a piece of planking, and turned to catch the firelight on the paper. He pondered a moment, then carefully began to write.

The 28th day of June, 1776

My dear Mother:

Important events have happened of which you will surely hear, and I write to let you know I am in good health and am sound.

Terrible plot to kill officers—discovered—caught some of the men—one was hanged this morning before entire army—city is divided, Tories and Patriots—four British men-of-war anchored to the south—waiting for more—great battle expected soon—women made cartridges—delivered them in a wagon—I am made corporal—will try to do my duty. Tell Margaret and Brigitte—have them tell Matthew—tell Trudy—I have not yet been paid and regret I cannot yet send money—no money available—food in short supply. Will write again soon.

> Faithfully your loving son,
> Billy Weems

He read the letter again, folded it, and stuffed it back into his knapsack, then turned back to sit cross-legged before his campfire and stare into the dancing, dwindling flames and the orange coals that were slowly turning black. He let his thoughts go where they would, and in his mind he once again saw a man standing on a gallows and then dropping through and the rope swinging, twisting. Terrified men in a front yard, held down while being smeared with tar. A dark-eyed woman expertly handling the long leather lines on a team of Percheron geldings, driving a heavy, expensive wagon into camp with 36,000 cartridges in 180 small pine boxes. Counting them into the regimental magazine. Corporal. Eli a scout. British men-of-war anchored to the south, waiting, watching.

He drew a great breath and exhaled it slowly. *Too much. Moving too fast. No time to tug at it and pull at it and make it all fit together. No time.*

A wistful smile crept. *Mother. Need to talk with Mother. Mother and Margaret. And Brigitte. Need to sit at the table after supper with hot custard and maple syrup sauce and talk with them.*

He reached for his knapsack and once again dug out his pad and pencil. *I wonder how things are with them. With Margaret and her family. Caleb. The twins. Brigitte. Would they read a letter? Would they have any interest?*

He pondered for a time before he turned the pad to the light and began.

My dear friends:

I sit at my campfire with pencil and pad in hand, hoping a letter will not intrude upon your busy lives. Many things have happened which I hope will be of interest to you. Sadly, this morning the entire army was required to witness the hanging of a man named Thos. Hickey, who was convicted of mutiny and corresponding with the enemy. I also witnessed Patriots tar some men who were Tories.

This afternoon the regiment commander, Colonel Israel Thompson, made me a corporal, though I do not know why, since I know nothing of being a soldier, except how to march and haul rocks to build a cannon battery.

He paused. *That should make her smile.* He continued writing.

Today we saw four British men-of-war in New York Harbor far to the south, and were told they are gathering to invade New York. We are very busy preparing to meet them. Today we received 36,000 more cartridges, which I was obliged to count into the regimental magazine. Women tied the cartridges, and a young widow delivered them in a splendid wagon. Women are doing many things to assist the army.

He re-read the last lines and his face fell in concern. *A young widow—will that concern her?* He considered for a moment, then continued.

Tonight my friend Eli Stroud brought quahaugs from the Hudson River for supper. That is an Iroquois word meaning hard-shelled clams. Cooked and salted they are edible, and better than the boiled fish with wild turnips from the regimental cooking kettles. However, none of the regimental meals compares with the bounties we have shared at

Billy suddenly stopped and slowly lowered the pad and re-read the letter, and his eyes widened. He read it again, and his face clouded as thoughts formed. *That should make her smile—will mention of a young widow concern her—the bounties we have shared . . .*

Make whom smile? Concern whom? Bounties shared with whom?

His breath came short as the answer moved to the front of his consciousness and every other thought faded.

Brigitte!

He did not know how long he sat before his dying fire, staring at the pad without seeing. The fire was dead and the camp was dark when he folded the unfinished letter and worked it into his knapsack, and then lay on his blanket and stared into the countless stars overhead for a long time before his eyes closed and he slept.

Notes

For his involvement in the plot to assassinate General Washington, Thomas Hickey was convicted of mutiny, sedition, and treachery, and was hanged in public June 28, 1776. Also involved in the plot were Governor Tryon of the colony of New York, and Mayor Matthews of New York City, among others. Matthews was arrested, but the evidence against him was insufficient and he was not convicted. The warrant for the hanging of Thomas Hickey, signed by General George Washington, is quoted verbatim in this chapter (see Godfrey, *The Commander-in-Chief's Guard*, p. 31). The dialogue between the chaplain and Thomas Hickey just prior to the hanging is taken from the letter appearing in Johnston, *The Campaign of 1776*, part 2, p. 129.

The practice of "Tory-riding" and of stripping Tories and abusing them with tar occurred frequently (see Johnston, *The Campaign of 1776*, part 1, p. 92, particularly the footnote).

There is a record of an Indian chief who saw George Washington miraculously unharmed in an Iroquois ambush and prophesied that he could not be harmed in battle and that he would found a great nation (see Parry and Allison, *The Real George Washington*, pp. 48–49).

Mary Flint is a fictitious character.

A "quahaug" is a hard-shelled clam that buries itself in mud. Soldiers who had too little food often dug them up and roasted them to eat (see Fitch, *New York Diary*, p. 45).

CHAPTER IX

★ ★ ★

*T*he general will see you now."

The deck of the *Greyhound* rose and fell slowly on the incoming swells of the Atlantic tides inside Sandy Hook Bay. Her sails were furled and her masts and yards thrust stark into the bright, clear New Jersey skies like skeletal ribs of a huge squat animal, with the British Union Jack fluttering high in the wind.

Ship's captain Averman Plessy led a cluster of five men to the rear of the main deck and rapped on the door of the quarters of General William Howe.

"Come."

He opened the door and led the group inside. For a moment they blinked, passing from the bright sunlight into the confines of the general's large, extravagantly appointed room. General Sir William Howe, in full uniform, sat in a decorated upholstered chair behind a large, ornately carved English walnut desk. He raised his face from half a dozen maps and documents and waited.

"Sir," Captain Plessy said, "may I present the honorable royal governor of the province of New York, William Tryon."

Tryon shifted a large, flat documents folder to his left hand, took a stride forward, bowed from the waist, and thrust his right hand forward. "I am deeply honored, General."

Howe rose and returned the bow. "My pleasure." Tryon turned to his entourage. "May I present Sergeant Graham and

Misters Rutledge, Ungerman, and Willet, who have been of great assistance in our work." They stepped forward in turn, exchanged bows with General Howe, and stepped back into line.

"Be seated, gentlemen." Howe waited, then settled back into his own chair and came directly to the point. "Governor Tryon, I understand you have some information?"

"Yes, sir."

"May I inquire?"

"Of course."

"What is the mix in the colonial forces, continental and militia?"

Tryon turned to Sergeant Graham. "Sir, Sergeant Graham has gathered that information and made diagrams and sketches, as you requested. He will answer."

Graham sat ramrod straight on his chair, facing Howe. "Nearly all undisciplined rabble. The Continental army is over ninety percent inexperienced citizens. Less than ten percent have been in battle."

"What are their numbers?"

"Nearing eighteen thousand, and more arriving regularly."

"Who are their officers?"

"George Washington, Israel Putnam, John Sullivan, Nathanael Greene, Charles Lee, Lord Stirling."

"I believe I know Lee and Stirling."

"Yes, sir. They are both traitors—formerly officers in the Royal Army."

Howe's eyes fell for a moment. "Any other officers I should be aware of?"

"Several lesser officers, but none of concern."

"Who commands in New York?"

"Mr. George Washington, of Virginia."

"Who on Long Island?"

"At the moment, Mr. Nathanael Greene."

"Who commands their cannon?"

"Mr. Henry Knox."

A crooked smile split Howe's face. "The, uh, fat printer?"

"Yes, sir."

Muffled laughter sounded and faded.

"How many cannon? Where?"

"About eighty-five at the moment, placed in batteries on both sides of Manhattan Island, with a heavy concentration in New York City. Several on Long Island in breastworks south of Brooklyn."

Howe sobered. "How are the troops dressed?"

"Very few uniforms, even among those calling themselves officers. Homespun, mostly in very poor condition."

"Describe their encampments."

Graham shook his head. "That's difficult, sir. They are generally in shambles. There is nothing suggesting military discipline of any kind."

"Their food?"

"Wormy hardtack, meat once a week, wild turnips, dried fish. They requisition or steal what they can from the local farms, but it is far too little. Dysentery is bad. Their infirmaries are full."

"How are they armed?"

"Badly. A few newer muskets taken from forces of the Crown, but mostly old colonial-made muskets used by farmers to shoot food for the table, some old French flint-locks, several fowling pieces from forty years ago, a few rifles."

"Can the troops shoot effectively?"

"A fair number shoot well, but few or none have ever fired a musket in a battle with an organized army such as yours. Several have not fired a musket more than ten times in their lives."

"Do they have powder and shot?"

"More arrives daily, but at this moment, far too little to engage in a major battle."

"Are they drilling daily?"

"No. Twice a week at the most. They're working dawn to dark building fortifications."

"Do they have the will to fight?"

"Judging from Concord and Bunker Hill, they probably do. But those battles were not typical. It's hard to judge what they'll do if they're facing an all-out assault."

"We learned many things at Concord and Bunker Hill, and we'll not repeat the mistakes. Are their fortifications good?"

"Yes, sir. One thing the colonial farmers understand is digging, sir. They can put up good breastworks faster than any army I ever saw."

"Are they mobile? How fast can they cross the Hudson, or the East River?"

"They have virtually no navy, sir. They would have to requisition civilian boats to cross either river. I have no way to know how they would cross, or how rapidly they could do it."

"Do I understand deepwater channels circle all three islands?"

"Yes, sir. Your gunboats can completely circumnavigate any of the islands."

"I need to know about New Jersey. Is Governor Franklin cooperating with you?"

Governor Tryon interrupted. "He is, sir. But I must warn, the New Jersey Provincial Congress has ordered his arrest. If that happens, we will have to take whatever steps necessary to continue without his support."

"Isn't he the son of Benjamin Franklin?"

"He is. The two are no longer on speaking terms."

Howe shook his head. "I'm sorry to hear that." He gestured towards the large, flat documents folder in Tryon's possession. "Do you have maps?"

"Yes, sir."

Tryon removed half a dozen maps and unfolded them onto Howe's desktop. His men crowded the front edge of the desk.

"Sergeant Graham made these from personal observations." Tryon stepped back, and Graham faced Howe across the desk.

For a time Howe studied the maps, one at a time, silently tracing lines and calculating distances. He pointed to ten positions on the shoreline of Manhattan Island. "Cannon batteries?"

"Yes, sir. And nearly every street leading to the water has a blockade, some with cannon."

Howe moved his finger to Long Island. "Brooklyn?"

"Yes, sir."

"Is General Greene building large fortifications?"

"Yes, sir. They consider that one place you may attack. There, or New York. They're fortifying both."

"Is this a ridge?"

"A long hill, sir. South of Brooklyn, running east-west. Their breastworks are on that hill."

"And here, farther south, another hill?"

"Yes, sir. Guana Heights. East-west, just like the one in front of Brooklyn, except not quite so high."

Howe tapped the map east of Brooklyn. "This is a road that runs north and south over or through both those hills?"

"Yes, sir. Bedford Road. There's a little valley that runs through both those hills."

"Is the road big enough to move troops?"

"Wide enough? Yes, sir."

Howe tapped the map again, farther east. "That's another north-south road through those two long hills?"

"Yes, sir. Jamaica Pass."

"How far from Brooklyn?"

"About four and one-half miles east."

"Large enough for heavy troop movements?"

"Yes, sir."

"I take it underbrush and foliage and the terrain would make it difficult to move, other than on the roads you've marked."

"Extremely difficult, sir. Nearly impossible with cannon and equipment."

Howe pointed again. "What's this?"

"Gowanus Marsh."

"What makes it a marsh? How big? How bad?"

"Gowanus Creek begins to the east, sir, from a natural spring on the island, and runs west. As it passes Brooklyn and empties into the East River at Gowanus Bay, it broadens into those flat plains and becomes a bog. A bad marsh, sir, fairly deep. Stagnant. Heavy mud. Impossible to move in it, or through it."

"This is marked Gravesend. A town?"

"Gravesend Bay and the town of Gravesend just east of it. And north of Gravesend is Flatbush, here." He pointed.

For half a minute Howe continued to pore over the map, fixing things in his mind, seeing Manhattan and Long Island through the eyes of one who had learned the brutal lessons of war from countless scars inside, taken in the hot cauldron of battles he had won and battles he had lost. He understood in his bones that the fortunes of war could hang on the simplest miscalculation of how well the enemy was armed, or their will to fight, or where a hill was, or a forgotten road, or a marsh, or how thick the trees and undergrowth were at a crucial place.

He moved his finger one more time. "What's that?" He tapped the map between Long Island and the mainland, in the middle of the East River where it widened into Long Island Sound.

"Hell Gate, sir. That's where the East River meets the Atlantic tides and they form a whirlpool that will wreck any ship that gets sucked in. Even your big men-of-war."

Howe's eyebrows rose. "That bad?"

"Yes, sir. I marked it so you wouldn't lose a ship finding out about it."

"Very good. Tell me what you can about Fort Washington."

"They're building it on the north end of Manhattan Island, sir, facing the Hudson. It's on the high ground and will have cannon covering all directions. Thick walls. They say it will be impregnable."

Howe's mouth narrowed for a moment. "What about Fort Lee?"

"They're going to build it facing Fort Washington from the New Jersey Palisades. It will also have cannon covering all approaches and a large number facing the Hudson. The colonials contend that the guns of Forts Lee and Washington will stop anything on the river."

Howe's eyes narrowed. "We'll see." He looked at Tryon. "May I keep these drawings?"

"Of course."

Howe ended the meeting as abruptly as he had begun. "Thank you, gentlemen, that will be all."

"One moment, sir," Tryon said, and the room fell silent. "The colonials uncovered our plan regarding Washington and Greene and the others. They've begun an investigation. Yesterday they hanged Thomas Hickey, our agent in Washington's headquarters. They've also detained Mayor Matthews, and they've been to my office. I doubt they have enough evidence to bring myself or the mayor to trial, but you should know we are presently altogether stopped in our plan."

Howe leaned back in his chair. "Are you in danger?"

"Not for the time being."

"Can you hold on for a few weeks? This entire affair should be concluded in the next several weeks in our favor."

"I believe I can, sir."

"Good. If not, get a message to me. I'll help."

"Thank you, sir."

"Anything else?" Howe stood.

"Nothing, sir."

"Thank you. My men will see you to your boat."

They shook hands, and General Howe remained standing until the door closed behind them, then settled back onto his chair. For a time he studied the maps they had left, committing to memory the cannon and battery locations at New York and on Long Island. Carefully he ran his finger over each of the roads, making calculations of distances and direction and of how long it would take to move troops who could average six miles in one hour in a forced march, five miles in one hour if they brought cannon.

He sighed and rose, dug a thumb and forefinger into weary eyes, then walked out the door into the bright sun, resenting the roll of the deck on the tide swells. He walked to the bow and leaned on the rail, arms stiff, palms flat, and let his thoughts run as he gazed north past the confines of Sandy Hook Bay to the east side of Staten Island and the Narrows leading to Manhattan Island.

Poor food, poor clothing, poor discipline, poor arms. Untried officers, untried troops. He shook his head. *I wonder what Washington is thinking right now.* His eyes narrowed as he pondered. *What will he think when the rest of our fleet sails into New York Harbor? Will he be willing to talk? work out an accommodation? If not, do we destroy him? And if we do, where do we strike? New York? Long Island?* He pursed his mouth and considered. *I'll wait for Sir Henry Clinton. He was raised on Long Island. He'll have something to say.*

Movement to his right caught his eye and he turned his head to look. White sails tight in the easterly Atlantic wind, the first ships in a column that reached out of sight were riding the Atlantic tides on a course that would pass between Sandy Hook and Gravesend Bay, towards the Narrows into New York Harbor. Howe turned to Captain Plessy standing admidships, his telescope extended, studying the incoming fleet intently.

"Whose are they?" Howe called.

"Ours."

"Do you have a count?"

"Forty-five."

"That should be the first of our troops and supplies."

"Shall I signal them to drop anchor here?"

Howe bowed his head in concentration. "No. I'll write a message. Send it out in a longboat."

"Yes, sir."

Howe walked rapidly back to his cabin and took quill in hand. He pondered for a moment, then wrote.

June 29, 1776

You will move through the Narrows into New York Harbor, remain there in sight of New York and Brooklyn for enough time to record the defenses that are visible to you, then return and join my squadron here at anchor in Sandy Hook Bay before nightfall. Do not open your cannon ports, and under no circumstance should you be provoked into firing your cannon. Should you be fired upon, reverse your course at once and come to Sandy Hook Bay.

Signed,
General Sir William Howe

To the north, on the island of Manhattan, where the Boston regiment was camped at the end of Reade Street, Billy scooped wet sand where the Hudson River met the bank and scrubbed his plate and utensils, while the sun, directly overhead, eight days past the summer solstice, bore down relentlessly. Billy dropped to his haunches to cup water in his hands and rinse the sweat from his face, then rinsed the plate and knife and fork, and stood, shaking water. He looked at the breastworks of the battery as he wiped his face on his sleeve, and a sense of satisfaction, pride, rose inside.

They had finished the breastworks and the inclined ramp behind them shortly before eleven o'clock, and half an hour later Brigadier General Thomas Mifflin of Pennsylvania, commanding officer of the brigade of which the Boston regiment was a part, had ridden in on a tall, nervous sorrel horse, with two other brigadier generals, to conduct the required inspection. Twenty minutes later they had shaken Colonel Thompson's hand and extended their congratulations.

The battery, breastworks, and recoil ramp were finished, and well done. A thirty-two-pound cannon would arrive within two days and be installed. General Mifflin would send written orders by evening directing Thompson where the regiment was needed next, but in the meantime the Boston regiment could stand down for the balance of the day. They had earned a rest.

Thompson had ordered the cooks to serve mutton and potatoes for the noon meal, and spirits soared. Banter and soldier talk flowed. Company Four caught Company One knee-deep in the river washing off sweat and dirt, and for twenty minutes the two companies were in the Hudson up to their waists, trying to drown each other while water and epithets and raucous laugher flew. Thompson took one look and retreated to the command tent.

Billy grinned at the remembrance of the wild, comic horseplay and was picking his way back to his blanket when he heard the shrill, urgent shout, "Look!" far to the south. All around him men stopped, turned, and fell silent as they stared, rooted to the ground.

A column of ships moved steadily forward into New York Harbor, against the New Jersey shore. The leaders were men-of-war, thick-hulled, three-masted, triple-decked, with sails furled except on the mainmast. They moved in a line, blunt bows plowing a white wake in the dark waters. Behind the men-of-war came the transports, fat, ponderous, broad in the beam. The entire fleet rode low in the water, heavily loaded.

The regiment moved toward the river for an unobstructed view, and Billy trotted to where Eli stood. Billy shaded his eyes with his hand, struggling to make out the flag flying from every mainmast. Thompson and the officers came trotting from the command tent to stand gaping with the troops.

The flagship continued north and then turned west, closing with the New Jersey cliffs, when the wind shifted and for a few seconds the flag was broadside to Billy. It was the red, white, and blue of the Union Jack.

"British," Billy muttered.

"Did you get a count?" Eli asked.

"Twenty-two so far. They're still coming."

The entire regiment remained motionless, silent, awestruck by the steadily growing number of British ships. For twenty minutes they counted, and then there were no more ships coming through the Narrows.

"Forty-five," Billy said, and his voice sounded too loud in the quiet. "Ten men-of-war, thirty-five transports." He turned towards Thompson, waiting for orders.

Thompson spoke. "Are their cannon ports open? I can't tell."

"No, sir. They're closed."

"I think they're putting on a show of strength." He paused for a moment, then spoke loudly. "Strike camp immediately. If they do begin an assault we aren't going to be caught here on the beach. Get ready to move, and we'll wait for orders or an attack, whichever comes first. I'll arrange some freight wagons. Get to it!"

Until that moment the soldiers of the Boston regiment had met the British enemy only in their imaginations, where the regulars wore their sparkling red coats and white breeches and black boots and marched to battle in immaculate straight lines. The British columns were invariably deep into a perfect colonial ambush before the signal was given and the regiment poured endless musket fire into them and they fell like ripe wheat before the scythe, and in the end the regulars struck their colors and laid down their arms.

Such vain imagery vanished without a trace in the harsh, chill reality of ten huge men-of-war with more than four hundred thirty-six-pound cannon, leading thirty-five fat transport ships loaded to the bulkheads with British regulars, powder, shot, horses, cannon, muskets, food, medicine. They sat ugly in the water on the New Jersey side of the harbor, insolent, contemptuous, so close men could be seen moving on their decks, telescopes extended, charting every cannon emplacement facing the Hudson, the breastworks, the barricades in the streets, and the contours of the land.

The regiment worked in silence, shaking and rolling and tying blankets, gathering damp clothing from bushes, stuffing them into knapsacks. Their eyes left the cannon ports on the British men-of-war only when necessary as they shoveled dirt to cover fire pits. Their minds were obsessed with but one thought: *How long would it take four hundred heavy cannon at point-blank range to blast New York City to rubble? One hour? Two?*

Time was forgotten as they worked on, eyes seldom leaving the harbor. The frames inside the command tent were pulled down, and the large, heavy canvas body collapsed and settled to the ground. Quick hands jerked the twenty-six tent pegs out of the ground, squared the limp canvas, tossed the twenty-six tension ropes onto it, folded it, tied it. The tall black iron cooking tripods and kettles were gathered in one place. The commissary tent was collapsed and folded and tied, while other men crated the surgeon's equipment, then collapsed and folded his tent. They left the infirmary tent in place to protect the sick from the sun until they were ready to leave.

Every man in the regiment started at the sound of calked iron horseshoes and iron-rimmed wheels on the cobblestones of Reade Street, and they looked to watch six freight wagons rumble off the end of the street into the dirt and stop. The first four wagons were military, hitched to teams of mules, while the last two wagons were larger, heavier, drawn by matched pairs of Percheron draft horses that stood mouthing their bits, throwing their heads, wanting to pull. Billy and Eli both recognized the flat-crowned straw hat that set level on the head of the driver of the fifth wagon, and they watched as Mary Flint worked with the reins and talked low to quiet the horses.

A lieutenant on the first wagon dropped to the ground and trotted to Colonel Thompson, saluted, and thrust a paper forward. The colonel unfolded it, read it quickly, drew the keys to the locks on the munitions magazine from his pocket, handed them to the lieutenant, and nodded. The lieutenant trotted back to his wagon and climbed back onto the seat and waited.

"Attention to orders," Thompson called, and the regiment crowded around. "General Washington has ordered this regiment to be ferried to Long Island under the command of General Nathanael Greene at Brooklyn. We are to assist there with constructing breastworks, and we are to undergo intensive drill and training with musket and cannon. Load what you cannot carry into the wagons. Make litters for the disabled. The sick who can, walk."

He paused and drew a deep breath. "We are to be on the docks south of Catherine Street by five o'clock, where we will be transported across the East River to Brooklyn on Long Island. That means we have to march completely across this island. We are to have our camp set up before nightfall. We have no time to lose. Officers, take charge of your companies. Get to it."

With the officers shouting orders and pointing directions, the various companies followed the wagons to the designated places where the regimental tents and equipment were stacked and bundled. Mary Flint took her orders, slapped the reins on the rumps of the big, prancing horses, and turned them towards the stacked iron kettles and cooking tripods, with Company Nine following.

Strong hands pulled the pins and dropped the tailgate, and half a dozen men climbed in, tossed the tie-down ropes to the ground, and waited. Others, two men at a time, seized the heavy black kettles and nine-foot three-legged iron tripods and began setting them inside the wagon bed to be moved forward and stacked by those inside. Billy and Eli worked shoulder to shoulder, Eli using only his right arm while keeping his left in the sling. The wagon bed steadily filled, and the last tripods were laid over the top of the kettles to lock them in place, and the tailgate was closed and the lock pins set. The tie-down ropes were laced back and forth through rings on the sides of the wagon and tied off, and the load was in place, secured.

Sergeant Turlock raised a hand to signal Mary, and she gigged the horses forward, then turned and lined the wagon towards Reade Street and pulled the horses to a stop, waiting to take her place in the column when the other wagons were ready. Company Nine walked to the riverbank once more to look with wide eyes and sober faces at the forty-five British ships, bright in the blaze of the afternoon sun. Their cannon ports remained closed.

Billy and Eli turned back. They passed Mary Flint's wagon and exchanged glances with her as they walked to the place where the infirmary had been dismantled. Men had rigged thirty-seven blanket-and-pole litters for the disabled, who were now in the heat of the sun. Twenty-two others sat cross-legged in the dirt, heads bowed, waiting. Each had insisted he could walk. Two were nearly out of their heads with fever.

"They're leaving!"

The shout brought every eye in the Boston regiment towards the harbor, and once more they stood rooted as they watched the line of British ships swing south, each in the white wake of the one before it as they threaded their way back through the Narrows.

Thompson's voice snapped the men back around. "Assemble into regimental formation. We leave in ten minutes. The regiment will lead and the wagons will follow."

Immediately the wagons began to roll towards Reade Street to form a line in the same order as they had arrived, while men went among the walking sick and helped them to their feet. One soldier would loop the arm of a faltering man over his shoulder for support while another took his musket, and they would move him to his place in his company. Billy and Eli dropped to their haunches beside the two who sat bowed, so fevered they were scarcely aware of what was happening around them. Billy lifted one to his feet and laid an arm over Eli's shoulders, and Eli caught the man about the waist with his right arm and turned him towards the column, nearly lifting him off the ground. Billy picked up the other man and carried him like a child, following Eli. They slowed to let a wagon pass and heard a woman's voice talk the horses to a stop, and they both looked up.

Mary Flint looked down at them from the high driver's seat. "Those two will never make it. Help me get them up here on the seat. There's room."

Eli leaned his man against the front wagon wheel, and the man's knees buckled and he sagged. Eli sat him on the ground, then quickly climbed to the driver's box. Billy lifted his man high, and Eli caught him under one arm, Mary under the other. They sat him on the driver's seat while Billy lifted the second one, and they settled him onto the seat.

Mary pressed her hand against each forehead for a moment,

then shook her head. "Fevered. Badly." She lifted a large canteen from the floor of the driver's box and looked for a cloth to soak, and there was none. She poured her hand full of cool water and gently bathed the face of each man, then spoke to Eli. "Help me give them a drink."

Eli cradled the head of each man in turn while Mary tipped the canteen to their lips, and each swallowed while she wiped at water that had spilled. Eli lifted a leg over the side of the wagon box to climb down, and Mary brought concerned eyes to meet his. "I don't know if I can drive this team and hold them both on the seat."

Eli looked down at Billy, and Billy handed up Eli's rifle, the two muskets of the disabled soldiers, and their knapsacks. "You stay. I've got to go with Sergeant Turlock—I'm his corporal. I'll tell him."

Eli sat on the load in the wagon bed behind the men and steadied them on the driver's seat, while Mary unwound the reins and slapped them on the hindquarters of the two horses, and the wagon lurched into motion and took its place in the column. Three minutes later Colonel Thompson took his position at the head of the regiment, turned his horse, shouted orders, and set a cadence. The regiment moved forward like a great serpent winding through the narrow turns of Reade Street towards Broadway, with the wagons rumbling heavy on the cobblestones behind.

While the regiment was yet five hundred yards from Broadway, carts and wagons began appearing in the streets, first a few, then many. Some were horse-drawn, some pushed or pulled by hand, but in all of them were clothing and food, hastily packed and loaded by wide-eyed, white-faced citizens who worked with mouths compressed, looking neither right nor left as they crowded bumping into the moving stream of humanity seeking the nearest street that would take them north, away from New York City.

Israel Thompson slowed the column to avoid colliding with carts and horses and wagons that would not yield, and suddenly understood and exclaimed, "They're running! Evacuating to avoid the battle!"

He ordered a halt and waited for the panic and the rush of people to stop, but it became worse. He ordered Company One ahead into the intersection, faced them south shoulder to shoulder against the oncoming mob, and ordered them to prime and load. He drew his sword, faced Company One, and bellowed, "If one of them moves north before the regiment has cleared the intersection, *level your muskets and shoot to kill!*"

The men primed the pans on their muskets, measured powder into the muzzles, rammed it home, jammed the ball down with the ramrod, raised their muskets to the ready, and faced the oncoming crowd. A dozen men bulled their way forward through the crowd and faced the line of soldiers, and ten of them walked straight towards them, defying the muskets. Every man in Company One pulled back the big hammer with the flint locked in place, raised the musket to his shoulder, and took dead aim, point-blank, on the advancing men. Gasps ran through the crowd, and instantly a dozen hands reached to grab those who were still doggedly advancing and pulled them back, held them cursing and kicking and fighting.

The regiment marched on through the intersection, watching the shouting crowd in disbelief. The wagons followed. Eli settled the stock of his rifle on his thigh, barrel pointed high, finger on the trigger, thumb hooked around the hammer, and his eyes did not stop moving. Mary held the horses at a steady pace, and the expression on her face did not change. With the last wagon past the cross street, Thompson halted the regiment, and Company One came trotting at double time back to their position at the front.

Thompson shouted orders. "Companies One and Two, move on ahead at double time and clear out the intersection at Broadway. When we're through it, move on to the next ones and keep them cleared until we reach the docks. Companies Nine and Ten, fall in behind the wagons and see to it nothing happens to them. Keep your muskets primed and loaded, and if anyone interferes, shoot to kill."

The regiment worked its way steadily westward through the Broadway intersection, with wagons and horses and shouting civilians backed up six blocks, while Companies One and Two formed a shoulder-to-shoulder line of cocked muskets to hold them until the regiment had passed through, then sprinted on to the next jammed intersection to clear it. The surging crowds and wagons and carts thinned as they came closer to the docks, and then Company One walked out onto the heavy black timbers where the tall ships were anchored and tied. Within minutes the Boston regiment was there, and Thompson again ordered a halt. The wagons rolled to a stop and waited while the incoming Atlantic tides lapped splashing against the great water-soaked pilings.

Thompson lifted his watch from the inside pocket of his tunic. It was about five minutes before five o'clock. He glanced anxiously up and down the waterfront, looking for a blue or a green officer's tunic of the New York militia, and there was none. The stamp of a horse on the heavy timbers and a familiar voice from behind brought him around.

General John Morin Scott reined in his horse facing Thompson. "Colonel, the ferry is waiting for the wagons, and we have boats ready for the troops. It'll take two crossings. You can be finished before dark."

Thompson called out orders, and the officers moved their companies to the waiting boats and barges and they clambered aboard. The wagons rolled to the ferry and stopped, waiting directions. The ferry crew gave hand signals, and two military wagons rolled aboard and stopped at the gate at the far end of the ferry, and the crew scrambled to set blocks to hold the wheels. Mary Flint held her team until the signal came and she gigged her horses forward, the stamp of the shod horses and the sound of the iron-rimmed wheels hollow on the heavy timbers. She lined her wagon behind one of those already locked in place and held the team until they had her wheels blocked, then turned to watch the other heavy wagon move in beside hers and watch the men jam the wheel blocks and drop the pins to lock them into place.

Loaded, the ferry and the boats with troops did not hesitate. In lengthening afternoon shadows they pushed off the docks into the East River, and the two wagons and the remainder of the regiment behind watched as the slow current caught them. They drifted south for a moment before the crews corrected and they swung back into line with the Long Island docks.

On the ferry, the horses and mules stuttered their feet and braced against the roll of the deck, and they threw their heads and rolled their eyes in fear until the white rims showed. Mary talked to the big draft horses and held the reins firm, and slowly they settled. She wrapped the leathers around the brake pole, turned to the man huddled next to her, and pressed the back of her hand against his forehead.

"Cooler," she said.

Eli answered, "Getting weaker. Needs to be in a bed."

Mary eased the man's head against her shoulder and again spoke to Eli. "Your arm all right?"

Eli nodded and said nothing.

For a time they remained still, quiet, watching the dark water roil white as the big square-nosed ferry plowed on. The sun setting behind them cast long shadows eastward before them.

"How did you hurt it?"

"It was nothing. A cut."

"An accident?"

Eli reflected for a moment. "In a way."

There was a question in her eyes as she glanced at him, then again fell silent.

The ferry pilot squared with the dock and the nose crunched into the sloped ramp, while practiced hands caught the thrown hawsers and dropped the loops over pilings. In golden twilight the ferry crew lowered the front gate onto the ramp. They pulled the wheel blocks from the wagons, and the driver of the first military wagon gigged his mules into motion. They leaned back and walked stiff-legged down the slanted gate onto the ramp, then lunged into their harnesses to pull the wagon up the ramp onto the dock. The second military wagon followed, then Mary, and finally the last larger, heavy wagon. The mules and horses snorted and threw their heads, glad to leave the undulating deck of the ferry behind, glad to feel solid land beneath their hooves.

The soldiers jumped splashing over the sides of the beached boats and barges and slogged ashore, while the boat crews reversed their oars and poles and drove their craft back into the river, headed back to the New York docks for the remainder of the regiment. The ferry crew raised the front gate, locked it into place, and worked the huge, cumbersome vessel back into the suck of the current, following the boats and barges.

The drivers and escorts on the four wagons just landed, and the troops dripping river water from wading ashore, all turned to watch the ferry and the cluster of small craft working its way back to the New York side. The mismatched boats and barges and the single ferry seemed dwarfed into insignificance in the brilliance of the great yellow ball of the sun touching the cliffs of the New Jersey shore. Strong, brilliant colors reached high into the heavens, casting the Hudson River valley into bronze and gold and red, and a strange feeling stole through the regiment as the soldiers stood still, faces glowing golden in the sunset, caught up for a moment in the unfathomable power of nature and of nature's God, and the sure knowledge that all of mankind combined could do absolutely nothing to change either.

Eli turned his head back to look down at the two men on the driver's seat next to Mary, and suddenly he thrust his hand forward and pressed his fingers against the throat of the man next to her. Mary turned her face from the sunset and looked at Eli, questioning. She recoiled at the flat look in his eyes, and her hand darted to the forehead of the man leaning against her shoulder, and it was cold.

Eli adjusted his fingertips against the man's throat, waited five more seconds, and then bowed his head for a moment. Gently he lifted the man from the seat and pulled him back onto the load, laying him out full length. He reached to close the half-open eyes, then the mouth, sagged open. Mary gasped, and Eli crossed the man's hands over his chest. He untied the man's blanket from his knapsack and spread it over the still body, then used the cord from the knapsack to tie the body onto the load. He looked at Mary and he saw deep pain. "He's gone on," he said quietly.

Mary swallowed and Eli saw her battle, and silent tears crept down her cheeks. He wanted to say more, but he did not know how to talk to her. She turned back in the driver's seat and bowed her head, and her shoulders shook with her silent sobs. Eli climbed into the driver's seat and touched the forehead of the remaining man, and it was hot. The man raised his head and his eyes slowly focused, and he swallowed against a parched throat and closed them again. Eli reached for the canteen in the bottom of the driver's box and poured cool water and washed the man's face, then forced him to drink.

Mary wiped her face and spoke. Her voice was firm. "Is he all right?"

"Fevered, but he's alive."

Eli sat with the sick man on the driver's seat beside him, cradled inside his arm. The glow of sunset faded to dusk, and he turned once to look at the river. He saw the black shapes on the water, with lanterns making points of light, moving steadily towards them in the gloom, and he saw the white water raised by the bow of the incoming ferry. Mary turned to look, then glanced at the sick man between them.

Eli spoke quietly. "I'm sorry for your pain. Truly."

In the gathering darkness she looked into Eli's eyes, and she saw tenderness and compassion that grow only from tragedy and pain, and she felt a stir inside and a need to know whence they came.

Eli continued. "You did all you could. You saved one."

The dock crew lighted lanterns and watched as the ferry lined up with the ramp and thumped to a stop and held while it was tied. The front gate opened slamming down, and the last two wagons rattled onto the docks. Thompson and the regimental officers followed, leading their six saddled horses stamping down the slanted gate, then up the dock ramp, prancing, hating the feel of a rocking boat deck. With Thompson were two New York militia officers with saddle mounts.

Thompson shouted orders in the darkness. "The regiment will assemble for the reading of orders."

Eli climbed down from the wagon and found Company Nine in the dark.

Three minutes later Thompson faced the regiment on the dock, with the sound of the river lapping at the pilings and the bullfrogs singing and the click and buzz of night insects. "These two officers from the New York militia will lead us to the battlements south of Brooklyn, under the command of General Nathanael Greene. We set up camp tonight, and in the morning we take drill and arms practice and our new work assignment."

He paused and drew a document from inside his tunic. "General Scott handed me this, and I am under orders to read it to you." He unfolded the document, straightened it, and read briefly.

" 'General Washington presents his compliments to Colonel Thompson and the men under his command, and advises that this date he had received advice from fishing boats returning from the Grand Banks that there is a fleet of British ships numbering 130 which will arrive in New York within two days. Fifteen of them are men-of-war with not less than forty-six cannon each. The balance are transports loaded with troops, provisions, arms, or horses. I am, &c., Gen. G. Washington.' "

For five seconds the regiment stood fixed, silent, and then quiet murmuring broke out and died as Thompson folded the letter and continued.

"That will bring the total known British ships in the New York campaign to one hundred seventy-nine. I need not remind you to watch constantly for spies and plots. Do not be far from your musket or rifle. Now, form into companies and follow these two officers."

Quickly Eli sought out Billy and Sergeant Turlock. "A man on Mary Flint's wagon died. We should get him down."

Turlock said, "No time. Can it wait?"

"It's not easy for Mary Flint."

Turlock's eyes dropped, and in the dark Eli could sense the pain as Turlock spoke. "We've got no place else to put him right now."

Eli nodded. "I'll take care of it."

The column started, and Eli swung up onto the seat and cradled the sick man inside his arm while Mary clucked the horses into motion. She moved her wagon into the line and took her interval as they moved steadily eastward on the rutted dirt road, Mary peering intently in the starlight to keep her horses from overrunning the tailgate of the wagon ahead. The regiment marched on in the darkness, stumbling on the rocks and ruts and holes in the road, unable to hold a cadence, and not caring. They moved on in silence, with one thought foremost in their brains: *One hundred seventy-nine ships. More than one thousand cannon.*

In the darkness their imaginations tried to create one hundred seventy-nine ships in New York Harbor, and they could not make that many ships, that many sails, that many cannon and soldiers. They marched on, fighting their own demons in the darkness.

The column angled north before Eli spoke. "I am sorry there was no time to move him."

"I know. It's all right."

Eli hesitated, then said quietly, "Colonel Thompson told us— Billy and me—about your husband and your baby. I wish I could say something. I surely do."

Startled that he knew, Mary turned her face directly to him to stare, while in the deepest chamber of her soul, where she lived alone with her pain, her heart leaped at the sure knowledge that somewhere in his life, this man too had felt inhuman tragedy. He knew the hot tortures of the pit, the soul-destroying desolation of a world in which there was nothing left but the cold ashes of all he held close and precious. The overpowering need to know welled up from within and she did not try to stop it, nor could she, and she spoke with an urgency and a need Eli had never heard in another human being. "How do you know about pain? Tell me."

There was no pretense, no barrier between them, nor at that strange moment did it seem proper there should be, and Eli spoke freely. "When I was two, the Iroquois came. I lost my family. The Iroquois took me and raised me. I think I have an older sister. I want to find her."

"What is your name?"

"Eli Stroud."

"Do you remember when the Iroquois came? what they did to your parents?"

"Yes. Both dead. Mother in the bedroom, Father in the kitchen with me."

"You were there? saw it?"

"Yes."

It was as though a dam burst inside Mary. Her sobbing was lost in the rumble of the wagons and the marching feet of the Boston regiment. Eli said nothing, and let it go on for a long time before he finally slipped his arm out of the sling and gently placed his hand on her shaking shoulder. After a time the trembling slowed, and then stopped. Words would have been a blasphemy, and neither of them spoke. Mary wiped at her eyes and face with her sleeve, and the wagon rolled on.

"There!"

The shout came from the front of the column, and in the distance they saw the faint points of light that became lanterns. Then they could make out men, and then they saw the tents and the blankets of a military camp scattered in the oak and maple and cedar trees and the underbrush. The pickets challenged, and the officers leading the column answered, and they marched on in.

With little talk, the bone-weary regiment followed directions to the bare ground where they were to make their camp. They built fires for light and began spreading their blankets by company. Eli and Billy moved the sick man from the wagon seat to the place where the regimental doctor was giving orders to men unfolding the infirmary tent. They sat the fevered man down and draped his blanket over his shoulders. The surgeon came to him while Billy and Eli brought the body from the top of Mary's loaded wagon.

Then they returned to the wagon, and while Mary held the horses in the firelight, Company Nine methodically unloaded the iron tripods and the round black cooking kettles clanking to the ground. It was approaching one A.M. when they coiled the tie-down ropes, laid them behind the driver's seat, and walked to their blankets, waiting further orders.

Mary began unsnapping the harnesses from the horses, and Billy and Eli came to help. They dropped the horse collars and unbuckled the trace chains, and Mary walked the horses forward away from the singletrees. She followed Billy and Eli to the stream at camp's edge, and the big geldings buried tired muzzles in the clear, cool water. She patted the animals on the neck while she listened to the suck of the water and the sound as it passed up the rings in their gullets. They raised their heads dripping once, eyes wine red in the firelight, then buried their muzzles again and finished while Mary smiled in the darkness.

They walked the horses to where the officers had picketed their saddle mounts, and the two men hobbled them where strong grass was high. Then, with Mary between them, they walked to Colonel Thompson, who was directing the setting of the frame for his command tent.

"Sir," Billy said, and Thompson stopped. "Is there a tent for Mrs. Flint?"

The colonel straightened and removed his hat and addressed Mary. "Mrs. Flint, did you assist in moving the regiment?"

"Yes, sir."

"I doubt I can thank you enough for all you've done. We have the wives of two New York militia officers staying the night. They have their own private tent, large enough for four, and there will be pickets throughout the night. I know the ladies would be honored by your presence. Would that be agreeable?"

"Of course."

"May I have the honor of escorting you?"

Thompson offered his arm and Mary slipped hers through his, and Billy and Eli fell in behind. Thompson walked Mary through the camp. Work slowed and men stood erect and removed their hats and silently nodded to her as she passed. Thompson spoke with the officer at the tent and he invited the ladies outside, where he introduced Mary. They exclaimed their delight and took her by the arm and were entering the tent flap when Mary stopped and turned.

She looked back at Thompson and Billy and Eli, and she said, "Thank you. So much." And she disappeared inside the tent with the two other women in a flood of questions and exclamations.

In darkness, exhausted cooks sliced cold mutton from their noon meal, and silent men gratefully ate it with hardtack, drank from their canteens, and dropped onto their blankets fully dressed, asleep the moment their heads came to rest on their arms.

Eli settled cross-legged onto his blanket, slipped the sling from his left arm, and drew his belt knife. For ten minutes he patiently worked the knifepoint under the stitches, cut them, and tugged them from his arm. He rinsed the tiny pinpoints of blood with canteen water and blew his arm dry, then clenched and unclenched his fist several times. The long pink scar held. Satisfied, he lay on his back for a time, hands behind his head, staring into the endless heavens, and his thoughts drifted back to the wagon and Mary Flint sobbing her heart out in the darkness at her own pain and the pain she felt for Eli when she understood what had been taken from him as an infant.

A deep sadness welled up to wrench inside, and he clenched his jaw against the remembrance of the need in her dark eyes. *Why the suffering? The common lot of mankind. Why? Why? Jesus talked against it but he suffered most. My people fought the Iroquois and suffered. The Iroquois fought the French and suffered. We're waiting on a battle right now, and men and women will suffer. Why does it have to be? The Good Twin and the Bad Twin. Is that the answer? There has to be bad? I don't know. I wish I knew. Jesus promises a place after this life where there is no suffering. How blessed. How blessed.*

He turned on his side and once again saw the dark eyes, open, frank, begging for help, relief. *I hope she can find peace. I hope so.*

Billy sat quietly on his blanket and finally, by force of will, dug his pad and pencil from his knapsack.

My dear Mother:

It is late and I have little time. Today forty-five more British ships arrived. We moved our camp from New York to Long Island, near Brooklyn. Gen. G. Washington said there are one hundred thirty more such ships coming to New York within two days. I believe the great battle is preparing. You are not to worry, for we will be ready. My health remains good, although fever is beginning in camp, and dysentery. However, I have not yet contracted either. I also mention that women here take a large and often heroic part in the Patriot cause by tying cartridges and gathering blankets, clothing, and so forth. One or two drive freight wagons with supplies and munitions. When you write, please tell me what you can about Matthew and Kathleen. Also, please share this with Margaret and Brigitte. I cannot send my pay because they have not paid us. I send my love to Trudy and ask her to help you all she can.

Faithfully your son,
Billy Weems

Billy sealed the letter, tucked it into his knapsack, shoved the pencil in beside it, and laid his head on his arms. His eyes closed, and the last thing he saw before he fell into exhausted sleep was his mother working in the kitchen at home, and Brigitte was there.

Notes

New York colony governor William Tryon, together with a Sergeant Graham, met with General William Howe and others on board the *Greyhound* anchored off Sandy Hook on the New Jersey coast and there gave Howe detailed information regarding the fortifications, deployment, roads, and passes on Manhattan and Long Islands (see Johnston, *The Campaign of 1776,* part I, p. 139, footnote; see also Higginbotham, *The War of American Independence,* p. 152).

The peculiar and deadly Hell Gate was a whirlpool that resulted from the meeting of the two tides of the East River and the Long Island Sound and was capable of sinking seagoing vessels (see Johnston, *The Campaign of 1776,* part I, p. 47).

On June 29, 1776, forty-five more British men-of-war and transport ships sailed into New York Harbor, then withdrew to Staten Island, and by July 3, 1776, the total number of British ships gathered at New York was 130, with more arriving regularly (see Johnston, *The Campaign of 1776,* part I, p. 94).

Averman Plessy is a fictional name for the captain of the *Greyhound,* General Howe's flagship.

CHAPTER X

*I*n the late afternoon a hot west wind came rippling the waters of the Back Bay and set waves lapping against the rocks and dock pilings of the northwest shore of the Boston Peninsula. The choppy waters and sea swells put every vessel on the leeward side of Boston Town in motion, rocking, and the masts of the tall ships began their erratic dance. Men of the sea cast concerned eyes west, then eastward past the harbor to the open Atlantic, judging whether the mix of hot inland wind and cooler ocean air would be strong enough to bring a storm.

In Boston Town, Margaret Dunson placed the butter crock on the shelf in the root cellar in her backyard, climbed the stairs, and lowered the door. She paused for a moment to gauge the hot wind on her face, then walked into the kitchen where Brigitte and Prissy were setting the last of the supper dishes, washed and dried, back into the cupboard.

"Wind's holding," she said. "Might have rain. When are your friends coming?"

"Seven. Captain Halliwell promised to come."

Margaret shook her head. "I swear, I don't know where you get these ideas. Gathering blankets, shoes, making cartridges, getting wagons."

"Mama, will you quit worrying?" Brigitte's voice was raised as she closed the cupboard and walked into the dining room. "We can do it! You'll see!"

Margaret followed her. "Make bullets at the church with gunpowder?" Her face was flushed, eyes flashing. "Silas must have been out of his mind! Do you have any idea what would happen if a barrel of gunpowder blew up at the church? One mistake! Just one!"

"We'll keep the gunpowder outside the building. No one is going to blow up the church."

"Brigitte! Wake up! You expect to bring in half a dozen girls who've never seen a cartridge in their lives, and get some army officer to come here to train them to make cartridges, sitting around our dining table?"

"There's no danger. Women do it in New York. You read Billy's letter."

"That's women in New York, not women in Boston who have never made a cartridge or worked with gunpowder."

"I asked Captain Halliwell. It's simple."

"Simple for him! And what's this nonsense about taking it to New York in freight wagons?"

"We can get wagons. Caleb put a notice in the newspaper and at the post house."

Margaret's mouth dropped open for a split second. "Newspaper? What kind of notice?"

"That we're gathering blankets and shoes and bandages and medicine at the church for the Continental army, and we're taking it to New York. We've got committees. We can do it."

"In the *newspaper?* Every Tory in Boston will sneak either here or up to the church at night to burn down the building."

"Don't be ridiculous. The Tories have all fled."

"Who drives the wagons?"

Brigitte set her jaw defiantly for a moment. "Me. Some of the women."

Margaret gasped. "Three hundred miles across Connecticut right in the middle of a war? Have you taken leave of your senses?"

"There's no war in New York yet. General Washington needs cartridges. If we all go together there will be no danger."

"You think you're going to drive wagons right into New York and find General Washington, with the British swarming down there?"

"They're *not swarming.*"

"They're not? How many British ships did Billy say? Forty? Fifty? And what about Richard Buchanan? What's your British captain going to think when he hears you've been loading cartridges to shoot at him and his army?"

It slowed Brigitte. Her eyes dropped and she lowered her hands. "He'll understand," she said quietly.

The front door swung open, and Caleb walked into the parlor towards his room to scrub the printer's ink from his hands.

"You're late," Margaret said. "Something happen?"

"We got news from New York. Had to set print and run some copies for tomorrow."

"Your supper's in the oven. What news?"

Caleb spoke excitedly. "The whole British navy is about to arrive in New York, clear from Halifax, and there's more on the way from England. There's going to be one big, final battle right there in New York City." He passed through the archway headed for his room.

Margaret turned to Brigitte, anger in her voice. "You see? You think you're going down there with bullets in the middle of a battle?"

Caleb barged back into the archway, eyes wide, voice high. "Brigitte's going to New York?"

"Not if I can help it," Margaret retorted.

Brigitte interrupted. "Mother, nothing bad will happen. I promise." She turned to Caleb. "Did you get the notice in the newspaper?"

Margaret shook her finger. "You're *not* going to New York!"

Caleb cut in. "*You're* going to New York?"

"Did you get the notice in the newspaper?"

Caleb's voice was loud, commanding. "If you go, I'm going." His mind raced wildly, framing the desperate, dramatic news story he would write about the battle of New York.

Brigitte bristled. "Caleb, *did you get the notice in the newspaper?*"

He sobered for a moment. "Yes. But if you take stuff to New York, I'm going."

Margaret raised a warning hand. "Caleb, forget it. Brigitte, stop this insanity about New York."

Brigitte closed her eyes in disgusted frustration, then looked at the mantel clock. Six-fifty P.M. "They'll be here in ten minutes. We'll talk later. Have Caleb read to Adam and Prissy in his room. I have to get ready."

At ten minutes past seven o'clock, Captain Bertram Halliwell stood at the head of the dining table, uncomfortable in the presence of Brigitte at the far end and three young ladies on each side. All seven faces were turned to him, waiting expectantly. He nervously dropped his right hand to a black leather satchel on the table before him and began his memorized recitation.

"Ladies, I was invited here to acquaint you with making cartridges for military muskets. There are a few fundamentals you must know before we begin. First, confined gunpowder explodes when touched by flame or a spark. Loose gunpowder will burn, but not explode, so working here at the table should not be dangerous. Keeping a keg of it nearby could be. I understand you intend making the cartridges at the church, and suggest the keg be kept somewhere outside and that an open pan of it be brought in to work with."

Heads bobbed in understanding and the ladies waited.

"Second, wet gunpowder is useless. Cartridges are made from paper. So once a cartridge is made, you must store it in a place that is dry so the paper does not absorb moisture. That usually means in a watertight building."

A momentary flurry of murmuring broke out, then subsided.

"Third, paper burns. So once a cartridge is made, it cannot be exposed to spark or flame. If it catches fire it could explode, and if it is stored with others, it could set them all off."

He waited a moment, then opened the black satchel and drew out a rectangular block of wood with three rows of holes drilled into it, ten holes per row, and held it up.

"This block will hold thirty finished cartridges. When filled, the block is put inside a waterproof leather case that is slung around the shoulder of a soldier and hangs at his side for use. Here's the leather case." He drew a black, scarred, stiff-leather case from inside the satchel and laid the block and the case on the table.

Margaret was in the dark kitchen, setting Caleb's warm dinner on a tray, shaking her head in disgust and fear as she listened. She covered the tray with a cloth, then quietly walked through the parlor to the archway and disappeared into Caleb's room, where Caleb was finished scrubbing and changing and the children waited.

Captain Halliwell continued. "The militia can supply you with cartridge papers and bullets, and at the moment we have some gunpowder. Later you may have to get your own lead and learn to cast the bullets, and somehow get your own gunpowder. They're all in short supply."

The ladies looked at each other in surprise, then turned back to Halliwell. He reached inside his satchel and laid several tools on the table, then a small wooden box of gunpowder and half a dozen .75-caliber balls.

"Watch carefully. These are the steps." He laid a patch of paper on the table before him. It was fairly large, and was square except for one side that had been cut at an angle. "This is the cartridge paper."

He laid a round six-inch stick of maple wood on it, along the edge leading to the angled side. One end of the stick was hollowed out, and that end was about one inch from the end of the paper. "This stick is called the 'former' because the paper is wrapped around it to form the cartridge."

He slowly, deliberately rolled the former inside the paper.

"You see that the hollowed end of the former is recessed

about one inch from the end of the rolled paper tube."

All the girls nodded, eyes large as they watched intently.

He picked up a lead bullet and inserted it in the open end of the paper tube, then pushed it with his finger until it was settled inside the hollowed end of the former. The bullet was out of sight, nearly an inch from the end of the paper tube.

"Now, please observe." He pinched the end of the paper tube to a point over the bullet, then reached for a ball of thread. He cut a piece about ten inches long and deftly wrapped it around the pinched end of the paper tube, three wraps, then tied it off, clipped the excess string, and held up the tube.

"Did you all see how that was done?"

Murmuring broke out and all heads nodded.

He carefully pulled the wooden former from the paper tube, put it aside, and laid the paper tube on the table before him. He then dipped a small, long, narrow scoop into the pewter powder box and carefully measured powder to an exact level. He inserted the scoop into the open end of the paper tube, carefully emptied it, then laid the scoop back on the table.

"Now, please watch." He jiggled the paper tube slightly between his fingers to settle the powder, then deftly twisted the paper at the open end of the tube several times, closing it firmly. He held the finished cartridge up before the girls.

"There it is, a finished cartridge." He waited while they exclaimed.

"Now let me show you how the soldier uses it."

He inserted the cartridge into one of the holes in the block of wood. "Cartridges are given to the soldier in these blocks. He draws one from the block of wood like this, sets the end with the bullet in the palm of his hand like this, grasps the twisted end between his fingers and pinches it off so powder cannot spill, like this."

He paused to be certain each girl had followed, then continued. "Then he bites off the twisted end with his teeth, like this." He grasped the twisted end in his teeth and ripped it from the cartridge, then removed the torn paper from his teeth with his left hand.

"Then he drops a small amount of the powder into the pan of his musket and the balance of it into the muzzle. That leaves the bullet in his hand, still wrapped in the paper. He simply thrusts that into the muzzle of his musket, both bullet and paper, and rams it down to the powder with his ramrod, and he's ready to fire. When the flint on his musket strikes a spark into the steel pan, the powder burns. The flame reaches through the touchhole into the powder inside the barrel. It explodes and shoots the bullet out of his musket while it burns the paper."

The girls around the table were ecstatic, exclaiming, pointing, and Halliwell waited for a time before he raised his hand and they quieted.

"I'll go through this all once again, and you stop me for questions any time. When I'm finished you can divide into two groups and try it yourselves. Be careful when you measure the powder. It has to be level to the top of the measure scoop and no more."

Once again he methodically worked through the steps and held up the finished cartridge. Then under his keen eye the girls gingerly began their first efforts at fashioning paper, lead balls, and gunpowder into acceptable cartridges, clumsily at first, biting their lips, silent, then giggling, then intense as they worked on. They rolled the papers badly, could not pinch the end to a peak, could not take three wraps with the thread without losing control of the former inside the paper, spilled gunpowder and recovered it, and did not twist the closure tight enough behind the powder.

Patiently Halliwell watched and corrected, and slowly the mistakes became fewer, and unaccustomed fingers became more nimble. At eight o'clock they finished their first cartridge that passed Halliwell's critical inspection. By eight-twenty the girls had six acceptable cartridges. By eight forty-five they had eighteen. By nine o'clock they had thirty acceptable cartridges in the wooden cartridge block, and they inserted it into the battered leather case and snapped the lid shut. Their eyes shined with excitement and pride in their newly learned craft, and their chatter filled the room.

Halliwell waited until they quieted before he continued.

"Now that you know how to do this, the question is, do you want me to leave enough equipment at the church tomorrow so you can make more cartridges?"

"Of course!"

Halliwell snapped the locks on the satchel and faced the girls. "Thank you. Would you let your minister know the wagon will be there about four o'clock?"

"I'll tell him."

Halliwell bowed and Brigitte walked him to the door. "Thank you."

The captain nodded as he reached for the door handle. "Good night." He walked out into the sultry, hot night air and glanced upward. The wind had died, and the black heavens were clear, star-studded.

Brigitte turned back to the girls, who were wrapping themselves in their shawls and tying on their bonnets, as required of all proper Bostonian girls before presenting themselves in public.

"It's past nine o'clock. We'll meet at the church tomorrow night at seven, and there will be at least twenty more women to make cartridges. We'll teach them, and in a few days we'll have enough to make a load, with the blankets and other things."

Brigitte opened the door and walked them all to the front gate, where they said their good-byes, then divided two and two to walk hurriedly home through the crooked, narrow cobblestone streets of Boston. Brigitte waved and waited until they were all out of sight, then turned and walked quickly back into the house and closed the door.

Margaret was waiting. "Get Caleb and the children for prayer."

Half an hour later Margaret sank onto a chair at the dining table, and for a long time she sat, working her hands together, staring at them in the yellow lamplight. Brigitte came dressed in her nightshirt, her hair down her back in a long single french braid.

Margaret came from deep thought to speak quietly. "Sit down."

Brigitte settled onto a chair and waited.

"It's all happening too fast." Margaret pursed her mouth for a moment. "The war. Your father gone. Matthew somewhere far, we don't know where, or even if he's alive. You working at the bakery. Caleb at the print shop, and wanting more every day to go to the fighting. Me trying to be both mother and father to the children." She shook her head.

An unexpected rush of compassion rose in Brigitte, and she reached to grasp Margaret's hand in hers.

Margaret raised eyes that mirrored her weary, exhausted, frightened soul. "Now you want to leave." She drew and released a great sigh. "Three hundred miles with bullets for war." She slowly shook her head. "I never dreamed these things could ever happen to all of us. Divided. Gone. Leaving."

Her eyes brimmed with silent tears and she wiped at them.

"You're young. You have no notion, not any, of what could happen to you if you go with wagons to New York. Our soldiers, their soldiers, any of them could use you for sport and you couldn't stop them. Accidents. Sickness. Taken by the British. I doubt they'd hang a girl, but I have no question they'd put you in prison."

Margaret faced her daughter and impulsively reached to tenderly touch her cheek for a moment. "Do you know what it would do to me if they damaged you? put you in prison? if you got sick and died? Do you know? I wouldn't want to live." A sob caught in Margaret's throat, and she swallowed hard and wiped her eyes.

Brigitte had never seen or heard her mother like this before. Her breathing constricted, and it seemed that a hidden door in her heart unexpectedly opened enough for her to sense the endless, selfless love of her mother, and with it for the first time in her life came flooding the bright understanding of the terrible price love demands of all true mothers. It humbled her to the core of her being, and she reached to seize her mother's arm. She tried to speak and could not. Her eyes brimmed with tears that slowly worked down her cheeks, and she wiped at them with the sleeve of her nightshirt.

The two women sat thus for a time in the yellow lantern light, silent, wordless, eyes locked, each silently speaking to the soul of the other in the purest language a mother and daughter can share.

In the magic of those moments Brigitte understood that her mother had accepted her as a grown woman, an equal. The child that had been was no more. Never again would Margaret speak down to her, order her, demand obedience. In the flash of understanding Brigitte felt both the thrill of full freedom and the grab in her heart that the precious time of childhood was past and gone.

Margaret sighed and broke off, then shrugged, and she spoke in matter-of-fact tones once again. "I know it's impossible to put old heads on young shoulders, but every generation has to have their try at it. You're going to have to follow the best that's in you and hope it's good enough, and take your bruises and learn your lessons, the same as all of us who came before."

Brigitte wiped her eyes and remained silent.

Once again Margaret's voice came with low intensity. "You'll have to follow your heart about your British captain. You feel what you feel. But remember, you're trying to live with one foot in each camp, ours and theirs, and eventually it will catch up. You'll choose him and England, or us and here. All I ask is, be very sure when you choose. You'll be a long, long time living with it."

Brigitte remained silent because there was nothing to be said.

Margaret stood. "We better go to bed. Tomorrow's going to be a long day for both of us." Arm in arm the two women walked through the archway and separated to their bedrooms.

Brigitte sat on her bed for a long time, staring at her hands, then at the yellow lantern glow, while her thoughts led her deep inside herself. *Am I wrong in helping the army fight for liberty? Daddy didn't think so. He died for liberty. Matthew's fighting for it. Billy. If it's right, then am I wrong about Richard? A cartridge I make could be the one that kills him.*

She shuddered at the thought, and in her mind she saw him once again—tall, strong, the deep scar in his eyebrow, the eyes that were gentle and strong and sensitive. She remembered the evening he shared supper with the family and won them over, as she knew he would. And once more she closed her eyes and recalled the few moments they shared together alone in the backyard before he left that night, near the bench that circled the old oak tree, when she had embraced him briefly and brushed her kiss on his cheek. She felt once again the few moments of magical transport from this world into a place where only he existed with her.

She sobered as Margaret's words echoed. *One foot in each camp, ours and theirs—him and England, or us and here.*

Words came to her. *A house divided against itself . . .*

She blew out the lamp, slipped between the sheets of her bed, and for a long time lay in the darkness beneath the great goose-down comforter, unable to force a reconciliation between helping the battle for liberty and the deep feelings in her heart for an enemy captain. The quarter moon was high in the heavens before she drifted into an uneasy sleep.

Three days later, in the evening, there were twenty-eight girls and women gathered at the church to make cartridges, among them Dorothy Weems and Margaret Dunson. On the fourth evening there were thirty-four, and the blankets and shoes and bandages filled the choir seats and first six rows of pews on the east side of the chapel.

On the fifth evening a blocky man in worn homespun appeared in the open doorway of the church, threadbare cap in hand. His long sandy-red hair was uncombed, and he forced a quick, shy, nervous smile as Brigitte approached him.

"Ma'am, a friend read me the notice in the newspaper. Might you be needin' strong, willin' men to help freight supplies to the army in New York?" His eyes were pleading as he spoke.

"Yes, we might."

"Sure, and I would be countin' it a blessin' if I could help."

Brigitte heard the decidedly Irish twang in his words and studied him briefly. "What's your name? your usual line of work?"

"Name's Cullen. Deckhand on a ship, ma'am. Earned my way here to Boston from Ireland, and I'll be wantin' to go to New York to join the fightin'."

"It's possible you could go with the wagons. How can we find you when we're ready?"

"If you'll be tellin' me when that might be, I'll come back here if I'm still around, ma'am."

"It might be three weeks or more."

"So long as that? Well, if I haven't already gone, I'll be back here, ma'am, and thankin' you for your kindness."

He smiled and backed out of the church, bowing his head to Brigitte before he cocked his cap over one ear and disappeared in the darkness. The man hurried to the corner, crossed the cobblestone street, and disappeared in the shadows of the maple trees lining the street. He stopped, looked furtively about, and whistled once, softly. From a black doorway the dark form of a taller man silently appeared and waited. The shorter man looked about once more, then quickly walked to him.

"They'll be leavin' in three weeks or so."

"You with them?"

"They said come back."

"Good. See to it you're with them."

In the dim light of a waxing quarter moon and the stars, the smile of the taller man could be seen in his full black beard, and he reached to pull the bill of his black seaman's cap lower as he turned on his heel and walked rapidly away from the church, with the shorter man hurrying beside him.

Notes

The process of making paper cartridges and cartridge boxes, including the necessary tools and materials, is well illustrated in Wilbur, *The Revolutionary Soldier*, pp. 22–24.

American women performed unnumbered acts of heroic patriotism during the Revolution, including melting pewter and lead for bullets; making cartridges; spinning flax for material to make clothing for the soldiers; making shirts for the soldiers; supplying food, clothing, and shoes; and serving as soldiers, spies, messengers, and nurses. The Daughters of the American Revolution very kindly provided the author with a number of articles and pamphlets recounting such inspiring deeds, including reference to a book in which the names of thousands of such women are listed and a brief sketch of their deeds given (see Claghorn, *Women Patriots of the American Revolution*, all pages, but specifically, 4, 10, 22, 117, 232, 246, 290).

CHAPTER XI

★ ★ ★

*G*ather round, you lovelies, and pay attention if you want to stay alive when the big guns start exchanging greetings."

Sergeant Alvin Turlock, Company Nine, Boston regiment, stood with feet spread as he slapped one hand on the touchhole of a cannon that was aimed point-blank into the sloped face of a great dirt breastwork forty feet distant. He glared at his men, who stood or squatted in the sweltering heat of midafternoon, with the sun bearing down, sweat running off their noses and chins, wet shirts clinging.

Since dawn they had set timbers and thrown dirt to build breastworks on a ridge nearly two miles south of Brooklyn. They paused only long enough to eat a noon meal of watery fish soup and wormy hardtack and weak coffee, then once again swung picks and axes and drove shovels into rocky soil to dig trenches in front of the breastworks, and fill the space between the parallel rows of timbers, sunk five feet into the ground. At two-thirty Sergeant Turlock had bawled out orders. "Gather for gunnery instruction," and Ninth Company laid down their tools and assembled.

"This is a cannon," he announced, and waited for the muffled murmuring to stop. "Cannon are made of brass or iron. This one's iron, a French Valliere six-pounder. This is one of those Colonel Knox brought from Fort Ticonderoga last winter."

He paused while Company Nine remembered and exclaimed

about the unbelievably daring and heroic epic of Colonel Henry Knox and his company of picked men who had crossed three hundred miles of hopeless wilderness in the dead of winter to reach the critically strategic Fort Ticonderoga that commanded the Hudson near the junction of Lake Champlain and Lake George. Earlier, Fort Ticonderoga had been held by the British, but on May 10, 1775, a scant three weeks after the battle of Concord, Ethan Allen and his Green Mountain Boys, with Benedict Arnold, had silently scaled the high eight-foot-thick stone and cement walls before dawn, taken the British pickets without a sound, then pounded on the door of the commanding officer's quarters just at daybreak. The groggy, half-dressed British commander opened the door with raised lantern to stare into the muzzles of pistols and muskets, while Ethan Allen loudly declared the mighty Fort Ticonderoga captured "in the name of the great Jehovah and the Continental Congress," not quite sure which had the more authority in the circumstances. The gaping British commander surrendered without so much as one shot being fired.

The following winter, Colonel Henry Knox, Washington's officer in command of all Continental army artillery, led an expedition from Boston to Fort Ticonderoga, dismantled nearly sixty cannon, mounted them and their carriages and accoutrements onto handmade skids and sleds, and with oxen dragged them cross-country through the deep mountain snows back to Boston, where General Washington positioned them in a ring around the city to lay siege to General Gage and General Howe and their British army within. The siege succeeded. On March 17, 1776, General Howe led the British from Boston north to New York. None had forgotten the ingenuity and gritty determination of Allen, Arnold, and Knox in capturing the guns of Fort Ticonderoga for the Patriot cause.

The talk subsided and Turlock continued. "Most cannon are the same, so if you can handle one, you can handle any of them. This one is mounted on a field carriage, which means that men, not horses, move it, by hand."

He paused to wipe sweat from his eyes.

"Now, listen close. I'll explain loading and firing from start to end, ten steps, one step at a time. When I finish, you will do it. You miss something, you could kill yourself or someone else."

He waited until no one was moving and all eyes were watching, and then began pointing.

"This is the muzzle, where everything goes in and everything comes out.

"First step. This is a budge barrel." He pointed to a barrel beside the cannon wheel, inside which was an open cloth sack with drawstrings to close it. "Inside the sack is gunpowder.

"Second. This is a powder ladle." He held up a heavy oak stick eight feet long with a large, open-faced scoop attached to one end. "You measure it level full of powder from the budge barrel and shove it down the cannon muzzle, like this. When you feel it hit bottom you back it up about three inches, then rotate the ladle to dump the load, back it up a little more, and shake it to be sure it's empty.

"Third. This is dried grass." He pointed to a stack of brittle dried sea grass. "Sometimes we use hay or straw, but dried grass will do. So will tow, just like the hemp or flax tow your women use to spin thread.

"Fourth. This is a rammer." He held up a second oak stick eight feet long, on the end of which was a heavy round block of wood. "You run the rammer down the muzzle and jam it against the powder to make sure it's packed tight, like this.

"Fifth. You take some of this dried grass, and you shove it in the muzzle, and then you push it on down with the rammer, against the powder, and pack it tight to be sure the powder stays in place.

"Sixth. This is a solid-shot six-pound cannonball. You put a little grass or straw or tow around it to make it fit snug, and you shove it in the muzzle and ram it down with the rammer.

"Seventh. This is the touchhole, and this is the priming flask. The priming flask is just like your powder horn. The touchhole leads to the powder you shoved down the muzzle, so you shake a little powder from the priming flask into the touchhole and leave some on top. You can do the same thing with your powder horn.

"Eighth." He held up a three-foot stick of wood with a small iron arm attached to the top. A cord was wound around the handle and held on the iron cross arm by a setscrew. "This is a linstock. The cord is cotton, soaked with saltpeter and lead acetate and lye to make it burn slow, maybe five inches an hour. It's burning right now."

He paused and took a deep breath. "This cannon is ready to be fired, and I'm going to fire it into the face of the breastwork over there. Get behind the muzzle, because the powder blast goes sideways as well as out. And cover your ears."

He waited until the company was behind the muzzle, blew on the smouldering end of the cord attached to the linstock until it was glowing red, then lowered it to the touchhole. A tiny white cloud erupted as the powder caught, and an instant later the cannon bucked and roared. White smoke leaped two feet out the touchhole and fifteen feet out the muzzle and formed a huge cloud, while dirt flew on the mound forty feet away.

Turlock waited until the shock had settled, then spoke once more.

"Ninth. This is a wormer." He held up another eight-foot heavy oak pole with a large corkscrew on the end. "After the shot, you drive this down the gun barrel to clean out all the grass and tow and anything else that's still inside.

"Tenth. And you better listen to this one." He held up another eight-foot heavy oak pole with a large sponge attached to one end. "This is a sponge. That bucket beneath the cannon is full of water and a little vinegar. You soak the sponge in the bucket and you ram it wet all the way down the barrel, and you twist it. This kills any smouldering powder grains still inside the barrel." He soaked the sponge and rammed it down the barrel, twisted it, withdrew it.

He paused for a moment and stared his men down until he had full attention, and he held the sponge high. "If you don't use the wet sponge, any powder that is left burning in the barrel will set off the powder in the ladle when you shove it in for the next shot, and that usually means we got one of two things. A one-armed cannoneer or a dead one."

He waited until he saw understanding grow in the eyes of his company before he lowered the sponge and leaned it against the cannon with the other equipment, and picked up a long, thin, tapered brass nail.

"This is a spike. If you have to abandon a cannon and the enemy is going to get it, you drive this in the touchhole with a musket butt, or a rock, or anything you can pound with. It goes clear through the chamber inside, hits the far wall, and bends back and makes a hook. That way it can't be pried out. It has to be cut out, and that usually can't be done in a hurry. That's what we mean when we say 'spike a cannon.' If you haven't got a spike, you can shove a cannonball down the barrel and a couple of wood wedges to lock it in, and they usually have to burn the wood wedges out to unplug the cannon. Or you can jam a couple of bayonets down the sides of a cannonball and lock it in. There are lots of ways to spike a cannon."

He held up the last eight-foot oak pole, which had four metal prongs on the end, spread, pointed. "This is a searcher. If something gets plugged in the barrel, you can feel around with this and try to work it out."

He set it down and picked up an L-shaped piece of brass with calibrations on both legs of it. "This is a sighting quadrant. You put the long leg of it inside the cannon barrel, short leg outside pointed down, and set the elevation according to marks on the curved piece that connects the two legs. If the cannon's level, it will tell you the angle to set the barrel to shoot measured distances. But over five hundred yards, you're pretty much left to guess, and that's called 'random shooting.' "

He paused to gather his thoughts. "We used a solid-shot cannonball just now, but there're all kinds. Chain shot, cannister, grape, bar, jointed-bar, incendiary, bomb. If you run out of shot, load 'er up with rocks or glass, nails, knives, forks, spoons—just about anything you can get down the barrel—and let 'er go."

He once again wiped at the sweat on his forehead, and the men moved and murmured for a moment before they all settled down.

"Sometimes you'll have cloth or paper pouches of measured gunpowder. If you do, ram them down the barrel, and then use a spike through the touchhole to punch through the paper or cloth so the spark can get to the power inside."

He stopped to gather his thoughts. "All right," he said. "When I point, you call out the name."

He pointed.

"Rammer," came the call.

He pointed.

"Wormer."

He continued, one item at a time, again and again, until the company went through it without error.

"All right, now two of you are going to load and fire, and you're going to count all ten steps, in order. If you make a mistake the company is going to tell you about it." He turned to Billy. "Corporal, you first. Pick a man and do it."

Billy nodded to Eli and they stepped to the cannon together and, calling out each numbered step, methodically loaded and fired, then rammed the wormer down the barrel, followed by the wet sponge, and moved back into the company. No one had called out a mistake.

Turlock nodded stern approval and pointed at the next two men. Slowly he worked through the entire company, two at a time, with men calling out the errors as they went. Four teams forgot to use the sponge, and Turlock was blasphemous in his instant correction. With the sun casting long shadows eastward, he stepped back to the cannon and raised his voice. "Now go dig all the cannonballs out of the dirt and stack them back here. We do it all again tomorrow afternoon, and then General Washington has ordered us to spend some time with muskets and rifles. We're through for the day. Dismissed for supper."

Company Nine turned, and to a man, each looked into the haze southwest towards Staten Island before they walked north to their blankets, each working pensively with his own thoughts. *Five days ago, another 130 British ships arrived, and they all unloaded troops and guns and supplies on Staten Island. Not a shot fired—welcomed like heroes—now over two hundred British ships down there—how many men, how many guns can two hundred ships bring? Who's in command?* And each man hesitantly asked himself the two questions that rode them heavy every minute, every second, of the day and night. *When do they attack? Where?*

Eli fell into step beside Billy and glanced east and west. As far as the eye could see in both directions, massive breastworks of timber and rock and earth had been formed on the high ground and trenches dug in front of them. Their orders had been terse, ominous. Build these lines to withstand heavy British attack. They must not fail.

They worked their way north, past the breastworks, to the campground where the Boston regimental flag hung limp in the dead air, bright in the setting sun, and sat down on their blankets to wait for supper call. Billy gestured west towards the camp hospital, hastily built of logs with mud and grass chinking. Inside, men sick with dysentery and fever lay everywhere a man could be bedded, and they spilled out into five great tents pegged down close to the hospital.

"Company Nine has five men over there," Billy said. "I'll have to go check on them later."

"Ague and dysentery." Eli shook his head. "Bad."

Billy's eyes dropped. "Buried twenty-six more yesterday. Doctors don't know how to stop it."

Eli pulled a long stem of grass and worked on the white root with his teeth. "Inside the hospital, you can smell it. Death." He shuddered.

They dug their plates and utensils from their knapsacks and settled back to wait.

Billy looked south. "I wonder how many more British ships will come before they start the battle."

Eli shrugged. "How many troops are down there now? How many cannon?"

There was no answer.

Then Billy said, "I've been asking around about your sister. A man came to me yesterday. Asked if there was a reward. I told him maybe, if he could describe her. He said she had dark eyes and dark hair. I sent him away."

Eli dropped his eyes for a moment, and Billy saw the wistful, needful look cross his face. "I've had that happen before," was all he said.

"Come get it." The call from the company cook brought them to their feet, and they walked to the cook fires and the iron tripods and the black, smoking kettles and stood in line for their share of stringy boiled pork from a dry sow that had been bartered from a nearby farmer that morning, a boiled potato smothered with lumpy gravy made from pork drippings and ground corn flour, coffee reheated from the noon meal, and hardtack from which they had to flick off the small worms. The gravy was salted heavily to replace the salt sweated out of their bodies since morning.

At the end of the line two men stood at two woven baskets and put a fresh peach on each plate and watched the eyes of the troops widen in amazed question as to how someone had bartered or stolen fresh peaches. The fruit had the pink blush that comes before full ripeness, mixed with green and yellow, and they had not yet begun to soften into full sugar. But they were peaches, and each man took his gratefully and thrust it into his pocket to be saved and eaten slowly after the meal was finished, the utensils had been washed, and late dusk had settled, and he had time to savor the small reminder of home and gentler times.

Billy and Eli ate in silence, drank long from their canteens against the thirst from the salty gravy, then walked back to the two great kettles filled with steaming water, one with strong lye soap, the other for rinse. They dipped their utensils, swabbed them with a two-foot wooden stick with burlap tied around one end, dipped again in the rinse water, and walked back to their blankets, fingering their hot plates until they cooled and dried. They buried them in their packs and settled back onto their blankets.

With shadows lengthening in the golden afterglow of a sun already set, Billy scraped together twigs and cut shavings and struck tinder to steel. He nursed the tiny spark and blew gently until it smouldered and then burst into a pinpoint of flame, and he worked it until a small campfire glowed in the early dusk. He dug to the bottom of his knapsack where he kept the brown packet, and slipped the worn letter from within. With a sense of tenderness he unfolded it and once more read the lines that he could now recite from memory.

Dear friend Billy:

I take pen in hand to tell you of strange occurrences . . .

He was reaching to touch the delicate handwriting when the high voice of Sergeant Turlock came calling in the dark. "Weems! Corporal Weems."

Billy and Eli both raised their heads, and Billy answered, "Here!"

A moment later Turlock hunkered down beside Billy, firelight making shadows on his small, craggy face. Eli silently sat on his blanket, listening.

"Weems, we got special orders from General Greene tonight. The regiment's to be on the parade ground at nine o'clock in the morning. Spread the word."

"What's happening?"

"Don't know. Says they want to read something to us."

"I'll spread the word."

"Is Stroud around?"

"Right behind you."

Turlock turned, surprised. "Stroud, Colonel Thompson sends this to you." He handed him a sealed paper.

Eli's eyes opened wide in the firelight. "What is it?"

Turlock shrugged. "He didn't say. I was told to deliver it."

Eli took it and waited.

Turlock stood and turned back to Billy. "That's all for now. Spread the word about tomorrow morning." He bobbed his head once and turned and was gone, working his way back through the small campfires.

Eli broke the seal on the paper, opened it, turned it towards the firelight, and silently read.

July 8th, A.D. 1776.
Pvt. Eli Stroud.

I need to know immediately if Indians have been, or are, scouting Long Island south of us, and if so, to what extent. Go there tonight to make that determination if possible. I leave the means and the details to you. Tell no one. Go alone. Avoid detection. Report to me directly upon your return, regardless of time. Present these orders to Captain Reynolds, and he will give you entrance to my quarters.

I am, &c.
Col. Israel Thompson

Eli rounded his lips and blew air.

Billy studied him for a moment, silently waiting.

"Looks like I'll be gone for a while," Eli said quietly.

"Now? Tonight?"

Eli nodded.

"Scout?"

Eli handed Billy the letter and Billy read it.

"It says you were supposed to share this with no one."

Eli shrugged. "You're no one."

Billy grinned in the darkness.

Eli said, "Watch the rifle."

"Be careful."

"Of which side? ours or theirs? I'm more likely to get shot by one of our nervous pickets than one of their scouts."

Eli tucked the small tin box holding his flint, steel, and tinder inside his shirt and stood. Billy folded the written orders and handed them up to him, and Eli folded them once more and slipped the paper inside the shirt with the tinderbox. He took a drink from his canteen, shoved the wooden stopper back in with the palm of his hand, and dropped the canteen on his blanket beside his rifle. He casually walked away, through the dwindling campfires, south towards the latrines on the downhill side of camp. Twenty minutes later he was five hundred yards south of the latrines, studying the distant campfires of the British patrols. No picket or patrol or scout had seen him or challenged.

He turned due west towards the East River, silently, rapidly working his way through the brush and growth. A waxing quarter moon rose above the New Jersey shore before he reached the rocky, sandy strip of shoreline of the river and turned due south once again, working through the sea grass and weeds that bordered the shoreline to avoid leaving a telltale moccasin print that would tell sharp Indian eyes he had passed. He paused every hundred yards and dropped to his haunches to watch and listen for any sound, any movement that was not natural to the night. The only sounds were the incessant song of the frogs and the murmur of the incoming tide against the rocks on the riverbank, mingled with the grating chirp of crickets and the hum of night insects, while night birds wheeled and darted in the faint moonlight.

He worked steadily southwest along the shoreline, and the campfires on the two ridges behind grew dim while those across the bay, on Staten Island, grew brighter. He paused at the Narrows, where the channel between the two islands was smallest, and for long minutes studied the lights on the ships and the campfires beyond, and his eyes narrowed in disbelief.

As far as he could see in both directions the lights on ships showed dozens of squadrons in order at anchor, while on shore it seemed there was no end to the campfires, laid out in straight rows, square upon square, regiment by regiment.

He continued south past Gravesend Bay, where the shoreline turned due east, and then angled slightly northward past Flatbush and Flatlands, and Bedford further inland. The moon was high when he stopped in his tracks. He closed his eyes and gently tested the incoming ocean breeze, and it was there—the unmistakable hint of tobacco smoke.

He dropped to his haunches, faced the Atlantic, and waited and watched, but there was nothing. No faint glow of a pipe, no murmur of human voice, no sound of oars in oarlocks.

They've put a scouting party ashore and they're waiting out there in a boat.

He slipped his tomahawk from his belt and moved silently backwards into the undergrowth and sat down.

I came in from the west and they weren't there. That leaves north or east. I wait.

Minutes became half an hour, then an hour, and Eli moved his legs to relieve cramped muscles, then settled again to listen to the sounds of the night. The moon reached its apex and began its journey back to the New Jersey coast, and still Eli waited, and then the sound came, a single whisper of brush on buckskin. Eli opened his mouth to breathe silently, and lowered his face to prevent the moonlight from reflecting off the flat planes of his forehead and cheeks. The sound came again, and Eli remained invisible and silent and waited while it passed in front of him and continued for the span of five breaths, then stopped, and the muted call of an owl came floating.

Owl? No. Indian!

Three minutes later he heard the rhythmic dip of oars in water, and then the sound of the bow of a small boat grating on the sand and stones of shore, and then the sounds of men climbing into a longboat. An errant oar rattled in an oarlock and someone hissed a curse, and then there were the sounds of feet slogging in the surf and then once again the rhythmic sound of oars backing the boat away from the shore.

Eli raised his face to look, and in the fading moonlight he saw the low, almost indiscernible outline of a longboat working its way south to clear the farthest reaches of Long Island, then west to Staten Island.

He counted two hundred breaths before he moved. He rose to his knees, with his back to the water, opened his tinderbox and placed it on the ground, shielded from the water by his body, and carefully struck flint to steel. He caught a spark in the tinder and patiently breathed on it until it caught, then quickly cupped a hand to shield it from being seen from the sea. He carefully walked, one slow step at a time, straight towards the water's edge, hunched low, looking for fresh tracks.

They were there. He counted three sets of moccasin tracks moving from east to west, fresh in the sand and grit of the shoreline, and he dropped to his knees and brought his face eight inches from the sand and earth to study each set. *Indian, all three. Two average size. One smaller. Walking in the sand, leaving tracks. Either they wanted to leave tracks or they don't care. Which? They don't care.*

He straightened and peered eastward in the darkness. *Went to the east and came from the east. What did they want to see east of here?*

Eli slipped his tomahawk back into his belt and judged the time to be an hour before midnight. *No time to waste, and I got to take a chance. If they left anyone behind I hope I find him before he finds me.*

He started east on the open shoreline at a trot, pausing at intervals to listen and watch, and there was nothing. He counted his paces and stopped at five thousand and waited while his heaving chest quieted. Then he once again struck flint to steel and lowered his tinderbox to peer at the narrow strip of sand, and the tracks were there, going east, then coming back west. One thousand yards farther east, his light showed no tracks, and he started back west. Three hundred yards later he found it. The tracks showed that the three men had turned north on a footpath through the brush and growth, and returned from the north on the same footpath, then turned west to return to their waiting boat.

Eli peered north into the darkness, then back west, making

calculations. *About five miles east of that big bay back there, then due north. No time to find out how far north. What's north of here? Brooklyn's back five miles west and about two, maybe three miles north. Does this trail lead back to Brooklyn? If not, where? Why did they come looking at this trail? No time to find out.*

It was past three o'clock when a startled, sleepy-eyed picket jerked erect at the sudden, silent appearance of a man before him dressed in Indian buckskins, hands held high, a paper clutched in one of them. Five minutes later Eli faced Colonel Israel Thompson across a table in his quarters.

"Report."

"They landed three Indians just east of that big bay down south of the Narrows about nine o'clock tonight. They worked their way east on the shore to a footpath about five miles from the big bay down there, then took the footpath due north. They came back on the same footpath and were picked up by a longboat."

"You saw them?"

"Yes."

"How do you know they were Indians?"

"Owl call. Moccasin tracks."

"Three? Not more?"

"Three. Two average size, one smaller."

"Did they see you?"

"No."

Thompson leaned forward on his forearms and for long seconds stared at his hands in deep thought.

Eli interrupted. "You got a map of that part of the island?"

Thompson spread a map on the tabletop and Eli leaned over it, moving his finger along the coastline of Long Island until he understood how the map lay.

He pointed. "This is the big bay?" He studied the printed name. "Gravesend?"

"Yes."

"They landed just east of there and worked on farther east." He traced with his finger and stopped. "What's that line?"

"Jamaica Road."

Eli followed the trail north where it slanted to the west to arrive behind the ridge where they were building the heaviest fortifications. He raised startled eyes. "That's a natural pass through the ridge?"

"Yes. Jamaica Pass."

Eli bent forward to continue poring over the map, and pointed to a second line that ran north from the bay to Jamaica Road. "What's that line?"

"An unnamed road."

"That one ties into Jamaica Road?"

"Yes."

Eli moved his finger farther west. "That line?"

"Bedford Road."

"That one ties right into Jamaica Road, north of Flatbush?"

"Yes."

Eli pointed once more at a line far to the west, near the shore of the Narrows. "That line?"

"Gowanus Road. It leads north to Brooklyn."

Eli straightened. "They're scouting every road they can to get behind us."

Again Thompson nodded but said nothing.

Eli looked back at the map. "Why don't they just take ships up the East River and unload troops north of Brooklyn? Our cannon couldn't stop them."

Thompson shrugged. "I don't know. Maybe they don't want to try putting that many ships through the Narrows or around through Hell Gate." He tapped the map with a finger.

"What's Hell Gate?"

"Right there." Thompson pointed. "Some sort of natural whirlpool where the tides meet. It will suck a ship down."

Eli's eyebrows arched in surprise. "I didn't know about it."

"They do."

Once more Eli leaned forward to study the map in the yellow light of a single lamp. He studied the Jamaica Road, then the Bedford Road, then moved his finger down the east bank of the East River, and suddenly sensed the deadly implications. He raised his head and for long moments stared into the intense eyes of Thompson as realization settled in. He spoke softly. "If the British use the Jamaica Road to get behind us, and then block us off from the east, that leaves us trapped against the East River with no way out."

Slowly Thompson nodded. "If that happens . . ." His voice trailed off and he did not finish the sentence.

Eli licked dry lips and for a moment stared at Thompson. "You going to tell General Greene, or General Washington?"

"As soon as I can." Thompson folded the map, placed it back on the pile at the edge of his table, and took charge of himself. "Thank you for your report. Go on to your bed. There's a little time before dawn, and by now you need sleep."

"One more thing. If those Indians I saw tonight are Mohawks, and Joseph Brant is their leader, General Washington has trouble he doesn't know about."

"Joseph Brant?"

"Smart. Dangerous."

"I'll be sure General Washington knows. Now, you go get what sleep you can. We have assembly on the parade ground at nine o'clock."

"I heard. What are they going to read to us?"

Thompson shrugged. "I don't know. Something from the Continental Congress, I was told. A declaration."

"Declaration about what?"

"No one said."

"See you in the morning." Eli walked out the flap, past the startled picket, and picked his way to his blanket, while Thompson stood in the yellow lamp glow for half a minute, staring at the folded maps. He drew a ragged breath and exhaled it slowly, then turned to look at the tent flap through which Eli had just disappeared. He shook his head, and despite himself a slow smile formed and he murmured, "I wonder if we'll ever teach that man to salute." He picked the lamp from the table, sat down on his cot to shed his tunic, then reached to turn the small brass wheel that trimmed the burning lamp wick and watched the lamp go black. He sat in the darkness for a moment, then quietly said, "Probably not." He lay down on his back to stare upward and added, "I hope not."

Eli drank from his canteen before he silently lay down on his back on his blanket and sighed. The tension began to drain and his muscles began to relax as weariness settled in, and he gave himself over to it and laid one arm across his closed eyes.

Billy's whispered words came quietly. "You all right?"

"Yes."

Nothing else was said, or needed, and Billy drifted into deep, dreamless sleep.

The tinny rattle of the regimental drum sounding reveille came clattering in the time before sunrise. In the east, the sun, not yet risen, set the undersides of a skiff of high clouds aflame, and the birds of morning chirped and warbled their challenges and answers. Raccoons and opossums moved away from streams and creeks and open places to disappear for the day, while beady-eyed squirrels with tails cocked over their backs came darting for berries and seeds, pausing now and again to scold those who had invaded their world to dig in the earth and destroy the bushes and trees.

The men of the Boston regiment rose silently from their blankets to swallow sour and begin their rotation at the latrines and at the washbasins to rinse their faces gasping in cold water and to wash their hands. Some stripped to the waist and quickly dashed water over their chests and wiped with soiled towels or cloths, while a few lathered and shaved. They straightened their stockings and breeches, tucked in shirttails, shook blankets and rolled or folded them for the day, then settled down for the monotony of assembling for morning inspection, roll call, and breakfast. Within minutes steam was rising from the great black kettles over cooking fires, and the men wrinkled their noses in passive disgust as the air filled with the bland aroma of thin cornmeal mush with no sorghum and of coffee from yesterday's grounds.

With breakfast finished, Sergeant Turlock called orders to Company Nine. "All right, you lovelies, bring your muskets and ammunition for practice." Ten minutes later they were gathered around him near the cannon they had used for drill, once again facing the sloped dirt breastwork.

"Each man take one of these wooden stakes and drive it into the dirt over there, and then come here and get five paper cartridges and line up with your musket."

He waited until the stakes were driven and the men were lined up facing the breastwork with muskets and paper cartridges in hand.

"General Washington says we're to prepare you men to meet British regulars, and to do that you need to know your weapon, and that takes drill. So today we drill."

He held up a musket. "Most of you have shot one of these before, but probably not with paper cartridges, and that's why we're here." He held up a cartridge box. "This is a cartridge box. Inside are thirty paper cartridges, like this one. Simple to use. Now, watch while I talk you through it."

He slowly took one cartridge in hand, bit off the end, primed the pan and closed it, poured the balance of the powder down the muzzle, stuffed the paper and ball in behind it, and drove it all down with the ramrod. He held it up. "Ready to fire." He cocked the hammer, shouldered he weapon, and pulled the trigger.

The flint in the huge hammer slammed into the frizzen and knocked it upward while it struck a spark downward into the powder in the pan. The powder caught and burned through the touchhole into the powder inside the barrel. It ignited and the musket blasted and kicked. The musket ball knocked dirt on the hillside next to one of the stakes.

"Simple," Turlock said. "Now, everybody pick out the stake you drove and do what I just did with one of those cartridges."

He watched as the men methodically went through the motions and knocked dirt all up and down the breastwork.

"All right, do it again."

He put them through the drill until all five cartridges were gone, and once again he raised the musket.

"Now, that's how you shoot with paper cartridges. Problem is, you won't always have paper cartridges. Then you have to work with a powder horn and a lead ball. Watch while I talk you through it.

"First, I've got to tell you I'm going to show you how to load what is called 'buck and ball.' That means after you put the powder in the barrel, you drop three large pieces of buckshot down, and then you put the ball on top. That gives you a ball, and behind it, three buckshot that spread after they leave the musket barrel, and you hit a lot more of what's in front of you that way. Now, watch."

Patiently he primed the pan with a powder horn, slapped it shut, set the butt of the stock on the ground, and measured powder from the horn down the muzzle. He used the ramrod to drive a patch down the barrel to lock the powder in, then dropped three large pieces of lead buckshot down the barrel, followed by the huge ball, and again used the ramrod to set it firm. He raised the musket, drew it to full cock, pointed it at a stake, and pulled the trigger. Dirt jumped over an area nearly two feet in diameter as the ball and buckshot plowed into the face of the breastwork.

"Buck and ball. Remember, muskets do not have a rear sight. They're not for accurate shooting. They're for rapid fire. Now, each of you come and get nine buckshot and three balls and load and fire three times."

Twenty minutes later he once again stepped before the men. "Now we're going to talk about rifles. First, we call them rifles because they have twisted ridges called riflings inside the barrel, and those ridges grab the ball and give it a spin that makes it fly straight for up to three hundred yards. Rifles have a gun sight at the rear of the barrel and at the front too, so you can line up the barrel with accuracy. That's good. But it takes three times longer to load a rifle than a musket. That's bad. A good man with a musket can get off three shots in one minute, sometimes four, while a rifle gets off one shot, two at best. So we mix the two. Muskets for fast firing, with rifles in between for longer range accurate firing."

He held up a rifle, longer and more delicate than the musket. "The loading and firing is like a musket except you have to seat the rifle bullet on a greased patch. Watch and I'll show you."

Methodically he primed the rifle and seated the powder in the barrel, then drew a greased patch from a brass-covered chamber carved into the rifle stock. He laid it over the muzzle, then forced a ball onto it firmly enough to lock it into place. He drew the ramrod and drove the ball and patch down the barrel, then faced the breastwork, and this time the bullet split a stake up the center as it drove through and ripped into the hillside.

He pointed at the splintered stake. "There's the difference. Accuracy. Muskets for rapid fire up close. Rifles for accurate fire long distance. Use both and you've got something."

He leaned the rifle against the cannon. "We don't have enough rifles to go around, but you'll all get training on them in the next two days. Right now we've got to get to the parade ground for the nine o'clock assembly."

Someone called, "What're they going to read to us?"

Turlock shook his head. "No one told me. I figger maybe terms of surrender by the British." He waited for nervous laughter to die. "All right, you lovelies, take your weapons back to your campsites and then assemble on the parade ground."

Shoulder to shoulder, Billy and Eli walked back to their blankets and covered their weapons, then picked their way to the place where trees and brush had been cleared to form a great parade and staging ground. To the north, at the edge of the clearing, the tents housing the entire Long Island command stood in bold relief against the green trees and shrubbery. A forty-foot flagpole stood before the command tent, proudly flying the New York colony flag. Beside the flagpole a platform twenty feet long and ten feet wide, built from fresh-cut maple, rose nine feet above the ground, with a waist-high railing all around. It faced south, with twelve steps from the back side.

At ten minutes before nine o'clock a regimental drummer in full uniform took his position before the stand, with his large snare drum hanging down his left leg on its shoulder strap, and began pounding out the familiar rhythm of assembly. Officers from every regiment on Long Island took their appointed positions facing the stand, and soldiers found their places in the rank and file, looking left and right, making adjustments to straighten the lines. At nine o'clock the entrance flaps of the command tent parted, and two officers dressed in New York green marched out, followed by the commander of the Long Island forces, General Nathanael Greene of Rhode Island, flanked by his staff and aides. Their uniforms were immaculate, and never had the soldiers in the ranks seen so much gold sparkling on the shoulders of so few men, as the officers marched rigidly up the back stairs and onto the platform to look out over the sea of expectant faces peering upwards at them.

The New York officer with the most gold on his shoulders stepped to the railing and the troops quieted. In the trees behind the command tent, a blue jay warbled. The warm July morning sun filtered through the leaves thick and green on the trees, unmoving in the still air, and behind the command tent the blue jay warbled again and another answered. Somewhere far to the west a camp dog barked and fell silent. Two red squirrels chased each other beneath the platform and disappeared.

"Attention to orders," the officer called. "General George Washington has lately received a document which he has ordered to be read to all soldiers of the Continental army and all militia under his command in New York and the New York area. General Nathanael Greene has ordered that I shall read it to you. When I am finished, you will hold your formations until copies of this document have been distributed to each regiment, following which the entire command will stand down for one hour while you acquaint yourselves more fully with the contents of the writing."

A surprised hush settled over the entire command as the officer unrolled a large scroll and began to read loudly, slowly, enunciating each word with careful precision.

" 'In Congress, July 4, 1776. The unanimous Declaration of the thirteen united States of America.' "

A thick silence settled over the parade ground, and no one moved.

" 'When in the Course of human events, it becomes necessary for one people to dissolve the political bands which have connected them with another, and to assume among the powers of the earth, the separate and equal station to which the Laws of Nature and of Nature's God entitle them, a decent respect to the opinions of mankind requires that they should declare the causes which impel them to the separation.' "

The officer paused, then continued.

" 'We hold these truths to be self-evident, that all men are created equal, that they are endowed by their Creator with certain unalienable Rights, that among these are Life, Liberty and the pursuit of Happiness.' "

Billy's breathing constricted as thoughts he had never heard struck into the very marrow of his being and awakened something that had long slumbered.

Eli stood ramrod straight, mesmerized, staring at the officer on the platform. Through the agony of his torn childhood, and an alien world ruled by tomahawk and rifle, he had hungered, searched for a life rooted in dignity, justice, compassion. And now, on this parade ground, on the brink of the greatest battle the colonies had ever seen, he had heard in three breaths that for which his heart had cried out from earliest memory. *"Endowed by their Creator . . . certain unalienable Rights . . . Life, Liberty and the pursuit of Happiness."* He dared not breathe as he waited for the officer to read on.

" 'That to secure these rights, Governments are instituted among Men, deriving their just powers from the consent of the governed, that whenever any Form of Government becomes destructive to these ends, it is the Right of the People to alter or to abolish it, and to institute new Government, laying its foundation on such principles and organizing its powers in such form, as to them shall seem most likely to effect their Safety and Happiness.' "

No one on the parade ground moved in the grip of the profound silence.

" 'Prudence, indeed, will dictate that Governments long established should not be changed for light and transient causes. . . . But when a long train of abuses and usurpations, pursuing invariably the same Object, evinces a design to reduce them under absolute Despotism, it is their right, it is their duty, to throw off such Government, and to provide new Guards for their future security. Such has been the patient sufferance of these Colonies. . . . To prove this, let Facts be submitted to a candid world.' "

Billy and Eli were scarcely breathing as the officer read on in the silence of sun in the trees and on the shoulders and heads of the Long Island command.

Despotism, denial of right to jury trial, taxes, confiscation of private property, corrupt government, denial of representation, burned towns, plundered coasts, fomented insurrection, the wrath of savages upon the citizenry—the list of grievances against King George continued on and on.

The officer paused for a moment, raised his eyes, and slowly finished.

" 'We, therefore, the Representatives of the united States of America, in General Congress, Assembled, appealing to the Supreme Judge of the world for the rectitude of our intentions, do, in the Name, and by Authority of the good People of these Colonies, solemnly publish and declare, That these United Colonies are, and of Right out to be Free and Independent States; that they are Absolved from all Allegiance to the British Crown, and that all political connection between them and the State of Great Britain, is and ought to be totally dissolved; and that as Free and Independent States, they have full Power to levy War, conclude Peace, contract Alliances, establish Commerce, and to do all other Acts and Things which Independent States may of right do. And for the support of this Declaration, with a firm reliance on the protection of divine Providence, we mutually pledge to each other our Lives, our Fortunes and our sacred Honor.' "

The officer stopped. For more than half a minute he stood there, hands trembling, swallowing against the great lump in his throat, eyes too shiny. Behind him, General Nathanael Greene worked his mouth and dropped his eyes to the clean yellow planking of the platform and did not look up for a time.

In the Long Island command, grizzled old veterans of the French and Indian wars, with battle scars on their weathered faces, wiped at their eyes without shame. Farmers and craftsmen who had left wives and children clamped their mouths shut and dropped their faces to stare at the ground. Young men stood white-faced, aware they had shared a moment that would shine forever in history but unable to understand the breadth and depth of it.

The officer took charge of himself, and once again his voice reached out over the parade ground. "This declaration has been signed by most members of our Continental Congress, and others will sign soon. At this moment, the Crown has uttered warrants for the arrest of many of these men for treason. May the Almighty grant us the will and the courage to move steadily forward in the course we have now so nobly begun."

He rolled the scroll and tucked it under his arm. "Regimental officers, come forward to receive copies of this document, and distribute them among your commands before you dismiss them to their campsites for one hour of further study. God bless you all."

For three seconds no one moved or spoke, and then the regimental officers marched to the stand, where the command staff divided out printed copies of the Declaration of Independence. The magic of the moment began to fade, and only then did murmuring rise in the rank and file of the command.

The regimental officers moved down the lines passing out copies of the declaration to reaching hands, took their positions at the front of their commands, called out "Dismissed," and stood in surprised amazement as the troops did not leave the parade ground. Instead they gathered into small groups exclaiming, groping to comprehend the unthinkable insult the Continental Congress had hurled in the face of King George and the British empire—the mightiest military force on the face of the earth. At once they were torn between fear of the wrath of the king and proud elation at openly defying him before the world.

Billy stood stock-still, oblivious to the soldiers and exclamations around him as he read again and again the words that pierced so deep. *"Truths . . . self-evident . . . endowed by their Creator . . . unalienable Rights . . . Life, Liberty and the pursuit of Happiness . . . to secure these rights . . . Governments . . . deriving their just powers from the consent of the governed."*

He was unaware when Eli came in from behind and stopped, eyes locked onto a copy of the declaration. Eli placed his finger on the paper and spoke. "What does this word mean?"

Billy started, then turned, and Eli showed him the marked place. *"Unalienable.* It means no one can take it away from you."

Eli raised his eyes to Billy's and swallowed. "Life. Liberty. A chance at happiness. Does this say I got them from God and no one should be able to take them away?"

"That's what it says."

"This part down here. The 'consent of the governed' part. Does that mean the ordinary people ought to have a say in who governs?"

Billy tried to speak and couldn't, and then answered. "That's what it says."

"Back up here. 'All men are created equal.' Does that mean nobody is born higher than someone else?"

Billy nodded his head and could not speak.

Eli swallowed hard and cleared his throat. "Who wrote this? These men whose names are at the bottom? They couldn't—not all of them."

Billy shook his head. "I don't know."

Eli turned on his heel and was gone, trotting, working his way to find Thompson. He returned in three minutes, breathless. "Thompson says a committee was told by Congress to write this. Benjamin Franklin and Thomas Jefferson were on the committee. Who's Jefferson?"

"I don't know. We'll find out."

A faraway look crept into Eli's eyes for a moment. "I don't think anybody ever wrote these thoughts the way they did, not even in the Bible."

The two walked back to their camp, reading the words slowly again and again, feeling the hair rise on their arms and the backs of their necks as the profound depth and breadth of the simple words reached ever deeper. They settled onto their blankets, and when they were finished they looked at each other, humbled, cowed, small in the bright light the words had brought into their minds and their hearts. For a long time they said nothing because it was beyond their power to speak words that would not diminish the thing that was spreading within, changing both of them.

They looked about the camp. Men sat or stood quietly, faces cast down as they read, and read again, the words that stirred their souls. A hush settled over the Boston regiment, and a spirit came quietly, surely, lifting them, binding them, raising their thoughts to heights never before known. It broke clear and shining in their minds that a hand mightier than any on earth had chosen them to fight the war that would change the history of the world forever, and it humbled them, frightened them.

Billy spoke quietly. "Do you feel it? We will answer to the Almighty if we fail him in this struggle."

Eli nodded, eyes bright as he whispered, "I know."

Half an hour later cannon and rocket fire erupted across the East River in New York City, and all faces in the Long Island command turned to stare in silence as the citizen Patriots across the black waters blew rocket after rocket arching into the brilliant blue sky in wild celebration of the declaration they had just received and that had been read to everyone on the common. Strong hands cast heavy ropes over the two-ton statue of King George mounted on a stylish horse that had been erected at Bowling Green on a six-foot-high marble base but three short years earlier. Willing citizens heaved their weight against the ropes. The statue held, and then it separated from the base, and then it came toppling from its lofty perch. The ground trembled as it struck, the head snapped from the statue, and the body broke into countless pieces.

Hundreds of hands gathered the shattered lead statue and loaded it into a wagon to be freighted off to the Oliver Wolcott home in Litchfield, Connecticut. There five women would see to it that 42,088 bullets were cast from the lead for Patriot muskets and rifles, to be fired at the red-coated soldiers of King George. The women were Mrs. Marvin, Ruth Marvin, Laura Wolcott, Mary Ann Wolcott, and Mrs. Beach, assisted by a few other Patriots.

They were certain there could be no better use for a statue of King George III.

Notes

Ethan Allen, with his Green Mountain Boys and Benedict Arnold, captured Fort Ticonderoga on the Hudson River on May 10, 1775, "in the name of the great Jehovah and the Continental Congress" (see Higginbotham, *The War of American Independence*, p. 67; Leckie, *George Washington's War*, pp. 120–21).

Colonel Henry Knox led the expedition that obtained the cannon from Fort Ticonderoga in the winter of 1775–76 and returned it on sleds three hundred miles to George Washington for the siege of Boston (see Higginbotham, *The War of American Independence*, p. 105; Stokesbury, *A Short History of the American Revolution*, pp. 60–61).

Illustrations and an explanation of the parts of a cannon and the process of loading and firing them can be found in Wilbur, *The Revolutionary Soldier*, pp. 44–46, and Peterson, *Round Shot and Rammers*, pp. 24–32.

Illustrations and an explanation of loading and firing the musket and the rifle can be found in Wilbur, *The Revolutionary Soldier*, pp. 29–31.

Hell Gate is described and the location explained in Johnston, *The Campaign of 1776*, part I, p. 47. A map identifies it in Stokesbury, *A Short History of the American Revolution*, p. 90.

The locations of the roads on Long Island that were involved in the imminent battle, including the critical Jamaica Road and Jamaica Pass, are described in Johnston, *The Campaign of 1776*, part I, pp. 154–61 (and see particularly the foldout map included in this source).

The arrival of the British armada at New York began on June 25 or 26, 1776, when General William Howe sailed in aboard the *Greyhound* with three other British ships, and it continued at intervals thereafter until August 15, 1776 (see Johnston, *The Campaign of 1776*, part I, p. 94; see also Higginbotham, *The War of American Independence*, p. 151, which gives the totals of men and ships).

General Washington had the Declaration of Independence printed and read to the entire Continental army in and around New York, as well as to the citizens, on July 9, 1776. In New York City the citizens celebrated by pulling down the statue of King George, which was melted down and cast into 42,088 bullets (see Johnston, *The Campaign of 1776*, part I, p. 93; Leckie, *George Washington's War*, p. 257).

CHAPTER XII

*S*ir, General William Howe has sent his adjutant general, who requests an audience with you."

General George Washington slowly raised his head, laid down the quill with which he had been writing, and settled back in his chair. Face a passive mask, he studied his adjutant general, Colonel Joseph Reed, for long moments before he spoke. "What name?"

"Lieutenant Colonel James Paterson, sir."

"Alone?"

"No, sir. Three other officers in his entourage."

"Where are they now?"

"In their boat, sir. We would not let them come ashore without your permission."

"Does he have a letter?"

"Yes, sir."

Washington rose and leaned forward on stiff arms, hands flat on the top of his massive walnut desk, which was half-covered with neat stacks of the never-ending paperwork that runs an army. His eyes sharpened, became penetrating. "To whom is this one addressed?"

"To 'George Washington, Esq., etc., etc.'"

A smile came and quickly passed as Washington spoke. "It appears General Howe has been somewhat educated since his last messenger came calling."

A proud grin flickered on Reed's face. "Yes, sir, it would appear so."

Both Reed and Washington were remembering the previous messenger sent by Admiral Richard Howe six days earlier, on July 14, 1776. Commodore Tupper of the nearly nonexistent Continental navy had rowed out in a barge to stop the British longboat as it approached the New York shores and demanded to know the purpose. The British officer in command stated he had been ordered to personally deliver a written document to General Washington and to exchange letters from prisoners. Tupper had reported to General Washington, who sent Colonel Henry Knox and Reed, with a bag of letters from prisoners, down to the bay to investigate. Reed had demanded to meet the British officer, who took hat in hand, bowed politely, and said, "I have a letter from Admiral Howe to Mr. Washington."

Reed's mouth had fallen open for a split second before he snapped it shut. *Mr. Washington! Mister Washington!* He had drawn himself up to full height and sucked in his chin. *Howe refuses to recognize we have an army, or that General Washington's the commander! How dare he!* He had brought his flared anger under control. "Sir, we have no person in our army with that address."

The British officer had gaped and stammered, "But . . . but will you look at the address?" as he thrust the sealed letter forward.

Reed had seized it and glanced at the address. " 'George Washington, Esq., New York.' " He had shoved it back at the British officer. "No, sir, I cannot receive that letter."

The stunned British officer had groped for a way to save his mission. "I, uh, I am very sorry, and so will be my commander, that any error in the superscription should prevent the letter being received by General Washington."

Reed had set his chin like a bulldog. "Why, sir, I must obey orders." Reed had relied on the cardinal rule of the British army, which was that orders would be obeyed first, last, and always. It worked.

The officer exclaimed, "Oh! Yes, sir, you must obey orders, to be sure."

Reed had handed him the bag of prisoners' letters, took the one from the British officer, and climbed from the British boat back into his own barge. The British boat had not gone ten yards before it turned and again approached Reed.

"Sir," the British officer had called, "by what particular title does Washington choose to be addressed?"

There had been fire in Reed's eyes as he spat, "You are sensible, sir, of the rank of *General* Washington in our *army?*"

"Oh, yes, sir, we are. I am sure Admiral Howe will lament exceedingly this affair, as the letter is quite of a civil nature, and not of a military one. He laments exceedingly that he was not here a little sooner."

Reed had glanced at Knox, and both men understood. Howe had gotten a copy of the Declaration of Independence, and realized that that single document had opened an irreconcilable separation of the fledgling colonies from Mother England. Howe was too late now in his desperate try at avoiding the holocaust that was coming. The American officers had said nothing, and the British boat had turned south once again, and was gone. Reed had looked at Knox, and both men turned their faces back to their own shore with grim satisfaction in the fact they had preserved the dignity of their young nation and the self-respect of their commander in chief.

Now, six days later, Washington was still smiling at the remembrance when he straightened and looked at Reed. "What's your advice? Should we receive this one?"

Reed thoughtfully stroked his chin. "Yes, sir, I believe the British commander now understands with whom he is dealing."

Washington glanced at the large, ornately carved clock on the mantel, then settled back into his great, upholstered chair. "Tell Colonel Paterson I will receive him in one hour, at eleven o'clock, in the offices of Colonel Knox at the Kennedy house. That address is Number One, Broadway. Show him every deference in the meantime. Refreshments—whatever he may want or need. And it will not be necessary to blindfold him. Have Colonel Knox provide a scribe who can copy what's said. Order my coach, and get two other officers, and prepare to come with me."

"No blindfold?"

Washington shrugged. "I doubt he'll see anything he doesn't already know."

"Yes, sir." Reed turned smartly on his heel and closed the door as he walked out.

General George Washington drew and exhaled a great breath, then turned in his chair and for a time peered out the west windows of his headquarters office in the second floor of the Mortier mansion in the northern section of New York City. The midmorning sun was bright, the trees and foliage a rich emerald green in the still air, and for a moment it seemed to Washington a profanity, a blasphemy, that at that moment two armies were gathering for a momentous battle that would shatter the profound beauty, the deep tranquility that lay all about.

In the quiet of his office he leaned back in his chair, elbows on the arms, fingers interlaced across his middle, and half closed his eyes in deep concentration. *What's Howe after? To get my reaction to a surrender proposal? Maybe. Not likely. Amnesty if we lay down our arms? Maybe. Exchange of prisoners? Probably not. A mercy request—medicine? Not likely—we have more sick than he does and he knows it.*

His eyes narrowed in question and his forehead wrinkled as he began preparing his mind, his thoughts, for the intense, critically sensitive duel of words and facial expressions, of nuance and shadings, of give and take, that occurs when two men charged with the duty of conducting war against each other meet to discuss the affairs that could result in the defeat of one nation or the other. He picked up the quill, dipped the split point into the inkwell, squared a fresh sheet of paper on his desktop, and methodically began making notes of dates and events that could become critical.

At half past ten Reed rapped on Washington's door. Five minutes later they sat opposite each other on upholstered cushions inside a swaying coach, listening to the click of iron horseshoes on cobblestones, peering out the windows at soldiers and civilians in the streets preparing for battle. At ten-fifty, less than two hundred yards from the waterfront, they entered the military headquarters of Colonel Henry Knox, commander of all cannon of the Continental army, at Number One, Broadway. At eleven o'clock Reed opened the door and ushered Lieutenant Colonel Paterson and his four support officers into the large, opulently furnished room.

General George Washington rose to his full six feet four inches, subtly the most dominant figure in the room. Strongly built, he moved with the natural grace of a born horseman, one of the best in the colony of Virginia. His pale blue and buff uniform was immaculate, his shoulder epaulets gleaming, his long hair brushed and tied behind his head. His mouth was thin, nose prominent, face noncommittal as he faced Lieutenant Colonel James Paterson.

Paterson looked into Washington's eyes, and for a moment his breathing slowed. In those blue-gray eyes he saw a resolve and a strength that chilled him, and he sensed perception and wisdom and judgment that were overpowering. Paterson stood silent in the presence of Washington, waiting.

Washington spoke and his voice was startlingly low, soft, his words simple. "I am honored by your presence, Colonel. Would you and your staff please be seated."

Paterson settled onto the front edge of his upholstered chair facing Washington's desk, back straight as a stick. Washington sat down in his own chair, while all other officers in the room took their designated chairs.

"I trust my staff treated you acceptably well?" Washington said cordially.

"Most graciously, Your Excellency," Paterson replied. He shifted his feet. "May I iterate my great personal gratitude for being allowed to confer with Your Excellency."

Washington nodded amiably. "The honor is mine. General Howe is well?"

"Indeed. Robust health, and the highest of spirits, Your Excellency."

Washington's facial expression did not change while he battled the inward need to laugh. *Your Excellency! Three times in two sentences! So much for "Mr. Washington."* "Your boat trip from Staten Island was agreeable?"

"Most agreeable. The weather is perfect, Your Excellency."

Washington could not contain a smile. "I understand General Howe wished to communicate a message to me?" He watched Paterson's eyes.

"Oh, yes, Your Excellency." He fumbled with a leather pouch. "Indeed. It is my honor to deliver this document to Your Excellency." Paterson rose to reach across the desk, and Washington accepted the letter.

Before he opened it, he casually read the inscription on the front and his eyebrows arched. "George Washington, Esq., etc., etc." He leaned back in his chair and thoughtfully tapped the letter against the thumb of his left hand, while his eyes bored into Paterson.

Paterson read Washington's expression perfectly, and his reaction was too abrupt, too forceful. "May it please Your Excellency," he exclaimed, "I would like to explain the inscription. You see, Your Excellency, General Howe had the greatest desire to address this letter properly in view of prior oversights, and thus he has included words intended to include all possible contingencies. The 'etc., etc.' means everything possible."

Washington's face remained passive while inside he was bursting with a great guffaw. He spoke quietly. "And the 'etc., etc.' could mean anything."

Paterson's face fell. He dropped his eyes, convinced Washington was going to return the letter unopened and terminate the meeting.

Washington turned the letter over and studied the large wax seal with the impression of the lion and the unicorn of Great Britain. He leaned back in his chair and dropped his face, and closed his eyes while he carefully calculated how he should react.

He raised his head and spoke to Paterson. "Are you acquainted with the contents of this document?"

"Your Excellency, I have not read the document. However, General Howe did share with me the general text."

Washington reached to thoughtfully rub his chin for a moment while he faced the decision whether or not the purpose of the letter should be made known to all the officers in the room, and he made up his mind. It should. He raised his eyes to Paterson. "What is the text of the letter?"

Paterson swallowed before he spoke. "If I understand General Howe correctly, he is offering a pardon to all who will lay down their arms and swear allegiance to the Crown." Paterson held his breath in desperate hope.

Washington leaned back and for long moments allowed the proposal to take root. *A pardon! Amnesty. Not terms of surrender. Lay down our arms and swear allegiance to the Crown, and all is forgiven and forgotten.* He drew and slowly exhaled a deep breath. *No reprisals. No arrests. Tens of thousands of lives would be saved, ours and theirs. Cities spared from fire and cannon. Untold suffering avoided.*

Paterson watched every expression on Washington's face, in his eyes, in a desperate hope of sensing which direction Washington's reactions were going. He saw nothing but those pale blue-gray eyes staring back at him, firm, solid, bottomless, without expression. Paterson plowed on, piling words on words rapidly.

"Your Excellency, His Excellency King George has anxiously and most benevolently appointed General Howe and his brother Lord Admiral Richard Howe of the Royal Navy as his special commissioners to approach Your Excellency with the proposal from the king that the Crown and the colonies accommodate the unhappy disputes lately developed between them. The king has empowered the general and the admiral to do so, by granting pardons."

It flashed in Washington's mind. *Unhappy disputes. Does that include the "unhappy dispute" of July twelfth—three days after Howe read the Declaration of Independence—when he sent those two men-of-war, the* ROSE *and the*

PHOENIX, *up the Hudson to shoot up gun emplacements and military bases and randomly blast private residences? Unhappy dispute? Closer to murder!*

Paterson hurried on. "It would give General and Lord Admiral Howe, and the king, great pleasure to accomplish such a result, and I am unable to fully express my personal great hope that Your Excellency would consider this visit as a preliminary to accomplish that great and most desirable result."

Once again Washington let his eyes fall to his desktop while he pondered, reached a conclusion, and then methodically reasoned through it once again to be certain of his own mind, his own convictions in the white heat of this fateful, pivotal decision. The room was silent as a tomb. No one moved. Muted street noises could be heard, with the buzzing of flies against the window glass. Washington's mind and heart settled and he raised his face.

"Colonel Paterson, the commission conferred upon me by the Continental Congress did not include authority to negotiate such a proposal with the Crown. That authority resides in the Congress, and the Congress only. Do General and Admiral Howe have authority to negotiate peace for the Crown?"

Paterson's eyes fell. "No, Your Excellency. To grant pardons only."

Washington drew a breath and spoke deliberately. "If the authority granted to the Howes is limited to granting pardons, they are not commissioned to negotiate terms of peace between two sovereigns. And since the Crown and the colonies are now two sovereigns, there is nothing to be accomplished in a meeting between the Howes and myself, since neither they nor I am empowered to negotiate any possible terms of peace. And as to being pardoned, the colonies have done nothing wrong, and are not in need of being pardoned."

Every officer in the room started at the profound simplicity, and Paterson swallowed hard. In Washington's eyes he saw something that turned him cold to the center of his being. He opened his mouth to speak and words would not come.

Washington leaned forward, amiable in countenance, but his

words cut to the core. "I am sensible of the fact that Lord Howe has read the Declaration of Independence, and I presume he understands the clear import of the words. I am also sensible of the fact that three days after the declaration was published in New York City, on July twelfth, General Howe sent the *Rose* and the *Phoenix* up the Hudson, and can only conclude their orders were to make the citizenry, and the army, keenly aware that our forces could not stop them. Our obstructions in the river failed, and six of our soldiers were killed that day, either by cannon from the men-of-war or by their own error in handling their pieces."

He paused long enough to see Paterson's face turn white.

"I am also sensible to the fact that on July fifteenth, Lord Admiral Richard Howe sailed his fleet into New York Harbor and disembarked troops and munitions and supplies on Staten Island, and they are there now, staging for battle. In all, there are in excess of three hundred British ships anchored off Long Island, and more than twenty thousand troops on Staten Island, preparing to attack. I have reliable intelligence that more such ships and men are to arrive soon."

Washington paused long enough to have the undivided attention of every man in the room before he leaned forward, eyes points of light, and finished. "It was not by accident that those unhappy disputes occurred prior to General Howe's sending a letter to propose a pardon. Rather, it occurs to my mind that that train of events was calculated by General Howe to raise great anxiety in the hearts and minds of the Continental army and the Patriot citizens concerning the overpowering might of the British military, and their firm determination to use it against us if necessary. Should that estimate of the intent of General Howe be accurate, then he has erred altogether in his hope, because his efforts not only have failed to intimidate but, to the contrary, have created an immutable resolve in the hearts of the Continental army and the Patriot citizens to fight for the rights enumerated in the Declaration of Independence. They will have their unalienable rights to life, liberty, and the pursuit of happiness."

For three seconds no one moved. Stunned, reeling, Paterson understood the matter was forever decided, closed. "Has Your Excellency no particular commands with which you would please to honor me to Lord and General Howe?" It was his last attempt to keep the negotiation possibility open.

Washington rose, and his face was placid. "Nothing, sir, but my particular compliments to them both." He gestured to a sterling silver tray with a decanter of wine and crystal glasses on a polished table against one wall. "Would you care for a refreshment?"

It was over. It had failed. And Paterson knew he had faced a man vastly superior in reach of thought and quality of judgment and depth of commitment.

He cleared his throat. "No, Your Excellency. For myself and on behalf of General Howe, I extend thanks for your gracious audience. With your permission I shall take my leave."

Paterson stood, struggling to maintain decorum. He tucked his hat under his arm and bowed to Washington, who returned his bow. He turned on his heel and led his four officers from the room without looking back.

Washington watched the door close and stood for a moment staring. *Was I too abrupt? too harsh? I pray I was not.*

He turned to the scribe. "At earliest opportunity make two copies of the proceedings of this meeting available to myself, one for my records, one for Congress. Use the exact words spoken in all places possible."

"Yes, sir."

Washington's eyes swept the room. "Gentlemen, I thank you for your presence. It seems we have rejected what I presume to be our last chance to escape from war. I trust the Almighty will continue to be aware of our struggles."

The coach ride back to Washington's headquarters was quiet, reflective, as each man worked with his own thoughts. Washington was escorted from his coach into the Mortier house, back to his command quarters, where he removed and hung his hat, then his officer's tunic, and sat down at his desk. He glanced at the clock, and started at the knock at his door. "Enter."

Reed carefully balanced a large, beautifully crafted silver tray to Washington's desk and carefully set it down, then removed the embroidered cloth. "Your lunch, sir."

"Thank you."

"And sir, you may be interested in this message that came in our absence."

Washington took the document, unfolded it, and read silently. His eyes widened. "Are you aware what this says?"

"From what I understand, the new governor of New Jersey has persuaded the New Jersey legislature to raise five battalions to serve in the Continental army until December first."

Washington nodded. "His name's William Livingston. He's stirred them up over there." He paused and his face fell for a moment. "Any word on what's happened to William Franklin? the governor before Livingston?"

"No, sir. Only that the legislature ordered his arrest, and he was taken into custody months ago. I haven't heard what's happened since." Reed's eyes saddened. "I feel sorry for Ben Franklin."

Washington pursed his mouth and shook his head. "I think it took something out of Mr. Franklin when his only son turned on the colonies—declared loyalty to the Crown. I understand it was some time before he'd talk with anyone about it. Maybe he still won't. He's never spoken to his son since. Swears he never will."

"So I'm told."

Washington shrugged. "Mr. Franklin will survive. He'll be all right."

"I'm sure, sir. Is there anything else, sir?"

"Not right now. Thank you for lunch."

"Not at all, sir." Reed turned to leave.

"Reed," Washington called, and Reed turned back, startled at the familiarity Washington had shown in not calling him by his rank.

"Yes, sir."

"Reed, I have a feeling that after supper I'm going to need a few spirited hands of whist. Gather up two more officers who consider themselves experts, and get them to my quarters along with a fresh deck of whist cards."

Reed's eyes crinkled. "Yes, sir."

"And Reed, share with them the standard rules of the game. Those caught cheating will face a court-martial prior to being shot."

"Yes, sir." Reed chuckled as he closed the door.

Notes

Around the third week of July 1776, two letters were written to George Washington by the Howes, one by Admiral Howe and the other by General Howe. The first letter was addressed to "George Washington, Esq." and was refused. The second was addressed to "George Washington, Esq., etc., etc." He did not receive the letter but discussed the contents with Lieutenant Colonel James Paterson, the British adjutant general with whom Washington met on July 20 (see Johnston, *The Campaign of 1776*, part I, pp. 96–99).

On July 12, 1776, General Howe ordered two British men-of-war, the *Phoenix* and the *Rose*, up the Hudson to bombard the town. The boats bombarded military and civilian targets on their way to Tappan Bay, where they remained six days, and returned unharmed, despite the efforts of American cannon to damage them (see Johnston, *The Campaign of 1776*, part I, pp. 99–100).

William Franklin, son of Benjamin Franklin, was governor of New Jersey and favored the Tories, remaining loyal to Britain. The New Jersey legislature ordered his arrest, and he was replaced by William Livingston, who was a patriot (see Johnston, *The Campaign of 1776*, part I, p. 111).

George Washington was fond of a card game named "whist," which is played by two sets of partners (see Leckie, *George Washington's War*, p. 129). The game is explained in Pool, *What Jane Austen Ate and Charles Dickens Knew*, p. 65.

CHAPTER XIII

★ ★ ★

*C*orporal Roy O'Malley of the Royal Fusiliers jerked erect, clacked his gaping mouth closed, dropped his axe, and reached to his right, groping for his musket while his eyes widened.

"'Ere, lookit what we got comin'," he breathed to Private Robert Willowby next to him. "Straight from the infernal pit, 'e is, just like all them savages, and fer my part we'd do well to send 'em all right back in the blink of an eye."

Willowby raised his head from stacking kindling in the wood yard where their company had been splitting firewood to heat water in the great, black kettles for wash day at the gigantic, sprawling British military base on Staten Island. He saw the four British soldiers in red coats with muskets, and he saw the swarthy skin and the partially shaved head and the feathered headgear of the man they were escorting, and the white man's shirt and coat over Indian leather breaches and beautifully beaded moccasins. Willowby slowly straightened, eyes narrowed as he studied the man walking steadily inside the square formed by the four soldiers towards the large command tent of General William Howe forty yards to the south. Others nearby slowed and stopped, looking.

Willowby pursed his mouth for a moment and reached to grasp O'Malley's arm. "Don't touch yer musket. A bloody officer see you, you'd be stood in front of a firin' squad before noon," he hissed. "That Indian's Joseph Brant, just back from a visit with the king. Right in London Town, 'e was, inside St. James's like 'e was the king of Spain, or France, talkin' with King George." Willowby shook his head in wonderment. "'Im an' George made some kind of treaty, and now 'e's on our side with all his warriors, helpin' us put down the rebels."

O'Malley grunted in disgust. "On our side, is 'e? Well, all the same I'm sleepin' with my bayonet under my blanket an' one eye open until I've seen the last of 'em."

The raucous shout from Sergeant Randall Ashcroft brought them both up short. "'Ere, you men, yer bein' paid to cut and stack firewood fer the laundry, not gawk an' talk. Now, get back to it, all of you."

This was a British military base for thirty-two thousand troops, under the command of General William Howe, one of the purest military minds in the world. Howe had established his reputation for leadership and absolute, selfless courage in the Seven Years' War when in 1759 he stripped off his officer's tunic and stood shoulder to shoulder with four hundred British regulars as they met and stopped two thousand French infantry in their tracks. Time and again he had marched at the head of his command without flinching as he led his men into withering musket and cannon fire. Thus it was that when General William Howe declared his camp would be orderly at all times, it was orderly at all times. All personnel would be in uniform at all appropriate times, and the uniforms would be clean. Clean uniforms meant washed, and washed meant hot water, and hot water meant firewood. Those who failed in performance of their duties would be warned once, confined on the second offence, flogged on the third.

The men took one last look at the Mohawk chief and once again settled into the rhythm of the wood yard. O'Malley picked up his axe and stood the next rung of pine on the battered chopping block, while Willowby began gathering another load of kindling to be stacked on a huge skid and dragged by ox team to feed the fires that would keep great kettles of laundry water boiling until sunset.

Joseph Brant strode on, eyes straight ahead, aware of those who slowed to stare as he passed, some from curiosity, others from fear, a few of the older soldiers from hatred at the bright, grotesque images burned into their memories in long-ago battles in which comrades in arms had fallen under the knives and hatchets of the Indians of the great northern confederation during the French and Indian wars.

The escort halted, facing the pickets stationed at the command tent entrance, and the picket on the right lifted the flap while Joseph entered. Inside he paused while his eyes swept the sparsely furnished room.

A large, long table stood in the center, with eight chairs on each side, two at the head, one at the foot. Four uniformed officers with gold braid on their shoulders sat on each side of the table, and all their heads turned towards him. They slowly rose to stand silently while he walked to the vacant chair at the near end of the table and sat down. No one spoke in the awkward silence while the eight men settled back onto their chairs, self-conscious, uncomfortable, trying too hard not to stare.

Minutes passed in the strained silence, and a cool midmorning east wind came gusting off the Atlantic and across the island to billow the sides and top of the great command tent and set the orderly rows of thousands of tents of the regulars flapping. The wind held, bringing a thin overcast from the sea that dimmed the August sun.

Twenty yards west of the command tent an orderly reached to lift the flap of the tent serving as living quarters for General Howe, and then came to full attention, waiting. The tall, angular general stooped to clear the top of the entrance and stepped out of his quarters, followed by his aide-de-camp, and glanced up at the overcast scudding westward. He held his gold-trimmed tricornered hat on his head as he walked steadily into the wind towards the command tent, coattails of his bright red tunic flapping.

The pickets at the entrance snapped to attention, chins sucked back, eyes locked straight ahead, and as the general approached, the one on the right reached to draw the flap, and the general again stooped to enter, followed by his aide-de-camp. Once inside he slowed and then stopped as all nine men at the table came to their feet facing him. Eight of them snapped their right hands to a salute and waited. He returned the salute, and they dropped their hands and stood at attention until he assumed his seat at the far end of the table. His chair was plain, like all others at the table.

"Be seated, gentlemen." His voice was deep, speech slow, direct, unsolicitous. He looked the length of the table at Chief Joseph Brant, nodded, and Joseph Brant nodded in return.

"Gentlemen, I am sure you're aware Chief Joseph Brant represents the sovereign Mohawk nation. He arrived from London July twenty-ninth on the *Lord Hyde* and agreed to remain here to help us deal with the rebellion." Howe paused, then added, "Chief Brant treated with King George, and the silver gorget he now wears at his throat was a gift of the king. He was also inducted into the Falcon Lodge of the Freemasons."

Howe stopped and watched to gauge the impact as the heads of all eight officers involuntarily pivoted, and for a moment they stared, surprised that a feathered, buckskinned warrior from an American Indian tribe could ever be granted audience with King George, and stunned that any lodge of the Freemasons would consider extending membership to anyone other than the high and the mighty in the ranks of blue-blooded English aristocracy. They instantly recovered their composure and turned back to General Howe.

He shifted his eyes to Brant. "Chief Brant, it would be appropriate for you to take a chair here at the head of the table."

Soundlessly Brant rose and walked to the head of the table and sat down on the chair next to Howe's, and waited.

Howe knew no other way than to plow straight into the meat of the conference without the formality of introductions or a recital of the credentials and military histories of the men whom he faced. If they didn't know each other at the start of the conference, they would when it finished.

"Gentlemen, General Washington refused my offer for a pardon, and that leaves us with no alternative."

He opened a large ledger. "For what follows, you will need to know the facts regarding the comparison between the strength of our army and that of the rebels." He dropped a finger to the open page in the ledger.

"August first, General Clinton arrived from Charleston with his ships and forces, and on August twelfth, General von Heister arrived with his Hessian forces. That brought us to full strength. At this time we have twenty-seven regiments of the line, four battalions of light infantry, four of grenadiers, two battalions of the king's guards, three brigades of artillery, and a regiment of light dragoons. Numerically we have close to thirty-two thousand troops. Of these, more than twenty-four thousand are battle ready. We will have a report on our naval forces directly, but I will say we have just over four hundred forty of our ships in and around New York Harbor at this moment."

He waited until the only sound was the wind humming in the tie-down ropes of the billowing tent. "Gentlemen, we have at our command the mightiest military armada ever gathered in the recorded history of the world."

A murmur rose and subsided.

"Governor Tryon of New York has furnished me with current estimates of the forces of the Continental army, which he has gathered through intelligence supplied him by a Sergeant Graham and a network of Tory spies. General Washington has seventy-one regiments or parts of regiments, twenty-five of which are in the Continental army. The total force is about twenty-nine thousand. However, their camps and facilities are rather, uh, rudimentary, and their forces are suffering badly from dysentery and fever. Just under ten thousand of their troops are disabled by illness. Their effective fighting force today is about twenty thousand. Mohawk scouts under the command of Chief Joseph Brant have confirmed this within the past twenty-four hours."

He closed the ledger. "I must further state, I am assured by Governor Tryon that we will be welcomed with open arms by the citizens of New York City the day we liberate them from the control of the rebels. It is probable they will vigorously help us in driving the rebels into submission."

He pursed his mouth and turned to his aide, who handed him a rolled document four feet long. With the officers assisting, they spread it out on the tabletop and anchored the corners and sides with small leather bags filled with buckshot. Instantly every man recognized the detailed, scaled map of the three islands forming New York, including the east shore of New Jersey and the western border of Connecticut. End to end, the map was eight feet long. A second, smaller map was unrolled and weighted down on top of it, and the officers recognized the scale drawing of Lake Champlain and the Hudson River valley.

"You know what these maps are. Take a few minutes and study them."

The eight officers pored over the maps in silence, occasionally tracing a line or a distance with a finger, and then each sat down.

Howe remained standing and picked up a three-foot maplewood pointer. "Let me start with first things first." He tapped the maps. "These colonies extend well over one thousand five hundred miles on the Atlantic coast. Logistically we simply cannot engage them all at one time. There aren't enough men and equipment and supplies in all England to accomplish that. For that reason, my orders are to establish a base in New York from which we can move up the Hudson River and meet General John Burgoyne coming down Lake Champlain from Canada, at Albany." He traced the river and the lake with his pointer. "When we control the Hudson River–Lake Champlain corridor, we can cut off the New England colonies from the middle and southern colonies and proceed to beat them in groups—northern, middle, southern."

He tapped the map to identify each section. "The king has

directed that we force the rebels into one great, decisive battle as soon as possible, and destroy the bulk of their army." He paused to consider. "I think the plan is militarily sound." He raised his eyes to the others, waiting for comments. There were none, and he continued.

"To execute the plan we must establish an operations base in New York, so the first problem is to decide how to take New York City with the least cost in time, lives, equipment, and supplies. In my view, Manhattan Island is indefensible because it's an island with open channels on all sides deep enough for heavy seagoing vessels. Our seaborne cannon can reach all parts from all sides." He turned to his brother Admiral Richard Howe. "What is our naval strength at this moment, and what is theirs?"

Richard Howe, equally as tall as William, equally unpolitical, blunt, with a mind keenly trained to the art of sea warfare, casually leaned back in his chair, relaxed, totally unimpressed with protocol, face unemotional as he laid it out. "We have seventy-three men-of-war, with a total of one thousand four hundred cannon, thirty-two- to thirty-six-pounders, all manned by thirteen thousand able seamen. Our guns can reach any of the fortifications on Manhattan Island, including Fort Washington, and Fort Lee on the New Jersey side. From Gowanus Bay and the East River, we can also reach all the fortifications now in place on Long Island. I estimate we could reduce Washington's fortifications on both islands to rubble in seventy-two hours of continuous day-and-night bombardment. The rebels have no navy—not one man-of-war and, so far as we know, not one seagoing ship available in or around New York." He could not repress a slow smile. "They move across the Hudson and the East River in longboats and ferries and garbage scows."

A muffled laugh rippled through the other officers.

General Howe smiled and continued. "It appears the first decision is whether we make our initial assault on New York City, here"—he tapped the map with the pointer—"or on the fortifications at Brooklyn, here." Again he tapped the map. "There are more men and more fortifications at New York than Brooklyn. If we destroyed or captured them, we would have the bigger part of the rebel army defeated and could move at our own pace to finish those on Long Island and at Fort Lee in New Jersey."

He paused and studied the map for half a minute. "The second option is Brooklyn. If we take Brooklyn first, we can establish cannon on Long Island that can reach across the East River well up the length of Manhattan, and control the east side of that island, including New York City. With Brooklyn secured, it would be little trouble to take the deep seaport and the docks and shipyards on the east side of New York City, and then the city itself. And if we move steadily, we could finish that part of the campaign before taking winter quarters in New York City."

The officers pursed their mouths as they tested the two proposals against their own hard-earned experiences of the making and breaking of massive battles, and they remained silent until General Henry Clinton interrupted.

"Seagoing cannon can destroy buildings and some fortifications, but not necessarily men. If there's one thing these rebels do better than any army I've ever seen, it's dig. They can make holes and hide in them faster than we can find them. If we're going to take their land, and hold it, we're going to have to do it with foot soldiers. Remember Bunker Hill."

He referred to June 17, 1775, when the British men-of-war in the Boston Back Bay and the Charles River blasted Charlestown to rubble and shelled the fortifications on Bunker Hill. Then they sent four thousand red-coated regulars up the hill to take it, and the rebel forces, appearing as by magic from the holes and trenches that had just been shelled, left one thousand of the British regulars dead on the grassy slopes before they ran out of ammunition and disappeared.

Howe's eyes narrowed as he considered. "Then perhaps the best thing would be to make our assault on New York City itself and avoid the risk of heavy losses taking the Brooklyn fortifications. That would give us the control we want of the entrance to the Hudson River. If we hold New York, we could lay Brooklyn under siege and starve them out. Winter's coming."

Again Clinton interrupted. "Do we have scouting reports on the roads and trails just west of Brooklyn?"

Howe turned to Joseph Brant and nodded.

Brant leaned forward. The other officers' eyes widened as he spoke in perfect English, with only the slightest hint of a Mohawk accent. None of them knew that as a younger man the fierce Mohawk warrior had received an excellent, full education in an English school in Connecticut. They listened as he spoke.

"All roads near Brooklyn are both fortified and patrolled. The Bedford Road farther east is partially patrolled. The Jamaica Road east of the Bedford Road is neither fortified nor patrolled."

Clinton leaned forward and all eyes fixed on him.

General Henry Clinton, short, stocky, one of the most experienced and respected officers in the British army, had arrived sixteen days earlier from his futile attempt to take Charleston, South Carolina, as ordered by Lord North. He had sailed the fleet under his command into the Charleston Harbor and was greeted by cannon fire from Fort Moultrie, built on Sullivan Island at the mouth of the harbor. He had ordered his men-of-war to destroy the fort, and for one day British cannon fought a close-range duel with rebel cannon.

What the British did not know was that the fort was built on soft, spongy sand, and the sixteen-foot-thick walls were built of soft palmetto logs backed by more sand. British cannonballs whistling over the walls and dropping inside the fort were burying themselves two feet into the stuff, and when they exploded, the only result was a muffled *thump* and a harmless spray of sand. Cannonballs hitting the soft palmetto logs simply disappeared. Good fortune had not smiled on Clinton that day. Three of his ships ran aground on uncharted sandbars. Two spent the day digging their way off, and the third had to be abandoned and was burned.

Rebel cannoneers in Fort Moultrie proved far superior to those on the British men-of-war, and when a well-aimed cannonball ripped the seat out of the breeches of Admiral Sir Peter Parker, commanding the fifty-gun flagship *Bristol,* he was left standing on the quarterdeck in his shredded underwear, his backside somewhat blackened, and him very much chagrined.

In the afternoon, Clinton had landed foot soldiers on the mainland with orders to march across the Breach, a narrow neck of water that had to be crossed to reach Charleston. Clinton's charts incorrectly showed the water depth at the Breach to be eighteen inches. It was in fact seven feet. When his first wave of foot soldiers dropped out of sight in the black waters of Charleston Harbor before his very eyes, to bob back to the surface fighting for air and thrashing around for something to cling to, Clinton decided the taking of Charleston could wait for another day. At eleven o'clock that night he sullenly sailed his command north to join the main force at New York.

Clinton spoke directly to Brant. "When was your last report?"

"This morning. My scouts returned at dawn."

"What is the rebel strength at Brooklyn? How much of their army is committed there?"

"Less than half. About ten thousand."

Clinton turned back to Howe. "May I make a suggestion."

Howe nodded.

"May I borrow the pointer."

Howe handed it to him and Clinton stood. "South of Brooklyn, two ridges just over a mile apart run east to west for many miles. They rise as high as one hundred fifty feet, and the south slope of those ridges, which we would have to climb, are steep—too steep to move men and artillery rapidly. Here they are." He ran the pointer the length of the two ridges. "Washington has committed the greater part of his army to defending the south ridge. He has heavy breastworks on the north ridge, about a mile behind it, but most of his troops are committed to the south."

Some officers moved in their chairs and Clinton waited until they settled. "There are four places where natural passes cut through those two ridges—Gowanus Road, here; Bedford Pass, here; Martense Lane, here where you see the Red Lion tavern; and Jamaica Pass, here." He pointed on the map as he spoke. "As you can see, the Jamaica Road and Pass are the farthest east from Brooklyn, and Chief Brant's scouts report it is not fortified or guarded."

He waited for a moment until no one was moving. "I suggest we land a sizeable force here, directly south of Brooklyn, at Gravesend Bay, and move them north." He tapped the map. "Make Washington believe we're coming at him just as we did at Bunker Hill. I think that's what he expects, by the way he's built his fortifications on the high ground. Have our force engage them and hold them there while another large force moves east under cover of darkness to the Jamaica Road, and then follows it back west, through the Jamaica Pass, to where the road comes in behind their heaviest fortifications on the south." On the map, he followed the route of the Jamaica Road, through the pass. "If we succeed, we'll have most of the rebel army in a trap, with large forces on three sides and the Gowanus Marsh and the East River on the fourth. Either they surrender, or we destroy them."

He waited while comments grew and dwindled. "We then move north and storm the north breastworks and take them. Then we set up our cannon along the west shore of Long Island for cover while we send in our second assault force on New York, which should meet little or no resistance, once we have defeated half their army at Brooklyn. The result will be exactly what the king has ordered—establish a base of operations in New York, and defeat this rebel army in one grand battle."

Howe's eyes bored into Clinton's. "You know the Jamaica Road and Pass?"

"Quite well. I spent part of my childhood on Long Island. The single place where they could cause a problem is at the pass. A small force of riflemen with one or two cannon could hold the pass for some time."

"And if the pass is unguarded?"

"We have a good road that will bring us in right behind

them on the south ridge. They won't have a chance."

Howe turned once again to Joseph Brant. "You're certain there are no fortifications at Jamaica Pass? It is unguarded?"

"Yes. As of this morning."

Howe turned back to Clinton. "Could you find the Jamaica Road and move large numbers of men over it in the dark?"

"Easily."

Howe's forehead wrinkled and his mouth narrowed as he considered. He studied the map, tapped it silently for a moment, then looked at General von Heister. "What is your opinion, sir?"

Blocky, fleshy, balding, heavy jowled, General Leopold Philip von Heister commanded the eight thousand Hessian mercenaries, among the most ruthless, feared soldiers of the time, hired for seven pounds per man per year. While von Heister could speak broken English, almost none of his troops could speak or understand one word of it, nor did they care to. This force of rented German soldiers knew nothing but the stark, brutal realities of army life, and held only contempt for what they had seen of the raw, ragtag, badly dressed, badly armed, undisciplined, misfit collection of rabble they had crossed the Atlantic to annihilate. In their blue-black and white uniforms, with their hair greased and braided down their backs, wearing their twenty-pound, hip-high thick leather military boots, and carrying their German muskets with the long bayonets, they were unable to understand why Howe did not simply land von Heister's command on either Manhattan Island or Long Island with orders to overrun the rebels and kill them all. In the Hessian opinion, they could do it themselves in two days, if Howe would but turn them loose.

Von Heister did not even look at the maps. His face was a blank, his words flat, without emotion, spoken with a heavy, clipped German accent. "Either way. Manhattan or Brooklyn. It makes little difference, because when we finish we will have them both."

Howe waited for a moment. "If we move on Brooklyn, where would you prefer to be with your command?"

Again von Heister did not look at the maps. "In the middle. Facing their largest force. The rebels cannot face our bayonets. They will run." His voice remained cold, unemotional. It was not a show of bravado. It was the only life he knew.

Howe turned to Colonel Carl Emil Kurt von Donop, second in command of the Hessians. "Colonel, what is your opinion?"

Von Donop shrugged indifferently. "I agree with Herr General von Heister. Either way. In the end, they shall be ours."

Howe turned to General Hugh, Earl Percy. "What is your opinion?"

This was the same Colonel Percy who had been sent by General Thomas Gage in response to the desperate plea from Lieutenant Colonel Francis Smith for reinforcements to save his command as their retreat from Concord on April 19, 1775, turned into a disorganized, blind, panic-driven rout clear back to Charlestown. Percy had aligned his cannon on a hill just south of Lexington and blasted shot after shot over the heads of the remains of the incoming British column, and it had slowed the swarming Patriots for a short time, but it did not stop them. Percy himself was forced to abandon his position and join the retreat. The humiliation of the battle was still bright in his memory, smarting, hurting.

He took his time answering. "If the flanking maneuver on the Jamaica Road described by General Clinton is feasible, and they do not hold the pass, it appears we should proceed against Brooklyn first. I really expect the entire campaign to be finished within two days of the time the first shots are fired."

Howe turned to General Charles, Lord Cornwallis. "Your views?"

The name Cornwallis had been identified with love and devotion to flag and king for four centuries. General Charles Cornwallis had distinguished himself as a strong leader, beloved, admired, over a long and distinguished career.

"Brooklyn." He said no more.

Howe raised a hand to slowly stroke his cheek, then his chin, while he concentrated on the maps, and considered the opinions of the men he had gathered to decide the fate of the recently declared United States of America.

America. Americans. No longer Englishmen. No longer of the family. Strangers. Yesterday our people. Today our enemy. He silently shook his head, hating the complicated politics of it, hating the sure knowledge he was going to have to unleash the greatest fighting force ever gathered by any country to do battle on foreign shores, sick in the realization his forces would be required to kill people who but short months ago had been his countrymen, his friends, his family.

In the loneliness of ultimate command, he made his decision.

"We will commence our attack on Brooklyn. This is Saturday. I am told the tides will be right next Wednesday and Thursday, August twenty-first and twenty-second. Weather permitting, we will load our troops and cross the harbor on the night of August twenty-first."

The die was cast.

Howe exhaled held breath. He unbuttoned his tunic, shrugged out of it, hung it on the back of his chair, and rolled up his sleeves. "All right, gentlemen. Now let's get down to the details."

To the north, across New York Harbor, in the northeast section of New York City, General George Washington sat in silence at the ornately carved oak table that served as his desk in the center of his private chambers on the second floor of his headquarters at the Montier house. His hands were spread flat on the desktop, head tipped forward, face pensive, somber, morose as he worked with his thoughts. The only sound was the whisper of the wind outside the windows and in the flue of the great fireplace along the wall to his left.

Idly he touched and reflected on some of the documents assembled before him. He picked up his letter of July 2, 1776, written to his army to bolster their courage as they daily watched the mighty armada of British ships gathering south of Manhattan Island.

The fate of unborn millions will now depend, under God, on the courage and conduct of this army.

He set it aside and looked at another document. August 8, 1776. General Orders to the Continental army.

As the movements of the enemy . . . give the utmost reason to believe, that the great struggle, in which we are contending for every thing dear to us, and our posterity, is near at hand—The General . . . does most anxiously exhort, both officers, and soldiers, not to be out of their quarters, or encampments, especially early in the morning, or upon the tide of flood.

He glanced at the letter he had finished and delivered only hours earlier, addressed to the New York Convention.

When I consider that the City of New York, will in all human probability very soon be the scene of a bloody conflict, I cannot but view the great numbers of women, children and infirm persons remaining in it, with the most melancholy concern. . . . Can no method be devised for their removal? . . . It would relieve me from great anxiety, if your honorable body would immediately deliberate upon it and form and execute some plan for their removal and relief; in which I will cooperate and assist to the utmost of my power.

He turned in his chair to peer out the bank of windows at the maple trees moving in the wind beneath the swirling overcast.

Outnumbered . . . out-gunned . . . untrained troops . . . unseasoned officers . . . no pay . . . poor food . . . no uniforms . . . no navy . . . a third of our army sick and disabled . . . bickering and fighting between the regiments from different regions . . . half the local citizenry ready to rise and join the British against us . . . no time left . . . Congress with no power to do anything about any of it.

He slowly stood and walked to the windows to clasp his hands behind his back and stare down at the beautiful grounds of the mansion.

Every known imperative of successful warfare is on their side . . . how do we rise above it? . . . how?

A brisk rap at the door turned him.

"Enter."

Adjutant Joseph Reed opened the door. "They're ready in the conference room, General."

"All of them?"

"Yes, sir, except General Greene, as you know."

"Thank you. I'll be along in a minute."

Reed closed the door and Washington listened as his footsteps faded down the hall, followed by the faint sound of the double doors to the conference room closing. Washington tugged his vest smooth, then the sleeves of the tunic of his blue and buff uniform, and assembled the documents into a packet. He straightened his spine, drew a long breath, raised his face, jaw set, mouth pursed, and strode steadily down the hall to the conference room, with the heels of his spurred boots tapping a solid cadence. He opened the doors without hesitation and walked into the room to the head of the great, polished conference table. Six uniformed officers stood to face him.

"Be seated, gentlemen."

While Washington laid down his packet and organized the documents before him, he glanced at the silent, expectant faces surrounding the table.

General Charles Lee. Thin, dour, cryptic, hatchet-faced, fond of strong drink, Lee had been born in England, where he rose to become one of the most respected officers in the British army before leaving England for the colonies. His military reputation followed him. It was Lee whom Washington had sent to South Carolina to meet Clinton at Charleston and thrash him at the brief battle of Fort Moultrie. He was considered by many, perhaps most, to be the best military mind in America, General George Washington not excepted, and Washington knew it. Lee himself shared the opinion, and on more than a few occasions brashly criticized his commander in chief, the Continental

Congress, and anyone else who stood in the way of his becoming the new commander of the army.

General Horatio Gates. Robust, fleshy, born in England as a descendant of Sir John Gates, privy councilor during the reign of Henry VIII, he had resigned a commission in the British army to marry into the family of a wealthy Virginia planter, a one-time neighbor to George Washington. He was considered among the most qualified officers in the Continental army.

General Israel Putnam. Ol' Put. Square, blunt, honest, simple, fearless, loved by his men, a bulldog in a battle. It was Ol' Put who had calmly stood on the breastworks at Bunker Hill and ordered his command to withhold their fire as they faced the oncoming British regulars. General Putnam knew his men had little ammunition, and he meant to make every single musket ball count. "Do not fire until you see the whites of their eyes." The first volley had been fired at less than twenty yards, and it decimated the oncoming regulars, devastated them, threw them into a panic-driven retreat, as did succeeding volleys, again and again.

Colonel Henry Knox. Young, short, rotund, a Boston bookseller who had fallen hopelessly, completely in love with cannon and had read everything available on the subject until he was clearly one of the leading authorities in the colonies. It was he who had rushed to Washington's side and volunteered to lead the expedition to Fort Ticonderoga in the dead of the winter of 1775, to bring the Ticonderoga cannon back three hundred miles to Boston and besiege General Gage's British regulars. Henry Knox had dedicated his life to two things: cannon and George Washington. Washington had appointed him commander in charge of artillery for the Continental army.

General Lord Stirling. Born in England as William Alexander, his father claimed the title of the earl of Stirling, and William had continued it, demanding he be called Lord Stirling. He had received his military experience in the British army. Balding, charismatic, mild mannered, vociferous in the field, Lord Stirling had been assigned to various lesser duties but not to a position of command in the New York campaign.

General John Sullivan. Garrulous, argumentative, somewhat charismatic, he had learned his military skills in the New Hampshire militia and been commissioned a general by Congress, not at Washington's request. Men competent in military matters were aware of gaps and lapses in Sullivan's comprehension of the fundamentals of battle.

Noticeably absent was General Nathanael Greene, whom Washington had placed in command of all military operations on Long Island.

Washington cleared his voice and came straight to it. "General Greene has been taken seriously ill with the fever and is not improving. If he is unable to continue in command, we will have to make adjustments in the Long Island command."

He waited while exclamations and strained glances were exchanged.

"Should it become necessary, General Sullivan will assume command in the place of General Greene. Lord Stirling will assume command of General Sullivan's forces. If that occurs, I will deliver written orders to all concerned."

General Sullivan's face blanched. Lord Stirling straightened, eyes wide in surprise. Lee's face clouded, and the other officers moved on their chairs and shifted their feet.

Washington continued. "Today I advised the New York Convention to evacuate the women and children and infirm from the city."

Every officer in the room knew the unwritten rule that required a commander to evacuate women, children, and infirm from their homes only if he was expecting a battle of such magnitude that the city could be demolished. For a moment they held their silence before exclamations broke out and then died, and they turned to Washington, waiting.

"I now share with you the facts regarding our situation as of today."

He picked documents from those before him and added one fact at a time, slowly, methodically building a comparison of the two forces now poised for battle. As the terrible imbalance took shape the room became increasingly quiet. When he laid the last document down the only sound in the room was the wind at the windows.

Washington stopped for a moment to organize his thoughts. "I am convinced they will attack within the next few days, and I'm inclined to believe it will come on New York City. The tides will be right on the twenty-first and the twenty-second, next Wednesday and Thursday. It will be imperative to do all we can between now and then to finish our fortifications and prepare our men."

Again he stopped to think. "I know in our previous councils we have had doubts—serious doubts—that we can defend these islands when the enemy's ships have absolute control of all sides, but we are past that now. Congress has directed us to defend New York City. Perhaps we can. We must clear our minds of all doubts, all reservations, and rise to meet this challenge."

From the documents before him, he selected the letter he had written to the army on July 2, 1776.

"I urge you strongly, each of you, to once again bring the message of my letter of July second to your commands." He raised the letter and read. " 'The fate of unborn millions will now depend, under God, on the courage and conduct of this army. Our cruel and unrelenting enemy leaves us no choice but a brave resistance, or the most abject submission; this is all we can expect. We have therefore to resolve to conquer or die: Our own country's honor, all call upon us for a vigorous and manly exertion, and if we now shamefully fail, we shall become infamous to the whole world. Let us therefore rely upon the goodness of the cause, and the aid of the Supreme Being, in whose hands victory is, to animate and encourage us to great and noble actions.' "

He stopped and laid the letter down, and no man moved as a quiet influence settled into the room. Every man present had dedicated his life to the art and science of warfare, and every man had been personal witness to destruction of cities and heart-wrenching scenes of soldier and civilian alike, torn, maimed, crippled, killed by cannon and musket shot and raging fire, and they had been hardened and calloused by it. None held any illusion about the holocaust that was coming. And yet, with the words of General Washington still in their ears, a strange, subtle influence crept into their souls to raise a quiet voice. *The Supreme Being is watching. This is his work.*

Washington cleared his throat, and the impression faded as all eyes came back to him. "If you need another copy of this letter, Adjutant Reed has them, and again I urge you, share it with your men. The British have military superiority. We have the Almighty."

He paused, and still no one moved.

"Now, gentlemen, you have questions. Let us begin."

With the sun touching the western skyline, casting long shadows across the East River towards Long Island and the Brooklyn fortifications, Billy and Eli sat on freshly mounded black dirt packed against the timbers of the breastworks. In bone-weary silence they spooned tasteless hot gruel from their bowls and chewed tough brown bread and washed it down with cold canteen water, while the wind fluttered their sweaty shirts and dried their hair, plastered to their foreheads. Finished, they sat for a time without moving, exhausted, gathering strength and the will to go wash their utensils and move to their blankets.

Billy stood and started towards the campground of the Boston regiment, and Eli followed. They dipped their bowls and spoons in the kettle of hot, cloudy, soapy water, then rinsed in the clear, and walked to their blankets, where they eased down, dropped their utensils, and rolled onto their backs, one arm thrown over their eyes.

Company Nine had begun work on a new section of breastworks at four A.M. in the light of lanterns. They paused at noon to stand by their shovels and eat stale cheese and black bread and drink from their canteens, then bowed their backs and worked until seven P.M. when Sergeant Turlock called them for supper. They had paid no attention to the wind and the overcast, nor had the wind prevented the sweat that soaked them, dripping from their chins and noses.

They lay without moving for twenty minutes before Billy spoke, arm still over his eyes. "Turlock asked me to check on our sick."

Eli could hear the dread in Billy's voice, and seconds passed before he moved his arm and rolled up to a sitting position and glanced at Billy. "Let's go."

They stopped at the cook tent to cut three loaves of the hard black bread into thick slices and drop it into a large fire-blackened bucket before they trudged across the camp to the sprawling hospital compound. The hastily built log hospital had long since been filled with men doubled over from dysentery and mumbling with fever dreams, and it was now surrounded by twenty-two huge tents. Inside each, cots were jammed wherever they would fit, and in some tents men were laid on blankets beneath the cots. The doctors and nurses had forgotten time in their endless rounds, and took snatches of sleep only when they could go no further.

The stench of unbathed bodies and unchanged bedding hung in the air like a wall, ten feet before Billy and Eli reached the tent where seven of the men of Company Nine were held. Eli lifted the flap while Billy entered, and Eli followed. They clamped their mouths shut and breathed shallow while they worked their way to their men.

Billy knelt beside a cot where an old man lay on his side beneath a ragged blanket, knees drawn up in pain. Billy touched his shoulders and the man's eyes opened to look up at Billy, trying to focus, to understand.

"It's me. Billy Weems from your company. I brought you some bread."

The craggy old head nodded, and the man again closed his eyes and settled back.

"I'll leave it here." Billy lifted the blanket and put a slice of the bread in the gnarled old hand, then rose and moved on to stop beside another cot, where a balding man lay on his back, breathing heavily, face flushed. Billy knelt and touched the man's forehead and glanced up at Eli, and the man looked at him, eyes wide as he spoke too loud through parched lips.

"I'll be reporting for duty in the morning, Captain. Just a touch of fever. Much better than yesterday—much better. Yes, sir, I'll be ready tomorrow. March for Boston. That's where the British are. Boston. I'll be ready, sir."

Billy nodded. "Good. We can use you. Thirsty?"

The man ran his swollen tongue over his cracked lips. "No, sir. Use the water for those who need it. I'll be ready to report in the morning, sir."

Eli moved quickly to the nearest water bucket and returned with the dipper and handed it to Billy.

Carefully Billy raised the man's head and lowered the dripping wooden dipper. "We've got a little extra water. Better not waste it."

"Are you sure, sir? Have the others got enough? I'll be ready in the morning, Captain."

"We have enough. Take a sip."

The man closed his eyes, and Billy patiently held the dipper to the pale lips, and the man sipped, then drank.

"Thank you, sir. What time do we leave for Boston in the morning? Early? If we leave early we'll get ahead of the heat. I'll be there, sir."

"We leave early. You'll need some bread for the march." Billy handed him a thick slice of the hard bread.

"I have my knapsack packed, sir. Plenty of rations. Plenty."

"I know. But you take that. The others have theirs."

The man's eyes were too bright, his expression too intense. "Are you sure, sir?"

"I'm sure. Go to sleep. You'll need rest for the march."

"Yes, sir. I'll do that, sir. Thank you, sir."

Once again Billy touched the man's forehead, burning with fever, then rose and walked on. Eli glanced back, then at Billy, and said nothing.

Five more times they stopped to kneel beside men too feeble to rise. They left bread, and held the water dipper, and made their best judgment on how many would recover, how many would not. In full dusk they walked out of the tent, away from the smell of sickness and death, breathing deep in the fresh wind and made their way to a second tent. Inside, nurses and men moved about in yellow lamplight, carrying water, bandages, carbolics, lime juice, soup, doing what they could to ease the suffering of men whom they did not know how to heal. The two men worked through the press of people to where two more of their company lay on cots.

Billy leaned forward to gently touch the shoulder of a boy lying on his side, doubled up, face to the tent wall, eyes closed. His long hair was matted, and his cheeks showed a growth of soft yellow hair. He had shaved but once in his life. He did not move at Billy's touch, and Billy shook his shoulder gently. One hand slipped from beneath the blanket to dangle limply.

Billy suddenly caught his breath and shoved two fingers against the young throat, and it was cold, lifeless, and Billy sucked air and bolted upright, white faced, struggling to recover from the shock. Eli stooped to touch the boy's throat, and all the air went out of him, and for a moment he did not move, eyes closed, face a mask of pain. Then he drew the blanket up and covered the face, and he and Billy turned away and stopped the nearest nurse.

"The boy over there on the cot. He's gone."

The portly nurse sighed and moved an errant wisp of hair from her face. "I'll see to it." She walked towards the cot, and Billy and Eli looked for the second man from their company.

He was not there. Billy stopped the nearest man carrying a water dipper. "The man that was over there this morning, from Company Nine? Black hair, black beard?"

The attendant shook his head. "We lost him last night, with three others. Are you kin?"

"No. Same company."

The man said nothing and moved on, and Billy and Eli turned to leave, when they were stopped in their tracks.

From behind someone shouted, "Catch her!"

The two men pivoted to see a nurse carrying a basin of steaming water stagger, stumbling, eyes downcast, struggling to keep her balance and hold the basin from spilling. Billy dropped the bread bucket and in two strides was there. He grabbed the basin with one hand and thrust his arm around the waist of the woman with his other and felt her full weight collapse against him, and then Eli was there and caught the unconscious woman up in his arms like a child, and he peered into her face and froze.

Mary Flint!

Billy's mouth dropped open, and he set the steaming basin on the dirt floor and reached to put his hand on her forehead as the doctor pushed through the crowded room.

"Fever! She's caught it," Billy exclaimed.

The doctor pushed Billy aside and placed the flat of his hand on her forehead, then on her cheek. His face clouded. "Bring her to my quarters at once."

"Where are your quarters?" Eli challenged without moving.

"At the rear of the tent."

Eli shook his head. "Not her. We're taking her out of here."

The doctor thrust his face forward, white, chin trembling. "I am a colonel in the Continental army and I am ordering you to bring that woman to my quarters immediately."

Eli turned on his heel and Billy moved ahead of him, clearing a way in the yellow lamplight as the two walked out the front of the tent into the darkness and fresh air, the doctor following, threatening them at every step. They paid him no heed as they marched through the center of the regimental camp in the flickering light of the evening campfires, while men stopped to stare at them. Billy stopped in front of the command tent of Colonel Israel Thompson and the picket challenged him.

"I'm Corporal Billy Weems, Ninth Company, Boston regiment. You know Eli Stroud by now. The woman he carries is Mary Flint, Patriot, and she's sick. The man behind Eli is a doctor. We're not going to leave her in the hospital compound. Tell Colonel Thompson."

"You're ordering me to interrupt the colonel over a sick woman?" The picket shook his head insolently.

Eli spoke. "You do it or I will."

The picket sobered and swallowed, and hesitated for a moment in indecision. Eli took a step and the picket turned and disappeared through the tent flap. Three minutes later Colonel Thompson stooped to clear the tent entrance and stood in his shirtsleeves in the firelight. "What's this about?"

Eli stepped forward with Mary in his arms. Her head was tipped forward, leaned against his chest. "Her. Mary Flint. She's sick. We're not going to leave her down there with the others."

Thompson looked at the doctor, who was fuming, eyes ablaze. "You're the doctor at the hospital compound?"

"Doctor Lemuel Hardesty. I want that woman in my quarters for treatment, immediately."

"Are your quarters in one of the hospital tents?"

"They are."

Thompson hesitated but for one moment. "How long has she been working with you?"

"Six days. I don't think she's slept in the last three."

"I appreciate your concern, Doctor. Would you have strong objection to allowing me to place her in the quarters of my personal physician, so he can attend her around the clock?"

Hardesty exhaled and his shoulders slumped and all the fight went out of him. "No." He rubbed his hand across tired eyes and looked at Thompson. "She'll be better off here. I'll come check from time to time. I'm, uh, sorry. I didn't know who these men were or where they were taking her. Things aren't good at the hospital and . . . I just didn't want . . ." The sentence trailed off unfinished.

"I know, Doctor. She'll have the best care we can give. Thank you for all you're doing. Come back any time."

Hardesty turned, and Billy watched him thread his way back

through the campfires, thin, pinched shoulders hunched forward, head down in the firelight.

Thompson motioned to Eli. "Bring her into my quarters for now, and then you two better get back to your duties." He turned to the picket. "Find my doctor and bring him here at once."

Ninety-seven miles east and north, in a small meadow beside a winding dirt road in the colony of Connecticut, Brigitte Dunson and thirteen other people sat cross-legged around a campfire, weary, exhausted, each clasping a pewter mug of steaming coffee, blowing to cool it as they stared at the dancing flames, letting their thoughts go where they would. Beside her sat Caleb, staring vacantly into the dancing flames as he blew on his coffee, then sipped noisily. Tucked under his leg was his ever-present tablet, half-filled with notes and impressions of the journey from which he was going to write an account of this small corner of the war and instantly change the world of journalism. He patted his coat pocket to be certain he had not lost his pencil, then again sipped at his coffee.

Six days earlier, with the morning star pale in the east, the fourteen of them, six women and eight men, had hitched sixteen horses to four wagons in the city of Boston, checked the heavy loads to be certain the boxed cartridges, blankets, medicine, shoes, and barrels of dried beef were tied down solid, and taken their places on the drivers' seats and on top of the loads. Two mounted, armed riders led, with the four wagons spaced out in a column behind.

Over the hot objections of the men, Brigitte had planted her feet, hands on her hips, and demanded she be allowed to drive one of the wagons, despite the fact she had never held the reins to a four-horse team in her life. In angry frustration the men had finally let her mount the driver's seat in the last wagon, showed her how to hold the reins, and warned her she would be relieved at her first mistake. Then they had put the rising sun at their backs and gigged the horses forward onto the rutted road running from

Boston, through Connecticut, to New York City, amid the cheers and tearful good-byes of friends and loved ones.

The first three days Brigitte had learned to thread the reins between her fingers and keep them tight, feeling the tug and rhythm of the rise and fall of the head of a pulling horse. The second three days she had learned to talk to them. Each morning she and Caleb had helped mount the horse collars, buckle on the harnesses, and snap the traces to the singletrees, and each night they had helped unhitch until they could do it all alone.

A look of grim satisfaction crossed her face. *If the weather holds, and we can keep the pace, we'll be in New York in five more days. Maybe four.*

Across the circle, a young man set his smoking coffee mug in the grass and rose. "I think I'll be makin' a round to be sure the horses are settled for the night." His Irish accent was marked. Quietly he walked away towards the stand of maple where the wagons stood with their wheels blocked for the night. The horses were hobbled just beyond, near a small stream and strong grass.

He had said his name was Cullen. He was quiet, did his share, kept to himself, and made a round of the wagons and horses each night alone, just before they all went to their blankets.

He was the same blocky young Irishman with the long sandy-red hair who had appeared at the South Church in Boston nearly a month ago, when Silas had allowed the women to use the church to tie cartridges. The shy young man had held his threadbare cap in his hand and offered his services for the trip through Connecticut so he could join the Continental army in New York, and Brigitte had said come back in about three weeks when we leave, perhaps we can use you.

Brigitte tracked him with narrowed eyes until he disappeared in the darkness. *What do we really know about him? Why did he join us? Where does he go when he walks out there at night?*

Notes

The Mohawk chief Joseph Brant visited King George III in England, treated with him, and received an engraved silver gorget as a gift from the king. He was admitted a member of the Falcon Lodge of the Freemasons. He and his Mohawk Indians assisted General Howe in the battle of Long Island (see Bolton and Wilson, *Joseph Brant*, pp. 10–17, 46; see also Leckie, *George Washington's War*, p. 298).

Dysentery and fever were near epidemic proportions and disabled about one-third of George Washington's army (see Johnston, *The Campaign of 1776*, part I, p. 125, footnote).

The numbers of British soldiers, sailors, and ships as given here are accurate. It was the mightiest armada in the history of the world, to that time (see Higginbotham, *The War of American Independence*, pp. 151–52).

General Henry Clinton was sent to Charleston, South Carolina, to attack and occupy the city. To do so he had to take Fort Moultrie on Sullivan Island at the mouth of Charleston Harbor. Fort Moultrie was built of palmetto logs and sand. Clinton failed. The American cannoneers blew the seat out of British admiral Peter Parker's breeches, leaving him on his flagship quarterdeck with his underwear blackened but otherwise not harmed. Clinton thought the water depth at the Breach was less than two feet, when it was actually seven, and many of his troops simply sank over their heads before his eyes. Three of his ships ran aground, one of which burned (see Leckie, *George Washington's War*, pp. 230–31).

General Henry Clinton was born and raised in New York, the son of a British admiral who was also governor of New York at one time (see Leckie, *George Wasghington's War*, p. 148).

General Charles Lee was sent by George Washington to Charleston, South Carolina, to engage and repulse General Clinton at the battle of Fort Moultrie. Lee participated, but his contribution was minimal (see Leckie, *George Washington's War*, p. 229).

For political purposes, Congress directed General Washington to defend New York (see Higginbotham, *The War of American Independence*, p. 151).

While General William Howe has generally been given credit for the plan by which the British forces attacked the Continental army on Long Island, the plan was actually Clinton's (see Higginbotham, *The War of American Independence*, p. 155).

CHAPTER XIV

★ ★ ★

*T*he screaming wind ripped great branches from the trees on the south side of Long Island and sent them hurtling north to smash against the rocks and brush and other trees inland, and against the barns and buildings of the farmers and the villagers of Utrecht and Gravesend and Flatbush and Bedford on the flat ground that sloped up from the sea to the first of the two high, wooded ridges south of Brooklyn.

Overhead, lightning leaped jagged through thick, low clouds that raced with the wind, and great bolts struck downward to shatter rocks or thrashing trees, or leave huge smoking trenches in the ground as the midnight storm reached the height of its fury. Six-foot sea swells, whipped to a white frenzy, rolled in from the Atlantic to crash into Gravesend Bay and through the Narrows, up the Hudson and East Rivers, tearing small craft from their moorings, battering them against the rocks and the great, black pilings of the wharves and docks on the east shore of Manhattan Island.

British regulars on Staten Island and American soldiers on Manhattan and Long Islands snatched their muskets and rifles and knapsacks and sought low ground, to crouch behind anything that would break the whistling wind while they clung to their hats and weapons, deafened by the roar of the wind, eyes clenched shut as the black world flashed white in the unending lightning, and thunderclaps shook them and the ground.

On the west shore of Long Island, just above the Narrows, Eli wedged himself in a crack between two great boulders and sat down. He leaned forward and jammed his hands over his ears, his long rifle locked between his knees, over his shoulder, muzzle plugged with a chunk of peeled maple branch. The wind tore at his hair and his shirt, and he clenched his eyes shut against the stinging, flying grit scoured from the beach. He dropped one hand to press the side of his shirt to be certain the pad and pencil and the telescope were still there, and then he clamped the hand over his ear once more.

In a world filled with blackness broken by brilliant light and with roaring wind and thunder that made the ground tremble, time blurred. It was after one o'clock when a great, crooked finger of lightning reached a thousand feet down to shatter a pitching maple tree eighty feet inland from Eli and leave it a shattered, smoking stump, and Eli felt the tingle in his feet and legs as the terrible power went to ground and spread. It was close to two o'clock when a second arcing lightning bolt flashed and struck a tall rock less than forty feet south and blew it into a million fragments, some small and molten hot, and they came pelting on the wind, and Eli hunched lower.

At half past two Eli felt a slackening in the wind, and at three o'clock it had softened to a gale. The overcast moved inland to the north, and the lightning dwindled to spasmodic flashes that grumbled on the far northern horizon, and then it was gone. At half past four, the wind was a breeze. A quarter moon was dropping towards the New Jersey coastline, and endless stars sprinkled the black velvet dome overhead.

Eli stood in the darkness and stretched cramped muscles, listening for a moment to the strangeness of near silence. He brushed the grit from his leather shirt and breeches, shook it from his hair, pulled the plug from the muzzle of his rifle, and walked to where the water lapped against the shore. Across the Narrows, on Staten Island, he watched as tiny points of light began to appear, randomly at first, then soon forming lines and then squares as the British army shook off the storm and lighted the fires they needed to start camp repairs. A little past five o'clock, with the pre-dawn gray at his back, Eli could make out the forest of masts of the British armada before him, sails furled and lashed against the storm, riding calmly at anchor.

With the first arc of the rising sun setting their sails afire, Eli watched five men-of-war hoist their anchors dripping from the water and slowly move south towards Gravesend Bay, to his left. He drew the telescope from inside his shirt, extended it, and concentrated to read the names on their bows. Then he reached for the pad and pencil and carefully printed, *Greyhound, Phoenix, Rose, Thunder,* and *Carcass.* The last two ships were smaller, and there was something different about their cannon ports. He made notes and a sketch.

While they were yet half a mile distant he retreated into the battered scrub oak and bushes, to higher ground where the Narrows were before him and the entire panorama of Gravesend Bay lay east, to his left. He settled into a stand of trees and rocks on a small knoll, where he could see everything and still remain invisible. He silently tracked the big men-of-war as they took up positions around the bay, opposite De Nyse's ferry, opened their cannon ports, and rolled the black muzzles of their guns forward into the brilliant sun.

His forehead wrinkled in question. *What are they doing? Those guns can't reach Gravesend or Flatbush.* Suddenly he realized, and his breath came short. *Those ships are for cover. They're going to bring the army over!*

The sun was an hour high when Eli rested the telescope over a rock and studied the beach on the near side of Staten Island. He watched tiny red dots assemble and then move down to waiting boats where they systematically boarded. The blades of the long oars were lowered into the water and then began their rhythmic stroking, and the boats swung around and took a heading directly across the Narrows, under the protection of the guns of the warships. Eli did not move as he watched them move towards Gravesend Bay, with the oar blades dripping water that sparkled in the bright morning sunlight. For a time it seemed the Narrows were covered with small, bobbing craft, filled with red-coated soldiers, and then they were at the bay, and slowly the detail of both the troops and the boats defined itself. Once again Eli drew out the pencil and pad and quickly made crude drawings, and began the crucial count of men, boats, and artillery.

The first of the boats were strung out nearly one mile when they reached the beach, and sailors dropped overboard into the knee-deep surf to throw their backs against ropes and drag the vessels scraping onto the sandy, rocky soil. The troops inside jumped onto the land and formed into regiments, with their officers barking orders and pointing directions.

Eli's eyes narrowed as he saw six men not wearing military uniforms draw off to themselves, and quickly he brought them into focus with the telescope.

Mohawks.

He watched them talking, gesturing among themselves for a few seconds, then walk to an officer and again talk, and then they turned east and fell into single file, trotting up the beach.

The thought flashed in Eli's mind, *Jamaica Pass!*

He remained where he was, hidden, methodically counting, making marks on his pad. With the boats empty, the sailors shoved them back into the water, scrambled on board, and once again began the stroking of oars to turn them and line out for Staten Island for the next wave of assault troops. It was approaching noon when Eli watched the flotilla disgorge their last loads and turn back to Staten Island, finished.

He stared in awe at what lay before him. Gravesend beach was a mass of red-coated soldiers, baggage, food in barrels and crates, cannon, arms, ammunition, medicine, all segregated, in great orderly stacks. While Eli watched and made rough sketches on his pad, the British spread north and east with their arms and supplies and cannon, establishing themselves on the great, broad plains sloping up from the water's edge of Gravesend Bay, six miles east to west, and five miles northward towards the first of the two long ridges on which the Americans had entrenched themselves. Their movements were organized, steady.

Four thousand of those first arrived had long since fallen into marching formation under the command of an officer and moved inland with six cannon, marching towards the village of Flatbush.

From the corner of his eye Eli caught movement to his left and brought his telescope to bear, and froze, startled. Scattered through the tangle of oak and maple he caught flashes of sunlight on homespun and buckskin and realized an American force of unknown size or origin was moving south, on a collision course with the four thousand British troops moving north towards Flatbush. The Americans stopped, then reversed themselves and began moving north, staying ahead of the British, just out of musket range, avoiding a fight as they continued north, testing the British intent. Within minutes, north of the Americans, dark smoke rose from the woods and spread against the blue sky as twenty men under orders of the American leader ran ahead of the main force, burning wheat fields and crops and outbuildings storing food supplies, and slaughtering animals belonging to the farmers of Flatbush, to keep them from falling into British hands.

The British ignored the Americans and continued north, to warily approach the outskirts of the small village, not knowing what to expect. They were welcomed with open arms by the Tories who had remained, while panic-stricken Patriots swiftly loaded their most precious belongings into wagons and disappeared northward on trails and paths through the thick brush and trees. Eli heard but one single cracking musket shot in the far distance before the village of Flatbush was occupied by the British.

He glanced upward. The sun was past its zenith, and he judged the time at about two o'clock in the afternoon. He brought his telescope to bear on the beach south and west of him and watched carefully to be certain no British forces were circling his position from the west. Satisfied, he continued to study the British movements, careful to keep mental track of movements into the dense trees and brush northward that could make an entire regiment of men invisible.

A little past three o'clock he jerked forward and adjusted the telescope, and they were there. The six Mohawk Indians came trotting single file along the shoreline and did not stop until they reached a British officer with much gold on his shoulder epaulets, sparkling in the sun. The Mohawk leader spoke for half a minute, pointing back towards the east, and the British officer stood with his hands clasped behind his back, listening intently. The officer said something, the Mohawk answered, they spoke for two or three minutes, and the British officer nodded, said something, and the Mohawk led his small command west to their tiny pile of belongings, laid down their muskets, and dug out their canteens.

By four o'clock half the British forces had their tents erected in orderly rows and squares on the slopes of Gravesend, segregated according to regiment. Their command tent was near the center, of modest size, not the great one requiring a center pole and sixty tie-downs. Before it the Union Jack fluttered proudly on a fifty-foot pole. Eli made a crude sketch of the command tent and once again went over the entire campsite with the telescope. Men were digging latrines and garbage pits and gathering rocks to build fire pits.

With the sun settling towards the New Jersey coast, Eli kept low as he backed off the low knoll, turned, and angled to the northwest towards the east shore of New York Harbor. He avoided the skyline, and paused every hundred yards to hold his breath and listen, but there were only the dwindling, distant sounds of a military camp and occasionally the scurry of some-thing small and furry dodging through the tangle of brush and brambles.

Once close to New York Harbor he followed the shoreline north, then angled back east past the great Gowanus marsh, with the stench of stagnant waters and dying things, to the fortifica-tions and breastworks of the Continental army that now reached nearly three miles inland, eastward. At dusk he stopped before the quarters of Colonel Israel Thompson and waited while the picket announced him, and one minute later was standing across the table from the colonel, notepad in hand.

Thompson was seated. "I was worried we'd lost you. Was the storm bad?"

"As bad as I've ever seen." Eli laid the notepad and then the telescope and pencil on the table.

"Any rain down there?"

"No. Wind. Lightning, thunder."

Thompson shook his head. "Killed four men here. Three were officers." He brought his eyes to Eli's, and Eli had never seen him so intensely focused. "What's going on down there?"

"I made some notes." He pointed to the pad, but Thompson did not immediately look at it. He wasted no time.

"How many troops?"

"About fifteen thousand."

Thompson rounded his mouth and blew air. "Where?"

"On the plains north of Gravesend Bay."

"Over how big an area?"

"Maybe six miles east to west, and over five to the north."

"Anyone move inland?" Thompson held his breath.

"About four thousand men. They took Flatbush without a fight. I heard only one musket shot and I think it was by accident."

Thompson exhaled and his shoulders dropped. "Any of their troops dressed in dark blue?"

Eli stopped for a moment, searching his memory. "No. All red coats."

Thompson's face clouded as he muttered to himself, "What's Howe doing with his Hessians? Holding them back for what? Are these troops on Long Island just a decoy while Howe attacks New York with the rest of his troops and Hessians?"

He spoke to Eli. "Did the British set up a camp?"

"Yes. Including a command tent and flagpole."

"Tell me about the command tent."

"Not big. There's a sketch in the notepad." Eli pointed to his pad.

"Sounds like a field tent, not a permanent one. Did they prepare to stay for a while? dig latrines? garbage pits?"

"Yes. And fire pits."

"How many boats to move their troops?"

"Eighty-eight."

"All the same kind?"

"No. Seventy-five flatboats, eleven squared off at both ends like I've never seen before, and two long ones with a dozen oars on each side."

"Flatboats, bateaux, and galleys," Thompson said quietly. "How many cannon?"

"The little boats didn't have any. There were five men-of-war and it looked like they—"

"I mean cannon with the ground troops. How many did they bring ashore?"

"Forty. The bunch that took Flatbush had six with them."

"How much time to move all that across the Narrows?"

"Three hours, maybe a little more."

Thompson's eyes widened in disbelief. "Three hours!" he exclaimed. "With all their supplies and luggage?"

Eli nodded but said nothing.

"Anyone move east?"

Eli leaned forward on stiff arms, palms flat on the table. "Six Mohawk. Gone for half a day and returned to report. I'm betting they scouted the Jamaica Pass. Do we have men there?"

Thompson shrugged, eyebrows arched, concern etched on his face. "I don't know. I presume we do."

Eli straightened. "Someone better find out. Those Mohawk were the first to leave and the first to report back. That wasn't by accident."

"I'll see to it General Washington hears. Is there anything else? Anything I missed?"

Eli shook his head. "Those notes might help."

Thompson stood. "You need to know about some things that happened while you were gone. General Greene was taken across to New York, out of his head with fever. General Sullivan's been given command here."

"He know this island?"

"No. Not very well."

"Somebody better tell him what's east of here. Jamaica Pass and those other roads."

"I'll give him your report." Thompson picked up the notepad. "When did you eat last?"

"Yesterday."

"Go eat and get some rest."

"One thing. How's Mary Flint?"

"Doing better. Her fever broke about noon. She's weak, but she's mending."

"Your surgeon still in charge?"

"She's in his quarters."

Eli nodded approval and turned to go.

Thompson called after him. "Would you like to see her?"

Eli paused for a moment in thought. "Does she know what happened? how she got to your surgeon's tent?"

"I told her."

"Maybe I'll go see her."

"Tell the doctor I sent you."

Eli ducked out the tent entrance into the darkness. Campfires flickered everywhere, and he shook his head at the havoc still showing from the storm. Wreckage from trees was still scattered, mixed with torn blankets and articles of clothing and knapsacks that had not yet been claimed. Weary men moved about, hunting.

Eli worked his way thirty yards south to the surgeon's tent. Inside, a single lantern glowed. He walked to the picket, who raised his musket.

"No admission here. This is the surgeon's tent."

"I know. Colonel Thompson sent me here to see Mary Flint."

The picket hesitated. "You know her?"

Eli nodded. "I brought her here."

"You got written orders from the colonel?"

"No. Is the doctor here?"

"Not right now." He dropped his eyes for a moment. "Only a minute?"

Eli nodded and handed the picket his rifle, and the picket drew back the flap and Eli ducked to enter.

She lay curled on her side beneath a blanket, her back to the canvas tent wall, and Eli went to one knee beside the cot. The dark eyes were closed, and small curls of dark hair were on her forehead, damp from light perspiration. Her face was peaceful, sallow in the yellow lantern light, and her breathing was slow and deep. For long moments Eli studied her quiet face and the hand that lay limp on the pillow, and he let his thoughts take him back to the night they had ferried the Boston regiment across the East River with a dead man on the top of her wagon, and he had told her of how he had lost his family, and she had wept.

I hope you find peace. I hope you find a good man who can give you children and make you forget all the pain. I hope so.

He rose soundlessly and had nearly reached the entrance when her quiet voice came from behind. "Eli? Is that you?"

He turned and retraced his steps and knelt again beside her cot. "I didn't mean to wake you."

"I'm glad you did. Colonel Thompson told me what happened. Thank you."

"It was Billy."

"Billy helped. You're the one who brought me here."

Eli dropped his eyes for a moment. "Go back to sleep. You need rest. The doctor said you'll be all right."

She smiled and her eyes lighted. "Thank you. Tell Billy."

Eli rose and smiled down at her and silently walked out the entrance of the tent into the night.

Sixty-two miles to the east, past the border of the colonies of Connecticut and New York, Cullen rose from the campfire and glanced around at the weary, exhausted faces of the others, lined by the dancing flames. He gestured towards the four wagons, standing beneath a quarter moon and the stars, twenty yards north on the edge of the small flat where they had stopped at dusk to make camp. The horses were hobbled just beyond, eyes glowing red in the firelight.

"I'm thinkin' I'll make a round of the livestock and wagons," he said quietly. No one moved or commented as he walked away to disappear in the darkness, as he had done every night since they left Boston.

Brigitte drew and released a great breath, then rose and gestured to Caleb. Together they walked to where their blankets were spread on two heavy tarps in the wild grass, five feet apart. They slumped down and pulled off their shoes and tucked them beneath the tarp to protect them from the heavy dews of morning, and watched as others, one and two at a time, rose to move to their blankets.

Caleb carefully pushed his notepad beneath his tarp and sat still, lost for a moment in his own thoughts. *Three more days . . . tonight and two more nights . . . our army and theirs . . . the greatest battle ever . . . I'll be there to record it . . . easy . . . just write down what I see . . . that's the secret . . . Mother will be surprised . . . proud . . . I wonder how she is tonight . . . Adam and Prissy . . . what they had for supper.*

Brigitte reached to pull the bandana from her hair, and paused to let her thoughts run. *A bath . . . hot water in a tub . . . in the kitchen . . . soap . . . sitting in the hot water . . . every muscle relaxing . . . the steam rising . . . rinsing . . . fresh hot water for my hair . . . the feel and smell of soap in my hair . . . the warm rinse cascading . . . Mother with a towel . . . a great, soft towel . . . warm and clean in a great, soft towel . . . my bed . . . my pillow . . . my thick comforter.*

She swallowed and pushed the thoughts away.

The six women in the small wagon column had had but one chance to bathe since they left Boston, in the dark following supper three days ago at a small, hidden pool fed by an icy mountain stream. With no soap, they had had but a few minutes to rinse themselves as best they could and briskly rub themselves dry with small hand towels from knapsacks. There had been no chance to wash their hair, and they had silently dressed themselves, teeth chattering in the chill of the night.

Brigitte motioned to Caleb, and they knelt facing each other and bowed their heads, and Brigitte spoke. "Almighty God, we thank thee . . ."

They said their "Amen" and then silently opened their blankets and slipped inside, fully dressed, in their stocking feet. They closed their eyes and in moments were lost in deep, dreamless sleep.

From deep inside an insistent command reached Brigitte's brain and she ignored it. It came again and she stirred, and it came again and she opened her eyes to narrowed slits in the blackness and battled to make sense of where she was and what was nudging her shoulder. She swallowed at the stale taste in her mouth and turned her head to stare upward, trying to focus, to understand the ball of yellow light suspended over her head in the black world.

She blinked and dug at her eyes with her hand, and once again tried to focus. The ball of light became a lantern, and above it was a face staring back at her, and above the face was a black tri-cornered hat edged with gold. The lantern rose and Brigitte saw the red coat and crossed white belts and the white breeches and polished black boots, and her forehead wrinkled as she puzzled at how a British officer got into her bedroom, and then she jerked upright and threw back her blanket, horrified, as understanding struck white-hot into her brain.

A strong hand clamped onto her shoulder. "Easy, miss. It'd be a bloody shame to do you harm when there's no need of it."

Brigitte swatted at the hand and tried to gather her legs to leap up, and the captain caught her by both arms and pinned them at her sides and jerked her upright and held her at arm's length. She kicked at him and he took it, and then he spun her around and locked her arms behind her.

To her right Caleb came from his blankets shouting at the captain, "You let her go," and a British regular caught him around the neck from behind and forced him to his knees, clawing at the arm around his throat, wild-eyed, frantic.

Brigitte wrenched against the hold on her arms and gasped at the pain in her elbows, and turned her head to scream, "Let go of me, let go of me."

The captain held her steady, firm. "Miss, you'll have to stop struggling or I'll order you bound and gagged."

"You wouldn't dare," Brigitte shouted, and the captain turned to two regulars standing behind him.

"Bind and gag her."

The two grasped her arms roughly and crossed her wrists behind her back, and one began wrapping them with rope.

She stopped struggling and her head slumped forward. "I'll stop. Don't tie me."

The captain raised a hand and the two regulars released her. She turned to face the captain, rubbing her arms. "What's the meaning of this?"

"In due time."

For the first time Brigitte looked about the camp. Half a dozen lanterns cast their small circle of yellow light, and suddenly she realized that everyone in the wagon column was captive, taken in their sleep. Two soldiers were gathering wood, while others forced the captives to the center of camp around the coals of last night's fire. Their muskets loomed larger than life in the dim light, and the bayonets reflected the golden glow.

Brigitte looked to the east, where the morning star still shined brightly. "What time is it?"

"About four A.M., ma'am."

"Do you know where you are? . . . that the Continental army will be here this morning?"

The captain smiled. "We're in Connecticut, ma'am, and your Continental army is in New York." He turned. "Gather them all by the fire."

They stood in stocking feet in the wet grass, feeling the cold morning dew soak through, white-faced, silent, ringed by twelve regulars, each with a musket and bayonet, faces impassive, eyes constantly moving, watching everything. The two who had gathered the wood stirred the ashes in the fire pit, blew on them until they glowed, set twigs and then sticks, then chunks of wood while the fire grew.

The captain clasped his hands behind his back and faced his captives. "I am Captain Gerald Hornaby of the British army. You are all prisoners of war. Each of you will continue in your daily duties. You will drive the wagons, make camp, prepare the meals, and tend the stock, just as you have done. I expect you will have thoughts of escape. I therefore order you now that there shall be no talking among you. Further, should you try to run, remember, we are mounted cavalry. You will be caught by men on horses and shot on sight. I'm sorry, but I have no other choice."

He dropped his hands to his sides and his face became severe. "Do each of you understand?"

He waited. No one uttered a word, and he continued. "I will lead the column and you will follow. My men will be on both sides and in the rear. We will leave this camp in one hour and a half. Get your blankets loaded, prepare enough breakfast for yourselves and my command, hitch up your teams, and be ready to leave by that time. You will change the order of the wagons. The one loaded with cartridges will be moved to the number three position, and the wagon with blankets and boots will move to the number two position. I'll change the order and the drivers again from time to time."

He stopped to survey them. "Are there any questions?"

There were none.

"Carry on."

For a moment Brigitte stood rooted, wide-eyed. *He knows what's in each of the wagons! How? How?* She groped for some explanation and there was none, and then it struck her. *He has a spy in this camp. An informer!* She turned startled to peer at those around her, unable to believe one of them could be a traitor, and her eyes came to Cullen and she gaped. *Him! Every night! Right before our eyes!*

Captain Hornaby pointed, and his clipped words cut her off. "Young lady, you had better be about your assignment."

Brigitte turned back towards her blankets, still rubbing her arms, Caleb by her side, frightened, angry, wanting to do something but not knowing what or how. They sat to put their shoes on over wet stockings, then stood and shook their blankets and rolled and tied them and loaded them in their wagon. They returned to the fire, where others had spread the three legs of the tripod and were hanging the large black kettle on the hook above the fire. Two men took four wooden buckets to the stream thirty yards south, followed by a regular with his musket at the ready, and returned with water to wash and cook, then made a second trip.

In strained silence they fried sliced sow belly on a griddle and made thick cornmeal mush in the kettle and black coffee in a two-gallon pot. The British ate first, then the captives, sullen, watching, fearful. They finished washing the utensils and packed them, and the drivers walked through the tall, dripping grass to their horses, hobbled, past the wagons, followed by four regulars.

Wet to the knees, they walked the horses to the small stream and waited while they lowered their heads and sucked water, then led them to the wagons, where they backed the two reluctant wheel horses astraddle of the tongue and started the task of mounting the horse collars and buckling the harnesses into place. They snapped the traces to the singletrees and then backed the lead horses into place ahead of the wheel horses, and again worked with the horse collars and the harnesses, then the traces and the singletrees. They held buckets of oats to the horses' noses and waited while they ground it down. Then they slipped the headstalls into place, buckled the straps under the jaws, adjusted the blinders, and ran the long lines back to the driver's seat and wrapped them around the brake pole. The men threw dirt on the campfire, and they all looked around to be certain they had finished striking camp.

The sky to the east was brilliant when they finished and the captain called them together once more, and Brigitte's eyes did not leave Cullen as the captain spoke.

"Well done. There will be no trouble if you make none. We will leave now."

Brigitte walked to her wagon, head turned, watching Cullen. He had not raised his eyes from his work, or from the ground, since daylight. He moved to the lead wagon and clambered up and crouched behind the driver's seat.

Brigitte raised her foot to the wheel hub of the fourth wagon, then onto the cleat, and climbed into the driver's seat. Caleb climbed the other side and took his place beside her, clutching his notepad to his chest. Brigitte unwound the reins from the brake pole, sorted them, threaded them through her fingers, and took up the slack.

She glanced at the red-coated soldier beside her, an older man, riding a heavy-boned dappled gray cavalry mount that was tossing its head, tugging at the bit, working its feet, nervous, wanting to go. On one side of the saddle hung a standard cavalryman's saber, on the other a large holster with the handle of a huge pistol protruding.

The captain loped his horse to the head of the column, stood in the stirrups for a last inspection, reined his mount around, and bawled out the order, "Forward." The lead driver gigged his horses and slapped the reins on their rumps, and their heads dropped as their hooves dug into the soft earth and the lead wagon lurched into motion. Brigitte waited her turn and leaned forward to shout to her horses while she smacked the reins down on their hindquarters, and she steadied herself as the wagon moved.

Less than one hour later the column left the twin ruts of the main road and turned south onto a trail through the heavy foliage and the clustered oak and maples. They rolled on until noon, pushing through the brush, the big wagon wheels cutting their own ruts while the horses and drivers avoided tree branches that reached to catch at their clothes and faces and hands.

A little past noon Hornaby called a halt near a stream, and they dropped the trace chains to lead the harnessed horses to drink, then wiped the sweated places with a burlap bag and turned them loose in tall grass, still harnessed. The red-coated regulars unsaddled and watered their mounts, rubbed them briefly, and hobbled them in the grass while their captives dug dried mutton and cheese and hardtack from a commissary chest, and they ate in silence and drank cold water from the stream. They packed the remaining food back into the chest, and the captain walked through the noon camp repeating, "One-half hour rest period. No talking."

They sought shade from the sun and settled into the cool grass to lie down or sit, letting tension drain from set muscles while they let their minds drift. At half past one they were back on the wagon seats, and on command swung the teams back onto the narrow footpath. The British cavalrymen were divided, half at the head of the column, half behind, all riding single file.

Caleb glanced back at the six following, then faced forward, speaking quietly to Brigitte beside him. "I'm going to try to get away and get help. They'll never catch me in these trees and bushes."

She did not turn her head when she spoke. "Don't you dare. With muskets and horses they'd catch you and shoot you. Besides, where would you go for help? If you got it, where would you find us? We don't even know where we're going."

Caleb set his chin stubbornly, fear and anger in his eyes. "Then what are we going to do? Be prisoners of war the rest of our lives?"

"I don't know. Wait. Somehow we'll find our chance."

A command came loud from behind. "'Ere, you 'eard the captain. Stop that talkin' or I'll have to bind and gag you."

Caleb turned and his face was a mask of insolence as he stared at the regular for a moment, then turned back and fell into silence.

They rolled on south, plowing through brush, then open meadows, swatting mosquitoes as blue jays cocked curious heads to watch them pass, and great hawks rode the thermals high overhead, circling, watching, waiting. They passed through small valleys carpeted with blue and yellow and red wildflowers, with bees thick in their endless work of gathering nectar for their hives. Twice, startled deer with great, soft brown eyes raised their heads and twitched their large ears, trying to identify the sounds of mounted riders and wagons, squeaking, groaning, rumbling through their domain, and they nervously drifted into groves of trees and vanished.

At dusk the captain stopped them on an open meadow, and with the regulars circled about them on their horses, muskets unslung and ready, they moved the wagons to one side, blocked the wheels, unhitched and watered and grained the horses, and hobbled them near the wagons, where there was grass. The British soldiers tended their horses while the captives built the evening cook fire and cut potatoes and carrots into the boiling kettle, browned diced beef on a griddle, then added it to the mix and sprinkled in salt. In full darkness they waited until the British soldiers had finished, then filled their pewter or wooden bowls with the smoking stew, took slices of dark bread, and water from the stream, and sat cross-legged in the grass to silently, gratefully eat.

While they were cleaning their utensils Brigitte glanced south and in the farthest distance saw a tiny cluster of lights. She did not know if it was a town or the British camp to which Hornaby was taking them. For the first time she caught the faintest taint of salt sea air in the breeze and knew they were approaching the Atlantic, or Long Island Sound, not knowing where or how far.

With supper cleared, Hornaby called them together by the dying fire. "You will sleep in one group. My men will stand watch on four-hour shifts with orders to shoot to kill anyone who tries to escape."

Brigitte faced him, feet slightly apart, hands on her hips. "Where are we going?"

Hornaby shook his head. "We'll be there in two days. Now, all of you get your blankets and spread them here, by the fire."

Brigitte did not move. "If we're prisoners of war, we have some rights. I demand the women be allowed to spread their blankets at a place separate from the men."

The captain laughed. "Get your blankets now, all of you, and have them spread here and be inside them within ten minutes."

"Did you hear my demand?" Brigitte spouted.

Hornaby shook his head, irritation apparent. "Miss, I have tolerated you until now, but no more. Test my orders one more time and you'll be tied on top of a wagon for the remainder of the trip."

By half past nine the campfire had dwindled to glowing embers with sparks drifting upward, and they were all in their blankets, with six soldiers sitting around them, muskets across their laps, watching their every move.

Brigitte stared into the stars and in weary exhaustion let her thoughts go where they would. *What have I done? . . . what did I do wrong? . . . lost it all . . . fourteen captured . . . prisoners of war . . . Caleb . . . I only meant good . . . what will Mother say? . . . what will they say in Boston? . . . what will they say?*

She drifted into troubled sleep, muttering and twisting as images of red-coated soldiers with evil grins and great muskets and bayonets riding on horses danced before her eyes.

She started and sat bolt upright, wide awake, staring in the darkness, and she jumped at the voice behind her.

"Time, miss. Breakfast and hitch up your team."

The first arc of the sun had cleared the eastern skyline when she climbed into the driver's seat and sorted the reins. The train continued on south, following the narrow footpath through woods and open meadows. She knew they were slowly descending a gradual slope, and again she caught the scent of salt air, so familiar to one born in Boston. They nooned at another small, open meadow, and by half past one were once again heading south, working through the brush and trees, while birds scolded and bees and mosquitoes and insects buzzed, and deer and rabbits scattered before them.

It was past four o'clock when sunlight flickered on something moving in the trees twenty yards to the east, and Brigitte glanced to look, and there was nothing.

Deer, she thought. The column plodded on.

East of the column, dressed in buckskin and moccasins, moving through the oak and maple silently, invisible, Corporal Allen Ramsey of the Connecticut militia paused for one more count. Satisfied, he remained motionless until the last mounted redcoat was thirty yards south of him, and he turned and headed east, down a gentle slope at a run, clearing low bushes, dodging rocks, his Pennsylvania rifle held high. Five minutes later he stopped in front of Captain Edgar Hoff, who was flanked by five more men dressed in buckskin and moccasins.

"Four wagons," Ramsey panted. "Fourteen civilians driving and handling the wagons and stock. They're probably Tories. I think some of them are women. Twelve red-coated cavalry escorting. A captain in command. Looks like a British ammunition train, maybe mixed with some supplies." His eyes were bright as he waited for Hoff's reply.

Hoff's mouth narrowed as he considered. "They'll likely make camp on the bluffs this side of Hamden. We'll get the others and set up the cannon there and take them. Try hard to not harm the women, and try to save the wagons. If the wagons break for it, destroy them with the cannon. Let's go." Without a word the seven men fell into single file, Hoff leading, and started south at a trot.

Twenty minutes later, after the last arc of the setting sun had disappeared and left the world in growing dusk, Captain Hornaby stood in his stirrups and pointed. "We camp there."

A quarter mile straight ahead the woods opened into a flat, open meadow with a small stream on the west side. They could see tall grasses and wildflowers in the fast-fading light. Between the column and the meadow, the path they followed passed between two large stands of trees, thirty yards apart, over two hundred yards long. The column moved steadily forward, their thoughts on camp and hot food and blankets.

They reached the halfway point in their passage between the two stands of trees, fifteen yards away on either side of them, before an inner instinct rose hot inside Hornaby and he suddenly realized they were in a perfect place for an ambush. Instantly he jerked his horse around while the startled regulars drew reign, waiting, and Hornaby raised his cupped hand to his mouth to shout, "Forward at a gallop," and those were his last words.

Twenty deadly, hidden Pennsylvania long rifles blasted from the east trees, their muzzle flashes orange in the dusky light, and Captain Hornaby threw his hands up and his head back and pitched from his horse, rolling, finished. Four regulars slumped in their saddles and toppled forward, and two others rocked backwards and fought to stay mounted as their horses pranced sideways, away from the white smoke drifting from the trees. The two civilian outriders from Boston grasped at their chests and slowly slid to the ground and did not move. The men driving the first two wagons jerked and collapsed sideways against the women next to them.

The red-coated regulars who were still mounted slammed their spurs into the flanks of their terrified mounts and leaned low over the necks, kicking them to stampede gait, trying to get past the trees, out onto the open meadow. As they streamed south, fifteen more rifles hidden in the west stand of trees erupted, and every regular jerked in his saddle. All but two slid from their running horses to hit the ground rolling, and the last two slowly buckled forward and toppled over the withers of their running horses and rolled to a stop in the wildflowers.

A lone figure leaped from the lead wagon and sprinted after the red-coated regulars, arms flailing, screaming, "Wait! Wait!" He made it forty yards before a single Pennsylvania rifle spoke, and Cullen grasped his chest and slowed and stumbled to his knees and fell forward on his face, and did not move.

When the first roaring blast erupted from the trees and men began dropping, and the drivers of the first two wagons collapsed and let their reins go slack, followed by red-coated riders streaking past into a second rolling blast of rifle fire from the west side, the wild-eyed teams of the first two wagons bolted. In ten yards they were at a full-out run, the women on the seats frantically straining to hold onto the dead drivers, while the reins flew free, dragging. The two teams behind knew nothing more than to follow, and in an instant what remained of the column was thundering south, wagons careening crazily as the big wheels hit rocks and mounds and holes.

Brigitte had her feet braced against the front of the wagon, frantically hauling back on her reins with all her strength, but her team had taken the bits in their teeth and were following the tailgate of the wagon ahead, heedless of where they were going. Caleb was hunched forward, hands locked onto the iron railing on the driver's seat, white-faced, mouth gaping, terrified.

From the left, the deafening roar of six cannon echoed for miles, and the front end of the lead wagon disappeared in a cloud of smoke and a million shards of shattered wood. The hindquarters of the wheel horses dropped and the horses fell in their traces, and the lead horses went berserk, bucking, jumping, tangled in their harnesses and chains.

At the same moment, the second wagon exploded in the center into two pieces. The dead driver and the women with him were blown forward, onto the rumps of the wheel horses and then onto the ground rolling, while the team continued in their wild run, dragging the front half of the wagon. The back half of the wagon cartwheeled and scattered blankets and shoes twenty yards in all directions.

The team of the third wagon jerked to the right to avoid the wreckage and Brigitte's team followed. They were closing with the trees on the right when the cannon hidden there opened up.

The first shot ripped through the side of the ammunition wagon just above the front wheels into the wooden cases of cartridges. The nearest cases ruptured and exploded instantly, and within one second the entire load of more than a ton of cartridges blew. Flame leaped one hundred feet upward, and burning cartridges arced in all directions, leaving fiery trails in the darkening sky. The driver and assistant were blown forward over the heads of the team. The wheel horses were killed in their tracks, the lead horses knocked unconscious to lie on their sides, legs still working back and forth.

The noses of Brigitte's lead horses were forty feet behind the tailgate of the ammunition wagon when it blew. Her lead horses were killed instantly, blown back into the wheel horses to jam them backwards over the singletrees, against the front of the wagon, and their screams echoed in the trees. Brigitte and Caleb were blown backwards, rolling over the top of the load of their wagon, off the back, to hit the ground stunned, hair singed, ears ringing, unable to focus their eyes for a moment or to rise or think. The wagon plowed into the wreckage of the ammunition wagon and the wheel horses, still alive, tangled in their own harnesses and trace chains and the shattered hulk of the burning ammunition wagon.

As quickly as it had erupted, the rifle fire and the cannon fell silent. Pieces and shards of the wagons, some burning, lay scattered for one hundred yards between the two stands of trees. Moans of the injured and dying rose in the silence, and the heartrending sounds of horses with broken legs and necks and backs came from the shattered remains of the wagons.

Caleb stirred and tried to rise, and Brigitte frantically shoved him back down. "Don't move," she hissed in his ear. All she knew was that for two minutes the world had been filled with rifle and cannon fire that had killed nearly everyone in the column and most of the horses, and blown the wagons to oblivion. Who had laid the ambush, and what they intended doing next, she had no idea. She lay beside Caleb in the tall grass, waiting in the falling darkness, frantic, unable to know what to do next.

She jumped at the lone crack of a rifle, and then another, and another, and she clamped her hand over her mouth to keep from screaming, certain the unseen enemy was moving among the wounded, shooting them. She did not know the shots were fired to mercifully end the suffering of the crippled horses. She lay perfectly still, breathing shallow, waiting for someone to loom above them to aim a rifle or musket.

Caleb touched her arm. "We better go see what happened."

She twisted her head and thrust her face close to his to stare into his eyes. They were wide, vacant, and she realized he was stunned out of his mind, in shock, and a wave of terror ran through her, followed by hot anger.

She clamped her jaw shut and hissed, "Can you hear me?"

For three seconds Caleb looked at her before he slowly nodded his head.

"Then turn around and start crawling. On your stomach. Don't get up. Just start crawling and don't stop until I say."

Again he looked at her without a change of expression, and she shook his shoulder and ordered him. "Move. Now."

He nodded and then slowly turned on his stomach and began crawling through the tall grass, away from the flickering fires and the sounds of men moving among the wreckage and the dead, and Brigitte followed him, watching, never rising.

The moon was up and they were dirty and their hands aching before Brigitte once again whispered to him. "Stop." She rose to one knee to peer south under the stars, looking for the light of a fire or a lantern. There was none. Caleb rose beside her, and they did not move for a full minute as they watched and listened.

Brigitte stood. "Let's go." Her whisper sounded loud in the darkness.

She led and he followed. They tried to find the ruts made by their wagon, and they could not see in the darkness. Brigitte got down on her hands and knees and felt, but the soft, spongy grass told her nothing. They walked on, driven by panic of what was behind.

At midnight they stopped to rest, and suddenly Caleb thrust his hand inside his shirt, and he exclaimed, "My notepad! It's gone! I have to go back."

Brigitte's shoulders slumped. "You're not going back."

The chill of night settled and they shivered, and Brigitte stood. "We'll have to walk to keep warm."

They trudged on in the darkness, stumbling on stones, with brush and tree limbs reaching to snag their clothes and scratch their hands. Half a dozen times they stopped at the sound of things moving in the brush, terrified, expecting the crack of a rifle. With the morning star fading in the east, Brigitte sat down on a rock, and Caleb slumped to the ground next to her. For ten minutes she let him rest, and then spoke to him. "Do you remember what happened?"

His forehead wrinkled as he struggled. "I think so."

"Tell me."

"We got shot at."

"What happened to our wagon?" She watched his eyes as he worked at remembering, and suddenly they opened wide and his face blanched and his voice rose.

"The ammunition wagon blew up and us with it."

"Do you know how we got here?"

He licked dry lips. "Crawled."

"Are you all right?"

"Why? Haven't I been?"

"It doesn't matter. Do you remember it all now?"

"Yes."

"How do you feel?"

"Scared. Mad. Mostly mad."

A smile flitted across Brigitte's face, and she continued. "Are you hurt anywhere?"

"Sore. Not hurt. Where's everybody else? Are we going back?"

Brigitte looked west, back from whence they had come, for a long time, and there was pain in her voice when she spoke. "No. I don't know where the rest are. Some are dead. I hope some got away. But we can't go back and get captured or killed."

Finally she set her jaw and stood and squared her shoulders and spoke with resolve. "We can't go back. We don't know where we are. We have no food, no blankets, no map, no coats. But we do have some things. We know that home is where the sun is going to come up, and we know we can find water. We can eat nuts and berries, and we're bound to find a farm. So we're going to walk home. Are you ready?"

Notes

The night of August 21, 1776, a tremendous wind and thunder and lightning storm struck the New York area, killing three American officers and one soldier (see Johnston, *The Campaign of 1776*, part I, p. 140, particularly the footnote).

The storm having quieted in the night, the morning of August 22, 1776, broke favorably, and the British executed the amphibious crossing from Staten Island to the southern portions of Long Island, and dispersed their troops to occupy the village of Flatbush and take up defensive positions, preparatory to moving north to Brooklyn (see Johnston, *The Campaign of 1776*, part I, p. 140 and following).

The incidents concerning Brigitte and Caleb Dunson and their efforts to bring supplies to the Continental army are fictional.

Part Two

★ ★ ★

AREA AROUND NEW YORK AND NEW JERSEY, 1776

Chatterton's Hill ▲
• White Plains

BRONX RIVER

HUTCHINSON RIVER

• New Rochelle

King's Bridge

Hackensack •

HACKENSACK RIVER

Fort Lee •

Fort Washington •

HARLEM RIVER

PELL'S POINT

Equacanaugh •

THROG'S NECK

PASSAIC RIVER

Harlem Heights

LONG ISLAND SOUND

NEW JERSEY

HUDSON RIVER

MANHATTAN ISLAND

HELL GATE

KIP'S BAY

EAST RIVER

NEWTON CREEK

• Newtown

PAULUS HOOK

New York •

Newark •

Fort George •

LONG ISLAND

• Jamaica

Brooklyn •

Bedford •

Jamaica Pass

Elizabethtown •

NEWARK BAY

NEW YORK BAY

GOWANUS BAY

Guana Heights

• Flatbush

STATEN ISLAND

THE NARROWS

New Utrecht •

Flatlands •

JAMAICA BAY

Gravesend •

GRAVESEND BAY

British Camp ▲

LOWER NEW YORK HARBOR

ATLANTIC OCEAN

N

Long Island
August 26, 1776

CHAPTER XV

★ ★ ★

*S*troud!"

Crusty little Sergeant Turlock slowed from a run to stand on the rim of the trench where the Boston regiment was dug in, south of the Brooklyn breastworks, looking down at Billy and Eli in the rose colors of dawn.

"General Washington's in Thompson's command tent," he panted. "Wants to talk with you."

Eli's eyebrows arched in surprise. "Me? What about?" His thoughts raced. *Washington! Why me?*

"That don't matter. Get out of there and move."

Eli vaulted out of the trench, Billy tossed his rifle up to him, and he broke for the command tent at a trot. The picket saw him coming, took his rifle, and without a word opened the flap. Eli stepped in and stopped, startled, not expecting the gathering into which he had been thrust. He stood still while his eyes swept the faces of the men who surrounded the large table.

Generals George Washington, Putnam, Sullivan, Stirling, Scott, and Colonels Thompson and Knowlton. Eli recognized Thompson and Scott by sight, and Washington by description, but no others. He did not salute but stood waiting for direction while the officers studied his buckskins and beaded moccasins.

Thompson took control. "General Washington, this is Eli

Stroud of the Boston regiment, Ninth Company. He has been acting as my scout."

General Washington was seated at the far end of the table. He stood and bowed. "Private Stroud, thank you for coming."

For a split second Eli stood silent, unsure of how he should respond in the presence of the most powerful assembly of men he had ever seen. Instinct rose. He stared steadily back into the blue-gray eyes of the tall figure at the head of the table. "Glad I could."

Washington gestured. "Would you like to be seated?"

"Could I stand? Thoughts come easier standing."

Washington smiled. "Mine come best sitting a good horse." He sobered. "Colonel Thompson informs me you were on scout yesterday."

"Yes."

Half the officers at the table shifted their eyes between Washington and Eli, aware that Eli was not addressing Washington as "sir" and wondering when Washington was going to correct him. They waited.

Washington pointed to the large map on the table. "Where did you scout?"

Eli stepped to the table and studied the Long Island map for a moment, then pointed. "Here."

Washington raised startled eyes. "Gravesend Bay?"

"Yes, and other places."

Washington glanced at Thompson, then back at Eli. "Below the battle lines, right in among the British?"

"Yes."

"How did you get in and out without getting caught?"

Eli shrugged. "Stay out of sight. Move quiet."

For three full seconds Washington locked eyes with Eli, and in those moments Eli knew Washington had probed deep, and he also knew that he had seen deeply enough into Washington to sense the steel in him.

Washington broke it off. "Do I understand more troops came ashore yesterday?"

"Yes. About six thousand. Their uniforms were dark blue, and they brought drums and fifes."

"Do you know who they are?"

"Hessians, I think."

"With the British, what is their total strength now?"

"Fifteen thousand four days ago, six thousand yesterday. Twenty-one thousand."

Washington pursed his mouth for a moment. "What can you tell us of their dispersion? Where are the British troops, and where are the Hessians?"

Eli pointed as he spoke. "Yesterday at sunset all the Hessians and some of the redcoats were here, at Flatbush, in the middle. To their south was the biggest body, all redcoats, here, near what's marked Flatlands. To the west, back over here, near the Narrows, the rest of them."

For ten seconds Washington studied the locations pointed out by Eli, mouth a thin, straight line, eyes narrowed in intense concentration. "Their cannon?"

"Divided up. They all had some."

"Horses?"

"Maybe seven hundred, scattered out on picket lines through all three of those places."

"Did any of these groups have tents set up? a camp?"

"Not many tents. Looked like they were expecting to move."

Washington nodded as he absorbed the implication, and he moved on. "How far east have you scouted?"

"About six miles."

"What did you see?" Washington was probing and testing, and Eli knew it.

He began pointing at the map. "We got fortifications at Brooklyn, and down on this ridge. I'll call it the south ridge. There are four natural passes through the south ridge. On the west there's Gowanus Road, here, and then there's Flatbush Road here that runs right through our breastworks, and then there's the Bedford Road, here, and farthest east, here, there's the Jamaica Road. Then there's this unnamed road, right here, that runs from Flatbush north up to the Jamaica Road."

He stopped to gather his thoughts. "Jamaica Road runs from here, nearly on the beach, north through Jamaica Pass, then swings back west, and Bedford Road joins it right here, and Flatbush Road joins it right here and goes right on into Brooklyn. The Jamaica Road passes *behind* all these trenches and breastworks that we've been building to stop the British, including where we are right now."

He stopped and raised his eyes to Washington's, and the room became so quiet they could hear the flies buzzing.

"Maybe we can stop them if they try to march up the south ridge straight at us, but if they send troops up to take the Jamaica Road and they get in behind us while we're fighting the rest of them coming up that south ridge straight at us, we're caught on three sides, and the swamp and river are on the fourth, over here. And the Gowanus Road leads up north from where the British are over there on the west, right to that swamp and the river. And the way these roads all tie in with the Jamaica Road, once they got that road they got a way to reach all of us, both here on the south ridge and north, up at Brooklyn."

Eli stopped and waited to see if Washington understood.

Washington slowly turned his head to Generals Putnam and Sullivan. "Gentlemen, I presume you are aware of the danger and will take appropriate actions to prevent a flanking movement through Jamaica Pass. At any cost."

Both generals nodded.

Washington turned back to Eli. "General Greene has taken seriously ill with the fever and has been moved to New York. General Putnam is in command of the Long Island forces. General Sullivan will be in command of our left, towards the Jamaica Road."

Washington looked at Sullivan and Sullivan bobbed his head once, and Washington turned back to Eli. "I intend going south today to personally observe the enemy lines. Any suggestions where I should and should not go?"

Eli considered for a moment. "Horseback?"

"Yes."

"How many of you?"

"Perhaps four."

"Yesterday I got a pretty good look at our own lines down there, and I know the British have sent scouts up to look at them, and we've had scouts out, and there's been a little shooting and a little shifting back and forth, so I don't know where the lines are today."

Sullivan's eyes dropped for a moment, and Eli caught it but did not understand what it meant, and continued. "I'd find out where our lines are today, and I wouldn't go past them." He tapped the map. "There's a little rise of ground right here that we held yesterday on our front line, and if we still hold it, four men on horses could see most of the center section of their forces and some of those at the Narrows and some of them over on the east, and not be seen if they're careful. You'd need telescopes."

Washington studied the place Eli had indicated, memorizing its location, and then straightened. "Thank you. Is there anything else you think important that I should know?"

"Yes. They have Mohawk Indians scouting. That likely means Chief Joseph Brant is with them. He's smart and tough. If he is you can expect them to hit hard and fast, mostly at night. You might want to warn your soldiers."

Washington thoughtfully raised a hand to stroke his chin. "Thank you, Private. I may call on you later. There is one more thing. Colonel Thompson told me the part you played in spoiling the plot to kill me—the Hickey affair. I understand I owe you my life. I am grateful."

His gaze was steady. His words were not protocol, not the standard phrase, not offered because they were required of him. They were sincere, from his heart, and Eli sensed it.

Washington continued. "If there is anything I can do in return, ask."

Eli cleared his throat and for a moment glanced at the other men, then spoke to Washington as though no one else were in the tent. "There is one thing. Do you have any officers in command of troops from New Hampshire or Vermont?"

"I do. General Sullivan. New Hampshire."

Sullivan turned his head to look directly at Eli, and Eli continued to speak to Washington. "Could I write out a message and have it spread among those troops?"

"What message?"

Eli didn't hesitate. "I lost track of my sister a long time ago. I searched but I couldn't find her. Maybe someone from up there will remember and know her and whether she's still alive, and maybe where I can find her."

Eli saw it in Washington's eyes. Compassion, understanding, and a sense of pain at Eli's loss. It rose above the war, the terrible imbalance he was facing, the fact he knew he would be fighting for the very survival of the Revolution within two days.

Washington spoke firmly. "You get the message to General Sullivan, and he'll deliver it to every company in his command." He turned to Sullivan. "Can you do that?"

"Yes, sir."

Washington turned back to Eli. "Anything else?"

"No."

"It is my great pleasure. You are dismissed."

Eli turned on his heel without saluting, and walked out the tent flap.

Washington's eyes followed him until the tent flap closed, and then he brought his eyes down to the map. For long moments he peered at it, considering, weighing, deciding, before he spoke.

"Gentlemen, the question is resolved. It's clear General Howe intends attacking here, to reach Brooklyn." He tapped the map. "I have been concerned he intended to use Brooklyn as a decoy, and strike at New York. But with six thousand Hessians arrived yesterday, he has committed over twenty-one thousand troops here on Long Island."

His face remained calm, unperturbed as he continued. "I will send a message to the New York command within the hour and order additional regiments to cross the river today, immediately, to strengthen our forces here." He looked at General Stirling. "The Delaware regiment and the Marylanders who were under your command will be among them, General." His eyes came back to the map. "And men from the Pennsylvania riflemen, some others from Maryland, and Connecticut. It will raise your strength to just over seven thousand."

He paused for a moment, until the tent was silent. There was no need for him to address the fact the British forces outnumbered the Americans three to one. The frightening imbalance was absolutely clear to every man at the table, and it haunted them, nagged at them.

Washington continued. "I want every small watercraft on the East River, civilian or military, to be taken and put under supervision of our Long Island command. I do not want the British to have one vessel available to them to cross the river, should things go wrong."

He looked at Generals Putnam and Sullivan, who nodded.

Washington referred to the map and his face grew solemn. "You must understand one thing. It is absolutely critical that we hold our breastworks and our trenches here, on this south ridge, at all costs. If we do not, and they do flank us, we could lose Brooklyn in one day, and most of the Continental army with it." He raised his eyes to theirs. "At all costs, gentlemen, we *must hold this south ridge.*"

General Sullivan felt the cut. Six days earlier, when General Greene had been taken from his tent on a stretcher, mumbling incoherently from fever dreams, Washington had given command of the Long Island forces to Sullivan, not Putnam. But when the British sent their first probing patrols north from Gravesend Bay to establish the position and strength of the American forces, Sullivan had sent a patrol south. The two small forces met, and Sullivan's command had opened fire and charged. The British patrol, acting under strict orders, retreated instantly and disappeared south to report they had contacted the Americans and to mark the location on a map for their superior officer. Their orders had not been to engage the Americans, only to locate them and return, without a fight if possible.

Sullivan's patrol had also reported instantly, that they had met the British and engaged them, and they had defeated them decisively. Sullivan had been jubilant. He had written a congratulatory letter to the officer in charge of the patrol, and immediately sent a letter to General Washington stating he had engaged the enemy and defeated them, which hopefully was but the first of many such glorious battles.

Washington had stood aghast when he finished reading Sullivan's letter. Didn't Sullivan realize the British patrol was never intended to engage the Americans, but only to find them and report back? If Sullivan had not realized that, but instead thought he had met a fighting force and won a significant victory, was he capable of commanding the entire Long Island command? Washington had quickly drafted new orders and sent them to Long Island by runner. General Sullivan was relieved of command on Long Island. General Israel Putnam was to assume that command, and Sullivan was to take subordinate command of the forces defending the American left, subject to General Putnam.

The change of command had been embarrassing to both Putnam and Sullivan, but in the critical stress of trying to arrange his officers in the best positions to meet a vastly superior British army, Washington did not have the luxury of politics. He had to call it as he saw it, and at that moment he was convinced that Putnam, the bulldog who followed orders to the letter and had demonstrated over and over again an absolute lack of fear for anything, was the man better suited for what was surely to come at the Brooklyn breastworks.

Sullivan remained silent, as did Putnam, and Washington moved on as though nothing had happened. "I'm going to return to New York tonight, so we have to leave now if we're going to inspect the lines. I have ordered four mounts. Generals Putnam,

Sullivan, and Stirling will accompany me. Gentlemen, are you ready?"

South of the command tent, beneath a clear sky and a hot, bright sun, Eli dropped back into the trench beside Billy. He cradled his rifle in his right arm and eased back to lean against the rear wall of the trench. Billy waited in silence, and Eli spoke. "Sullivan's no longer in command here. Putnam is."

Billy's forehead creased. "Why? Since when?"

"Two days ago. I don't know why. I think Sullivan might have done something Washington didn't like."

"Was Washington there?"

"Yes."

"Did you talk to him?"

"Nearly the whole time."

"What about?"

"The redcoats and the Hessians, and the Jamaica Pass."

"Jamaica Pass?"

"Yes. East of here. If the British come up through it they can get right in behind where we are and we're trapped against the river."

"Did Washington understand?"

Eli nodded. "Told Sullivan and Putnam to take care of it."

Billy paused to choose his words. "What did you make of him?"

Eli drew a breath and worked with his thoughts. "I think he'd rather talk straight than pretty. I think he understands. And I know he listens to little things if they concern his troops."

Billy reflected for a moment. "Little things?"

"I told him about my sister. He said I should write a message and get it to Sullivan. Sullivan commands men from New Hampshire."

Billy gaped. "You told General Washington about that?"

"Yes. He said he knew about the Hickey business over in New York, and he thought he owed me—was there anything he could do for me. I told him."

"And he listened?"

"He listened, but more, he felt it and he understood. I saw it in his eyes. When he told me to write the letter, he turned to Sullivan and told him to handle it, and Sullivan said yes. It was as important to Washington as anything else we talked about."

Billy settled for a moment. "Did you feel anything? about Washington?"

A little time passed before Eli answered quietly, with measured words. "Yes, as far as he went. I don't know yet what will happen in battle, but what I've seen so far . . . he's a rare man."

The sound of troops coming in from their right interrupted and both men turned their heads to look. A young lieutenant halted a company of infantry behind them and faced them, rigid, officious, self-conscious and a little awed by the fact he was an officer. "Your watch is over. We're your replacements."

Ninth Company had been on duty since midnight, watching through the night, tense, nervous, listening to every sound, certain half a dozen times the dreaded Hessians were upon them. Gratefully they climbed out of the trench while the fresh, uniformed company dropped in and took their positions, muskets in hand.

Billy and Eli made their way to the breakfast line and with the rest of Company Nine stood with their plates and cups to get their ration of what had become their standard breakfast—lumpy cornmeal mush and fried sow belly, with bitter, hot coffee. They sat nearby to silently eat it, then washed their utensils and walked to their blankets. They sat down, and Billy dug his pad and pencil from his knapsack. "What's the message?"

Ten minutes later he read aloud what he had written. Eli nodded and left with the folded paper in his hand. He stopped at the command tent of Israel Thompson and waited while the picket disappeared inside for a few moments, then returned, and Eli entered.

"This is the letter General Washington said I could write for Sullivan, about my sister."

It took Thompson a moment to remember. "Good. I'll see it's delivered. Mind if I read it?"

"No. Go ahead."

"Anything else?"

"No." Eli turned to leave and Thompson stopped him.

"You did fine this morning."

"You had something to do with that."

Thompson smiled. "Get back to your post."

Eli walked steadily back to Billy, and they lay down on their separate blankets in the mounting heat of midmorning, with one arm over their eyes, and shut out the sounds of an army, and slept.

A little past one o'clock they were awakened by the piercing voice of Sergeant Turlock. "All right, you lovelies. General Putnam's given orders that we're going to move. Get your meal and then get your blankets and knapsacks packed and be ready."

By half past two Company Nine and the Boston regiment were sitting on their blanket rolls, awaiting orders. At three o'clock they watched four thousand troops arrive from the north to bolster the fighting force they had in the trenches and breastworks. Their orders were to form a line east as far as they could, to try to block any British coming north on the Bedford or Jamaica Roads.

By four o'clock the newly arrived reinforcements were dug in, stretched thin over three miles, facing south. Their line ended over one mile short of Jamaica Pass. There were simply not enough men to maintain the line farther. At the pass, five mounted American officers had been assigned to take up a position from which they could see any forces coming north on the road. If any appeared, they were to ride at stampede gait back to report to General Sullivan or Putnam.

The Boston regiment remained at the breastworks on the south ridge, but their position was shifted two hundred yards west, directly in the center of the lines. If the British overran them, they had a clear field of approach to the fortifications on the ridge to the north bordering Brooklyn.

Billy and Eli, and Company Nine, stacked their blankets and knapsacks on the ground and took up their positions looking south over the great logs and compacted earth. It was past five o'clock.

Billy swatted at mosquitoes and watched and waited in silence, sweat rolling down his cheeks. Eli wiped his leather sleeve across his forehead and remained still, watching. A little past six o'clock they took their rotation at the supper line, washed their utensils, and resumed their positions. They watched General Washington and the three who rode with him return to camp at a canter on sweated horses and disappear into the command tent for a short time, while aides stripped the saddles and bridles and walked the mounts until they were cooled out, then rubbed them down and watered and fed them.

The sun settled onto the New Jersey skyline and cast long shadows eastward before General Washington emerged from the command tent. A carriage with four armed men led, with Washington's carriage behind, traveling west towards the river and the Brooklyn ferry.

The sun disappeared, and the men in the breastworks licked dry lips and settled in for the night, watching, waiting, listening to every sound. Dusk settled. Campfires were lighted all along the lines, dancing, casting shadows moving in the trees, illuminating the eyes of small creatures that paused in their hunt for food to peer and then vanish in the brush. Great owls blinked in trees and their muted calls caused edgy men to cock their muskets and wait, only to uncock them and wipe the backs of their hands across their mouths and wait again.

Far to the south, past the battle lines, near Flatbush, with dusk settling, General William Howe leaned forward over the council table in his command tent, yellow in the light of two lanterns. He glanced at the faces around him before he spoke.

"General Grant, tomorrow morning at five-thirty A.M. your command will advance on our left, here." He tapped the map. "Engage the Americans when you find them, but do not penetrate their lines or overrun them. Hold them right where they are. Our last report says General Lord Stirling commands the Americans you will be facing. He will fight, but you will not push them back until I give my signal."

General James Grant, whose hatred of Americans had driven him to boast he could march from one end of America to the other with only five thousand troops, nodded his head, eyes glittering, impatient. "When do I get your signal?"

"I will come to that."

Grant remained silent, waiting.

Howe turned to General Philip von Heister. "General, tomorrow morning at five-thirty A.M. when General Grant moves north, you will take your forces north also, directly up the center, to engage the American lines here." He pointed. "Your orders are to engage them and hold them there, the same as General Grant. Do not overrun them or push them back until you hear my signal. I'll explain the signal in a short time." He paused for a moment, then added, "Do you understand?"

Von Heister grunted, "Ja." His face was passive, without emotion, all business. He and his command were professional mercenary soldiers. Which side they fought on, or the reason for the war, meant absolutely nothing to them, since they fought for pay, not a cause. In von Heister's view, the rebellion of the Americans against the British Crown was a matter of profound stupidity. In his judgment, the American army was the most disorganized collection of disgusting rabble he had ever seen, and it was incomprehensible to him that they would ever think of challenging the power of England for any reason. That they would do so solely for an abstraction they called "liberty" left him shaking his head in wonder. Given a choice, he and his Hessians would simply march forward until they had killed them all, collect their pay, and return to their homeland to wait for the next call for their services.

Howe turned to Joseph Brant, and his eyes narrowed and he slowed his speech. Brant stopped all movement, focused.

"Five of your best Mohawks will lead a squad of ten British cavalry east to the road that leads north through the Jamaica Pass and proceed north on that road. The Mohawks will leave the cavalry one-quarter of a mile this side of the pass and proceed to scout out the pass. If the Americans have a force there and it is too large for the Mohawks and the cavalry, they will count the number of Americans and the number of their cannon, as best they can, and return to the squad of cavalry, and they shall all wait there, one-quarter of a mile south of the pass."

Howe broke it off for a moment. "But if the American force is small, and your men with the cavalry can take it with little or no trouble, you shall do so, alive if you can because I will want to question them. If you take the American force, you will simply wait there at the pass. Under any circumstance, your men and the cavalry must not be captured. If they are, we will not know it and could fall into our own trap."

He stopped. "Do you understand so far?"

Brant nodded but did not speak.

"I will come back to your orders in a moment."

Howe turned to Cornwallis, Clinton, and Percy, clustered together.

"You will accompany me. We will take ten thousand troops and proceed east to the road that turns north to the Jamaica Pass and proceed through the pass." He pointed on the map. "When our entire command is through the pass, we will continue north to the Jamaica Road and turn west. We will continue west until we approach the rear of the American fortifications on the ridge south of Brooklyn."

He stopped and waited for total silence.

"Now listen carefully to the timing of when each of you moves."

He turned back to Brant. "Your Mohawks with the cavalry will leave immediately when we finish here."

He turned to Cornwallis, Clinton, and Percy. "In one hour, about nine o'clock, you will leave with me and our command of ten thousand. That will give Brant's men and the squad of cavalry time to get to the pass and either take it and wait there or count the Americans and meet us a quarter mile this side of the pass. Either way, we will take the pass and move through it. We should be on the other side of the pass before dawn tomorrow morning and moving back west towards the rear of the Americans on the south ridge."

He turned back to von Heister and Grant. "When we're within striking distance of the rear of the American fortifications, we will fire the cannon, and that's your signal. When you hear our two cannon shots, timed at three seconds, you will no longer simply hold the American forces in the engagement, you will move forward with all strength and vigor. Push the Americans back. Force them to concentrate on you, coming at them from the south. While you're doing that, I and the forces with me will come west on the Jamaica Road and arrive behind the Americans and beside them. They will be trapped with our forces on three sides and the Gowanus Marsh and the East River on the fourth side. Either they surrender or we destroy them as we see fit."

He stopped and took a deep breath. "Have I missed anything? Do you all understand the time you are to move, where you are to move, and what the other parts of our forces will be doing at the same time?"

All heads nodded. No one spoke.

He turned to Grant and von Heister. "If anything goes wrong and you do not hear the cannon signal, break off the engagement at twelve o'clock noon and return to this camp."

Again he paused before he finished. "All right. I am going to go through it one more time to be certain, and then Brant's Mohawks will leave."

With the evening star high and bright, Joseph Brant stood before five Mohawk scouts dressed in buckskin hunting shirts and breeches. Behind them, ten British cavalrymen sat on horses that tossed their heads and stuttered their feet, nervous at being forced to move on unfamiliar ground at night.

Quickly, quietly, signing with his hands as he spoke, Brant gave the Mohawks their orders one more time. They nodded understanding, and he nodded back. Brant turned to the captain in command of the cavalry squad and he nodded, and Brant led his group trotting east in single file. Fifteen seconds later they vanished, swallowed in the blackness and the small sounds of the night. The cavalry had muskets slung over their backs and pistols and sabers in saddle holsters. The Mohawks carried neither musket nor rifle. Each had a belt knife and an iron-headed tomahawk thrust through his weapons belt.

One hour later Howe leaned from his saddle to shake hands with Grant and von Heister, then spurred his mount to the head of the column of ten thousand red-coated British regulars. They were strung out six abreast for well over one mile in the darkness. Like a great, creeping caterpillar they wound over the rises and through the swales and twists and turns of the dirt road, each rank straining to see the white belts on the one before it to keep their interval in the black of night.

To the north of the great column, and a little east, five American officers, spaced ten yards apart at the south edge of the entrance into the Jamaica Pass, crouched hidden in the heavy brush and tangled oak and maple trees. Their mounts were tied a few feet behind each, nervous, ears pricked as they listened to the night sounds in strange territory. The officers—Van Wagenen, Troup, Dunscomb, Gilliland, and Hoogland—sat motionless, peering south through the tangled growth, jumpy, nervous, hearing British cavalry and infantry in every sound of the night. The inquiring "Whoooo" of an owl became a signal to attack. The scurry of an opossum leading her young through the brush to water became infantry advancing. The far-off sudden bark of a fox became the voice of a British officer barking orders.

None of them heard or sensed the silent infiltration of five Mohawks who moved slowly among them until they scented the horses. The Mohawks followed the scent until they could outline the saddled mounts in the dim light. They counted them, then withdrew back to the south as silently as they had come.

Five minutes later they stopped in the road and softly called to the British cavalry squad, who led their horses onto the narrow dirt strip and gathered to listen.

The Mohawk leader spoke in hushed tones "Five. With horses. Leave yours here. They will talk to the American horses if they get close. Follow us. Walk only where we walk."

The cavalry squad tied their horses in the brush and returned to the road with their muskets unslung, ready, wide-eyed in the darkness. When they were formed into a single-file column, the Mohawks led them north on the road, walking carefully in the soft dirt, making no sound.

Twenty minutes later Officer Troup's horse shied behind him and stuttered its feet. He ignored it, then suddenly spun to look. At the same moment Officer Gilliland looked sideways at the sound of something brushing against the tangle of bushes to his right. Both officers suddenly rose to their feet and jerked their muskets upward, thumbs clawing for the hammer, when a British bayonet was thrust within three inches of their throats, and they froze.

At the muffled sounds, the other three American officers hissed, "Are you all right?" and there was no answer. They bolted to their feet, muskets raised, and saw the pale moonlight glint off British bayonets and the iron heads of Mohawk tomahawks within two feet of their faces, and they stopped and slowly lowered their muskets.

Notes

On August 25, 1776, General Howe crossed six thousand Hessians from Staten Island to the Long Island camps under the command of German lieutenant general Philip von Heister. That raised the British forces to twenty-one thousand (see Johnston, *The Campaign of 1776*, part I, p. 160).

General Nathanael Greene was taken seriously ill with fever and General Washington relieved him of his command on Long Island until he could recover. General Sullivan was first appointed to replace him. However, General Sullivan's troops encountered a British probing patrol, which they attacked, and the patrol withdrew to report to General Howe where the Americans were. Sullivan believed he had met and defeated a sizeable portion of the British army, and jubilantly reported such to Washington. Washington realized Sullivan had badly misunderstood the event, and deeply concerned, he immediately replaced Sullivan with Putnam. It caused some embarrassment to all concerned (see Johnston, *The Campaign of 1776*, part I, pp. 103, 149, 150, particularly the footnote; Leckie, *George Washington's War*, p. 260).

On August 26, 1776, General Washington crossed from New York to Long Island and personally inspected the American fortifications and forces, remaining until evening (see Johnston, *The Campaign of 1776*, part I, p. 153). On that same day, reinforcements were sent from New York to Long Island, including regiments from Maryland and Delaware and a regiment of Pennsylvania riflemen (see Johnston, *The Campaign of 1776*, part I, p. 154).

The names given here of the five American officers who were assigned to cover the Jamaica Pass are as they appear in Johnston, *The Campaign of 1776*, part I, p. 159.

CHAPTER XVI

★ ★ ★

he turnips and carrots will be getting ready . . . potatoes . . . done with the peaches . . . apricots . . . apples starting to blush . . . they'll be waking up about now . . . Tuesday . . . breakfast . . . wonder what . . . maybe griddle cakes and maple syrup . . . Trudy will help with the apples . . . time to make soap . . . they can do it . . . they'll be all right . . .

The black of the eastern sky had given way to purple, and with each passing moment the gray preceding sunrise was creeping. Billy stood leaning against the center breastworks on the south ridge, eyes wide, peering down the slope towards the woods and brush, his musket laid on top of the dirt mound. He ran a hand over his dry mouth and drew and released a great breath.

Sometime in the night Putnam had ordered General Stirling down towards the Narrows. The British had overrun a small advance outpost, and Putnam's orders were very clear. The Gowanus Road was to be blocked at the Narrows and held at all costs. Stirling had left in the dark with Haslet's and Smallwood's regiments, moving at a trot.

Then Putnam had ordered the Boston regiment to the major breastworks on the south ridge with two thousand other American troops. Again his orders were blunt, clear. The Hessians are forming south of us, near Flatbush. If they come, stop them. At any cost.

In pitch black the troops had left their blankets and taken their positions at the entrenchments, shivering in their light summer clothing, teeth chattering, silent, peering south over the top of the earth-and-timber mound. Fear rode them like a great ugly animal, robbing them of reason, crowding them into an unreal world where their thoughts were fragmented abstractions of things and places unrelated to standing at a breastwork in the dark, waiting an eternity for an enemy to come with cannon and musket and bayonet to kill. Home, mother, family, the sea, the farm, harvest-time, childhood, wife, children, sweetheart—their thoughts ran and they could not control them, nor did they try. They stood at the breastwork and they peered south in the darkness, waiting, watching, listening.

More than two hours before dawn they had heard the faint popping of muskets and then the deep-throated boom of a few cannon far down to the right, near the Narrows. It stopped for a moment, and then it grew hot and it did not stop, and the men looked at each other in the dark, silent, fearing, asking themselves questions and inventing answers. Which side was attacking, Stirling or the British? Who was winning, losing? Are they coming here? When? Where? How many? Twenty thousand. Coming here. Now. At sunset which of us will be dead, crippled? Which army will be holding these breastworks?

Then sporadic musket fire sounded farther to the east, away from the Narrows, and died, and then a few muskets popped closer, and stopped, and the men at the breastworks swallowed dry and wiped at their mouths with their hands, and waited.

Billy glanced up and down at the line of men standing against the dirt and timber nearly shoulder to shoulder, weapons laid over the top. Their clothing was worn, patched, dirty. Their hats were tricorns, or coonskins, or knit caps, or leather hats from the sea, or no hats at all. They wore cartridge boxes on their belts or slung around their necks on a leather strap, and they had canteens. Their faces were old and weathered and wrinkled, or younger and smooth and innocent, some bearded, some not, most with a four-day growth of whiskers, and their dialects were different. Their weapons were muskets or rifles, and there were not fifty bayonets in the entire line. Bayonets were hand tooled to fit a standard military musket, and few of them had standard military muskets. No bayonet would fit the long rifles.

Once again they stood quiet with the taste of fear in their mouths, while their minds drifted back to places where people loved them and times when they were doing the happy things of life. They let it go unchecked, welcoming the fleeting release from fear.

"You all right?"

Billy jerked, then turned to Eli, standing next to him, and nodded. "Yes. You?"

Eli shrugged and said nothing.

A few moments passed and Billy spoke quietly. "Ever think much about killing men?"

Eli turned his head to study Billy's face in the gray light and realized Billy was searching for something. "Yes."

"Is it right or wrong?"

Eli considered. "Like everything else, I guess. Sometimes right, sometimes wrong. Like in your Bible where it says there's a time for everything."

"When is it right?"

Eli searched long and hard. "When they mean to take away something important."

"Like what?"

"Life. Family. Country."

"Liberty?"

"I think so. It bothers you? having to kill for liberty?"

"I hate killing for any reason. I wish it never had to be."

Eli heard the deep revulsion in Billy's voice.

Billy continued. "But sometimes . . ."

A moment passed and Eli spoke. "Ever think about dying?"

"Yes." For a moment Billy hesitated, weighing whether he should share his innermost fears with another man. He decided. "I'm afraid."

He waited, hoping he had not reached too deeply into the inner core of fears and weaknesses common to all mankind, the revealing of which undercuts the need of society to hide them, to continue the necessary facade of inner strength when there is none.

Eli didn't hesitate. "So am I."

A sense of relief welled up inside Billy.

A moment passed before Eli spoke again. "Ever think of what's there waiting when a person dies?"

Billy pursed his mouth in thought. "Heaven. The Bible says heaven."

"You believe it?"

"Yes. What do the Iroquois teach?"

"A lot like your Bible. Peace for those who were good, no peace for the others. Iroquois don't much fear dying. They just hate dying badly."

Billy nodded, and for a time they remained quiet, each working with his own thoughts before Billy changed direction. He pointed over the breastwork, to the south and west. "What do you think's going on over there?"

"Stirling's in a fight down at the Narrows, holding the Gowanus Road. There's someone coming straight up the Flatbush Road at us." He turned inquiring eyes to Billy. "Do you know who's to our left, watching the Jamaica Road?"

"Colonel Miles with about five hundred men."

Eli said nothing, and they both turned back to peer into the gray, straining to catch the first movement of red in the trees to the south. Jays and robins and crows began their morning cacophony, and it sounded strangely loud, unreal. A slight mist rose from the wet grass on the slope, and in it trees became men and bushes became cannon.

They heard them long before they saw them. With the first streaks of rose and gold in the eastern sky, the faint lilt of fifes and rattle of drums hammering out a martial tune came drifting, and the men at the breastworks narrowed their eyes in disbelief as the sound grew. Half a dozen musket shots popped and then fell silent as some American patrol fired and fell back.

Far to the right, from the Narrows, came the sudden thudding of cannon and then the sound of a few muskets and then a continuous, ongoing blasting of cannon and volley after volley of musketry.

The men licked dry lips and reached for their weapons, and flinched at the sudden shout from the officers.

"Don't fire until the command!"

They exhaled breath and settled.

It seemed the sound of the fifes and drums was right up on them before it stopped, and the men tensed in the first arc of the rising sun. As the sunlight reached slanting into the trees, they saw the first flash of movement all along the tree line, directly south of the center of the breastworks. For a moment they gaped as they looked east and west, and for a quarter of a mile each direction they saw the patches of sunlight on uniformed men, still in the trees. The uniforms were deep blue, not red.

"Hessians!" The gasped word went up and down the lines.

They saw the ugly snouts of cannons inside the tree line and the brush and they knew it was coming, but they jumped as a dozen cannon opened up. They saw the white smoke blossom, and then the cannonballs smashed low into the breastworks and dirt flew as they exploded, and then the thundering sound rolled past. They ducked, then raised their heads to peer over the breastworks once more.

"Fire!" shouted the American officers, and the cannon emplacements in the breastworks boomed and the cannonballs ripped smashing into the trees.

The smoke cloud from the Hessian cannon rolled a second time, and now the cannonballs slammed high into the breastworks and a few cleared the top and exploded and a few men groaned and slumped.

"Steady!" The officers stood resolute, swords in their hands, eyes flashing.

Suddenly a long line of blue uniforms appeared before the tree line, and the first wave of Hessians resolutely lowered their bayonets and began their steady, relentless march straight ahead.

Once again the American cannon blasted, and a few holes appeared in the oncoming line.

Then came the order from the American officers. "Hold your musket fire!"

The Hessians stopped at two hundred yards, knelt, took aim, and fired their first musket volley. A thousand musket balls smacked into the breastworks and whistled over, and a few more Americans jerked and sat down.

All along the American breastworks came the heavy click of musket hammers being drawn back to full cock.

The order boomed. "Uncock your muskets. Hold your fire. Fire on command. Fire on command."

They uncocked their weapons and again waited.

The Hessians stood calmly and dug cartridges from their cartridge boxes, ripped off the ends with their teeth, primed their pans, jammed the paper and ball into the muzzle, slammed the ramrods home, cocked, and once again began their forward march.

They went to one knee at one hundred yards, and once again their muskets blasted and again dirt jumped all along the breastworks and musket balls whistled over, and more men dropped.

Billy and Eli raised their heads, and suddenly they felt a deadly calm come creeping through the American line. Nerves settled. Trembling hands became firm, resolute. Eyes narrowed and became calculating, sure. The waiting was over.

They watched the Hessians reload once more, and their breathing slowed as the blue uniforms continued their steady ascent up the incline, directly towards the breastworks. They could now see the buttons on the tunics, the build of the black hip-high boots, the buckles on their cartridge boxes, and most of all, the dead eyes and vacant faces of the oncoming soldiers.

"Cock your weapons!"

The muskets clicked.

At fifty yards they heard the command for the Hessians to kneel for their next volley, and before the Hessians could go to one knee the American officers screamed, *"Fire!"*

A thousand muskets and rifles kicked and roared over the breastworks, and a cloud of white smoke half a mile long leaped and rose. All up and down the Hessian lines, men in blue uniforms staggered backwards and fell, some to rise, others not. Calmly the Hessian officers shouted orders, and the blue line began a slow retreat, pausing at one hundred yards to fire their last harmless volley and then continue back down to the tree line and disappear in the shadows and patches of sunlight.

A resounding cheer rose from a thousand voices behind the breastworks as a giddy sensation of relief, of confidence, of victory surged through the Americans.

"Reload! Reload!" The officers walked back and forth, shouting, pointing. "They'll come back! Reload."

The men reached for their cartridge boxes.

The Hessian cannon blasted and dirt and timber shards flew on the American entrenchments, while American cannon answered, and trees disintegrated and branches exploded among the Hessians. Then once again the long blue line emerged from the trees, this time to stop at two hundred yards, fire another harmless volley, and retreat back to the trees.

The sun was three hours high before the Hessian guns fell silent and movement stopped in the trees. The American officers cautiously looked over the fortifications to study the tree line with their telescopes, watching for movement. The Hessians did not mount a white flag and send patrols out onto the slope to get their dead and wounded, and the American officers puzzled, with growing concern.

Behind the mounded dirt and timbers, the American troops gently removed their fallen and their wounded back to the field hospital, where strong hands received them and went to work, and then they walked back to their posts at the fortifications and continued watching down the slope in the strange stillness of the lull in the battle.

Twenty minutes later the distant thumping of cannon and popping of muskets down at the Narrows became intense, furious.

Eli reached to scratch his cheek thoughtfully. "Stirling's in a fight, and we're in one. But I haven't heard a cannon or a musket to our left."

Billy nodded his head. "I was thinking the same thing. What happened to Miles? Something's wrong over there."

To their left, in the woods near Jamaica Road, Miles had heard the first musket pops at Flatbush when an American patrol had unexpectedly walked into the Hessians. He assumed that was where Howe was advancing, and eager to obey his orders to engage Howe, Miles had instantly marched his command southwest, towards the Bedford Road, intending to work his way down to Flatbush. Within two miles he had met Colonel Wyllys, who was under orders to guard the Bedford Pass, and Wyllys had told him there was no need for his troops there. Miles had puzzled on it for one minute before it dawned on him what had happened, and in near panic he turned his troops around and started back to the position he had left unguarded at the Jamaica Road.

Eli hunkered down for a few moments, pondering, then stood. "I'm going to take a look."

Billy shook his head. "You could be shot for deserting."

Eli drank long from his canteen, smacked the stopper back into the hole, tossed it onto the dirt mound, and replied, "I'm not deserting. My corporal told me to go find out." He watched Billy's eyes grow wide, and a smile tugged as he turned and was gone, running.

He cut through the trees and brush due east, towards the Bedford Road. Once on the road, he followed it north to the tiny hamlet of Bedford, then turned east on the Jamaica Road, moving steadily at a ground-eating trot, rifle held loosely in his right hand, watching everything before him as he worked his way east. Twice he stopped for two minutes to catch his wind, and each time he turned his ear into the gentle east breeze to listen for sounds of battle, either east or west, and there was only the sound of the birds. It seemed a hush had settled in and everyone was waiting for something that was yet unknown. A deep dread began in his breast.

He passed heavy woods on his right, and half a mile ahead, to the east, he saw a draw between two low rises, and he knew the road angled, and then he heard the sounds he most feared, and felt the vibrations in the soles of his feet. Many men marching, and heavy cannon moving! In ten seconds he was off the road, hidden, moving on east, watching, listening, and then they were there on the road to the north of him and he gasped when he saw the column.

It was strung out for more than a mile. Thousands upon thousands of red-coated British regulars led by mounted officers with more gold braid on their hats and uniforms than he had ever seen. The soldiers' uniforms were dusty from marching all night on a dirt road, four abreast. They showed no fear, no concern of being seen. He waited only long enough to make a hasty count, including their cannon, and then he turned and raced south for the trees and cover. Once past the tree line he turned west, running, flying over low bushes, reckless, not caring if a sharp-eyed British officer or regular saw him, certain they could never catch him and that no sharpshooter alive could hit him as he dodged through the trees.

He crested a small rise and plowed into Miles's command, which had just arrived from their forced march, returning from their mistaken advance down to the Bedford Road. They were exhausted, sweated out, and they did not raise a musket or challenge him as Eli slowed, looking for Miles with the gold on his shoulders.

Eli pulled up face-to-face with him, sweating, fighting for wind, and he pointed. "They're right up there on the Jamaica Road. Ten thousand. With cannon. We're flanked!"

Miles's head jerked forward and his face drained of blood. "What? Who are you?"

Eli's patience snapped. "Listen! It don't matter who I am. You're flanked! Ten thousand British regulars are over there less than half a mile east, headed this way on the Jamaica Road."

Miles recoiled, mind numb, and he stared for a moment before he spun on his heel and exploded, shouting orders. "Battle formation. We'll cut due north and fight our way through to Long Island Sound. Battle formations. Mount your bayonets."

Miles's command stared, unable to grasp what was happening. North? To the Long Island Sound? They shook their heads in confusion as they began to fall into rank and file, dumbstruck by Miles's orders that they were going to Long Island Sound.

Miles turned back to Eli and started to speak, when behind him less than half a mile one British cannon blasted, and three seconds later a second one. For two seconds no one in the command moved or made a sound while the echoes died. There were no more shots. Murmuring broke out and became loud.

Once again Miles spun towards his troops and pointed at a young captain. "You. Leave immediately. Find General Putnam. Tell him ten thousand British troops are coming west on the Jamaica Road."

The captain stood riveted to the spot, disbelieving of what he had just heard.

"Go. Now. *Move!*" Miles shouted, and the captain bolted west, angling for the Jamaica Road.

Eli turned and was gone, while Miles shouted after him, and Eli ignored him as he sprinted through the undergrowth, back to the Jamaica Road one hundred yards ahead of the captain whom Miles had ordered to go find Putnam, and turned west. He had not gone five hundred yards when from the west the distant *whump* of cannon and the popping rattle of muskets came clear. It rose to drown out all other sounds, and Eli slowed for a moment in puzzlement and then the realization sunk in.

The Hessians were waiting for those two cannon shots to signal! They're attacking to hold Sullivan and Stirling while the British column on the Jamaica Road comes in behind!

He set a pace he hoped he could hold for four miles, while his mind raced and he fought to control the panic that rose each time he thought of two thousand Americans at the breastworks caught between six thousand Hessians and ten thousand British regulars, with only one way out—west through the Gowanus swamp.

With the sun barely above the eastern skyline, General Lord Stirling stopped his sixteen-hundred-man command just north of the Narrows, nearly on the beaches of Gowanus Bay to his right. For long minutes he studied the hills and gullies and the wild growth of oak and maples and the dense foliage to his left, and then he addressed his officers and troops. His face was dark, scowling.

"General Parsons and what's left of his command are just to our left, over that rise, dug in, waiting. About half a mile south of us, that pompous fool General Grant is in command of about six thousand British regulars, and he means to come up this road to get to our fortifications." He paused, hating the need to even say the name of General Grant. It was Grant who had bragged to the world that if he had five thousand regulars, he could march from one end of America to the other. Stirling continued. "Our orders, and Parsons' orders, are to stop him. We are to hold this road at all costs."

He pointed. "We're going to form up our three regiments in a line right here. Gist next to the road, then McDonough, then Kachlein. Use natural cover—every rock, gully, tree, ditch, and bush—to hide your men. When the shooting starts, listen for my commands to fire. I'll be right here among you. All right. Move."

Ten minutes later the American line was in place, with hardly a man visible from the road. At least twenty riflemen had climbed to the tops of trees to wedge themselves into a fork or on a branch where they commanded an open field of fire southward, down the road. The entire line quieted, waiting in tense silence.

From the south came the distant sounds of an army marching, and it grew louder as the long minutes ticked by. Then they could hear the voices of the officers, and then they saw their red coats and crossed white belts gleaming in the warm morning sun as they came on, four abreast, up the Gowanus Road. Just over the ridge to their left, they could hear more British regulars moving parallel to the road, on a collision course with Parsons's command.

Stirling stood resolutely behind a shamble of rocks, partly hidden by scrub oak, watching, gauging distance carefully. He turned to the officer next to him. "Cock your muskets. Spread the word." The order went quietly up and down the American line, and the clicks could be heard for two hundred yards.

The British came on without showing a sign of hesitation. Stirling picked out a smooth, worn boulder on the seaward side of the road and gauged it's distance at seventy yards. *When the first regiment is past that rock.*

The first regiment reached the rock, and Stirling could see the sweat and hear the clank of canteens on cartridge boxes as they came on. They had nearly cleared the huge stone when the leading officer caught his first glimpse of an American rifleman behind rocks, and he instantly raised his hand and started to shout an order.

Stirling shouted first. *"Fire!"*

Sound and smoke erupted all along the road and red-coated regulars staggered and slumped in confusion, and then their officers barked orders and they began to fall back, organized, firing as they did, covering their retreat. Stirling could hear the muskets and rifles blasting over the ridge where the regulars had stumbled into Parsons's command.

Minutes passed while Stirling's men reloaded and waited.

The British regrouped and their officers formed them into skirmishing squads, and once again they advanced, this time off the road, in the brush, coming in short bursts of speed, probing, watching to see where the smoke and sound came from.

"Hold your fire," Stirling shouted. "Wait. Wait for my command."

The British were eighty yards away when they stopped and

raised their muskets, and Stirling again shouted, "Fire!" Once again smoke and flame leaped from the tops of trees and from behind rocks and bushes, and .75-caliber American musket balls tore into the British line. Red-coated regulars groaned and dropped and staggered back, and again the British command echoed, "Fall back."

The Americans reloaded and held their positions. Slowly, cautiously, a feeling of confidence bordering on bravado began to creep into them, and they smiled and made small talk. *We turned them. They came and we engaged them, and we held and they retreated.*

With the sun climbing high, the British advanced twice more, and both times their regulars delivered a volley, and some of the Americans sagged at their hiding places and sat down and toppled over as the British again retreated to regroup and reload. They were in plain sight, half a mile south of Stirling's position, and he studied them through his telescope.

There are six thousand of them standing down there, doing nothing. What are they up to? What have I overlooked?

He called for his officers, and Gist and Kachlein and McDonough came trotting, red-faced, sweating.

Stirling pointed south. "They're down there doing nothing. Six thousand of them. Can you suggest what's holding them back?"

"No, sir. I've wondered the same thing. With a little help from Parsons we might hold them if they formed ranks and came at us head-on, but so far they've only been probing with squads and skirmish lines."

"One more thing," Stirling said. "The shooting at the breastworks has stopped. Did you notice?"

McDonough looked at Kachlein. "I noticed, but didn't think about it."

The four officers stood for a moment, puzzled, unable to make sense of the British maneuvers and the sudden silence when there should be shooting.

Stirling shook his head, dark suspicion mounting. "Our orders are to stay here and hold this road. We can't be concerned about what's happening with Sullivan back at the breastworks. We'll follow our orders and wait here until the British show their hand. Return to your troops."

Kachlein and McDonough and Gist turned to go, when from the distance, far to their left and behind them, came the clear sound of one shot from a heavy cannon, and then three seconds later, a second shot, and then silence. They turned to peer back to Stirling, searching to understand the oddity of two timed cannon shots in the midst of an unexplained silence.

South of Stirling, General Grant raised his head and turned to a colonel and a captain standing next to him. "Did you hear those two cannon?"

"Yes, sir."

"Three seconds apart?"

"Yes, sir."

"I believe those shots were General Howe's signal. He's taken Jamaica Pass and he's in position behind Sullivan at the breastworks. Do you both agree?"

Without hesitation both officers said, "Yes, sir."

Grant removed his tricornered hat and wiped the sweat from the hatband, and settled it back onto his head. The gold braid sparkled in the sunlight. His face showed utter contempt as he spoke. "Form your men according to the plan I showed you. Move the artillery up. In exactly fifteen minutes our infantry moves north against Stirling." As an afterthought he added, "Crushing that popinjay shouldn't take long."

Grant watched as the officers called orders and their regiments moved into their positions. The road was cleared while horse-drawn cannon and mortars came rumbling forward and took up positions three hundred yards from the trees and gullies and rocks where the Americans were hidden. Grant waited until the officer in charge of the big guns nodded, and he called to them, "Fire!"

The cannon blasted hot and heavy for ten minutes, blowing grape and cannister shot to shred the trees and pepper the gullies that hid the American lines, before Grant issued his next order. "Cease fire. Infantry, forward."

The officers barked orders and nearly six thousand regulars stepped out, marching steadily, bayonets gleaming.

North of them, General Stirling's eyes narrowed and his breathing slowed as he studied them through his telescope. He turned to his officers. "Don't fire until you hear my command."

At seventy yards he gave the order and the American muskets and rifles fired, and British soldiers went down but those behind did not slow. They marched over their own fallen and continued forward while the Americans reloaded. At fifty yards the first rank went to its knees and the second rank stood behind it, muskets cocked, aimed.

"Fire!" shouted Grant, and a thousand muskets cracked, and Americans went down while the British continued in their steady, relentless march, with the first two ranks falling back to reload while two fresh ranks moved to replace them.

Reloaded, the Americans waited for Stirling's command. At thirty yards he gave it, and the Americans fired their second volley, and great gaps appeared in the leading rank of the advancing redcoats, and for a moment they hesitated and then they began to withdraw.

Stirling exhaled held breath and wiped his hand across his mouth. "Reload."

Too many. If they come again like that, can we hold? He straightened his spine and set his jaw, and watched.

Far to the east, in the woods to the south of the Jamaica Road, Miles sobered and by force of will calmed his shattered thoughts and impulses. He stood for ten seconds, studying the column of British troops marching west on the road, and took charge of himself.

Ten thousand! No chance! We can help Sullivan if we can reach the breastworks in time.

He called his officers. "Form ranks for a march. We're not

going north to Long Island Sound. We're going west to help Sullivan. We have to move at double time."

He led his eight hundred men west, parallel to the Jamaica Road, working through the trees, hoping to get ahead of the advancing British. He made it five hundred yards before a British officer towards the head of the column on the road sent a patrol to see what was advancing through the woods.

"Halt," Miles ordered, and the Americans stopped in the trees, waiting, hoping the patrol would remain short of them and return to the road.

The young lieutenant in command of the patrol marched on, slowing, uncertain, peering into the filigree of light and shadow in the trees, waiting for movement. There was nothing, and he halted the squad. For half a minute he studied the woods before he raised his hand to signal the squad to return to the column, when his sergeant suddenly pointed. "There, sir. Someone tryin' to 'ide with a musket."

The young lieutenant hesitated, caught between whether to go into the woods or to send back for reinforcements. He turned to his corporal. "Go back and report something's here. Tell them to send a large force."

Miles was close enough to hear their voices but too far to hear their words. He watched the corporal trot back to the column, where a mounted officer reined in his horse to listen. The officer turned and gave orders, and an entire regiment followed him from the road towards the trees.

Miles gave hushed orders and his men cocked their muskets.

Ten minutes later five hundred British regulars moved into the trees cautiously, watching, muskets at the ready. Five hundred more formed a line twenty yards from the trees and went to one knee, ready.

Inside the woods, a red-coated private nearly stepped on one of Miles's men crouched in the heavy foliage, and the American stood up, facing the regular not three feet away. The startled regular jerked back and stumbled and went down and his musket fired, and one second later muskets on both sides were blasting all through the woods.

In the momentary lull while both sides were reloading Miles shouted, "Cease fire, cease fire!" Quickly he stripped his saber from his belt and sprinted to the edge of the woods, out into the sunlight, facing the long line of British infantry. He carried his saber in both hands, high over his head, shouting frantically. "We are your prisoners. Cease fire."

With the sun climbing higher at his back, Eli left the Jamaica Road to cut south on the Flatbush Road, down towards the breastworks, listening to the sounds of a furious cannon-and-musket battle grow louder with each step. He crested the last low rise and stopped in his tracks, sweat running, fighting for wind, and a low moan escaped him.

The Hessians were no longer coming up the hill in a long blue line. They were coming in six long blue lines, thousands of them, marching into the American cannon and musket fire, bayonets glittering in the warm August morning. Half a dozen of their cannon were fifty yards north of the tree line, firing as fast as the cannoneers could reload, blasting cannister shot over the heads of their own infantry to burst all over the American lines. Behind them, from the trees, a dozen more cannon had the range and maintained an unending fire of solid thirty-two-pound cannonballs that were blowing the timbers and dirt of the great mound fifty feet in all directions with each hit. On both ends of the fortifications, Hessians had scaled the front and reached the top, only to be thrown back in desperate hand-to-hand fighting, leaving their dead and wounded on top of the breastworks, and a few on the American side.

Eli plunged on, eyes searching for Putnam or Sullivan, and he could see neither as he dodged and darted through the cannon shot and the dead and wounded and the confusion behind the lines. He reached the center where he had left Billy and the Boston regiment, and they were there, sweating, smoke-stained, white-faced as they mechanically fired and ducked behind the dirt mound to reload while cannister shot blasted downward from overhead to kick dirt all around them, and musket balls whirred past and cannonballs shook the front of the breastworks.

He crouched beside Billy, and Billy looked at him and his head sagged forward for a moment in relief. "You're alive!"

"Where's Putnam or Sullivan?"

"I don't know."

"Where's Thompson?"

Billy pointed. "Over there somewhere a minute ago. Why? What's happening?"

"They got the Jamaica Road." He jerked a thumb over his shoulder, pointing. "Ten thousand. They'll be here in ten minutes."

Billy froze and went wide-eyed. "*What?*"

"We're flanked. Trapped. Help me find Putnam or Sullivan, or even Thompson."

Billy stood and his eyes swept the lines and suddenly he pointed. "There!"

Eli lunged to his feet and sprinted to the west towards Putnam, still giving orders to load and fire. He stopped, panting, face-to-face with the startled old general, nearly shouting to be heard above the blasting guns. He pointed east. "We're flanked. Howe is coming on the Jamaica Road with ten thousand troops. They're less than ten minutes from us right now. We're in a trap."

Putnam blinked and slowly formed words. "Who are you? How do you know?"

"Eli Stroud, Boston regiment. I went to look." Eli contained himself, waiting for understanding to show in Putnam's face.

"Why hasn't Miles sent word?"

"He sent an officer. He's coming."

"Where?"

"I don't know. Behind me somewhere."

Putnam studied Eli for long seconds. "I'll wait for word from Miles."

"That officer might not make it. What if he doesn't?"

Putnam shrugged. "I'll wait."

Eli lost his patience, shouting, pointing. "General, in five minutes you're going to have ten thousand British regulars right in here among your men, behind these breastworks, and you won't have a chance. Everybody here could be dead in half an hour. *Do something!*"

Putnam stared, then turned to the nearest officer. "Have this man restrained."

Eli groaned and spun on his heel, running, looking for Sullivan. He saw the back of a uniform with gold on the shoulders, on the lines, near the Boston regiment, and he angled towards the man and stopped, facing him.

Thompson!

"We're flanked!" Eli shouted, pointing. "Howe took the Jamaica Road. He's less than five minutes from here leading ten thousand redcoats. We're trapped."

Thompson's face went white. "*What?*"

"They're coming! We got less than five minutes."

For five seconds Thompson stood stock-still, mind racing, groping. "Did you tell Putnam?"

"I did. He wants to wait for word from Miles. He was going to arrest me."

"What happened to Miles?"

"He's back there somewhere. He sent an officer to tell Putnam."

"Where's the officer?"

"I don't know. I distanced him."

"Did you tell Sullivan?"

"Can't find him. I'm telling you."

Thompson shook his head as if he were coming out of a dream and he barked, "Come on!"

He set out at a trot, working east, looking frantically for Sullivan's uniform, Eli at his side. They had gone twenty yards when Eli grabbed his shoulder and pointed, excited. "There! There's Miles's officer."

A blonde-haired uniformed man was staggering towards the east end of the lines, gasping, hat gone, musket gone, uniform dirty, sweat running. Eli sprinted, with Thompson following as fast as he could. Eli lifted the man's arm over his shoulder and turned, starting back, as Thompson came to a stop.

"Captain," Thompson shouted above the din, "where's Miles?"

The man formed words between gasps. "Back there. I saw them. Ten thousand. I saw them."

Thompson spun on his heel and started back west, looking for Putnam, Eli behind, half carrying the captain who was muttering, wide-eyed, half out of his mind. Eli shouted to Thompson, "Over there," and Thompson veered towards Putnam, to stop in front of him.

"Sir, we have a messenger from Miles." He pointed.

Putnam eyed Eli, then the captain, who stared back at him with blank eyes.

"Your name?"

"I saw them. So many."

Putnam's forehead wrinkled. "Who are you?"

The man swallowed and shook his head and tried to take control. "Captain James Adamson, under the command of General Miles."

"Where's Miles?"

"East."

"What's the message?"

"Howe has taken the Jamaica Road. He's coming here. Ten thousand regulars. Cannon."

Putnam's mouth sagged open for a split second. "How close?"

"Close. I don't know."

Putnam looked at Thompson. "Do you believe it?"

"I do. My man Eli Stroud got to me first. Said he told you."

Putnam looked at Eli. "He did." He turned back to Thompson. "Can you find Sullivan?"

"I can try."

"If it's true we're flanked, we've got to send word immediately to Stirling and Parsons to fall back to the Brooklyn lines."

"I agree."

"I'll start here. You get Sullivan and have him report to me. Then get your command under control and get ready for an orderly withdrawal back to Brooklyn."

"Yes, sir."

At that moment the four men involuntarily ducked as a cannonball whistled ten feet over their heads to plow into the ground eighty feet west of them and explode, throwing dirt and debris, and knock two running soldiers rolling, and then the boom of the cannon came rolling in from the east.

Instantly all four men pivoted, and for a moment they stood stock-still, gaping. Five hundred yards to the east were six mounted British officers, and behind them was an ocean of red coats with crossed white belts as far as they could see. For a moment they stood in shock, minds numb as the sick truth tore their hearts. Miles and his command were gone. Every American patrol to the east was gone, and the village of Bedford was overrun and lost.

They did not move, and white smoke rolled from three more cannon and an instant later the cannonballs whistled overhead to rip trenches five feet long in the earth before they exploded, and all four officers ducked and flinched as grains of sand and dirt pelted their backs and stung their necks and the sounds of the blasts rolled past.

Putnam straightened and knew he should give a command, but he could not force his mind to invent one. Sullivan stammered but could not form a coherent sentence, and he simply raised an arm to point. Eli spun on his heel and sprinted for the center of the line where he had left Billy and what was left of the Boston regiment. Thompson waited three more seconds for orders from either of his commanding officers and realized they were not capable of giving one, and he turned and ran after Eli in the desperate hope he might save some of his command.

At that moment every British regular behind Howe raised his voice in a sustained battle cry, knowing they had sprung the trap to perfection and that the core of the Continental army would be dead or captured before midafternoon. Their voices became a crescendo that rose above the sounds of battle, and the Americans at the breastworks all turned their heads to look. For an instant they did not move, eyes wide and mouths fallen open in unbelief that turned to stark horror.

Frantically they looked for their officers and they saw none, and in an instant they broke from the breastworks in wild chaos, running any direction their instincts took them, a terrified mob without leadership, without direction, without thought. The leading British regiment streamed straight on through, led by Cornwallis, and continued west to the Gowanus Road, where Cornwallis led them south. His orders were to proceed with all haste to trap and crush Stirling's command, which was being held in position by Grant.

Immediately south of the breastworks, von Heister heard the cannon from the east and then the oncoming shouting, and turned to von Donop, his second in command. "Howe is in behind them. Now is the time we storm the breastworks. When we have reached the other side, immediately send two regiments to the Gowanus Road with orders to move south with Cornwallis, where they will find Stirling and trap him against Grant's forces." He shrugged indifferently. "Kill or capture all of Stirling's forces." He paused to be sure he had given the correct order, and concluded. "That is all. Give the orders."

"Ja, Herr General," von Donop said in clipped German. Three minutes later the Hessians surged over the breastworks, nearly six thousand strong, into the wildest melee any of them had ever seen. It seemed the world was filled with men running and dodging in every direction, alone, in twos and threes, shouting, while British regulars held their lines, running west, closing off the escape routes into the woods or north to Brooklyn. They did not stop to reload their muskets. Five thousand bayonets were doing their work.

★ ★ ★

To the west, on Manhattan Island, at his headquarters in New York City, General George Washington paced in his private quarters, waiting, tenuously maintaining an appearance of controlled calm. He started at the rap on the door. "Enter."

Colonel Joseph Reed opened the door instantly. "Sir, we've received word there is heavy fighting at our lines on Long Island."

Washington's eyes flashed as he instantly asked, "Have the British sent any ships up either the Hudson or the East River? Are they preparing to attack us here at New York?"

"No, sir."

Washington swept up his hat and cape. "Saddle my horse."

"She's saddled, sir, and the staff is waiting."

Ten minutes later Washington reined in his winded mare on the flagstones surrounding the Fort George Battery on the water's edge at the south end of town. He leaped from the saddle, jerked his telescope full length, and held his breath as he swept the Brooklyn Peninsula, while his staff dismounted and waited.

He saw the pall of white smoke hanging low over the American lines, and then he saw flashes of blue, and then red, and he sucked air. He paused and by force of will slowly glassed the coast once again, and then he cocked his head to listen to the sustained sounds of cannon and musketry and rifles and, most of all, the throaty roar of soldiers in the full flush of victory.

He rammed the telescope closed, jammed it into its scarred leather case, and turned to Reed. "We're going over."

Reed recoiled. "You're going over there, sir? Dare you risk it?"

Washington swung up onto his mare, who stuttered her feet and shied, and Washington took a tight rein and spoke back to Reed. "Dare I not?"

Forty minutes later Washington hauled his mare to a stiff-legged halt at the crest of Cobble Hill, near the west end of the American lines, and again extended his telescope to study the action to the south, while his staff caught up, winded, on horses that showed sweat where the bridle straps had worked. One of them drew a pocket watch to check the time. It was half past eleven o'clock. The sun had not yet reached its zenith.

Washington sat his horse like a statue, face set, as he studied the movements of Stirling's command, and then he lowered the telescope and picked up the red-coated regulars moving south on the Gowanus Road under Cornwallis, and coming in right behind Cornwallis, the blue coats of the Hessians.

Washington inwardly groaned at the realization that Stirling was trapped.

To the south, General Lord Stirling gritted his teeth and turned to his nearest officers. "We're under orders to hold this road, and by heaven, we're going to do it! Order your lines in towards the road. Regroup. Time your fire. Don't waste cartridges. Keep up your spirits. We've held so far, and we can hold through the day."

The officers barked orders and the outer reaches of the lines moved in towards the Gowanus Road, moving slowly but surely, firing, reloading as they walked, controlled, taking the enemy fire cooly, keeping their heads.

Then from the north came the sounds of a great body of advancing troops, and Stirling's men turned and their breath came short. Half a mile up the road, moving south at a trot, were a thousand British redcoats, followed by the hated blue coats of the Hessians. Stirling's officers instantly turned to him, silently waiting for orders that surely must come.

For ten seconds Stirling stared while his mind accepted it, and then he made his decision. "My orders were to hold here, but if the British and Hessians are coming behind us, that means they've overrun the breastworks. I'm exercising my rights to initiate my own orders." He stared long and hard at the great expanse of the Gowanus marsh, spread out to his left and slightly ahead of him. In the history of Long Island, no one had ever tried to cross the muck and quicksand and stench of the great, dead swamp.

Stirling sucked air and turned to the officer in command of

his Maryland regiment and gave the orders that would forever shine in the annals of brave men doing brave deeds. "Major Gist, you and I and half of your Marylanders are going to attack the British and the Hessians to the north. When we do, all the rest of this command is going to cross that swamp." He pointed to his left, and his officers looked and their eyes dropped and they said nothing as he spoke loudly. "When you're past the swamp, move on north to the lines at Brooklyn. Reform there and await orders."

Every man in the command knew that Stirling was committing his own life and those of Major Gist and a small group of men to a fight they could not win and from which too many of them would not return.

Gist turned and gave terse orders. A section of his Marylanders fell out of their regiment and formed behind him, heads high, ready. Not a man among them flinched.

Stirling faced the remainder of his command. "When we start north, the rest of you wait until we engage the column coming down, and then move into the swamp, and don't stop." He wanted to say more but could think of nothing, and he quietly said, "God bless you all."

He turned back to Gist and wiped the back of his hand across his mouth. His eyes were bright, his face clear. "All right. Follow me." Stirling drew his saber and took a deep breath and started up the road at a trot. Gist was right behind, and following Gist was the small group of Marylanders, matching their leaders step for step, not one man wavering.

Four hundred yards from the oncoming British, Stirling slowed and raised his telescope. "*Cornwallis!* We're facing Cornwallis!" He continued forward at a trot, and at two hundred yards suddenly veered off the road into the brush and trees, and with hand signals spread his small command along the road.

Cornwallis watched him with an expression akin to amusement and ordered his command to continue. They marched on towards the place where Stirling had disappeared, unaware that Stirling and his men had moved forward and were waiting behind anything that would hide a man. Stirling waited until the British were nearly abreast before he rose from the brush and, with his saber raised, shouted the order. "Fire!"

The muskets cracked and the smoke rose, and some British regulars staggered and went down.

Instantly Cornwallis ordered the lead regiment to face the smoke, and the first British volley rang out.

South of the shooting, the remainder of Stirling's command heard the popping of the muskets, and grim faced, the remaining officers led them at a run to the edge of the Gowanus swamp, and they plowed in, black sticky muck flying. They plunged on, into their waists, then their chests, and they struggled on with their muskets held high and the putrid stench of dead and decaying things rank in their nostrils.

Cornwallis waited a moment; then, satisfied that Stirling's small group had run away, he continued south. He had gone two hundred yards when, without warning, from as close as thirty yards from the road, a second volley came whistling and more of his regulars crumpled. Again Cornwallis stopped, ordered his first regiment to face the smoke, and answered the volley. And again Cornwallis waited until there was nothing moving in the brush, and continued on south.

Stirling left seven of his Marylanders lying in the brush and trees as he led his men silently south, dodging, running low, and suddenly they appeared on the road eighty yards in front of Cornwallis's column. The Americans fired without command and again dodged into the brush.

To the north, at the top of Cobble Hill, Washington watched the action develop from the beginning. Stirling marching straight into the great British column—firing—hiding—exchanging volleys—moving—firing—refusing to run—stopping the oncoming British time and again in his desperate try at saving the bulk of his command as they plowed onward through the swamp.

Washington lowered his telescope for a moment and Reed looked at him. Washington's eyes were too shiny, his voice too high, his chin trembling as he uttered, "What brave fellows I must this day lose."

Behind him, Colonel Smallwood, recently returned from New York City, spurred his horse forward, unable any longer to watch his men cut down in their heroic stand. "General, I'm begging. Let me take a regiment and go down there. I can't . . . I've never seen anything like that. Someone has to go save Stirling."

Washington's voice caught for a moment and he cleared his throat and spoke. "No. We can't save him, and we can't sacrifice men trying."

South of Stirling, General Grant watched the small group move north to meet Cornwallis and then the main group break for the Gowanus swamp, and he stood still, unable to believe what he was seeing. No one had ever tried to cross the swamp. And a handful of Americans stood no chance in a fight with Cornwallis. Had they all lost their minds?

To Grant's right, over the ridge, Parsons had suddenly realized he was hemmed in, surrounded, and ordered his men to scatter, find any out they could, and to make their own way north to the breastworks, unaware they were walking into the worst holocaust they had ever seen.

Grant shrugged and gave his orders. "Forward." He started up the road to close the trap that Stirling now found himself in, with Cornwallis coming from the north and Grant from the south.

The little band of Marylanders divided, half facing one way, half the other, and they moved into the trees, dodging, loading, firing, running, loading, firing, while the British sent volley after volley after them, and slowly, one at a time, one here and one there, the Americans were dropping, most of them to remain, a few to rise to try to struggle on with their wounds.

Once more Stirling rallied his men and gave orders. "Scatter. Go separately, any way you can. Try to get back to the breastworks or to the Brooklyn lines. Good luck to you all." He stared into their faces for a moment. "It has been my great honor to fight by your side."

In ten seconds the tiny group was gone, having disappeared in the trees and brush. Stirling remained only long enough to be certain they were gone, then paused one moment to look south at Grant's command moving in on him. His lip curled in contempt. *I'll die before I'll surrender to that man. Or, for that matter, to Cornwallis.* Resolutely he moved out into the trees, headed north and east towards the breastworks. If he was going to be killed or captured, he would be certain it was by someone other than Grant. Anyone but Grant, even the Hessians.

To the north, the Hessians who were with Cornwallis's regulars angled to their right, off Gowanus Road, to the swamp where the bulk of Stirling's command was working its way north, struggling, fighting their way through the black slime that reached to their waists, desperately trying to reach the safety of the Brooklyn lines. From their right came running the Americans who had broken through the British and Hessian trap at the breastworks, one or two at a time, and they plunged into the Gowanus swamp and the woods, driven by blind terror. The Hessians trotted along the eastern edge of the swamp, forming a long line, and then they stopped. With relentless precision they picked their targets and they fired and reloaded and fired again, in a steady stream. The nearest Americans held their muskets high over their heads and turned towards the shore, screaming, "We surrender! We surrender!" but the Hessians did not understand one word of English, nor did they care. They shot them, and those that made it out of the muck they bayonetted, and the screams of the wounded and the dying meant nothing to them. They had come to destroy the impertinent, ragged, foolish Americans, and they were doing it. They would finish by nightfall and collect their pay and go home to Germany.

Washington could take no more. He turned to his staff. "We're going to the breastworks." He reined his horse around and tapped his spurs to its flanks.

The breastworks were a chaotic bedlam. American officers shouted orders that were instantly lost in the deafening roar of muskets and cannon, and of men screaming as bayonets struck, and of British and Hessian soldiers in full battle cry, slowly tightening their circle. In their blind panic the American soldiers heard no orders, nor did they try, and their officers drew their sabers and pounded their own troops on the back and legs with the flat side, trying to rally them, regroup them, organize them into a defensive unit.

Then the Hessians began seeking out the American officers, and in twos and threes they ringed them and drove their bayonets home and watched the officers topple, and moved on, seeking the next one.

After Eli broke from a stammering Putnam, in the wild jumble of sound and men, he sprinted, dodging, towards the center of the breastworks, empty rifle slung over his back on its strap, tomahawk in hand, searching for Billy. A redcoat swung around with his bayonet lowered, and Eli slapped it aside and swung the tomahawk once and leaped over the body and continued on, watching, head turning in his desperate hunt, unable to hear anything above the deafening din. He saw only the hated Hessians at the place the Boston regiment had been, mechanically thrusting with their bayonets as they worked their way towards the British. He plunged into them, tomahawk swinging, knocking aside their muskets, and he broke through and Billy was not there, nor was his body among those lying on the ground, bloody and broken and dead.

He vaulted to the top of the breastworks and spun around, frantic, and then he saw Billy thirty yards north and east. In the mindless heat of battle, with no time for either Billy or the British to reload, Billy had thrown down his useless musket and swept up the sword of a fallen officer and was swinging with all his strength, hacking his way, leading half a dozen of the regiment in a do-or-die fight to break through for a desperate run to the Brooklyn defenses. The British were using their overpowering numbers, their bayonets, and their musket butts as they systematically continued in their deadly work of annihilating or capturing the American forces.

A Hessian rushed at Eli with his rifle butt raised, and Eli ducked and swung the tomahawk in the same motion and the Hessian dropped. Eli leaped from the breastworks and ran, jumping over bodies, striking with his tomahawk, dodging bayonets, until he reached the tiny group led by Billy, and then he was beside Billy, and they surged forward into the wall of red-coated regulars.

A British officer spread his feet squarely in front of Billy and raised a huge pistol directly into his face. Billy swung the sword and he saw the officer jerk the trigger and the hammer fell—and the thought flashed in Billy's mind, *Too late, too late*—and the flint struck the frizzen and the powder in the pan flared just as Billy's sword struck the side of the pistol. In the fleck of time it took for the fire to burn through the touchhole, the pistol muzzle was knocked four inches to Billy's left, and he twisted his head to the right just as it went off. The blast blackened Billy's shirt around his upper left side and the ball tore through the cloth to leave a black streak on the crown of his left shoulder and leave his ear ringing.

The officer gasped and stumbled backwards, and Billy swung his fist with the sword handle in it and struck the officer over the right ear and he hit the ground in a heap. In one movement Billy swept him up and draped him over his left shoulder and once again walked straight into the red-coated regulars, sword poised, ready.

The British soldiers blinked and then they raised their bayonets and began backing away, confused about how to attack a man who had a British officer slung over his shoulder. None of them wanted to be the one court-martialed and shot for wounding or killing one of their own officers.

There were four regulars in front of Billy and Eli, and then two, and then there were none, and then they were past the British lines, past the edge of their own camp, running free in the brush and foliage towards the tree line. Billy threw the officer from his shoulder, rolling in the dirt as they plunged into the trees and ran, not looking back. They ran until the sounds behind them were fading, and they stopped, panting, trying to catch their wind.

Sweat ran, and their faces were streaked and dirty from gun smoke. Billy looked at the men who had followed him away from the breastworks. There were six when they started. Three remained.

Without a word Eli pointed and started west at a trot. Five minutes later the trees gave way to grass and brush, and then they were on the Flatbush Road. They stopped to look, and to listen. The only sounds were those of the unending battle behind them, and they turned their faces north and started up the rutted dirt road towards the Brooklyn lines. Eli turned once to look back.

What did they do with the nurses? Did they move her out before the fight? Is she back in New York, safe?

They continued on in the heat of the August sun, silent, without speaking, their minds struggling to leave behind the world filled with soldiers in blue and red uniforms, and guns and bayonets, and screaming men maimed and dead.

To the west, past the breastworks, General Washington rode to the sound of the guns. It led him south, where he suddenly found himself among Americans running headlong from all directions, through the trees and brush, driven by panic. There were officers scattered among them, but they were making no attempt to halt the fragmented troops. Washington jerked his saber from its scabbard and rode spurring his horse back and forth, slamming into his own men, shouting, "Remember what you are contending for. Wives, families, liberty." If they heard his words, and if they recognized who he was, it did not slow them. They streamed past him, not stopping, not caring.

They pushed past him and around him, and they paid no heed. He began smacking them with the flat of his sword, his voice raised, shouting at them to stop, and they did not. He singled out an officer and reined his horse directly in front of the man and shouted, "Halt! Take command of your troops." The man paused half a second to stare up at him white-faced, and he dodged around the horse and was gone.

For a long time Washington spurred his horse into the midst

of his beaten army, waving his sword, shouting, striking officers and troops alike, and they ignored him in their headlong stampede.

Panting, angry, watching his army disintegrate before his eyes, Washington slowed and then he stopped. The air went out of him and his shoulders slumped and he sat there, head bowed, sword dangling from his hand. A hundred Hessians burst from the brush and trees eighty yards to the south and came trotting, bayonets lowered. One of Washington's aides gasped and reached from his own mount to grasp the bit of Washington's horse and jerk the animal around, and he raised the two horses to a gallop, running with the decimated, retreating army, trying for the safety of the Brooklyn lines.

It was a few minutes past three o'clock in the afternoon when Billy and Eli, with the three survivors who had followed them, caught their first glimpse of the Brooklyn defenses in the distance. The open ground sloped steadily upwards to the lines, which were anchored on the right by Fort Putnam and on the left by Fort Box, with Fort Greene and a great breastwork spaced between them. The Flatbush Road ran through the center, dividing Brooklyn nearly in half. The structures were connected by trenches, where men had dug in with their muskets.

Billy and Eli plodded forward, silent, watching others, one or two at a time, stumbling towards the road. Slowly the survivors of the beaten army entered onto the roadbed, some limping, some helping others, all of them filthy, ragged, most of them bloodied, all with but one thought: Brooklyn—safety.

Billy stared hard as they neared the lines, looking for smoke or men in red coats, wondering whether the British had sent men-of-war and troops up the East River and taken Brooklyn from behind. They had not. The exhausted men plodded on.

By four o'clock small groups of men from all commands had passed through the lines to gather on the ground, waiting, watching in silence as others came in, grim faced, looking for their officers or any familiar face. By four-thirty most of those who could had gathered, and dropped into the grass to lie as they fell, drained, body and soul.

A little past five o'clock the shout from the lines came echoing, "They're coming."

And then General Washington was there among them, on the ground, leading his horse. He spoke a word here, gave a helping hand there, constantly moving, encouraging. There were no incriminations, no accusations of who had failed. He shook the hands of the officers, asked what they needed, circled their shoulders with his long arm, knelt beside a private with one leg missing to cover him with his cape and touch his forehead.

Slowly he rallied his battered army, and they rose to their feet one more time and grimly made their way to the trenches. They brought anything they could for weapons—muskets if they had them, swords, axes, sticks, rocks—and they lowered themselves into the trenches and peered down the slope at the Flatbush Road. They saw the flood of red and blue coats fanning out from east to west in lines a mile long, and they saw the cannon. In the warm late afternoon sunlight, with shadows slanting to the east, the officers in the forts silently made their count and sent word to General Washington.

A little over twenty thousand British regulars and Hessians were forming in regiments, with over one hundred cannon in a line, less than one mile away. Washington stoically accepted the reports, then ordered his staff to count his officers and if possible his men, and report.

Sullivan, Miles, Stirling, Parsons, Putnam—all missing, either dead or captured, and no one knew the count of the lesser officers. Nor did anyone know how many men were crouched in the trenches and in the forts and breastworks. Perhaps two thousand, perhaps more, or less.

Every officer, every man at the lines knew their small beaten huddle of men would be overrun in minutes when the British and Hessians came marching. The Continental army would be annihilated, crushed, and in their hearts they knew their dream of

America, and of liberty, would pass into history barely noticed, remembered as foolishness by only a few. They set their jaws and they gripped their weapons, and they waited.

"They halted! They stopped!" The shout came from a dozen throats.

Every head on the lines jerked up and eyes opened wide, afraid to look, afraid to believe, and the men slowly stood in the trenches, dumbstruck as they saw the long British lines standing still, waiting.

Behind the massive lines, General Howe called for consultation with his officers. Clinton, Cornwallis, Percy, von Heister, and Grant all faced him, their faces alive, eyes keen, their blood hot for a final attack, and they wanted it before dark.

Howe turned and studied the terrain—the open slope up to the trenches, the Americans dug in at the top. Was he seeing Bunker Hill all over again—a few Americans cutting the redcoats to pieces, stacking the dead row upon row as they marched up a hill? Was it true—his sympathies were stronger for the Americans than for the Crown? Was he calculating the time it would take to put Brooklyn under siege and starve them out, with no battle at all? His officers could not tell.

He turned back to them. "We wait. Tonight they have a lot to think about, and tomorrow we'll move on them. I expect Washington will offer terms of surrender. I don't think he'll sacrifice the last of his army for a lost cause." He pursed his mouth for a moment. "So we wait."

Clinton's mouth fell open. "*What?*" He pointed north, animated, and his words coming hot. "They're right there, in the palm of our hand. In one hour this entire idiotic revolution can be over, finished, and we can be on our way back to England. I've never seen an army so close to total annihilation!"

The other officers held their breath, waiting, covertly watching Howe. Seldom had they seen any general officer address his commander so sharply.

Howe's expression did not change as he turned to Clinton. His voice was calm. "We will wait."

Cornwallis exhaled. "Sir, respectfully I must point out that a delay will only give them time to regroup, organize, re-arm, plan something. At this moment they have no semblance of command, half of them are not armed, their spirit is broken, they're sitting right there, ours for the taking."

Howe remained passive and silent.

Percy spoke. "If it's the forts that concern you, sir, give me half an hour with the cannon and they won't be standing."

Howe raised a hand. "We wait. Issue orders that we camp here tonight."

It was finished.

The sun touched the western rim of the world and shadows lengthened, and suddenly the shout came once again from the American lines. "They're building cook fires—bedding down for the night."

Again the Americans stood in the trenches and fortifications to peer south into the first shades of dusk. Fires winked on. They could hear the clatter of iron tripods being spread and the clank of huge black kettles being hung on chains as the regimental cooks started supper. The Americans stood still, staring, afraid to hope.

Billy turned to Eli, standing in the trench next to him. "Do you believe it?"

Eli rubbed a grimy hand over tired eyes. "I don't know. It could be a trick for a night attack. In a while I'll go look." He glanced back at Billy. "Seen Thompson? Turlock?"

"No."

"Do you know if Thompson got our sick out before the British hit us?"

"Mary?"

"Yes."

"I don't know. I doubt it. It happened too fast."

"What do the British usually do with sick prisoners?"

"No one ever said. I suppose they take care of them. It's the only way to be sure we'll do the same for them." He looked at Eli and saw the need. "Mary's not a soldier. She'll be all right."

Ten minutes later Washington set up his meager command post out in the open, in full sight of his tattered army. It was only a table and a few chairs, with a lantern, but from it a sense of sanity, of organization, of focus seemed to spread. He put out a call for all officers of the rank of captain or above and ordered them to search out their own men and assemble them in one place and report back. He issued orders to the regiments to set up cook fires, while he sent runners to Forts Putnam, Greene, and Box with orders to empty their commissaries immediately of all smoked meat, flour, and fresh vegetables and bring them to his command post within the hour to be distributed at once. All medicines, all clothing, all utensils, all blankets, all available muskets and cartridges were to be stockpiled behind him. The able were to do what they could for the wounded. Pickets were assigned on a four-hour rotation. At all times the trenches and breastworks and forts were to be fully manned, prepared to defend against a night attack, which was surely coming. Men were to take sleep in four shifts, two hours each, so at all times at least three-fourths of the army would be ready in the trenches.

It crept outward. *He's here. He's in command. It will be all right.*

In full darkness the regiments collected around their cook fires, taking their portion of stew steaming in wooden bowls they had just been given, to sit on blankets that had been passed out, and work at their stew with wooden spoons while they drank scalding coffee from pewter mugs they were handed. They tore chunks of black bread and ate in silence. They finished and put down their utensils dirty and walked back to take their positions in the trenches, listening, watching.

A little after nine o'clock Eli slipped past the pickets and disappeared in the darkness, traveling south. At nine-thirty a drummer softly pounded out tattoo, and one-fourth of the men sought their blankets for their two hours of sleep, exhausted, weary to the bone, gone before their heads were down.

Just after ten o'clock Eli returned unseen and dropped beside Billy. "They're not coming for a night attack."

"Think Washington should know?"

Eli thought for a moment. "Maybe."

The two wearily made their way to the command table to find General Washington sitting erect, working in the dim yellow lantern light with pen and quill, writing orders. His personal bodyguard faced the two, hand on his sword. Washington raised his face as they approached and waved his hand to his bodyguard, who stepped back.

"Sir," Billy said, "Corporal Billy Weems, Boston regiment. This is Private Eli Stroud. We haven't found our officers yet, but I thought we should report to you."

Washington squinted to see Eli clearly. "Have we met?"

"Yes. I scouted the British lines and reported to you yesterday."

"I remember. What can I do for you?"

Eli spoke. "I just came back from the British lines. They're in for the night. There won't be a night attack."

Washington's eyes widened. "Who sent you down there?"

"No one."

"What did you see?"

"They got their tents up. Horses tied. Pickets out. Cannon blocked. Lights out."

Washington released his breath, and for a moment Billy saw profound relief in his face. "Are you certain?"

"Certain."

Washington stared long and hard, judging whether he dared accept this report from a man he had met but once. He made his decision. "Thank you. That will give us precious time to get ready for their attack tomorrow morning. Go back to your regiment and carry on."

"Yes, sir."

They were turning to leave, when Washington rose to his full height. His face shined in the lantern light, and his eyes were like flecks of pale gray obsidian. He spoke once more, softly. "Gentlemen, it was a privilege to be one of you today. Our losses were not the fault of how our men fought. I have never seen such courage." He paused for a moment, then finished. "Get some rest. We have much to do to see this thing through. God bless you both."

Notes

One of the most thorough, competent historical reports of the battle of Long Island—which includes the geography of the battle area, the officers involved, the troop movements, and the results—is found in Johnston, *The Campaign of 1776*, part I, pp. 139–206. The narrative given by Johnston, together with the battle map that accompanies his book, supports the general text of this chapter. See also Higginbotham, *The War of American Independence*, pp. 152–59, and Leckie, *George Washington's War*, pp. 258–67.

CHAPTER XVII

★ ★ ★

*P*elting rain fell straight down drumming in the black an hour before dawn, and the Continental army stood shivering in the Brooklyn trenches in mud and water up to their ankles. Chill water dripped from their noses and chins and drenched their clothing and matted their hair, and soaked the powder in their musket pans. They watched south in the rain, straining to hear sounds of slogging feet or the guttural cursings of soldiers trying to move cannon up the incline, with wheels sunk ten inches into the sticky muck. There was nothing.

Sunrise came to change the blackness to a pall of gray gloom. There were no lights in either camp; every campfire had been drowned to lifeless heaps of soaked ashes. Hunger came gnawing, and the men took rotation by the regiment to go to the commissary and get their ration of two hard biscuits and four ounces of raw pork for the day. The officers stood in line with their men, George Washington leading. He received his two hard biscuits and chunk of pork with the others, and walked dripping back to his command table in plain sight of his men. They returned to drop splashing into the mud and water in the trenches. They broke their biscuits with wet rocks and shoved pieces between chattering teeth and slowly began to work it. They used their belt knives to cut small chunks of raw pork. And they looked at their commander, working on his ration with a pocketknife, soaked, muddy, fatigued just like them, without rest since the battle of yesterday, and they took heart.

A little before eight o'clock the first British cannonballs came whistling to plow into the mud thirty yards in front of the breastworks and disappear, and then the rain-muffled sound of the distant cannon came rolling. The buried cannonballs exploded with a nearly soundless *thump* and did little more than raise half a ton of mud eight inches before it settled back.

American cannoneers peered intently down the incline with narrowed eyes until they saw the orange wink of the British cannon in the blur, and then they held heavy tarps over the touchholes of their own heavy guns and loaded and returned fire. One of the first ten shots hit something in the British camp filled with gunpowder, and flame spurtled fifty feet upward. A moment later the resounding blast rolled past, and the American cannoneers stood in their trenches and raised their fists and shouted their defiance.

A little before nine o'clock the rattle of sporadic musket fire came from the left and then stopped, and Billy and Eli and the others in the front trenches turned anxious faces to peer, expecting an ocean of red and blue coats to suddenly walk from the rain with bayonets at the ready. But there was no one. Twenty minutes later written orders to all regiments arrived from General Washington.

"Each regiment will select a squad of men and send them towards the British lines, where they shall proceed until they make contact with the British forces. They will not engage them, but will return at once to report their position and their movements. It is vital that we know their location and, if possible, their preparations to move against our defenses in force. I am, &c., Gen. G. Washington."

Five minutes later Corporal Billy Weems led a squad of eleven men over the lip of the trench, moving south, using brush and rocks for what cover they could find. Beside him, Eli's head was constantly moving, watching everything in front of them and counting the paces. Eleven hundred yards south of the lines they walked into a water-soaked British patrol that stopped dead in its tracks, staring in disbelief at the Americans twenty yards away.

Billy gave a hand signal and his patrol vanished into the brush before the young British lieutenant in charge shouted orders. "Fire!"

All fifteen redcoats in his patrol instantly pulled back the hammers on their heavy Brown Bess muskets, pointed them at the place the Americans had been, and pulled the triggers. Not one of the soaked powder pans took the spark.

The young lieutenant swallowed hard and for a moment stood as if in a trance before he shouted his next order. "Mount bayonets."

Billy gave a hand signal and his squad turned and started back, staying low, moving in the brush.

The startled British squad jerked their bayonets from their scabbards and fumbled with wet, cold fingers to slip them over the muzzles of their muskets and lock them in place, then stand waiting for the next order.

"Charge!" shouted the young officer, and the squad lowered their bayonets and trotted faithfully into the soaked brush for twenty yards before they slowed and stared at the lieutenant.

He cleared his throat. "Uh, fall back. We, uh, must return and report this contact with the Americans."

Billy's weary squad stood upright as they approached the Brooklyn lines and dropped back splashing into the trenches to once again wait for the inevitable British assault, while Billy made his way to the command post. A captain he had never seen took his report and then searched for a rain-soaked report of the missing from the battle twenty-four hours earlier. For several seconds he read from it before he stopped, and Billy saluted and returned to his regiment.

He turned to Eli to speak quietly. "A captain back there has a written report. They can't find Stirling, or Miles, or Sullivan. Maybe dead, maybe captured. And they can't find Thompson or Turlock."

They stood for long moments, dripping in the steady rain, eyes downcast as they worked with their thoughts.

"Did he say what happened to the nurses back at the hospital?"

Billy saw the haunted look in Eli's eyes. "They were left there with the sick. The British won't harm them."

Eli remained silent, and both men turned to once again watch and listen and wait in the mounting tension for the surging attack that was certain to come.

By nine o'clock the ground could absorb no more water, and the rain began filling the trenches and running in rivulets down the slope towards the British lines. By ten-thirty the Americans were standing in water to their knees, holding their muskets and rifles over the lip of the trench, no longer making an effort to keep their powder dry, because it was impossible. Those relieved from the trenches for sleeping sat cross-legged in the mud behind the trenches, soggy blankets draped over their heads and shoulders, staring down, making no pretense of trying to sleep. With no cook fires and no way of making one, they broke cold pieces from their biscuits and cut small chunks from their pieces of raw pork, and their jaws worked slowly, methodically, to appease the hunger pangs.

Eli whittled a chunk of wood and jammed it in the muzzle of his rifle to keep the rain out, and once again raised his eyes to probe the slope, and there was nothing, and he murmured to Billy, "I'd like to know what Howe's thinking. Looks like his horses and cannon will have trouble moving up the slope, and his foot soldiers won't be able to keep their powder dry. They're going to move slow until the weather changes."

"Sooner or later they'll come."

One and one-half miles south, General Howe sat at the conference table in his field tent that had been erected before dawn and ditched against the rain. He rose, dour, impatient, frustrated, and paced, then settled back down in his chair, waiting. His orderly walked to the tent flap. "They're here, sir."

"Bring them in."

Howe stood as Clinton ducked to enter the tent, followed by Cornwallis, Percy, and Grant. They all removed their hats to throw water on the tent floor, and stood waiting, eyes dead, water dripping from their cloaks.

"Be seated." Howe waited for them to take their chairs at the table according to rank, then stood at the end of the table. He had neither the ability nor the inclination to do other than speak his mind bluntly, without the slightest hint of concern for those whom he might offend.

"I was advised less than an hour ago that Washington has reinforcements coming today from New York, perhaps thousands."

The tent fell silent, save for the steady hum of the rain.

Howe continued, slowly. "I cannot understand what Washington is thinking. His Long Island command is trapped against the East River, and he's bringing more men over, right into the trap with them! If he brings his entire New York command over here, there won't be enough to change the outcome. All we have to do is wait for them to arrive, then have the navy move gunboats up the East River behind Brooklyn and bombard it, while we wait for the weather to change enough to give us full use of our cannon from this side and then storm their trenches with infantry. We can annihilate the whole Continental army in less than one day." Howe paused, his forehead wrinkled in puzzlement. "Why isn't Washington moving his men away from the trap rather than into it?"

He stopped, unaccustomed to saying so much at one time, then shrugged and concluded. "Until I can see good reason to do otherwise, we wait until he gets his reinforcements over here, and our men-of-war are in place, and the weather breaks. In the meantime, I'm sending some of Brant's Mohawks up there to take a count of men, and find their powder magazine, and count the cannon covering the Brooklyn Harbor."

A little before eleven o'clock the rain slackened for a short time, then resumed the drenching downpour. At eleven-fifteen Billy and Eli and every man in the breastworks and trenches flinched and turned, white-faced, at the sound of a thousand shouting voices coming in directly behind them. They gripped their muskets white-knuckled, or their swords, or the axe handles, or the rocks they held for weapons, while bright images of the endless horde of red-coated regulars coming in behind them just twenty-four hours earlier flashed in their minds.

Then they saw the blurred figures through the rain and they became American soldiers. A shout went up from the trenches as the incoming column marched on into camp, with General Mifflin leading his two Pennsylvania regiments under Colonels Magaw and Shee, with others following.

Behind came General Mercer with his New Jersey forces.

Last came Colonel John Glover with his Marblehead regiment of fishermen. They marched in silence, with the rolling gait of men grown accustomed to a pitching deck beneath their feet. Their hands were curled from salt seawater and hawsers, and their faces were weathered, wrinkled, eyes narrowed. They wore the white breeches and blue blazers of men of the sea and the flat-brimmed, flat-topped black hats that mark the sailor. They spoke with the twang and dialect of fishermen, and did not worry if those unfamiliar with the ways of the sea could not understand that a "hord-horted" man was a "hard-hearted" man or that a "tor barl" was a "tar barrel."

Their leader was small, thin, wiry, and could not remember a day when he had been other than a fisherman out of the port of Marblehead, Massachusetts. The men in his command were gathered from Marblehead and had known him, and each other, for most of their rememberable lives. No regiment in the American army stood closer to each other and to their revered commander, nor were any more dedicated to the cause of liberty than the Marblehead regiment. With the hardheaded practicality of New Englanders and the inborn confidence of men of the sea, they assumed they could do whatever had to be done.

Washington was instantly among them, handing out written orders, encouraging, directing, seeming to be everywhere. The incoming regiments moved to the locations shown on their orders and settled in.

As he watched, Eli spoke to Billy. "Looks like we got enough now to make a respectable fight of it."

"I estimate we should have over nine thousand now."

"Howe has twenty thousand, and more cannon, but we have the high ground and the breastworks. Should be interesting." Eli's next words were slow, deliberate. "See any doctors or nurses come in with them?"

"No. They could have. I just didn't see them."

Eli remained silent for a moment. "I'll go see later, maybe when the rain stops."

"She'll be all right."

The afternoon wore on, gray, chill, the downpour steady, neither side able to see one hundred yards. Patrols from both sides clashed and retreated, under orders to locate the enemy and retreat and report. In the gloom of late afternoon, once again the British opened up with their cannon firing blind, and the solid shot balls sent mud flying as they sank in two feet, to explode with nothing more than a rise in the soaked earth. Americans returned fire without ever knowing where their shots were hitting, and fifteen minutes later the cannon fell silent.

Fires were impossible. The day ended, and the gray gloom gave way to a thick blackness in which the sole sound was the drumming of the rain into puddles and onto drenched blankets. General Washington had not erected a command tent, but sat at his table with a lantern, continuing to write orders and directives under a tarp set up to cover the paper and quill. He remained available to any man, officer or foot soldier, who had reason to seek him, and he was muddy, hungry, soaked to the bone just as they were.

It was past nine o'clock when Eli suddenly stiffened and turned to Billy. "If I was Howe, I'd have some of Brant's Mohawks up here taking a look about now."

Billy raised his head. "In this? They couldn't see their hands in front of their faces."

"That's just the time to send them." He handed his rifle to Billy. "Watch that. I'll be back in a while." He eased out of the trench headed back into camp. Billy listened, but heard no one challenge Eli in the pitch black. Billy turned back to once again take up the vigil of watching south, waiting for the attack that was bound to come. He found his thoughts running and he was too weary to care, and he let them go.

My knapsack's gone—Brigitte's letter, everything. No razor, no soap, nothing. Nothing to write on—I've got to write Mother. When she hears about yesterday she'll worry. Is Brigitte all right? Matthew? Kathleen? I wish someone would write and tell me. I wonder what Mother had for supper tonight. Mutton roast. And peas. The peas are on. She had fresh peas.

A longing ache rose in his breast and he pushed away all thoughts of home.

Behind him, Eli worked his way north through camp, plowing through water and mud, pausing to peer into the blackness, listening, avoiding the huddled soldiers and the pickets. He cleared the rear of the camp and dropped to his haunches to consider.

If they come, they'll likely take the high ground around the east end where Fort Putnam is, away from the river and the swamp.

He turned east, working through the brush and trees, then cut back towards the rear of the American lines and came up behind Fort Putnam. He walked to the northeast corner, then paced twenty yards due north and sat down in the brush and bowed his head to concentrate on any sound, any hint that broke the rhythm of the sound of the steady rain.

If they circle to the back of the fort, they should come within a few yards of me.

He lost track of time as he sat in the rain, head down, intense in his concentration on sound, and then it was there, too close, and the thought flashed through his brain—*somehow they heard me, they're looking for me*—and in that instant a foot hit water three feet to his right and Eli threw himself violently towards the sound and struck the knees of a man. He felt the bite of a tomahawk on his right shoulder blade as he rolled on through the legs to sweep them from beneath the man, and he pivoted and dived to grapple with the body as it struggled to rise in the slippery mud. Then they were locked in a death struggle, and Eli was desperately grasping for the tomahawk he could not see. His hand closed on the iron head and he jerked the handle free and threw it blind into the blackness while he groped for the man's throat. The man's fingers came clawing for his eyes and Eli turned his head, and then he found the throat and his left hand closed on the windpipe and jugular. He wrenched them and the man gagged and jerked back and Eli did not release, and the man grabbed his arm with both hands to tear him loose as Eli brought his own tomahawk up and struck once, twice, and the man relaxed.

Instantly Eli dived away and tried to control his heaving breath to listen for a second man. He heard the whispered name, and he waited until the sound was close and he stood. For a stunned moment the dark shape faced him. In that instant Eli dived into him and he went over backwards splashing in the mud with Eli on top of him. Eli found the soft throat and the man strangled and reached for Eli's arm as Eli struck him just above the ear with the flat side of his tomahawk, and the man groaned and settled.

Eli rolled away, poised, waiting, counting twenty breaths, but there were no sounds other than the steady rhythm of the rain.

Quickly he found the body of the first man and tucked his fingers under the jaw and there was nothing. He turned to the second body, and he felt for a sign of life and there was the steady, slow pulse and deep breathing. He felt for the man's weapons belt and threw it away, then lifted the man to his feet and draped him over his shoulder and turned towards the fort.

Ten minutes later he was challenged in the dark by a picket whose eyes opened wide when Eli answered and then walked past him. The startled picket muttered, "One Indian carrying another one." Eli had disappeared before it occurred to the picket he should have held him and called for help.

Eli walked on towards the center of camp until a picket stopped him at bayonet point. "Who comes there?"

"Eli Stroud. Boston regiment. I got a Mohawk spy. Where's the nearest officer?"

The man's head jerked forward. "You got a *what?*"

"Get an officer!"

Thirty seconds later a major appeared before him, staring at the rare sight. "You want an officer?"

"This is a Mohawk Indian sent to scout out this camp. I think General Washington might want to talk to him."

Five minutes later Eli settled the man onto a chair at the command table of General Washington, with the single lantern hissing in the rain, casting great, grotesque shadows into the blackness.

General Washington stared for a moment, then spoke to Eli. "Didn't you report to me about General Howe last night?"

"Yes."

"Who is this man?" Washington peered at the buckskin hunting shirt and breeches, and the moccasins, and the high roached hair.

"A Mohawk scout sent by Howe. I caught him over by Fort Putnam. There's a second one over there, dead. I think there might be others."

Washington looked closely. "Is he alive?"

"Yes."

"Can you talk with him?"

"I can if he wakes up. Got some alcohol?"

Two minutes later Eli tipped the man's head back and held his nose until his mouth opened, then poured half a cup of medicinal alcohol into the gaping mouth. The man choked at the bitter bite of the raw liquid and threw his head sideways and gagged and spat onto the ground. He blinked his eyes and raised his head, and Eli dropped to one knee beside him. He drew his belt knife and laid it gently at the man's throat.

The man's eyes grew wide as he heard Eli's words spoken in perfect Mohawk. "Why are you here?"

The man raised his eyes to look around, trying to understand where he was, and Eli continued. "This is General George Washington. You are in his camp. Your companion is dead. We know

Joseph Brant sent you here because General Howe told him to. We want to know why you are here. What were you sent to find out?"

The man turned defiant eyes to Eli and clamped his mouth shut.

George Washington interrupted. "What have you said?"

"I told him where he was. I asked him what he was sent here to find out."

"Do you think he'll answer?"

"Maybe." Eli turned back to the Indian. "If you do not answer, you will be hanged, here, tonight. I will ask you one more time. What were you sent to find out?"

The man stared defiantly into Eli's eyes and said nothing.

Again Washington interrupted. "What did you say?"

"We'd hang him if he didn't answer. Indians don't much fear being dead, but they don't like being hanged. It disgraces them. I got one more thing to tell him."

He turned back to the Indian. "If you tell us what we need to know we will let you go."

Eli understood one thing. Being caught had shamed, humiliated the Mohawk badly. If given his freedom, his pride would not let him return to the British camp. He would go north, eventually to rejoin his own people after a time had passed for him to purge himself of his guilt and for his people to have forgotten it.

The Indian spoke. "Brant said count soldiers. Find gunpowder."

"You came to count our army and find our gunpowder?"

"Yes."

"That's not enough. What else?"

The Indian's eyes flashed defiance in the yellow lantern light, and then they softened and he continued. "Blow up gunpowder."

Eli's eyes narrowed. "What else?"

"Count cannon at river."

"At river? Why?"

"I do not know."

"What is Howe going to do at the river?"

The Indian shook his head.

Eli continued. "How many did Brant send with you?"

The Indian held up four fingers.

"Where are the other two?"

The Indian shrugged.

Eli rose to his feet and faced Washington. "He was sent to count our soldiers, and find our powder magazine if he could and blow it up, and to count our cannon at the river. He says Howe sent four Mohawk. He doesn't know where the other two are."

Washington's eyes narrowed. "Where do you think the other two are?"

"No way to know. Might be good to double the pickets at the powder magazine, and send a company of men down to the river."

"What's this about counting cannon at the river?"

"He doesn't know why."

Washington's forehead wrinkled. "What's at the river? Howe's got maps. He's seen our gun placements. Why would he want to count our cannon when he already knows?"

The two men stood stock-still for ten seconds while their minds ran with the question, and slowly it came to both of them. Washington spoke first. "He wants to know if we've added cannon on the waterfront, because he plans to send their gunboats up the river to bombard Brooklyn from the river!"

Slowly Eli nodded. "Sounds like yesterday all over again."

Washington straightened. "What did you promise this man for this information?"

"Freedom."

Washington's eyes widened. "Let him go? to return to Howe?"

"He won't go there. He's disgraced by being caught. Finished. He'll go north, back to his people. I'll take him a mile north of camp and turn him loose."

Half an hour later Eli dropped splashing into the trench beside Billy.

"Find anything?"

For three minutes Eli spoke in the rain while Billy listened, eyes narrowed when Eli finished.

"Is Howe going to trap us again?"

Eli pursed his mouth for a moment. "I doubt it. But I'll tell you one thing. We better hope this storm gets worse. If Howe gets his gunboats up the East River off the Brooklyn shore, some of those heavy guns can probably reach us here. We can't stop them, but the weather can."

Eli raised his right arm and flexed it, shrugging his right shoulder.

Billy caught the grimace on his face. "You hurt?"

"Barely broke the skin."

"What? Where?"

"Tomahawk. Back of my shoulder."

Billy laid his musket on the lip of the trench. "Pull off that shirt." He helped Eli shrug out of the soaked buckskin, and in the blackness he leaned close to look and to feel.

"You're cut, but not bad." Billy used Eli's belt knife to cut both sleeves of his own shirt off at the elbow and fold them into a compress. Eli tugged the shirt back on and Billy positioned the compress in place.

"It'll stop the bleeding if you'll try not to move."

Behind them, General Washington sat at his command table, staring at his folded hands in the pale lantern light. By force of an iron will, he slowed his racing thoughts and began to put them in order.

I missed it—too caught up in yesterday—could only think of stopping Howe from the land side—didn't think of the men-of-war down south—How many? Seventy-three. If they come up the river, Brooklyn is lost and so are we. How could I miss it? How?

Minutes passed before he suddenly stiffened and his head snapped up.

What have I done? We're in a trap and I ordered thousands of more men to walk into it! Backwards—all backwards. I should have gotten every man out of the trap, not into it. Have I lost it all? The revolution? America? Have I? Have I?

Half an hour later he called to his aide. Ten minutes later, well past midnight, Colonel John Glover stood before him, rain dripping from the flat brim of his black hat. His eyes glittered in the lantern light as he raised them to Washington's, who stood one foot taller than Glover, and John Glover took his measure of General George Washington. He wasn't sure how much he could like a Virginia aristocrat who had spent a fair part of his life riding high-bred horses, chasing small red foxes in green meadows, wearing costly uniforms covered with gold braid and gold buttons, and attending seasonal balls and great banquets for the rich and powerful. He wasn't sure if such a man had the common sense and grit to make the hard decisions, and enough steel in his backbone to drive himself and his men to make the right things happen. One thing Glover did know. This man was his commanding officer, and the rule on which he had built one of the finest fighting units in the American states was obedience to superior officers and to orders.

He came to attention. "Colonel Glover reporting as ordered, sir."

Washington stared into his gray eyes and for a moment studied the small bandy-legged man before him. He saw the clear, perceptive eyes, the leathery face that had seen a thousand violent storms on the sea, the set of the mouth and chin, and he saw the hands that were hard and callused. "Colonel, I've been in error. I need your help."

Glover covered his surprise. "Help, sir?"

"I've assembled nine thousand men here to oppose General Howe, who has twenty thousand. If he now brings his gunboats up the East River, he can cut Brooklyn to shreds from the river, and some of his heavy guns can reach us here. We'll be in a trap with no way out."

Glover nodded. "I know, sir."

Washington paused at the frank statement, then continued. "I'm told your regiment is composed of men who know boats and water."

"We do."

Washington selected his words carefully. "Can you transport this army across the East River to Manhattan Island in one night?"

Glover neither moved nor spoke for nearly half a minute while his mind raced, making calculations. "Yes, sir, we can, if we can get the boats."

"What kind of boats?"

Glover's answer was simple. "Anything that floats, sir. It makes no difference to us."

Washington stopped for a moment and stared into the steady eyes. "I gathered up a great many boats when we crossed over to Long Island."

"How many?"

"Maybe one hundred."

"A good start. We'll need more. Give me the order and my men can get them in twelve hours."

Washington's mouth dropped open for a split second. "Where?"

"Here. Across the river. Down on Gravesend. Up on the sound. Wherever we find them. My men know where to find boats."

"What if this storm holds?"

"We can make the crossing in this storm, but if a heavy wind moves up the river we'll have to wait. If we have to wait, so will the British gunboats."

"If the storm quiets?"

Glover shook his head. "If it quiets and the British bring their gunboats up the river, we'll have trouble."

"Wait." Washington sat at his table and his aide held the tarp while he wrote orders to Glover. He folded them and stood and handed them to the colonel. "There's my written authority to get the boats. If you need anything else from me, I am at your service. Bring the boats near the Brooklyn ferry, and try to do so with as little notice as possible. We must keep this from Howe as long as we can."

Glover shoved the written orders inside his sodden tunic. "Yes, sir." He saluted and started to turn, when Washington stopped him.

"Colonel, I, uh . . . Do you believe . . ." Washington's voice trailed off.

Glover's eyes were steady, his voice matter-of-fact. "I do, General. We're in His hands. Anything else, sir?"

Seldom had Washington felt the surge that filled his breast. He swallowed hard before he could answer. "No, Colonel. Thank you. Carry on."

The rains held throughout the night. Dawn changed the black pall to a gray pall, and the rain continued relentlessly. The men in the trenches and behind the breastworks mixed with the officers at the commissary tents to take their rations for the day, which were exactly the same as the day before—two hard biscuits and four ounces of raw pork. They had had nothing hot for forty-eight hours, nor had they slept, nor felt the warmth of a fire. They moved about in silence, doing only what had to be done, taking their rotation in the trenches that had four feet of water and mud, and rising.

Quietly the Marblehead regiment had scattered throughout the night and were returning with boats from everywhere. Flat-bottomed boats, longboats, barges, rowboats, whaleboats—anything they could find. Twice Glover asked Washington for specific orders and Washington gave them.

One was to General Mifflin and on to General Heath at King's Bridge. The message was terse. Get everything that will float and deliver it to New York, now. Glover's sailors crossed the East River and brought the boats across to the Brooklyn shore under cover of the rain.

The second one was to Assistant Quartermaster Hughes at New York, with the same blunt message. Anything that floats, oar or sail. Get it. For twenty-two hours Hughes never dismounted his horse, but rode the New York shoreline relentlessly commandeering everything he could find that would make it across the East

River, and Glover's men, along with sailors from Salem, brought them to Brooklyn.

In the midst of it all, Washington sat at his command table, poring over a plan that would move the entire army across the river in one night.

In their condition, if they know what we're doing, there's the strong risk of panic that could cripple the whole operation. And if Howe's scouts discover it, he'll be on us instantly.

Calmly he worked out the orders that would be made known to the troops and which would seem to them normal, unremarkable, certainly not part of a plan to move an entire army across a river in one night.

The sick, who were a burden on the army, were to be taken to the hospital and from there across to New York to report to Surgeon General Morgan. Entirely normal procedure. The newly arrived troops from New York had come to replace the men who had survived the disaster of August 27. Who could question it? Further, certain other regiments were to be transported back to New York according to their condition and need, but it had not yet been determined which ones they were. Therefore, all regiments were to be packed and prepared to leave by seven P.M.

Washington went over the plan again and again, then sent out written orders and waited. Not one officer, not one soldier questioned the orders. Not a man in the Brooklyn command realized they were participating in a full night retreat.

In the gloom of six o'clock, Washington convened a council of war with his officers, who needed to know that the real plan was a full evacuation of Long Island—not a rotation of troops as had been told the troops. They did not meet at the fortifications. Rather, they met secretly in the home of Philip Livingston on Hicks Street, near Joralemon in Brooklyn. Livingston was away attending his duties in the Continental Congress, and the house was vacant.

The officers came in ones and twos, to shed dripping capes and hats in the grand entryway, try to remove the mud from their boots, and take their places at the great, polished table in the library. Putnam, Spencer, Mifflin, McDougall, Parsons, Scott, Wadsworth, and Fellows all sat silent, unsure why they were there, fearful they were going to hear the word *surrender.*

"Gentlemen, I propose wasting no time. Tonight I have decided to evacuate the entire army across the East River to Manhattan Island."

Every man at the table reared back in his chair, eyes wide, questioning, and Washington continued.

"I tell you this with my strongest admonition that it must not be made known to the soldiers. Should they find out, I fear they will think we are in imminent danger and slip into a panic. If we will remain calm, there is no danger."

Washington left no room for debate, nor did he ask for their advice. He asked only for their approval. They gave it, he thanked them, and the brief, critical conference ended.

At seven o'clock Colonel Little moved his regiment down near the ferry, and with deadly efficiency the Marblehead fishermen, with the Twenty-seventh Massachusetts Regiment, all under command of General McDougall, loaded them into the waiting boats and pushed off into the black waters of the East River in heavy rain and deep gloom. Colonel Douglas followed. Hitchcock's Rhode Islanders hoisted their baggage to their shoulders and marched through the mud with no light left, and minutes later the third flotilla of sailboats, longboats, barges, whaleboats, sloops, flatboats, and pettiaugers pushed off into the swollen river.

At nine o'clock heavy winds came pushing high tides. Glover's fishermen cast worried eyes upward, knowing what was coming, but they did not slow. Half an hour later a howling nor'easter came in behind the winds, and the Marbleheaders furled all sails and anchored the sailboats but continued moving the men in the longboats and barges and whaleboats. But they knew; if the nor'easter held, and they had nothing but the longboats and whaleboats and barges to move the entire army, they would not be finished by morning. And if that happened, those remaining on the Brooklyn side would be annihilated by Howe's redcoats. The Marbleheaders set their jaws doggedly and kept working.

At eleven o'clock the nor'easter suddenly dwindled and in minutes it died. Seconds later a gentle breeze set in from the southwest, and Glover and his Marbleheaders peered at each other in disbelief. They had sailed the open seas and every river on the American coast, but never had they known a nor'easter to blow itself out in minutes, to be followed in seconds by a steady, quiet breeze from the opposite direction. They said nothing and kept working with their steady efficiency, loading the boats, some of them so heavy the water was within three inches of the gunnels when they pushed off into a river that was smooth as glass.

By two o'clock half the army was on the New York side. By four o'clock, two-thirds were standing on the New York docks.

At the trenches and breastworks on the Brooklyn side, General Mifflin remained with his selected command, who had been assigned by Washington to cover the retreat should Howe find out what was happening and make a night attack. They were to raise the alarm at the first sight of the British advancing and then retreat to the Brooklyn church to make their defense. If any of Washington's troops were to be lost in the retreat, it would be Mifflin's command, left behind to cover the silent boats.

In the dead of the night, Major Scammel misunderstood an order from General Washington and rode to General Mifflin. "Sir, you are to bring your command to the boats, now."

Within minutes Mifflin had his entire command marching through the mud, the breastworks and trenches behind, to the boats in the East River ahead. The sudden sound of horse hooves in the mud slowed Mifflin, and his eyes widened as General Washington reined in his mud-splattered, steaming horse.

"What are you doing?" Washington demanded.

"Sir, Scammel brought an order from you to move down to the boats."

Washington raised his voice. "Then Scammel has mightily misunderstood. Turn around. Return to the breastworks. You might be all that stands between the remainder of the army and destruction if the British attack."

"Yes, sir." Mifflin spun and barked orders, and his men headed back for the trenches and breastworks at a trot.

Towards dawn the rain slackened, and then stopped, and the rolling clouds parted to show countless stars for the first time in three days. Mifflin ran a hand across his mouth, searching for what to do when sunrise came and Howe realized the American breastworks and camp were nearly deserted.

He drew a deep breath and cracked out orders. "All right. Get anything that will burn. Break down the doors and the walls inside the forts. Bring out the dry blankets, tables, chairs, bunks—anything inside that's dry enough to burn—and set up a row of campfires along the breastworks and trenches. Get fires going. The British are going to have to believe we're still here in force when it's light enough to see. Move."

Desperate hands grasped axes and sledges and stripped doors and furniture out of the three forts while other hands seized dry blankets and trotted outside. With the morning star fading, they heaped the shattered wood onto the blankets in thirty places and struck flint to steel, nursed the spark, and set the fires. Then they climbed the towers into the fort where they could be seen, and took up what positions they could behind the breastworks, but avoided the trenches that were nearly filled with water.

Mifflin walked among his men, talking, encouraging. "If they come, fire until they're fifty yards from the trenches, then retreat to the church. Fall back twenty paces, reload, fire, fall back, reload, fire. Do not panic. We'll make it."

The unanswered question that was foremost in the fears of every man in his command was simple. How do we slow down twenty thousand seasoned British troops and still escape? They said nothing as they obeyed their orders and took up their positions.

At half past five the eastern sky was glorious as the sun caught the breaking clouds and turned them into a thousand colors of reds and golds and yellows. Mifflin's command licked at dry lips and watched and listened and waited, and then they saw the British a mile down the slope, preparing to advance.

And as they watched in absolute disbelief, a fog bank moved up the East River and began to spread, and within five minutes Brooklyn and the East River and the British army were smothered in a thick, wet fog. From behind came the sound of a horse, and Mifflin's men turned and heard the command, "Come to the boats. Everyone is across. You're the last."

With the sound of British pickaxes at work and of Howe's army advancing, they broke from their positions and ran. They reached the steps down to the boats and General Washington was there, giving them his hand to steady them as they pounded down the slippery, wet stone steps, and the Marbleheaders grasped their arms to help them aboard the boats, rocking gently in the black water.

Behind them they heard a cannon blast, and then a continuous roll of cannon fire, and then two rapid volleys of a thousand muskets, and then silence. For one moment they paused and looked back, and in their minds they saw it. The British charging into the abandoned fires, blasting with their cannon and muskets, only to find the American camp deserted, empty.

They grinned as the Marbleheaders shoved the boats out into the river.

Lieutenant Benjamin Tallmadge of Connecticut peered back at the last boat, and he saw the last man to step in, tall, with a tri-cornered hat and a cape, and Tallmadge watched as Washington turned to peer back at the Brooklyn shore.

General Howe, with Cornwallis and Clinton at his sides, reined his winded horse to a sliding stop on the banks of the East River, mud flying, and leaned forward in the stirrups to stare through narrowed eyes as the last boat disappeared in the fog. Standing in the rear of the boat was the tall silhouette of General Washington.

Howe gritted his teeth and pounded his fist on the pommel of his saddle, while Clinton threw both hands upward and hurled curses into the fog-filled heavens.

Notes

The novel's depiction of the events and circumstances during the two days following the defeat of the Americans on August 27, 1776—including the weather conditions, George Washington's presence among his troops, the council of war held at the home of Philip Livingston, and the retreat across the East River—is based on the account given in Johnston, *The Campaign of 1776*, part I, pp. 208–24 (see also Leckie, *George Washington's War*, pp. 265–67; Higginbotham, *The War of American Independence*, pp. 158–59). Eli Stroud's involvement in these events is, of course, fictional.

CHAPTER XVIII

★ ★ ★

*D*on't you worry. The Almighty's watching. They'll be home soon."

Margaret Dunson tucked the comforter under Prissy's chin and touched her cheek as she peered into the worried eyes. "If you get scared, call. I'll leave the lamp on and the door open." She turned the wheel and the lamp dimmed, and she rose and walked from the bedroom into the hall leading to the parlor. Three steps short of the archway a feeling began in her heart and surged to become an overpowering conviction. She stopped, wide-eyed in the dim light, and her hand flew to cover her mouth.

They're alive! They'll be here tonight!

With the sureness born of a mother's intuition she set large brass kettles of water on the stove and poked huge chunks of coal into the glowing embers of the firebox. Then she carried the supper remains of ham and potatoes from the root cellar and set them in the oven, and went back for a pitcher of cider and a jar of butter.

While the water heated she strung the lines in the kitchen for baths and draped them with blankets, then cut bread onto a plate and took the honey pot from a cupboard. She walked back to the bedrooms and silently stole to the bedside of both Prissy and Adam, and for a moment leaned to study the innocence in their faces and listen to their deep, slow breathing. She laid fresh underwear and nightshirts and towels on Caleb's bed, then on Brigitte's, and went back to the kitchen to check the water. It was heating but not yet steaming. She went outside to drag the huge wooden bathtub into the kitchen, then back out to the well to carry in two buckets of cold water and set them against the wall.

With the water kettles steaming, she moved them off the stove onto the black top of the oven and set the lids clattering on top to hold the heat. She jiggled the grate to the firebox, reset the draft, looked around to satisfy herself, and walked back to the parlor. She set two more large kindling sticks on the fire in the great fireplace, then settled down into her rocking chair to wait.

At eleven o'clock a light southeasterly breeze came off the Atlantic, and she heard it soft in the chimney. She got her knitting basket and settled back into her chair, fingers working without thought, eyes bright, waiting for what she knew would come. At half past twelve she rose, stretched, and walked back into the kitchen to lift the lids to the kettles. Steam rose and she set them back, then returned to her rocking chair and once again picked up her knitting needles.

A little past one o'clock her hands stopped and her eyes dropped as she concentrated on a faint sound at the front gate, and then she heard footsteps on the brick walkway, and she bolted for the door and threw it open. Brigitte blinked and squinted as the irregular rectangle of yellow lamplight flooded out from the open door, and she saw the black silhouette of Margaret in the same instant Margaret saw her, with Caleb slightly behind her to one side. Margaret uttered a sound, and in two lunging steps the women were in each other's arms, Margaret holding Brigitte to her breast with all her strength, Brigitte murmuring, "Mother, Mother." Caleb reached to touch his mother's arm, and she seized his hand and pulled him to her, and they stood in the dooryard for a time, the three of them clinging, while the many days of dark fears faded.

Margaret pushed them back and stared into their faces, dirty, gaunt, and then at their clothes, filthy and frayed. "You're both a mess!" she exclaimed. "Come in and wash while I set the table, and then you're both getting out of those clothes and taking a bath!"

For a long time the two sat leaned over their plates while they ate steadily in silence, possessed only by the thought they had never tasted anything so wonderful. Margaret watched in the lamp glow, taking satisfaction in their voracious appetites, waiting for the talk to start.

Brigitte set her buttermilk glass on the table and Margaret spoke. "What happened?"

Brigitte looked into her eyes. "I'm not sure. Did anyone else make it back?"

"Charles Johannesen. Three days ago. He tried to get Donald Hughes home but his leg was broken. He died. Charles buried him."

Brigitte's face blanched. "Just Charles? No one else got home?"

Margaret shook her head. "Not yet."

Brigitte's chin quivered and she dropped her eyes to the table.

Caleb spoke, angry, bitter. "Cannon shot us to pieces. We don't know who did it."

Margaret drew a deep breath. "The Connecticut militia did it. They said they saw British soldiers and Tories moving wagons with supplies to the British army and they shot at them."

Caleb's face turned white and Brigitte's head jerked up as he exclaimed, "Connecticut militia? They're the ones? Our own army?"

Margaret nodded once, her face grim, noncommittal.

Caleb tried to speak again but could find nothing to say.

Brigitte's face was white when she turned again to Margaret, and Margaret saw the desperate need in her eyes as Brigitte spoke. "Eleven dead by our own army? Because of me?"

Margaret chose her words carefully. "No. Eleven dead because they chose to join the work of the Almighty in the fight for liberty. Like your father, and Matthew, and Billy. In war people make mistakes. The Connecticut soldiers thought they were doing their duty. No one meant it to happen."

Caleb's lip curled in a sneer, and Margaret glanced at him, and he turned his face away while Margaret's eyes narrowed. She turned back to Brigitte. "Tell me about it."

Margaret saw the horror come into Brigitte's eyes as she recalled the scenes, and suddenly she swallowed and said, "Oh, Mama, I can't. I can't. It was . . . the British took us by surprise and . . ." By force of will she had not cried since the blasting cannon had filled the world with exploding wagons and rifles had knocked men from their horses dead in the twilight in that faraway Connecticut meadow, but now the dam had burst and she could not stop it. She buried her face in her arms on the table and her body shook with her sobs as the long days of grief and guilt, hiding and walking, eating nuts and berries, and stealing from farm granaries and fields and orchards came flooding.

Margaret placed her arm about Brigitte's shoulders and spoke softly to Caleb. "Get your bath. There're towels and a nightshirt on your bed." Caleb rose and walked through the archway into the bedroom wing.

Slowly the bitter tears slowed, and then stopped, and Margaret waited.

"We had a traitor. Remember the young Irish boy? Cullen? He was in with the British, and they woke us up in the night with muskets and bayonets." Margaret watched the haunted terror in Brigitte's eyes as she continued, words coming faster and then spilling out in a rush.

Forced to drive on—leaving the main road—dusk coming on—driving through the gap between two groves of trees—the cracking of rifles from ambush—the British redcoats knocked from their horses, dead—the drivers of the advance wagons, tumbling—the horses bolting—the cannon blasting nearly in their faces—the lead wagon hit—the next one blown in two pieces—then the ammunition wagon exploding—the hot blast killing the horses—knocked backwards off the wagon—in the grass—terrified—hearing shots—not knowing who it was—crawling backwards in the dark—Caleb out of his head—walking—eating anything they could find—a farm—being chased by a man with a hoe—sleeping in haystacks, fields, ditches, anyplace they could find—eating peaches left rotting on the ground in an orchard—corn from a corncrib—turnips stolen from a garden—no meat—diarrhea—vomiting—endless walking . . .

Margaret sat silent, face set like stone as she listened, and then Brigitte was finished and raised her tear-stained face to her mother.

"Did Charles Johannesen tell all this? Our people who were killed? Does everyone hate me?"

Margaret saw the searing fear in her eyes, and took time in choosing her words. "Charles told it the way he remembered it. He thought you and Caleb were both killed when the ammunition blew up. He tried to help Donald Hughes, but his leg was broken too bad. It went rotten and Charles tried to cut it off, but Mr. Hughes died. Charles came on back. He thought he was the only one who survived."

The pain leaped into Brigitte's face. "You thought we were dead?"

Margaret did not flinch. "No. I never did. I knew you were alive."

Brigitte's shoulders slumped in relief; then she straightened. "Was it in the newspaper?"

"Yes. I saved a copy for you."

"Does it say I killed them? I got them to go, and I killed them?" Brigitte held her breath, waiting.

Margaret spoke evenly. "No. It says you and Caleb are heroes. You tried to help the Patriot cause and gave your lives."

Brigitte groaned and she closed her eyes in pain. "Not heroes. Fools. Fools! We got our people captured by the British and then killed by Connecticut militia! We lost everything we worked for since July. Lost it all! Heroes?" She shook her head and silent tears trickled down her cheeks onto her dress.

Margaret straightened her spine and squared her shoulders. "We'll talk about that later." She turned and called quietly into the kitchen. "Are you finished?"

Caleb walked through the kitchen door in his fresh nightshirt, still working his hair with his towel.

Margaret turned back to Brigitte. "Get your towel and night-shirt from your bed."

Brigitte rose and walked silently through the archway into the bedroom wing while Margaret gave Caleb a hand sign to sit down at the table, and Caleb sat down, waiting, while Brigitte passed back through, towel and nightshirt in hand, into the kitchen.

Margaret turned to Caleb. "Brigitte told me most of it. Were you out of your head, at the first?"

"She said I was. I didn't think so."

"Are you all right now?"

"I'm not hurt."

Margaret caught the shaded answer. "I don't mean hurt. I mean, are you all right inside?"

Caleb licked his lips and his eyes dropped for a moment. "I'm all right."

Margaret's eyes narrowed but she went on. "You're both thinner. Are you sick?"

"No. We couldn't find enough to eat."

"You had diarrhea? vomiting?"

"Yes. Bad peaches."

"Charles Johannesen got home."

"I heard you tell Brigitte."

"It was in the newspaper. You and Brigitte are heroes."

A cynical look crept over Caleb's face and turned to a contemptuous sneer, and he turned away from Margaret and said nothing.

She spoke with a firm authority. "Are you all right?"

He turned back, eyes flat, defensive. "I said I was all right. I'm not hurt."

"I don't mean that. I mean inside. Are you all right inside?"

Caleb leaned back, studying his mother's face, for the first time in his life unwilling to speak the truth from his heart. Margaret saw it and her breath came short at the realization she was seeing a gulf between them for the first time, and she felt the instant stab in her breast and the white-hot questions came leaping. *What did I do wrong? When did it start? How did I miss it? Who?* And then the fear she lived with every moment of her life came welling up. *He needs John or Matthew—If John were here, or Matthew—I can't go on without John—can't—can't—I'm going to lose him without John.*

She raised her chin and faced him. "Answer me."

For a long moment he stared into her eyes before he spoke. "I'm all right."

She leaned forward. "You sure?"

His eyes were evasive. "I'm sure."

She clutched his arm. "Caleb, something's wrong. You're going to tell me."

He looked down at her hand on his arm, and slowly raised his eyes and his words came sharp. "When those rifles shot, I saw twenty people die. When the cannon came, there were people blown to pieces—horses—right there in front of me. I washed blood off myself the next day—not mine—I don't know whose it was— maybe from someone on the wagon ahead of us, maybe from our own horses—I don't know. We thought we were on the side of the Almighty, but with all the dead people and horses it didn't make any difference whose side we were on or how right we were. Most of us were just plain dead. If we were doing the work of the Almighty, where was he when we all got blown up and shot? Where?"

His eyes were points of light, his anger so deep it struck Margaret like something physical and she recoiled and gasped, then struggled for control and thrust her head forward, eyes flashing. "Caleb! Don't you ever speak like that again! One of the dead who willingly gave his life *is your father!*" Her chin trembled for a moment and then she went on, boring into him. "That afternoon, twenty minutes before he died he told me he knew this was the work of the Almighty. He *knew* it! Don't you ever forget!"

For a moment he continued to stare at her, unmoved, defiant, and then he softened, and for a moment she caught a glimpse of the boy who had left home only weeks earlier, eager, anxious to take his place in the battle for freedom, liberty. He dropped his eyes and murmured, "I'm sorry, Mother. Truly. I'm sorry."

Margaret folded her hands on the table and worked them together, groping for what to say, when Brigitte's voice came from the kitchen. "Mother, would you do something for me? Would you help me wash my hair?"

Margaret stood. "In a minute." She turned back to Caleb. "No need for you to wait. Let's go to your room and have our evening prayer."

He had no choice. He rose and followed her, toes raised from the chill of the polished hardwood floors. She knelt in the lamplight beside his bed and waited for him to kneel beside her, and she turned to him. "You offer it for us."

He hesitated for a long moment, then clasped his hands before his face and closed his eyes. "Almighty God, for all things we thank thee . . ."

He rose and slid between the crisp, clean sheets and pulled the comforter up, and settled his head onto the pillow. Margaret could not resist. She leaned over him and kissed him on the cheek, and touched his damp hair. "It's good to have you home, son."

He reached up and pulled her down and held her close. "I love you, Mother."

Her breath caught and she straightened and her eyes were too shiny, and she smiled down at him. She turned the wheel on the lamp and the light died, and she walked out and closed the door behind her, then walked into the kitchen.

Brigitte sat in the tub and gasped as Margaret poured warm water over her head, then worked in the soap, rinsed, lathered, rinsed again, and once more. Margaret handed her the large, clean white towel and walked back into the living room while Brigitte dried, slipped on her nightshirt, then went to work on her long hair with the towel. She came out into the parlor, where Margaret was sitting at the table, waiting.

Brigitte spoke as she worked with the towel in her hair. "Oh, Mama, that feels so good."

Margaret smiled as she watched her daughter take joy. "When was the last time you had a bath?"

Brigitte shook her head. "A few days before the attack. I've forgotten."

Margaret shook her head, then sobered. "Come sit for a minute." She waited until Brigitte was seated beside her at the table, hair wrapped in the towel.

Margaret's stare was direct. "Did you have prayers with Caleb each night?"

"Yes."

"Did he take his turns?"

"Most of the time."

"Notice anything wrong?"

Brigitte leaned back in her chair and pursed her mouth for a moment. "What makes you ask that?"

Margaret avoided the question. "Did you?"

Slowly Brigitte nodded her head. "I thought it was him trying to forget the killing. It was horrible."

"Has he said anything that made you think he's questioning God?"

Brigitte's eyes widened as she realized the implication. "He said some things, but I didn't think about them that way."

"What did he say?"

Brigitte paused while she pushed her memory. "A remark about where was God when all our people were killed. Why? Has he said something to you?"

"The same thing." Margaret began working her hands together on the tabletop. "I'm terrified he's questioning the Almighty. He's only fifteen. His father's gone, Matthew, Billy. He needs them so badly. He's had to grow up too fast—too fast. He wasn't ready for the hard things of life, and now he's seen the worst of it—the senseless killing of war—and he's too young to know how to handle it."

Margaret raised tortured eyes to Brigitte. "I can accept death, and war, but I cannot accept him turning on the Almighty.

Losing his immortal soul. I can't. I can't." She began rocking back and forth, sobbing quietly, tears trickling down her cheeks.

Brigitte could not bear it, and she knelt before her mother and threw her arms about her, and held her close until the shaking slowed and stopped and Margaret pulled away to wipe at her eyes.

"He'll be all right, Mother. He'll find his way through it."

Margaret looked into her eyes. "Watch for a chance to talk to him. Help him. I'll ask Silas to talk with him."

Brigitte rose. "Help me dry my hair, and then we must go to bed."

Later, with the house dark, Margaret went to her knees beside her bed. She clasped her hands and her words came from her soul. "Our Father who art in heaven, hallowed be thy name. I thank thee for the blessings of my life. I beg of thee, with all my heart, do not abandon Caleb. Forgive him his youth and strengthen him . . ."

CHAPTER XIX

★ ★ ★

*G*one! *Six thousand of the Connecticut regiments gone—deserted—captured—killed—others deserting every day—murmuring in the ranks that they were sold out on Long Island—how close are they to mutiny? My letters to Congress ignored—Congress beginning to question—army shrinking every day—morale gone.*

Washington sighed and rose from the table in the spacious library and walked slowly to the bank of windows, morose, troubled, filled with self-condemnation. He hated the anger he felt towards officers who had broken and run in the soul-wrenching defeat on Long Island, and soldiers who had thrown down their arms in their blind, mindless stampede. His eyes wandered over the lush gardens and courtyard without seeing as his thoughts ran.

The army thought this would be over in time for harvest—they meant to be home in time to prepare for winter—didn't realize this will go on—not soldiers, citizens.

He parted a lace curtain to peer towards the street in front of the great mansion.

How does one deal with men who are citizens first, soldiers second? who despise authority? who hold their independence so dear? How does one reach them?

He flinched at the sudden rap at the door. "Enter."

Colonel Joseph Reed swung the door open. "They're waiting in the conference room, sir."

General Washington nodded, straightened his vest, walked to

the table, and picked up a thin valise of documents. He followed his adjutant down the hall, boot heels clicking on the polished hardwood floor. Reed opened the door and Washington walked into the large room, and his eyes swept the men seated at the great, polished table.

Generals Putnam, Spencer, Heath, Greene, Scott, and eight others watched him take his place, then leaned forward, intense, waiting.

"Thank you for your attendance. General Greene, how is your health?"

General Nathanael Greene, hollow cheeked and sallow from eighteen days with a raging fever, answered, clear-eyed, strong. "Very good, thank you. The surgeon says I'm fit for duty."

Washington nodded approval. "There are some matters I must review before I reach the purpose of calling you to this council." He took a great breath, then continued.

"You know that Lord Admiral Howe sent General Sullivan, after his capture on Long Island, to arrange a negotiation with Congress, and Congress sent Franklin and Adams and Rutledge to Staten Island to see what Howe proposed. Nothing came of it."

Washington glanced at handmade notes. "You will recall that on September second we agreed to divide Manhattan Island into three sections, under the command of Generals Putnam, Spencer, and Heath—lower, middle, and northern sections, respectively. You will also recall the warm debate we held that day concerning whether we should abandon everything below Harlem Heights and, if so, whether we should destroy New York City, on which question I personally wrote to Congress."

He selected a document from the valise. "Congress instructed us not to damage New York City." He looked at General Greene and a smile flickered for an instant. "General Greene advised us to abandon it and burn it to keep the British from using it as a base through the winter. John Jay said the same. General Scott agreed."

He laid the letter back on the valise. "September seventh we held a war council and made our decision. Having been led to suspect that Congress wished the city to be maintained, and contrary to the instincts of some, we decided to try to hold New York, and we left General Putnam and his command here. At that time it was clear that this island was critically vulnerable to invasion by British troops coming across the East River, and we left our troops remaining in strong fortifications from Corlear's Hook, just above New York City, clear up to Horn's Hook, just south of the plains of Harlem. Those regiments were under Generals Scott and Wadsworth and Colonels Douglas, Chester, and Sargent. At Kip's Bay, we left Fellows and Parsons with strong commands to support Colonel Douglas. On the Hudson River side, we left Colonel Silliman in command of fortifications near Greenwich and on up towards Bloomingdale."

He opened the valise and removed a large folded document and laid it on the table without unfolding it.

"Now I must review with you what else has happened since September second." He again referred to handwritten notes. "September third the British man-of-war *Rose* convoyed thirty ships up the East River, and they are anchored at Wallabout Bay. Our artillery was unable to do them any appreciable damage. Today thirty-six more gunboats sailed up the river. This morning I am reliably informed that tomorrow, forty more will go up, and the next day, ten more, including six transports."

The men at the table leaned back in their chairs, eyes set as they made calculations at the picture Washington was developing, and Washington waited until their muted remarks quieted. He unfolded the large document and laid it on the table before them.

"This is a detailed map of Manhattan Island and the surrounding area, including Westchester on the mainland, east of this island and north of Long Island Sound." He waited while they oriented themselves. "Over here, directly across the East River from Kip's Bay on Manhattan Island, is Newton's Creek on Long Island. Howe has assembled eighty-four troop transports over there under the command of Cornwallis and Clinton. He is also assembling massive numbers of both British regulars and Hessians."

Open exclamations of surprise edged with heavy concern erupted and Washington raised a hand to quiet them.

"North of Kip's Bay, up here above Hell Gate, on Montressor's Island, within rifle shot of Harlem, they have another large camp of troops ready to move. All told, the British will have over one hundred six ships in the East River, many of them men-of-war, and eighty-four troop transports ready to move from Newton's Creek and Montressor's Island. They can reach any point on this island with twenty thousand troops, from New York City on the south tip of the island clear up to King's Bridge at the north tip, within hours, under cover of over twelve hundred cannon."

He waited while his officers gave vent to their growing fears.

"Now look at the Hudson. That string of obstructions we built from Fort Washington across the river to Fort Lee to stop their boats has totally failed. No one knows why. They move ships up and down the Hudson freely, and their cannon outnumber ours many times over."

Again he waited for quiet.

"I received information less than an hour ago that Howe is sending squads of men into Westchester on the mainland to find out what they will meet if they decide to move north there. Howe wants New York because of its docks and shipyards. With those facilities he can bring his naval power against us along the entire Atlantic coast, and can reach any major city we have in any state, either from the sea or from the major rivers."

He was pointing as he spoke, and the men at the council table were watching, dread beginning to show as Washington continued. Then, suddenly, most of them straightened, wide-eyed as they caught the implication.

"Now may I make the point." Washington tapped the map. "I think Howe is getting poised to do again what he did at Long Island. If he moves men up through Westchester just above King's Bridge, then sends gunboats up both the Hudson and the East River to bombard our positions, and then lands sizeable forces at Kip's Bay and Harlem, or other places, he has us trapped on all sides with no way out. We will lose our entire Continental army."

The room went dead silent.

Washington straightened. "Gentlemen, for these reasons I am abandoning New York City. I am drawing those troops up to Harlem Heights, to the high ground around Fort Washington, and probably on north, across King's Bridge to White Plains on the mainland, where we will be out in the open and can maneuver. The fortifications and breastworks on the east shore and the troops we have in place there will remain until New York is evacuated, and they will follow when I give the orders. I am not going to allow Howe to trap us here the way he did at Long Island."

Every general leaned back in his chair, startled into silence at the swift, unexpected, radical change in the plan of defending Manhattan Island, their minds groping to work it, understand it, accept it.

Putnam dropped his eyes to the tabletop, feeling the sting of his monstrous failure on Long Island. He had known of Jamaica Pass and the terrible consequence that could come if it were left unguarded, and had thought that General Sullivan had sent men to block the pass. Washington saw his pain.

"The Jamaica Pass mistake is as much on my shoulders as anyone else's. I inspected our lines the day before they took the pass and I did nothing. I was disappointed in the panic that seized some of our men, and our officers, and said so in my letters to Congress, but it's all behind us and forgotten. The real value of the error is, did we learn our lesson?"

Putnam raised grateful eyes.

"I repeat. Howe is not going to trap us again. I am abandoning New York City first, then Manhattan Island. The single exception might be Fort Washington. With a strong command there, we might hold it, and that would force the British to leave a considerable number of their troops there. The rest of our army is going to the mainland where we cannot be trapped, probably to White Plains."

Scott brought his racing thoughts under control. "Did Congress agree?"

Washington spoke with measured words. "I understand Congress has said I should not remain in New York City longer than I think prudent, and in my view that time has arrived. I'm expecting their letter at any time. So, we abandon New York and move north. We might be able to hold Fort Washington, but whether we do or not, my intention is to move on over King's Bridge to the mainland and get out in the open. I regret giving New York City to Howe, but in the balance, I prefer having an army rather than losing it trying to hold New York, when it is obvious it cannot be held."

Putnam raised a hand. "Are you asking our opinion?"

The blue-gray eyes narrowed and the generals saw the lightning as Washington spoke. "No. Only your approval. If any of you disapprove, say so now."

Ten officers approved at once. Three pondered a moment, then chose to stand by the earlier decision to try to hold New York. General Washington accepted it, and moved on.

"We have a major hospital in New York City, with over ten thousand sick and wounded. I will order their evacuation as soon as wagons can be arranged. I soon will be moving my headquarters to the Morris house, just south and east of Fort Washington in Harlem Heights. Get your commands ready to march, and wait for my written orders to move north. Does everyone understand?"

They did. Washington refolded his map and assembled his valise.

"Take charge of your troops. Dismissed."

By four o'clock in the afternoon, wagons were rolling into New York City on every road from the north. By sunset they were parked in every field and lot in and around the city, horses fed and watered and hobbled, with the drivers gathered around the cooking fires for supper.

At five-thirty A.M. the regimental drummers pounded out reveille, and the Continental army in New York City began moving their ten thousand sick and wounded out of the hospital tents to the waiting wagons, and then began crating all medicines, all bandages and surgical and medical equipment. Last they began the task of striking the great tents as they emptied of the disabled, while the first of the loaded wagons moved north, winding like a great, long snake on the twists and turns in the dust and dirt of Bowery Lane and the Post Road.

Company Nine of the Boston regiment, assigned to load wagons at the military hospital directly behind the Jersey Battery on the Hudson, answered the twelve o'clock call for their midday meal and lined up for their ration of boiled fish and cabbage, with stale black bread and warm canteen water that tasted of pine pitch. Sweaty, dirty, they sat down in the nearest shade to get out of the sweltering noon heat of the September sun, to eat in silence, lost in their own thoughts.

Moving the sick and wounded out—getting ready for another retreat—run rather than fight—if all those British ships start with their cannon . . .

Billy sat cross-legged with his back against a wagon wheel in the thin line of shade cast by the wagon. He finished, wiped the pewter plate clean with his last piece of bread, and thrust it into his mouth. He drank from his canteen and leaned back against the wagon wheel and closed his eyes.

Eli sat on the ground at the end of the wagon, hunched over his plate, finishing. He drank long, set his plate in the sandy dirt, and shifted out of the direct sun. Ten minutes later a young lieutenant neither of them had ever seen shouted orders, and Company Nine came to its feet. They took their dirty plates and forks back to the cook fire and dropped them into a steaming kettle, and walked on to the huge pile of canvas that was one-half of a great hospital tent.

The company formed on all four sides, grasped the canvas, and backed up, stretching it flat. They folded the rounded top back over the rectangular wall, again straightened and stretched it, then began the work of folding it. They sweated with the bulky, awkward canvas for half an hour, continually folding, walking on it to push out the captive air, folding again, walking on it, until it was a rectangle, twelve feet long, six feet wide, five feet high. It weighed twelve hundred pounds.

Patiently they worked ropes under it, threw them over the top, jerked them tight, tied them off, and signaled the next wagon. It rolled three feet past the huge bundle and stopped, and ten men of Company Nine lined up on each side, Billy and Eli among them. With Billy calling the steps, they bent, grasped the bottom layer of canvas, stood, and slid the great package into the wagon bed. Others tied it down and then signaled the driver, and he gigged the horses forward to the next station to finish loading his wagon with blankets bound into bundles.

Company Nine turned to the other half of the tent and again grasped all sides to stretch it flat. Forty-five minutes later they stood, finished, and Billy waved to the next driver to come in, and froze. Eli turned to look, and he started and his breath came short as he saw the flat-topped, flat-brimmed straw hat with the chin string, and the heavy Percheron draft horses pulling a heavy, high-walled wagon, and he did not expect the relief that flooded through his being.

Mary Flint!

The two waited while she gigged the horses and the wagon rumbled forward, to stop three feet past the great, tied bundle of canvas, and then the two were there beside the driver's box, staring up at her, grinning, and she was smiling down at them, eyes bright. A civilian sat beside her, musket between his knees, watching everything around.

Eli spoke first. "You got over the fever?"

"Eight days ago."

He saw the slight hollow in her cheeks, the pinch around her mouth, and the lack of bloom in her face, and there was concern in his voice and his eyes. "You look pale, thin. You shouldn't be working like this."

She beamed. "I'm gaining my strength back. I feel fine. Right now work is the best thing for me."

Billy broke in. "We worried." He pointed at the bundled tent.

"You know where this load is going?"

"North. Harlem Heights."

"You're driving it up there?"

"Yes."

Billy glanced back at the men waiting to load, and Eli spoke. "We have to get you loaded and moving. We'll try to find you up there."

They started back to the waiting men as she called, "I was so frightened when they told me you were in the fighting at Long Island. I'll see you up north."

The crew heaved the bundle into the wagon, and Mary once again slapped the reins on the rumps of the big horses. They settled into the horse collars and the wagon moved on to the next station to finish out the load with blankets. Billy and Eli watched for a moment, and waved when Mary turned to look back. Eli watched her until she was out of sight, while Billy waved to the next wagon and gave hand signals, and the driver clucked his horses forward towards the stacked sections of tent frame.

Company Nine worked on, sweating, steadily loading the wagons and watching them wind their way north, each man silent in his own thoughts. At six o'clock they slowed and stopped at the call to supper, and took their places in line. The soup was thin and the biscuits hard, but they took them and floated the biscuits on the top of the greasy, steaming gruel and stirred them in and broke them.

They drank from their canteens and walked one hundred yards to the west, to the bank of the Hudson River, and they waded in to their knees and sat down, gasping at the bite of the cold, dark water. They ducked their heads under and threw water when they jerked them out, then did it again, and again. They rose and sloshed back to the store, water streaming from their clothes and hair and beards, digging at their eyes with the butts of their hands, smoothing their hair back.

They made their way to their own blankets, and sat down, exhausted, feeling a sense of frustration, anger, knowing they were all but encircled by a vastly superior army with enough cannon to blast them to oblivion in one day, but not knowing by what plan their own officers intended saving them.

With the setting sun casting long shadows, the pounding rumble of distant cannon came rolling from the east, and every American on the southwest side of Manhattan Island stopped dead in his tracks and turned his head to peer east, eyes wide. The thunder came again, and then it continued in a steady roll, and the Americans swallowed dry. They looked at each other in question, fear creeping as the thudding blasts continued for twenty minutes, and then they slowed and stopped. All of the Americans stood stock-still with one thought driving everything else out of their minds. *Have they begun the bombardment that will destroy everything we have and all of us along with it?*

Billy ran a hand over his mouth and spoke quietly. "I don't think they attacked, or they'd still be shooting. I wonder what it was."

Eli shook his head. "Maybe a skirmish. Maybe more ships going up the East River. I don't think it's the big attack."

Slowly the men moved back to their blankets and carefully inspected their muskets, then their cartridge boxes, and laid them where they could be reached instantly. Then they finished cleaning their dirty utensils and settled down for the evening, glancing eastward in the gathering twilight. At full dark they were silent, sitting near campfires, saying little, constantly turning to listen and peer into the darkness to the east.

At half past nine o'clock a mounted messenger reined in a lathered bay gelding and handed written orders to the officers. Ten minutes later they walked among the troops, stopping at each regiment in the flickering firelight to repeat the message.

"The British sent forty more gunboats and transports up the East River. We traded cannon fire with them. Get packed, ready to march north in the morning."

At ten o'clock the regimental drummers tapped out tattoo and the campfires winked out. An eerie silence crept into the camp while every soldier settled onto his blanket with his musket by his side, ready, and every ear strained to hear the first sound of a night attack. They dreaded nothing more than the sudden blasting of British cannon in the middle of the night, blowing grapeshot and cannister into the sleeping camp, and the fifes and drums of thousands of blue-coated Hessians in a full charge, bayonets leveled.

Pickets began the battle of nerves, jerking at night sounds in the brush, hearing the creak of cannon wheels where there were no cannon, certain the calls of night birds were signals to attack.

At eleven o'clock Eli spoke quietly to Billy in the dark. "I'm glad we saw Mary—that she's all right."

Billy heard something in Eli's voice. "It was good." He waited for Eli to answer.

"Yes. It was."

It was there again, a softness in the way he said the words. Billy clasped his hands behind his head. "Maybe we'll see her again up north."

"Maybe. I hope so."

For a time they lay in silence, peering at the endless scatter of stars in the black heavens before Eli spoke again. "You said this war is for liberty—that it's the Almighty's work."

"It is."

"Was he there at Long Island?"

For a long time they lay in silence before Billy answered. "He was there."

"We got beat bad. Nearly lost the whole thing."

"I know."

"Is that how he works?"

"Sometimes. We don't see what he sees. What do you think?"

Minutes passed in silence, and Billy raised his head. "Eli?" He heard the intake of breath.

"He was there. I doubt he could stop us from our own foolishness at Jamaica Pass. But after, when we were at Brooklyn, I don't think it was an accident the heavy rains stopped the British for two days, and then when the winds came from the northeast and changed so fast to the southwest and Glover moved our whole army across the river in one night—I never heard of anything like that. And when the rain stopped and our last boats were caught out in the open, and that fog came up the river until Glover got us all across . . ." A time passed before Eli concluded. "He was there."

They fell into silence for a time while they worked with their separate thoughts, and Billy spoke again. "Anyone say anything yet about your sister?"

"Two or three. Nothing came of it."

"Keep asking."

"I will. Someday I'll know."

Neither man knew when they drifted into a restless sleep, and both awoke instantly at four A.M. when someone with a lantern nudged their feet and they took their rotation on the picket line. The drums sounded reveille at five-thirty A.M. and the camp came to life, tense, quiet, watching, listening. At eight-thirty a mounted messenger galloped into camp with written orders. At nine o'clock the last of the wounded and the medical supplies rolled north in loaded wagons, and the first of the regiments fell into marching formation.

Their loaded wagons rumbled east towards Bowery Lane, then left, due north, with the soldiers following, four abreast. Their eyes seldom left the low ground swells and draws and brush to their right, towards the East River, from where an attack would come, if it came at all. Where the road forked at Madison Square, they held to the right, angling east, then north, past Kip's Bay, on north towards the plains of Harlem, then onto the high ground at Harlem Heights, and westward towards Fort Washington.

Steadily, slowly, the regiments under Putnam's command took their place in the great column, wagons first, horse-drawn cannon next, troops following. Dust rose. By noon every man was sweated out, and all the horses showed sweat streaks on their hides and white lather where the bridle leather and saddles worked. The Boston regiment remained behind with the dwindling command of General Israel Putnam to cover the rear of the retreat.

By seven o'clock, with the sun setting, they had evacuated all but four of the regiments, when a messenger rode in on a lathered horse with a folded paper for General Putnam. At seven-thirty Putnam's adjutant general read the message to the remaining troops.

" 'Approximately six-thirty this evening five more British transports sailed up the East River. They appear bound to join the *Rose, Phoenix, Roebuck, Orpheus,* and *Carysfort* anchored at the mouth of Bushwick Creek, just below Newton Creek. They did not engage in cannon fire with our batteries. It appears the British are preparing for a troop movement from Montressor's Island. Continue the evacuation with all due deliberation. Do not destroy New York by fire. Repeat. Do not destroy New York by fire.' "

By midnight there remained but two regiments to evacuate, and Putnam ordered a halt to their work. Should his command have to fight, they would have to be rested. The Americans went to their blankets hungry, dirty, in clothes damp with sweat, and were asleep the moment their heads were down. At five-thirty A.M. the drummers pounded out reveille, and at six o'clock the last of the remaining troops were ready to evacuate. General Putnam called their officers together. His round, plain, bulldog face was set, his words blunt.

"I will stay here with the last two regiments while the rest of you evacuate. If the British attack, it will come from the East River. So do not take the road east to Bowery Lane. Take the road west of here, up towards Greenwich and continue north. Stay against the Hudson River. Pick up the Bloomingdale Road and continue as far as you can, then go on across the plains of Harlem to the Post Road. It will take you to Harlem Heights and Fort Washington."

He paused until he saw understanding in the eyes of all the officers.

"When you are all evacuated, I'll wait three hours, then follow with the last two regiments. If they come at us from the rear, you keep moving. I'll fall back and stop them. Any questions?"

At seven-thirty Putnam's two remaining regiments watched the dust settle from the last ranks of those already gone, and they stood in silence, tense, nervous, counting the minutes for the three-hour wait to pass, listening for the cannon fire that was certain to come. Among those remaining was the Boston regiment.

At ten A.M., across the island, the Americans standing behind the breastworks and in the trenches at Kip's Bay on the east shores of Manhattan Island suddenly stiffened and their eyes opened wide as they watched five great British gunboats emerge from Newton's Creek, directly across the river on Long Island. The Union Jack fluttered from their mainmasts, and their sails were full, tight in the morning breeze. The ships quartered south, then turned back and ran with the wind to stop in a line that bottled up Kip's Bay, in easy musket range. They were so close the Americans could see the faces of the sailors and read the names on the prows of the ships.

Behind the gunboats, at the mouth of Newton's Creek, a troop transport filled with blue-coated Hessians appeared, moved slightly south, and stopped. The Americans gaped as the next one appeared, filled with British redcoats, and for long minutes they watched as the boats kept coming, to fill the mouth of Newton's Creek, and spill out along the Long Island shore. When they stopped coming, a white-faced American soldier counted eighty-four of them filled with blue and red, and muttered, "They look like a clover field in bloom."

At ten-twenty the gun ports on the men-of-war opened, and the black snouts of the dreaded heavy cannon rolled forward into the bright sunlight at near point-blank range. The Americans could see the smoke from the linstocks.

At ten-thirty, the Americans heard the shouted command from the gunnery officers on all five gunboats.

"*Fire!*"

Notes

Much of the material in this chapter is based on information found in Johnston, *The Campaign of 1776*, part I, pp. 227–33 (see also Higginbotham *The War of American Independence*, pp. 157–61; Leckie, *George Washington's War*, pp. 268–69, 277).

CHAPTER XX

★ ★ ★

*T*he orange flame leaped from the cannon muzzles and the white smoke billowed and the thunder came rolling over the Americans, crouched behind the fortifications and in the trenches at Kip's Bay. The cannonballs smashed into the breastworks, throwing a cloud of dirt and shredded timbers fifty feet into the air as the British rolled the cannon back from the gun ports to reload. One minute later the second salvo came ripping, and then the deadly barrage settled into a continuous, unending roar that splattered grape and cannister shot over every American fortification while solid shot began tearing large holes in the breastworks, and a white cloud of gun smoke settled between the British ships and the American fortification.

Then, from out of the smoke and the storm of shot, the Americans saw the bows of the eighty-four troop transports come poking, and then they saw the red and blue coats and the faces of the eager enemy, and bayonets glistening in the clear, warm Sunday morning sun. Grapeshot was kicking up dirt all around them, and men were groaning and dropping. Their breastworks were becoming death traps. The entire American force seemed paralyzed. The superior officers were not giving orders. No one was moving. They stood there as though dumb, unable to think, to move. And then the lesser officers nearest the boats shouted, "Retreat!" and they turned and ran. Those behind them turned and followed, and within seconds the entire American force was running away from the hail of shot and the Hessian bayonets. Generals Scott, Wadsworth, and Douglas rode desperately among their own men, cursing them, trying to turn them, to form them into ranks and make a line, but the panic-stricken soldiers were deaf, blind, in their fear.

Four miles north and west, at Harlem Heights, Washington stopped dead in his tracks at the first sound of the distant bombardment. He listened for two minutes while the sound of the cannon became a continuous rumble, and then without a word he leaped onto his dappled mare and smacked his spurs into her flanks. In two jumps she was on the Post Road headed south at stampede gait, Washington leaning low over her neck, kicking her in the ribs at every stride.

South and west, at the Hudson River fortifications, General Israel Putnam's head swung around to the northeast at the first sound of the cannon, and he froze, listening, then pivoted and barked orders to General Parsons. "They're attacking somewhere around Kip's Bay. Send Prescott, Tyler, Huntington, and Fellows with their commands to reinforce them."

Parsons spun his horse and was gone, and two minutes later Putnam's command was split as Prescott led his men eastward, followed by Tyler, then Huntington, and finally Fellows with their troops.

Prescott, Tyler, Huntington, and Fellows had not gone half a mile when Putnam heard the first cannon volley come rolling from behind, and he and every man left as the New York City command turned, stunned, to watch British gunboats moving steadily up the Hudson, not two hundred yards from shore, their mainmast sails full, gun ports open, empty, like great vacant eye sockets. And then the black cannon muzzles rolled forward to fill the gun ports, reloaded, and they bucked and roared once more and grapeshot came whistling to kick dirt all around the troops, and some groaned and dropped. Solid shot followed, tearing into the breastworks at the Jersey Battery.

The officers shouted, "Get back! Get off the roads where they can see you! Move back. Back."

The backward movement was disorganized, hectic, but not yet a panic, as the troops moved away from the shores of the Hudson, away from their breastworks and trenches, and waited for further orders. The leading gunboats continued north, directly in front of the breastworks on the south edge of Greenwich, to form a continuous line, and then they stopped dead in the water. Moments later their cannon blasted a deadly, continuous, unrelenting fire of grape, cannister, and solid shot that steadily opened great holes in the Greenwich breastworks and the Jersey Battery defenses, and sprayed above the heads of the terrified Americans.

They pulled further back, into the brush, hiding behind whatever they could, waiting for orders that did not come. The officers of the Boston regiment shouted at their men, and Billy and Eli joined in, "Stay together, don't run, stay together," but the men, in mortal panic, heard only what they wished to hear, and the Boston Regiment began to disintegrate along with the others.

Across the island, at Kip's Bay, the British transports met no resistance as they scraped to a stop on the Manhattan shores of the East River, and the blue-coated Hessians shook their heads in disgust at the sight of the backs of the Americans running into the trees and brush, heedless of where they were going, so long as it was away from the cannon and grapeshot and bayonets behind.

The running Americans hit the Post Road and instinctively turned north, towards the high ground and Fort Washington at Harlem Heights, throwing aside their blankets and canteens, abandoning their wagons and carts with their baggage and food, leaving behind anything that slowed them. They had not gone two hundred yards when the first of the Hessians filled the roadway ahead, and without hesitation the Americans plunged off the road to their left to run across the huge farm of Robert Murray, a Quaker.

At that moment Washington came galloping onto the farm from the west and in one second understood that the Americans were in a wild rout, with the Hessians right behind them. In the next second Washington saw the great cornfield behind the house and the stone walls lining the huge farm, and knew what had to be done. The Hessians would not be anxious to storm into a cornfield with American muskets hidden everywhere, or to walk into stone walls behind which American riflemen were crouched, waiting.

He kicked his horse into the leaders of the retreat and began shouting, "Take the cornfield! Take the walls!"

But the Americans refused! They stopped momentarily, then surged on past, not listening, avoiding Washington as he reined his horse back and forth, riding in amongst them. He drew his sword and began striking them with the flat of the blade, on their backs and arms and legs, shouting, cursing, ordering them to stop and form in the cornfield and at the walls, but they would not stop. Behind him, Generals Parsons and Fellows arrived with their commands, and following Putnam's orders they immediately tried to stop the rout, but their own men saw the red and blue coats swarming within one hundred fifty yards and were caught up in the panic and turned to run.

Washington stood his ground until most of the American forces had streamed past him, and then the air went out of him and he slumped in his saddle, sword dangling from his hand, and he sat there, head down, face a blank, unmoving.

An aide reined up beside him, fighting his own wild-eyed horse, and shouted at Washington, "Sir, the Hessians are only eighty yards away. You must save yourself."

Washington looked at him as though he had heard nothing, and the aide gasped as he saw the vacant eyes. He leaned from his saddle to grab the reins to Washington's lathered, sweated horse, and he reined his own mount to the west and set his spurs. His horse lunged forward and the aide clung to the reins of Washington's mount, and with musket balls whistling, he made the run that saved George Washington's life.

Far to the south, at the breastworks near Corlear's Hook on

the East River, below Kip's Bay, Colonels Henry Knox and Gold Silliman saw the red-coated British regulars and the Hessians take the shores, and gaped as the realization sunk in. With British cannon blasting the American defenses to rubble on both sides of the island, and their forces coming ashore with no resistance, Knox and Silliman were cut off, trapped!

Knox sucked in air and turned to his men. "We fight right here, to the end." Silliman swallowed dry and began making calculations as to how many men he would lose if he made a run for it, when a man came galloping on a bay gelding and reined in the nervous, prancing mount.

"I'm Aaron Burr, aide to General Putnam. I have his orders. I know this island. I can lead you out of here, and he sent me to do it. You're to follow me." Burr, short, slight, dark headed and dark eyed, sat his saddle straight, instantly a commanding figure.

Knox looked up at him in doubt. "I'm staying here. My command will fight to the last."

Burr saw the glassy look in the upturned eyes. "You wish me to report that you refused to obey an order from General Putnam?"

It took five full seconds for Henry Knox to understand what he was threatening to do. "No. I'll obey the order."

"Get your men into marching formation. Tell them we're going to get out of here all right. Tell them."

Knox and Silliman turned and shouted orders, and five minutes later Burr was leading them on back roads and across fields and through trees and brush and up draws and gullies and ditches, always to the north.

At that moment, north, where the Post Road ran past the Robert Murray farm due east of Kip's Bay, General William Howe, with New York governor William Tryon mounted at his side, broke into the clearing just east of the winding Post Road. With an almost detached interest, Howe watched the Hessians steadily moving ahead, and beyond them he caught sight of the distant backs of the Americans in full, disorganized, panic-driven retreat. A look of passing disgust crossed his face for a moment, and he reined in his horse and studied the scene before him.

The Murray home was huge, opulent, the yards well kept, the outbuildings painted, the fences white. Inside, Mrs. Murray stood at the bank of windows that faced east towards the road, feet spread slightly, face a study in determination.

When the sounds of the distant British cannon had begun at Kip's Bay two hours earlier, she had gasped and thrown her hand to cover her mouth, aware what was beginning. Then when the cannons had cut loose in the Hudson River, she realized the British attack was massive—they meant to take the island. She watched at her windows until she saw the Americans break from the trees east of the road, running, wild, and she ran to watch to the south, down towards New York. When the first of the retreating Americans appeared from the south, she knew. The British intended setting a line across Manhattan Island and trapping those still coming from the south, to destroy them.

Within minutes she had decided what she was going to do, and she had shouted for her house servants. They had gathered in the great parlor, eyes wide, frightened.

"Bring wine. Twenty bottles. Get all the cakes we have in the house. Nut cakes, pumpkin cakes—all of them. Set up this parlor to receive high-ranking guests. We're going to entertain whatever British officers arrive here."

The servants recoiled in astonishment. Robert Murray and his wife were Quakers! They had long since declared their strong stand in favor of the American quest for liberty. And now, she was going to receive and entertain *British* officers?

Without a word the servants disappeared into the cellar for the wine and into the pantry for the cakes, while Mrs. Murray ran to her bedroom to change into one of her finest gowns.

To the south, Burr had led Silliman and Knox and their commands north, where they stumbled into Putnam's command, also heading north in full retreat, and the two groups merged, but with no clear leader in command, because Putnam had left his subordinate officers in charge while he rode to the aid of Washington. Burr began shouting, "Follow me," and as they continued north, they found themselves following him simply because he was the sole person who seemed to know where he was going. He led them to a road that skirted the east side of Greenwich, out of sight of the British gunboats six hundred yards to the west, and they continued north.

John Glover's Marblehead regiment had arrived to lead, because they were the only command that remained cool, organized, silently following every command given by their commander. Glover saw the Americans coming in from the east, chaotic, in twos and threes, no one in command, and he raised a hand and his regiment paused. He saw the hated bluecoats move out of the trees and brush behind the Americans, in a line, bayonets gleaming.

Instantly Glover gave hand signals and his men turned east and formed into two lines. He gave another signal and they all started forward, Glover leading. They let the Americans pass them, and then Glover marched his men straight out in front of the oncoming Hessians, and gave another hand signal. The first line knelt and cocked their muskets. The second line spaced itself two feet behind those kneeling in front, cocked their muskets, and they waited.

The Hessians were fifty yards away when Glover shouted his first audible command. "Fire!"

Those kneeling pulled the triggers and close to five hundred muskets blasted. Hessians all up and down the line staggered backwards and sat down and toppled over. Those behind kept coming. Instantly the kneeling line began to reload.

Glover shouted his second command. "Fire!"

The second line, standing, cut loose and another five hundred muskets bucked, and again Hessians groaned and fell backwards, and still those behind kept coming.

The kneeling line was reloaded, and they waited.

Again Glover shouted, "Fire!"

And again the kneeling line pulled the triggers and the third volley in as many minutes ripped into the Hessians, and more of them dropped and staggered backwards.

The standing line was reloaded, and as Glover watched, the Hessians stopped, and they stared, and they turned and ran!

"Fire!"

The fourth volley blasted out and Hessians dropped as the rest of them disappeared in the trees and brush to hide, their relentless attack stalled temporarily.

Glover turned to look at the Americans behind, and they had slowed, mesmerized by the Marblehead sailors, dressed in their white trousers and blue jackets and black flat-topped hats.

"Follow me," Glover shouted to his regiment, and they turned and fell into a column behind him, and he led them to the front of the Americans and turned them north, silent, calm, orderly, and once again they led the retreat towards Harlem Heights.

At the Murray farm, Howe turned to Governor Tryon. "I believe we'll stop at the house for a refreshment."

Tryon reflected for a moment. "If they have American troops hidden inside?"

Howe shrugged. "The nearest American troops are right over there"—he pointed—"leaving as fast as they can."

He walked his horse across the road, watching every building for movement that might suggest a trap. There was nothing.

Howe had reached the front gate when Mrs. Murray walked boldly out onto the long covered porch. "Gentlemen, how kind of you to stop."

Howe slowed and studied her for a moment. "I'm General William Howe of the Royal Army. This is Governor Tryon of New York. My staff is with us."

Mrs. Murray gasped expertly, then covered her mouth with her hand and dropped her eyes demurely. "Why, I hadn't expected such distinguished visitors in the midst of all this . . . interesting commotion. The day is hot and you must have come a long way.

We would be most *honored* to share our house and some refreshment with you before you move on."

Howe glanced at Tryon, then his staff. "We would be most appreciative." He spoke to one of his aides. "Ride to tell our officers to hold our troops at this farm for a while. They need a rest before the final push."

The aide spurred his horse around the fenced house and galloped towards the front of the British line.

Howe and his entourage dismounted at the fence and pushed through the gate and walked to the three steps leading up to the porch. "May I speak with your husband?"

"I regret that he's away on business, sir. He's a merchant. I'm certain he would count it a high honor to have you take a rest here with us."

Howe removed his hat and bowed. "I thank you, ma'am."

"Mrs. Robert Murray," she corrected.

"Mrs. Murray," Howe repeated.

She gave a hand signal and servants walked rapidly to the horses tied at the hitch rack at the gate, and walked them towards the barn, to be unsaddled, rubbed down, fed, and watered.

Mrs. Murray led Howe into the house to the great parlor. Her servants took the capes and hats of the guests. She gestured to the large, polished oak table, set in front of the windows with crystal wine goblets and cakes on silver platters, and white linen napkins and porcelain plates and shining wine bottles.

"Please," she said, "would you help yourselves to the wine and cakes while you rest?"

Howe was totally captivated. In the midst of cannon and musket fire, with soldiers from both sides swarming throughout the countryside, five hundred of them visible from the windows of the house at that very moment, this gentlewoman was offering a refreshment more befitting the gentilities of a cotillion than a war!

"Absolutely delighted," Howe responded, and stepped to pick up a china plate with hand-painted winged cherubs around the edge. He selected four slices of cakes, poured white wine from a decanter into a sparkling goblet, picked a fresh white linen napkin, and sat down on an upholstered chair with a high back. Governor Tryon followed, then each of their staff. Howe tasted the first cake and he closed his eyes and for long moments he sat still, savoring the sweet nut flavors. "Madam," he said, "I assure you, this general has never tasted better. My utmost compliments."

"Oh, my, I am *so* pleased. You will take more, won't you."

Indeed they would.

Minutes passed to half an hour, and still they sat, savoring the moist sweet cakes while the sounds of battle continued to the west. They sipped the wine, and they talked.

Governor Tryon turned to Mrs. Murray. "Madam, I can't help but comment on how surprising it is to have you receive us so royally, when it is known your sympathies are with the Americans."

Mrs. Murray didn't bat an eye. "We are Quakers. You're as welcome here as any of God's children."

Howe looked steadfastly at his plate while he smiled, charmed by the political expertise with which Mrs. Murray had handled Governor Tryon.

Half an hour became an hour, and still General Howe sat, unconcerned about finishing the taking of Manhattan Island, secure in the knowledge he could complete the task any time he pleased. At length he set his plate back on the table and rose. "Madam, it has been a great treat and delight to—"

Mrs. Murray was on her feet instantly. "Oh, General, surely you can't mean to leave. We've prepared a musical presentation of songs with the harpsichord in the music room. You absolutely *must* spend a few more moments." She laid her hand gently on his arm and gazed upwards into his face, eyes pleading.

He sighed. "All right. Just a few moments."

"Oh, wonderful! Please bring your wine glasses."

One hour became two as they sat in the music room and a servant played every song she knew on the harpsichord, while Mrs. Murray joined with her clear, clean soprano voice, engaging if not professionally trained.

Finally General Howe raised a hand. "Madam, were circumstances different we would be delighted to remain longer, but we cannot. Our troops are rested, and we must move on. Would you be certain to give my compliments to your husband, and thank him for the graciousness of the Murray house?"

"I shall. And our compliments to you, sir, and your companions. You know you will be welcome here any time, should you pass by again."

She spoke to her servants and several of them hurried out the back door to saddle and lead the general's horses from the barn to the front gate, while others fetched the hats and cloaks of the visitors. She followed the general down the stairs to the gate, and watched as he and his entourage mounted their horses.

Howe gallantly swept his hat across his breast and bowed deeply to her from the saddle. "Good-bye, madam. We shall not forget your hospitality."

She curtsied. "Nor shall I forget your most welcome visit."

The general reined his horse smartly to the left, around the house, and raised it to a rocking lope out towards the cornfield, and Mrs. Murray watched them disappear behind the buildings and a line of trees.

She turned her head and stood still, holding her finger to her mouth to silence her servants. For more than three minutes she stood listening, without moving. There was no rattle of musket fire from the direction in which General Howe had disappeared, and she exhaled held breath and her shoulders dropped. She gave orders and one of her servants saddled his horse and loped out towards the west, to return in less than one-half hour.

"Madam, it appears all the Americans got past while you held the general here. The only sounds are muskets once in a while, at least a mile to the north, up by Bloomingdale."

Her head rolled back and she closed her eyes and a great breath escaped her as the realization sunk in. Had Howe pushed on westward but ten minutes earlier than he did, he would have cut off most of Putnam's command coming north and had them trapped against the British coming from the south. Under her breath, Mrs. Robert Murray said quietly, "Almighty God, I thank thee."

The afternoon became a cauldron of humid, sweltering heat. Aaron Burr led the Americans steadily north, through draws and gullies unknown to the British, staying ahead of them, out of sight. In the heat, the sweating men began seeing dancing spots before their eyes. Occasionally some would drop, unconscious from heat exhaustion. Helping hands lifted them, then laid them back down when they discovered they were dead.

Billy and Eli picked twenty men from the Boston regiment and fell back to slow down the pursuing British. Eli rested his Pennsylvania rifle over a tree limb, steadied it, and waited. When the first mounted British officer came riding from the trees one hundred eighty yards behind, he pulled the trigger. The officer sagged in his saddle, then folded over frontwards and tumbled to the ground, finished. Billy fired, and the men beside him fired their muskets, and the advancing British line slowed and stopped, and Eli and Billy led their small group back two hundred more yards and settled to their haunches behind rocks and trees, waiting for the British to follow.

The afternoon wore on, with the Americans working their way north, slowed by the twists and turns and the thick brush and trees. Burr led them places where there were no trails, but neither were there cannon or Hessians. With Burr and Glover's Marbleheaders leading, and Billy and Eli and their small group at the rear harassing, they plowed on, with the sun reaching for the western horizon.

They came to a creek and marched through, and Billy and Eli and their men fell to their bellies to drink. When they stood, Billy glanced at the man to his left, still on his stomach, head submerged in the cold, clear water. Billy reached to nudge him with his foot, and the man did not move, and Billy seized him by the back of his shirt and rolled him over. His eyes were open, vacant, dead.

There was no time. Billy folded the limp arms over the still chest, bowed his head for a moment, and quietly repeated, "Almighty Creator of us all, receive this good man, one of thy sons." Then he waded gasping into the cold, chest-high water of the creek, holding his musket and cartridge box above his head as he kept moving with Eli and the small detachment from the Boston regiment. With abrupt suddenness a rainsquall swept up the island, drenching everyone before it moved on north and the sun drew steam from everything as it quickly dried.

The sun set and dusk settled as they walked out of the trees onto Harlem Plains. In full darkness Major Burr found the Post Road and continued on past the Hollow Way to their left, as the sounds of musket fire from the rear stopped. The road ran along the east edge of Harlem Heights, and then it led upward in a steady incline, to crest out on top. They passed the lights of the Morris house to their right, where Washington was setting up his new headquarters, and a mile ahead they saw the blessed lights of Fort Washington and in the starlight could make out the dim, stark outline of the thick walls, five-sided and solid against the stars, and knew they were under the cover of the cannon and muskets of the regiments stationed there.

They marched on and Burr slowed at the first challenge of a hidden picket.

"Who comes there?"

"Burr, under orders of General Israel Putnam. We're coming in."

"Come ahead." Two minutes later a lantern beamed ahead, and then another, and then they came on by the dozens as the regiments of Fort Washington came pouring out the heavy gates to meet them, jubilant, venting their fear that they had all been trapped and killed or captured in the chaotic retreat.

Billy slowed and stopped and sat down on a rock to wait for orders. Eli came up beside him, and Billy spoke, weary, sweated out, hungry. "We nearly got trapped again today. Close. Too close."

Eli stared down at him for a time. "They didn't get us. We're here."

"For now. What happens tomorrow?"

"It couldn't be worse than today." He shook his head sadly. "It was pretty sorry, the way the regiments broke and ran."

Billy heaved a sigh. "We better start looking for firewood. Maybe they got something to eat inside the fort."

Notes

Much of the novel's depiction of events and people associated with the battle of Kip's Bay (September 15, 1776)—including the landing of the British and Hessian soldiers, the Americans' retreat, the brave actions of Colonel John Glover and his Marblehead regiment, and so on—follows the account given in Johnston, *The Campaign of 1776*, part I, pp. 233–42 (see also Carrington, *Battles of the American Revolution*, p. 225; Leckie, *George Washington's War*, pp. 277–79; Higginbotham, *The War of American Independence*, p. 160). As shown here, General Washington met the retreating Americans near the farm of Robert Murray and rode among his own troops ordering them to "Take the cornfield! Take the walls!" but was essentially ignored. He continued his efforts without effect, and finally he slumped in his saddle in near collapse. One of his aides led his horse away, probably saving the general's life.

Regarding the participation of Mrs. Murray, who allegedly delayed General Howe long enough to allow the fleeing Americans to escape, historians are not unanimous on the facts of the event, some denying it happened. The report of it in this chapter is taken from Johnston, *The Campaign of 1776*, part I, 239–40. In his later works, Johnston was less convinced of the accuracy of it. Thus, while the facts are controversial, the story is included herein for the human-interest value.

CHAPTER XXI

★ ★ ★

In the black before dawn, General Washington eased himself onto the chair at his desk in the Morris house, still in his dirty uniform, damp from the sweat and rain of the chaotic retreat and the battle of yesterday. Unshaved, unbathed, he fumbled to light the lamp, then trimmed the wick, and the yellow glow reached to fill the room and cast shadows. With deliberation, he squared a piece of paper on the desktop and picked up the goose-feather quill, then paused, slowly twisting it in his fingers while he pondered the first words of the harsh, bitter letter he must write.

He exhaled a deep breath and his shoulders settled as he dipped the quill tip into the ink bottle. The scratching of the pen sounded too loud in the stillness of the room.

To: John Hancock
Head Qrs. At Col. Roger Morris's House
Septr. 16th, 1776

Sir:

On Saturday about sunset, six more of the enemy's ships, one or two of which were men-of-war, passed between Governor's Island and Red Hook and went up the East River to the station taken by those mentioned in my last. In half an hour, I received two expresses, one from Col. Sarjent at Horn's Hook (Hell Gate) giving an account that the enemy to the amount of three or four thousand . . .

He paused to dip his pen again, then described the movement of the British and Hessians that evening before he moved on to the disaster of the following morning.

But in the morning they began their operations. Three ships of war came up the North River as high as Bloomingdale, which put a total stop to the removal by water of any more of our provisions, etc., and about eleven o'clock those in the East River began a most severe and heavy cannonade to scour the grounds and cover the landing of their troops between Turtle Bay and the city, where breastworks had been thrown up to oppose them.

He laid the quill down and flexed his fingers, then continued.

As soon as I heard the firing, I rode with all possible dispatch towards the place of landing, when to my great surprise and mortification I found the troops that had been posted in the lines retreating with the utmost precipitation and those ordered to support them, Parsons's and Fellows's brigades, flying in every direction and in the greatest confusion, notwithstanding the exertions of their generals to form them. I used every means in my power to rally and get them into some order, but my attempts were fruitless and ineffectual, and on the appearance of a small party of the enemy, not more than sixty or seventy, their disorder increased and they ran away in the greatest confusion without firing a single shot . . .

With the battle scene and the shameless retreat running before his eyes, he wrote rapidly, describing it in blunt detail, struggling to bridle the anger that was driving his words and his pen. He continued.

We are now encamped with the main body of the army on the Heights of Harlem, where I should hope the enemy would meet with a defeat in case of an attack, if the generality of our troops would behave with tolerable bravery. But experience, to my extreme affliction, has convinced me that this is rather to be wished for than expected. However, I trust that there are many who will act like men and show themselves worthy of the blessings of freedom . . .

Once again he stopped and by force of will brought his raging feelings under control. He wrote one more line advising that he had sent out scouting patrols, then closed.

I have the honor to be with the highest respect, sir, your most obedt. sert.

With the rose colors of dawn breaking in the eastern sky, he tossed the quill aimlessly onto the desk and leaned back. He dug the heels of his hands into weary eyes, then hunched forward to read what he had written, weighing the delicate question of how the politicians, with whom he must contend in the Congress, would respond to his blunt, sharp criticism of the troops who had fallen into the shameful, headlong plunge from their assigned battle positions and run blindly north, defying their officers, including himself, the commander in chief. Would his letter divide Congress along the same lines as his army was now divided, New Englanders against the middle colonies, each throwing hot, divisive accusations of cowardice and desertion against the other?

For a long time he stared out the east bank of windows at the beauty of a sun rising over the rolling emerald hills across the Harlem River, on the Westchester County mainland, and he sighed as he struggled with his own thoughts. Suddenly he straightened and folded the letter.

They are the politicians. I am the commander in chief of the Continental army. It is my duty to tell them the truth. Let them do with it what they will.

He folded the flap into place and dropped the wax on it, and pressed the seal of his command into the warm wax.

"Adjutant!"

A moment later Colonel Joseph Reed was in the doorway. He was in his dirty uniform, unshaved, unbathed. The entire staff had worked until three o'clock in the morning to move the records and the furniture and bedding into the Morris house before Washington ordered them all to take a rest. They had lain down wherever they could, hungry, dirty, unbathed, for two hours, and then they were back at their duties. Fatigue showed in their faces, in their movements, their demeanor.

"Yes, sir."

"This dispatch should go out by special messenger today to Congress."

"Yes, sir."

Reed took the message and turned to go, when Washington stopped him.

"Colonel, yesterday your behavior was exemplary. I regret I am unable to say that of many of our officers, but yourself, and Glover, and a few others conducted yourselves in the best military tradition. Should further engagements require it, would you take a command in the field?"

"I would be honored, sir."

"Thank you. Would you tell the rest of the staff to heat water for—"

The pounding of an incoming horse at full gallop sounded at the front of the house, and Washington came off his chair in one fluid move and was out the door, striding down the long hardwood hallway towards the great entryway. At that moment the door burst open, and one of the pickets entered, pulled up abruptly, and saluted.

"There's a Lieutenant Geisler on the front porch, sir. Says he was sent back by Lieutenant Colonel Knowlton. They ran into a British regiment coming this way."

Washington brushed past the man, out onto the porch, and the young, smooth-cheeked, blonde lieutenant snapped to rigid attention, spine like a steel rod, chin sucked in. His hand hit his forehead hard in his ambitious salute. He was sweating, panting, and behind him his sorrel horse was standing spraddle-legged, fighting for wind.

"Sir," he gasped, "Colonel Knowlton sent me." His words came tumbling. "Sir, we ran into a regiment or a brigade or a company of British coming this way, sir. We engaged them, sir. Sir, Knowlton says he thinks we got them drawn out and—"

"Settle down, son." Washington took him by the shoulder. "You're doing fine. Just talk to me. What happened?"

The young man's shoulders dropped and he looked up gratefully into the blue-gray eyes and his speech slowed. "There's a pretty good body of them, sir. Colonel Knowlton has only twenty men, so we dropped off to one side and ambushed them, and we hit them pretty hard. Then he led them north, up towards the plains, and he thinks if we act fast we can get in behind them and trap them. He sent me to tell you."

Washington spun on his heel and called orders to Reed, and ten minutes later he led Reed, the young lieutenant mounted on a fresh horse, and four other members of his staff south on the Post Road at a gallop. They rode down the incline and broke out onto the Harlem Plains and galloped straight ahead, cross-country, down towards Bloomingdale. They reined in at the sound of musket fire ahead.

Washington spoke. "I wanted to be certain they weren't coming in force across the plains. It sounds like they're down near the Apthorpe home or the Vandewater place, by the Bloomingdale Road."

Reed's response was instant. "Sir, I ask permission to lead a probing party down there to find out what's going on."

Washington nodded. "Granted. I'll go back to headquarters. Report as soon as you can."

Twenty minutes later Reed and the lieutenant, with two other members of Washington's staff, pulled their horses to a halt at the sight of Americans crouched behind trees and rocks two hundred yards ahead, north of the Bloomingdale Ridge. They waited only long enough to see them fire a volley and fall back one hundred yards, and they spurred their horses ahead at a canter, shouting, "We're friendly, coming in behind."

Five minutes later Reed was facing Colonel Knowlton behind a stand of oak. Knowlton was intently watching all movements to the south, bright-eyed, his blood up as he spoke quickly to Reed. "We ran into them three miles south. Three hundred of them. We got them to follow. If a company of our troops can get behind them, we can trap them."

Suddenly Knowlton raised a hand for silence, and they watched the flashes of red in the trees one hundred fifty yards away, and then the first of the British pursuers were out in the brush and foliage, low, working forward. Knowlton's command did not move. They waited, poised, behind trees and rocks and bushes, Reed and his men with them, waiting for the command from Knowlton, who was like a statue, gauging distance. He waited until the leaders were seventy yards away.

"Fire!" he shouted, and the American muskets erupted and British redcoats groaned and dropped from sight.

"Fall back and reload," Knowlton continued, and the Americans dropped from sight and moved north, working with their cartridge boxes and ramrods as they moved.

Reed grasped Knowlton's arm. "I'll go back for help."

"Know what to do?"

"Circle around them without being seen and box them in."

"Good. I'll try to keep them coming."

Reed swung up onto his mount and three minutes later burst out onto the Harlem Plains, his men in a line behind, past Snake Hill, and he held his mount to a full-out gallop until they hit the incline from the plains up to Harlem Heights. He slowed and stopped for a moment, and dismounted to give the horses time to catch their wind, then remounted and climbed the hill at a trot. Once on top of the heights, he again raised the horses to a gallop and pulled them to a skidding stop, dust flying in the morning sun, in front of the Morris house. One minute later he stood across the desk from General Washington.

"Sir, there are three hundred of them coming this way. Knowlton's doing a master's job of retreating one hundred yards at a time with his twenty men, but they'll soon reach our lines at the foot of the heights. If we act now, we can probably circle and trap them."

Washington was on his feet instantly. "Take command of this operation. Get Major Leitch and one hundred twenty of his men to go with Knowlton to circle to their right flank and get in behind them. Get Colonel Crary and his Rhode Islanders to meet them at the Hollow Way and hold them. Capture or destroy them if you can."

"Yes, sir." Reed spun and was gone, pounding across the front porch. He mounted his horse and swung it around headed north, towards the sprawling camp surrounding Fort Washington, his three men following at a gallop.

Billy raised his head at the sound of the running horses passing forty yards away. He spoke quietly to Eli. "Know who they are?"

Eli watched them for a moment. "I've seen two of them. I think the one in the lead helps Washington." He shrugged. "Wonder what's got them moving so fast."

They both broke off watching the mounted detail disappear in a cloud of dust when a lanky, soft-spoken sergeant came striding into Company Nine, inquiring. "Anyone here named Stroud? Anyone know someone named Stroud?"

Eli walked to meet him. "I'm Stroud."

For several moments the man eyed Eli, surprise showing. "You're Stroud?"

Eli said nothing and waited, hands locked over the muzzle of his rifle.

"You're supposed to come with me."

"Where to?"

"Inside the fort. There's a nurse says it's urgent."

Eli dropped his hands, eyes instantly alive. "A woman?"

The man nodded. "Name's Flint, I think. Pretty thing."

Eli turned to Billy and Billy gave him a hand signal, and Eli turned back to the man. "Let's go."

They walked north through the haphazard camps of those who had arrived in the night and dropped where they stood. They passed a few fires and men who wore bloody bandages and sat staring at the ground. They climbed the steep incline up to Fort Washington, and the front gates were open, with pickets keeping a loose watch on who came and went. The sergeant led Eli inside the high, thick walls with the cannon covering all fields of fire, and made his way through the sea of faces inside, towards a door with the word "INFIRMARY" carved above.

Inside, Eli breathed shallow in the poor light and the smells and sounds of hundreds of wounded, crammed into a space made for one-third their number. He peered through the gloom, searching, and then the sergeant pointed and Eli looked, and she was there, near one corner, leaning over a cot on which a man lay with one arm missing below the elbow. Sweat drenched his pillow and he was constantly moving his legs, feet, arms, head, anything to relieve the pain and the shock of being a one-armed man for the rest of his life.

Mary Flint leaned over him, blotting with a cool, damp towel at the sweat running from his face. Eli was walking up behind her before she sensed his presence and turned. She gasped and relief flooded over her face. "Eli! They found you!"

His face was intense, eyes alive. "Are you all right? They said it was urgent."

"I'm fine."

He released held breath as she continued.

"Come with me where we can talk for a minute."

She led him to a small room in the corner with the word "APOTHECARY" on the door, and closed it behind them. A lantern glowed, and light filtered in through a small window near the ceiling of one wall. The medicine smell was strong.

"While I had the fever someone told me General Sullivan was looking for anyone who might know of a woman who had been orphaned by the Indians a long time ago. They said a soldier named Stroud was looking for her. Was it you?"

Instantly Eli's breathing constricted. "Yes." He waited, eyes points of light boring into Mary.

"I asked wherever I could. An old man in the hospital remembered something."

Eli started, waiting.

"He lived north, on a river or a lake. He had a family. He said the Iroquois came raiding and they killed his wife and two of his five children. They also attacked the neighbors eight miles away. They killed the parents and a small boy, but they left a girl alive because they thought she was insane. He thought the family name was Stroud. Could that have been your family?"

"Maybe. Where's the girl? Did he say?"

"Who was the boy they killed?"

"Me, only they didn't kill me. They took me. He must have thought I was dead because he couldn't find me. Did he say what happened to the girl?"

"He took her to a reverend. She stayed there with his family. The reverend moved four years later."

"Where? Where did he move?"

"South and east was all this man knew. Away from the Indians, towards New York."

"Did he see the girl? Eyes? Hair? How old?"

"Blue eyes and golden brown hair. About six years old at the time of the raid."

"That's my sister." Eli asked the next question and held his breath. "Did he remember her first name?"

"No."

The air went out of him and for a moment his eyes dropped. "Where is this man now?"

"I lost track of him when they moved all the wounded up here. I've tried to find him but I can't. I'll keep trying."

"What regiment? Who was his commander?"

"A New Hampshire or Vermont regiment. Militia. His commander was missing after the Long Island battle. He didn't know who the new one was."

"Do you know his name?"

"Josephus Tanner."

For a time Eli stood, committing to memory every word Mary had told him. Finally he raised his eyes to hers. "I've been looking for my sister for four years. It's part of the reason I left the Iroquois. I don't know how to thank you. Someday I'll find a way to pay you back."

"No need. I'll keep trying to find him again."

Eli nodded. "Mary, it means more to me than you know. I thank you. I surely do."

He stood facing her, and he wanted to say more but he could think of nothing that would sound proper. He raised his eyes to hers and for a long moment studied her upturned face, and then he turned and walked out the door of the small room. He made his way through the rows of wounded and the acrid smells of carbolics and the sounds of men in agony. He stopped at the big hospital door to look back, and she was standing in the door frame of the apothecary, watching. She raised a hand to wave, and he raised his and stepped out blinking into the bright sunshine.

She was alive! A minister! She was going to be tall and handsome. Blue eyed. Brown hair. Maybe married by now. Josephus Tanner. Must find him.

"Eli!"

The shout came from the south and Eli raised narrowed eyes, squinting to see. It was Billy, two hundred yards away, motioning frantically, and Eli broke into a run, his rifle in his right hand. Billy was talking loud as he slowed and stopped.

"There's a party of redcoats on the plains just south of us and we've been ordered to get down there and help. Let's go."

They ran to catch up with Company Nine and take their positions, and they continued at a trot down the inclined Post Road from Harlem Heights to the plains, and stopped. To their right, at the Hollow Way, they saw the small force led by Lieutenant Colonel Archibald Crary, stopped in the trees and partially hidden, and then they saw the British on the ridge, waiting for them.

In the moment they waited on Crary, Billy turned to Eli. "Was it Mary at the hospital? Is she all right?"

"She's all right. She heard about my sister. She talked to an old man named Josephus Tanner who remembered something. My sister lived. She was given to a minister." His eyes narrowed. "I'll find her. Sometime I'll find her."

Crary took a long look at the flat ground of the Hollow Way between his command and the British, and he looked at the British gathered on the Bloomingdale Ridge on the far side, and he divided his force. He sent a small part of his Rhode Islanders forward out into the open, and they formed a line and on his command fired a long-range volley into the British. It fell short, as Crary knew it would. The British regiment, five times larger than the small group of Crary's command, fired back a volley that fell short, and then they charged forward off the ridge, down towards the open Hollow Way, ready to engage and crush Crary's tiny command.

Crary's face came alive. *It worked! They're coming after us, right out in the open.*

Instantly Knowlton and Leitch and Reed ordered their commands to the left, then straight south, out of sight of the British.

The Virginia rifles led in a hard run to get behind the British before they were seen and trap them against the larger body of Crary's Rhode Island command still waiting unseen in the trees.

The timing was slightly flawed, but close enough. Crary watched until the British reached a rail fence in the Hollow Way, and then he stood and shouted to those hiding behind, in the trees. "Follow me! Charge!"

He spun and sprinted straight at the British, sword high, waving, shouting as he came, and his men came out of hiding hot on his heels, muskets and rifles high, voices raised in a sustained battle cry.

Suddenly the advancing British understood they were facing a much larger force than they had seen, plunging straight at them shouting, screaming, a swarming horde. They stopped dead in their tracks and for a brief moment they stared in confusion. Then from behind came the shout, "They've flanked us!" and they turned their heads to see Knowlton and Leitch and Reed breaking out of the brush deep on their right flank.

Knowlton raised his sword and shouted, "Follow me," and plunged straight at the nearest redcoats, followed by Leitch, who shouted to his command, "Follow me," and their men appeared as if by magic from behind rocks and trees and ditches.

The British turned and the Scottish Black Watch bolted for Knowlton's flank, and then the British buglers sounded a fox-hunter's call. Loud and clear it came, an open, deep insult to every American facing them, and a seething rage instantly filled every man in the American lines. Knowlton slowed for a moment to give Reed time, and Reed shouted orders and without hesitating came storming with his sword in his hand. "Follow me!" he bellowed, and the Virginia rifles surged behind him, straight towards the oncoming Scottish Black Watch. On command they stopped at one hundred yards and knelt, and Reed waited for one split second while they cocked their long rifles, and he shouted, "Fire!"

One hundred fifty long rifles blasted. Every man in Reed's command could hit a teacup at one hundred yards with his long rifle, and they had aimed at where the white belts crossed on the chests of the British soldiers. A hundred of the redcoats grunted and gasped as the rifle balls ripped into them, and they went over backwards, and more than half of them did not move again.

The remaining British desperately returned fire, stunned that the Americans had not broken and run as they had just twenty-four hours earlier. They reloaded while they waited for the smoke to clear, and they swallowed hard as they saw the Americans running towards them with those deadly rifles, to crouch again, sixty yards away. Before the British could once again shoulder their muskets for a second volley, Reed had his command on one knee, taking sure aim, and shouted, "Fire," for the second time.

The rifles cracked and the front ranks of the British regulars wilted. Men were knocked backwards, dead, dying, wounded, and those behind saw Reed's Americans running through their own rifle smoke, straight at them, while Knowlton and Leitch, with the threat to their flank removed by Reed's Virginians and Bostonians, came on once again, swords high and voices raised in chorus with their men.

The British regulars turned on their heels and ran into the trees and around them and through the brush, never stopping to look back. Their officers shouted and cursed them and they paid no heed. They lost their muskets and they didn't care as they scrambled on their hands and knees back up the Bloomingdale Ridge, with Knowlton and Leitch on their heels.

Reed followed them, and this time it was the Americans shouting, "Hallooo, Hallooo," taunting the British, telling them it was the day of the Americans, and the British were the ones who had broken to run.

Knowlton and Leitch stormed over the lip of the Bloomingdale Ridge in hot pursuit, still leading their men, swords high, when suddenly Leitch grabbed his side and pitched forward, hit hard by three bullets, almost at the same instant. Within minutes Knowlton threw an arm across his middle and stumbled and went down with a musket ball deep in the small of his back.

But still the Americans surged on. Behind the redcoats, a company of Hessians sent forward to save the retreating British from total annihilation quickly formed a line and set up two cannon, three-pounders, and as the Americans came into view they opened fire. Billy and Eli led Company Nine forward through the hail of whistling musket balls and grapeshot, and they stopped in a line. Eli went to one knee with his rifle and buried the front sight in the middle of the Hessian commanding the first cannon and squeezed the trigger, and the officer went down backwards and the cannon crew scattered. Billy and twenty others fired their muskets and more enemy soldiers went down, and then Company Nine was on its feet again, working forward, slowed but not stopped.

The Hessians fired more than fifty cannon rounds as rapidly

as they could, and then they were out of ammunition, and once again Billy and Eli led Company Nine forward at a run, shouting, and then the Virginians were with them, and the Rhode Islanders. The Hessians took one look at the screaming scourge and they grabbed their cannon and fell in with the retreating redcoats.

Billy and Eli and the Americans never slowed. They pressed on, firing as they ran, straining to catch up with the backs of the routed, panic-driven enemy, who were dropping in twos and threes all along their rear lines.

The Hessians and British ran until they reached their main lines, and they continued right on past. Billy and Eli raised their hands and slowed enough to realize they had pushed the enemy back into their own main camp, and they were facing thousands of British under the command of General Cornwallis.

They signaled, and the troops slowed and stopped, and for one long minute they looked at the British main lines, four hundred yards to the south. They stood there, sweaty, faces dirty from gun smoke, but they were grinning and shaking their fists, and the Rhode Islanders and the Connecticut and Massachusetts and Virginia commands were pounding each other on the back, jubilant, all barriers, all differences forgotten.

Their withdrawal was slow, steady, controlled, and the British did not follow. They worked their way back towards the Bloomingdale Ridge, and the call came, "Colonel Knowlton! Over here!"

They gathered around him, lying on his side, eyes closed, breathing fast and shallow. Reed was on his knees in an instant, and he lifted Knowlton's head to his chest while Billy and Eli and some officers held back the gathering troops to give Reed room and air.

Knowlton's eyes fluttered open, too bright. He blinked to focus and then he recognized Reed. The gray lips moved as he tried to speak, but no sound would come, and he tried once more. Reed leaned close.

"Did we drive them? Did we carry the day?"

Reed nodded. "Don't talk. We're taking you to the fort."

Knowlton's breathing became ragged. "I won't make it. Did we carry the day?"

Reed choked out, "We did. You led. Your men were among the finest."

Knowlton's eyes closed for a moment and a faint smile formed on his lips. He tried to make his dry mouth work once more, but could not, and slowly his eyes closed and his head settled against Reed's chest, and Reed raised a hand to smooth the sweaty, matted hair.

Captain Stephen Brown knelt beside him, tears streaming. "He was my superior officer. I was right beside him when he went down. I caught him. He said he didn't value his life much, if we could but carry the day. I'm glad we got back to tell him. I never saw the like of what he did. May I help put him on a horse? take him back?"

Reed wiped his eyes. "Use my horse."

Billy and Eli turned away and they stood for a time, silent, and with a hundred other men wiped at their eyes unashamed.

A hushed voice called, "Leitch! Over here."

Leitch was sitting with his back against a rock. He was wrapped tight with a bandage around his middle, showing a great gout of blood on his right side. Reed went to one knee. "Can you stand?"

"I don't think so, but I can ride if you can get me on a horse." His face was showing gray, but his voice was strong, his breathing regular, his eyes clear, focused.

Strong hands lifted him onto a horse, and within minutes his feet were tied to the stirrups and he was laced to the saddle. A mounted captain took the reins of his horse while two more reined in on either side to reach for his arms to steady him. They raised their mounts to an easy lope and headed down the slope of the Bloomingdale Ridge, onto the Harlem Plains, towards the Post Road up to the fort. At that moment, reinforcements sent by Washington came pounding up, including Generals Putnam and Greene and a large company of Marylanders.

General Putnam, the ranking general, quickly called for a council, and the officers gathered. The sun was still high.

"Shall we wait and meet them here and make a stand?"

Just then Tench Tilghman, an aide to Washington, galloped up on his lathered horse and handed a sealed message to Putnam. The signature was that of George Washington.

"Under any circumstance do not commit to a major engagement in the open field. At such time as you have destroyed the British that were on Bloomingdale Ridge, or they have retreated to their main lines, break it off and return to the fort. I repeat, do not become entangled in a major engagement."

Led by their officers, the Americans gathered their dead and their wounded, and they fell into regimental formations and marched down the north slope of the ridge, onto the plains. They marched with their heads high, their muskets over their shoulders, and no one was calling criticisms to any other command as they moved north, shoulder to shoulder, up the Post Road onto Harlem Heights and to the fort. Gentle hands helped the wounded to the hospital, while others began the solemn process of laying the dead in a line, covered, to be prepared for burial.

In the late afternoon sun, the generals and Colonel Reed sat facing General Washington in his new quarters at the Morris home.

"Report."

General Nathanael Greene spoke. "I believe it would be fitting for Colonel Reed to make the report. He's the only one here who was there through the entire action."

For five minutes Reed systematically laid out the events as they had occurred, and then he paused, and General Washington waited for a moment. "Yes. Go on."

"Sir, when we were in the crucible, it was Colonels Knowlton and Leitch who turned it. They did not order their men, 'Forward.' They shouted, 'Follow me!' and they led them. They led them. I can't tell you, sir, the effect on the men. I believe they would have followed those two officers straight into the infernal pit if that's

where they had led them. Never have two officers acquitted themselves so gallantly. I hope the general sees fit to give them their
due."

Washington sat still, fascinated, as Reed went on.

"One more thing, sir. Not one command performed better
than another. Connecticut, Maryland, Rhode Island, Virginia—it
made no difference. And when it was over, they thought of themselves as one army, no longer divided. There was a feeling as they
marched back up the Post Road, their wounded and dead with
them, shoulder to shoulder."

The generals looked at each other and said nothing. For several seconds the room remained silent.

Washington said quietly, "Excellent. Would you all submit a
brief written report of your individual observations and conduct
for the permanent records. You are all dismissed."

The group rose to leave, and Washington reached to take
Reed's arm. "Colonel, there's hot water. Get a bath. I'll have a hot
supper waiting. Then take a rest. After, I need your help."

It was past eight o'clock when Reed rapped on the door of
Washington's private quarters.

"Enter."

Reed stepped into the room. "There was something I could
do for you, sir?"

"Sit down." Washington was seated at his corner desk, and he
turned to face Reed. "I need you in command of troops in battle.
I need someone to replace you here. Do you have any suggestions?"

Reed dropped his face in thought. "I haven't considered it. I'll
need a little time."

"What would you think of Alexander Hamilton? He's a captain,
with a command. He is recommended to me as bright, decisive."

"I've heard of him, but I am not informed enough to speak to
his qualifications."

"Would you do some investigating?"

"Of course. Was there anything else?"

"In the morning, early, I intend writing a letter commending all the officers and all the troops who were in today's action. I'd like your help."

"Very good, sir."

"Could you make arrangements for the burial of Colonel Knowlton? Full military honors. I would like a few minutes in the service to speak about what that brave man did. This army needs to hear it."

"I would be honored."

"One last thing. I doubt General Howe has an appetite to try to dislodge us from this hill by a direct attack from the south. I expect him to send troops ashore on Westchester, probably across Long Island Sound, to come in behind us at King's Bridge and trap us. He might cross at Pelham Bay, or Throg's Neck. I sent a spy from Westchester County whose presence will not raise suspicion. I assigned him to sketch all the British troop disbursements and their defenses on Long Island Sound, immediately. I expected to hear from him before now. Has anything come to your attention about this?"

"No, sir. I'll report immediately should I hear."

"That's all for now, Colonel. You have distinguished yourself today. I am deeply grateful."

"Not at all, sir."

"You are dismissed."

Tattoo had sounded and the campfires had gone out when the pickets on the Post Road heard the muffled sounds of a small body of men moving directly up the incline towards Harlem Heights.

"Who comes there?"

"Lieutenant Robert Marshall. Connecticut militia. I've got wounded. We're coming in."

Half an hour later three exhausted men watched the doctor in the infirmary lay two wounded men on makeshift cots on the floor at the rear of the hospital. He shook his head and turned to Marshall. "I'll do all I can. Were there any more?"

"Two. We lost them. Buried in a cellar down in New York City."

"Go get something to eat."

Marshall led his two men out of the hospital, into the clear, starry night, and took his bearings inside Fort Washington. He worked his way through men in their blankets to the commissary. It was dark and no one answered his knock. He shook his head and stood with his shoulders slumped, unable to force his numb brain to make another decision.

A lantern approached from behind and a voice asked quietly, "You the party that just arrived?"

"Yes."

"I'm Major O'Connell. Maryland Brigade. Where did you come from?"

"New York City. Been hiding down there with wounded since yesterday morning."

"When did you leave?"

"This morning around ten o'clock."

There was surprise in O'Connell's voice. "You got out of New York in daylight?"

Marshall's head dropped forward and he spoke quietly. "Some of us were sent into New York to get all the bells in town to melt down for cannon, under General Washington's orders. We got them, but my detail was last getting out and we got trapped. We hid in a cellar. This morning Howe sent General Patterson to occupy New York City."

The exhausted lieutenant's face fell forward. "You should have seen it. Patterson lined his troops out in a column and marched up Broadway and stopped. Seemed like the whole town turned out. Singing, dancing in the streets, fireworks. Welcomed the British with open arms. Hoisted Patterson onto their shoulders and carried him around like a hero. Went door to door looking for Patriots, and they were beating them. Killed some of them."

Marshall paused. "We were hiding in that cellar up towards the top of Broadway. Two of our wounded died in the night and we buried them right there. The British and Tories didn't even notice this morning when we slipped out and went north, up past Bayard Hill Fort with our other two wounded."

He raised his face, yellow in the lantern glow. "You should have seen it."

"Follow me. I'll help with food and blankets and a place for the night."

Marshall fell in behind O'Connell, his stumble-footed men following, and Marshall mumbled once more, "You should have seen it."

Notes

The unexpected meeting between a force of British and Hessian soldiers probing north towards Harlem Heights and a small force of American soldiers, with the resulting Battle of Harlem Heights, in which the Americans badly beat the British forces, is chronicled in Johnston, *The Campaign of 1776*, part I, pp. 248–58. This battle also saw the tragic loss of two gallant American officers, Lieutenant Colonel Thomas Knowlton and Major Andrew Leitch.

This time it was the Americans calling "Halloo" mockingly after the retreating British (see Leckie, *George Washington's War*, p. 280).

The American officers did not order their commands into battle; they led them (see Leckie, *George Washington's War*, p. 281).

All American commands performed with bravery and emerged from this battle more united than ever before (see Johnston, *The Campaign of 1776*, part I, p. 261; Leckie, *George Washington's War*, p. 281).

New York City

September 21, 1776

CHAPTER XXII

★ ★ ★

*T*he acrid bite of smoke came creeping in the blackness to sting in the nostrils of the sleeping in New York City. The Reverend Ewald Gustav Schaukirk of the Moravian Church on Fair Street twisted in his bed and coughed, and from deep inside a tiny voice of alarm grew and suddenly he opened his eyes and jerked bolt upright. Dull orange reflections played on the outside of the drawn window shade, casting his small bedroom in a strange, deep gloom. For a moment he sat still, with the wind and the glow at the window, while the sleep fog lifted from his brain, and then he threw back the bedcovers.

He shoved hasty feet into his slippers and they slapped on the hardwood floor as he trotted to the door at the rear of his church and threw it open. Instantly he was caught in a swirl of wind and smoke, and he dug at his watering eyes, struggling to focus. He gasped and coughed as he stared.

It seemed at first as though the entire city were caught in smoke and a red glow that reached into the black heavens to blot out the stars. He hurried out to the street, not caring that he was in his nightshirt and slippers, and watched as the windows in the houses began to glow and people ventured out, candles and lamps held high as they peered, then ran back inside their homes to throw off their nightshirts and scramble into clothes to return to the streets, running towards the red that was leaping into the night sky along the Hudson waterfront, fanned by the wind.

Schaukirk stood long enough to realize the fire was only to the west and south of him—the entire city was not in flames. Then he ran as hard as he could inside his church and threw open the door to the belfry and seized the ropes, and pulled downward with all his weight. There was no sound, and only then did he remember the American army had stripped every bell from every tower as they deserted New York City and ran north in panic. For a moment he stood, unable to grasp the fact there was no way to raise a city-wide alarm, and then he ran back to his bedroom to throw off his nightshirt and thrust on his street clothes.

He trotted northwest along Fair Street for two blocks, then headed down Broadway, working his way through the gathering crowds in the street, and nearly collided with Sister Sykes of his congregation, carrying a large child and a bundle, leading her children away from the fire. Her legs buckled and he caught her and took the child and the bundle and led them back to his own quarters and left them there while he went back outside. He quickly gathered two buckets from the toolshed behind the church and once again started towards the red glow spreading to the west and north.

The heavy wind was quartering in from the southeast, and the reverend silently prayed, "God of us all, please do not let the wind shift, or it is all lost." The wind held, blowing toward the north and west, up the Hudson River.

"It started at Whitehall Slip," someone shouted, and someone answered, "It's moving up Broad."

Within minutes the streets were locked in chaos, people with buckets running from one place to another, red-coated soldiers among them, disorganized, wasting precious time as the fire worked north along the Hudson riverfront. No one had expected the inferno, and the fire wagons had not been filled with water. The men of the fire brigade seemed unable to understand they should fill the wagons, and they backed away to mix with the milling mobs in the street.

The wind spun spirals of sparks high in the skies, and they settled back among the trees and houses on Stone Street, Beaver Street, and finally Broadway. Wisps of smoke appeared among the shingles on the rooftops, and fanned by the winds, sparks came alive and then points of flame flickered and caught. There was no way to move water from the ground to the rooftops and the fire leaped north from one rooftop to another, as far as King's College.

The shout arose, "Save the church!"

Hundreds ran to the Trinity Church, the revered shrine on Broadway, oldest and largest of the English churches, but there was no way to reach the roof. People stood on the ground helpless as they watched the great tower begin to smoke, and then flames licked, and the old, weathered shingles caught, and the steeple, so long a landmark and a symbol, became a great flaming pyre thrust into the night sky, visible for miles. Slowly the ancient timbers burned through, and then the steeple tottered and came crashing down on the roof of the church, driving a million sparks a hundred feet into the blackness above while the roof caved in, and within minutes the old church was a burned-out hulk. A scant one block away, the old Lutheran church followed.

The spreading flames gave no quarter as hovels, small homes, mansions, churches, landmarks, wharves, docks, warehouses—all were swept up in the raging inferno to become blackened ashes as the night wore on. Women led screaming children east to the common, where they gathered in the center, away from anything that could burn, and clustered together, wrapped in each other's arms as they wept, watching the western half of their city disintegrate to charred rubble before their eyes.

Reverend Schaukirk was driven back, back, finally to his own street. The roof of the corner house caught and the reverend shouted orders. "Fetch the ladders from the church belfry and the cemetery!" Minutes later strong hands slammed the ladders against the walls of the home and young men scaled them at a run while others followed, and they began passing water buckets upwards. Seconds passed to minutes as they threw water as far as they could, and slowly, slowly the fire began to sputter, and then it dwindled, and then it went out. They remained on the ladders, throwing water, drenching the entire rooftop, before they dropped the buckets to the ground and descended.

In the black hour before dawn the reverend went among his people, comforting, encouraging, inquiring of their losses. Sister Kilburn had lost two houses, her only support in her old age. The Pell family had lost three houses, everything they owned. Widow Zoeller had escaped with only what she wore; her tiny home and everything she had treasured from her long life was black rubble. Lepper and Eastman Company had lost their entire warehouse. The heartbreaking count went on and on.

With gray showing in the eastern sky, and the ashes still smouldering black into the dawn sky, the pain and suffering of the people turned to anger.

"Who started it?"

"The Patriots!"

"Incendiaries! Hang them!"

Mobs combed through the city, knocking down doors of the known Patriots, beating them, smashing everything inside their homes. Two hundred were arrested on no more evidence than an accusatory finger pointing at them. Four were hanged before seven o'clock, without a hint of a chance to defend themselves or a trial.

The wind died two hours after sunrise, and for the first time the people gathered themselves, smoke blackened, exhausted, devastated, and faced the hard, stark facts. More than one-fourth of their city was gone. A large part of the rest of it was damaged. They had lost treasured artifacts going back to the foundations of their very beginnings, including a building and irreplaceable objects from Peter Stuyvesant, the governor who had to surrender New Amsterdam to the English more than twelve decades earlier. The Hudson River wharves and docks were closed down, burned, with many ships anchored there.

Silently they accepted it. Those who had, shared with those who had not. Doors were thrown open to receive any who needed beds. Root cellars and storehouses were opened, and lines formed for food, with no one asking questions. Blankets were gathered on the common, with clothing and shoes, and handed out to waiting hands. It went on into the day as the wounded city took its first stumbling steps towards healing itself.

It was noon before General Patterson had a written report on the damage suffered from the fire, and by one o'clock General Howe was sitting at his command desk, mouth clenched, reading the report. The Hudson River wharves and docks had been largely destroyed and damaged. Buildings and homes used to billet British soldiers were burned-out hulks. Warehouses along the waterfront were charred, with hundreds of tons of food, blankets, clothing, medicines. By three o'clock General Howe was pacing in his private quarters, clinging to a fragile hold on his rage.

The waterfront! We had to have the wharves and docks for our navy, and they're gone. More than two thousand of our troops now forced to set up tents. At least one hundred tons of foodstuffs—blankets—uniforms—gone.

At half past five o'clock a rap came at his door and he turned on his heel and barked, "Enter."

"Sir, one of Roger's Rangers captured a spy in our camp on Long Island. You may want to interrogate him."

"A spy? Civilian?"

"No, sir. A captain in the rebel army."

Howe recoiled in surprise. "What? A rebel captain, in our camp?"

"Yes, sir. As I said, sir, you may want to interrogate him."

"Bring him here."

One hour later Howe stood as his aides led a man into his conference room. He was of average height, well built, well groomed, solid, good features, dressed in civilian clothing. He faced Howe with a calm demeanor, blue eyes steady.

"Untie his hands," Howe ordered, and an aide removed the ropes binding the hands.

Howe sat down but required the man opposite his desk to remain standing.

"Your name?"

"Nathan Hale."

"Are you a soldier?"

"Captain in Colonel Knowlton's rangers."

Howe looked at the youthful face. "Your age?"

"Twenty-one."

"Where are you from? What town?"

"Coventry, Connecticut."

"I'm told you were captured in a British camp on Long Island."

"I was."

"You're dressed as a civilian, a spy. Do you know the penalty for spying during war?"

"Yes, sir. I do."

"Were you spying?"

"I was."

"Looking for what?"

"It's all there in my sketch pad, sir. I was sent to get information on your troop positions and your strength. I was to make sketches."

"Let me see the pad."

An aide laid it on his desk, and Howe spent minutes going over each of the drawings, eyes widening from time to time. He closed the pad and raised his face. "Excellent work. You did well."

Hale stood silent.

"I could use your talents. Would you be interested?"

The answer was calm but immediate. "No, sir."

"It would save your being hanged."

"I know."

"Are you educated?"

"Yale College."

"Your profession?"

"Teacher."

"You freely admit you were spying for the Continental army?"

"I do."

Howe shook his head and a sad expression came across his face for a moment. "What a waste." He swallowed. "I'll give you overnight to change your mind. If you cooperate with me, I promise you safety and high reward. I'll talk to you again in the morning."

The aide began working the rope back onto Hale's wrists when Howe spoke. "Never mind that. Put him under lock and key for the night, but leave him alone."

The dawn came calm, with rose and gold light flooding from the eastern sky. At eight o'clock Nathan Hale once again stood facing Howe across the large maple desk.

Howe raised hard eyes to Hale. "Have you had time to consider my offer?"

"I have."

For a moment Howe hesitated before he asked the question. "Have you changed your mind?"

Hale's gaze was steady. "No, sir."

Howe's head dropped forward and for a moment his shoulders lowered. He raised his face and the two men stared into each other's eyes, and Hale saw the frustration, the anger in Howe.

"The execution will take place in one hour." Howe clamped his mouth shut and turned away.

They loaded Hale into an army freight wagon with four armed soldiers, and drove him north on the Post Road. People in the street stopped to stare until they understood, and then they fell in behind, following in an ever-growing crowd. The wagon rumbled on in the bright, warm sunshine of a clear, calm September morning. The driver reined the team of horses into the road of the Rutger farm, and stopped at the near edge of an apple orchard, where the scaffolding had been hastily hammered together. The leaves were changing colors, and the birds and squirrels were busily flitting.

Rough hands helped Hale to the ground, and the four soldiers held their muskets at the ready as they took him to the steps. They bound his wrists behind his back and walked him to the top of the stairs, to the trap, and tied his ankles. They slipped the rope over his head and pulled the slack out of the noose.

General Howe marched up the steps and faced him. "Do you have anything you wish to say?"

"I presume I will not have a trial?"

"You have confessed. There will be no trial."

"May I speak with a clergyman?"

"You may not."

Hale's voice was steady, calm. "Then may I see a Bible?"

"You may not." Howe paused for a moment. "You can still save yourself with one word."

Hale reflected for one moment. "I cannot do that." He paused and looked down into the faces of the mob that had collected in the beauty of the simple surroundings. For a moment he glanced into the orchard, and listened to the sounds of life in the trees. Then he turned his eyes back to Howe. His voice was as calm and gentle as the morning. "I regret that I have but one life to give for my country."

A hush fell. Howe nodded to the man behind Hale, and he reached for the lever to the trap.

Notes

The accidental fire of September 21, 1776, that burned more than one-fourth of New York City is competently described in the diary of the Reverend Ewald Gustav Schaukirk (Shewkirk) of the Moravian Church on Fair Street (see Johnston, *The Campaign of 1776*, part 2, pp. 118–19).

While acting as a spy under orders of General Washington, Nathan Hale was captured and publicly hanged by the British pursuant to orders of General William Howe (see Johnston, *The Campaign of 1776*, part 1, p. 262; see also the brief biography of Nathan Hale in the same book, part 2, p. 188). General William Howe would not allow a trial of Nathan Hale (see Leckie, *George Washington's War*, p. 282).

CHAPTER XXIII

★ ★ ★

*I*n the warm, late afternoon October sun, General Washington leaned forward in his chair to move the lace curtain and stare west out the window of his private quarters at the Morris house. Frost had touched Harlem Heights, and the trees were alive with color as the leaves turned in their eternal cycle of birth, life, death, and rebirth. He stared at them, morose, unseeing, filled with dark foreboding.

I've misjudged too many times—Brooklyn—Long Island—New York— and now here—can't defend Harlem Heights—gunboats in the rivers on both sides—our obstructions in the Hudson failed to stop them—British to the south—and now they're moving on the mainland—will they come in from the north? surrounded us? trap us again? Congress paralyzed—no power to raise an army or pay for one—nothing but committees who know nothing, do nothing— won't or can't send troops—my own officers murmuring—General Lee— resign, he said—threaten Congress with your resignation if they don't meet your demands—resign—with him next in line to take my command.

He suddenly stood, as though the physical movement would somehow dispel the somber spirit, and he paced aimlessly, hands clasped behind his back.

He started at the sudden rap at his door.

"Enter."

Colonel Joseph Reed opened the door. "The generals are in the conference room, sir."

Washington considered. "Hold them. Notify me when the two scouts are here to report."

"Yes, sir."

Washington returned to the windows to peer out at the great cornfield, harvested a month earlier, with the full, golden ears stored in the stone granary twenty yards from the huge white barn. The cornstalks, cured and dried, stood tall and white, and rustled when the errant breezes of fall ruffled the brittle leaves. For a moment Washington's thoughts reached for his beloved Mount Vernon, and he turned away from the windows at the sudden overwhelming need to be home with his wife, in his own fields, looking with deep satisfaction at his own granaries and herds and flocks and orchards. He did not know how long he stood, remembering, seeing in his mind what had once been, and then the second rap came at the door.

"The scouts are here, sir."

"Wait until I am in the conference room, and then bring them."

He straightened, set his face, paced down the hall to the large double doors, and strode into the conference room. Generals Lee, Putnam, Sullivan, Scott, Greene, and Colonel Henry Knox rose to their feet at the table and stood while he walked to his place at the head before they turned their faces to him, waiting his pleasure.

"Thank you. Be seated. We are here to receive the report of two scouts just returned from Westchester on the mainland. It is my belief they will have critically important news."

At that moment Reed appeared in the doorway and Washington nodded, and Reed stepped aside.

Dirty, with a week's growth of beard, Billy entered the room, followed by Eli, and they stopped in the presence of the clean uniforms and the gold braid. Billy saluted General Washington while Eli glanced at the officers. He recognized all but one. He had never seen hawk-faced, dour General Charles Lee.

Washington stood and spoke, his words echoing slightly. "Were you able to complete your mission?"

"Yes, sir," Billy replied. "We came straight here."

Not one of the officers moved, and Eli sensed a tension, a prickly, disjointed feeling among them as he waited.

"Make your report."

Billy glanced downward at his clothes, his appearance. "Sir," he said, embarrassed, "we didn't stop to clean up. I'm sorry for how we look."

"Don't be concerned. Go ahead with your report."

"It was Private Stroud's scout. I went along only so one of us would get back if the other was caught. I believe he can make the best report."

Billy stepped back and Washington faced Eli. Recognition flickered and a faint smile formed as he spoke. "Report."

Eli stepped to the end of the table and spoke to Washington as though no one else were in the room. "Do you have a map from over there?"

Washington unfolded a map and anchored it with leather pouches filled with buckshot. Eli studied it for a time before he pointed at an irregular line running north and south on the mainland, ending at Long Island Sound, the sizeable body of water separating Long Island from Westchester County on the mainland. "What river is that?"

"The Bronx River."

Eli shifted his finger slightly to the east. "That river?"

"The Hutchinson River."

"What's this, down here?" His finger was on a tiny, irregular-shaped peninsula jutting from the mainland into Long Island Sound.

"Throg's Neck. An island with a bridge to the mainland."

"Here?" His finger had shifted farther north, to the irregular coastline of the mainland, on Long Island Sound.

"Pell's Point, at Pelham Bay."

Again he shifted his finger farther north. "Here?"

"White Plains. A town."

"Here?"

"New Rochelle. A town."

Eli's finger shifted to the west side of the Bronx River. "Here, and here?"

"Valentine's Hill and Mile Square."

Eli nodded, peered at the map for several moments, then began, shifting his hand, pointing as he identified the locations. "We have troops and fortifications here and here, at Valentine's Hill and Mile Square, west of the Bronx River."

Washington nodded. He had ordered troops to those locations days earlier, to assure keeping the all-important communications open between his headquarters and the mainland. Above all, he had to know of every troop movement by Howe in Westchester County. The overriding fear of the entire Continental command was that Howe would suddenly move troops on the mainland and appear undetected at King's Bridge to close the Americans' only way off Manhattan Island.

Eli shifted his hand and continued. "Six days ago the British moved ships up the East River, here, past Hell Gate, then turned east into Long Island Sound. They landed here, at Throg's Neck, but a company of riflemen stopped them on the bridge, and then tore the planks up."

He straightened. "I don't know why, but the British waited six days after they landed before they moved from Throg's Neck up north about three miles to Pell's Point." He tapped the map. "They came ashore here early this morning."

Every general at the table leaned forward and Washington's response was instant. "How many?"

"About eight thousand. Nearly half Hessians."

There was a sharp intake of breath around the table.

"Cannon?"

"Not less than one hundred, horse drawn."

"Supplies?"

"A long line of wagons with everything they'll need for a while."

"Did you recognize any officers?"

"Howe's in command."

Washington paused for a moment before he asked the single most critical question. "Which way did they move from Pell's Point?"

Eli sensed the deep urgency. "I thought Howe would move north and west, across the Bronx River to King's Bridge, and cut us off." He shook his head, deeply puzzled. "But he didn't. He headed up towards New Rochelle. Above that is White Plains. I can't see much to be gained by that unless he plans to burn all the food and kill all the livestock to keep it from us." Eli shook his head. "But he wasn't doing that."

He stopped. For long seconds the room was locked in dead silence while every man struggled to explain Howe's laconic attitude. Billy could hear the flies buzzing at the windows.

Washington leaned slightly forward. "How fast were they moving?"

Eli shrugged, mystified. "Slow. Not paying much attention to anything I could see. I don't understand Howe. He could have his whole army up at King's Bridge by tomorrow afternoon if that's what he means to do, but at the pace he held this morning, he'll be days getting there. I can't figure him."

Washington pressed on. "What condition are the barns and granaries in over there?"

"Full. Good harvest. An army can live off the land a long time over there."

"Is any of the militia or the population harassing Howe? resisting?"

"No. Some are opening their homes and their barns and granaries to him."

Washington stopped and dropped his face forward while he gathered his thoughts. Satisfied he had what he needed, he asked, "Is there anything else this council should know?"

"Yes. Brant's Mohawks have scouted all around us, here, on this island. Howe probably knows everything about us he needs."

The face of every officer turned to Eli, eyebrows arched.

"How do you know?"

"Moccasin tracks. At least five sets. Some two, three days old, some fresh this morning. I saw them coming in."

"Anything else?"

Eli reached to scratch under his chin. "No, not exactly."

Washington cocked his head. "I don't understand your answer, Private."

Eli drew a breath and released it. "Only this. We had frost over there the last three nights. Winter's coming. If they hold the mainland, come spring what's left of us here will be pretty cold and hungry."

Billy glanced at Eli, then at Washington, fearful Eli had gone too far. Privates do not instruct the commander in chief, particularly with five other generals and the colonel in charge of artillery listening.

Washington did not flinch; nor did the expression on his face change. "Thank you. Both of you. You have done well. You are dismissed."

Billy saluted, Washington returned his salute, and Billy walked out of the room, Eli following. Reed closed the double doors and Washington settled onto his chair, mouth pursed as he gathered his racing thoughts. "It is obvious to me we must get the army off this island, starting now, tonight."

Every man at the table leaned back, stunned.

"The single question is, do we abandon Fort Washington?"

Greene spoke firmly. "We can hold it. As long as we do, they'll have to leave a sizeable command here to contain it. It will reduce their available forces."

Lee shook his head violently. "Abandon it. It's useless. Both Fort Washington and Fort Lee."

Scott interrupted. "Congress says we should hold the two forts."

Lee stood, palms flat on the table, arms stiff, and his words rang off the walls. "Congress! Politicians! Bumbling fools! There's only one way to deal with them." He stood erect and faced Washington, eyes blazing. "Make a list of your demands and tell them unless they meet them, you resign your command! *That's* how you deal with fools."

For a moment no one moved, and Washington stared at Lee, eyes narrowed as he realized for the first time that he had never seen or understood what was in Lee's heart and head. Lee's military education, probably the best and most complete of anyone's in the entire Continental army, including that of Washington himself, had been drilled into Lee in the *British* army, not the American. Everything Lee had learned rested on the foundation of complete power in the king, not the people. His solution to everything that lay in his path was to crush it under authority of the king. Lacking such authority, Lee was floundering, groping, lost, unable to understand how to deal with a Congress that had the power to dictate military policy but not the power to raise the money or the army to support it.

Suddenly Washington's breathing slowed as his thoughts went deeper. *Resign! He's said it twice! He wants me out so he can take my command! He wants power! His ambition knows no limits!* For a split second Washington's mouth narrowed as the conviction knifed into his heart. Then by force of a will that knew no peer, he spoke calmly.

"We will hold both forts. Colonel Magaw will take command of Fort Washington with one thousand five hundred troops, and General Greene will take command of Fort Lee with three thousand five hundred troops. I will take the balance of our forces across King's Bridge to White Plains. There are strong positions there. If we can fortify them before winter, we can stall Howe until spring. In the meantime, through the winter, we can petition Congress for more troops, more supplies, more money, and prepare for a decisive battle."

Lee's face was a study in disgust as he dropped back onto his chair, fist clenched on the tabletop.

Outside the Morris house, with the sun touching the western rim and the chill of evening coming on, Billy and Eli walked to the camp of Company Nine. They laid down their rifle and musket and settled onto their blankets for a time, to let the weariness and tension of seven days in the bowels of enemy territory, with British redcoats swarming, settle and begin to drain. Billy raised his head at the sound of a young captain calling.

"Weems. Is Weems back yet?"

"Here."

"Mail." The captain handed him a letter and walked away while Billy seized the document and instantly read the return address. Dorothy Weems. He ripped the flap from the wax seal and brought his racing thoughts and fears under control as he read.

Monday, Sept. 23, 1776

My dear son:

We are well. We have dried fruit and salted meat and fresh vegetables in the root cellar sufficient for winter. We are warm and happy and I beg of you, please do not spend useless time worrying about us.

However, I am constrained to relate a sad story. Brigitte and Caleb were part of a group of fourteen Patriots who undertook to transport food, supplies, and munitions to your army at New York. Unknown was the fact one of their number was a traitor. He betrayed the entire train of four wagons into British hands.

Billy gasped and Eli rose to one elbow, looking, while Billy skimmed on through the letter.

Taken prisoner—forced to drive for the British—Connecticut militia mistook them for British and Tories—shot at them—cannon and rifles—every wagon destroyed.

Billy choked and Eli sat up, staring, waiting, as Billy continued with trembling hands.

All lost except Charles Johannesen and Brigitte and Caleb— saved by the grace of the Almighty—they were blown from their wagon into the grass—could not be seen. Walked three hundred miles back to Boston—untold hardships—little food—slept in the open.

Home—recovered—Brigitte suffering from self-condemnation—Caleb struggling to understand that such terrible things do happen in times of war.

> I have heard terrible things about our losses at Long Island and at New York. I have not received a letter from you in many weeks, but in my heart I know you are all right. Please write to me when you can. I place you in the hands of Almighty God and know you are serving him.
>
> With every tender affection,
> Your loving mother,
> Dorothy Weems

All the air went out of Billy and he sat for a moment, mind reeling, heart pounding.

"You all right?" Eli waited. "What's wrong?"

"My mother."

Eli started, focused. "Is she all right?"

Billy nodded. "Brigitte and Caleb were nearly killed."

"Brigitte? The sister of your friend Matthew?"

"Yes, and her younger brother."

"What happened?"

Billy handed him the letter, and Eli turned it towards the setting sun to read it. He laid it on his blanket and sat for a time before he spoke. "That was a bad thing." He looked at Billy. "Will you be all right?"

"Yes. It was just . . . a surprise."

"A bad one. But neither one of them was harmed."

Billy refolded the letter and held it in his hands for a moment. "I've got to find a pencil and paper."

"I'll help, but first we better get a bath and something to eat. I think we'll be leaving this camp soon."

At half past eight o'clock, in deep dusk, the orders came. At ten o'clock General Washington led the first regiment marching north up the Post Road to King's Bridge. They crossed in the darkness and angled eastward, towards the Bronx River and White Plains. Behind them weary troopers moved horses hitched to cannon onto the dirt road, and when there were no more horses, ten men were assigned to drag the two-thousand-pound guns and carriages. They crammed their pitifully small supply of food and blankets and ammunition into the few wagons they had, and on George Washington's command rumbled into the blackness, vapor trailing from their heads, dressed in their light summer clothing, without coats, shoes loose at the seams, holes in the soles. By two o'clock the hoarfrost reflected sparkling on the grass and ground. By four o'clock it showed on the hair and eyebrows and beards of the trudging, weary army, slowly, painfully making its way through the black of night.

In the gray of half past six o'clock a mounted rider galloped up to George Washington and reined in his blowing horse, steam rising from the hot hide and flared nostrils. He wore the uniform of a captain. Washington raised his hand and the column stopped.

"Sir, General Howe and his first division are not more than three miles to the east, moving north and west. His column will be directly across your path within two hours, and he's ready for a fight."

"How many men?"

The captain hesitated for a moment. "Four thousand."

Washington paused for a moment, then turned to his aide. "Go bring Colonel John Glover here, immediately."

Five minutes later John Glover was facing General Washington. Streaks of morning sun were showing in the high clouds to the east.

Washington spoke crisply. "Colonel, General Howe is less than three miles to the east on a line of march that will put him directly across our path in the next few miles. If he attacks this column, strung out as it is, he will destroy us all. He must be stopped."

Washington paused for a moment, knowing what he was about to ask Glover.

"Can your command slow him for one day? I can be on high ground and organized if I can have one day."

Glover, one full foot shorter than Washington, peered upward into the granite face in the breaking dawn. "How many men are with him?"

Washington swallowed. "Four thousand."

Glover did not flinch. "Do we have anyone who knows the ground over there?"

"We do." He turned to his aide once more. "Get Corporal Weems and Private Eli Stroud, Boston regiment, now."

Three minutes later Billy and Eli pulled up beside John Glover, winded, panting, their breath rising in a cloud of vapor. There were no formalities as Washington spoke.

"General Howe is three miles east, trying to cut off our line of march and destroy us. Did you learn the ground over there well enough on your scout to serve Colonel Glover if he tries to stop them?"

Eli's answer was instant. "We know the ground. There are some wheat fields over there, with stone fences. The right men behind those stone fences can do it."

Washington looked down at the lined, weathered face and the steady eyes of Glover, and he searched for the words that would say how he loathed ordering the Massachusetts men into open battle in broad daylight against four thousand of the finest of the world-renowned British army. He spoke slowly. "I will not order you. In the name of the Continental army, and for the sake of the liberty we are fighting for, I ask you. Will you try to give me one day?"

Glover's answer was simple, quiet. "We'll stop them. Give me ten minutes."

Five minutes later Billy and Eli watched as Glover gathered his regimental officers around him and spoke briefly, pointing. The officers nodded and trotted to their different companies. Three minutes later, seven hundred fifty men of the Massachusetts regiments had formed beside the road. Two hundred fifty remained with Washington's column. Two minutes later Glover gave the order and started north at a trot, Billy and Eli beside him, his hand-picked companies behind him, following.

They turned due east and left the road, working through fields of grass wet with the morning dew. One hour later, soaked to the knees, they crested a rise and slowed, and stopped. Before them was a valley filled with wheat fields that had been harvested two months earlier. Stone fences, waist high, nearly a mile long, ran from east to west at intervals of about one hundred yards, with lesser, irregular fences and paths running from north to south. The white stubble and the straight stone fences turned the floor of the shallow valley into a gigantic checkerboard. From far to the south the first distant sounds of fifes and drums drifted into the valley.

Billy and Eli pointed. Glover nodded and turned to his officers and gave orders and hand signals, and led them into the valley at a trot. With Billy and Eli showing the way, the fishermen took measured intervals behind a waist-high stone fence in the center of the valley and strung out for half a mile. When they were in position, every man in Glover's command could see him at the extreme east end of the line. Glover removed his black hat and waved it, and a captain at the west end of the line waved back and immediately the entire command crouched behind the stone wall. Billy was beside Glover, while Eli was in the center of the line, where a small opening in the stone fence allowed passage of a road large enough for a two-wheeled farm cart.

The sound of fifes and drums grew, and then came the sounds of four thousand foot soldiers and two hundred horses marching north, and then they were there at the south end of the valley, red coats and white belts bright in the sun as they marched steadily on, scaling the stone fences as they came.

Eli felt the ground vibrations in the soles of his moccasins as the clatter of scabbards and cartridge boxes and canteens, mixed with the first sounds of voices, reached over the stone fence. Eli glanced to his left and right, and every man in the Massachusetts regiments had his face turned east, waiting for the signal from Glover. The rustle of feet moving through the wheat stubble came clear, and it seemed the British were right on top of the stone fence, and still Glover waited.

When the crouched Americans heard the drums in the first rank cease, and the drummers prepare to scale the fence, Glover suddenly rose from behind the stone wall. The British captain leading the advance caught the movement from the corner of his eye, looked at Glover one hundred yards to his right, and did nothing, dumbstruck at the sudden appearance of a man where none had been, fumbling in his own mind to understand who Glover was and what he was doing behind a stone fence in a wheat field.

When Glover stood, every man in his command cocked his musket and every third man stood bolt upright, face-to-face with the British less than fifteen feet south of the stone fence. The British troops stopped dead in their tracks, staring, minds blank.

The first volley thundered at point-blank range, and more than one hundred red-coated soldiers staggered back and buckled. The second two hundred fifty Massachusetts soldiers stood as those who had fired squatted down behind the fence and drew fresh cartridges from their cartridge boxes and ripped the ends out of them with their teeth, reloading, while the second volley blasted. Blind panic seized every British soldier within fifty feet of the wall as more than seventy of those in the lead ranks gasped and dropped. The third two hundred fifty Americans stood as the second two hundred fifty crouched down and began reloading, and the third volley echoed through the valley, and again more than seventy of the British soldiers toppled.

The first two hundred fifty, now reloaded, stood as those who had just fired crouched, and they picked their targets and the fourth thundering volley ripped into the running British. They were throwing down their muskets, canteens, cartridge boxes, anything that slowed them in their blind stampede back towards the stone fences to the south, to hide wherever they could to escape the holocaust behind.

Glover's men fired two more volleys before the British threw themselves over the stone fence one hundred thirty yards to the south. They lay in the wheat stubble, gasping for breath, not moving while their officers crouched behind the fence, daring to raise their heads enough to see the thick white cloud of gun smoke obscuring the fence to the north. The wheat field seemed filled with patches of red, and the officers gaped, white-faced, as they quickly estimated their dead. More than two hundred, in less than six minutes. And they had not heard a single cannon!

Eli reloaded his long rifle, cocked it, and rested it over the stone fence, waiting.

One hundred eighty yards to the south a British major, incensed at the catastrophic rout of his command, kicked his horse in among his own men, shouting at them, sword drawn, cursing, threatening, rallying them for a charge.

Eli glanced at the drifting smoke, gauging the speed and direction of the wind, laid his cheek against the worn stock of his rifle, lined the sights, raised the muzzle to compensate for distance, and squeezed off his shot.

One-half second later the British major grabbed his chest and his sword went spinning. He buckled forward, clawing for the pommel, trying to stay mounted, and he could not. His men caught his body as he fell.

Eli and the Americans settled down once more behind the stone fence, watching Glover at the east end. Glover extended his telescope and raised his head enough to study the British movements, and they waited.

Minutes became half an hour, while the British struggled to regain their shattered composure. The men in the front ranks who had faced the devastation swore that more than five thousand Americans had risen from nowhere and the musket balls had come thicker than hail. Half an hour became an hour while the officers walked among them, trying to reason with them, finally ordering them under threat of execution to form ranks.

They came again in two ranks, one thousand strong, muskets lowered, bayonets flashing, stepping over their own dead as they trotted north across the field.

They were ten yards from the fence when Glover gave his command, and this time the Americans did not stand. They laid their muskets over the top of the fence and showed only the tops of their heads as they aimed and fired in rotation, each group firing while the previous one reloaded. The relentless musket balls ripped large holes in the front rank of the oncoming British, then the second rank. The British still standing fired their muskets without aiming, and turned and ran. Most of the musket balls whistled high, some slammed into the stone fence, others tore dirt in front of it, and a very few hit the Americans.

Twice more the British regrouped and came across the open field, and twice more the Americans patiently rotated their volleys with calm, deadly precision, and twice more the British broke and ran.

The sun passed its zenith and settled towards the west. The British sent regiments east and west to flank the men behind the stone fences, and Glover sent companies of his command to stop them.

In the late afternoon Glover watched the British officers form two thousand men into five ranks and face them north. Glover closed his telescope, gave orders, and his regiment crouched low and silently moved back one hundred ten yards to the next stone wall and took up positions.

The British came marching across the field, stepping over their dead, and their faces were a mix of surprise and great hope as they breached the first stone fence to find nothing more than tracks headed north through the stubble. They were fifteen yards from the next fence when the dreaded muzzles of the American muskets suddenly appeared above the stones, and an instant later the deadly rotation of volleys blasted in their faces. The front ranks collapsed back on those behind, who pushed their dead aside and marched on, only to be sent reeling back by the succeeding volleys, less than thirty seconds apart. The British were ten feet from the stones when their ranks broke and fled.

The Massachusetts men reloaded and waited. The sun cast long shadows eastward, and then settled behind the western rim.

Dusk came creeping, and the shades of night deepened. Three hundred yards to the south, campfires flickered. Eli crept east, found Glover, and they talked quietly for twenty seconds before Eli slipped over the wall. Fifteen minutes later he silently scaled the fence and dropped beside Glover to report.

"They're making camp for the night. It's over."

Glover gave orders and his command quietly moved due north a quarter mile, carrying their dead and wounded, then turned west in the darkness, Billy and Eli leading with Glover between them. Behind them, in the dark stubble fields, lay one thousand red-coated British casualties.

It was midnight when Billy and Eli raised their arms to point at the distant pinpoints of light that marked the campfires of Washington's army, and it was past one A.M. when the south picket challenged Glover, then let him and his command pass. It was two o'clock when the Americans had delivered their dead and wounded to the infirmary, and gathered back at the campfires to gratefully wrap their hands around hot pewter mugs of steaming coffee, and sit down on blankets, or logs, or knapsacks, or in the dirt, teeth chattering in the hard cold, and work at smoking strips of crisped sowbelly and black bread while they gingerly sipped at the steaming cups. Their noses began dripping, and they wiped at them as they continued, and the warmth in their stomachs spread.

Glover tapped Billy and Eli on the shoulder, and they followed him to a tent glowing with lantern light. The picket held the flap and they entered and faced General Washington. He was seated at his table in full uniform, quill in his hand. He turned in his chair to face them, then stood. He said nothing as he waited for Glover's report.

"We met them, sir. They stopped."

Washington drew breath and cleared his throat. "Casualties?"

"We left about one thousand of them in the stubble fields."

Washington started in astonishment. "Your casualties?"

"Eight dead, as far as I know. About thirteen wounded. They're at the infirmary. I expect nearly all of them to recover."

Glover gestured to Billy and Eli. "We have these two soldiers to thank for knowing where and how to meet them."

Washington's face filled with unexpected emotion and for a moment he could not speak. Then he took charge of himself and his spine straightened. "I will include this in my report to Congress. Tomorrow we continue on to White Plains to prepare for battle. Thank you. Dismissed."

General Howe sat his big-boned sorrel horse for a long time in the crisp cold of early morning, working his telescope back and forth across the massive American breastworks fifteen hundred yards ahead, north. Six hundred yards in front of the breastworks, three country dirt roads crossed, with the hamlet of White Plains surrounding the intersection. Howe glassed the tiny village with rooftops and fields sparkling from countless frost crystals until he was satisfied there were no Americans hidden in the trees or ditches, then raised his telescope once more and again counted the cannon and the regimental flags at the breastworks beyond. He shook his head, again amazed at the magic the Americans could perform with pick and shovel and one day's time.

The heavily fortified center of Washington's defenses was flanked on Washington's right by a crook in the Bronx River and on Washington's left by lowlands that would be nearly impossible to gain and hold under the muzzles of the Americans' cannon.

Howe twisted in his saddle and focused his telescope west, to his left, where the Bronx River, four hundred yards distant, ran south. The far bank of the river was a steep incline of ninety feet, and again Howe worked his telescope back and forth, counting the cannon muzzles on the rim of the incline. He was swinging the telescope back to peer north once more when he hesitated, then brought it back to look past the steep incline bordering the Bronx to a hill half a mile farther west. There were cannon on the hill, and suddenly he stood in his stirrups and studied it carefully.

He abruptly turned to his aide. "What's that second hill?" He pointed.

The aide glanced at his map. "Chatterton Hill, sir."

"Do you have an elevation on it?"

"Not in feet, sir. It is just identified as the highest hill in this neighborhood."

Howe studied Chatterton Hill once more, and then with the eye of one whose life had been spent gaining priceless wisdom in the brutal cauldron of battles, both won and lost, he gauged distances and directions, and once again turned to his aide, pointing. "If we take that incline just across the river, then move straight north around Washington's right flank, the cannon on that second hill—Chatterton Hill—can reach us easily. Is that correct?"

"That is correct, sir."

Howe sat for a time, studying the breastworks dead ahead, trying to work himself inside Washington's mind. He turned once more to his aide. "What's behind Washington?"

"Sir, our report says he has prepared more breastworks about three or four miles back, at North Castle. With the Croton River right there, those fortifications are very good. It is our guess he will fall back to them if things do not go well where he is."

"How much of his army did he bring with him?"

"Fourteen thousand five hundred, sir. He left fifteen hundred men at Fort Washington under Colonel Magaw, and three thousand five hundred at Fort Lee under General Nathanael Greene. The rest are here."

Howe pursed his mouth and dropped his eyes for a time in deep thought.

He has superior numbers and good fortifications on the high ground, and he's ready to fall back to strong positions if he has to. He's inviting me into a decisive battle, with most of the advantages in his favor.

He shook his head and pushed his thoughts to a conclusion.

He wants another Bunker Hill—us walking through White Plains onto the open ground in front of his breastworks while his long rifles and muskets cut us down, and he brings his forces from the incline and Chatterton Hill in behind to trap us. What will he do if we take both the incline and Chatterton Hill away from him first?

He turned to his aide. "Get General Leslie and the Hessian officers."

Five minutes later Leslie reined in his horse, with the Hessian colonels von Donop and Rall following on their nervous horses, wisps of steam rising from their heated hides and clouds of vapor trailing from their flared nostrils. Facing Howe, they stopped and waited.

Howe spoke with expressionless authority. "General Leslie, take your brigade along with the commands of Colonel von Donop and Colonel Rall across the Bronx River and up the incline. Take it and go on past and take the next hill—Chatterton Hill. We will give you cover with cannon. Any questions?"

One hour later, behind the breastworks in the center of the American fortifications, Billy and Eli flinched and instinctively ducked at the thundering sound of fifty cannon blasting out a volley nearly one mile distant. They braced for the shock of cannonballs ripping into the breastworks, counted three, then looked at each other in puzzled silence before they cautiously raised their eyes above the breastworks to peer south in the morning sun.

In the haze, past the clumped trees of White Plains, a cloud of white smoke hung in the still air above the frosted ground. Ten seconds later a second cloud of white smoke erupted, and then the roar of the second volley rolled past the American lines, and Billy and Eli watched the cannonballs blow dirt and rocks just below the rim of the incline west of the Bronx River.

Billy raised a hand to wipe at his dripping nose. "They're not coming here. They're going after the rim on the river."

"And that second hill behind it," Eli added.

The Americans behind the breastworks stood bolt upright, entranced at the deadly drama unfolding before their eyes. Dots appeared on the east shore of the Bronx River and they became boats filled with red or blue specks as the British and Hessians pushed off into the open water to make the crossing. From the rim of the hill opposite, American rifles and muskets began their deadly work, and then in the center of the American defenses,

Captain Alexander Hamilton barked orders to two American cannon crews. They depressed the muzzles of their three-pound cannon downward, point-blank at the river, blocked up the rear of the cannon carriage, and cut loose on the boats coming straight at them. The first volley raised waterspouts thirty feet high among the boats. The second volley blasted holes through the bottoms of two boats, but the British doggedly kept coming.

The first wave of British and Hessians hit the American side of the river and started up the incline, clawing their way. At the top of the ridge, Americans leaped over their own breastworks and stood at the rim, firing downward at men less than ninety feet away. The red-coated bodies fell backwards, sliding, tumbling down the steep incline, and those below let them fall past as they kept their faces upward and climbed.

Across the river the British cannoneers rammed bar shot and chain shot down the muzzles of their guns and set up a continuous barrage, holding their gun muzzles high enough to clear their own forces on the face of the incline. Americans staggered back and went down, while others came leaping over the breastworks to replace them. With grim determination the British and Hessians refused to break, to retreat as they doggedly clawed their way up the hill into the guns above.

Then an American turned and shouted something, and leaped from the rim, plunging downhill, and one followed him, and then another, and then hundreds as they slammed into the enemy below in a wild hand-to-hand fight, swinging their muskets or a rock or anything they had as they tore into the British and Hessians with their battle cry echoing up the river to the Americans at the White Plains breastworks.

And the British and Hessians broke! Those in the lead turned and slid downhill into those beneath, and they became a red and blue avalanche that hit the riverbank and spilled into the dark winter waters.

Billy and Eli and a thousand Americans did not realize they had leaped atop their own fortifications with their fists clenched above their heads, shouting their own battle cry as they watched the Americans clear the face of the incline and then turn to scramble back to the top while the British cannon blasted at them.

For long moments the cannon fell silent. Hope leaped in the hearts of the Americans that the British were withdrawing, and then the long line of redcoats started up the steep incline once more. Again they clawed up, fifty feet, seventy feet, and again the Americans leaped over the rim, down among them, face-to-face, clubbing, grappling, kicking, and once again the British were swept off the incline.

The Americans stood on the White Plains breastworks silent, wide-eyed, with one desperate question, one great hope. *Will they try again? Let it be over.*

Suddenly Billy's arm jerked up, pointing, and he shouted, "To the left! Look left! They're climbing up!" as though the Americans nearly a mile away, on the rim, could hear him.

While the red-coated British had held the Americans directly on the face of the incline, Colonel Johann Rall had led his Hessians farther south, and while the Americans had swept the British back, Rall and his blue-coated troops had surged up nearly to the top of the rim before the Americans saw them.

Flanked, with the howling Hessians coming in behind them, the Americans broke. They fell back, west and north, unable to stop and load as the Hessians came with their muskets banging and their bayonets lowered. Behind them, Colonel von Donop led his Hessian command towards Chatterton Hill at a run, and up the hill without stopping. The Americans at the top realized that with the British forces now able to bring their cannon to the top of the incline to the east, the Chatterton Hill defense would be rubble within twenty-four hours. They fell back in full retreat to join the main American forces with George Washington at the White Plains fortifications. They met General Israel Putnam leading his command to reinforce them, but too late, too late. The battle had already been lost.

With the broken and retreating defenders streaming into his

main camp, Washington sat alone in his tent, staring at his hands clasped on the table before him. He raised them to dig at weary eyes.

He refused the bait and sprung the trap. I've lost the advantage. We will have to move back to our lines at North Castle and hope he comes after us.

Reluctantly he assembled his officers.

"Prepare your commands and wait for my orders to move back to North Castle."

He saw the blank look creep into their eyes, and sensed the thinly veiled anger, the frustration seething in them as they silently stood and walked back out into the cold sunlight. One hour later Washington rose and fastened his cape about his shoulders and walked out among his troops, watching, listening. He saw the sullen, narrowed eyes glancing at him, and was aware of the silence that fell as he passed. He returned to his tent and slumped onto his chair and he leaned forward on his elbows, face buried in his hands.

South one mile, the setting sun shined through barren tree branches to cast delicate designs on the ground as the picket at the flap of Howe's command tent entered.

"Sir, you have a messenger."

Howe rose. "Send him in."

A stocky sergeant entered and saluted. "From General Percy."

Howe unfolded the document and read. "Thank you. There will be no return message. Dismissed."

Howe sat down at his table and read the message again, slowly, then leaned back in thought.

He's preparing to fall back to North Castle. All right, so be it. We'll follow to be sure he's set there, and then we withdraw back to Manhattan Island. When he discovers we intend to take Fort Washington and Fort Lee, he'll come quick enough, and I will pick the time, and the place, for the battle. He will fight me on my terms, not his.

It was full dark when Howe gathered his generals to his tent.

"Washington is going to retreat to North Castle soon. We'll follow only long enough to be certain he's established there, and then we leave for Manhattan Island. We will take Fort Washington and Fort Lee, and if he follows, we will fight him at the time and the place we choose."

Clinton shook his head. "Finish him right now. We beat him today, and we can beat him at North Castle. We've cornered him twice and let him go. That's enough. Go after him right now."

Howe slowly shook his head. "We will have one-half the casualties if we make him come to us and fight on our terms. I won't trade good British troops for a few days' time. We wait and make him come to us."

Six days later, at North Castle, with dawn breaking, General Washington raised his head from his breakfast of bitter coffee and fried corn mush and faced his picket, who had thrust his head inside the command tent.

"Sir, you have a messenger."

Washington read the message, then read it once more. "Thank you. There will be no reply. Dismissed."

He tossed the message onto the tabletop and leaned back in his chair. Half an hour passed before he summoned his officers.

"General Howe left in the night, moving his army south and west. I believe he is going to attack Fort Washington and Fort Lee. If he succeeds, I think he intends moving west through New Jersey to take Philadelphia. I am convinced he wants to take our Continental Congress."

The officers moved, but said nothing.

"General Lee, you will remain here at North Castle with five thousand men until I send you written orders. General Heath, you will take three thousand and hold them at Peekskill until I call for them. I will gather two thousand and go to Manhattan Island to repulse Howe."

He watched his officers rise and file out of his tent, and he watched as they walked away, heads down, without looking back. He returned to his table and picked up his empty coffee cup, with the cold dregs in the bottom, and he stared at them for a long time.

Notes

The fortifications of the Americans and the location of the British troops in the area of White Plains, New York, including Chatterton Hill, are well identified in Carrington, *Battles of the American Revolution*, maps section, p. 19.

On October 12, 1776, the British passed through Hell Gate and landed troops at Throg's Neck but failed to move onto the mainland in the face of American resistance, then moved on to land at Pell's Point six days later. Thence they moved to New Rochelle and stopped for several days (see Higginbotham, *The War of American Independence*, p. 160; Johnston, *The Campaign of 1776*, part I, pp. 265–71).

General Charles Lee advised Washington to make his demands of the Continental Congress and threaten to resign if they failed to meet them (see Leckie, *George Washington's War*, p. 283). General Lee was probably the best and most completely trained military mind in the American forces, albeit his training was by the British army, from which he defected prior to the beginning of the Revolution to take up residence in the colonies (see Leckie, *George Washington's War*, pp. 116–17).

General Nathanael Greene was given command of Fort Lee with 3,500 troops; Colonel Robert Magaw was given command of Fort Washington with 1,500 men (see Leckie, *George Washington's War*, p. 284).

General Washington called on Colonel John Glover and three of the Massachusetts regiments under his command to stop the British during the American retreat to White Plains. Colonel Glover did it by using a series of stone walls in open fields (see Higginbotham, *The War of American Independence*, p. 161; Johnston, *The Campaign of 1776*, part I, p. 271).

General Washington had prepared defensive fortifications at North Castle in the curve of the Croton River, about four miles north of White Plains, in the event of a defeat at White Plains. When the British forces captured Chatterton Hill, Washington retreated to the North Castle position (see Leckie, *George Washington's War*, p. 287; Johnston, *The Campaign of 1776*, part I, p. 276).

The battle at Chatterton Hill became known as the Battle of White Plains. Again, the Americans lost and had to retreat to North Castle. Thereupon Howe decided to wait long enough to be assured Washington was not moving, and then march back to take Fort Washington and Fort Lee, thence on to take Philadelphia, where the Continental Congress was then sitting. Alexander Hamilton, later to become aide-de-camp to General Washington, commanded cannon in this battle (see Johnston, *The Campaign of 1776*, part I, pp. 274, 276; Leckie, *George Washington's War,* pp. 285, 287; Carrington, *Battles of the American Revolution,* p. 243).

General Washington ordered General Lee to remain at North Castle with five thousand men, and General Health to remain at Peekskill with three thousand men, while Washington took the remainder of the army back to Fort Washington (see Higginbotham, *The War of American Independence,* p. 162).

CHAPTER XXIV

*I*n bright, cold mid-November afternoon sunlight, Captain Zachariah Blaisdell stopped on the parapet of the east wall of Fort Washington and raised a hand to shade his eyes. Suddenly he dropped his hand, spun, and leaped to the ground, sprinting to find Colonel Robert Magaw, commanding officer.

He found him at the powder magazine and pulled up, gasping for breath. "Colonel, there's a British officer approaching the main gates under a white flag. What are your orders?"

Colonel Robert Magaw studied his aide for a moment. "Let him enter."

"Blindfolded?"

"No. I'll receive him in my quarters."

The pickets swung the huge gates open, and Blaisdell passed through to march ten yards ahead and stop, waiting for the British officer and his aide to approach.

Inside the fort, Colonel Magaw glanced about the fort for a moment, wondering if he should have had the messenger and his aide blindfolded. The interior was jammed with nearly double the number of soldiers for which it was designed, with sick and wounded visible outside the hospital, and supplies and munitions stacked out in the open.

It makes no difference. They know what we have inside.

He strode to his quarters, straightened his uniform, and sat down at his desk, puzzled at what a British officer intended doing under a white flag. He flinched at the sudden rap at his door. "Enter."

Blaisdell entered. "Sir, Adjutant General Paterson of His Majesty's army has a sealed message for you."

"Bring him in."

A moment later Paterson and his aide were inside, at rigid attention, facing Magaw.

"Sir," Paterson said, "it is my honor to deliver this message to you."

"Would you care to be seated?"

"No, thank you, sir. It is not intended that we remain for any length of time."

"What's the message?"

"An offer, sir. A generous offer."

Magaw received the message, broke the wax seal, and read it carefully.

> Every consideration will be extended to yourself and your command at Fort Washington, including pardon, should you accept this offer to surrender immediately. Should the offer not be acceptable, we regretfully advise that the entire garrison will be put to the sword at once.

Magaw read the letter once again with a growing anger at the threat of a massacre, and then he spoke. "I presume you know the contents of this message."

"I do, sir."

"Howe intends putting this entire command to the sword?"

"I am aware that is what he said."

Magaw pursed his mouth for a moment. "I'll need some time—maybe six hours—to consider this."

"I deeply regret, sir, that I must have your answer within the hour. I am under orders to wait for it."

Seething, barely maintaining control, Magaw left Paterson

standing while he sat down at his table and for a time worked with quill and paper. He dusted the finished message, read it once, then stood and handed it to Paterson. It was neither sealed nor folded.

Paterson looked at Magaw for an explanation.

"Go ahead and read it," Magaw said.

15 November, 1776

Sir: If I rightly understand the purport of your message from General Howe communicated to Colonel Swoope, this post is to be immediately surrendered or the garrison put to the sword. I rather think it a mistake than a settled resolution in General Howe to act a part so unworthy of himself and the British Nation. But give me leave to assure his Excellency that actuated by the most glorious cause that mankind ever fought in, I am determined to defend this post to the last extremity.

Rob't Magaw, Colonel Commanding

Paterson's mouth dropped open for a moment before he clacked it shut. "This is the reply you wish me to deliver?"

"It is."

Paterson snapped to attention and saluted. "Thank you, sir." He turned stiffly and marched out the door, with Blaisdell following to escort him through the gate and out to safe return to his own lines.

The sun had set when Magaw called his officers together in the small, austere command headquarters of Fort Washington. They came with their capes drawn about them, vapor trailing behind their heads, to sit on plain pinewood chairs in yellow lamplight.

"The British are going to mount a sustained attack in the morning. My scouts tell me there are more than two thousand Hessians north at King's Bridge, under Colonel Rall and General Knyphausen, and there are two thousand British south on Harlem Plains under General Percy. I don't know from which direction the attack will come, so this is how we are going to prepare."

He leaned forward, facing each officer as he spoke their names.

"Colonel Rawlings, you take the north quadrant where the Hessians will be coming. Colonel Baxter, you prepare to command the east wall. Colonel Cadwalader, you prepare to meet the British to the south. It's clear they can't scale the cliffs on the west, so we don't have to prepare a defense there unless they send gunboats up the Hudson to bombard us. If that happens, our cannon will answer. Any questions?"

There were none. The officers rose, each lost in his own calculations and plans to mount the defenses that had fallen on him, and they walked out into the sharp air, across the dark compound to their separate quarters to begin writing the orders that would be delivered in the dark to the companies that would defend Fort Washington.

Campfires burned into the night as the men moved munitions and food and water to their battle stations while others huddled around the flames, blankets drawn over their heads as they warmed fingers and toes numbed by the biting cold. Towards morning, frost crystals came to reflect a million points of light and turn the world white.

With mist rising from the river in the gray before dawn, anxious pickets on the west wall pointed and then shouted, "Gunboat on the Hudson!"

Across the river, on the New Jersey side, below Fort Lee, General Washington led Generals Putnam, Greene, and Mercer into a longboat and settled down for the trip across the river to make their final inspection of the fortifications before the battle they knew was coming. They worked through the thin crust of shore ice out into the current, when suddenly Washington sat straight up and pointed. Dead ahead in the mist was the British gunboat, the Union Jack on the mainmast, anchored one hundred yards from the hill leading up to Fort Washington.

"A British gunboat! Are we too late? Has it begun?"

Greene extended his telescope. "She's the *Pearl.* If she's come to—"

Greene got no further. Twenty-two cannon on the *Pearl* blasted and the white smoke billowed. Half a second later the cannonballs punched into the west wall of Fort Washington and exploded. Dirt and shards of timber flew eighty feet into the air. With the echo still rolling across the Hudson, the American cannon on the wall of the fort answered.

Five seconds later, cannon at the foot of the steep inclines on both the north and south ends of the fort set up a rolling thunder that reached across the river and echoed off the granite face of the Palisades and the walls of Fort Lee. The four American generals sat in the longboat, silent, spellbound as the battle unfolded before their eyes. Each had his telescope, and they shifted from one place to another as they watched the troop movements and the grape and cannister shot whistle.

At the north end of the fort, Sergeant William Corbin leaped over the wall and down the hill, sliding, falling, to an American cannon emplacement that was exposed to Colonel Rall's Hessians, battling their way up the one-hundred-foot incline to reach the north wall of the fort.

Corbin tipped the cannon muzzle down the hill and slapped the linstock against the touchhole and the gun bucked and blasted. The first rank of Hessians threw their hands high and fell backwards while Corbin grabbed the sponge to ram down the barrel, and for the first time realized that his wife, Margaret, had followed him. He dropped the sponge and reached for the powder ladle, slammed it home and twisted it, then jerked it out as his wife crammed straw into the muzzle and shoved the ramrod home to lock the powder in place. Corbin pushed the next cannonball into the muzzle, and again his wife drove the ramrod home. Corbin touched linstock to touchhole and the gun roared, and the Hessian lines wavered.

Then, at the bottom of the incline, two Hessian cannons answered, and Corbin threw his wife down and fell partially on her as the cannonballs struck and dirt and rocks showered them. The smoke and dust settled and they leaped to their feet again, loading and firing down at point-blank range into the oncoming Hessians.

At the south end of the fort, Percy's redcoats waited until the freezing air was filled with cannon smoke, then surged forward into Cadwalader's command, trading cannon volleys, then musket volleys. Howe, watching and waiting on the east bank of the Harlem River, waited until the right moment, then shouted orders above the roar of the ongoing cannonade.

"Sterling, take the Forty-second Highlanders and get between Cadwalader and the fort."

Twenty minutes later the Highlanders lowered their bayonets and marched up the steep incline from the Harlem River to the level ground leading to Fort Washington, and plowed into the rear of Cadwalader's command in fierce, hot, mindless, hand-to-hand fighting, bayonets against clubbed muskets and axes and pitchforks. The chaotic battle teetered, and then the British surged forward and within minutes Cadwalader's command was caught, Sterling on the north, Percy on the south.

Cadwalader cursed as he watched one hundred fifty of his advance company surrounded, and he groaned as they threw down their arms and huddled in surrender. Percy's command continued on, rank upon rank, firing as they advanced. Cadwalader paused long enough to realize that within minutes he would lose his entire command if he remained where he was. He turned and shouted to his men, "Fall back, fall back."

On the river, Greene turned to Washington in the longboat. "We should get you back to the New Jersey side. If the *Pearl* sees us, her cannon can sink us in minutes. I'll go back over to help Magaw."

Washington slowly shook his head. "No, we'll all go back to the New Jersey side, and we'll stay there."

The generals looked at each other and said nothing, aware that their commander in chief already understood that Fort Washington was going to fall. Fort Washington—the one bastion they had thought was invincible, indestructible.

As the oarsmen turned the boat and dug their oars into the

dark Hudson waters, Washington watched, face set like stone, as the Hessians once more clawed their way up the north incline towards the cannon of Sergeant Corbin. Once more the cannon fired, and the leading rank of blue-coated soldiers fell back on those below. As Corbin grabbed the sponge to ram down the hot, smoking gun barrel, a Hessian laid his musket over a rock, steadied it, and fired. The huge ball struck Corbin just beneath his ribs and he grabbed his chest and moaned and fell backwards and did not move.

Margaret screamed and clasped both hands over her mouth, then crouched beside her dead husband, cradling his head against her for a moment, and then the next volley of musket balls came whistling, tearing dirt and whanging off the cannon.

Margaret tenderly laid her husband's head down and spun on her heel. She loaded the powder and the straw and the cannonball, grabbed the linstock, and laid it on the touchhole. The blast knocked the leading ranks of the Hessians thirty feet downhill, and Margaret grabbed the sponge. Ninety seconds later she touched off the next shot and again the Hessians fell back.

On the east side of the fort, Colonel Baxter watched helplessly as the unrelenting bombardment of grape and cannon shot ripped holes in his command. "Fall back. Fall back to the fort."

To the south, Cadwalader was desperately trying to lead a controlled retreat, shouting, "Fire and fall back. Reload. Walk. Don't run."

On the north, the Hessians once again angled the muzzles of their two cannon upwards at the gun emplacement where Margaret Corbin, face smudged with cannon smoke, hands blistered by the heated gun barrel, was still loading and firing. On command the two big guns blasted and an instant later both cannonballs ripped through what was left of the thin breastworks of the gun emplacement. One hit the wooden carriage of the American cannon and blew one wheel to pieces to leave the cannon pointing into the dirt. The other cannonball tore the left sleeve of Margaret's dress before it smashed into the hillside directly behind her and exploded. It blew her forward, rolling, her left shoulder torn and bleeding, and she came to rest against the wrecked cannon, unconscious, blood soaking into the dirt beneath her shoulder.

One minute later the shouting Hessians stormed the gun emplacement and the leaders continued on past, up the hill, to the north wall of Fort Washington. Those behind traded musket volleys with the Americans on the top of the wall while the first two ranks threw up their ladders and scaling ropes and went up, those behind taking the place of those above who fell.

Behind them, at the gun emplacement, a Hessian slowed and stared as he passed Margaret, and he stopped, unable to believe he was looking at a woman. He called to his captain, who walked to him and looked down, wide-eyed. The captain barked orders and strong hands lifted her up while a trooper ran for the regimental surgeon. Minutes later they had her shoulder washed clean, bound up, and they were gently moving her down the hill to be taken to their infirmary. Whatever their reputation, whatever their shortcomings, the Hessians had respect for a courageous soldier, and this one—a woman—they meant to save if they could.

To the south, Cadwalader's command came streaming in through the main gates of the fort, followed by Baxter's decimated ranks, crowding two thousand nine hundred soldiers into a space built for one thousand. Magaw shook his head in disbelief. He was no longer in command of a fighting force inside a fort. He was in command of a death trap.

Within three minutes the Hessians held the north wall of the fort, and it was then that Colonel Johann Rall, proud, contemptuous, sent his demand to Colonel Magaw.

"Surrender or die."

Slowly Magaw lowered his face. In his heart he knew. Quietly he told his aide, "Strike our colors."

It was over. Fort Washington had fallen. In less than one day the British forces had stormed and taken the one American position that none thought could be conquered.

On the New Jersey side, in cold wintry sunlight, Washington

stared stoically as the American colors were lowered and the British Union Jack made its way up the once-proud flagpole, and he turned cold inside as the realization sunk in.

Two thousand nine hundred men. Two hundred nineteen cannon. Two thousand five hundred muskets. Four hundred thousand cartridges. Thousands of blankets. Tons of food. Irreplaceable. Gone. Lost in one day.

Washington folded his telescope and turned to his officers. Their faces were blank, eyes flat as they struggled to accept the staggering loss they had witnessed across the river, and to make calculations of how deep an impact it would have on the war they had so eagerly started just over one year earlier. For the first time it broke clear in their minds that the loss of the men and munitions and supplies at Fort Washington could trigger mass desertions from the army, and the withdrawal of congressional support, without which the battle for liberty was doomed.

Was it all over? finished? an illusion? a dream doomed from the beginning? They silently asked the question and then they backed away from it, unwilling to force an answer they did not want.

Washington spoke with deliberation to Putnam and Greene. "You remain here at Fort Lee. I'm going on to my camp at the Hackensack River. I'll be back when I know what to expect from Howe."

Head bowed, Washington put foot to stirrup and, with his aide Tench Tilghman at his side, turned his mare west. They rode in silence, both grappling to comprehend the soul-wrenching disaster they had witnessed across the Hudson River. In the late afternoon sun they worked their way through the scattered camp on the banks of the Hackensack River to Washington's command tent, and Tilghman took charge of Washington's horse as the commander in chief walked inside and closed the tent flap. He removed neither his hat nor his cape as he sat down on the chair facing his desk, and for a long time he did not move as he gathered his thoughts that had been shattered by the loss of Fort Washington. Twilight came and Tilghman brought his supper.

R.G. MICHAELS

Washington nodded his thanks and gestured to the table, and Tilghman set the tray down.

"General," he ventured, "Thomas Paine walked into camp about an hour ago. He's carrying a musket. I thought you should know."

Washington turned, surprised. "The writer? Common Sense?"

"The same."

"Is he here now?"

"Yes, sir."

"Ask him if he would share supper with me. Bring him, and a second tray."

Ten minutes later Tilghman returned and set a second tray of smoking coffee and food on the table. "Mr. Paine is outside."

Washington stood. "Bring him in."

Tall, wiry, slightly round-shouldered, long nosed, with bushy brows and piercing eyes, Paine followed Tilghman into the tent.

"Sir, may I present Thomas Paine."

The tall Virginian grasped the firm hand of Paine. "I believe we met once before while I was serving in the Second Continental Congress," Washington said. "In any event, I am honored at your visit, Mr. Paine. Please take a seat and share my table."

Paine removed his hat and cape, and they sat at the table opposite each other. Washington bowed his head and returned thanks for their food, and they reached for their forks and began. Paine worked his food slowly, savoring it.

Washington spoke. "It's good to see you again. To what do I owe this honor?"

Paine broke heavy brown bread and thoughtfully chewed for a moment. "General, I've heard some troubling things. I wanted to find out for myself."

Washington slowed. "What things?"

Paine stopped and raised his eyes, clear, sharp, penetrating. He studied Washington for a time. "Your losses. Your army near mutiny. Officers murmuring. Congress considering replacing you."

Washington put down his fork and locked eyes with Paine,

waiting. Sitting there in the yellow lantern light, they were just two men, carefully speaking the hard truth as best their understandings would permit.

"You know about these things?"

"It's my business to know. That's why I'm here. To find out for myself."

"You're carrying a musket?"

"Yes."

"What regiment?"

"None. I joined the Pennsylvania Associators regiment back in July—then General Greene appointed me his aide-de-camp in September, at Fort Lee, as you know. I left there to join you. I belong here with your army to find out what I can. I'll go with whatever regiment you say."

"You've been among the men?"

"Here and back at Fort Lee."

"You've heard talk of mutiny?"

"Open talk. Desertions are wholesale. Their enlistments are up on New Year's Day, and right now I expect you'll lose at least seventy-five percent of your army, maybe more."

"The officers?"

Paine shook his head and sipped at his steaming coffee. "There's a rising clamor to have Congress appoint Lee in your place. Your adjutant general—Reed, I think—wrote a letter that's being circulated. He sees Lee as the savior of the Continental army, if it can be saved at all."

Paine paused and looked directly into Washington's eyes to see how violent the reaction would be.

Washington leaned back, struggling to hide his profound surprise. "Reed?" he whispered.

"Reed." Paine scooped stew into his mouth and chewed. "There's a cabal now forming to unseat you as commander in chief."

"Who's forming it?"

"Some men in Congress. A few officers."

"Can you name names?"

"That's not important. What's important is they're beginning to talk about some sort of terms with England to end the rebellion."

"How strong is it?"

Paine shrugged and dipped bread in his stew and bit it off. "Growing. But that's not important either."

A minute passed in silence before Washington asked, "What *is* important?"

Paine slowed, and laid his bread on the side of his plate. He sipped at his smoking coffee cup for a moment, then set it down, and with an intensity that was nearly tangible brought his face square with Washington's. He leaned slightly forward and spoke.

"That someone stand and shout down these naysayers. Did they think breaking from the British would be easy, simply because it was right? Did they think they could give birth to a new nation without walking through the valley of the shadow? The fools! The need is not for brilliant generals. The need is for men who know in their souls that this is the work of God, and have dedicated themselves to it!"

He stopped, eyes blazing, and the force of his will seemed to reach into every corner of the chill tent. Washington sat silent, unmoving, as the power of Paine's words reached inside him and took root, and spread.

Paine leaned back and his face softened. "I'd like your permission to move among your men. I need to talk with them, eat with them, share with them. I'd like to take notes. Maybe write something. Maybe it will help."

Washington cleared this throat. "This camp is open to you. Would you like me to sign an order?"

Paine shook his head. "No. They need to see me as one of them—a common citizen."

They finished their meal in near silence, and stood. Paine picked up his hat and cloak. "Could we talk again sometime?"

"I would treasure it."

It was freezing as Paine strode out into the campground. Men huddled around fires, blankets clutched around them, vapor rising from their faces to disappear as it rose. He walked among them, watching, listening, nodding a silent greeting. At half past nine o'clock Paine approached the fire where the regimental drummer was seated, blanket held about his shoulders, shivering.

"Could I use your drum for a time?" he asked.

"For what?"

"To write on. I have some things to write."

The drummer shrugged indifferently. "Go ahead."

At ten-thirty the drummer interrupted Paine to sound tattoo, then returned the drum and Paine once again laid his writing pad on top of it. He drew his pencil from within the folds of his cape, and in the flickering yellow light of a campfire he continued to write. His fingers became numb in the cold, and still he continued. He laid the pencil down and clamped his hands beneath his arms for a time until feeling came again, and he once again picked up his pencil and wrote, pausing thoughtfully, continuing, pausing, adding to, taking from. It was past midnight before the fire had burned down to glowing embers, and Paine slipped his pad and pencil back inside his cape, and gathered his blanket about him.

The dawn broke clear in a world white with frost. Shivering men blew on coals in fire pits until wisps of smoke curled, and then added dry wood shavings, then twigs, then sticks until fires were going, and they broke through the shore ice on the Hackensack River to get water for cooking. Tench Tilghman was bringing a tray to the tent of General Washington when the sound of an incoming rider spurring his horse at full gallop turned him around and he stared at a soldier, cape flying, thundering straight through camp while men leaped out of his path, and he reined in before Washington's tent. He leaped from his sweated, steaming horse and stopped at the tent flap only long enough for the picket to challenge him. Then he was inside.

"Sir, General Howe just landed about four thousand regulars six miles north, on the Hackensack. They're coming this way."

Washington was outside his tent in four strides, sprinting for the rope line where the horses were tied and the saddles were racked. He saddled his own mount in ninety seconds and vaulted into the saddle, then looked at the nearest officer and barked orders.

"Get these men across the Hackensack Bridge and move them on west at least one mile. Do it right now. Take muskets and ammunition, and whatever else you can gather in a few minutes, and leave. Take the cannon if you can but don't delay. Do you understand?"

The major stammered, "Yes, sir," and Washington socked his spurs into the flanks of his mare and in two jumps she was pounding through camp at a gallop. Washington swept out onto the dirt road leading east to Fort Lee, holding her in to save sufficient strength for the nine-mile run to Fort Lee. Five minutes later Tilghman caught up with him, and together they held their mounts at a steady, ground-eating lope, feeling the rhythm of the breathing and the reach and gather of the driving legs as they rode on into the rising sun. Twice they slowed and stopped to let their horses blow, then remounted and went on, carefully spending their horses in their desperate run to reach Fort Lee.

The pickets on the ramparts recognized the tall figure, cape flying, while Washington was still half a mile away, and had the gates open for him, and he passed on through and reined in his lathered, sweated mount, then leaped to the ground. He thrust the reins into the hands of the nearest officer and demanded, "Where's General Greene?"

"In his quarters, sir," the startled lieutenant replied.

Washington broke into a run, Tilghman on his heels, and pounded once on the door, then threw it open. Startled, Greene turned to see who had the impertinence to burst into his quarters without invitation. His mouth fell open when he recognized the tall figure in the doorway. "General! In the name of heaven what—"

Washington cut him off. "Get the men moving. Now."

Greene grabbed his tunic and threw it on and began fumbling with the buttons. "What's happened?"

"Howe! He's six miles above the Hackensack bridge and moving south. If he gets to that bridge before we do, we're cut off. With Howe in front of us and Cornwallis behind, we're finished! Get moving."

"Sir, we've got munitions and food and—"

"Forget it! The men and their muskets. That's all."

"They have kettles with hot food cooking for—"

"Forget the kettles. The men and their muskets. Leave everything else. We can get food and blankets, but we cannot get more men and muskets."

Washington spun on his heel and ran outside and shouted orders. "Stop whatever you're doing. Stop it right now. Assemble into your regimental units immediately. This instant. Get your muskets and your ammunition and your knapsacks if you have any, and start out the gates of the fort now. Move due west to the Hackensack Bridge, and do not stop until you cross it."

The entire camp stopped dead in its tracks. Soldiers looked at each other, astonished at the sight of their commander in chief shouting direct orders, overriding his subordinate officers. They looked at their officers in question, and their officers looked at Washington, dumbstruck.

The man to whom Washington had thrust the reins of his horse had walked the horse in a circle to cool it out in the freezing air, and Washington ran to him, seized the reins, and swung up. As his right foot caught the stirrup he drew his saber and spun the horse towards the nearest cluster of men. He smacked the first one he came to on the back with the flat of his sword. "Move! Out the gate."

He swung his sword again and the second man felt the sting as the flat of it raised a welt one foot long across his shoulders. "*Move!*"

Only then did the camp come to life. Men sprinted to their blankets to sweep them off the ground, then their muskets, and their knapsacks if they had any. They left their breakfast cooking pots boiling and fled out the gates, looking for others in their company or regiment, Washington riding among them, shouting, swinging his saber. Down the dirt road they streamed, across meadows, past neat Dutch farmhouses, through orchards and pastures, scrambling across stone fences. They dropped their knapsacks when they could go no further, then their blankets, and they struggled on. The sick stumbled and went down, panting, sweating, and could not rise, and others paused to lift them, carry them, as they worked on west.

And then they crested a gentle rise, and before them was the Hackensack River and the broad wooden bridge. They pushed on through the abandoned knapsacks and blankets and camp litter left behind by the regiments that had retreated that morning, and the first of them crowded onto the bridge and moved across. The few wagons loaded with muskets and cartridges followed, the horses' hooves and the wagon wheels ringing hollow on the wooden planks. They passed on to the open ground west and collapsed to lie panting, fighting for breath, exhausted in body and soul, not caring if the British caught them. The last of the fleeing army was on the bridge when they heard the shouts of Howe's army from the north, and they looked to see the Scottish plaid kilts of the Highlanders coming at a trot.

Quickly Henry Knox and Alexander Hamilton reined their horses down, and from the wreckage of the abandoned camp they dragged two cannon clattering over the bridge and swung them around, muzzles pointing east. With the Highlanders less than eight hundred yards away they jammed powder, straw, then grapeshot down the muzzles of the two cannon, and struck flint to steel and lighted two linstocks.

They stood there, two lone men, tears of rage streaming down their cheeks, linstocks hovering above the touchholes of their cannon, waiting, silently challenging the Highlanders to come take the bridge if they could. The Highlanders stopped, out of grapeshot range, and they began to play their fifes and rattle their drums, and then they stopped, and began shouting insults at the dirty, ragged, filthy Americans who knew only one thing about war.

How to run.

Washington gave his men one hour to rest, and then he was back among them, driving them, pushing them on farther west and south. Day became night and then day again, and then time became a blur of nights filled with cold that cut to the bone and days filled with no food as they pushed on—Equacanaugh—Springfield—Newark—Boundbrook—run—run until you drop —New Brunswick—Cornwallis is behind us—don't stop.

Winter rains came and they slogged through freezing mud in the daytime and shivered in it at night—ice on the road cutting bare feet—run—can you see them behind? Princeton—Trenton—there's a great river ahead—what river? the Delaware.

Get Humpton and Maxwell—send them to get the big ore boats—Durham boats at Riegelsville ten miles up the river—used to carry iron ore down to Philadelphia. Do we pay for them? no money, give them American script—give them my note—give them anything but get the boats—in two days—and smash every other boat you find within thirty miles of here—leave the British nothing they can use to follow us.

And get John Glover—we've got to cross the river—can you take this army across the Delaware in one day? if Cornwallis traps us on this side we're finished—if he catches us crossing, his cannon will pick us off like ducks on a pond—can my Marbleheaders and I move this army across in one day? yes—if Humpton and Maxwell get those Durham boats I'll take your army across the Delaware in one day.

"Thank you, Colonel."

Glover saluted and turned, and Washington watched the small man's rigid back disappear. Washington paused only long enough to get pen and quill and paper, write a message, seal it with wax, and turn to Tench Tilghman. "Get Private Eli Stroud, Boston regiment, as fast as you can."

He impatiently paced for five minutes before Eli came running. Washington drew him aside, handed him the message and spoke quietly. "That message is for a man named John Honeyman. He lives near Princeton. He's been posing as a Tory spy. You must find him and deliver it to him at any cost. Do not read it, and let no one else read it. If you're captured, swallow it—that message *cannot* fall into the hands of the British."

Washington was watching Eli's eyes intently, waiting for understanding to creep in. It came, and Washington continued. "Leave quietly tonight, and tell absolutely no one—no officer, no friend, no one—you've done this. Do you understand?"

"Yes. How do I find Honeyman?"

Washington shook his head. "At a small village just north of Princeton named Griggstown is all I can tell you. I leave it to you."

Eli nodded his head, carefully folded the message into his bullet pouch, nodded to Washington, and walked away. With anxious eyes Washington watch him disappear in the mass of bewildered, exhausted men, then remounted his horse and once again raised the shout, "Move! We must keep moving!"

Slowly, mechanically, the men shouldered their muskets and once again plodded southwest, not knowing their destination, not asking.

Suddenly at the great river—from daybreak to dark—the entire army across the river—stopping in a grove of trees with a barn and a large stone house nearby.

They no longer cared where the British were, or where they themselves were. They only knew that General Washington was no longer riding everywhere among them, whipping them with the flat of his sword, driving them like a demon until they dropped. When they could they slowly gathered firewood and built great fires. They cut the last of their raw pork and stuck it on sticks and thrust it into the flames, and they ate it when it was black, dripping, and it seared their mouths and they did not care.

With dusk settling, a major hesitantly approached George Washington. "Sir, the men don't know where we are."

Washington looked at him. "Pennsylvania. Opposite Trenton. Bordentown is down the river and Philadelphia is beyond that."

Notes

On November 15, 1776, the British forces sent a messenger under a white flag to offer terms of surrender to Colonel Robert Magaw, commander of Fort Washington. Colonel Magaw refused the offer, and the message he wrote in return appears in this chapter verbatim (see Leckie, *George Washington's War*, p. 291; Johnston, *The Campaign of 1776*, part I, p. 278).

Colonel Magaw assigned Colonels Rawlings, Baxter, and Cadwalader to defend designated areas around Fort Washington (see Johnston, *The Campaign of 1776*, part I, pp. 277–80).

General Washington, with Generals Putnam, Greene, and Mercer, left Fort Lee in New Jersey to cross the Hudson River to inspect Fort Washington, and while their boat was in midstream the British commenced the bombardment of Fort Washington. The British gunboat *Pearl* was in the Hudson just below Fort Washington, and exchanged cannon fire with the fort (see Johnston, *The Campaign of 1776*, part I, pp. 278–79; Leckie, *George Washington's War*, p. 291; Higginbotham, *The War of American Independence*, p. 162; Carrington, *Battles of the American Revolution*, p. 249).

In the battle of Fort Washington, Margaret Corbin, wife of William (John in some sources) Corbin, continued firing the American cannon at the north end of the fort after her husband was killed, holding the attacking Hessians at bay for some time. A Hessian cannonball injured her badly, but British doctors saved her life; however, her left arm was permanently disabled. She survived and was returned to the Americans, and in 1779 the Continental Congress voted her a veteran's pension, the first woman to receive that honor, and she became known as "Captain Molly." A bronze plaque on a granite stone at West Point commemorates her brave and gallant deed. It was not uncommon for wives to go with their husbands to the army in the Revolutionary War (see Claghorn, *Women Patriots of the American Revolution*, pp. 55–56).

General Howe ordered the Forty-second Highlanders to get between Cadwalader's command and the fort, which they partially accomplished, sending Cadwalader's command running back to Fort Washington (see Johnston, *The Campaign of 1776*, part I, p. 280).

The losses of the Continental army were 219 cannon, 2,500 muskets,

400,000 cartridges, tons of food, and thousands of blankets, a catastrophic loss (see Leckie, *George Washington's War*, p. 294; Higginbotham, *The War of American Independence*, p. 162; Carrington, *Battles of the American Revolution*, p. 251).

Thomas Paine arrived in General Washington's camp carrying a musket, and requested he be allowed to mingle with the soldiers that he might see the war through their eyes. He enjoyed close conversations with General Washington and reputedly wrote most of *The American Crisis* on a drumhead in freezing weather (see Leckie, *George Washington's War*, p. 318; Higginbotham, *The War of American Independence*, p. 165).

General Howe landed a major force on the Hackensack River in New Jersey about six miles north of General Washington's army, and Washington left immediately to move his army from Fort Lee across the Hackensack bridge before Howe's forces arrived to cut them off (see Leckie, *George Washington's War*, p. 294; Fast, *The Crossing*, pp. 19–20).

The last of the American army was crossing the Hackensack Bridge when the Scottish Highlanders appeared in the distance. Weeping with rage and anger, Colonel Henry Knox and Captain Alexander Hamilton turned two cannon against the British troops, loaded them with grapeshot, and waited for them to come. However, they remained out of cannon range (see Fast, *The Crossing*, p. 20).

General Washington assigned two officers, Humpton and Maxwell, to get Durham boats to transport his army across the Delaware River from New Jersey to Pennsylvania. They were ordered to get the boats in two days, but performed a miracle in getting them back to the crossing place in five days. He requested Colonel John Glover to move the entire army across the Delaware River in one day. With the boats, Colonel John Glover and his Marblehead regiment accomplished this unbelieveable task (see Fast, *The Crossing*, pp. 24, 26, 28).

General Washington sent a secret message to an American spy masquerading as a Tory loyal to the British Crown (see Higginbotham, *The War of American Independence*, p. 168; Leckie, *George Washington's War*, pp. 317–18).

McKonkey's Ferry, Pennsylvania
December 19, 1776

CHAPTER XXV

★ ★ ★

*R*eveille came too loud in the darkness. Slowly Billy pushed aside the cover of dried leaves heaped over the shallow trench where he had lain. Shaking with cold he stirred the ashes of last night's fire until he felt heat. Then he blew and added wood shavings until smoke and then a flicker of flame came, and he carefully laid small sticks.

Eli rose from his cover of leaves, picked up his cup, and walked away while Billy emptied the last water from his canteen into a small, fire-blackened pot and set it in the low flames. Billy glanced around as men worked with their fires, stiff, grimy, bearded, teeth chattering in the freezing air. Across the Delaware River he saw the glow of hundreds of campfires where the Hessians had set up their tents in orderly rows to keep the Americans pinned down, content to wait while bitter cold and the lack of food destroyed what was left of the decimated American army. Colonel Johann Rall saw no need to waste his Hessians on what the winter would do for him without firing a shot.

Sunrise came stark through the frigid, bare branches of the trees at McKonkey's Ferry. It turned the outlying meadows to sparkling fields of diamonds as it caught the thick blanket of frost crystals. Hundreds of thin columns of smoke rose from campfires on both sides of the river, bright in the sunlight against the clear blue sky.

A captain with a blanket wrapped about his shoulders stopped twenty yards away from Billy and read the morning orders. "The regiment will stand down and rest throughout this day."

Billy's head dropped forward and his eyes closed in blessed relief. Eli returned and dropped to his haunches beside the fire. In his cup was a handful of coffee beans. He crushed them with a rock, then poured them into the steaming water. From within his shirt he drew out two square pieces of hardtack, wormy, moldy.

"Our rations for today," he said quietly.

They sat cross-legged for a time, watching the water boil in the small pot, and then they divided the steaming, bitter coffee. They held it in pewter mugs and sipped at it while they dug worms and shaved mold off the hardtack, and they broke pieces and stuffed them in their mouths to soften while they worked on the scalding coffee.

They finished and set their cups down, and Eli rose. "I'll be back."

Billy watched him go, then reached beneath his blanket, inside his shirt, and drew out a notepad and a short stub of pencil. He laid the pad on his knee and for a time looked about, gathering his thoughts. Then he began to write, slowly, numb fingers clumsy from the cold.

December 19th, 1776

My dear Brigitte:

I take first opportunity to write you of the many things that have happened in such a short time. I am with General Washington at a place called McKonkey's Ferry on the Pennsylvania side of the Delaware River. It is some distance above Philadelphia, and across the river the Hessians are camped in plain sight. The pencil and paper I use were given to me by Thomas Paine, of whom you know. He was with us for many days, but left a short time ago.

I have never supposed an army could survive what we have experienced the last many days . . . badly beaten at Long Island . . . again at New York . . . retreated from White Plains back to Fort Washington on Manhattan Island . . . the British and Hessians attacked and occupied in less than one day . . . lost 3,000 men dead and captured there, with much of our winter supply of food and blankets, and most of our cannon, muskets, and ammunition . . . surrendered Fort Lee without a battle . . . scarcely avoided total defeat at the Hackensack Bridge . . . ran completely across the state of New Jersey with the British at our heels, and crossed into Pennsylvania to save ourselves.

General Washington left most of the army behind under Generals Lee and Heath for reasons I do not know . . . numbers he has here are growing fewer daily . . . rash, sickness, cold, and hunger take a daily toll . . . men deserting every night. Today I received bitter coffee and one piece of moldy hardtack for my rations. Yesterday we had one half cup of dried peas. I am also recently recovered from a severe fever that robbed me of much strength and substance, since I am quite thin.

I am still wearing the summer clothing I wore leaving Boston. My shoes are in pieces, but I have tied them on with strong cord. My good friend Eli Stroud, who was raised by the Iroquois Indians, has taught me how to dig a shallow depression at night, and to line it with dry leaves and then cover myself with more dry leaves, to avoid freezing to death. Last week we lost nine men to freezing.

I am sorry to say there is open murmuring among the troops against General Washington, and even the officers are beginning to show disaffection. I was also informed four days ago that our men who were taken prisoner have been placed on prison ships in New York Harbor, where they are dying daily, and their bodies dropped overboard every morning.

I believe that General Washington would find it difficult to find five hundred men in this part of his army who today could be called fit for duty. I do wish to tell you, however, that my spirits remain high. I know we are in the right.

Billy stopped and re-read what he had written, and his heart began to race as he continued.

I took a terrible start when I learned of your sad experience in trying to bring food and ammunition to the army. I feel great warmth in my heart for all you tried to do and can only regret that it turned out so badly. I am grateful to the Almighty that you, and Caleb, escaped. I trust you will learn from the experience.

Please give my highest regards to your mother and family. Know that I think of you each day, and that I pray the Almighty will protect you.

> With every tender and loving thought,
> Billy Weems

His heart was pounding with an excitement he never knew existed. He was seeing her as she was that morning so long ago in the Dunson parlor in Boston when he came to bid them good-bye, when he had embraced Margaret, and then Brigitte had thrown her arms about him and held him, and he had held her, and she had wept for a reason she could not explain. He was seeing her face and the color of her eyes and hair, and he was remembering the smell and the feel of her.

He re-read the last few lines of his letter again and again, not knowing or caring where he had found the courage to speak from the depths of his heart of his feelings for her, aware only that his being was alive, singing, overflowing as it never had before. He reached to wipe at his eyes, and then slowly brought his surging feelings under control.

He did not tear the letter from the pad. He was fumbling to put the notepad back inside his blanket when Eli strode up behind him and went to one knee beside the fire. Eli thrust his hand inside his shirt and drew out a handful of acorns and laid them on the ground.

"Wrote a letter?"

Billy nodded and Eli dropped a second handful of acorns on top of the first.

"Mother?"

"Friend."

Eli dropped another handful of acorns, mixed with hickory nuts. "The Dunson family?"

Billy looked at him, deciding. "Brigitte."

Eli slowed. "Matthew's sister?"

"Yes."

Eli continued unloading acorns and hickory nuts from his shirt while Billy's eyes grew wider.

Billy asked, "Where did you find those?"

"Followed a squirrel."

"Was that his winter storage?"

"Part of it. He has about three more hollow trees half filled."

"Where's the squirrel?"

"I expect right now he's sitting in one of those other hollow trees cursing me."

Billy smiled and shoved the notepad inside his shirt.

Eli stopped and looked at him. "Aren't you going to mail it?"

Billy shook his head.

"What's wrong? Bad letter?"

Billy stared at the fire for a time, shy, embarrassed at the thought of opening his innermost thoughts about a girl to another man.

He cleared his throat. "No. I have no right to send it. I said things that will trouble her."

Eli settled down, sitting cross-legged. "You have feelings for her?"

"I do."

"You said that in the letter?"

"Not that way. But it's there."

"That will give her trouble?"

"She has already given her heart to another. A British officer. A fine man." Billy shook his head. "Look at me. I know what I am. She has found someone befitting a girl like her—an officer, a fine gentleman, not someone like me. I can't interfere. I won't. For her sake."

Eli dropped acorns into the coals of the fire. A passing soldier slowed to eye them wistfully, and Eli reached to give him a handful, and he continued on to his own fire.

Finally Eli spoke, quietly, without raising his eyes. "You've got two problems. You're ugly, and you're dumb, and I can't figure which is the worst." He raised his face and spoke with sudden intensity. *"Send the letter!"*

Billy's mouth dropped open in astonishment, and he stared at Eli, and Eli looked at him in disgust, and then Eli grinned, and a chuckle rolled out of Billy, and then they both threw back their heads and laughed. Men fifty feet away paused to stare at the first sound of laughter they had heard in weeks.

At the south end of the camp, General Washington had established his headquarters on the main floor of the gray thick-walled stone house that stood in a clearing near the ferry dock. The door to his private chambers was locked, as it had been for most of the daylight hours for two days. The heavy curtains were drawn against the sunlight and any who would peer in.

Inside, General Washington sat at his desk, hands clasped before him, hunched forward, head bowed, racked body and mind and soul by the searing white heat of the knowledge that he had led the Continental army to the brink of its destruction. He could not control the sharp images that came flashing again and again. Hessians—the Gowanus swamp—muskets and bayonets—the Americans trapped in the black muck—ten thousand redcoats—the Jamaica Road—behind Sullivan—the night retreat from Brooklyn back to Manhattan Island—Glover's boats—the torrential rain and fog sent by the Almighty—Chatterton Hill—wiped clean by the British in one morning—a second desperate night retreat—Fort Washington—three thousand troops and their food and guns for a year—gone—Fort Lee gone without firing a shot—the shameless, headlong running, running across New Jersey, driven like sheep before the British.

He slammed his clenched first down on the desk and rose to his feet to pace, back and forth across the room, in an attempt to escape the endless battering that was destroying him, and he could not stop it.

General Lee openly soliciting Congress—his own adjutant

general, Reed, begging him to do something to reverse the months of shameful retreat—favoring Lee—a proposal to reconsider his appointment as commander in chief—desertions by the hundreds from his army every day—sickness everywhere—men without shoes—medicine—clothing—food—muskets—powder—men sleeping in holes like animals at night to avoid freezing—eating anything they could find—rats—crows—anything.

It rang in his brain like an unending refrain—It was my error, my error. I'm responsible, responsible, responsible. Me, me, me.

He wiped at his eyes and he could not stop the tears. He stood on the carpet in the center of the room, head bowed, shoulders slumped, and he wept. He did not know how long he stood there, desolate, beaten, but suddenly he could bear it no longer. Head bowed, hands clasped before him, he spoke.

"Almighty Creator of all, in my anguish I come to thee . . ."

For a long time he remained thus, tears streaming down onto his tunic, despairing, pouring out his heart, baring his soul to his God, pleading, pleading. "This is thy work. Help me in my weakness."

He fell silent and for a time was unable to move. Then he slowly walked back to his desk and dropped onto his chair, exhausted. He turned to look at the west bank of windows where the curtains were bright with the afternoon sun. He stood and started towards them, when a rap came at the door.

"What is it?"

"A letter, sir."

"From whom?"

"John Adams."

Washington's breath came short. *John Adams. From Congress. It was Adams who nominated my appointment. Has he now written to take it away?*

"Slide it under the door."

He watched as the folded document appeared, and he walked to stoop and pick it up. He sat down at his desk and broke the seal.

Philada. 15 Decr. 1776

My dear sir:

I steal a moment's opportunity to send you a few lines of encouragement. Congress is, as ever, convuls'd by tumult and alarm, but never so much as to do anything of purpose or effect for our cause. Some upbraid you, some defend you, and the result is a deadlock.

I take the liberty of copying out a passage of a letter that my dear wife has sent me from Massachusetts. You will see in it the spirit that animates the people—would that Congress felt it as strongly.

I am, with every assurance of esteem and respect,
Your obed't serv't,
John Adams

With trembling fingers Washington quietly read the words Abigail Adams had written to her beloved husband.

We have had many stories concerning engagements upon Long Island this week, of our lines being forced and of our troops retreating to New York. Particulars we have not yet obtained. All we can learn is that we have been unsuccessful there; having lost many men as prisoners, among whom are Lord Stirling and General Sullivan.

But if we should be defeated, I think we shall not be conquered. A people fired, like the Romans, with love of their country and of liberty, a zeal for the public good, and a noble emulation of glory, will not be disheartened or dispirited by a succession of unfortunate events. But, like them, may we learn by defeat the power of becoming invincible.

Washington jerked erect in his chair.

Not be disheartened or dispirited by a succession of unfortunate events— learn by defeat the power of becoming invincible!

He read it again, and he felt a tiny ray of light struggling through the black clouds of anguish in his soul.

Learn by defeat.

A tingle began.

He heard the muffled pounding of a horse at the front gate, and the opening of the front door, and brief words were spoken. Running footsteps came up the hall and his aide knocked sharply.

"Yes."

"Sir, a messenger is here. Thomas Paine sent him from Philadelphia. He has two bags filled with papers he insists you must see at once."

Washington came off the chair in one fluid move and jerked the door open. "Where is he?"

"Waiting in the parlor, sir."

Washington strode down the hall and turned through the archway into the parlor, where the man stood between two large canvas sacks on the floor.

"Thomas Paine sent you?"

"Yes, sir, from Philadelphia. He said to tell you that you might want to read these."

"You've come from Philadelphia today?" Washington was incredulous.

"Yes, sir."

"What are they?"

"Newspapers, sir."

Washington's head dropped forward. "Newspapers? About what? What's happened? Has Congress done something? Has he published more of his writings?"

"I don't know, sir."

"Thank you." He turned to his aide. "I'll take the sacks. See to it this man gets food and refreshment and his horse is tended. Use my stores if necessary."

He grasped one sack in each big hand and walked rapidly back up the hall. He dropped them on the floor of his quarters, and jerked the knot out of the first one. From within he drew out half a dozen copies of the *Pennsylvania Journal,* dated December 19, 1776, together with a brief note from Paine. The messenger had covered nearly forty miles in less than six hours. Washington unfolded and read the note.

Philada., 19 Decr. 1776

My dear sir,

I write in haste so that the courier can bear this note with the enclos'd newspapers. I hope that the essay printed there may be of use to the glorious cause to which we are devoted.

> God bless you and have you in his keeping,
> Your obed't,
> Thos. Paine

Washington took the top copy of the newspaper and sat down at his desk and spread it before him, searching for what it was that would drive Thomas Paine to send a horseman such a distance to deliver.

It covered most of the second page and finished on page three, and Washington brought his racing thoughts under control as he read.

The American Crisis.
Number I.
By the Author of COMMON SENSE.

These are the times that try men's souls: The summer soldier and the sunshine patriot will, in this crisis, shrink from the service of his country; but he that stands it NOW, deserves the love and thanks of man and woman. Tyranny, like hell, is not easily conquered; yet we have this consolation with us, that the harder the conflict, the more glorious the triumph.

Washington's breath came short as he continued.

What we obtain too cheap, we esteem too lightly:—'Tis dearness only that gives every thing its value. Heaven knows how to set a proper price upon its goods; and it would be strange indeed, if so celestial an article as FREEDOM should not be highly rated.

The tingle that had begun when Washington read Abigail Adams's letter came strong and he felt it spreading through his breast.

Britain, with an army to enforce her tyranny, has declared, that she has a right (*not only to* TAX) but "*to* BIND *us in* ALL CASES WHATSO-EVER," and if being *bound in that manner* is not slavery, then is there not such a thing as slavery upon earth. Even the expression is impious, for so unlimited a power can belong only to GOD.

The deep black cloud that had for so long seized Washington's soul was gone. Never had he felt the light and the power that were now upon him.

I have as little superstition in me as any man living, but my secret opinion has ever been, and still is, that GOD Almighty will not give up a people to military destruction, or leave them unsupportedly to perish, who had so earnestly and so repeatedly sought to avoid the calamities of war, by every decent method which wisdom could invent.

Washington stopped. His eyes misted. He could not speak. He raised a hand and then dropped it back onto the newspaper and continued.

By perseverance and fortitude we have the prospect of a glorious issue; by cowardice and submission, the sad choice of a variety of evils—a ravaged country—a depopulated city—habitations without safety, and slavery without hope—our homes turned into barracks and baudy-houses for Hessians, and a future race to provide for whose fathers we shall doubt of.

He finished reading and he sat in his chair unable to move. He had never supposed that a man could be plunged into light so brilliant and power so potent as to rob him of all natural strength of mind and body, strip him of every human foible, everything he had ever supposed, to leave him helpless, able only to know that the Almighty had touched him and that he would never be the same. He was aware a strange feeling of light had filled the room, reached every corner, and he dared not look. He remained motionless for a time—he did not know how long—and then slowly the spirit in the room faded, and his natural strength crept back into his body and his soul.

He turned to look, and the room appeared as normal.

When he could, he stood and rushed to the door and threw it open.

"Lieutenant Brewster!"

The man came running. "Yes, sir."

"Deliver a copy of this to every corporal's guard in this command. Do it now. Have every officer read the article styled *The American Crisis* aloud to every soldier in this camp. Make them listen. Am I clear?"

The man's eyes were wide. "Yes, sir." He seized the two bags and dragged them down the hall.

Washington approached the windows and threw back the curtains and stared long and hard at the Delaware River, running full with winter rains, sheet ice forming near the banks. He could see the fires of the British camp on the far shore and the red, white, and blue of the Union Jack flying high, an open insult to the huddled Americans.

In his soul, a resolve formed and it grew until it filled him. He turned on his heel and strode rapidly down the hall to catch Brewster, who was just loading the two canvas sacks onto a cart.

Washington called to him. "And bring Colonel John Glover back here. We've got a river to cross!"

Notes

The description of General Washington's despondency at the condition of his army and of the Revolution in mid-December at McKonkey's Ferry can hardly be overstated (see Ketchum, *The Winter Soldiers*, pp. 209–10; see also Fast, *The Crossing*, pp. 64–69). His own adjutant general, Joseph Reed, had written a letter praising General Lee at the expense of General Washington (see Leckie, *George Washington's War*, p. 293).

The passage from the letter written by Abigail Adams to her husband, John Adams, that, in the novel, is forwarded on to General Washington appears verbatim in this chapter (see Johnston, *The Campaign of 1776*, part I, p. 201).

The American Crisis by Thomas Paine was printed in Philadelphia by a newspaper named the *Pennsylvania Journal* on December 19, 1776. Thomas Paine hired a rider to carry several copies of the newspaper to General Washington's camp at McKonkey's Ferry, which he did that same day. Selected portions of this famous writing are quoted herein (see Ketchum, *The Winter Soldiers*, p. 211; see also Fast, *The Crossing*, pp. 76–78).

SELECTED BIBLIOGRAPHY

★ ★ ★

Bolton, Jonathan, and Claire Wilson. *Joseph Brant: Mohawk Chief.* New York: Chelsea House, 1992.

Carrington, Henry B. *Battles of the American Revolution: Battle Maps and Charts of the American Revolution.* New York: New York Times, 1968.

Claghorn, Charles E. *Women Patriots of the American Revolution: A Biographical Dictionary.* Metuchen, N.J.: Scarecrow Press, 1991.

Earle, Alice Morse. *Home Life in Colonial Days.* 1898. Reprint, Williamstown, Mass.: Corner House Publishers, 1975.

Fast, Howard Melvin. *The Crossing.* New York: William Morrow and Co., 1971.

Fitch, Jabez. *The New York Diary of Lieutenant Jabez Fitch.* Edited by W.H.W. Sabine. New York: New York Times, 1954.

Flint, Edward F. and Gwendolyn S. *Flint Family History of the Adventuresome Seven.* Baltimore, Md.: Gateway Press, 1984.

Godfrey, Carlos E. *The Commander-in-Chief's Guard: Revolutionary War.* Baltimore, Md.: Genealogical Publishing Co., 1972.

Graymont, Barbara. *The Iroquois.* New York: Chelsea House Publishers, 1988.

————. *The Iroquois in the American Revolution.* Syracuse, N.Y.: Syracuse University Press, 1972.

Hale, Horatio, ed. *The Iroquois Book of Rites.* 1883. Reprint, New York: AMS Press, 1969.

Higginbotham, Don. *The War of American Independence: Military Attitudes, Policies, and Practice, 1763-1789.* New York: Macmillan, 1971.

Johnston, Henry P. *The Campaign of 1776 Around New York and Brooklyn.* 1878. Reprint, New York: Da Capo Press, 1971.

Ketchum, Richard M. *The Winter Soldiers.* Garden City, N.Y.: Doubleday, 1973.

Leckie, Robert. *George Washington's War: The Saga of the American Revolution.* New York: HarperCollins, 1992.

Mackesy, Piers. *The War for America, 1775–1783.* 1964. Reprint, Lincoln: University of Nebraska Press, 1993.

Martin, Joseph Plumb. *Private Yankee Doodle.* Edited by George F. Scheer. Boston: Little, Brown and Co., 1962.

Parry, Jay A., and Andrew M. Allison. *The Real George Washington.* Washington, D.C.: National Center for Constitutional Studies, 1990.

Peterson, Harold L. *Round Shot and Rammers.* Harrisburg, Pa.: Stackpole Books, 1969.

Pool, Daniel. *What Jane Austen Ate and Charles Dickens Knew: From Fox Hunting to Whist—the Facts of Daily Life in 19th-Century England.* New York: Simon & Schuster, 1993.

Stokesbury, James L. *A Short History of the American Revolution.* New York: William Morrow and Company, 1991.

Ulrich, Laurel Thatcher. *Good Wives: Image and Reality in the Lives of Women in Northern New England, 1650–1750.* New York: Vintage Press, 1991.

Wilbur, C. Keith, *The Revolutionary Soldier, 1775-1783: An Illustrated Sourcebook of Authentic Details About Everyday Life for Revolutionary War Soldiers.* Old Saybrook, Conn.: Globe Pequot Press, 1993.

ACKNOWLEDGMENTS

★ ★ ★

Richard B. Bernstein, a constitutional historian specializing in the Revolutionary generation, made a tremendous contribution to the historical accuracy of this work, for which the writer is deeply grateful. The staff of the publisher, Bookcraft, most notably Garry Garff, editor, and Jana Erickson, art director, spent many hours immersed in the details of preparing the manuscript for publication. Harriette Abels, consultant and mentor, graced this volume with her wisdom and encouragement and, ultimately, her approval.

And finally, the spirit of those heroes of so long ago seemed to reach across time and touch the words as they formed on the pages.

Without all of these, this volume would have been lacking.